E. V. Thompson wa_____
nine years in the Na_____
police. He is now _____
writer.

Also by E. V. Thompson

THE MUSIC MAKERS
THE DREAM TRADERS
CRY ONCE ALONE
BECKY
GOD'S HIGHLANDER
CASSIE
WYCHWOOD
BLUE DRESS GIRL
TOLPUDDLE WOMAN
LEWIN'S MEAD
MOONTIDE
CAST NO SHADOWS
SOMEWHERE A BIRD IS SINGING
THE LOST YEARS
PATHS OF DESTINY
TOMORROW IS FOR EVER
THE VAGRANT KING

The Retallick Saga

BEN RETALLICK
CHASE THE WIND
HARVEST OF THE SUN
SINGING SPEARS
THE STRICKEN LAND
LOTTIE TRAGO
RUDDLEMOOR
FIRES OF EVENING
BROTHERS IN WAR

The Jagos of Cornwall

THE RESTLESS SEA
POLRUDDEN
MISTRESS OF POLRUDDEN

As James Munro

HOMELAND

E. V. THOMPSON OMNIBUS

Seek a New Dawn

Winds of Fortune

sphere

SPHERE

This omnibus edition first published in Great Britain by
Sphere in 2007
E. V. Thompson Omnibus copyright © E. V. Thompson 2007

Previously published separately:
Seek a New Dawn first published in Great Britain in 2001
by Little, Brown and Company
Published by Time Warner Paperbacks in 2002
Reprinted 2002 (twice), 2004
Reprinted by Sphere in 2006
Copyright © 2001 by E. V. Thompson

Winds of Fortune first published in Great Britain in 2000
by Little, Brown and Company
Published by Warner Books in 2001
Copyright © 2000 by E. V. Thompson

A CIP catalogue record for this book is
available from the British Library.

ISBN 978-0-7515-4008-6

Papers used by Sphere are natural, recyclable products made from
wood grown in sustainable forests and certified in accordance with
the rules of the Forest Stewardship Council.

Printed and bound in Great Britain by Mackays of Chatham Ltd.
Paper supplied by Hellefoss AS, Norway

Sphere
An imprint of
Little, Brown Book Group
Brettenham House
Lancaster Place
London WC2E 7EN

A Member of the Hachette Livre Group of Companies

www.littlebrown.co.uk

Seek a New Dawn

To the many friends who introduced me to Australia and the splendour of the Adelaide Hills and the Flinders Ranges

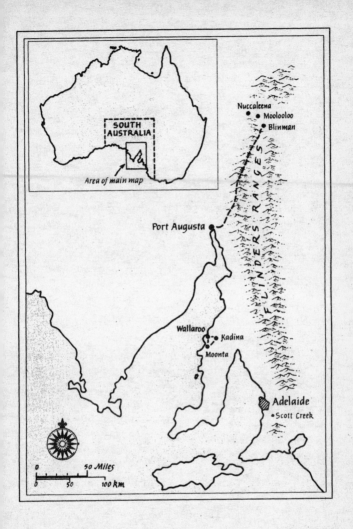

BOOK ONE

1

I

'Emily! Where have you been, girl? Your father has been waiting for you for almost an hour. You are to go to his study – immediately!'

Emily had entered the vicarage happily humming 'All Things Bright and Beautiful', only to be confronted by the housekeeper, Maude Rowe, standing in the hallway, hands on hips, wearing an expression of stern disapproval.

Her happiness disappearing with the warm sunshine as the door swung closed behind her, Emily asked wearily, 'What am I supposed to have done now, Maude?'

'For a start I expect he'll want to know where you've been since you left church. The service has been over for an hour and a half but no one's been able to find you anywhere. You're in trouble and you've no one to blame but yourself. The number of times you've been told . . .'

'Emily, is that you? Come in here, this minute.'

The voice of Reverend Arthur Boyce reached them from beyond the partially open door of his study, situated on the far side of the large hall.

Emily knew there was about to be yet another confrontation between herself and her strict parson father. As she turned and, with a heavy heart, made her way towards her father's study, she noted that Maude's expression was a combination of smug satisfaction and I-told-you-so righteousness.

Life in the vicarage had not been happy since the death of her mother many years before. The Reverend Arthur Boyce had taken his wife's death very badly, unable to come to terms with his loss.

Emily and her sister Caroline both lived at home, but Caroline was currently away. Twenty-two years of age and older than Emily by two years, she was paying a visit to relatives, near Bristol.

Maude ran the household with the help of house servants. Responsibility for performing charitable duties in Reverend Boyce's parish rested with the two young sisters.

Inside his study, Reverend Arthur Boyce, a tall and gaunt-featured figure, sat stiffly upright behind a desk, facing the door. Light from the window behind him fell upon the fine quality grained leather, stretched to provide a smooth surface for the desk that formed a barrier between him and his errant daughter.

On the desk-top lay sheets of paper covered with evenly spaced lines of impeccably neat handwriting. It was the sermon the reverend had delivered that morning from the pulpit of his St Cleer church.

Arthur Boyce had married late in life and was

fifty-three years of age when Emily came along. Now over seventy, his shock of pure white hair and a tired expression were visible manifestations of a man who believed he had experienced more than a fair share of the troubles the Lord sent to try those who served His cause.

Parson Boyce was also inclined to view young people with the unequivocal intolerance of age. Emily deeply resented that she and Caroline were made to bear the brunt of his disapproval – she especially.

While she had been alive and before she took to her bed, their mother had been able to deflect her husband's irritability. Unfortunately, there had been no one to champion the girls for some years now, Maude invariably siding with her employer.

'Where have you been, Emily?' Arthur Boyce put the question to his petite, fair-haired daughter as she stepped through the doorway of the study. 'It was my intention to walk home with you, but you had left the church even before I began my farewells to the congregation. I did not leave the church until late and arrived home in expectation of finding you here, helping Maude to prepare the dinner. However, it seems your plans took no account of duty. I would like to know what they were.'

'I had no plans, Father,' Emily replied, gazing through the window at the lawn beyond, where a black-bird was successfully tugging an elastic-bodied worm free from the tight-packed earth. There was a wooden-armed chair on her side of the desk but she remained standing. She knew better than to sit down without her father's permission.

'Well, girl, where have you been?' he demanded impatiently.

'I went to see some kittens that had been born only yesterday. We all went to see them. All the choir.'

'I presume Samuel Hooper went too?'

'Of course. He's one of the choir. Besides, the kittens were in a barn on his father's farm.'

Arthur Boyce's lips tightened to a thin, pink line of disapproval. 'Emily, how many times do I have to tell you that you and Caroline must keep yourselves aloof from the villagers? Young Samuel is a *miner* and miners are ... well, let us say that they have "a certain reputation". As my daughters – and nieces of a peer of the realm who is also one of Her Majesty's most trusted ministers – you and Caroline are expected to set an example to others and have morals that are beyond reproach.'

'I wouldn't have thought there was anything immoral in going with others to look at a litter of kittens, Father. Certainly nothing to put Uncle Percy's reputation in danger.'

'Do not be obtuse, Emily. You are well aware of my meaning – and although those with whom you have unfortunately been associating may say "wouldn't" in their speech, I expect you to say "would not". Your poor, dear mother would agree with me, were she still alive.'

It was unfair of her father to bring her mother into the argument and tears suddenly burned Emily's eyes. Nevertheless, she had done nothing of which to be ashamed. She believed her mother, at least, would have agreed with her.

For over an hour Emily argued her case, although she knew from bitter experience there was no hope of persuading her father that he was wrong. Arthur Boyce regularly reminded his children that the Boyces were a family of considerable breeding; his brother a peer of the realm. He himself was a local magistrate and had been educated at Eton college, the most exclusive and prestigious school in England, his fees paid by another relative, knighted for diplomatic services in India.

Reverend Boyce had always insisted on his children remaining aloof from parishioners, even when carrying out the charitable duties expected of them.

Emily, perhaps more than her sister, found her father's narrow-minded bigotry intolerable, which *might* have had something to do with Sam Hooper. Emily was far more attracted to Sam Hooper than she was willing to admit to anyone – including Sam himself.

The outcome of today's argument between father and daughter was never in doubt. Arthur Boyce's strength in debate had been lauded at university. More recently it had been recognised by his bishop with an archdeaconship.

Nevertheless, Emily could be extremely stubborn when she believed right to be on her side and she refused to admit defeat until her father brought the argument to an end with a statement that left her stunned.

'I am deeply saddened that you should choose to defy me on a matter of such importance, Emily. As the youngest of my daughters I feel you have unfortunately been showered with more affection than is good for you. Perhaps there should have been less affection and a little more discipline. Fortunately, your regrettable indiscretion in this particular matter will soon be brought to an end and village gossip silenced once and for all.'

'What do you mean?' demanded Emily. Still angry

she was nevertheless puzzled by his statement. 'If you intend dismissing Sam from the church choir for being a friend to me, tongues will wag even more. It will certainly not prevent me from speaking to him whenever we chance to meet.'

Before the reverend could reply, there came an urgent knocking on the study door and Maude called out to her employer. Arthur Boyce frowned angrily, but before he could tell the housekeeper to go away, she opened the door.

Looking flustered, Maude said, 'Young Donald Rowse has just run here from the village. There's been an accident up at the South Caradon mine. He doesn't know how serious it is, but says they're calling in miners to go and help. He said you'd want to know. I sent Donald off to catch the pony, then get out the trap and harness-up for you.'

The dramatic news brought Emily a respite from her father's displeasure. As the parson of a copper-mining parish it was his duty to attend the scene of a mine accident. There would undoubtedly be a number of Methodist ministers and lay preachers there and competition was keen between Church and Chapel in Cornwall. A Church of England vicar could not be seen to be tardy when such disasters occurred.

Emily knew her father would not forget the matter of Samuel Hooper. He would return to the subject of her innocent indiscretion as soon as an opportunity presented itself. However, right now there were far more important matters to be addressed. Even the smallest mine accident affected a disproportionate number of households in an area where so many families were connected by marriage. In the difficult times currently being experienced in the mining industry, an accident might decide the future of a whole community.

The South Caradon mine was where Sam worked. Because he had been at church that morning Emily knew he would not have been caught up in the accident, but he would be one of those going underground to help in the rescue work. She would be concerned for him until she knew he was safely back on the surface.

II

Riding in the pony-trap, Emily and her father overtook many women and children, all hurrying in the direction of the South Caradon mine. No one yet knew what they would find when they arrived, but few were making the journey for the first time. Such tragedies had always been a part of mining life, but recently they had been occurring with a frightening frequency.

One reason was that the copper mines of Bodmin Moor were going through a lean period. The price of copper had slumped and men were being laid off. Mine 'adventurers' – the shareholders who owned the mines – were not willing to deplete dwindling profits by throwing away money on safety measures for a dying mine.

As a result, Emily had found herself playing an increasing role in such tragedies. When a body was brought to the surface, she would try to provide what comfort she could to the women and children of the dead miner's family. This was a duty she found more harrowing than any other.

Nevertheless, despite her aversion to the task, it was one she performed well, possessing as she did a genuine and natural sympathy for the bereaved.

Not all the women they passed had men working at the South Caradon mine. Nevertheless, their presence at the scene of a tragedy was expected. In return they would receive similar sympathy and support from others should their own menfolk become involved in a mine accident.

As the pony and trap reduced speed to pass through a knot of villagers who were slow to move off the road, Reverend Boyce momentarily forgot his displeasure with his daughter.

Annoyed with the women, he made the observation that if the miners of the South Caradon mine had observed the Sabbath in an appropriate way, such an accident might never have occurred.

Emily's own opinion was that had the adventurers been less concerned with profit-making there would have been no need for Sunday working. However, she kept such thoughts to herself. She did not want to become involved in yet another argument with her bigoted father.

A rapidly growing crowd, comprised mainly of women and children, was gathered around the head of the main mine shaft. Many men from the area had emigrated in recent years, leaving their families behind to cope as best they could. The few men present today were mainly aged or invalids, unable to either work or emigrate.

Bringing the pony to a halt, Reverend Arthur Boyce handed the reins to a young boy from St Cleer before making his way to where the mine captain stood talking to two adventurers, both of whom were local landowners.

Emily hurried to where she could see Rose Holman, the young wife of the Methodist minister, standing among a group of silent, anxious women. These, Emily knew, would be women who had men working underground.

'Is the news bad?'

Emily put the question to Rose in a low voice. Despite their allegiances to different religions, each woman knew and respected the other. Sadly, their mutual respect had grown from just such occasions as this.

'We don't know.'

Pretty and dark haired, Rose had been born and brought up in a moorland mining community. She had witnessed many mine tragedies, even before meeting and marrying her preacher husband.

'There's been a roof fall, but nobody's yet come up to grass to tell us how bad it is. 'Tis fortunate it's happened on a Sunday, I suppose. There are still many men who won't work on a Sunday, even though they might need to tighten their belts a notch or two because of it.'

The two women conversed quietly for a few minutes before Emily hurried to the aid of a distraught and heavily pregnant woman. Her three-year-old daughter had just fallen and grazed an elbow and both knees.

The mother, no older than Emily, was close to tears and seemed unable to cope with the child. Taking charge of the small girl, who parted tearfully and reluctantly with the information that her name was

Primrose, Emily brushed off the grazed joints, before tying her own handkerchief around a knee that was dribbling blood.

'There, that's better, isn't it?' When the young child looked at Emily doubtfully, she added, 'You've been such a brave girl that when your knee is better Mummy can wash the handkerchief and you may have it for your very own.'

Primrose gave Emily a fleeting smile before limping away stiff-legged to proudly show off the makeshift bandage to a young friend.

'Thank you kindly, Miss Boyce,' the child's mother said gratefully. 'I'd have tended to her myself, but I'm finding bending down a bit difficult right now. I've only got another two weeks to go – that's if all this don't bring it on quicker.'

The woman looked frightened. Emily was aware her name was Jean Spargo, but she knew very little else about her. 'Is your husband down there?' she asked sympathetically.

Jean Spargo nodded. 'Him and his brother. It's the first Sunday they've ever worked. We're Methodist, you see. Their father's a lay preacher.'

She spoke apologetically, as though half expecting Emily to walk away because she was not a member of Reverend Boyce's congregation.

When there was no immediate reaction to her disclosure, she added, 'Phillip's pa told him he'd offend the Lord by working on the Sabbath.' Her voice broke as she continued, '"Six days may work be done, but in the seventh is the sabbath of rest, holy to the Lord. Whosoever doeth any work in the sabbath day, he shall surely be put to death." That's what his pa told him. I remember every word, but Phillip wouldn't listen. He told his pa he had a family to provide for and the Lord would understand.' Brokenly, she added, 'I hope he was right.'

'Hush! You must not upset yourself. We don't know what's happened down there, or who – if anyone – has been hurt.'

Even as she spoke there was a stir among those crowding around the head of the shaft. The man-engine had clanked into action. The women pressed forward as the wheel commenced to spin, winding on cable attached to a cage designed to carry men to and from their work below ground.

When the cage came into view and stopped, it disgorged three passengers. Emily realised with a start that one of them was Sam. He was so filthy she had not immediately recognised him.

All three men stood squinting uncomfortably as the light of the early summer afternoon replaced the gloom of the underground mine.

One of the first people Sam saw when his eyes became accustomed to the light was Emily. His expression softened momentarily and he began to walk towards her.

The mine captain was pushing his way through the crowd towards the shaft but Emily noted that her father was still talking to the adventurers. He did not appear to have noticed Sam.

She returned her gaze to the young miner just as he saw Jean Spargo and came to a sudden, uncertain halt. It was immediately apparent to Emily that the two knew each other. Rose Holman knew Sam too and it was she who spoke first.

'What's happening down below, Sam? Has anyone been hurt?'

'I'm afraid so.' He spoke carefully, avoiding the eyes of the pregnant woman. 'There are two dead, but no one else seems to be hurt.'

'Is my Phillip all right?'

It was a direct question and desperately though Sam wished he could avoid giving an answer, he could not.

'I . . . I'm sorry, Jean. He was caught by the roof fall. Him and Wesley . . .' Wesley was Phillip's brother. 'They would have known nothing . . .'

It was doubtful whether the young pregnant woman heard his final sentence. Swaying alarmingly for a moment or two, her head suddenly fell back and she crumpled to the ground.

Emily succeeded in preventing her head from striking the muddy ground, but she could not avoid falling to the ground with her.

The next few minutes were filled with confusion. As Primrose screamed, she, her mother, Rose and Emily were hemmed in by a crowd of concerned women.

While some attempted to revive their cruelly widowed neighbour, others offered loud and contradictory advice on how best this might be achieved.

Holding the thoroughly frightened child to her, Emily struggled free of the crowd – and came face-to-face with her father.

Before he could speak, she said, 'The wife of one of the men who has been killed has fainted. She's heavily pregnant. This is her little girl. I am taking care of her while her mother is revived and helped to her home.'

Arthur Boyce was not an altogether unfeeling man,

but he felt uncomfortable surrounded by noisy, grieving women. 'Very well, Emily. Er ... my pony and
trap are at the woman's disposal should it be of help,
but I need to be back at St Cleer for the evening
service ...'

The pony and trap were not needed. The women
acquired a stretcher upon which Jean Spargo was
placed. Then, carried by two men and two women, it
was hurried away to her home in a nearby hamlet.

Primrose seemed to have been overlooked in the
general commotion. Thoroughly confused by everything happening about her she clung to Emily, sobbing
uncontrollably. Holding her close, Emily hurried after
those carrying Jean Spargo.

The home of Primrose and her mother was a one-
up, one-down terraced house beside the mineral railway line, along which was carried ore from the mines
to the small South Cornish port of Looe.

Although small, the house was clean and well-kept
and Emily saw sad little domestic traces of the dead
miner. One was a home-made pipe rack, fastened to
the wall beside the fireplace, containing a variety of
clay pipes. Another was a half-completed carved
wooden doll lying on a shelf.

Primrose had ceased crying now and wanted to be
reunited with her mother, who had been taken upstairs
to the only bedroom. However, there was so much
coming-and-going in the house that Emily felt obliged
to keep the child downstairs with her for the time being.

Suddenly there was the sound of raised voices from
the bedroom, followed by a cry of, 'Quick! The baby's
coming!', and Rose came hurrying down the stairs to
organise a supply of hot water.

Seeing Emily, she said, 'This is no place for an unmarried girl, Emily. You'd best be getting on home.'

'What about Primrose?' The child had become frightened by the increased activity and raised voices. 'She's asking for her mother.'

'It's no place for her either,' declared Rose. 'My sister lives not far away. She has two children of her own. Primrose will be all right with her. I'll send someone round there with her right away.'

From upstairs there came the sound of a woman's voice crying out with pain and Rose said hurriedly, 'Here, give her to me. I'll take her now, before she becomes even more frightened. Jean's baby is pushing hard to come into the world, even though she's not ready for it yet. It won't be easy for her. Come on, Primrose. You get off home right away, Emily. If you stay here listening to what's going on up there you'll be put off for ever from having a family of your own.'

III

Leaving the terraced cottage behind her, Emily chose a path that would take her around the side of the hill that had given its name to the mine. Caradon hill stood guard overlooking Bodmin Moor's southern boundary. It had been the site chosen by King Charles the first to muster his army before he led it to a notable victory against Parliamentarian forces during the Civil War, more than two hundred years before.

The course of the path along which Emily was walking had been trodden by the feet of countless generations of Cornish miners, men who would have witnessed many such tragedies as she had just left behind her.

Eyes cast down, she was wondering what the future held for Jean Spargo and her young daughter. Then, passing a large clump of yellow-flowering gorse, Emily looked up and saw Sam.

He was seated on a large rock of freestone granite scarred by long-dead hard-rock miners. They had practised their rock-drilling skills on it, using a hammer and spade-ended boring tools.

Sam was still as dirty as when he appeared on the surface of the man-engine shaft at the South Caradon mine. He looked weary and despondent.

'Hello, Emily. Is Jean all right?'

'Not really. She's gone into labour, although Rose doesn't think it's her time just yet.'

'Poor Jean.' When Sam shook his head his weariness was more pronounced. Unhappily, he added, 'She's going to have a hard time of it with two young 'uns and no man to take care of her.'

'Do you know her well?' Emily didn't know why she asked this question.

He nodded. 'There was a time when her ma and mine thought we would marry. Then Phillip came along and she had eyes for no one else from then on. They thought the world of each other.'

'Now she has lost Phillip and will have two young children to support. Perhaps she will turn to you once more.'

Sam shook his head. 'We're neither of us the person we were all those years ago. Besides, even if I did feel that way about her, I couldn't bear to spend the rest of my life knowing I was second best to the ghost of a man who had been my best friend.' He gave her a wan smile. 'I was pleased to see you there helping her, though. She needed someone around who could show some commonsense when it was wanted. I hope everything goes well for her with the baby. It's all very, very sad. She and Phillip were so looking forward to the birth. Primrose was too, but, fortunately, she's too small to know very much about what's going on.'

'She's a delightful little girl,' said Emily. Her concern shifting to Sam, she said, 'It must have been horrible for you to be among those who found her father.'

'It was . . . but let's not talk about it any more. I saw Parson Boyce go home alone with the pony and trap and waited here hoping you might take this way home. I've got a special reason for wanting to speak to you.'

As they began to walk along the path together, Sam continued, 'Things have been bad at the South Caradon mine for weeks now. I reckon this accident has put the seal on its fate. Cap'n Rowe told me before I came away just now that the adventurers will probably be shutting the mine down.'

Emily looked at him in concern. 'What will you do?' She was aware that none of the other mines were taking on men. Those mines still working had a hundred men chasing every vacancy.

Sam looked unhappy. 'Pa was talking to me about that only today, Emily, just before the accident happened. In fact, we've spoken about it many times before. We've all known the mine didn't have much life left in it, what with the price of copper being so low. Pa wants me to go to Australia. My Uncle Wilf is there, at a place called Kadina. His letters are full of the marvellous life he has. He says it's a great new country where a man can carve out a good future for himself if he's willing to work hard – and I've never been afraid of hard work.'

'You are not *seriously* considering going all the way to Australia?' Emily was dismayed. Regardless of her father's ban she had been quite determined that she would not stop seeing Sam – and there was much more to her determination than natural stubbornness. If he emigrated to Australia there was little possibility they would ever meet again.

'I have very little choice, Emily.'

'Of course you have! There are other mines. You are a good miner – and a local man. You'll find work.' She spoke with an optimism she knew was ill-founded.

Sam knew it too and he shook his head. 'By the end of the year almost all the Bodmin Moor copper mines will have shut down. There'll be hundreds of men – married men, most of them – chasing every job that's on offer.'

'But ... you don't need to depend entirely upon mining. Your father has a farm. He can find work for you.'

Despite her resolve not to let Sam realise how much she thought of him, Emily now came close to desperation as the knowledge that he was likely to go out of her life for ever sank in. In truth, he was the only really close friend she had. Being the daughter of a vicar, especially one who was a social snob, was a lonely life in such a poverty-stricken area.

'There's no money to be made from farming in these parts unless miners are making money and buying farm produce. As it is, half the wage-earners have emigrated. The families they've left behind are only half a step ahead of starvation. Pa is a caring man, Emily, he's already giving away more than the farm is making. I'd be just an extra burden for him to bear.'

Emily realised that nothing she could say to Sam was going to make any difference. It seemed his mind was made up. She would need to face up to the fact she was going to lose him.

'When do you think you will be leaving?'

'As soon as a passage can be arranged and that won't be very long. Pa had me do all the paperwork and get references some time ago – just in case. He says ships are leaving from Falmouth and Plymouth every week and Cornish miners and their families are being offered free passages. He's offered to give me enough money to see me started there. I've managed to put a little by too. It should see me all right for a while.'

As he unfolded his plans, Emily realised she was likely to lose him even sooner than she had anticipated. Somewhat bitterly, she said, 'You seem to have everything well worked out and are wasting no time about this.'

'That's Pa, not me. He's been thinking about it for a very long time. I believe he's even discussed it with Parson Boyce.'

Emily suddenly recalled the conversation she was having with her father when the news of the mine tragedy reached the vicarage; her father was smugly asserting that her friendship with Sam would soon be at an end. She wondered now whether the suggestion that Sam should go to Australia might have originated from her father and not from Sam's.

'When did your pa speak to my father about this?'

'I don't know. It must have been mentioned again

this morning though, because Pa had a list of sailings Parson Boyce gave him straight after church.'

Emily said nothing to Sam of her belief that her father had put the idea into Farmer Hooper's head. She remained silent for much of the remainder of the walk to the village. Nevertheless, inside she was very, very angry – and extremely hurt. It was even possible that her father had provided the money to finance Sam in his new life there.

IV

'I'm going to miss you, Sam. I know the whole choir will, but I feel I will miss you most of all. You are the only one I am able to really talk to about things.'

When he made no immediate reply, she added, 'It's not too late to change your mind, you know.'

Emily and Sam were seated side by side in the porch of St Cleer's ancient church. Choir practice had ended twenty minutes before and darkness was lowering over the village, yet neither Sam nor Emily was in a hurry to go to their respective home.

It was a Friday evening, almost five weeks after the accident at the South Caradon mine. Sam was to leave for the emigration depot at Plymouth on Sunday, and would be setting sail for Australia only a day or two later.

'I couldn't change my mind now, Emily. Besides, three more mines have closed this week. Mining has collapsed in the whole of Cornwall. It's finished – and this time I'm convinced it's for good. Miners will be fighting for places on emigrant ships before long.'

Despite the misery she felt because he was leaving, Emily knew Sam was right. Things were so bad she had been helping her father write letters to Church leaders and prominent businessmen in other parts of the country. Arthur Boyce was calling for donations to help feed the impoverished families of thousands of out-of-work Cornish miners.

'Why did you come to choir practice tonight, Sam? You won't be singing in church on Sunday – or any other day.'

'I don't really know. I suppose it's because I've got so used to coming here every Friday. Anyway, although I'd said "goodbye" to most of the others, I hadn't been able to see you. I couldn't go off without speaking to you.'

'I would never have forgiven you if you had!' Emily tried to make a joke but failed miserably.

'I'll miss you, especially,' he suddenly blurted out.

'Will you? Will you really?' she seized upon his words eagerly. 'You'll write to me?'

Sam fidgeted uncomfortably. 'My writing's not very good, Emily. I didn't get much schooling.'

This was an understatement of the facts. He could write his name, but little more than that.

Emily should have been aware of this and she was angry with herself for causing him embarrassment. 'But . . . you'll be keeping in touch with your parents somehow. Will you ask whoever writes letters for you to include a message for me, please?'

'If you'd really like me to.'

'I would, Sam. I *really* would.'

'Will Parson Boyce allow you to have a message from me?'

'Why shouldn't he?' she replied sharply.

He shrugged his shoulders, the gesture barely visible in the gathering darkness. 'Pa said the parson had spoken to him about village gossip. It seems he made it very clear he doesn't approve of me.'

'Father disapproves of most people – *me* especially – but when did this conversation take place?'

'I don't know exactly. A few months ago, at least.'

'About the time when your father first suggested you should go to Australia?'

'It might have been . . .' Sam suddenly realised why she was asking the questions. 'You're not suggesting the two things are connected? I'm sure they're not. Pa has said many times that there's nothing in Cornwall for a young man, especially if he works on the mines.'

Emily was less convinced than Sam that her father had nothing to do with his forthcoming exile, but she realised she would probably never learn the truth of it.

'At what time on Sunday are you actually leaving St Cleer?'

'About ten in the morning. Pa's taking me in the light farmcart as far as Liskeard. I'll be catching a train from there to Plymouth to board the boat.'

'That's very early,' Emily said unhappily. 'I was hoping I might be able to see you before you left.'

'Why don't you come to see me tomorrow?' Sam suggested eagerly. 'Friends and family will be dropping in at the farm all day to have a drink, a bite to eat, and to wish me well. You'd be made very welcome if you could come.'

Emily shook her head, a gesture that was lost in the darkness. 'I couldn't get away. My sister Caroline is returning home tomorrow and Maude has been given the day off to visit her sister. Besides, my father will be home all day. I'm only able to stay talking to you this evening because he is at a diocesan meeting in Bodmin. Even so, I had better go now, or Maude will tell him I was late returning from choir practice and I'll be in trouble once again.'

She rose to her feet and Sam followed suit. As they stood close together in the narrow church porch, he said, 'I'll walk home with you.'

'No!' Emily had not intended to sound quite so vehement and she quickly added, 'The chapel meeting will be turning out about now. Preacher Garland would love to be able to tell Father I had been seen walking in the dark with you.'

Preacher Garland was a lay preacher who had taken it upon himself to crusade against the twin evils of alcohol and a reprehensible lack of morals among the young.

'Then I suppose I'd better say goodbye to you here and now.'

Sam held out his hand to her but Emily could not see it. Beside, she had other plans. Her heart beating alarmingly fast, she said, 'You may kiss me, if you wish.'

His feet shuffled on the stone-paved floor as he moved towards her, then his breath brushed against her cheek as he gave her a glancing kiss.

Emily's experience of kissing had so far been restricted to perfunctory greetings given to her by older family members. Not certain exactly what she had been expecting from Sam, she was yet aware of a feeling of disappointment.

With a boldness that would have horrified her father, she said quietly, 'Is that the best you can do, Sam

Hooper? Is that how your Daniel would have kissed Bessie Mitchell?'

The questions were extremely provocative, as Emily well knew. Daniel was Sam's older brother. His passion for Bessie had been the talk of the village, providing a subject for more than one of Preacher Garland's highly critical sermons.

It had come as no surprise to anyone when Bessie became pregnant and the young couple were obliged to marry. They had been married for little more than three years now and had three young children, yet none of the passion had faded from their relationship.

Sam was standing very close to Emily and instead of replying he reached out and pulled her to him.

This time the kiss was all she had anticipated – and more. It seemed to her that every nerve and fibre she possessed was responding to the nearness of his body as she strained against him.

Suddenly, they heard the sound of voices and the spell was broken.

Guiltily, they stood back from each other as the voices drew nearer. Emily's confused emotions untangled themselves and she felt a very real fear. If the voices belonged to her father's churchwardens, coming to the church for some reason, she would be in serious trouble. Not merely for being here alone with Sam, but also for deliberately flouting her father's explicit order that she was not to have anything more to do with him.

Holding her breath, she sensed that Sam was doing the same.

Then the owners of the voices passed by the porch entrance – two miners from a nearby hamlet, taking a shortcut through the churchyard on their way to work on the nightshift at one of Bodmin Moor's few remaining working mines.

Emily and Sam breathed out their relief, yet both were aware it would be impossible to recapture the magic of the moment they had just experienced.

'You'd better be getting home before someone comes looking for you.' Sam spoke the words reluctantly. 'I suppose I should be on my way too, it's going to be a busy day tomorrow.'

'Yes,' Emily agreed, with equal reluctance. Miserably, she added, 'I know I won't be able to see you again, Sam, but take care of yourself and please find some way of letting me know where you are and what you are doing.'

'I'll try,' he promised. 'But let me walk you home . . .'

'No,' she said, more firmly than she felt. 'We've said our goodbyes now. We must not risk having villagers see us together and causing more trouble than they have already. Take care, Sam – and God go with you.'

She kissed him once more, but this time it was a brief, almost perfunctory gesture.

Before he could make a move to stop her, she turned and fled into the darkness, taking a path that would lead her to the vicarage.

Left alone, Sam listened to the sound of her running feet until he could hear them no more. Then, feeling very confused and experiencing an increasing sense of frustration and unhappiness, he reluctantly turned his back on the church and made his way home, but he went far more slowly than had Emily.

V

For much of the day before Sam left St Cleer, members of his large family came from miles around, joining with many friends to bid him farewell and wish him a safe journey and success on the far side of the world.

All considered it highly unlikely they would ever meet with him again. The advent of steam had made crossing the oceans of the world less hazardous than in earlier years, but they knew from their experience of the many men who had emigrated from Cornwall during the recent lean years that very few returned to resume life in their native land. Most either sent for their families to join them or regularly remitted money to those they had left behind. Others were never heard from again.

Among those who flocked to the farm were women who had seen loved ones depart never to return, and, ignorant of the vastness of the country to which Sam was voyaging, they pressed letters upon him, urging him to deliver them personally, to places as far apart as Tasmania, Queensland and Kalgoorlie.

They brought presents for him too. Small and simple gifts for the most part. A kerchief, belt, pencil, socks – and a book, for which he gave polite thanks to the donor, even though he could not read it. There was also a hairbrush, a razor – and even a cake, baked for him by a great-aunt. She declared that the farther a man travelled, the more he would appreciate good whole-some home-cooking.

Sam would have been quite content to forego the farewells of both family and friends. Most, after a few solemn words, stood around in small, mildly embarrassed groups, food and drink in hand, talking loudly to each other.

Many of the more distantly related members of the family had not seen him since he was a small child. However, saying farewell to an emigrating relative, no matter how distant, was a duty that could not be shirked. It was as important an occasion as a birth, christening or funeral.

Sam was about to leave Cornwall and all he had ever known, crossing the ocean to make a new life among strangers. It was incumbent upon them to come to his home and offer good wishes.

Their numbers took Sam by surprise and spoiled his own plans. He had been hoping there would be an opportunity to spend a little time at the church, and that Emily might be there. Or that she would see him from the vicarage and find an excuse to sneak away from the house and meet him, if only for a few minutes.

Their parting the previous evening had left him in a very confused state of mind. A strong, unspoken bond between him and Emily had gradually grown up over the months – perhaps years, even – yet he had always been painfully aware of their vastly different stations in life.

For this reason he had thought it impossible there could ever be anything more than friendship between them.

Until last night.

In the church porch, Emily had done what he had never dared contemplate. Her actions had been so unexpected he still found it difficult to believe it had really happened.

Since then she had occupied as much of his thoughts

as the forthcoming voyage to Australia and the events of the day would allow. He wondered whether she would ever have behaved in such a manner had his imminent departure not meant their relationship could never go any further.

He dismissed such thoughts. She had made him promise to get news to her of where he was and what he was doing. Why should she do that if nothing was likely to come of it?

Had Emily been anyone else and not the daughter of Parson Boyce, he would have called on her today and asked her how she *really* felt about him.

Had her reply promised a future together he would have deferred his emigration . . .

But this was no more than foolish conjecture. Emily was . . . who she was. Emily Boyce, daughter of the Reverend Arthur Boyce, vicar of St Cleer and niece of Lord Boyce, an important minister in the government of England. He, Sam, was the son of a poor moorland farmer. A miner, unable to read or write . . .

'Hello, Sam.'

A soft voice broke into his thoughts. He turned to see Jean Spargo standing beside him, holding the hand of Primrose.

'Jean! It's very nice of you to come here.' Suddenly remembering, he said, 'I was sorry to hear about the baby . . .'

The child, a boy, had lived for only a few hours.

'I was at Phillip's funeral, but never had an opportunity to speak to you.'

'I saw you, Sam, but was still feeling so ill I didn't want to talk to anyone – but I haven't come to say good-bye.'

'No?' Her statement puzzled him. 'What then?'

'I'm going to Australia too, me and Primrose – and to the same place as you, to Kadina, although I didn't know *you* were going there until last night.'

'But ... why are *you* going there? I would have thought you would have wanted to stay here, in Cornwall, where you know people.'

'I have no one here in Cornwall, Sam – not now. At least, no one who's close. Besides, everywhere I turn I'm reminded of Phillip. I decided I'd go to Australia to my pa. If you remember, when my ma died at the same time as your aunt, he and your uncle Wilf went off to Australia together. I had letters from him saying how well he's doing and what a wonderful place Australia is. There haven't been any letters just lately, but I'd have heard if anything had happened to him. He always wanted me and Phillip to go out there and join him, but Phillip didn't want to leave Cornwall. Now he's dead there's nothing to keep me here.'

Her news was so unexpected Sam hardly knew what to say. 'It's an incredible coincidence that we should be going to the same place, Jean, but ... when are *you* leaving?'

'Tomorrow, Sam. We're sailing for Port Adelaide on the *Bonython*, the same as you. I was just talking to your pa about it. He's said that if me and Primrose are here by ten o'clock in the morning he'll take us to Liskeard with you in the cart to catch the train.'

At that moment Primrose pulled away from her mother. She ran to where two children, a year or two older than herself, were being shown one of the kittens that had been the cause of Emily's confrontation with her father some weeks before.

After satisfying herself that Primrose would come to no harm with the other children and the kitten, Jean turned back to Sam once more. 'You don't know what a relief it will be having you close at hand on the ship, Sam. I was dreading the thought of going all that way with Primrose, knowing no one. I'm not sure you'll be as pleased to have *us* travelling with *you*, but I promise I'll not allow Primrose and me to be a burden ...'

At that moment Primrose let out a scream as the kitten, pulled from one child to another, put out its claws and scratched the little girl.

As Jean hurried to her daughter, Sam watched her go with mixed feelings. It *would* be nice to travel with someone he knew – and he and Jean had been friends for a very long time. However, despite Jean's assurance, he had an uneasy feeling that she and Primrose *would* prove to be an unexpected and not entirely welcome responsibility on the long journey to South Australia.

VI

Jean and Primrose arrived at the Hooper farm more than an hour before Sam and his immediate family were due to leave for Liskeard.

Although Jean protested that she and Primrose were not hungry, they did full justice to the meal placed in front of them by Sam's mother.

In truth, they were unused to eating well. Raising money for the expenses they would incur on a voyage to Australia had not been easy for the young widow. The sale of her household effects and those of her late husband had not fetched as much as she had expected and Phillip's workmates had been able to spare little for the collection made on her behalf.

In the recent uncertain times, she and Primrose had often gone short of food. Being hungry was no new experience for either of them. However, the little money she carried with her would have to last for at least three months – more if they did not immediately locate her father.

But Jean tried not to think of the hardships that lay ahead. She and Primrose were setting off to begin a new life. One devoid of poverty and despair – or so her father had declared in his letters.

Eventually, it was time to set off. Clutching their pitifully scant possessions, mother and daughter settled themselves on the farm wagon, together with Sam, his luggage and members of his family.

Many friends had gathered to wave them on their way, but Sam was deeply disappointed that Emily was not included among their number. He realised it would have been very difficult for her, but he had hoped she might find a way to come and see him off.

Other friends were also absent. Good friends he had known for many years and who had sung with him and Emily in the choir. He tried, unsuccessfully, not to be too hurt by their absence.

Sam's father called for the well-wishers to stand clear. When they obeyed, he shook out the reins and urged the horse into motion.

The wagon creaked away to the cheers of the friends Sam was leaving behind and with a number of excited young children running beside it.

The journey took them through St Cleer village. As they approached the church, Farmer Hooper was forced to bring the wagon to a halt, the road blocked by a group of people – the church choir.

As wagon and horse stopped, the choir started to sing a hymn that began 'For the dear ones parted from us'. Listening to the words, tears stung Sam's eyes, but when the hymn came to an end and the members of the choir gathered around the farm wagon to voice their farewells, he had eyes for only one of their number – and Emily held his gaze.

She was the last person to grasp his hand. Remembering the previous occasion on which they had met, he would have wished for something more demonstrative than a handshake. However, he realised she dared make no show of affection in front of so many witnesses.

As it was, she held his hand for a dangerously long time, at the same time pressing something into it.

'Take care of yourself, Sam, and don't forget to let us know how things are going for you in Australia.'

Closing his hand upon the as-yet-unseen object she had placed there, he said, 'I won't forget, Emily. I won't forget anything.'

His low-spoken words gave Emily more pleasure than he would ever know; at the same time she hoped that none of those hearing them would detect their hidden meaning.

'All right, everybody, stand clear, we have to be on our way,' Farmer Hooper called out to the choir. Moments later horse and wagon were on the move once more.

Sam and the others in the wagon waved furiously until the well-wishers disappeared from view.

Not until now did Sam open his hand to discover he was holding a gold crucifix. It was one Emily had frequently worn on a delicate gold chain about her neck. It had been a present from her late mother.

Sam was aware how much Emily valued the crucifix. It was proof, beyond any doubt, that Emily's feelings for him went far beyond friendship. He wished there was some way he could have thanked her properly for giving him such a valuable and treasured farewell present.

He had thought the gift had gone unnoticed by the others, but Jean caught a glimpse of it when he unclenched his hand. Now she said quietly, 'That's a very nice thing to be given, Sam.'

'It's very generous,' he agreed. 'Far too generous, she shouldn't have done it.'

'Is Emily Boyce your sweetheart?'

The direct question was so unexpected that for a few moments Sam floundered for a reply. Finally, he said, 'She's a friend. A very good friend, that's all. She couldn't be anything else when she's the daughter of the parson, could she?'

He was saved from further questioning because at that moment the wagon came up with a party comprising two women and five children, trudging along the road. Each, including the smallest child, was struggling with a bundle of possessions.

Bringing horse and wagon to a halt, Farmer Hooper called out, 'Are you all going to Liskeard?'

When the women said they were, he invited them to accept a ride on the wagon.

They clambered on board eagerly and a small boy settled himself beside Sam. Hugging a lumpy bundle, the child glanced at Sam uncertainly once or twice before suddenly blurting out, 'I'm going to see my dad.'

'Are you now?' Sam smiled at him. 'And where is he?'

The answer to this simple question seemed beyond the capabilities of the small boy and he looked to one of the girls, perhaps twice his age, for an answer.

'He's in Australia,' she replied. 'Him and our uncle. They're working on a mine. We're going to live with them again. These are our cousins . . .'

She indicated the other children, who were all within a year or two of her own age.

'Why, that's where we're going too,' said Sam. 'Where in Australia are you bound?'

It was the beginning of an excited conversation which soon involved children and adults. The newcomers had walked from North Hill, a village some miles distant, on the edge of Bodmin Moor. They too were sailing from Plymouth, but on a different ship, their destination mines on the eastern side of Australia.

It seemed to Jean that if the present exodus continued there would be no one left in Cornwall in a few years' time.

2

'I wonder what Jean Spargo and Primrose were doing in the wagon with Sam?'

When the Hooper farm wagon passed from view Emily put the question to a choir member as they filed into church to prepare for the Sunday morning service.

'They're off to Australia too,' said the girl to whom she had spoken. 'Jean's father's out there. He's all the family she has now. There's her husband's family, of course, but it's not the same. Mind you, I think she'd have done better to stay here, but it's none of my business and blood's thicker than water, or so they say.'

'I'm surprised Sam never said anything when he came to choir practice,' Emily persisted.

The thought of Sam travelling all the way to Australia in the company of Jean Spargo troubled her. Sam and the young widow had once been close – and Jean was a very attractive woman.

'To tell you the truth, I don't think he knew,' said another of the choir members who had overheard the brief conversation. 'Jean was at the farewell party given at the Hooper farm yesterday. I believe he learned only then. Mind you, I doubt if he'll mind too much, Jean's a fine-looking woman. Any red-blooded man would be happy to spend a few months in her company.'

'Sam will need to watch himself,' another choir member chipped in. 'Jean Spargo's "chapel". If he shows too much of an interest she'll have him standing with her in front of the altar before he knows what's happening.'

The talk moved on from Jean Spargo. Minutes later the choir began to prepare for the service, but for the remainder of that morning Emily found it very difficult to concentrate on spiritual matters.

After the service Emily waited for her father and they walked back to the vicarage together.

Arthur Boyce said very little until they neared the vicarage gate. Then, well out of hearing of members of the congregation walking in a similar direction, he said sternly, 'Did I see you talking to Samuel Hooper before the service?'

Emily started guiltily. Her thoughts at that very moment had been of Sam. Defensively, she said, 'Yes, the choir sang a hymn for him, to wish him well on his long journey.'

'Very laudable,' said her father with unashamed insincerity. 'However, it might have been more judicious of you to have allowed the other choir members to say their farewells without you.'

Stopping in her tracks, Emily looked at her father in

disbelief. 'Are you saying I must distance myself from the other members of the choir now?'

'Of course not . . . Well, not when they are singing for my services. The choir is much admired by the congregation and I am, of course, delighted that you play such an active part in church activities. However, you need to remain aloof from the others when you are outside the church. After all . . .'

'I know . . .' Emily's bitterness spilled into the open, 'they are not suitable companions for the daughter of the vicar of the parish.'

'Not just because I am the parish priest, Emily, but also because you are the niece of one of Her Majesty's ministers . . .'

As he spoke, Emily silently mouthed the oft-repeated words in time with her father.

'We must remember at all times that we are all of us joint guardians of Uncle Percy's reputation.'

'I doubt whether Uncle Percy's reputation is so fragile that it would be endangered by my singing with a village church choir to bid farewell to a fellow member who was emigrating to Australia,' Emily said scornfully.

'Gossip is an insidious thing, Emily, believe me. It will linger on long after Samuel Hooper has left these shores. I assure you that the reputation of one of my daughters is just as important to me as that of Uncle Percy.'

'Is it?' Emily's anger and frustration suddenly overtook caution. 'Is it really, Father? Is that why you sent John packing when he began to show an interest in Caroline? *He* was not damaging her reputation. Indeed, the villagers thought of the situation as highly romantic.

Everyone was delighted for both of them. Everyone but you.'

John Kavanagh had served as a young curate at St Cleer for some eighteen months, during which time he and Caroline had become increasingly fond of one another.

Reverend Boyce had been slow to observe such things for himself, but when a churchwarden made an innocent remark about Caroline and the young curate making 'a handsome couple', Arthur Boyce was quick to act.

There had been a stormy confrontation with the young curate, as a result of which John Kavanagh made a hurried departure. He took up a curacy in Yorkshire, after promising Parson Boyce he would make no attempt to contact Caroline for at least a year.

Caroline had been inconsolable for weeks after the departure of the young curate. Arthur Boyce had forbidden the mention of his name in the vicarage, but Caroline spoke of little else to her sister when their father was absent.

The year-long ban was almost at an end, but it seemed Arthur Boyce's unreasonable ruling had brought the innocent relationship to an end. No word had been received from him since his leaving. Although Emily knew her sister still pined for him, she had not mentioned his name for some months now.

'Is it really our reputation that is of concern to you, Father? Or is it the thought that both Caroline and I might find happiness elsewhere and leave you with only a housekeeper to take care of you in your bitter old age? If so, it is a very short-sighted view – and a selfish one. We could both provide you with grandchildren to bring a great deal of pleasure into your life.'

'How dare you make such an outrageous accusation, Emily! Your welfare, and that of Caroline, has always been my major concern since I lost your dear mother. I cannot even begin to imagine her distress were she alive to hear you speak to me in such a manner. I declare I am quite unable to face you across the dining table. You will go to your room immediately and remain there for the rest of the day.'

Angry that he had once again used a reference to her late mother in an attempt to deflect her, Emily said defiantly, 'Does that mean I am excused choir this evening?'

'It means you will do as I say and go to your room – *now*! If I have any more to say to you today I will say it there. Go!'

Still defiant, Emily entered the vicarage ahead of her father and made her way to her room.

In the kitchen, where she was preparing lunch in the absence of the housekeeper, Caroline heard Emily stomp her way up the stairs to her room and slam the door noisily. Then she heard the quieter sound of the closing of the study door and she knew her father had gone to have his pre-Sunday-lunch sherry.

Caroline realised there must have been words between her father and sister yet again. She guessed correctly it would have had to do with the departure from St Cleer of Sam Hooper. Caroline had hoped the relationship between Emily and their father might improve during her absence on holiday. She now realised it had been too much to hope for. Both possessed strong characters and each was too stubborn to give way to the other.

Caroline felt sorry for Emily. Despite her sister's reticence on the subject, she was aware of her feelings for Sam Hooper – and now he had gone from St Cleer for ever.

In common with Emily – and most of the villagers – Caroline did not doubt that Sam's departure had been engineered by their snobbish and domineering father, just as he had more openly sent John Kavanagh packing.

But John was still in England. Although he had kept his word to her father not to contact her for a year, he had ensured that mutual acquaintances kept her informed of all that was happening in his life.

She firmly believed that when the year's banishment came to an end John would return and provide her with the means of escaping from the unreasonable discipline imposed by the vicar of St Cleer upon his two daughters.

3

I

There was a number of departing emigrants waiting on the platform of Liskeard railway station by the time the train that would take them to Plymouth wheezed to a halt.

Tears mingled with blessings and good wishes as the departing miners and a few dependants struggled to escape from well-wishing friends and relatives and seek a seat on board.

Hanging precariously out of a carriage window, Sam's last memory of Liskeard station was of tearful faces gazing after the departing train and a forest of waving arms still bidding farewell when the train passed from view.

As Sam tugged on a leather strap to close the compartment window, Jean said, 'Now I feel we're *really* on our way.' Hugging Primrose to her, she added, 'Your ma and pa were very nice to us, Sam. I felt as though they were waving Primrose and me on our way too.'

'So they were,' said Sam. 'They know we're all travelling to Australia together and will be sharing whatever adventures happen along the way.'

Jean shivered. It was partly excitement, but there was apprehension too. 'It's an awful long way, Sam. I'm sure that if I'd had longer to think about it – I mean *really* think about it – I'd never have dared to make such a journey. I would probably pull out even now if you weren't travelling with us.'

'You'll be fine, Jean – you and Primrose,' he added hastily, embarrassed by the look she was giving him.

He was quite ready to give Jean all the help she needed on the long journey to Australia. Indeed, it was a great pleasure to have someone he knew so well travelling with him – but he had grown used to her in the role of wife to his friend Phillip. He had liked things that way. Besides, he had some thinking to do – about Emily.

There was a very wide gulf between their stations in life. Such a difference would have remained an insurmountable barrier in Cornwall, but he had been told that such social barriers did not exist in Australia.

If he worked hard and made good there, who knew what might be achieved?

When Sam, Jean and Primrose left the train at Plymouth they were at a loss about where they should go. However, the young boys of the busy seaport had long ago learned to turn the stream of emigrants passing through the city to their advantage. They crowded about the railway station in droves, offering to carry the baggage of the bewildered new arrivals to the migrants' transit depot – for a price.

However, such was the fierce competition for custom

that Sam was able to strike a bargain with a young lad who said his name was William, halving the asking price from a shilling and sixpence to ninepence.

The price agreed, their baggage was loaded on a small home-made handcart and they were soon walking through the streets of Plymouth in the company of the cheerful young Plymothian.

After telling them of the 'hundreds' of emigrants he had assisted on their way, William asked their destination. When told they were travelling to the port of Wallaroo, in South Australia, he commented, 'Then you'll be travelling on the *Bonython*. You'll find it's pretty crowded for families on this voyage.'

'Then it's just as well we're not a family,' Sam corrected him. 'Jean and Primrose will be in the family accommodation. I'm just a friend and will be in the single men's part of the ship.'

'That's going to be even more crowded,' William said. 'You'll need to be sure you find a good bunk for the voyage.'

'Do you know the ship?' Jean asked.

"Course I know her,' the boy declared scornfully. 'I knows all the ships that come in to Plymouth.'

Glancing speculatively at Sam, he added, 'Mind you, I know the *Bonython* better than most.'

'Oh, and why is that?' Sam was only mildly interested, being wrapped up in his own thoughts.

'Because the first mate is my uncle and the watchman who looks after the ship while it's in port is my grandad.'

Sam became more interested. 'If we tell this uncle of yours that we've met you, will we be given better treatment during the time we're on board?'

'That depends,' William replied obtusely.

'Depends on what?' Sam asked, aware the boy had a proposition in mind.

'On whether you'd like to put this baggage on board right away and choose your bunks before any of the others go on board.'

Sam had heard disconcerting rumours about the conditions they were likely to encounter on board a migrant ship. All the reports suggested the great advantage to be gained from knowing someone on board and becoming a 'privileged' passenger, but he remained cautious.

'How much is all this likely to cost?'

'Ten shillings. Five for my uncle and half a crown each for Grandad and me,' the boy said immediately.

Sam shook his head. 'I'm sorry, William, you're far too expensive for the likes of me. I'm just a poor, out-of-work Cornish miner – and Jean's a widow. We neither of us can afford to hand out such money. I can understand your uncle wanting five shillings, he's an important person, but two-and-six each for you and your grandpa is far too much. I suppose I could manage a shilling each for you, but that's all.'

William realised he had a prospective 'customer', albeit one inclined to haggle. However, he knew his uncle would give him a commission of sixpence for arranging the deal. He eventually agreed a price of seven shillings and sixpence, being five shillings for the mate and two-and-sixpence to be shared between himself and his grandfather.

It was money Sam would rather not have spent at this stage of the voyage, but he believed it would prove to be a worthwhile investment.

Content that he had concluded a profitable deal, William chatted happily to Sam and Jean for the remainder of the walk to the dock area where the *Bonython* was moored alongside a quay in Plymouth's Millbay Dock.

The ship was not yet ready to take on passengers. Until it was, prospective emigrants were being housed in a holding depot a short distance from where the ship, a barque of about eight hundred tons, was moored.

Jean looked at the three-masted wooden barque apprehensively. 'It's a lot smaller than I imagined it would be,' she said tremulously.

'She's bigger than a lot of ships sailing to Australia,' William declared defensively. 'A whole lot faster, too. Some of the ships take four months or more to get there. The *Bonython* can get there in three – more or less.'

Jean was appalled at the thought of her and Primrose spending three months of their life incarcerated in such a small vessel, but she kept such thoughts to herself.

At that moment William's grandfather came across the gangway from the ship to greet them.

When he heard they wished to choose their berths now, and the price they were willing to pay, the old man made a half-hearted attempt to increase his share from the arrangement. Fortunately, as Sam had correctly anticipated, there had been a dearth of emigrants with sufficient money to take advantage of William's offer.

The three prospective emigrants were taken on board to be introduced to the mate, a bluff Cornishman named Henry Hunkin.

After a whispered conversation with William, during the course of which money changed hands, the mate beamed at Sam and Jean and tweaked the cheek of

Primrose. After promising to help them in any way possible during the long voyage ahead, he left them in the care of the aged watchman and young William.

While Sam helped William bring their luggage on board, Jean and Primrose were taken below by the watchman to the centrehold where the families would be accommodated. Returning alone, the old man then preceded Sam down a steep ladder to the rear hold. Divided into two sections, with separate ladders leading to each part, this was where he and the other single men would be accommodated, single women being carried in the hold forward of the families.

Leading Sam to a bunk adjacent to a temporary bulkhead that separated the single men's accommodation from that occupied by families, the watchman said, 'Take the top bunk here, son.' Giving him a lewd wink, he added, 'Your friend and the young girl have the top bunk on the other side. As you can see, there's a gap between the deckhead and the partition. You'll be able to speak to each other through there. The gap's big enough for you to hold hands too if that's what you want, though you won't be able to get up to any mischief. Put what you'll need for the voyage on the bunk to stake your claim. William and I will take the rest of your things down below and make sure they're stowed clear of any bilge water.'

Sam was not entirely happy at trusting, on the recommendation of a Plymouth street urchin, all his worldly possessions to the care of a man he had not met before today and would probably never meet again but the die was cast. Besides, there was already property on some of the other bunks. He slung his bags on to the top bunk beside the bulkhead.

Half an hour later, their bunks reserved and their belongings safely stowed away, Sam, Jean and Primrose walked together towards the huge transit shed. Here they would spend the night after completing emigration formalities.

Jean was complaining of the accommodation on board the *Bonython*. 'It's so *cramped*!' she wailed. 'Primrose and me will be occupying the same bunk for all that time – and it's hardly the size of a single bed!'

'You're only entitled to a space of six feet by eighteen inches,' Sam explained. 'It's a good thing Primrose is no bigger than she is, or you'd have even less room.'

'It's so dark down there too,' Jean said unhappily. 'I don't know how we're going to survive such a long voyage, I really don't.'

'Do you want to return home?' Sam asked her. 'It's not too late. I'll give you the money for your train fare to Liskeard.'

Jean considered his offer for only a few moments. Then, shaking her head, she said miserably, 'There's nothing for us back on the moor. We'd likely starve if we were to go back there. At least we have the chance of some sort of future in Australia, although I wish I knew more about the country and the place we're going to.'

Sam felt much the same. It was an unknown country, but he said, 'We'll find out soon enough. My uncle says in his letters that with all the mines there are around Kadina, it's easy to imagine you're still in Cornwall – except that the pay's a whole lot better.'

II

The transit shed was a large, overcrowded building, where a couple of overworked men were kept busy checking the documents of would-be emigrants. Their task was to ensure that the departing men, women and children fulfilled conditions laid down by the South Australian immigration authorities.

Some of the prospective emigrants had been in the depot for four or five days. They were complaining that they should now be allowed on board the ship, which had almost completed taking on provisions for the voyage.

Jean did not strictly conform to the stated requirements, having no husband. However, her letters of suitability had been carefully worded to make it appear she would be joining a family already established in South Australia.

This in itself gave Sam a small niggle of concern. If Jean's father was not where Jean expected to find him – and miners had a habit of moving to other mines whenever the mood for a change took them – Sam had an uncomfortable feeling he would need to accept responsibility for her and Primrose for longer than planned.

It was not how he wanted to begin life in Australia.

In truth, he had given little thought to the details of what he would do in the new land. He knew there were mines there but his plans did not extend beyond finding work in the one where his uncle was working. All reports reaching England from South Australia indicated that the mine captains, most of whom were Cornish, were eager to employ miners arriving from the land they themselves had left behind.

* * *

By noon the following day, the last of the emigrants had arrived, all formalities were completed and the emigration officer declared they could embark on the *Bonython*.

The announcement was the signal for a frantic exodus from the transit shed and a dash to the ship in an effort to secure a favourable berth.

Sam and Jean followed more slowly with Primrose. Boarding the ship they stood back from the holds where emigrants scurried back and forth with their belongings.

It was a dull grey day with a light drizzle falling on the docks. The three travellers from Bodmin Moor were glad to take advantage of the shelter of a tarpaulin, rigged on the deck of the *Bonython* to protect the extended cooking area of the upper-deck galley.

This was where food would be prepared and cooked for the three hundred and fifty or so passengers. The ship's cook would be assisted by some of the women emigrants. They would be paid for their work and the *Bonython*'s mate had already promised Jean she would be included in their number.

'There seems to be an awful lot of people travelling on the ship,' Jean said, watching the men, women and children swarming over the *Bonython*.

'There's likely to be more by the time we reach Australia,' Sam said. 'I've seen at least half a dozen women whose time will come before we arrive.'

Remembering her own recent traumatic experience of childbirth, Jean shuddered. 'I should hate to give birth to a baby on board here. It's so cramped and gloomy down below and there's no privacy at all.

Heaven only knows what it is going to be like if we run into bad weather.'

'You'll be all right,' Sam said, with more confidence than he felt. 'Treat it as a great adventure. That's what we're going to do, aren't we, Primrose?'

Primrose's response was to cling to her mother's skirt and say tremulously, 'No . . . I want to go home. It *stinks* down there.'

The accommodation for emigrants on board the ship might generously have been described as spartan. The holds of what was essentially a merchantman had been fitted out with bunks, arranged in such a way that the ship could carry the maximum number of passengers in a minimum of space.

It was apparent to Sam that with such cramped accommodation, inadequate sanitary arrangements and no privacy whatsoever, the voyage would not be an enjoyable experience, but he did not pass on such thoughts to Jean.

So much would depend upon the weather, even their eating habits. If the weather proved too bad for cooking to be carried out on the upper deck the emigrants would need to manage as best they could with whatever food they could prepare in the crowded holds.

By the time things had settled down a little, with less movement between deck and hold, the rain had become heavier and was dripping through the canvas awning. Despite her aversion to the accommodation hold, Jean said she would take Primrose below. Sam decided to follow her example.

Climbing down the ladder, Sam made his way to the

bunk he had chosen. When he reached it, he was startled to see a fully clothed man lying there, apparently asleep. The belongings Sam had placed on the bunk had been removed and thrown to the deck.

Suddenly angry, Sam took the man by the shoulder and shook him vigorously.

The man reacted like someone waking from a deep sleep. When he turned over to face Sam, the miner caught the strong smell of stale ale on his breath.

'Go away! I'm tired.'

'Then find somewhere else to sleep, this is my bunk. Get up and out of it.'

The man was probably in his early thirties, unshaven and heavily built. Sitting up in the bunk he looked down at Sam through bloodshot eyes.

He saw a young man, almost six feet tall and with the muscular build of a man who earned his living by physical labour. But so too did he – and Ira Moyle had a reputation as a 'hard' man in the community whence he had come.

'I didn't see any sign that someone else had taken this bunk,' he lied. 'As far as I'm concerned I was the first one here.'

'Is that why my gear has been thrown on the floor?' Sam snapped. 'You're in my bed-space. Get down and find somewhere else, or I'll haul you down.'

Sam was aware that others in the hold were taking a keen interest in the argument, but he was angry and did not care. He had never gone out of his way to look for trouble, but violence was never far away in the community in which he had grown up and he had been involved in more than one fight.

Drink was readily available close to the mines and

incoming miners without family or community ties tended to drink sufficient to make them aggressive.

'There are plenty of spare bed-spaces down here—'

'That's right,' Sam broke in upon the man's argument. 'So get down and find one of your own. This is where I'm sleeping.'

At that moment Sam saw Jean peering through the gap between partition and deckhead above the bunk. From her side of the partition she had overheard much of the conversation between Sam and the stranger. She appeared scared.

The older man swung his legs over the side of the bunk, as though about to concede Sam's right to the bunk. Then, instead of lowering himself to the floor, he suddenly lashed out at Sam's head with a heavy, steel-tipped boot.

Had it connected, the fight would have been over before it began, but Sam had seen too many pay-night fights between rival miners to be caught out in such a simple fashion.

A swerve of his body was sufficient to avoid the kick, then he grabbed the man's foot and twisted hard, bringing the other man crashing heavily to the deck at his feet.

As he hit the floor the man screamed in pain as his knee was twisted painfully. Nevertheless, he came up fighting, only to be sent back to the deck by a kick from Sam which caught him between the eyes and left him dazed and confused.

Standing over him, Sam said, 'We can carry on with this argument if it's what you want, but things are going to be hard enough during this voyage without one or both of us coping with injuries as well. What's it to be?'

Ira Moyle rose unsteadily to his feet, seeking support from the tier of bunks closest to him.

'Where I sleep isn't important to me, but there's unfinished business between you and me, son. It'll be settled before we get to where we're going, I promise you that.'

Reaching up to the bunk from which he had so recently been ignominiously ejected, he grabbed the bundle containing his belongings. Limping unsteadily, he made his way between the bunks, nursing a painful leg and heading for the ladder leading to the upper deck. He would seek accommodation in the other half of the divided hold.

His departure was the signal for a series of cat-calls and applause from those who had witnessed the brief altercation.

One of the men sitting on a nearby bunk said, 'You did well there, young 'un, but keep a sharp look-out for Ira Moyle while the two of you are on this ship together. He's not the best of men to cross.'

'Ira Moyle? Is that his name?'

'That's right, you might have heard of him. He's well known in Cornwall and has earned himself a reputation as a hard man among the miners down Camborne way. You've put a dent in his image that he'll neither forgive nor forget.'

'I'm not looking for trouble,' declared Sam, 'but he'll find that Bodmin Moor miners are just as tough as the Camborne men.'

The man who had given Sam the information about the man with whom he had just fought grinned wryly. 'I reckon Ira Moyle has just learned that lesson for himself. No doubt you'll be able to prove it again should the need arise, but be wary of him. Ira's not a man I'd choose as a friend, but neither would I be happy knowing I had him as an enemy.'

Sam was left with an uneasy feeling that he had not heard the last of Ira Moyle, but there were other things to think of right now. The *Bonython* was preparing to put to sea, setting out on the long voyage to Australia.

4

I

Hardly a day went by in the St Cleer vicarage when Emily did not think of Sam and wonder where he was and what he was doing. She hoped it would not be too long before he was able to send news of his safe arrival in Australia to his family.

However, two months after his departure an event occurred that would have a profound influence upon Emily's life and her aspirations for the future.

She and Caroline spent much of the day in the vicarage kitchen helping to prepare food for a dinner party. It was to celebrate the visit to Cornwall of Lord Percy Boyce, Minister of the Crown and brother to Reverend Arthur Boyce, and extra servants had been engaged for this special occasion.

The guest list included Sheriff John Williams of Caerhays Castle, the Lord Lieutenant, two of Cornwall's Members of Parliament and a number of other notable local gentry.

Emily and Caroline had been up since dawn, supervising an augmented kitchen staff, which included Lord Boyce's own cook, brought to Cornwall by her employer especially for this occasion.

'I don't know what all the fuss is about, I'm sure,' declared the peer's cook, with a scornful sniff. 'I've cooked for ten times the number we're expecting tonight – and with half the kitchen staff.'

It was a comment the Bristolian cook had repeated at least four times during that evening. Standing hardly taller than Emily's shoulder she must have weighed at least fifteen stone. Her ability to organise an incredible variety of dishes ready for pot or oven with a minimum of effort on her part added credence to her words.

'Well, Ada, Caroline and I have tasted your wonderful cooking on our visits to Uncle Percy. We were convinced that nothing short of a whole army of kitchen staff would be required to help you.'

Ada looked sharply at Emily, suspecting she was being mocked.

She saw only Emily's open smile and said, 'Well . . . as Cornish kitchenmaids seem to work at only a quarter the speed of Bristol maids, you were probably wise, but when I'm working I like to have space enough to move around in me kitchen without tripping over them as seem more used to farm work than cooking.'

'You have only to say who you want removed and we will send them off to carry out other duties about the house, won't we, Caroline?'

The older of the two Boyce sisters failed to respond to the question and Emily realised she had not been listening. In truth, she had been preoccupied for weeks. Aware of the reason, Emily felt deeply sorry for her.

The twelve-month ban their father had imposed on John Kavanagh had expired a month before, but there had been no word from the young curate. As the days passed, Caroline became increasingly depressed by his failure to put in an appearance.

Emily had tried to reassure her sister by pointing out that John would have clerical duties to perform that could not be put aside at a moment's notice.

Despite her earlier unshakeable faith that once the ban came to an end, John would immediately return to Cornwall to claim her, Caroline was now convinced her father had succeeded in his aim of driving away the man she had hoped one day to marry.

'If you don't keep your mind on what you're doing in the kitchen you're going to burn something and incur the wrath of Ada – and I don't doubt she can strike a blow that would fell a miner.'

Emily spoke jocularly to her sister in a bid to shake her from her melancholy, speaking quietly so her words would not carry to the ears of the formidable cook. However, Caroline was not ready to be prised free of her misery quite so easily.

Caroline was less discreet. 'I really don't care if everything is burned to a cinder and father's dinner party is a total disaster.'

Her words startled two of the temporary servants and Emily hurriedly bustled her sister out of the kitchen to the garden.

Once out of hearing, she said, 'What are you thinking of, Caroline? It was unforgivable to speak like that within hearing of the servants.'

'I don't care,' Caroline declared defiantly. 'It is how I feel and I don't care who hears me.'

'You *have* to care. We have a position to uphold in the community . . .'

Even as the words came out, Emily realised what she was saying and broke off.

'You sound just like Father,' Caroline said accusingly.

'You're right, I do,' agreed Emily. 'But you're not the only one to feel bitter about the way he's behaved towards us, you know.'

Emily had never spoken to Caroline about Sam before. She did so now, voicing for the first time her suspicion that their father had been instrumental in sending Sam to Australia in order to avoid any hint of a scandal.

'I wouldn't put it past him,' agreed Caroline. 'He would do anything to prevent a family scandal, but although you were friends, losing Sam hasn't broken your heart. I mean, it was not as though you hoped to *marry* him. That is the difference between what Father did to you and what he has done to me and John.'

For an unguarded moment Emily thought of revealing to Caroline just how much she cared for Sam, but she stopped herself in time. Caroline despised their father right now, but would share his horror if she confessed to having such feelings for a miner.

'That's not the point, Caroline. He had no right to have Sam sent away just because he did not approve of our friendship.'

'No, of course not. Any more than he had the right to send John away. I will never forgive him. *Never!*'

Despite the smouldering resentment of the two sisters, dinner at the St Cleer vicarage was a grand affair. It was also highly successful. The food was excellent, the drink plentiful and the company in good humour.

Emily had been concerned about Caroline, fearing she might voice some of the resentment she felt and embarrass her father and the guests. However, Caroline had been seated next to the Bishop of Exeter's chaplain, a man of considerable humour, who had happened to be in the area with his wife.

He was successful in temporarily lifting Caroline free of her depression, telling her stories that met with the disapproval of his wife, seated across the table from him. She had heard many of the stories before and when he neared the end of one that was risqué, albeit mildly so, she would cough loudly in a vain attempt to attract his attention and show her disapproval. When he ignored her she would talk embarrassingly loudly in a bid to drown out the punchline. But by so doing she only encouraged her husband to raise his voice further, which meant that far more guests caught the end of his story than would otherwise have been the case.

Nevertheless, the meal was declared a most enjoyable occasion. When it came to an end and the women had remained in the room for a suitable length of time, Emily, as her father's joint hostess with Caroline, announced that the ladies would now withdraw to the drawing room for coffee. The men would remain at the table to enjoy coffee and brandy and discuss current news and events.

As the men pushed back their chairs and rose politely to their feet – some more steadily than others – a maid hurried into the room and crossed to where Reverend Arthur Boyce stood.

'Excuse me, sir, but you have a visitor.'

'A visitor? In the middle of a dinner party?' Arthur

Boyce frowned in deep annoyance. Visitors did not come calling in the middle of a formal dinner party. 'Tell whoever it is to come back at a more convenient time.'

'I did tell him you had guests, sir, but he said—'

'I do not care what he said. Tell him to go away,' Reverend Boyce thundered in his best pulpit voice and the words carried far beyond the dining room.

'Yes . . . Yes, sir.'

The maid was clearly unhappy, but she knew better than to argue with her employer. Dropping a quick curtsy, she fled from the room.

The interruption had delayed the departure of the ladies, but they now moved towards the door. As they did so a figure appeared in the doorway.

It was a tall, dark-haired young man wearing clerical garb and carrying a black, wide-brimmed, shallow-crowned hat in his hands.

At sight of him, the blood drained from Caroline's face and she began shaking uncontrollably.

II

'What the devil do you mean by coming here uninvited when I have guests – important guests – and frightening Caroline nigh to death? When I sent you packing I thought we had all seen the last of you.'

Flushed with an almost uncontrollable rage, Arthur Boyce confronted John Kavanagh. Caroline had been taken to her room and was being tended by Maude and a couple of women guests. The remainder of the women had been shepherded to the drawing room by Emily, who was explaining John to those who did not know him.

In the dining room, the effect of the arrival of Reverend Boyce's one-time curate provided an excuse, if one was needed, for a more than usually determined attack on the contents of the brandy decanter. It was currently making its second circuit of the dining table.

'I am deeply sorry, Reverend Boyce, but you knew I *would* come back. The arrangement was that I should go away and make no attempt to communicate with Caroline for a twelve month. I have kept my word. It is now thirteen months since I left St Cleer.'

'All right, so you have kept your word, but, dammit man, could you not have sent a letter instead of barging in to my house in the middle of a party, like some ill-bred young ruffian?'

'Once again, I can only offer my sincere apologies to you and your guests, Reverend Boyce – and especially to poor Caroline. I am very much afraid that in my euphoria at being appointed to my own parish and what it could mean for Caroline and me, everything else was driven from my mind. Besides, I have to be back in Yorkshire tomorrow night in order to officiate at two funerals in my present parish the following day. It left me just enough time to pay a fleeting call upon you—'

'Nothing you have said excuses such behaviour,' snapped Arthur Boyce. 'And what is all this nonsense about your appointment being meaningful to Caroline? I have agreed to nothing. Neither, as far as I am aware, has Caroline.'

'That is my reason for calling here today,' said the younger man. 'As for not informing you I was coming,

I could say nothing in case my interview with the patron of my intended parish proved unsuccessful.'

Listening to the young cleric, Lord Boyce felt genuinely sorry for him. In a bid to dissipate some of his brother's anger, he spoke to John for the first time. 'What is the parish to which you are being presented, young man?'

Grateful for his intercession, John Kavanagh said, 'Winterbourne Abbas, in Dorset, sir. My family home is nearby.'

'Winterbourne Abbas, eh?' This from Brigadier Sir Gilbert Ashley, a veteran of the Indian Mutiny who lived in a grand but run-down mansion on the eastern fringe of St Cleer parish. 'My commanding officer in India came from there. Major General Sir Sinclair Rose. A fine soldier. Doubt if he's still alive though, it was a long time ago.'

'He is still very much alive, sir. Not only that, he is now *Lord* Rose. He is my uncle.'

'Is he, by jove? Here, Arthur, allow the boy to sit down and have a drink, at least. It seems he has travelled a damned long way to get here.'

Frowning but less angry than before, Arthur Boyce waved John to a seat. The brigadier poured him a large brandy, taking the opportunity to top up his own glass.

When John had taken the glass, Arthur Boyce said, 'You never mentioned to me that you had an uncle with a peerage.'

'It was given to him very recently,' John explained, grateful for the toning down of the parson's anger. 'He has been performing duties for Her Majesty, in London, for some years.'

'Comptroller of the Royal Household, no less,' said

Lord Boyce. 'I know Henry well, please give him my regards when next you see him – and by the sound of it you will be seeing a great deal more of him now you have been appointed as his parson.'

'It's still subject to the bishop's approval, of course,' John replied. 'But I can think of no reason why he should object.'

'He had better not,' Lord Boyce said jovially. 'Her Majesty is Head of the Church and your uncle is very highly regarded in Court circles. It would be a brave bishop indeed who chose to oppose your appointment without a very good reason.'

'I wholeheartedly agree with his Lordship,' declared the brigadier, who had consumed more than his quite considerable daily intake of brandy. 'But I still do not understand exactly what you are doing here this evening.'

'He was my curate for a while,' Arthur explained. 'We treated him as one of the family.'

This was not quite the truth, but John allowed it to pass unchallenged.

'That doesn't explain why poor Caroline was so upset when she saw him,' persisted the brigadier.

'Why don't we allow this young man to explain it to us,' said Lord Boyce. 'What exactly has brought you back here?'

Instead of giving the assembled men an explanation, John looked at Arthur Boyce before licking his lips and saying, 'I feel I should speak privately with Reverend Boyce before I say any more, sir.'

Lord Boyce smiled and said to his brother, 'This young man has come a long way to speak to you, Arthur. If the purpose of his visit is what I believe it to be I trust you will give him a sympathetic hearing, at least.'

'Thank you for your understanding, Percy. If you gentlemen will excuse me, I will ask John to accompany me to my study. You understand, of course, that this situation is not of my making . . .'

Arthur Boyce and John Kavanagh had been absent from the room for about fifteen minutes when Caroline burst into the dining room with two women guests in close attendance.

Looking around the room agitatedly, she demanded, 'Where is he? Where is John? Oh, don't tell me Father has sent him away again.'

She appeared so close to tears that Lord Boyce jumped to his feet and, taking her arm, steered her to the chair he had just vacated at the head of the table.

'The young man is still in the house, my dear. He and your father are having a serious discussion in the study. One in which I have no doubt you figure largely . . . No, my dear, please sit down and be patient. If my reading of the situation is correct, you have shown admirable restraint for more than a year. It is my firm belief that your patience is about to reap its reward. Here, allow me to pour you a small brandy – no, please don't argue. It will do you good.'

Turning to the women who had accompanied Caroline, one of whom was his wife, he said, 'Jennifer, would you inform the ladies in the sitting room that Caroline has recovered and will no doubt be joining them in due course . . . But here is Arthur. You may be able to convey something of even more importance to them.'

Arthur Boyce re-entered the room, accompanied by

John. When the younger man saw Caroline, his face lit
up with delight and relief. He would have hurried to
her, but the St Cleer vicar put a restraining hand on his
arm.

'One minute, if you please, John.'

Looking across the room to his daughter, he said,
'John and I have discussed at some length the reason
for his most unexpected visit here this evening. We are
in agreement on a number of very important matters,
but before I make any official announcement it will be
necessary for you and he to talk together. You may
accompany John to my study. When you have arrived
at a decision please come to the sitting room. We will
be there with the ladies.'

John and Caroline were absent in the study for some
ten minutes. When they entered the sitting room
Caroline's cheeks were flushed, but Emily thought she
had never seen her sister look so happy.

Their arrival was a signal for all conversation to
cease. An uncertain, expectant hush fell upon the room
as the young couple paused close to the doorway.

Caroline's hand sought that of the young curate.
Taking her hand, John held it very tightly.

'My Lord, ladies and gentlemen,' John spoke confidently, 'I apologise for my unexpected arrival earlier
tonight, which caused an unforgivable disruption to
your dinner party. However, I trust you will forgive me
when I tell you the reason.' He smiled at Caroline before
continuing. 'Caroline and I have been parted for more
than a year, but this evening I returned to St Cleer to
fulfil a promise I made to her before I went away. Soon
after my arrival I asked Reverend Boyce for the hand
of Caroline in marriage.' Pausing until the burst of

applause died away, John continued, 'He was agreeable, but said any decision had to be made by Caroline herself. I have just asked her to be my wife – and she has agreed.'

There was another outburst of applause but, holding up his hand for silence, John said, 'I would just like to add that at this moment I am the happiest man in the whole of Cornwall ... No, in the whole of Her Majesty's kingdom. I thank you for your understanding.'

The guests of Reverend Arthur Boyce crowded around Caroline and John to congratulate them on their engagement and Emily was the first to hug them both.

Yet, even while she was giving them her congratulations, Emily was aware what this meant for her. She would be the sole daughter living at the vicarage with her elderly father. Full responsibility for him would now rest with her.

He could live for another twenty – or even *thirty* years. By the end of that time she would be fifty years of age. It seemed she was doomed to a life of spinsterhood.

It was not what she had envisaged for herself.

5

I

When the *Bonython* was three days out of Plymouth it ran into a strong north-westerly wind and the ship's movements became alarmingly violent. Emigrants moving about the ship were thrown heavily against bulkhead and bunks, running a very real risk of injury.

The pitching and rolling of the ship was so violent that the captain decided it was far too risky for the women to come on deck and attempt to cook. Not that the majority of those on board could even think of eating. So few could face cooked food that the ship's cook was able to cope single-handed with those who retained an appetite.

It was not long before seasickness struck and conditions below deck deteriorated rapidly.

Sam was as sick as anyone. Doing his best to ignore the overpowering stench of the passenger hold, he sought the solace of his turbulent bunk.

Making a mumbled inquiry through the gap above

the partition about the well-being of Jean and Primrose, he was told by a bilious mother that she and her daughter were lying down and waiting for death to put an end to their abject misery.

The bad weather lasted for a full forty-eight hours before, slowly, the wind eased and veered to the north-east.

Now the wind was astern of the *Bonython* conditions on board became far more bearable. All hatches were thrown open to allow in fresh sea air, holds were scrubbed and bedding and soiled clothing fluttered on long washing-lines criss-crossing the upper deck.

The appetites of those on board returned and Jean was kept busy cooking for stomachs that had rebelled against food for two days and nights.

Soon the ship turned on a more southerly course and as it eased slowly down the coast of Portugal the weather became warmer.

However, as the days passed, it was neither the sea nor the weather that became the enemy, but boredom. Games were organised and dozens of fishing lines trailed in the wake of the ship, but as each passing day became a repetition of the day before, tempers became frayed. Quarrels were frequent among the women and there were two fights between the men – both involving Ira Moyle.

'It's this heat, Sam. It's unbearable down below.'

Jean spoke as one of the men involved in the latest fight was helped aft to the cabin occupied by the ship's doctor, although there would be little he could do to treat the man's broken nose.

'You can't blame the weather for the behaviour of men like Moyle,' Sam replied. 'He'd be trouble anywhere.'

Moyle had twice tried to draw Sam into an argument, but he refused to be provoked by the violent miner.

'Isn't he the man you had trouble with on the first day we were on board?' Jean asked.

'That's right – and he hasn't forgotten it. He'll try to get his own back before we reach Australia.'

'If it's the man I think it is, he's spoken to Primrose a couple of times and always says "Hello" very politely to me when we meet on deck.'

Sam was surprised. He was also vaguely uneasy. 'I suppose there *might* be some good in the man, but be careful, Jean, he might be trying to get at me through you.'

That evening another fight broke out among the men on board, but this time Ira Moyle was not involved. The fight was between Cornish miners and a number of Welsh smelters.

On this occasion a knife was wielded and one of the men received a knife wound to his stomach. Although not life-threatening, the wound bled a great deal and women and children in the vicinity were terrified.

This time the ship's mate had the men who had taken part in the brawl escorted to the ship's captain and they returned considerably subdued.

Shortly after this the captain mustered the migrants on deck and warned them that he would tolerate no more fighting on board his ship. If anyone else caused trouble they would be placed in irons until the ship reached Australia, or sent back to England on board the next British warship they encountered. This was not an unrealistic threat; the *Bonython* had passed three

Royal Naval vessels since leaving Plymouth and would no doubt meet with more before Australia was reached.

The captain's warning had the desired effect and, soon afterwards, the boredom of life on board was broken by a raucous ceremony to mark the crossing of the equator.

Two days later the *Bonython* was becalmed and the mate had a boat lowered and manned by some of the migrants. They were encouraged to expend their excess energy towing the ship across a calm sea.

Only a week after crossing the equator, the ship experienced the heaviest weather met with since leaving the English Channel.

For eight days the *Bonython* was buffeted by wind and sea. Those on board were kept far too busy maintaining their balance and avoiding injury to think of quarrelling – and soon there was something far more serious to worry about.

The ship began to take in water.

At first it was not thought to be too serious. The pumps were able to cope, even though it meant a great deal more work for the ship's crew. But then it became frighteningly apparent that the pumps were barely holding their own with the incoming water.

The mate called for volunteers among the migrants to help the weary crew to work the pumps. They quickly formed teams, each vying with the others in a bid to pump out more water during their stint on the pumps. Camborne men vied with Bodmin Moor men – and both were determined to outstrip the Welsh.

The ship's carpenters did their best to stem the water entering the ship, but their efforts met with little success. It seemed that shortly before arriving at

Plymouth to take on the emigrants, the *Bonython* had run aground on a short voyage to Ireland. Quickly refloated, it was believed at the time that no serious damage had been caused. It now seemed possible that a rock had caused damage to the hull, below the water-line.

Word went around the ship that the captain had decided to head for Cape Town. There were facilities there to careen the ship and effect repairs. It was unusual for an emigrant ship to break its journey in such a manner, but the ship's carpenters needed to work from the outside of the hull.

Unless repairs were effected – and very quickly – the captain feared he might lose his ship and the lives of everyone on board.

II

Because the *Bonython* was an emigrant ship the author-ities in Cape Town kept it anchored in Table Bay for a frustrating twenty-four hours before they were satis-fied there was no contagious illness on board.

The migrants found this a fascinating time. The harbour was situated at the crossroads of two great oceans. Although the opening of the Suez Canal only a few years before had resulted in a reduction in the amount of shipping using Cape Town, it was still a very busy port.

It was also a beautiful one. The town itself was built on flat land about the harbour but houses of the wealthy stretched back to the slopes of the flat-topped moun-tain that dominated both town and bay.

Named Table Mountain, the plateau-like peak was covered for much of the day by a 'tablecloth' of fluffy white cloud.

During the time the *Bonython* was prevented from berthing alongside the harbour wall, the pumps on board were in constant operation and the captain bombarded the port authorities with angry protests that his ship was likely to founder with great loss of life if they did not allow him to bring it alongside and take immediate steps to stem the leak in the vessel's hull.

Fortunately, once a clean bill of health was given to the ship the port authorities moved quickly. A steam tug came out to tow the barque and it was moored alongside a quay. Here, a team of African workers careened the ship over to one side, supported by ropes and stout timbers.

When this was done the ship's carpenters waited for low tide when, aided by shore-based shipwrights, they hoped to be able to assess and repair the damage to the *Bonython*'s hull.

Due to the uncomfortable but unavoidable angle of the ship and the proximity of the town, with all its attractions, the *Bonython*'s captain felt he had no alternative but to allow his passengers to go ashore and a gangway was put in place to link ship and land.

After almost two months spent on board their never-still 'home' most of the emigrants were eager to set foot on land again. Once there, they staggered about as though drunk, much to the amusement of the harbour-side workers.

Watching from the deck of the *Bonython* with Jean beside him, Sam saw Ira Moyle and some of his friends weaving their way towards the town and its many grog-shops.

'I've no doubt some of the men will be staggering just as much when they return to the ship tonight,' he commented. 'Will you be going ashore, Jean?'

'I'm not sure,' she said. 'I'd like to – but only if you're going. But perhaps you'd rather go with the other miners and find a place where you can have a few drinks. I wouldn't blame you if you did. It's not been an easy voyage.'

'I don't have money to waste on drink,' replied Sam, 'but I would like to stretch my legs on dry land for a while. I'm sure Primrose would enjoy it too.'

'Oh, good!' Jean said eagerly. 'I'll just go and clean Primrose up a little. We won't be a few minutes . . .'

Half an hour later Sam, Jean and Primrose were walking towards the town. They too had experienced the nauseous sensation of a lack of balance when they set foot upon land. It had largely worn off now, but Primrose complained that her legs still wanted to 'go for a walk by themselves'.

The trio spent a couple of hours ashore, during which time they bought sweets for Primrose and a number of small items that would help to make life on board a little more bearable.

Using some of the money she had earned by cooking for the other emigrants, Jean purchased some perfumed soap which she hoped might keep some of the odours of shipboard life at bay.

Sam bought a large bag of oranges, which he thought would make a welcome addition to the bland diet available on the ship. He also bought paper, pencils and a book in which to write. During the long voyage he had begun taking writing lessons from Jean. When they reached Australia, he hoped to be proficient enough to pen a letter to his family – with a message for Emily – to inform them of his safe arrival and to surprise them with his newly acquired skill.

Passing through the area close to the harbour there was ample evidence that Sam's fears about the single men travelling on the *Bonython* were fully justified. There seemed to be a party going on in every grog-shop and the uncertain gait of many of the men who made their way from one to another was induced by alcohol and not water.

When they reached the ship they discovered that work had been suspended for the day because the tide was rising. The ropes connecting ship to the shore had been eased to enable the vessel to assume an upright position and make it more comfortable for those on board to sleep. In the morning it would be careened once more for repairs to the hull to continue.

In the meantime, in order to save time when work resumed the following day, some of the great beams that held the ship clear of the harbour wall had been left in place. This meant there was a consid-erable distance between the *Bonython* and the harbour wall.

The gangway linking the two was narrow and had only a single rope handrail on either side. It was highly dangerous and Sam lifted Primrose and carried her on board rather than run the risk of having her slip and fall in the water.

Sleep was hard to come by that night. Those men who did not return to the ship singing stumbled about in the lamp-lit hold alternately cursing and laughing at their drunken clumsiness.

Eventually, when one of the men in a nearby bunk began noisily retching, Sam decided that sleep would not be possible for a while yet. Rising from his bunk he pulled on his trousers and climbed the ladder to the upper deck.

It was warm up here but a light breeze made it quite pleasant. Standing in the shadow of the cookhouse, Sam took out his pipe, lit it and gazed at the town.

There was an almost full moon climbing in the sky to the north-east and Sam moved towards the guardrail to look at the lights that could be seen twinkling far into the distance on the shore.

'Couldn't you sleep either, Sam?'

He was deep in thought, thinking of Cornwall, of St Cleer – and of Emily – when Jean's voice broke in upon his thoughts and startled him. She had emerged from the hatch that led from the family hold without him noticing.

'No . . . no, it's pretty noisy down below and stifling hot.'

'It's the heat that's been keeping me awake.'

'What about Primrose? Where is she?'

'Walking around Cape Town today tired her out. I left her asleep. The woman in the next bunk is feeding her baby. She said she'd keep an eye on her for me. It isn't often I have a few minutes to myself, Sam.'

'No,' Sam agreed. 'She's a lovely little girl, but having to look after her on your own must be a big responsibility.'

'It might have been worse. Had things turned out differently I would have had two of them to look after on the voyage.'

Remembering the grim day when Jean had lost both husband and baby, Sam's teeth clamped more tightly on the pipe stem, but he said nothing. It was not a day he enjoyed talking about.

'I don't think I could have coped on board with only *one* had it not been for you, Sam.'

Jean was standing close and Sam could smell the perfumed soap she had bought earlier that day. The showers in a washroom on the harbourside had been allocated to the women for the duration of their stay in Cape Town and she and Primrose had made use of them.

'You'd have managed,' he said. His mouth felt unnaturally dry, his throat tight. Jean was standing very close to him, the perfume of her soap strong. 'Phillip would have been proud of you.'

'He'd be proud of you too, Sam. You've been a true friend and looked after Primrose and me really well. I'm more grateful than I'll ever be able to tell you.'

She reached out a hand to him and he was acutely conscious of the fact that he was not wearing anything above the waist.

Jean was aware of it too. Her hand rested on his arm for a few moments then travelled upwards, to his bare shoulder . . .

Suddenly there was shouting on the harbourside. It was immediately apparent that a fight was in progress. As the shouting grew louder, a whistle was blown and Sam and Jean heard the sound of laughter and running feet.

Jean's hand slipped away from Sam's shoulder and they both looked shorewards. A number of men ran unsteadily along the quay towards the gangway leading to the *Bonython*.

There were lanterns strung along the quayside and by their pale yellow light Sam could see the men but he was unable to make out their faces.

As they approached the gangway one of the men slipped and two of the others began to half-carry, half-drag him towards the boat.

'I'd say some of the men who've been drinking have settled their grudges while they've been ashore,' Sam said.

'Yes.' Jean sounded disapproving. 'It's a pity we can't leave all the troublemakers here.'

The men had reached the gangway now but were having difficulty in helping the almost unconscious man on board.

One of those in the forefront of the group turned to say something to the man behind him. As he did so he lost his balance and clutched at the slack rope-rail for support. The rope sagged alarmingly beneath his weight and before anyone could do anything to save him, he pitched forward, plunging into the water that occupied the large gap between ship and shore.

The accident provoked great merriment from the drunken men, but Sam was aware of the cries of the man in the water. They were coming now from the stern of the *Bonython*, whence the current in the bay had taken him.

Hurrying to where the other men were still crowded around the gangway, Sam called, 'The man in the water – can he swim?'

In the sudden hush that followed his question, one of the men, apparently more sober than the others, replied, 'I doubt it. I grew up with 'im and there was nowhere we could learn to swim on the Wheal Druid.'

Sam ran to the stern of the *Bonython*. The light from the lamps on the quayside was too feeble to illuminate the water, but the sea sparkled silver in the bright moonlight.

He could see no one.

Suddenly and unexpectedly, there was a thrashing of water and an arm and a head broke the surface behind the ship. The man in the water uttered a choking cry of distress as he was swept still farther away.

Without a moment's thought, Sam clambered on to the raised stern of the *Bonython* and dived headfirst into the waters of Table Bay, hearing Jean's scream before he plunged beneath the water.

What the Camborne miner had said was true of most miners. There were few places close to inland mines where a boy could learn to swim. However, Sam, and the boys who lived or worked in the Caradon mining area, were fortunate. Nearby was a deep pool which had formed in an ancient working known as the 'gold diggings'. Generations of moorland boys had learned to swim here, Sam amongst them.

With powerful strokes he reached the spot where he had last seen the desperately struggling man, but he was nowhere to be seen now.

There was a strong current. Sam felt himself being drawn with it – away from the harbour and the *Bonython*. Suddenly there was a sound from nearby and the man he was seeking rose to the surface once more.

His struggles were feebler now but a couple of strokes brought Sam to him and he managed to grab the man's shirt as he went under yet again for what would probably have been the last time.

Hauling him to the surface, Sam said, 'It's all right,

I've got you. Just don't struggle and we'll soon have you out of here.'

It was doubtful whether the man heard him. He had certainly stopped struggling and appeared to be unconscious. Sam prayed his condition had not gone beyond that stage.

His main concern now was to get the man out of the water as soon as possible. This was a matter of some urgency, but the *Bonython* was far behind them now as Sam and his deadweight burden were swept out into the bay.

Meanwhile, back on the ship, a panic-stricken Jean had found Henry Hunkin and told him what had happened. The ship's mate took immediate steps to launch one of the *Bonython*'s boats and ordered its crew to search for Sam and the man who had fallen overboard. He also despatched a seaman to inform the harbour authorities and urge them to send out as many boats as could be manned to scour the bay.

None of this was known to Sam and he began to think that both he and the man he was holding were doomed to die. Then he realised the current was carrying them in the direction of a large steamship, which had only recently arrived and was anchored in the bay.

From the number of lights showing on the vessel it was clear that it was a passenger ship.

By kicking out and paddling desperately with his free arm, Sam managed to maintain a course towards the unknown vessel, at the same time shouting as loudly as he could.

Soon he was close enough to observe that his cries had been heard. He could see people running around on the deck, trying to ascertain whence the cries were coming. Even so, he was likely to be carried past the bow of the anchored vessel before help was forthcoming.

Suddenly he was swept against something painfully hard. He grabbed at it instinctively and realised that by sheer good fortune he had bumped against the ship's anchor chain.

Pulling the unconscious man towards him, Sam crooked an arm about the chain. By gripping with his legs too, he was able to hold his burden above water.

Safe for the moment, he redoubled his shouting, able now to tell anyone who was listening exactly where he was.

It seemed to Sam he was clinging to the chain for an age, but he was receiving encouragement from those on board now, as they urged him to hold on, crying out that help was coming.

The current was strong, imposing considerable strain upon Sam's arms and legs. When he was beginning to think he would be able to hold on for only a few more minutes, a boat moved out from the shadow of the ship and edged towards him.

Moments later arms reached out. Taking the rescued man from him they dragged him inside the boat. Next it was Sam's turn. As he was being pulled in to the boat, he gasped, 'He needs a doctor . . . urgently!'

'Don't worry, we've got a good doctor waiting at the gangway. If he can be saved, our doctor's the man to do it.'

A few minutes later Sam and the rescued man were being lifted on to a platform at the foot of the gangway that led up to the ship's deck. Above him a crowd of excited passengers crowded around the guardrail and set up a cheer as Sam was helped on board.

At the top of the gangway one of the ship's crew held a lantern close to the man Sam had saved and who had been carried on deck.

It was now that Sam saw the man's face clearly for the first time and the countenance shocked him. The man he had risked his life to save was Ira Moyle!

III

While the doctor worked swiftly in a desperate attempt to revive Ira Moyle, Sam told the first mate of the steamer, SS *Eastern Prince*, what had occurred. Around him, a circle of passengers listened in respectful silence.

The first mate said nothing for a few moments, then he spoke gravely, 'You were very, very lucky, son. There is nothing but ocean out there between the *Eastern Prince* and America. If you hadn't bumped against our anchor chain and managed to hold on . . .' He shrugged. 'Not that you'd have suffered for very long, the seas about here are full of sharks. I reckon you are the luckiest man alive right now.'

While the mate was talking, the ship's doctor came upon the scene, unnoticed. It was he who spoke now. 'No, Mr Gordon, it's the *other* man who is the luckiest man alive. This one's a hero. Knowing about those sharks of which you're talking it would take a very brave man to dive into the sea to rescue a drowning man in daytime, let alone take such a risk at night.'

There were murmurs of agreement from the listening passengers, but Sam hardly heard them. He had not given a thought to sharks when he dived in the

water, although he knew they were in the area. They
had been following the *Bonython* for days before the
ship put into Cape Town.

Shaking off the thought of what might have
happened, he asked, 'Ira Moyle . . . the man who fell
into the water. Is he going to be all right?'

'I think so, although it's more than he deserves. Salt
water is a very efficient emetic. It has effectively cleared
his stomach of enough alcohol to kill a man not used
to it. I'd say that, one way or another, he owes his life
to you.'

The passengers crowded around Sam now, congratu-
lating him on his courageous act. A few minutes later
the ship was hailed by the coxswain of one of the boats
that had put out to search for the two missing men and
he was informed that both were on board.

Before the boat came alongside, one of the passengers was able to provide Sam with dry clothing, of a
quality finer than any he had ever possessed before.

As he was led to the gangway he asked after Ira
Moyle once more and was told the doctor would keep
him under observation until morning. Then, if he was
well enough, he would be sent back to the *Bonython*.

As Sam was about to descend the gangway, one of
the passengers came forward. To general applause, he
pressed a small leather satchel into Sam's hands, saying,
'We have had a collection among ourselves to show our
admiration for your bravery.'

Before the astonished Sam could stutter out his
thanks, the donor of the gift had backed away to be
swallowed up in the crowd of applauding well-
wishers.

Sam encountered more adulation when he arrived

back on board the *Bonython*. Jean was the first to greet him, hugging him warmly and clinging to him when he stepped on board.

She had thought him dead and her tears were of genuine relief. Others reached out to touch him and call out their praises as he crossed the deck.

All Sam wanted to do now was make his way to his bunk space and escape from the fuss that was being made about something he had done instinctively, but he was not to escape so easily.

The captain wished to speak to him and Sam was ushered into his presence by the mate.

Shaking Sam's hand warmly, the captain pressed him to accept a drink of Cape brandy.

Sam was not a drinking man, but he had seen the eager look on the mate's face when the invitation was extended to him too. He decided it would be churlish to refuse.

Waving him to a seat, the captain said, 'The mate has told me what you did, Mr Hooper. I am grateful to you, very grateful indeed. It is my proud boast that in all the years I have commanded the *Bonython* I have never lost a passenger through misadventure – and none from illness during the last two voyages to Australia. Had it not been for your courage and resourcefulness that record would have gone. Do you know the name of the man you rescued?'

Sam nodded. 'Yes, sir. He's Ira Moyle, a miner from Camborne.'

'Is he a friend of yours, Mr Hooper?'

'No.' Sam did not choose to amplify his reply, but the mate did.

'Moyle is a troublemaker. He is one of the men you

warned about their future conduct. Probably the ring-leader of all the trouble we've had on board.'

'Was Moyle drunk at the time he fell into the sea?' the captain asked Sam.

Sam remembered what the *Eastern Prince*'s doctor had said. He owed Moyle nothing and could have repeated the medical man's words. Instead, he said, 'I saw him fall and I think it was probably an unfortunate accident. He lost his balance, grabbed for the rope at the side of the gangway, and missed. Had he been able to swim he'd have got out of the water by himself and no one would have known of his accident.'

'But he could *not* swim,' the captain said. 'He was damned lucky that you could – and that you had the guts to go in after him. I hope he realises just how lucky he is. Did he come back on board with you?'

'No,' Sam replied. 'I managed to get him to a steamer, the *Eastern Prince*, anchored out in the bay. The doctor on board said he wanted to keep Moyle there overnight, just to make sure he is all right.'

The captain returned his attention to the mate. 'When Moyle comes back on board I want to see him. He may have been sober, as Mr Hooper seems to think, but he's caused enough trouble since he came on board. I'll warn him that if he so much as sneezes too noisily while he's on my ship, I'll have him clapped in irons for the remainder of the voyage.'

It took three tides for the leak in the hull of the *Bonython* to be repaired and caulked in a manner that satisfied the captain. Once this was done he set sail on the next rising tide – but with fifteen fewer passengers than had set out on the voyage from Plymouth.

Eight Cornish miners, lured by the talk of diamond finds in the Kimberley region, had decided South Africa had more to offer them than the copper mines of Australia. They deserted the ship.

Another seven members of a family from Wales, unable to cope with conditions on board the emigrant ship, had taken advantage of the unexpected landfall and abandoned the *Bonython*, choosing to take their chance in a country about which they knew absolutely nothing.

Although they were now at sea once more, Sam had made no attempt to check on the well-being of Ira Moyle. He had risked his life for the Camborne miner, but his bravery had been very well rewarded.

The purse given to him on board the *Eastern Prince* contained the astonishing sum of ninety-seven pounds – in gold coin. It was as much as Sam might have expected to earn in a good year in the mines of Bodmin Moor.

Added to the money he already carried, it would ensure him a sound start in the new land.

When the ship cleared Table Bay, Jean went to the galley to help in preparing the evening meal, leaving Primrose in Sam's care.

He was playing a string game with her, crouching down and helping her to make interesting patterns on her small fingers, when she suddenly looked up and smiled at someone who had come to stand behind Sam.

Glancing over his shoulder he saw it was Ira Moyle. Standing up slowly, he turned to face the Camborne man.

Ira seemed to be having difficulty in finding words and Sam said, 'I'm glad to see you up and about. It was by no means a certainty when they carried you on board the *Eastern Prince*.'

Finding his voice at last, Ira said, 'The only thing that's certain is that if it hadn't been for you, I'd be a dead man now. There's no one else would have done what you did. I owe you my life, Sam Hooper. I promise you I'll never forget that, not as long as I live.'

He held out his hand and when Sam took it Ira gripped it so hard that Sam felt the Camborne man's gratitude was likely to cost him crushed fingers.

'It's not only the rescuing of me I have to thank you for, either,' Ira continued. 'By telling the captain that I wasn't drunk when I went overboard, you saved me a whole lot of grief.'

'Well, you weren't the worst of 'em,' Sam said, embarrassed by Ira's declaration of gratitude. But there was more to come.

'I'm sorry you and I got off to a bad start when we first came on board. It was entirely my fault. If there's any way I can make it up to you ... ?'

'Forget it,' Sam said. 'We're both grown men – and Cornishmen, at that. What's past is best forgotten. We're heading for a new life in Australia. Let's look forward to it.'

Still grasping Sam's hand, Ira said, 'You're a good man, Sam Hooper, and I like the company you're keeping on board.'

He nodded his head in the direction of Primrose. Despite intense concentration, she had managed to allow a string 'cradle' to slip from her fingers and now, frowningly, was attempting to untangle it.

'I've noticed you're not travelling as a family. Is the child on her way to join her father?'

Sam shook his head. 'Her father was my best friend. He was killed in a mine accident at the South Caradon mine on Bodmin Moor a couple of months ago. Primrose is on her way to join her grandfather at Kadina, on the Yorke Peninsula, in South Australia.'

Ira Moyle looked duly sympathetic. 'Is that where you're heading too?'

'Yes, I have an uncle there.'

'I'm going to Kadina too,' said the Camborne man. 'I don't know anyone there, but lots of Camborne men are working there. The letters they've sent home talk of there being plenty of work for Cornishmen in the mines in that area.'

'I've heard the same. Let's hope they're right and there's still work to be done. A lot of Cornish miners have gone out there in recent months.'

Ira nodded, but he was looking at Primrose. Suddenly looking up, he asked, 'Do you and the girl's mother have an understanding?'

The question took Sam by surprise. He was about to tell Ira it was none of his business, but something in the other man's expression caused him to change his mind. 'We've known each other since we were small children. Like I said, her husband was my best friend. I'm happy to do what I can to help her on such a long voyage.'

For a few moments Ira mulled over what Sam had said. He seemed uncertain of Sam's reply but instead of pursuing the matter, he asked, 'Would you mind if I played "Cat's Cradle" with Primrose and her string?'

'Of course not, go ahead.'

Ira crouched down beside the small girl and after a few words took the string from her. Untying it, he proceeded to demonstrate more variations of the game than were known to Sam. He made the string patterns skilfully and was able to show Primrose how to copy them, which delighted the young girl.

Watching Ira's patience with Primrose, Sam realised he was seeing a facet of the Camborne miner's character that was not usually shown to the men with whom he associated.

Ira was still entertaining Primrose when Jean came from the ship's galley with a pasty she had cooked for Sam in advance of the main meal.

Seeing Ira crouched down with Primrose, their heads close together, she was horrified and looked to Sam for an explanation.

'He's showing Primrose how to make a cat's cradle,' Sam said. 'And he's a sight better than I am at it.'

Looking up, Ira saw Jean. Standing up hurriedly, he left Primrose protesting that he had not completed the string pattern he was weaving on her fingers.

Snatching the cap from his head, he stammered, 'I . . . I'm Ira Moyle. I . . . was just teaching Primrose a few little tricks with an old piece of string.'

Aware that this was the man who might so easily have cost Sam his life, Jean said frostily, 'It seems you have more success with a piece of string than with a rope, Mr Moyle. Had you been capable of keeping hold of the gangway rope when you returned on board at Cape Town, Sam wouldn't have needed to risk his life for you. It would also have saved everyone involved a great deal of trouble.'

'That's perfectly true, ma'am. I've just been thanking Mr Hooper. I realise I owe him my life. It's something I shall never forget as long as I live.'

Ira's apologetic manner successfully blunted the edge of Jean's anger. In a less brusque manner she said, 'No matter how long your life may be, Mr Moyle, you'll owe every single day of it to Sam.'

Looking to where Primrose squatted, frowning in concentration and frustration at the web of string wrapped around her fingers, she said, 'You seem to have the knack of entertaining young children, Mr Moyle. Have you left a family behind in Cornwall?'

As though she had struck him a physical blow, an expression of acute pain crossed Ira's face. He said, quietly, 'I had a little 'un, once. She was about the same age as Primrose when both she and my wife were carried off by smallpox. That was a couple of years since. My wife was the daughter of a lay preacher, down by Camborne, and we were both strong for chapel. When they were taken away from me I lost my faith. Lost my way too, I reckon. Perhaps the fact that I was saved when by rights I should've drowned is God's way of telling me he still has work for me to do. As the hymn says, "God moves in a mysterious way".'

As though suddenly embarrassed, Ira said, 'That's the first pious thought I've had since I saw my wife and daughter buried. I thank you for giving me that. Perhaps you'll let me speak with Primrose again?'

Ira walked away, leaving Sam and Jean staring after him, momentarily lost for words.

'Well, the world is full of surprises!' Sam said, shaking his head in disbelief. 'Who'd have thought of Ira Moyle as a staunch Methodist? Will you let him have anything more to do with Primrose?'

'Why . . . yes. Yes, of course I will. It sounds as though Ira Moyle has suffered quite enough for one man's lifetime. Perhaps he's right in thinking that God has decided He has need of him again.'

When Jean had returned to the galley, Sam remembered that she too was a Methodist and her late husband's father a lay preacher.

Seating himself on the deck beside Primrose, Sam offered the child a piece of the pasty Jean had cooked for him. Primrose declined it.

Holding up two hands, with the string wound around her fingers, she said, 'I want to do this ... but you're not as clever as the man. When will he come back?'

6

I

The marriage of Reverend John Kavanagh to Caroline Boyce took place in the St Cleer church of St Clarus at Easter, 1873, seven months after the young couple's dramatic reunion.

John's family travelled from Dorset to Cornwall for the wedding. It caused a great stir in the vicarage when it was learned that Lord Rose was among them and had asked if he and his wife might stay at the vicarage with other members of the family.

Arthur Boyce need not have been concerned about accommodating the peer. Lord Rose was not a difficult man to please. Indeed, he seemed delighted with all that was done for him.

The wedding was a memorable occasion and passed off smoothly. Packed with well-wishers, the church was fragrant with the perfume of a plethora of spring flowers, donated by parishioners.

Outside, even those villagers who worshipped

elsewhere were gathered to catch a glimpse of the bride and groom as they left, many calling out messages of goodwill.

It was a wonderful day for everyone. Everyone, that is, except Emily.

Watching her sister, the new Mrs Kavanagh, drive away in a carriage, bound for Liskeard railway station and a journey that was taking her to a married life outside Cornwall, Emily felt very alone, very vulnerable – and hopelessly trapped.

Her feeling of loneliness deepened the next day when family and guests departed from St Cleer. She began gathering about her the threads of a new and more inhibiting way of life that was destined to be her lot for as long as her father lived.

That evening, when Arthur Boyce was attending a meeting of his churchwardens, Emily went upstairs to the bedroom that had been occupied by Caroline since they were both small children.

Standing in the doorway she contemplated the blankets, folded neatly on the bare mattress of a stripped bed, and the dressing table and shelves now devoid of Caroline's personal toiletries and knick-knacks, collected during the childhood and early adult lives of the two sisters.

The only sign of the lately departed occupant was a small vase containing primroses, gathered by Emily and given to Caroline on the eve of her wedding.

Suddenly overcome by the depth of her feelings, Emily burst out crying and fled along the corridor to her own room. Here, flinging herself face down on her bed, she wept as she had not cried since the death of her mother.

* * *

During the ensuing weeks, Emily missed her elder
sister far more than she could ever have imagined. Not
only was there now no one to share the social duties
undertaken on behalf of their father, but there was no
one with whom she could discuss his constant irritability.

Maude too was becoming increasingly difficult. It
seemed to Emily that the housekeeper was intent upon
taking advantage of the fact that Emily now had no
one else with whom to discuss household matters. The
housekeeper began making decisions without consulting her.

Emily was aware that Maude was throwing down
a challenge but it was one she was hesitant to do
anything about. In the past, Reverend Arthur Boyce
had always sided with the housekeeper and not with
his daughter in any dispute about household matters.
Emily doubted whether he would change his attitude
now.

About a month after Caroline's wedding, Emily was
leaving the outlying home of a sick and elderly parishioner when she saw Oliver Hooper, Sam's father, on his
way back from Liskeard market, driving a farm wagon.
It was the first time they had met for some months.

It was perfectly natural for the farmer to offer her a
ride to the village and she accepted readily, hoping he
might have some news of Sam.

After inquiring about the health of Oliver Hooper's
wife, she asked if he had heard from Sam, hoping the
question sounded more casual than it really was.

'As a matter of fact we had a letter from him only a
week ago,' the farmer said, adding, with considerable

pride, 'written in his very own hand, it was.'

Taken aback, Emily said, 'I thought Sam couldn't write?'

When Oliver Hooper threw her a look of surprise that she should know of Sam's lack of learning, she said hastily, 'He mentioned it once – at choir.'

'That's why we're so proud of him,' declared the farmer. 'That Jean Spargo started teaching him on the ship to Australia – and he's kept it up since they arrived, it seems. He's still not a great writer, mind, but he's learned enough to put a short letter together for us.'

Emily felt a sharp stab of jealousy at the mention of the pretty young widow.

'I had forgotten Jean and Primrose were travelling with Sam,' she lied. 'Are they both well too?'

'I suppose so. He didn't say anything about them, except to say Jean was learning him to read and write, no more than that. He doesn't mention young Primrose either, but then, it's his very first letter. I don't doubt it took him a long while to write.'

'Is he settling down in Australia?'

'I expect so. He doesn't say anything about life there, and there's not a mention of his uncle.'

'I wonder if he still thinks of his friends in the choir?' Emily said hopefully. It was always possible there might have been some message for her in the letter, perhaps hidden in an allusion to choir members.

'I'm sure he does,' said Oliver Hooper. 'A great one for the choir was our Sam. He used to enjoy his singing.'

'When you and Mrs Hooper write to him you must tell him you've met me and that I was asking after him. Tell him he's missed by everyone in the choir.'

'I will and it's kind of you to say so – but how about

Miss Caroline, or Mrs Kavanagh as I suppose I must call her now? Have you heard from her? I wasn't in church myself to see the wedding, but Mrs Hooper was. She said it was one of the loveliest weddings she'd ever been to. Cried her eyes out, she did. Our Sam would have loved to have sung for that service, I don't doubt.'

For the remainder of the journey to St Cleer the conversation was of Caroline's marriage and of local happenings. Sam's name never entered the conversation again.

Emily knew it would have been very difficult for Sam to have sent a direct message for her in his letter, but she was disappointed that he had not managed to convey even an oblique reference to her. The thought of Jean Spargo being with him also disturbed her.

When she thanked Oliver Hooper for the ride and waved farewell to him she entered the vicarage in a very depressed state of mind.

She would have felt very different had she known that Sam _had_ mentioned her in the letter he had sent to his family. Oliver Hooper had been asked to thank Emily for the generous gift she had given to him on his departure. He was to tell her he carried it with him at all times.

During their journey Oliver Hooper had wrestled with his conscience about whether or not to pass on the message to her, but practical considerations prevailed.

Because of the current perilous state of agriculture in general, when harvest time came around Oliver Hooper would need to plead with Parson Boyce in the hope that he would forego some of the tithes due to him.

He could not afford to antagonise the man who held the balance between ruin and survival for the Hooper family.

II

For a while during the summer of 1873 it seemed that mining on Bodmin might make a welcome recovery. The price of copper rose, making it once more a viable commodity. As a result, mines were re-opened and new shafts sunk.

Once again the clatter of steam crushers rent the air over wide areas of Bodmin Moor and families began making tentative plans for the future.

News of a resurgence in the fortunes of copper travelled fast. Out-of-work miners from the traditional tin-mining region centred on Camborne and Redruth flocked to the Caradon area.

Sadly, the euphoria lasted only a few months. As autumn approached, the price of copper plummeted yet again and the mining 'boom' died with the warmth of the summer sun.

Miners were laid off in their thousands and this time the plight of the men and their families was worse than ever before. By coming to Bodmin Moor many had cut their ties with the rest of the county, where they had been born. As a result, they had no family roots on the moor to cushion them against this latest disastrous mining recession.

Miners had the reputation of being proud and independent, but with starving families to support they were forced to swallow their pride and become beggars in a desperate effort to survive. But when their own efforts failed they realised that their wives and children possessed more appeal, and they were sent out to beg in place of their menfolk.

The moorland communities did what they could for the unfortunate newcomers, but their resources were limited. Finally, some of the miners – remarkably few in view of their desperation – took to stealing in order to survive.

One day, when Reverend Boyce had ridden off to attend a meeting in Bodmin, Rose Holman came to the St Cleer vicarage and related a harrowing tale to Emily.

A copper miner from the Caradon mine had left for Australia the previous year, leaving behind his wife and two sons, aged nine and seven. Nothing had since been heard from him.

Desperately short of money and unable to pay even the nominal rent asked for the cottage they occupied, the family had been evicted. For weeks they had made their home in a ditch, with only a rough latticework of sticks and grass to serve as a roof against the elements.

One day the woman fainted from a lack of food. Frantic with worry, the two young boys raided a nearby farmyard and stole half a dozen eggs, which they intended to cook for their starving mother. But their luck was out. They were caught by the farmer and promptly handed over to the local constable.

'They're coming up in Liskeard magistrates' court tomorrow,' Rose explained. 'I shall be in court to see what happens to them, but they really need someone to stand up and speak on their behalf. I'd do it myself but, as you know, most of the magistrates are either parsons, like your father, or else prominent members of the Church of England. If I were to do it I'd probably make matters worse. I thought, with Reverend Boyce being a Justice of the Peace you might speak to him on behalf of the boys. They're only children, Emily, two *good* boys, I promise you.'

When Emily hesitated, Rose added, 'It really is a deserving case – but before you make up your mind let me take you to meet Margaret Minns, the boys' mother.'

'All right, but you mustn't raise your hopes too high, Rose. I will not be able to raise the matter with my father. He never discusses his magisterial duties with me – and he would not dream of trying to influence a case being heard by another magistrate.'

When Rose appeared crestfallen, Emily asked, 'Where is the boys' mother now?'

'Staying with the wife of another out-of-work miner, a woman hardly better off than Margaret, but she does at least have a roof over her head. Others have donated what food they can spare in a bid to put some strength into Margaret before tomorrow's court hearing. She's determined to be in court when her boys are brought before the magistrate. To be honest with you, the way she is at the moment she'll probably drop dead along the way.'

Making up her mind, Emily said, 'Call back here in about half an hour. I'll come with you to see her and bring some food with me.'

As Emily walked through the house to the kitchen, she met with the tight-lipped and disapproving house-keeper and realised Maude had overheard the conversation. Emily was uncomfortably aware that her father would be informed the wife of the Methodist minister had called at the vicarage – and he would be given a highly biased reason for her visit.

It would undoubtedly cause another argument, but Emily decided she did not care.

Still in her twenties, Margaret Minns must once have been a very attractive woman. Sadly, years of hardship and uncertainty, culminating in the harrowing events of recent months, had taken their toll. She looked frail, tired, and old beyond her years.

Despite this, when Emily and Rose entered the room where she was lying, Margaret made an attempt to sit up to greet them.

When Emily protested that she must lie still and rest, Margaret Minns said feebly, 'I've been lying down for far too long, Miss Boyce. I need to find strength enough to get to court for my boys in the morning. It won't come back to me if I spend my time lying abed.'

Struggling to a position that was half lying and half resting against the brass bedhead, she looked eagerly at Emily. 'Rose says you're going to help get Tom and Albert set free tomorrow?'

'I'm afraid it isn't quite as simple as that,' said Emily. 'The magistrate will make up his own mind about what to do with them.'

She looked accusingly at Rose. It was unfair of her to build up this woman's hopes in such a fashion.

'Margaret was asleep when I came back from speaking to you,' Rose said apologetically, 'I haven't spoken to her since.'

Margaret looked from Emily to Rose and back again, her expression registering dismay. 'But . . . you *can* help them? Your father . . . the parson . . . he's a magistrate.'

'He will not be trying your two boys, Margaret. Even if he were, I doubt if I would be able to influence the outcome of the case in their favour.'

'Oh! I thought . . .' Tears suddenly welled up in the young mother's eyes and overflowed, to run unheeded down her cheeks. Alternately clutching and releasing the bedcover, she said brokenly, 'They're good boys, Miss Boyce, especially Albert. He's only nine, but he's tried hard to behave like a man since his pa's been gone. He only did what he did because he couldn't bear to see me so ill and weak. It's all my fault. What can be done for them, Miss Boyce? I really don't know what I'll do if they take the boys away from me. I love them both so much!'

'Now, now, Margaret, don't upset yourself any more. The boys won't be taken away from you.' Rose tried to reassure the weak and ill woman.

'Of course they won't,' said Emily, with more conviction than she felt. One of the area magistrates, Sir Richard Jane, had recently committed brothers, aged five and seven, to prison for an offence of fouling the water in a well!

Hopefully, he would not be trying the case of Albert and Thomas Minns and at this moment Margaret Minns urgently needed reassurance. Despite having grave misgivings about the wisdom of becoming involved, Emily said, 'I will go to court tomorrow morning and speak on their behalf, Margaret. In the meantime, you must not worry.'

The two women left Margaret Minns still crying, but with at least a glimmer of hope for her two young sons.

Outside the bedroom, Emily asked, 'Who was the

farmer who handed Margaret's two boys over to the police?'

'Farmer Norris, of Tor Farm, over by Tremar.'

'Oh!' Emily's hopes sank. She knew Farmer Jacob Norris. He was an irascible bachelor farmer who had fallen out with his neighbours on many occasions over the years. Now a virtual recluse, he claimed he owed allegiance to no religious denomination.

The two Minns boys could not have chosen a more intransigent farmer from whom to steal.

'I doubt very much whether I will be able to persuade him to drop charges against the boys, but I will go to the farm and speak with him.'

III

Tor Farm was neither the most readily accessible nor the best kept of moorland habitations. The approach was by way of a rough track that had once been regularly surfaced using granite waste from a moorland quarry. That had been before Jacob Norris inherited the farm from his father at the age of twenty-three, almost fifty years before. Little maintainance had been carried out to the track since that time.

As Emily neared the farm she was forced to hoist the long skirt she wore clear of her ankles. Picking her way carefully through the mud, she tried to avoid the most obvious potholes.

Sited in a natural hollow, cleverly sheltered from the prevailing westerly wind, the farmhouse was no better maintained than the track. As Emily drew nearer she looked down upon a thatched roof in sore need of repair; a garden choked with brambles, and paths that were barely discernible beneath a variegated carpet of weeds.

When prolonged knocking at the farmhouse door brought no response, Emily searched the outhouses for Jacob Norris.

She eventually located him cleaning out a chicken house, the same one from which the Minns boys had stolen the eggs.

Norris was wearing filthy moleskin trousers, a collarless shirt and a coat made from the hide of a heifer. Complete with hair, the hide had holes cut in it for the reclusive farmer's arms.

Emily had visited the farmer on previous occasions, usually to check on his well-being when he had not been seen for some time by his farming neighbours. None would check for themselves, having suffered the abuse he invariably directed at them when all proved to be well.

Emily had never fared any better and this visit was no different. She was greeted with the words, 'What you doing 'ere, eh? Them nosey neighbours been minding my business again? Pity they ain't got nothing better to do with their time.'

'My visit has nothing to do with the neighbours, Mr Norris. I've come to speak to you about the two small boys you handed over to the police.'

Detecting a note of sympathy in her voice, Norris said aggressively, 'Small they may have been, but they was big enough to know how to steal my eggs.'

'Stealing anything is wrong, Mr Norris, and the boys have been brought up by their mother to know that Unfortunately, the family has fallen on hard times -

very hard times indeed. When the boys' father left to
find work in Australia they and their mother were
turned out of their home. They have been living
outdoors ever since. Food was so scarce the mother
starved herself, giving any food she obtained to the
boys. As a result she became seriously ill. It was desperation that drove the two children to steal, Mr Norris.
They could think of no other way to save the life of
their mother.'

'If God had decided it was time for her to die, then
so be it. I shouldn't have to remind *you* that it's *His*
commandment that says "Thou shalt not steal".'

'But it couldn't have been His will she should die,
Mr Norris. What has happened to the boys has
brought her the sympathy she was never given before.
She has been taken into someone's home. Given such
a chance, she will hopefully recover, but the boys are
her whole life. Her recovery depends largely upon
you, Mr Norris. You seem to have forgotten there are
another nine commandments. One of them calls for
us to honour our parents and those little boys have
certainly honoured their mother. Another commandment says "Thou shalt not kill" and I can tell you that
the boys' mother is so desperately ill that if the magistrate deals harshly with her two children it will surely
kill her.'

'What the magistrate does is up to him, not me. I
was doing no more than any other man would have
done,' Jacob Norris insisted defensively. 'What I have
every right to do. Protect my own property. Besides,
what do you mean by coming here and telling me what
I should or shouldn't be doing? For all either of us
know, these two have been going around like so many

of their kind, thieving from them as has little more than themselves.'

Turning his back on her, the cantankerous farmer said, 'You've wasted enough of my time, now you can go about your business and leave me to tend to mine. Them whose job it is will decide what's to happen to those as can't keep their hands off what rightfully belongs to others. No doubt they'll do no more than pat 'em on the head, tell 'em not to be naughty boys and send 'em back home. Then they'll go straight back to stealing from someone else who's struggling to earn an honest living.'

Emily left the farm disappointed but not surprised at her lack of success. There had been a very brief moment when, as she spoke about the illness of Margaret Minns, she thought she detected a glimmer of sympathy in the expression of the farmer, but she had probably been mistaken. Jacob Norris was not known to be a compassionate man.

Thinking about this, she wondered how the farmer would react if the two young boys *were* let off with a light sentence? There was the chance that, in a fit of pique, he would report her for trying to persuade him to drop charges against them.

It was a serious possibility, yet she allowed herself a wry smile at the thought of her father's outraged reaction were *she* to be the subject of a police investigation and criminal charge!

IV

Despite Margaret Minns' determination to attend the Liskeard magistrates' court in support of her two young sons, she was too weak to stand unaided when she tried to leave her bed.

Nevertheless, she wept and pleaded with Emily and Rose to be allowed to accompany them to Liskeard. Rose was immovably firm. Margaret was unfit to leave the house and needed to remain confined to bed for a few more days.

Emily and Rose travelled to court in Reverend Boyce's pony-trap. In order to borrow the small vehicle Emily had made the excuse to her father that she had shopping to do in the mid-Cornwall market town. Preoccupied with the problem of removing the church bells from the tower for much-needed restoration work, Arthur Boyce gave her trip his distracted approval.

Had shopping really been the purpose of her journey Emily would have left pony and trap with the incumbent at the Liskeard vicarage, as she usually did. Instead, she placed it in the care of the ostler at the Webb's hotel in the town centre, and the two women made their way together to the courtroom.

The court officials recognised Emily immediately and she and Rose were given seats in the front row of the public gallery.

The court was crowded almost to capacity and Jacob Norris was among those present. He was seated, looking down at his feet. Emily was not certain whether or not he had seen her.

When the court was called to order and the

magistrate and his clerk entered the room, Emily had a moment of despair. The magistrate *was* Sir Richard Jane, the least compassionate of those authorised to dispense justice in the courts of the area.

Seating himself on his high-backed seat, Sir Richard cast his gaze about the courtroom. He recognised Emily immediately. Although surprised, he acknowledged her presence with a cursory nod of his head. Then, with a similar gesture to his clerk, he signalled for the day's proceedings to commence.

It was soon apparent to Emily that Sir Richard's reputation was fully justified.

The first case involved a young woman who had stolen a neckerchief from a market stall. She pleaded that, having no money, she had stolen it as a birthday present for her desperately ill husband. They had been married for only a few months but he was not expected to live to see the year out.

Commenting that her husband would have been better served with an honest wife rather than a stolen neckerchief, Sir Richard sentenced her to six months' imprisonment.

Unperturbed as she was dragged to the cells screaming and pleading for mercy, he called for the next case to be brought before him.

Two miners were led from the court cells and stood in the dock accused of stealing and killing a sheep on Bodmin Moor. Both men admitted the offence, but claimed to have believed the sheep had no owner. They had killed it to provide meat for more than a dozen hungry families.

Sir Richard informed the prisoners that they were liable to be imprisoned for fourteen years, and pointed out that earlier in his lifetime they would have both been hung for the crime they had committed. He then ordered for them to remain in custody to face trial at the next Assizes.

When the two miners had been taken below it was the turn of Albert and Thomas Minns to be tried.

A murmur of sympathy arose from those in court when the boys were brought up from the cells. Emily's heart, too, went out to them.

Poorly clad and tousle-haired, both boys seemed thoroughly confused and frightened by what was happening to them. Standing side by side in the dock, Tom had to raise himself on tiptoe to peer over the edge. Albert was somewhat taller, but only the top half of his face could be seen as he peered wide-eyed at the impassive magistrate.

The charge was read out that they had feloniously and unlawfully stolen six eggs, the property of Jacob Norris, from a hen house on the farmer's farm. The clerk then asked Tom whether he pleaded 'Guilty' or 'Not guilty' to the charge.

Tom seemed confused but when Sir Richard said impatiently 'Come along, speak up, boy,' his confusion turned to fear and he turned to his brother for support.

'He doesn't know what you mean, sir,' explained Albert.

'Then for goodness' sake tell him,' snapped the magistrate.

'I . . . I'm not sure I know neither,' Albert confessed.

Before Sir Richard could say anything more, the clerk of the court said, more kindly, 'Thomas Minns, I am asking whether or not you took the eggs from the chicken house?'

Over the edge of the dock it was just possible to see Tom shake his head.

'Are you saying you did *not* take them?' asked the surprised clerk.

'No, sir. It was Albert who went into the chicken house. He handed them out to me – but I couldn't hold all of 'em. I dropped two and they broke, so he had to take two more.'

There was a moment of hastily stifled laughter in the court and, looking up at Sir Richard, the clerk said, 'I think we might accept that as a guilty plea, your worship.'

Sir Richard's reply was too low to carry to Emily, but the clerk turned immediately to Albert. 'Is what your brother said true? Did you take the eggs?'

Albert nodded his head vigorously, but the clerk said, 'You must *tell* me, Albert. Yes or no?'

'Yes, sir. I took them.'

'Thank you.'

Turning to the magistrate, the clerk said, 'I will record it as two guilty pleas.'

'Good! May we now have the facts, please?'

A police inspector stood up and presented the facts of the case. They were quite straightforward. Albert and Tom had gone to the farm, taken the eggs and been apprehended by Jacob Norris, who had then handed the boys over to the police.

The brief summary took only a few minutes. When the inspector had concluded he sat down and Sir Richard Jane fixed a stern gaze on the boys in the dock.

'Albert and Thomas Minns, you have heard the case against you, is there anything you wish to say to this court?'

Thomas was as confused as before, but Albert said, 'No, sir.'

It was at this moment that Emily stood up and said, 'If it pleases, your worship, I would like to say something on their behalf.'

Frowning, Sir Richard asked, 'Do you know the two defendants, Miss Boyce?'

'No, Sir Richard, but I have met their mother and I am familiar with their background. I feel it has an important bearing on this case.'

Sir Richard's frown deepened, but he said, 'Very well, you may come forward to the witness box and address the court – but please be brief. I have a very full list to deal with today.'

As Emily made her way to the witness box she was aware of the two young boys peering at her over the top of the dock. Young Tom was clutching the edge of the woodwork, pulling himself up to see the stranger who was going to speak on behalf of him and his brother.

Nervously at first, but with increasing confidence, Emily made an impassioned plea on behalf of the two brothers, pointing out their tender years, the absence of their father, the loss of their home and, latterly, the illness of Margaret Minns.

She referred to the intolerable burden that had been placed upon nine-year-old Albert, forced to take on the responsibility for his mother and younger brother, with no one to turn to for help or to ask advice.

Emily had the rapt and sympathetic attention of every man and woman in the courtroom who heard her speak.

All except one.

Sir Richard Jane listened attentively to what Emily had to say for perhaps two minutes. Then, apparently losing interest, he began studying a document that was lying on the bench in front of him.

Aware of the magistrate's lack of interest in what she was saying, Emily brought her plea to an end. Deeply disappointed, she realised she had achieved nothing.

It was a full half-minute after she had ceased talking before Sir Richard looked up in apparent surprise and said, 'Thank you, Miss Boyce. You waxed most eloquent. Your father would be proud of you. However, I regret you felt it necessary to make such an impassioned plea on behalf of two young scoundrels. By their own admission they chose to steal the property of an honest and hard-working member of our community.'

Emily opened her mouth to speak, but Sir Richard pre-empted her. '*Chose*, I say – and that is exactly what I mean. I have heard nothing in this court today to suggest that Albert and Thomas Minns ever contemplated any other means of solving the problems of their family. Their first thought was to steal. To take what did not belong to them . . .'

Meanwhile, Jacob Norris had listened with great concentration to what Emily had to say. Wrestling with his conscience, he sprang to his feet as Sir Richard dismissed Emily's plea and blurted out, 'Sir Richard, I want to withdraw the charges I laid against the two boys. What they done wasn't right, but neither is punishing 'em for trying to save their sick mother. I want 'em sent back to her. Miss Boyce is right what she said to me yesterday, punishing them is only going to punish their mother more.'

'Mr Norris!' Sir Richard snapped at the farmer. 'You

will ask permission before you address this court. As for withdrawing charges . . . it is too late for that. What happens to the two defendants is no longer a matter for your concern. You will sit down and remain silent.'

'But it was *my* eggs they took, not the court's. *I* should be the one to say whether anyone gets in trouble for taking 'em . . .'

'Mr Norris!' Sir Richard's voice thundered out. 'You have been told to remain silent. Another word from you and I will have you detained for contempt of my court. Then you will be able to personally express your sympathy to these two young law-breakers – but I warn you, Mr Norris, *you* will still be there when they are released.'

Emily's hopes of securing the immediate release of the two young boys sank at the magistrate's words. It was apparent he had decided to send Albert and Tom to prison. Nothing she had said in mitigation had made any difference. Sir Richard Jane was living up to his reputation.

When Jacob Norris remained standing, a constable hurried across the courtroom to him. Taking the stubborn farmer by the arm, he led him through the door to the street outside.

When he had gone, Sir Richard brought the case to a swift conclusion.

Looking at the two young boys with a stern expression, he said, 'Albert and Thomas Minns, you have both pleaded guilty to the crime for which you have been brought before me. By so doing you have avoided wasting this court's time. For that I give you due credit. However, thefts by miners and the families of miners have reached alarming proportions. It is my duty to pass sentences upon you that reflect the concern of law-abiding citizens for such unacceptable behaviour. Thomas Minns, you will pay a fine of twenty shillings, or, in default of the same, go to prison for one month. Albert Minns, you are the older of the two and should have set your brother an example. Instead, you were the leader in this dishonest escapade. You will pay a fine of three pounds, or, in default, go to prison for three months.'

Emily's spirits lifted. She had brought with her more than enough money to pay the two fines and have the boys released that morning. For a brief, misguided moment she believed that for all his stern words Sir Richard had shown compassion, knowing she would probably pay the fines.

His next words gave her a rude awakening.

'In addition, as the instigator of this crime, I order you, Albert Minns, to receive six strokes of the birch, to be administered before your release, whether that be from this court today, or from prison on completion of your sentence.'

V

The sentence imposed upon the two young brothers provoked an eruption of outrage from the members of the public inside the Liskeard courtroom.

Sir Richard Jane called in vain for silence, his efforts seeming only to increase the anger of those who had witnessed his 'justice'. Eventually, his face purple with anger, he announced that he was suspending proceedings for thirty minutes and called for the court to be cleared.

Most of those who had watched proceedings inside the courtroom were miners. The heartless sentencing of Albert and Thomas Minns unleashed some of the anger, resentment and frustration felt by the out-of-work men.

Their noisy protests continued when they spilled from the court building to the street outside and quickly spread around the town.

Many miners and their families were in the habit of spending their empty days in Liskeard, preferring the bustle and illusion of wealth found in the town to the silent and wind-swept loneliness of the mine-dotted moor. Attracted by the noise of the ejected courtroom crowd they added their own anger to that of their colleagues when word went around of the sentences passed on the two small boys.

Emily, who had remained in the courtroom with Rose until the last of the crowd had gone, now emerged from the building. She was immediately recognised and loud applause broke out. As she walked through the crowd, hands reached out to touch her and there were shouts of approval for her support of the two Minns boys.

Before leaving the court, Emily had spoken to the senior policeman on duty, a man she knew by sight. She asked him who would carry out the birching of Albert.

'That depends whether his fine is paid or whether he goes to prison.'

'I shall pay the fine of both boys right away,' Emily declared firmly.

Ill at ease, the policeman said, 'Then I'm afraid the

distasteful task of flogging the boy will fall to me, Miss Boyce.'

'I trust the blows will land lightly. After all, he's only a child and should never have been convicted in the first place.'

'It's a view as is held by many, Miss Boyce. I'll not hurt the boy any more than is necessary, but Sir Richard likes to be present when a flogging is taking place. If he thinks I'm holding back he's as likely as not to order someone else to step in and do the job instead of me.'

'Your understanding of the situation does you credit, officer. Perhaps you can tell me when the boys will be freed, once I have paid their fines?'

'The flogging will take place at the end of this morning's court, Miss Boyce – though with all this trouble, there's no telling when that will be. It certainly won't be before one o'clock.'

'Then I shall pay the fines and return at that time.'

After hurrying away from the angry scene outside the magistrates' court, Emily took Rose to the hotel where the pony was stabled. Here, she ordered tea before speaking of the events of the morning and deploring the punishment meted out by Sir Richard Jane.

Aware that Emily was extremely angry and upset, Rose did her best to be conciliatory. 'I don't think the magistrate had any alternative,' she said. 'After all, the boys did admit to stealing the eggs.'

'I know that, Rose, and he gave them the option of a fine – which I am happy to have paid – but having heard the circumstances leading to the theft he should not have added a whipping to poor Albert's punishment.'

'The crowd thought so too,' said Rose. 'That was what upset them so much.'

'Sir Richard will never accept any blame for the disturbance,' Emily said bitterly. 'He will regard it as proof that the miners are becoming increasingly lawless and hand out even harsher sentences in the future.'

'Who would your father support – you or Sir Richard?'

Rose's question was unexpected and Emily needed to think for a moment how best to phrase her reply. 'My father has a great deal of sympathy for the miners and their families,' she said eventually, 'but he would never accept hardship as an excuse for breaking the law.'

'Is he likely to be understanding when he hears you spoke up in court today on behalf of Albert and Tom?' Rose asked shrewdly.

Emily shook her head. 'No, but somebody needed to speak up for them – and pay their fines. Can you imagine what their life would have been like in a prison?'

'Only too well!' came the grim reply. 'I've met with children who have been to prison. They're never the same again. But it wouldn't only have been the boys who suffered. I truly believe it would have killed Margaret had they gone to gaol.'

'What do you know of Margaret?' Emily asked. 'She was far too ill for me to form an accurate impression of her but I would not have thought she came from a mining family.'

'She doesn't. Before Margaret married she was a lady's maid in the house of the Earl of St Germans. I don't know how she met up with her husband but she could have done a lot better for herself. Between you and me, he's always been a bit shiftless, never remaining at a mine for long, even when work was available. I doubt whether she or the boys will ever see anything of him again, although she's fully convinced he'll send for them when he's made some money.' Rose shrugged. 'Hopefully I'll be proven wrong. I've never been a good judge of men. It was lucky for me that William came along when he did, or I'd have probably ended up just like Margaret and the many others around here who are in a similar situation.'

Looking at Emily, she asked, 'Have you heard anything of Sam Hooper since he went away?'

The question took Emily by surprise and she said defensively, 'No. Is there any reason why he should write to me?'

Rose leaned towards Emily and rested a hand on her arm for a moment. 'I'm sorry, Emily, that was unforgivably rude of me. It was just . . . Oh, I don't know. I saw you together once or twice and thought that if things had been different . . . I mean, had you come from similar backgrounds, what a lovely couple you'd have made. He's a very nice young man. I believe that if his pa had given him a chance in life instead of sending him out to work as soon as he was big enough to pick up a shovel, he'd have made something of himself.'

Aware of how easy it was for the most straightforward statement to be distorted by village gossip, Emily said cautiously, 'Sam is missed by the choir. He had a fine voice.'

'I wasn't thinking only of the choir . . . You know he has asked after you in his letters?'

'How do you know that?' Emily demanded, startled

by this news. 'When I spoke to Sam's father he said he
had received only one letter from Sam and that it
contained hardly anything at all. Of course, that was
some months ago.'

'He has had at least two letters since then, although
one was little more than a note. You were mentioned
in all of them. At least, that's what Bessie told me and
she has no reason to lie.'

Bessie was the wife of Sam's brother Daniel. Her
father was a staunch Methodist and she and Rose knew
each other quite well.

Emily was hurt that Sam's father should have lied
to her, but Rose's words gave her a warm glow.

Keeping her feelings to herself, she put down her
cup and said, 'Come along, let's see if we might have
the boys released so we can take them home. Poor
Margaret must be desperate for news of them . . .'

VI

Returning to St Cleer in the trap pulled by Reverend
Boyce's high-stepping pony, it was Tom and not his
older brother who was shedding tears.

On the instruction of Sir Richard Jane, the young boy
had been forced to watch as Albert, the brother he
revered, received six strokes of the birch at the hands
of the burly police officer.

Albert took his punishment manfully, letting out an
involuntary gasp of pain only when the first blow
landed, but when he was released and Emily saw his
pale and drawn face, she could have wept for him.

* * *

Margaret Minns had become increasingly anxious as the morning passed with no sign of her two sons. At midday she insisted upon being helped out of bed and into a chair close to a window, from where she could see the lane along which the boys would be coming.

She had a long wait. It was almost three o'clock before she saw a trap pulled by a trotting pony bowling along the lane. Inside were two women – and two small boys.

'It's them!' she cried. 'The boys . . . they've got them free! Help me up . . . please. I want to meet them at the door.'

The woman who occupied the cottage, assisted by her daughter, helped Margaret to the door. They stayed near and would have supported her, but she shook them off and when the boys reached the garden gate she was standing, unsupported, in the doorway.

'Ma!'

Delighted, Tom ran along the garden path and flung himself at his mother, almost knocking her off balance.

Albert came along the path more slowly, but his expression showed that he too was delighted to see his mother on her feet.

With an arm about Tom, she held the other out to Albert, saying, 'You're taking your time, Albert. Come here quickly, so I can hug you too.'

'He can't hurry, Ma,' Tom cried. 'His back hurts. They flogged him – and they made me watch.'

Margaret's jaw sagged and she looked to Albert for confirmation, but it was Rose who replied as she came along the path behind Albert, with Emily by her side.

'Albert has been a very brave boy, Margaret. The constable who had to birch him said as much.'

'But why was he flogged?' In tears now, Margaret said, 'Oh, Albert, come here, my son . . .'

Reaching out, she pulled him to her but he winced and she released him immediately.

'I'm sorry, Albert, it's all my fault . . .'

It was too much for Margaret in her weakened state and she began to cry uncontrollably.

In a bid to comfort her, Albert said, 'It's all right, Ma. It didn't really hurt me . . . well, not *too* much.'

'It could have been a whole lot worse, Margaret,' said Rose. 'Albert was given a three-pound fine, or three months in prison, and Tom a pound, or a month in prison. Miss Boyce paid their fines. She also spoke up for them in court.'

Margaret switched her tear-filled gaze to Emily. 'Thank you. Thank you very, very much. I'll try to repay you one day. They're not really bad boys. If only I'd been more able to cope with things.'

Emily thought she had never seen a woman more broken in spirit and she said sympathetically, 'It's *not* your fault, Margaret. Albert should not have done what he did, but he is young and had no one to turn to for help. Even Jacob Norris realised it. He actually came up to me afterwards and said he was sorry for turning the boys over to the police. An apology from Mr Norris is without precedent. He would not condone what they did and said they deserved to be fined, but he was horrified that the magistrate ordered a young boy to be flogged for trying to help his sick mother. Others agreed with him. They created such a fuss in court over the sentence that the magistrate could not continue. He had to order the court cleared.'

Margaret began crying once more and Emily said

hastily, 'We must put this in the past, Margaret. The important thing now is to get you well, find somewhere for you and the boys to live and see if we can obtain work for you.'

'There are thousands of women looking for the same thing,' Margaret said bitterly. 'I'm not in this state because I haven't tried to find work. It just isn't around to be had.'

'We'll see about that,' Emily said determinedly. 'You leave it to me.'

Once outside the cottage, Rose said to Emily, 'I know you were just trying to cheer up Margaret – and there's no one who needs it more – but she's going to be very disappointed if nothing comes of the promise you've made to her.'

'Something *will* come of it,' Emily declared. 'I intend taking the first steps towards a solution to Margaret's problems immediately.'

Despite her assurance to Rose, it was a slightly less self-assured Emily who picked her way through the mud of Jacob Norris's farmyard half an hour later, her skirts raised halfway up the calves of her legs.

The quarrelsome old farmer saw her coming and prepared himself for the tirade he felt certain she was about to deliver. But Emily's opening words took him by surprise.

'Mr Norris, outside the Liskeard magistrates' court this morning you expressed regret for having Albert and Tom Minns brought before the magistrate. Did you mean that?'

'I don't say things I don't mean. Not like some folks I could name.'

'Good! Then perhaps you would like to make amends for having a nine-year-old flogged and he and his seven-year-old brother branded as thieves for the remainder of their lives?'

'If it's money you're after, you'll need to think again. I feel sorry for 'em, yes, but I've no money to spare for the likes of they.'

'I'm not asking you for money, Mr Norris, but I believe you own that old cottage along the lane. The one I passed on my way here. I looked in through the windows and noticed a piece or two of furniture in there as well.'

'That's right. My ma's brother lived there until he died. That was nigh on ten years ago. It hasn't been touched since then.'

'As it's been empty for so long, why not allow the Minns family to move in? It would give them a roof over their heads, at least.'

'Ah well,' Norris said cautiously, 'folk'd pay good rent for a cottage the likes of that.'

'The Minnses *have* no money, as well you know,' Emily retorted. 'Letting them move into the cottage would be an act of contrition on your part for what happened to the two boys. Nevertheless, Margaret Minns will be happy to carry out some domestic work for you when she is well enough. The boys could help around the farm for a few coppers too. I have no doubt you could manage that without any hardship. On my last visit I watched you straightening up after you had been working in the chicken house. You are not getting any younger, Mr Norris. A little help around the farm would not come amiss.'

'*I'll* be the one to decide whether or not I need help

around the place, not you. There'll be no one poking about my house and nosing into my affairs. No, I'll not have it.'

'Do I take it then that you will allow the Minnses to move into your cottage and ask for nothing in return? That would be a *most* charitable act indeed.'

Emily was aware she was forcing the issue and when a long silence ensued, she feared she might have pushed the eccentric farmer too far, too quickly.

To her relief and delight, he growled, 'There's no one gets anything for nothing in this life. If they're going to move into the old cottage rent free I'll expect the boys to help about the farm and not look for any pay. Their mother too, sometimes.'

'Margaret Minns will need to have money coming in in order to feed her family,' Emily said. 'I am hoping to find more suitable work for her, but I have no doubt the boys will be happy to help you in any way they can.'

Emily left Jacob Norris's farm well pleased with herself. The first part of her plan had been more success-ful than she had dared hope.

The next would not be quite so easy. Of this she was certain.

VII

Reverend Arthur Boyce travelled to Liskeard to carry out his magisterial duties two days after the trial of Albert and Tom Minns. In St Cleer, Emily awaited his return with considerable trepidation. She had not told her father of her own eventful visit to the magistrates' court, afraid of his predictable reaction. Nevertheless, she was aware he would be given details by the court officials – and would be furious at her involvement.

All went very much as she had anticipated – except that it was Sir Richard Jane and not a court official who told Arthur Boyce of the role played by Emily in the near-riot that had erupted when the two young sons of Margaret Minns were sentenced for theft.

'I am angry beyond words that I should have learned of this matter from Sir Richard and not from my own daughter.'

Arthur Boyce and Emily faced each other across the width of his desk, as they had on so many occasions before. 'Maude told me that Rose Holman had called at the house and spoken to you, but I thought it most probably concerned some simple village matter. To think I even allowed you to use the pony and trap! Had I known I would have forbidden you to leave the house.'

Emily had been dreading this confrontation, but she was ready for it and determined not to allow her father to browbeat her into submission on this occasion.

'I *wanted* you to hear about it from others first. Then I could be certain that you would come to me, hear the *full* story and it could be laid to rest, once and for all.'

Her reply took Arthur Boyce by surprise. He had been expecting her to make excuses for not telling him what had taken place in the Liskeard magistrates' court.

'If what I have heard is true – and I have no reason to doubt the word of Sir Richard Jane – then it is not a matter that may be dismissed quite so easily. According to Sir Richard you must take responsibility for much of the outrageous behaviour that took place because of your decision to defend the actions of the two young thieves in an open court.'

'No, Father,' Emily said determinedly. 'Responsibility for the genuine outburst of anger from those in the public gallery lies with Sir Richard, as it was the direct result of the sentences handed out by him to children aged nine and seven. It was his actions that were disgraceful.'

'Sir Richard was carrying out his magisterial duties,' Arthur Boyce said pompously. 'Punishing lawbreakers—'

'*Punishing!* You talk of punishment for a seven-year-old? Not that Sir Richard has ever shown compassion for children, whatever their age. The sentences he metes out to them are certainly not in keeping with the teachings of Our Lord . . . but I hardly need to remind you of His words. Nor do I believe *you* would commit a five-year-old to prison, as Sir Richard has on occasion, or sentence a nine-year-old to a flogging because in sheer desperation he stole a few eggs in order to save the life of his starving mother. I, and others in court, were incensed that Sir Richard chose to add a flogging to an already severe sentence. It is my sincere belief that had you been on the bench you would have tempered justice with mercy.'

'Not knowing all the facts of the case it is impossible to say what *I* would have done – but that is not the issue here.'

'I know. You are angry because I became involved in a case held in the court where you sit as a magistrate.' Emily was determined not to sound apologetic, but neither did she wish to further antagonise her father if it could be avoided. 'I had little choice, Father. Rose Holman came to the house to see me, explained the details of the case, and asked for my assistance. I could not refuse.'

Momentarily forgetting his anger, Arthur Boyce exclaimed, 'The wife of the Methodist minister came here seeking your help? Are you telling me these two boys are from a Methodist family?'

'I don't know, Father. The question of the poor woman's religion has never been raised, but I have good reason to believe she and the boys belong to the Established Church. For this reason alone I could hardly have refused to help and have it said we lacked the compassion of the Methodists.'

Somewhat mollified, but by no means fully satisfied with Emily's explanation, the parson said, 'Nevertheless, did it not occur to you that the sympathy you were to show to those two young thieves might have been misplaced?'

'Of course.' Emily believed she was on firmer ground now. 'That is why I visited their mother before agreeing to help. Sadly, I found the story told to me by Rose was all too true. The mother is a good woman who has come desperately close to death. Before her marriage she was a lady's maid, for the family of the Earl of St Germans.'

As Emily had anticipated, this latter piece of information impressed her father more than anything else that had so far been said in defence of Margaret Minns and her two children.

'What of her husband?' he asked.

'He worked in the mines, but when he was put out of work he went to Australia, promising to send for the family as soon as he was able.'

Arthur Boyce was fully aware of the problems beset-
ting the Cornish mining industry. Nevertheless, his next
words were less than sympathetic.

'I cannot understand any man abandoning his family
and going off to a strange land without first making
adequate provision for those he leaves behind.'

Observing Emily's momentary unguarded expression, he added, 'Oh yes, I know things are bad for
miners at the moment, very bad indeed, but there have
been good years too. A prudent man would have put
money aside when it was available.'

When Emily made no reply, he continued, 'I am
extremely disappointed by the manner in which you
have conducted yourself over this matter, Emily. You
should have consulted me before taking such foolish
action. You must have known it would prove a great
embarrassment to me – and might well have brought
discredit upon more important members of the family.
However, I am prepared to accept that, however
misguided, your actions were prompted by charitable
motives. I will therefore overlook your indiscretion on
this occasion – on condition that your work on behalf
of the needy is in future conducted along more conventional lines.'

Emily nodded, as though agreeing with her father's
condescending statement. 'Thank you, Father, but with
so much need in the parish right now I am finding it
very difficult to cope with the many demands upon my
time. I have decided I need to take on a personal maid,
to help me both in and outside the house.'

'A personal maid . . . ?'

Arthur Boyce looked at his daughter with growing

disbelief. 'I trust you are not talking of the mother of those two convicted young thieves? Oh no, that would be carrying charity too far!'

'What you really mean is that it would be bringing it too close to home. That is hypocritical, Father.'

Emily braced herself for yet another of their long and acrimonious arguments, but she was determined to stand her ground on this occasion. 'I want a personal maid and Margaret Minns desperately needs employment. What is more, she has all the qualifications for such a post.'

'Are you not forgetting something, Emily? She also has two sons who have both been convicted of theft. I refuse to have them living beneath my roof.'

'Margaret would be a living-out maid.'

'Really? I thought that one of the mitigating facts produced to the court was that the family *has* no home.'

'When the case was heard that was quite true, but Jacob Norris has allowed them to move into the empty cottage on his land.'

'Norris? The man from whom the boys stole the eggs?' Arthur Boyce was well aware of Jacob Norris's anti-social reputation.

'That's right, Father. When he heard of the family's circumstances he tried to withdraw the charges he had laid against the boys. Sir Richard refused to allow it.'

'By the time the case reached court it was too late for Jacob Norris to change his mind,' said her father, less belligerently. 'But I am amazed that he, of all people, should even have tried – and then to give the family a home too . . .'

'Indeed, but it is an act of charity that should be used as a yardstick for us all, should it not?'

Arthur Boyce realised belatedly that he had walked into the trap so neatly set by his daughter and there was no escape. The Wesleyans would make much of the fact that Jacob Norris had been shown to be more charitable than the vicar of the parish. He had no doubt that if Emily, his own daughter, did not get her way, it *would* become known that he had refused to employ the mother of the two boys.

'Do you have any proof that this woman *was* a maid in the St Germans household?'

'Rose Holman told me she was. I would not doubt her word.'

'The word of a third party, however credible, is not sufficient in such matters,' Arthur Boyce snapped. 'A satisfactory reference will be required. If one is forthcoming, Maude will interview the woman to ascertain whether or not she is suitable for the post.'

'No, Father, Maude will *not* interview her. If Margaret is to be employed here as *my* personal maid it will be because *I* think she is suitable. *I* will employ her and decide on her duties within the household.'

Emily knew that if Maude became involved Margaret Minns would not be taken on.

For a moment it seemed Arthur Boyce would insist upon Maude's right to interview Margaret. Instead, he shrugged in the manner of a weary man. 'Very well, but if she proves unsatisfactory in any way the responsibility will lie with you. I will leave it to you to inform Maude. You will also ensure that this woman conforms to the routine of the household.'

Slumping down in his chair, Arthur Boyce waved Emily from his presence. For the first time Emily could remember, she actually felt sorry for him. She wanted to go to him, give him a hug and say 'Thank you'.

'Go now, Emily, before I change my mind.'

Emily turned and left the study. As she closed the door behind her she realised this was the first time she had ever won a serious argument with her father.

VIII

Margaret Minns began work at the vicarage three weeks after Emily gained the parson's less than enthusiastic consent to employ her.

The miner's wife was still not fully recovered from her months of near-starvation but she was determined her weak state would not prevent her from carrying out her new duties. Emily had provided her with an opportunity to regain respectability and she was determined not to allow it to slip from her grasp.

The first thing she did was to inspect Emily's clothing, re-ironing much of it and sending some back to the laundry-maid, supervising the girl as she worked and explaining how a lady's clothes *should* be treated.

Maude did not take kindly to what she considered to be 'interference' with the household she controlled and she swiftly took Margaret to task.

Margaret Minns was not a hot-headed person and she refused to be drawn into an argument with the resentful housekeeper. However, she stood her ground over this particular issue, with the result that Maude complained to Reverend Boyce that the new maid was 'disrupting the smooth running of the household'.

Arthur Boyce did his best to placate the indignant housekeeper, but he would not agree that Margaret should be dismissed. The reason was that Emily had received a letter from the Countess of St Germans, praising Margaret as the best personal maid she had ever employed and expressing a wish to call in and speak with her when she was next in the vicinity. The St Cleer vicar would never pass up the opportunity to meet with a leading member of the aristocracy. However, his refusal to act did nothing to lessen Maude's animosity towards Emily's maid.

Emily discussed the housekeeper's attitude with Margaret when they were carrying baskets of newly baked bread to the soup kitchen set up for miners' families in the changing room of one of the recently closed mines.

'You mustn't take anything she says to heart, Margaret. She has been in charge of the household since my mother died and resents anyone else taking decisions she feels should be hers.'

'It doesn't really bother me,' Margaret said easily. 'I'm aware that she's being spiteful because you took me on without consulting her. It's understandable, I suppose. She sees it as undermining her authority. But I'm in work and grateful to you for it. I'll not be upset by the resentment of a woman who's seen marriage pass her by – and with it the chance of a family of her own. Take away the little bit of power she wields over the other servants in the vicarage and she's left with nothing. I have a husband – even though he's the Lord only knows where – and I have the boys. I wouldn't be without them for the world.'

They spoke about the boys and the work they were doing on the farm of Mr Norris until they arrived at the improvised soup kitchen. There they found a

frighteningly large queue of women and children waiting for them, together with a few men.

It was the men for whom Emily felt particular
sympathy. When soup and bread was being distributed
they shuffled forward in abject misery, ashamed of
being out of work, seemingly convinced that their present condition was their fault.

The soup kitchen was a non-denominational venture
and Rose Holman and a band of helpers had been at
the mine for most of the morning. Using coal supplied
by the mine owners they had built up a fire and, in a
huge cauldron, made up a soup comprising anything
edible the women had been able to obtain.

As the hungry families began to eat, Margaret went
among them. Remembering how ill she had been
herself, she chastised any mother she saw giving away
her own food to her children.

Emily worked in the soup kitchen with a growing
feeling of anger and frustration; anger that miners and
their families should be reduced to such dire straits
through no fault of their own, and frustration that there
was so little that could be done to find a long-term
answer to their problems.

She expressed her thoughts as she, Margaret and
Rose made their way back to St Cleer once the soup
and bread had all been distributed.

Rose was surprisingly philosophical. 'Mining is a
hard way to earn a living. It always has been. A miner
spends his working life underground with death lurking at his elbow. Yet if he's forced to spend too much
time above ground he's restless to be down below
again.'

'That's right,' Margaret agreed. 'And when he's

working his family can never settle, no matter how hard they try, or however long he does the job.'

'That's true,' Rose added. 'A mine closure is a mixed blessing for a miner's wife. Part of her will be pleased to have him above ground but, particularly if there are children, she'll be worrying how she's going to feed them. I know my mother used to say as much on many occasions.'

'It's even worse when your husband is forced to go abroad to try to earn a living,' said Margaret, with considerable feeling. 'You're never certain that things *are* going to get better, or whether you're going to need to make a new life for yourself and the children.'

'Don't give up hope,' said Emily. 'With any luck you'll hear from your husband before too long and he'll send you money to pay the fare for you and the boys to go to Australia.'

Pretending not to notice the sceptical glance Rose gave her, Emily continued, 'Once you're together again, with someone to share your problems, you'll feel on top of the world.'

'That's right,' Rose said encouragingly. 'I've heard a great many good things said about life out there.'

'I sometimes think that Charlie probably doesn't want us out there with him.' Margaret spoke with a hint of bitterness that Emily had never heard from her before. 'It's been more than a year now since he went away. I can't help feeling that life must be better for him without the burden of a wife and a couple of children.'

'You mustn't think like that,' Emily tried to reassure her, even as she remembered what Rose had told her about Margaret's husband. 'The mail takes a long time to reach England. He's probably working in some remote place there and even when the mail arrives at a port it needs to be put on board a ship and I believe the voyage sometimes takes three months or more.'

She was trying to cheer up Margaret, but at the same time she remembered that Sam's family had received a number of letters from him during the time he had been in Australia.

She feared that Rose might be correct in her assessment of Charlie Minns.

7

I

The last, long leg of the voyage of the *Bonython* from Plymouth to South Australia passed almost without incident, although the vessel arrived at its destination with two extra passengers. Both girls, they had been born during the last weeks of the voyage.

There had, in fact, been four births on board. However, despite the earlier proud boast of the ship's captain that he had never lost a passenger on his ship, two of the newly born children died when each was less than a day old and they were buried at sea.

Nevertheless, the record of the *Bonython* compared very favourably with those of the other ships engaged in carrying migrants to Australia.

The latter part of the voyage had also seen Ira Moyle spending a great deal of time with Sam, Primrose – and with Jean. He was now included among the men for whom she prepared meals. He never tired of telling her how much better was her cooking than that of the woman who had provided his meals on the earlier part of the voyage.

Jean was pleased to earn the extra few shillings that cooking for Ira brought her and she was always polite towards him, but she rarely extended to him the same warmth that was part of her relationship with Sam.

However, Ira and Primrose were happy in each other's company and Ira would spend hours playing simple games with the child that would have tried the patience of most men. For this Jean was grateful.

It meant she was able to devote more time to taking classes in reading, writing and simple arithmetic and so was able to add a few extra shillings to the money she was putting aside to give herself and Primrose a secure start in the new land.

When the *Bonython* had been at sea for a hundred and five days, word went around that they might expect to sight Australia at any time.

For the remainder of that day the excited passengers crowded the upper deck, each hoping to be the first to glimpse the land that was to be their new home.

The passengers had spent enough time at sea now. All wanted to leave the ship and face the challenge of the new land where they could begin to rebuild their lives.

When dusk fell over an empty ocean and the wind began to pick up, the disappointed migrants slowly dispersed and made their way below deck to their bunks.

There were numerous remarks about the crew causing them to 'get all excited about nothing', but they knew that land could not be too far away.

Sam would have gone below with the others, but

the mate struck up a conversation with him. Soon, Sam was the only passenger left on the upper deck. The two men were standing in the lee of the galley, sheltering from the wind, when the mate said to him, 'Well, son, we'll not be enjoying each other's company for very much longer now. How have you enjoyed the voyage?'

'I won't be sorry to get off the *Bonython*,' Sam admitted. 'But that's not saying anything against the ship, in many ways the voyage has been better than I thought it would be. It's just that I want to be back mining again.'

'You won't find a finer ship than the *Bonython*,' the mate said with pride. 'Or a finer skipper than Captain Carver. I couldn't name you more than two other ships that have ever made this voyage without losing a passenger – a passenger who boarded the ship in England, that is. I'm not counting the babies who died. They'd have probably been lost if they'd been born on land – and a ship's no place for a woman to give birth. It's not natural.'

Sam felt unable to argue with the mate's logic. Jean had lost her baby on land. 'I'm sure you're right,' he said. 'Most of the passengers feel the way I do, too, but tonight they're going to their bunks disappointed. We were all expecting to have our first sighting of Australia before the day was out.'

'Then they should have had a little more patience,' declared the mate. 'Take a look for'd, on the starboard side.'

Puzzled, Sam nevertheless did as the mate suggested. At first he could see nothing. Then, far away where the unseen horizon merged with the sky, a

pin-point of light winked at him for a brief moment
before vanishing once more.

'What is it . . . ? That light . . . ?' he exclaimed excitedly.

'It's the lighthouse at Cape Borda, on Kangaroo
Island,' the mate replied. 'That's Australian territory,
son. You're almost there.'

II

The mate's statement that the *Bonython* had almost
reached its destination proved somewhat optimistic. It
was not until early morning of the fourth day after
sighting the Cape Borda lighthouse that the rattle of
the anchor chain signalled the arrival of the ship off the
busy Wallaroo dockside.

It was the nearest port to Kadina and served the
copper mines of South Australia's Yorke Peninsula.

There was great excitement on board and on the
harbourside too. News of the imminent arrival of the
migrant ship from Plymouth had reached the three
copper mining towns of Wallaroo, Moonta and Kadina
only hours after it had been first sighted beating its
way along the coastline, miles to the south.

Of those living in the mining towns, many were
Cornish and were awaiting friends and relatives.
Hurrying to the port they hired boats and put out to
meet the ship in the hope of seeing a familiar face on
board.

There would be a great number of reunions that day,
most eagerly anticipated, but some that were not.

Those migrants with friends and relatives waiting

for them were almost frantic in their efforts to be among the first to go ashore.

As no one was expecting Sam or Jean, they stayed back, waiting for the excitement to die down. As a result they were among the few who spent an extra night on board.

The following morning, Sam rose early and went on deck to enjoy the quiet of the early morning, before others woke and before work began in earnest on the dockside.

Gazing out at what could be seen, it was something of a disappointment. Beyond the ships and warehouses the land was flat with not a hill of note to be seen anywhere.

Even houses were not immediately in evidence, although smoke rose from a sufficient number of chimneys to give some indication of the extent of the port of Wallaroo.

He had just lit his pipe when he was joined by Jean, carrying a still-sleepy Primrose.

'I thought I might find you here,' she said, by way of a greeting.

'It was too hot down below without a sea breeze to cool things down. I thought I'd come up here to enjoy the peace and quiet for a while.'

'Primrose and I couldn't sleep either – so we've come up here to disturb your peace and quiet.'

Sam smiled. 'That's all right, Jean. I don't find you and Primrose disturbing.'

Giving Sam a strange look, Jean said, 'No, you don't, do you?'

Unsure what his reply should be to this unexpected interpretation of his words, Sam said nothing.

The silence stood between them for some three or four minutes, before the strangled note from a steam whistle announced the first very early departure of a steamship from the busy port.

It served to break their silence and Jean said, 'It doesn't look to be very exciting out there, Sam.'

'I agree, Jean, but we won't be staying here very long. Once ashore we'll head inland to Kadina and the mines. We'll feel at home there, I'm quite sure.'

'What's going to happen when we reach Kadina, Sam? What will we both do?'

'I'll find work in the mines, hopefully in the big Kadina mine and you'll find your father. That's what we said we'd do.' They had spoken of this so many times he could not understand the reason for her questions now.

'We've travelled all the way from St Cleer together and have known each for so many years. Where do we go now, Sam – you and I?'

When he did not reply immediately, Jean asked, 'How do you see me, Sam? Just as a girl you've grown up with . . . or is there more to us than that?'

When he still did not reply, she added softly, 'Do you still see me as the woman who was the wife of your best friend, Sam? Phillip's dead now and no amount of grieving is going to bring him back. I'm no longer his wife, Sam – I'm not *anybody*'s wife. I'm just a very lonely woman who has a young daughter to care for – and who's desperately afraid of facing a future on her own. Do you understand what I'm trying to say, Sam?'

'I . . . I think so.'

Sam knew very well what she was saying. She was

telling him in as obvious a manner as she could, that she was available – if he wanted her.

'Is there anything you want to say to me, Sam?'

He wished he could say the words he knew she wanted to hear. To tell her there was a future for them – together. But he could not. He thought too much of her to be dishonest.

Lamely, he said, 'We're going to enjoy a good life out here, Jean. When you and Primrose find your pa you'll have someone to take care of you. Someone who's family. If he's still working on the Kadina mine we'll all see quite a lot of each other, because that's where I expect to be working. It'll be good to be below grass again, winning ore.'

Jean said nothing for a long while. Then she said, 'I think I'll go below and make certain I've packed all our things.'

Sam was aware Jean was hurt by his response, but he did not know what else he could have said.

'Jean . . .'

She turned back to him expectantly, but he said, 'Let me know when you're ready. I'll bring your things up on deck, ready to put in the boat.'

'There's no need, Sam, Ira said he'll do it for us, if I wanted him to.'

'Oh! Well then . . . I'll see you when we're all ready. The mate says the easiest way to get to Kadina is by the horse-train. I'll find out a bit more about it before we go ashore.'

'All right, Sam. I'll tell Ira what's happening.'

It should have been a relief to him that Jean understood he would not be assuming long-term responsibility for her and Primrose. It *was* a relief, he told himself. Yet he felt he had somehow let them both down.

Trying hard to shake off the feeling, he went below to the single men's hold to complete his own packing and bring his baggage up on deck.

8

I

When Margaret Minns had been working for Emily for only two months, a tragedy occurred that would lead to a dramatic change in both their lives.

It was a Sunday and Emily had been to the morning service in the village church, singing in the choir, as usual. Margaret had unexpectedly attended the service, leaving the boys to put in a morning's work on the Norris farm.

Emily was talking to Margaret while she waited for her father to finish bidding farewell to his congregation.

His duty completed, Parson Boyce made his way to where the two young women stood. Margaret immediately broke off her conversation. Nodding farewell to Emily and her father, she turned to make her way home.

Looking closely at her father, Emily asked anxiously, 'Are you all right, Father? You don't look very well.'

'I confess I do not feel too well, Emily . . .' His reply

was breathless and his eyes appeared to find difficulty in focusing on her. 'I . . . I have a pain . . . a dreadful pain . . .'

Suddenly, Arthur Boyce fell to his knees, then pitched forward on to his face.

Emily let out a cry of horror and crouched beside her prostrate father. As she struggled to turn him over she was aware of the sound of running feet along the path. Soon others were helping her and someone was calling for Dr Kittow. He had been in the congregation and was now making his way towards his pony and trap, left in the lane outside the church.

'Parson's still breathing,' said one of the church- wardens who had helped to turn Arthur Boyce on his back.

Emily took some consolation from his words, but her father was quite unconscious, his forehead bleeding where it had struck the ground.

Taking out a handkerchief, she was wiping away the blood when the doctor reached the scene, the small crowd parting to allow him through.

After only a cursory glance at the parson, the doctor took the unconscious man's hand and felt for a pulse. Nodding his head gravely, he spoke to the crowd. 'Some of you men carry him to the vicarage. Two take his shoulders, two more get a firm grip on his cassock and one of you support his head. Quickly now.'

As some of the village men gathered around their parson, Emily asked the doctor, 'What is wrong with him? Has he fainted?'

The doctor shook his head. 'It is rather more serious than that I'm afraid, Miss Emily. It's your father's heart. He has suffered a seizure.'

Wide-eyed and suddenly afraid, Emily asked hesitantly, 'He . . . he's not going to die?'

'I'll know a little more when we have him at the vicarage and I am able to examine him more thoroughly.'

The doctor was being deliberately evasive. The realisation that he thought this necessary frightened Emily more than if he had told her the truth.

At the vicarage, Arthur Boyce was carried upstairs with some difficulty and placed gently upon his bed. Dr Kittow then sent everyone from the room, declaring he would undress his patient, examine him and put on his night attire.

Emily thanked the men who had carried her father home. After promising to keep them informed of her father's condition, she sent them away.

As it was Sunday, the servants had the day off, but Maude was in the house and had come from the kitchen when the party entered the house. Emily repeated the doctor's brief diagnosis to her, adding, 'We should know more when Dr Kittow has completed his examination, Maude.'

'Heaven help us all if anything happens to poor Parson Boyce,' lamented the housekeeper. 'He works himself too hard, as I've told him many times. He has too much on his mind right now, what with all the changes that have gone on in his own house since dear Miss Caroline married and went away. Poor man, he's reached an age where he should have peace and quiet.'

'I'll go and make some tea,' said Margaret, who had come to the vicarage instead of returning to the Norris farm. 'No doubt the doctor would like a cup when he's finished his examination.'

'*I'll* do that, if you don't mind,' Maude said indignantly. 'I'll not have you taking over the kitchen as well.'

When Maude had gone, Margaret said apologetically, 'I'm sorry, Miss Emily. I should have known better than to suggest I did something in the kitchen when Maude was around.'

'Maude is upset because of what has happened to my father,' Emily replied. 'She has looked after him for very many years. I am quite certain she did not mean to be rude.'

Margaret thought otherwise, but she said nothing. Emily had more to worry about than animosity between two servants.

'Why not go home to the boys?' Emily said. 'You see little enough of them in the week.'

'I'll wait with you until the doctor has examined Parson Boyce. The boys have been working this morning. If I'm not home when they finish, Albert will get something for him and young Tom. He's a good boy that way.'

'You are lucky to have them, Margaret. No matter what happens in your life you have them to support and care for you. That must mean a great deal.'

'Yes, I have them with me – thanks to you. But you mustn't feel *you* have no one to turn to right now – whatever happens. I'll be here – twenty-four hours a day, if need be. The boys will be ready to give you any help they can, too. They both know how much they owe to you.'

Touched by the other woman's declaration of

support, Emily said, 'Thank you, Margaret. I appreciate your loyalty. Hopefully, my father will make a full recovery and things will soon return to normal.'

'Of course. I just don't want you thinking there's no one who cares – really cares, that is. Now, Maude seems to be taking her time with that tea. I'll go down to the kitchen and see what's keeping her.'

Margaret had been gone for no more than a couple of minutes when the door to Arthur Boyce's bedroom opened and Dr Kittow came from the room, closing the door quietly behind him.

'My father . . . he is all right?' Emily was alarmed by the doctor's grave expression.

'He is still unconscious, Miss Emily, and likely to remain so for quite some time. He has had a rather serious seizure, I'm afraid.'

'But he *will* recover in time?' Emily suddenly felt more vulnerable than at any time in her life.

'It would please me beyond measure were I able to give you a categorical "yes" to that question, my dear, but it would be less than honest of me. Your father's life is in the hands of one with whom he has a much closer relationship than I.'

Tea was served to Emily and Dr Kittow in the sitting room by a sullen housekeeper. Maude had taken offence when Margaret had come to the kitchen and offered to serve the tea for Maude, since she must be busily engaged in preparing lunch in the absence of the maids.

Muttering darkly about 'them as can only think of their stomachs at such a time as this', Maude told Margaret she had always been able to manage things on a Sunday, '. . . and could do so well enough now.'

Placing the tea on a tray, with cups, sugar and milk, Maude brushed past Margaret and bore the tea off to the sitting room.

Emily, used to the housekeeper's moods, realised she was angry and knew it probably had something to do with Margaret, but she had more important matters to worry about right now.

'What course can I expect my father's condition to take, Dr Kittow?'

The doctor was little more forthcoming than before. 'In cases such as this it is very difficult to make an accurate prognosis, Miss Emily. Sometimes a patient will regain consciousness – sometimes not. If your father regains consciousness in the near future his chances of recovery will be higher, but by no means assured. He is seriously ill. I am afraid I will be a frequent visitor to your home in the weeks ahead.'

While Emily was still mulling over his words she heard a click as the door to the sitting room was closed. She realised the doctor's words of warning had been overheard by Maude.

It made little difference to her at the time, but she would recall this moment later.

II

Reverend Arthur Boyce lay in a coma in his room for almost seven weeks, during which time Caroline, summoned by Emily, arrived at the vicarage and stayed for eight days.

While she was there Dr Kittow called daily, occasionally twice a day. Eventually, convinced her father would never regain consciousness and might lie in a coma for weeks, even years, Caroline decided she would return to her Dorset vicarage home. Now four months pregnant, she could not bear to be separated from her husband.

She departed after assuring Emily she would return immediately should their father regain consciousness, or if Emily felt her presence could serve any useful purpose.

Emily was left feeling that Caroline was reluctant to spend one hour longer than was absolutely necessary in the sprawling vicarage.

She did not blame her sister. Caroline now had a husband she adored, a home of her own and was about to start a family. The gloomy old vicarage was a reminder of unhappier times; the place where her mother had died leaving the two sisters to be brought up by a despotic father and an implacable housekeeper.

Even now, with Reverend Arthur Boyce lying so gravely ill, Maude seemed more concerned with maintaining her status in the household than in trying to make Emily's burden lighter. She and Margaret had another of their frequent arguments, this time about the carelessness of the laundry-maid, who had torn one of Emily's dresses in the wash and failed to say anything about it.

Margaret discovered the tear when she set out Emily's clothes one morning. She wasted no time in taking the maid to task, first for her carelessness and, secondly, for not reporting the matter in order that the dress might be mended immediately.

Maude overheard the admonition and angrily confronted Margaret, declaring that the manner in

which the servants carried out their duties was *her*
responsibility and not that of a 'jumped-up miner's
wife' who was incapable of controlling her own two
thieving children!

Hiding the anger she felt at the housekeeper's words,
Margaret calmly suggested that if the laundry-maid
was the responsibility of the housekeeper, Maude
should take steps to ensure she took adequate care of
Emily's clothes.

Maude's angry tirade in response to Margaret's carefully controlled criticism brought Emily hurrying from
an upstairs room.

'Maude! What on earth is going on? How dare you
shout in such a manner? Control yourself immediately!'

'Don't you tell me to control myself, Miss Emily!'
Maude's anger had gone beyond the bounds of reason.
'You may have taken on this hussy, but *you're* not my
employer.'

'My father is lying seriously ill upstairs, Maude.
Until he is well enough to take charge of his affairs once
more I *am* your employer and I have no intention of
standing here arguing with you. Kindly show some
respect for my father.'

'Respect, you say? I'm the one who should be calling for respect around here. Haven't I looked after
your father for all these years – your mother too when
she was ill? Yes, and you and your sister when you
were left without anyone else? I've sacrificed any
chance of a family of my own for you all – and what
thanks do I get for it? My authority is undermined
and I'm left with no say about who is put to work in
the house. I'm not prepared to stay under such conditions, Miss Emily. If you're going to be in charge of

the house I shall leave. Your ways are not my ways.'

'It would be very inconsiderate of you to leave just now, Maude, as you are fully aware. Besides, it would be foolish to make such a decision in a spirit of anger. Sleep on it. If you wish, we will talk more about it tomorrow.'

Believing her threat to leave had seriously alarmed Emily, Maude said, 'It's become quite obvious that me and your so-called "personal maid" are never going to see eye to eye, so, as I see it, either she goes or I do. It's as simple as that. The choice is yours.'

Margaret was standing to one side of Maude and Emily could see her stricken face. Margaret believed that, called upon to make such a decision, Emily would not allow the housekeeper to leave.

'This is foolish, Maude. I refuse to accept such an ultimatum made, as it is, in the heat of the moment. We will talk about it again tomorrow.'

'There's nothing foolish about it, Miss Emily. If the parson recovers I shall be happy to return to take care of him. If he doesn't . . . ? Well, he told me a long time ago that I'll be remembered in his will. I suggest you think about *that*, Miss Emily. If you want me to stay then *she'll* have to go.' And with a maliciously triumphant glance at Margaret, Maude turned and left, heading for her own room.

Margaret was desperately unhappy. 'I . . . I'll leave, Miss Emily. I don't want to cause you any more trouble – but I'd like to be given time to find somewhere else. I don't want me and the boys going back to the way of life we had before.'

'There is no question of you going, Margaret, so we'l hear no more of it. I doubt if Maude will leave, either once she has had time to think about it in a rational manner.'

It would be extremely inconvenient were Maude to leave right now, but Emily was aware this was a confrontation she could not afford to lose. If Maude stayed – on her own terms – Emily would lose all credibility with the other servants. She was not prepared to allow such a situation to arise.

III

Early the following morning the tension in the Boyce household was almost tangible. Aware of the confrontation that had taken place between Emily and Maude, there was much speculation among the servants about which of the two women would emerge as the victor. The balance of opinion was tilted in favour of the housekeeper, but Emily had her champions.

When Margaret arrived for work earlier than usual, she found servants who had previously ignored her eager to seek her opinion on the imminent show-down between Emily and the housekeeper who had ruled Parson Boyce's household for so many years.

'I don't think Miss Emily will dare let her leave,' declared a maid who had been employed at the vicarage for almost as many years as the housekeeper. 'She's been here for so long the household couldn't manage without her.'

'That's absolute nonsense,' Margaret said heatedly. 'No one is indispensable. True, there would need to be changes, but I don't doubt that most would be for the better.'

'Especially for Miss Emily,' said a more recently employed maid. 'From what I hear, Maude has made her life a misery ever since she was a small girl.'

'That's the truth!' said a longer-serving maid. 'There have been times when I could have wept for Miss Emily. If I was her, I'd jump at the chance of getting rid of Maude.'

'Well, we're none of us Miss Emily,' Margaret said firmly. 'And I suggest you mind what you're saying. Maude has had all night to think about her situation. If she's got any sense she'll stay on and try to put things right between them. She'll not find another household prepared to put up with her ways.'

As the morning wore on without Maude putting in an appearance it became evident the housekeeper was not prepared to contemplate a compromise with the daughter of her employer.

Emily herself went about her daily business aware of the air of expectancy prevailing among the servants, but she said nothing. She felt all that needed saying had been said. The next move was up to the housekeeper.

It was eleven thirty that morning before a tight-faced housekeeper came downstairs and knocked at the door of the study of Parson Boyce, where Emily was going through the household accounts.

Maude was dressed for outdoors in a long black dress, black coat, shoes and hat, and a pair of black gloves. It seemed to Emily that the housekeeper had already decided her father was not going to recover and had gone into premature mourning.

Wasting no time with any form of greeting, Maude

said, 'I see you're going through the accounts. You'll no doubt be able to work out what I'm owed. I'll take it with me, if you don't mind.'

'I have it all ready for you, Maude ... here.'

Emily opened a desk drawer, took out some banknotes and coins and handed them to the black-clad woman, saying, 'You will find it correct. Unfortunately, in view of the suddenness of your decision to leave I feel unable to offer you a reference.'

'I don't need a reference – or anything else from *you*, Miss Emily. If the parson recovers he'll want me back here. If he doesn't then I won't ever need to work again.'

'His generosity towards you doesn't surprise me, Maude. He always thought a great deal of you. Your decision to leave now, when he probably needs you more than ever before, will come as a great disappointment to him.'

'If he recovers I'll explain my reasons to him. He'll understand.'

'Try explaining them to me, Maude, so *I* can understand. I know you don't like me very much and never have, but for my father's sake you might have tried to put your grievances to one side for a little while longer.'

'You just don't know how I feel, do you? You and your sister never have. I thought once upon a time that *he* did, but I was fooling myself. You talk of loyalty, but you don't know what real loyalty is – or the sacrifice it calls for. Well, I'll tell you. Many years ago I met a man who wanted to marry me. A shop-keeper, he was, who'd have given me a good life. Then your mother's health began to fail and the parson begged me to stay on and help him bring up you and your sister. Said you all needed me. That *he* needed me. I'd never regret staying, was what he said. He led me to believe ... But never mind what he led me to believe. I did what was asked of me, turned down the shopkeeper and stayed here at the vicarage – and for what?'

Maude gave an unnecessary tug at one of her gloves. 'Well, I *have* lived to regret listening to him. I see women of my age with children and grandchildren of their own to care for them in their old age – and what have *I* to look forward to? I'll tell you, a life with a sister who's a spinster like me, with no one to look after either of us. Oh, we'll both manage on what the parson will leave me, I don't doubt that, but there'll be no one to really care what happens to me.'

Emily felt sympathy for Maude welling up inside her. Then she remembered the times *she* had cried herself to sleep, when a hug from the cold and spiteful housekeeper would have made a huge difference to the loneliness she felt; when even a kind word or a warm glance would have been enough to break the cocoon of despair that had her trapped for so much of her young life.

'The decision is yours to make, Maude. I will not beg you to stay, but for my father's sake ...'

'You should have thought about all that when you brought that woman into the house against my wishes. It gave me a good idea of what I could expect when you took over the running of the vicarage, as you were bound to, one day. I suppose I should have known, really, seeing as how fond you are of miners and their families.'

'You are being impertinent, Maude. I think you had better leave before you say any more.'

'I'm leaving, but as for being "impertinent", it doesn't really matter any more. I can say what I think – and what I think is that the parson would have been better off if he'd let you run off with that Sam Hooper, instead of having him packed off to Australia.' Having delivered what she hoped would be a revelation, Maude finished, 'I'll send someone to collect my belongings as soon as I can. They're all packed up in my room.'

With this, the ex-housekeeper to Parson Arthur Boyce swept out of the study, leaving Emily fighting back tears.

It was not so much that Maude had confirmed what Emily already believed about Sam's departure from St Cleer, but that the housekeeper should have nurtured so much hatred and resentment inside her all these years.

Emily had accepted long ago that Maude did not really like Caroline and herself, but the depth of her dislike came as a great shock.

She also wondered how much happier life in the vicarage might have been had Maude married her shopkeeper and her father taken on a kindlier house-keeper.

Emily was quite certain of one thing. If, as she sincerely hoped, her father *did* recover, Maude would never return to work at the St Cleer vicarage.

IV

Only minutes after Maude's departure from the vicarage, Margaret entered the study with tea for Emily.

'I thought you might be in need of this. Maude hasn't

spoken to me, of course, but the maids say she was in a vicious mood.'

'They were not exaggerating,' Emily agreed, still shaken up by the vitriolic confrontation with the ex-housekeeper. 'I never realised just how much bitterness she harboured towards us all.'

'I fear she isn't entirely normal,' Margaret said sympathetically. 'The other maids are saying so quite openly now. No one dared say anything against her while she was still employed here.'

'If only she had told us years ago how she felt,' Emily said unhappily, 'we might have been able to resolve some of her problems and avoid the many years of unhappiness we have all suffered at her hands.'

Margaret could see that Emily had been deeply upset by the ex-housekeeper. She said comfortingly, 'Well, she's gone now. From what the servants have been saying, there's not one of them who's sorry to see the back of her, but it does leave a gap in the household. Will you take over her work?'

'I can't, Margaret. There are still many duties to be carried out around the parish – even more with my father so ill, and I must care for him too. I will need to find another housekeeper – and quickly. Unfortunately, I don't think any of the servants are up to the job, unless ...' Looking speculatively at Margaret, she asked, 'Do you think *you* could take it on, Margaret?'

'Me ... ?' Margaret's incredulity was unfeigned. 'I couldn't do it! Well, I *could* but you need someone to live in and I have the boys to think of.'

'That need pose no problems,' Emily declared, her enthusiasm growing as the spur-of-the-moment idea began to take shape. 'The annexe attached to the vicarage is empty. Adam, the gardener, lived there until he married Widow James, who has a house in the village. He moved in with her and her children and the annexe has been empty ever since.'

'What of your father? We're all hoping he'll recover, of course, but, when he does, will he allow us to stay there?'

'That's something I will deal with when the time comes,' Emily assured her. 'If you take on the post of housekeeper it will be permanent, I promise you. What's more, you will be paid a housekeeper's salary. What do you say?'

Margaret gave it some thought, then she said, hesitantly, 'I don't want to sound pessimistic, Miss Emily, but what if Parson Boyce *doesn't* get better? The Church will want to put another vicar in and we will have to move out – you as well.'

'That's quite true, Margaret, and I fully understand your concern. No doubt the new incumbent will need servants, but if you didn't suit each other ... well, I will have to find somewhere to live too and will need household staff. Whatever happens, I promise you you will not lose by becoming the housekeeper here.'

Satisfied, Margaret nodded. 'In that case I will be delighted to become your housekeeper, Miss Emily.'

In truth, the offer could not have come at a better time for her. Jacob Norris had lived alone for so long that he was unaccustomed to having others about him. Although at first he seemed pleased to have Margaret clean his house once a week, he was beginning to find fault with her for being *too* tidy. The house of the eccentric farmer had not been properly cleaned for half a lifetime and it seemed he preferred it that way.

With the boys, too, he was a hard taskmaster, expecting them to take on tasks more suited to grown men.

Margaret had decided to put her trust in Emily for whatever the future held in store for them all. It would be more secure than relying upon the whims of Jacob Norris.

When Reverend Arthur Boyce regained consciousness it came as a complete surprise. Dr Kittow, apparently resigned to the belief that his ecclesiastical patient would never regain his faculties, reduced the frequency of his visits to two a week. The last had been only the day before, when he reported that there was no change in his patient's condition.

Emily was in the parson's bedroom, arranging some flowers in a vase that stood on a sideboard. The window was open and from a side lawn came the sound of Albert and Tom's laughter as they played with a ball.

She had her back to the bed and was startled by a barely discernible, hoarse whisper from her father.

'I can hear children playing.'

'Father! Oh, Father, thank the Lord! You have come back to us.'

'Is that Caroline and Emily I can hear in the garden?'

He did not appear to have heard her. Aware that he had not fully regained consciousness, Emily took one of his hands in both of hers and said, tearfully, 'Yes. Yes, Father, it's Caroline and Emily.'

The ghost of a smile crossed Arthur Boyce's face and he said, 'It is a delightful sound, my dear. A truly joyful sound.'

He had not opened his eyes and now he ceased talking and seemed to relax.

Releasing his hand, Emily rushed from the bedroom. In the hallway outside she bumped into Margaret.

'Margaret, my father . . . he just spoke. He heard the boys laughing as they played in the garden and said what a delightful sound it was. He thought it was Caroline and me. I must send someone to Dr Kittow!'

Emily was so excited that before Margaret had time to say that *she* would send someone for the doctor, Emily was running downstairs to tell the good news to the servants and to send someone hurrying to fetch the doctor.

There was a babble of excitement coming from the servants gathered in the hallway when Margaret made her way slowly downstairs.

'Margaret, I have sent Albert to fetch the doctor,' Emily said as soon as she saw her. 'He can run faster than anyone else here. I will give him a shilling as a reward—'

Her excited chatter came to a sudden halt when she saw Margaret's eyes fill with tears. 'Margaret . . . ! What's the matter?'

'I'm sorry, Miss Emily. It was wonderful that your father was able to speak to you one last time, but . . . I just put my head around the door to see if there was anything he wanted. He was lying so still I went in to check him. He's gone, Miss Emily. The parson is dead.'

V

When the funeral service was over and Arthur Boyce had been laid to rest in the St Cleer churchyard, his family gathered in the vicarage study to hear solicitor Benedict Goldsworthy read the vicar's will.

Caroline and her husband were present, as were Lord and Lady Boyce, together with five nieces and nephews and two cousins. It seemed that each would receive a bequest.

Elsewhere in the house were many of Cornwall's churchmen, local gentry – and the Bishop of Exeter. On a visit to the county, he had caused a stir in the community by putting in an appearance at the funeral and delivering a eulogy to the late vicar of St Cleer.

Benedict Goldsworthy was seated behind Arthur Boyce's desk, preparing to read the will he had drawn up on the instructions of his late client. He was the archetypal English country solicitor. He even wore a pair of gold-rimmed pince-nez, perched low enough on his nose to enable him to peer over the rim at the gathered family as he coughed to gain their attention.

When those present fell silent he began to read from the document on the desk in front of him. There was a number of minor bequests to be distributed among the assembled family, but the bulk of his substantial estate was to be shared out equally between Emily and Caroline, making them both wealthy women.

Lord Boyce and a couple of the cousins murmured their approval of the monies inherited by Arthur Boyce's two daughters when, suddenly, there came the sound of raised voices from the direction of the hall. The door was thrown open and Maude entered the room so quickly she stumbled and almost fell.

Behind her Margaret hesitated in the open doorway, an expression of consternation on her face.

'Miss Rowe! What is the meaning of this unseemly interruption? This is a solemn occasion for the reading of your late employer's will. You are the last person I would have expected to show such unforgivable disrespect!' Benedict Goldsworthy fairly bristled with indignation.

'I am here to claim what's rightfully mine. I know I wasn't invited here for the reading of the will, but I don't intend to be cheated out of my rights by her!'

Maude jabbed a finger at Emily and one of the Boyce nieces closest to the ex-housekeeper started back, as though fearing lightning was about to issue forth from Maude's fingertip.

'My dear Miss Rowe, had you possessed any "rights", as you call them, in the will of the late Reverend Boyce, I assure you I would have notified you and requested your presence here today. Now, will you kindly leave, in order that I might conclude what is a purely private affair?'

'Are you telling me Parson Boyce never mentioned me in his will? If you are then I'll call you a liar. I know I'm in there. He came back from Liskeard one day and told me he'd left me money in his will. Enough to see me comfortable for the rest of my days, he said. I can even tell you the date if you like, because I wrote it down at the time. It was not many months before he sent that Sam Hooper off to Australia.'

'I have no doubt your recollection of the date is perfectly accurate,' said the solicitor. 'So, too, is the fact that you are mentioned in the will of the late Reverend Boyce. However, you are *not* a beneficiary.'

'What do you mean?' Maude demanded. 'If I'm in Parson Boyce's will then I'm entitled to what he promised me.'

'No, Miss Rowe,' Benedict Goldsworthy said firmly. 'Am I correct in saying that you left Reverend

Boyce's employ prior to his death?'

'She didn't give me no alternative.' Once again the finger was extended in Emily's direction. 'Taking on that miner's woman against my advice—'

'Your reasons for leaving Reverend Boyce's employ do not matter. The terms of the will are perfectly clear. Reverend Boyce did bequeath you a sum of money – a very *generous* sum, but it was conditional upon you being in his employment at the time of his death. I am sorry, you have no entitlement, so I must ask you once again to leave this room. Immediately, if you please, Miss Rowe.'

One of the churchwardens had been standing outside the door and heard what was said. He now stepped inside the study and led the stunned ex-housekeeper outside, closing the door behind him.

'Poor Maude, I could almost feel sorry for her,' Caroline whispered to her sister as the somewhat ruffled Benedict Goldsworthy rearranged the papers and documents he had inadvertently placed in the wrong order during the initial confusion caused by Maude's unexpected dramatic entrance.

'My Christian instincts are to feel the same,' Emily whispered in return, 'but, try as I might, I can find no compassion in me for her. I wish I could, truly I do.'

'Shall we proceed?' Benedict Goldsworthy peered disapprovingly over his pince-nez at the two sisters. 'I must apologise for the interruption. It was most unfortunate and not a little upsetting, but the formalities will take only a few more minutes of your time . . .'

The following evening, when the last of the funeral guests had departed, the house felt strangely quiet.

Emily was in her father's study, writing acknowledgements of the many letters of condolence she had received, when there was a soft knock on the door.

'Come in!'

The door opened and Margaret entered the room. In her hand she carried a mug of steaming milk. Placing it on the desk in front of Emily, she said, 'I've put the boys to bed and was heating some milk for myself. I thought I'd bring some for you. It will do you good and help you sleep after the strain of the past few days.'

'Thank you, Margaret, it is very thoughtful of you. Did you heat it in the kitchen?'

'Yes, Miss Emily, I hope you don't mind, but the stove was still hot.'

'Of course I don't mind . . .' Emily paused. She was still looking at Margaret, but appeared to be thinking. 'Look, why don't you fetch your milk and bring it in here? I think we should have a chat about the future.'

It was a despondent housekeeper who went off to do Emily's bidding. Margaret felt that nothing good could come from the forthcoming discussion. She had already spent many sleepless nights thinking about what the future held. Albert too was mature enough to realise they could not remain at the vicarage now Parson Boyce was dead. He had said he hoped they would not return to living in a ditch and risk her becoming seriously ill again.

Despite Emily's earlier promise, Margaret was aware that Caroline had asked her sister to go and live with her. She hoped Emily might be able to find employment for her elsewhere, but it was unlikely to be as either a housekeeper or a lady's maid. Not with two young sons to support – and she was determined never to give them up.

* * *

'Sit down, Margaret.'

Emily indicated the chair on which she herself had so rarely been allowed to sit on the occasions when she had been summoned to this room. Aware of Margaret's apprehension, she did not delay.

'I am quite certain you realise the reason I want to talk to you, Margaret. The death of my father means there will be changes – great changes – in all our lives. Not least of them, of course, is that I will shortly need to vacate the vicarage.'

Nodding acknowledgement of her employer's words, Margaret asked, 'Do you know when that will be?'

'As soon as they appoint another vicar. Probably in some two or three months' time.'

Margaret relaxed a little. At least she and the boys were not in imminent danger of being made homeless. 'Perhaps Mr Norris will let us move back to the cottage. The fact that I'm now well enough to work on the farm might make a difference. There wouldn't be any pay, of course, but it would mean we had a roof over our heads.'

A pained expression crossed Emily's face. 'I would not allow that, Margaret. You and the boys deserve better than that. I have grown very fond of you all during the time you have been living here.'

'What will *you* do?' Margaret asked. 'Will you go and live with Mrs Kavanagh? I know she's asked you to.'

'No,' Emily replied emphatically. 'Caroline is very happily married with a home of her own and expecting her first child. The last thing she really wants is to have another woman about the house. No, Margaret. There's something else I have had in mind for quite some time. It was no more than a forlorn dream while I was taking care of my father, but now ...'

Leaning back in her chair and looking speculatively at Margaret, she asked, 'Have you heard from your husband since you have been at the vicarage?'

The question took Margaret by surprise but, shaking her head, she replied, 'I've heard nothing from him since he left Cornwall, that's more than a year ago, now.'

'Would you care if you *never* heard from him, or ever saw him again?'

Startled by the question, Margaret replied indignantly, 'Of course I would. He's the boys' father.' Recovering her composure, Margaret's expression softened. 'Besides, he's my husband. Yes, I'd care very much.'

'Good! That's exactly what I hoped you might say, Margaret. Do you care enough to travel to Australia and try to find him?'

Emily's earlier questions had taken Margaret by surprise. This one left her dumbfounded.

Recovering, she asked, 'You mean ... me and the boys ... travelling alone?'

'No, Margaret. I am suggesting we all travel together. You as my personal maid and travelling companion – and the boys coming along with us.'

Margaret looked at Emily as though she had suggested they should fly off to the moon together.

Emily smiled. 'I spoke to my uncle and the bishop about it while they were both here. My uncle has a number of friends and acquaintances in Australia and the bishop said the Church was greatly concerned about the danger posed to the morals of young men in the mining camps of South Australia – many of them

Cornishmen. He feels there is great scope there for someone who knows and understands the problems of a mining community. Someone like myself. He believes I might be able to help those wives and families who are suffering hardship under the primitive conditions of some of the camps too. He suggests I might help organise social activities to wean the men away from more sinful pursuits.'

'From what I've heard about some of the places out there, that won't be easy,' Margaret said doubtfully.

'Of course it won't,' Emily agreed enthusiastically. 'But just think what a wonderful challenge it poses! I intend taking up that challenge, Margaret. Will you come with me?'

'I'd like a little while to think about it, Miss Emily. I'll talk it over with Albert, he's a very sensible boy for his age.'

Hiding her disappointment that Margaret had not shown more enthusiasm for her proposal, Emily said, 'Of course, you need to give it a great deal of thought, but it would give you an opportunity to look for your husband – and offer the boys a new start in life. Now, I think I'll take this milk off to bed with me. These last few days *have* been something of a strain.'

As she climbed the stairs a few minutes later, Emily felt excited at the thought of the future she had mapped out for herself.

The excitement was not entirely due to the challenge she knew she would face in the mining communities of Australia.

There was the hope that in Australia she would meet with Sam once more.

BOOK TWO

1

I

The last passengers from the *Bonython* were taken ashore by lighters, together with their belongings. Once on land, the excited but apprehensive immigrants said emotional farewells to those with whom they had shared danger and cramped quarters for more than a quarter of the year, before going their separate ways.

Wallaroo was one of three towns marking the angles of the so-called 'Copper Triangle', the others being Moonta and Kadina. A great many mines of vastly differing sizes existed within this area, all producing copper, and most employing Cornishmen.

Many of those who arrived at Wallaroo on the *Bonython* had friends, relatives, or, at the very least, a contact in one or more of the mines within this 'triangle' of mining activity.

Ira was in possession of the names of a number of Camborne men who might be able to help him to find work. However, for now he was content to go along with Sam – and with Jean.

The remaining migrants from the ship were travelling to their destinations by various means, but Sam, Ira, Jean and Primrose were the only ones to use the horse-drawn train to travel to Kadina. The fare of a shilling for each passenger might have deterred some of them, especially those with large families, or it could have been the lack of comfort in this mode of transport. The carriages were no more than empty ore trucks returning to the mines, with the addition of logs, sawn in half lengthways, serving as primitive seating.

Primrose thought it fun at first, but the novelty soon wore off.

'When are we going to see Grandad?' she queried for the third time in ten minutes after the small 'train', pulled by three horses in line, had been travelling for an hour.

'It won't be long now,' Ira reassured her, knowing he had to be proved right very soon. The distance between Wallaroo and Kadina was no more than six miles.

Pulling from his pocket the string with which he had kept Primrose amused on board the ship, he said, 'I think I might have a new cradle for you to try. Come and sit by me.'

Jean threw him a grateful smile as Primrose eagerly scrambled from her place beside her mother and went to sit beside him.

Seeing Jean's smile, Sam felt a fleeting twinge of unexpected and unreasonable jealousy. He berated himself silently, knowing that he had been given every opportunity by Jean to take his own relationship with her forward. The fact that he had not done so meant he could hardly complain now that she was looking elsewhere. She was a young woman with her future to consider – and a young daughter to support.

Nevertheless, he had grown accustomed to having her depend upon him. Although such responsibility had sometimes troubled him, there had also been a vague comfort inherent in the unspoken arrangement. Now Jean had shifted her dependency to Ira it left an unexpected gap in Sam's life. He found himself thinking of the home and family he had left behind in Cornwall – and of Emily. He wondered whether she too might find herself a new 'friend'.

He felt in his pocket and his fingers closed about the crucifix she had given to him as he was leaving. Their final moments in the church porch had been proof that her feelings for him went beyond friendship. Such a generous and highly personal present had provided additional proof, if such were needed.

He reminded himself that others had been aware of her feelings for him too – especially her father, and therein lay the barrier to taking their relationship beyond friendship.

Had Emily not been the parson's daughter, had she been, say, the daughter of a farmer, or a miner, Sam had no doubt they could have married and been very happy together.

As it was . . . he fingered the crucifix once more. They could hardly be farther apart than they were at this moment, with little chance they would ever meet again. And yet . . . ?

'You're not saying very much, Sam.'

At the sound of Jean's voice, Ira looked up from his

game with Primrose and smiled at each of them in turn, his fingers entwined in a complicated pattern of string.

'Were you thinking of home? Of St Cleer?'

Sam nodded. 'It seems an awfully long way away right now.'

Jean flapped her hand vigorously in front of her face in a vain hope that the action would produce a hint of cool air.

'Do you think it might be raining there? Cool, wet, lovely rain?'

'Most probably,' Sam said shortly.

'Are you disappointed with what you've seen of Australia so far?' she persisted.

'We've hardly seen any of the country yet, although I must admit it's different to what I was expecting. But if there's work to be had here – underground work – then it's where I want to be.' He stood up to look over the edge of the high-sided truck. 'Talking of mines . . . look what I can see, up ahead.'

Both Ira and Jean rose to their feet, Ira holding Primrose with one arm and supporting himself with the other.

'It's a mine!' Jean exclaimed excitedly.

'More than one by the look of it,' Sam said. 'It must be Kadina.'

There was one other passenger in the truck. They had given up trying to talk to him early on the journey because it was evident that he spoke hardly any English. Now, at mention of 'Kadina', he smiled, showing yellowing teeth, and nodded vigorously. 'Is Kadina,' he said. 'Is Kadina.'

II

After Sam and Ira had unloaded the luggage, the two men accompanied Jean and Primrose to the office of the mine captain, close to where the train had been stopped especially for their benefit.

They stood back, not making their own requirements known while Jean inquired after her father from a heavily bearded mine captain with a strong Cornish accent.

'Jeremiah Hodge?'

The captain scratched his head and tried to concentrate. 'As I recall we have seven or eight Hodges at work on the Kadina mine, but I can't recall a Jeremiah. How long ago is it that he came to work here?'

'It was some years ago now,' Jean admitted unhappily. 'Before I married and had Primrose. I suppose it must be at least five, possibly six years, since he left Cornwall to come here.'

'Well, his name should be in one of the employment books . . .' He nodded at the office clerk, who selected a large leather-bound ledger from a shelf above his desk and lifted it down for the captain.

'Here we are, here's a book that begins in eighteen sixty-eight. It should be in here. Let's see . . .' Poring through the book, he suddenly jabbed a finger at the page in front of him. 'Here are the Hodges. Hodge, Brian . . . , Hodge, David . . . , Frederick . . . Ah! Here we are, Hodge, Jeremiah. He worked on a pare with a number of other Cornishmen. But he's not working at Kadina now. None of them are. They've been gone for quite some time.'

A 'pare' was a group of miners who worked together as a team.

'Oh!' The mine captain's words brought Jean very close to tears. The reunion she had been so eagerly anticipating was not about to take place after all. 'But . . . I've come all the way from Cornwall to be with him. I've brought Primrose . . .'

She was utterly demoralised and Sam asked, 'Is there any record of where he went after he left Kadina?'

The captain shook his head. He could add little that would be of further help. 'None at all. We don't ask the men where they're going when they leave us. Most wouldn't tell me the truth if I did. If I was asked to *guess*, I'd say he went off to the Northern Territory. That's where most miners went about that time. There was a gold find up there and we lost more than a quarter of the workforce. I've no doubt he was one of them. Whether he's still there – and where *exactly* he went to – is a very different matter. As far as I can recall, the gold strike didn't amount to very much on that occasion.'

Jean was absolutely devastated and Ira moved closer to her, murmuring, 'Don't upset yourself, Jean. We'll find him.'

'Well, if that's all I can do for you . . .' the mine captain began.

'It isn't,' Sam said quickly. 'We've all just arrived from Cornwall. Ira and I are both experienced copper miners and we're looking for work.'

The mine captain shrugged his shoulders. 'I only wish I could be of help to you. Had you arrived here only six months ago I'd have taken you on, there and then, but the way things are right now . . .' He shrugged again. 'The price of copper is falling and we're having to go deeper to find ore. As a miner you'll know that the deeper we need to go, the more it's going to cost to win ore. In fact, we're about to put out a notice telling the men they'll need to take a cut in pay if they want to stay in work. I'm sorry, but we're looking to cut down on the numbers of the men working at Kadina, not taking on more.'

His words stunned the two Cornishmen. They had come to South Australia in the firm belief that this was the promised land for all Cornish miners. To be told there was no work for them was a major calamity!

'But . . . what can we do? We're here because we've been told there would be work waiting for us – and because Jean and I thought we had family here. Now you're telling us there's no more work in South Australia than there was in Cornwall!'

'No. What I'm saying is that there's no work at the Kadina mine – and that Jeremiah Hodge is no longer here either. But you mention having family in the area – would I know them?'

'My uncle, Wilf Hooper. He came to Kadina at the same time as Jean's pa, or thereabouts.'

'Ah, yes, *Captain* Wilf. I have no need to look him up in the ledger. He went north to the Blinman mine, up in the Flinders Ranges, to take a job as underground captain. As far as I know he's still there. They were lucky to get him. Captain Wilf is a good man.'

'The Blinman mine . . . ? Flinders Ranges . . . ? Where are they?' Sam's knowledge of South Australian geography was virtually non-existent and he admitted it to the Kadina mine captain.

'Blinman is probably about three hundred miles north – as the crow flies. The best way to get there is to take a boat to Port Augusta, then pay for a ride on one of the bullock carts. They bring ore to the port and return to Blinman with supplies.'

Sam looked at the Kadina mine captain with an expression of dismay. 'How long is it likely to take to get there?'

'If you wait for the steamer from Wallaroo you can get to Port Augusta within twenty-four hours. From there? Ten, fifteen days ... maybe twenty. I couldn't tell you exactly, I've never made the trip myself and haven't spoken to anyone who has.'

Sam and Ira exchanged concerned glances. Meanwhile, Jean sat in a chair and stared down at the floor. She looked utterly defeated.

'The steamer's not due in here for a few days – that's if you want to catch it. If not, well, you could always stay around in the hope that things will pick up and you find someone to take you on. It's happened before.'

Sam shook his head. 'We'll most likely move on – but are things likely to be any better at Blinman?'

'Probably. It's a long way from anywhere. Men who go that far out to find work are usually looking to make money in a gold mine, not in copper. Besides, Captain Wilf's your uncle. He'll probably take you on whether or not the mine really needs men. I'd say that's certainly your best bet.'

'What about me?' Jean asked plaintively. 'What can I do? I've got Primrose to think of and was expecting my pa to be here ...' Her voice broke and she could say no more.

Embarrassed, the mine captain could offer her no words of comfort. He remained silent.

'We'll need to find a place to stay while we think this over,' Sam said to the mine captain. 'Do you know anywhere we could put up for a few days?'

'Well, there's the Miners' Arms Hotel, but that might prove a bit pricey if you're looking to watch your spending. If you don't mind being a bit cramped for space I can recommend you to Widow Pengelly – Florence Pengelly. She's from Cornwall and is always looking to take in boarders to make herself a bit of extra money. She's a fine cook too and will look after you. She lives in Goyder Street. I'll send a man ahead to tell her you're on your way, then give you directions to get there.'

Looking sympathetically at Jean, he added, 'I'll get one of the drivers to take your baggage there in a donkey cart. I'm sorry I haven't been able to be of more help to you, but I wish you luck.'

III

With Primrose riding on Ira's broad shoulders, the dejected new arrivals walked away from the mine, following the directions given to them by the Kadina mine captain.

All were concerned about what the future held for them. Jean, very close to tears, kept shaking her head in disbelief at their misfortune.

Aware of her deep unhappiness, Ira moved closer to her. 'Don't despair, Jean. Everything will turn out all right, you'll see.'

'How *can* it?' Jean demanded fiercely. 'I've brought Primrose all this way in the belief that her grandpa would be here to take care of the two of us, only to find that he's apparently disappeared off the face of the earth and there's no more work here than there was in

Cornwall. We're worse off than we were.'

'Don't distress yourself, Jean,' Sam tried to reassure her. 'Ira and I aren't going to desert you. We'll make certain you and Primrose are all right before either of us moves on.'

'That's right,' Ira agreed. 'Whatever happens, we won't leave you and Primrose to fend for yourselves.'

Jean's eyes were brimming with tears as she looked from one to the other gratefully. 'Thank you. Thank you both.'

'Why is Mummy crying?' Primrose asked.

'She's upset because we haven't been able to find your grandad yet,' Sam explained. 'I expect you're unhappy about it, too.'

'Is he dead, like my daddy?'

The question was so unexpected that for a few moments no one could think of a suitable reply. As Jean turned away, no longer able to control her tears, Sam said, 'No, he's not dead, Primrose. He's gone off somewhere to earn lots of money, so that when you *do* meet, he'll be able to buy you lots of nice things. Tell me, what is it you'd most like to have?'

Sam had put the question to her in a bid to change the subject to something that would be less upsetting for Jean, but Primrose's reply had the opposite effect.

'I'd like to have a daddy again, so that Mummy won't cry so much.'

Sam saw Jean's shoulders begin to heave. Reaching her as the first sob broke free, he signalled urgently for Ira to take Primrose on ahead.

Jean had regained control of herself by the time they reached the home of Florence Pengelly. As they were ushered into her home, she told them with great delight that she had been born in the hamlet of Tremar, in Cornwall, a very short distance from St Cleer.

She chatted happily to Sam and, to a lesser extent, Jean, as they discovered mutual acquaintances. However, her delight at having guests in the house who were familiar with her old home did not impair her perception.

After showing Jean and Primrose to their room, she returned to fix Sam and Ira in turn with a stern, thin-lipped gaze.

'That young woman's been crying. Why? I don't want any trouble or goings on while you're in this house. If there's something I ought to know then you'd better tell me now.'

'There's no trouble, Mrs Pengelly,' Sam said. 'It's just that something Primrose said on the way here touched a raw nerve at a time when Jean's feeling particularly low.'

He told the landlady briefly about the death of Jean's husband and the loss of her baby, which had prompted her to leave Cornwall, and of her dismay at not finding her father here, in Kadina.

Florence had been scrutinising Sam's face unnervingly as he related Jean's story. Now, satisfied he was telling her the truth, her expression softened.

'My dear soul!' she exclaimed, with great feeling. 'I know what it's like for a woman to lose her man, but at least the Lord gave us a long and happy life together. To have him taken away like that – and a baby too! 'Tis enough to turn a young woman's mind. Then to come all this way with a young child to be with her father, only to find he's no longer here ... I'm not given to questioning the actions of the Lord, but He does seem to give some folk greater burdens to carry through life than He does others.'

'Don't worry, Mrs Pengelly,' said Ira. 'We'll see that Jean and Primrose are properly looked after.'

Giving him a searching look, Florence said, 'Will you now? Well, I hope you've told her. There's nothing worse when things are going wrong than the feeling that no one cares. Now, I don't doubt you'll all be wanting something to eat – and you've chosen a good time to arrive. I've a whole batch of pasties almost ready to come out of the oven. They're for the Miners' Arms, but it doesn't matter how many they get. They're pleased to take as many as I care to cook. You won't find a finer pasty anywhere outside of Cornwall – and not many can better them there neither.'

Florence Pengelly was convinced that food was the answer to most of life's problems. Her paying guests were treated to meals they had not dared to even dream about during the months they had spent on board the *Bonython*.

If there was one tiny complaint Sam might have made about their sojourn in the widow's home, it was that they were given no time together to discuss plans for the future. He had hoped they might be able to arrive at a decision during their first evening there, but it was not to be. News of the new arrivals from Cornwall had spread rapidly among the closely knit community of Kadina and there was a steady stream of visitors to the Pengelly house. Many came in the hope that Sam, Ira or Jean might have news of friends and relatives they had left 'back home' in Cornwall.

Although delighted to be able to talk about Cornwall, most went away disappointed. But a few were given comparatively up-to-date news of those they had left behind them – some as long as twenty years before.

Because of the manner in which Florence had welcomed him and the others into her home, Sam felt that by chatting to her friends he and the others were repaying her in a small way for her generous hospitality. However, when Florence asked Sam the following morning to accompany her to visit a house-bound woman named Polly Luck, who had left St Cleer many years before, he protested. He told her that he and the others needed to have a serious discussion about their future plans, as a matter of some urgency. The monies given to him for his act of bravery at Cape Town meant he would not immediately be pressed for money – and he would take care of Jean where money matters were concerned – but he and Ira both wanted to find work as soon as possible.

'I can understand your concern,' said Florence, 'but you come out with me now and I'll make certain no one disturbs you this evening. One or two matters might very well have resolved themselves by then and you'll have a much better idea of what everyone wants to do.'

'What do you mean by that?' Sam was puzzled by her statement.

'If you *really* don't know then you wouldn't believe me if I was to tell you what I'm thinking,' Florence said. 'Now, if you're ready you can go and fetch Primrose. We'll take her with us. It'll do the child good to get away from her mother for an hour or two and Polly will enjoy meeting her. She has umpteen grandchildren and great-grandchildren, so there'll no doubt be a few toys round to keep Primrose amused.'

Polly Luck turned out to be a garrulous, meandering old woman who certainly knew St Cleer and the families who lived there. She had known Sam's father when he was a small boy, but she kept confusing Sam with others she had known. By the time he, Primrose and Florence left the house, his brain was almost as scrambled as Polly's talk had been.

However, Primrose had been given a doll to which she had formed a particular attachment and she, at least, was extremely happy.

On the way back to Goyder Street, Sam said to Florence, 'When you were talking earlier about things sorting themselves out, were you thinking of Ira and Jean getting together?'

'I was – so it seems the idea doesn't come as so much of a surprise to you as you made it out to be.'

'I've known for some time that Ira is sweet on Jean, but I've never been quite sure how serious it is – and I doubt very much whether Jean looks upon Ira as a potential husband.'

Florence snorted derisively. 'When a woman who's been widowed has a young child to support and there's no other way of doing it, all single men are a potential lifeline. Not that I'm saying that's *all* he is to her. I've seen the way she's looked at him once or twice. They weren't calculating looks. Those two have quite a lot to offer each other.'

Fixing him with a direct look, she continued, 'From what I've gathered it was you and Jean who set out from Cornwall together. How would you feel if the two of them decided they wanted to make a go of things?'

Choosing his words carefully, Sam said, 'Jean and I have known each other since we were both Primrose's age. I was best man to her husband when she married him. If Jean feels she can be just as happy with Ira I'll willingly stand as best man again.' He grimaced. 'Mind you, had you asked me that question after Ira and I had met for the first time you'd have got a very different answer. We both know each other a lot better now. Even so, it will come as a big surprise to me if I learn that Jean feels the same about him as he does about her.'

'If Jean can still surprise someone who's known her all her life there's not much wrong with the girl. At times like this I wish I wasn't prevented by my Methodist upbringing from having a small wager with you.'

When Sam entered the house it was immediately apparent that Florence had read the situation between Jean and Ira far more accurately than he.

They were both in the kitchen, standing as far apart as was possible in such a small space. Jean looked flustered and Ira seemed to be finding it difficult to stand still.

Oblivious to anything but the doll she was carrying, Primrose ran to Jean, holding out the toy given to her by Polly Luck.

'Look what I've got! The lady said her name is Rose. She's got a flower's name, just like me.'

'It's lovely, darling. Very nice indeed. Aren't you a lucky girl?'

Pulling the doll back from her mother, Primrose held it up for Ira's inspection. 'Do you like her too?'

'She's beautiful,' Ira agreed enthusiastically. 'But not as beautiful as you. Here, come and let me give both of you a great big hug.'

As Ira scooped up the small girl and the doll in his arms, Florence gave Sam a triumphant look that said clearly, 'I told you so!'

Intercepting the other woman's glance, Jean blushed and said, 'Me and Ira have had a long talk while you were out . . .'

Aware of what she was about to say, Ira's cheek, pressed against Primrose's face, turned a bright scarlet.

'We spoke of the situation we're all in out here, in South Australia. Ira is particularly concerned about me and Primrose. He wants to take on responsibility for us . . .'

Ira saw the uncertain expression that fleetingly crossed Sam's face. Aware that Jean had not made his intentions as clear as was intended, he said hurriedly, 'I've asked Jean to marry me, Sam – and she's said "yes".'

'I trust there's more to the pair of you getting married than uncertainty about the future,' Florence said before Sam could reply. 'There's nothing more uncertain in life than marriage.'

'We both know that,' Ira replied. 'It's not the only reason we want to marry. I've grown to admire Jean more and more since we first met on the boat. Sam knows that's true. It's taken Jean a bit longer to feel the same way about me, but that's hardly surprising. I wasn't any woman's idea of an ideal husband or father when she first saw me. I'm not proud of the man I was then. But she's given me a reason to put my life back together again. I want to share that life with her – and to be the daddy that Primrose said would be the best present anyone could give her.'

It was the longest speech Sam had ever heard the Camborne miner make and he did not doubt his sincerity.

Neither did Jean. Moving to stand beside Ira, she shyly took his hand. 'Primrose and me are lucky to have found Ira. I'll do my best to be a good wife to him.'

'That sounds far more promising.' Florence's approval was accompanied by a warm smile. 'What do you have to say about it, Sam?'

'I'm very, very happy for everyone concerned,' Sam said, with the utmost sincerity. 'Ira and Jean came to South Australia looking for a new life. They couldn't have got off to a better start than this.'

After kissing Jean warmly, he shook hands with Ira and said, 'Does this mean you and Jean will be going off following a trail of your own now?'

The happy smile left Ira's face for a moment and he said, 'I hope not, Sam. It's not what either Jean or me want. We'd both like it if the three of us and Primrose could stay together. It's just . . . well, when we decide what we're going to do it will be with me and Jean coming along as a married couple, that's all.'

'That's fine with me,' Sam said. 'Let's hope Uncle Wilf can still be found. I believe our best hope of finding work will be with him, at the Blinman mine.'

IV

When Sam made inquiries the following day he learned that the paddle-steamer *Marquess* was not due to make the journey from Wallaroo to Port Augusta for another four days.

During the wait, the newcomers to South Australia were given the benefit of Florence's knowledge of the country and her views on what *she* thought they ought to be doing.

'If you really want to make some money for yourselves you should go up into the Adelaide Hills searching for gold,' she said at breakfast one morning. 'It's there – my William found it. I went with him to a gold diggings when I first came out here to join him. I can tell you that some of those gold camps were rough places. There were no Methodist preachers around then to stop a man – or a woman – from enjoying a drink at the end of a hard day's work, or to celebrate a rich strike. Things are very different on a copper mine. You'll be lucky to be given work in any of 'em if you don't go to chapel at least twice every Sunday and if your "Hallelujah" isn't louder than the next man's. I was brought up a Methodist, but I don't hold with a lot of what they teach these days. They seem to have made up most of it along the way. It certainly isn't what John Wesley intended them to teach. It wasn't the life for my William, neither. We worked hard and played hard. By the time we'd done we'd made enough money to buy this place, where we could put up folk like yourselves and advise them on what they ought to be doing.'

'We're very grateful for your advice, Mrs Pengelly, we really are,' Sam said, 'but I know that Ira wants to have a little money put by so that Jean will be comfortable, come what may, and I'm looking to find my Uncle Wilf, up at Blinman, so it looks as though it's going to be copper for us.'

'You know what's best for you, of course,' Florence said, unconvinced. 'But don't let anyone put you off seeking gold if you think it might be there. Copper may keep you from starving, but it's gold that will make you rich.'

The few days spent in the house of Florence Pengelly proved a welcome period of recuperation for the immigrants from Cornwall. During this time they met with more of Florence's friends who had benefited from gold finds in various parts of Australia.

Sam was impressed by the stories of the wealth that finding gold had brought to these people. However, such success stories were counterbalanced by the stories of failure he heard a couple of days later.

Jean, Ira and Primrose had left the house with Florence to visit the shops to buy a few things that Primrose was likely to need when they reached Blinman. Florence had warned them that Blinman was so remote it might not be possible to buy all the things they might need there.

It had been Sam's intention to remain in the house, but as it was a very hot day he decided to go for a walk in the hope of finding a breeze on the streets of Kadina.

On a street corner, he was accosted by a grizzled old man, who asked Sam to spare a coin or two for 'an old man, down on his luck'.

Recognising the man's dialect as that of a Cornish moorland man, Sam chatted to him for a while before accompanying him to a shanty bar, sited amidst scrubland, beyond the perimeter of the bustling township that was Kadina.

Here, in a bar constructed of uncut timber and

corrugated iron, Sam met others like his grizzled companion. He spent more money than he had intended, buying rounds of 'swanky', the locally brewed beer, while listening to tales of woe. Many of the men here were ex-goldminers, down on their luck, who had returned to the Copper Triangle hoping in vain to find work.

The stories they told were depressingly similar. All had originally come to South Australia from Cornwall to take work in the copper mines that had sprung up on many parts of the country, with varying degrees of success.

In due course, lured by stories of miners who had become rich men overnight, they deserted the copper mines and set off in search of gold.

Some went to the hills just outside Adelaide, South Australia's capital, where gold was being found in varying quantities. Others sought their personal Eldorado farther afield. All had the same story to tell.

For every man who found gold there were hundreds who discovered anew the anguish of the poverty they had known in Cornwall.

Some travelled from claim to claim in the vain hope of changing their luck. Many actually discovered gold, but never in sufficient quantities to halt the downward slide their life was taking.

Most of those here had returned to their original work places in the vicinity of Kadina, only to learn that their places had been taken by younger, more energetic men, deemed by the mine captains to be more dependable than those lured away by the prospect of instant riches.

Now, penniless and without hope, they lived in makeshift hovels in the countryside surrounding what had become for them an uncaring community. Scrounging and begging, and occasionally killing wild or even domestic animals, they contrived to stay alive.

Sam returned to Florence's house sobered in spirit if not in body. He found the household in a state of high excitement.

Whilst out with the others, Ira had become the township's hero by stopping a runaway horse that was pulling a baker's van in one of Kadina's busiest streets.

'Ira was *marvellous*,' Jean gushed. 'The baker was just stepping down from his van when a dog suddenly rushed at the horse, snapping at its legs. When it took off the baker was knocked down by the cart and lucky not to be run over. There was chaos on the street, with people screaming and running to get out of its way. Then Ira jumped out and caught the horse's bridle. He was dragged for a long way and I thought he might be killed himself, but he managed to bring the horse to a halt without anyone being hurt. You should have been there to see all the people crowding around to congratulate him.'

'Well done, Ira,' said Sam, shaking the other man by the hand. 'I wish I'd been there to see it for myself.'

'I was *frightened*!' Primrose added. 'I *cried*.'

'There would have been tears from a great many people had Ira not had the courage to jump out and stop the horse,' Florence declared. 'He was a hero today.'

'Someone would have been killed for certain,' Jean agreed.

'It was a very brave thing to do, to jump out in front of a horse like that,' Sam said. 'I doubt if I could have done it.'

Ira looked embarrassed. 'That isn't true, Sam. I did nothing that you wouldn't have done had you been there – as we all know. Besides, I grew up with horses. My pa used to break in the ponies used on the mines, and I'd help him. Horses have no fear for me, whatever mood they're in – and this horse wasn't bad, only frightened.'

'It was a bold enough thing to do, whatever Ira says,' declared the Cornish landlady. 'What's more, it didn't go unnoticed. Councillor Mintoff was in the street and saw what happened. He came across to congratulate Ira, wanting to know who he is and where he's staying. He says he intends organising an official presentation to him for his bravery. I'm sure he will. He's trying to win nomination to the state parliament but folk around here are lukewarm about it. If he doesn't get nominated he'll probably have to stay with local politics and there's likely to be too much dirt raked up about him, given time. I don't like Mintoff and wouldn't trust him any farther than I could throw him, but that needn't concern any of you too much. What's certain is that Ira will leave Kadina richer than when he arrived.'

'It's no more than he deserves,' Jean said vehemently. Giving Sam a sidelong glance, she added, 'I think Primrose and me are very lucky to have two such brave men taking care of us.'

She then needed to explain to Florence how Sam had saved Ira's life when he fell into the sea at Cape Town.

'Well I never.' Florence's admiration now encompassed both men. 'There have been more than one occasion in the goldfields when I've prayed that men like you two would come along to help me out. There were always plenty of the wrong sort who offered, but none who could be depended upon when things got tough. The pair of you are a bit late for me now.'

Turning to Jean, she said, 'Make certain you hang on to at least one of them, my dear, there aren't too many like them around.'

'I will, Florence,' Jean said, smiling warmly at Ira.

'Now, let's all go into the front room,' said Florence. 'I think I might be able to find something that's more suitable than swanky for a small celebration.'

The following day, at a private ceremony to which local officials and the editor of the local newspaper had been invited, Councillor Stefan Mintoff presented Ira with a 'bravery award' of twenty-five pounds, donated, as he pointed out, from his own pocket.

Florence commented, unkindly, that had Ira's deed been witnessed by any other member of the city council, there would have been an official presentation in front of a full council. The absence of such recognition was indicative of Mintoff's unpopularity.

However, aware of none of this, Ira was delighted with the money. He acknowledged it with a stammering modesty that was in marked contrast to the long and highly political speech given by Stefan Mintoff.

Later that evening, when Jean was putting Primrose to bed and Florence was in the kitchen preparing an evening meal for her lodgers, Sam and Ira sat in the 'front room' enjoying the Cape brandy Florence had first produced as a celebratory drink the previous day.

It had been apparent to Sam for many minutes that Ira wanted to say something to him but could not quite muster the courage to express himself.

Eventually, Sam said to him, 'You're as fidgety as a stoat in a chicken run, Ira. Is there something on your mind?'

'Yes . . . yes, there is, Sam. Jean and me would like to be married before setting off for Blinman, but it will mean staying here for a few more weeks, while we arrange everything and have the banns read.'

'That shouldn't be too much of a problem, Ira. Not now that you've been given the money from this Councillor Mintoff.'

'Are you quite sure, Sam? After all, it will mean that while we're here you too will be spending money instead of earning it.'

'Your marriage to Jean is a lot more important than a couple of weeks' pay, Ira. You go ahead with the arrangements, I'll happily fall in with them.'

V

Jean and Ira's hopes of marrying at Kadina were dashed when a measles epidemic swept through the township. By the end of a week it had claimed the lives of a score of young children. Schools were closed and mothers were afraid of taking their children out on the streets.

After a discussion on the increasing seriousness of the outbreak, Ira and Jean reluctantly decided that for Primrose's sake they must catch the first boat out of Wallaroo, putting off their marriage until they reached Blinman.

After bidding Florence an emotional farewell, they were fortunate to catch a paddle-steamer that day. It would carry them north on the Spencer Gulf to Port

Augusta. Although this was the nearest seaport to Blinman, they still faced an overland journey of a hundred and fifty miles. The mine was situated in the heart of the Flinders Ranges, a spectacular series of mountain ranges which ran parallel to the course their steamer was taking.

Jean was thankful that on this occasion they would be spending only a single night on the boat. She and Primrose had spent enough time afloat to last them a lifetime. She hoped that their arrival at Blinman would mark the end of their travels. Certainly the end of journeys by boat.

In fact, the short voyage on the steamship turned out to be a very enjoyable experience. The accommodation was certainly a great improvement on the vessel that had brought them from England, the men sharing one cabin and Jean and Primrose having another to themselves.

It was a welcome experience too not to be at the mercy of winds and tides. With its great paddle-wheels threshing the water, the steady throb of the engines was reminiscent of the mine-engines that had been an ever-present feature of moorland life in Cornwall during the good years of copper mining, and the men, in particular, found the sound strangely comforting.

They did not have sufficient time on the steamship to become bored. Primrose was the only child on the vessel and during daylight hours the crew delighted in pointing out interesting features on ship and shore to her. In turn, she repeated the information to her doll, embellishing each piece of information with childhood fantasies.

The travellers went to their beds that night happy

in the knowledge that when they woke the next morning they would have reached Port Augusta.

Soon after dawn the passengers were awoken by the sound of men calling from the decks of the ship to the shore. At the same time the engines were continually changing speed as the telegraphs rang out a stream of instructions to the sweating men in the engine room.

They had arrived at Port Augusta and the ship was edging towards a berth at a small jetty.

This was a very busy seaport. In addition to copper ore and smelted copper, there was an ever-growing variety of farm produce passing out through the docks. Arriving ships brought in manufactured goods and foodstuffs from all over the world.

The town of Port Augusta spread inland from the docks and in the distance could be seen the dark grey mountain ranges of the Flinders. Somewhere among them, far to the north, nestled the mining community of Blinman.

Finding a bullock cart and driver willing to take the small party to its destination proved to be no problem; there was a number readily available.

A price for the long journey was eventually agreed with Piet van Roos, owner and driver of a bullock team and dray. A South African by birth, he had arrived in Australia almost forty years before. Small and heavily bearded, his skin had the dried-up, leathery texture of a man who had spent a lifetime out of doors.

They had not been travelling for long before the immigrants learned that Piet had been a prospector for much of his life. He informed them that although his labours had not netted him a fortune, he had found gold in sufficient quantity to buy himself a dray and a team of bullocks.

'Is there gold to be found in the Flinders Ranges?' Sam put the question to the teamster as he and the old man plodded along beside the lead animal, following a track that had little more than the ruts of many wagons to mark it out as the main thoroughfare between Port Augusta and the copper mines of the Ranges.

'Gold, silver, copper ... a man can find whatever he's looking for in the Ranges if he keeps his eyes open when he's walking around. Mind you, most of those who call themselves "prospectors" wouldn't recognise gold if they tripped over it. Would you?'

Sam shook his head. 'Copper and tin, yes. We've never had much gold in Cornwall.'

Spitting to one side of the track with scornful abandon, the old man said, 'How would you know, if you don't know what it looks like?'

It was a good question and one to which Sam had no answer.

There were many such conversations with Piet van Roos during the days and nights they were on the trail. He particularly enjoyed talking of his early days in South Australia, once they were seated about a campfire at night and the contents of the whisky jar he kept on the dray had loosened his tongue.

Piet told them there was much gold to be found in the country, adding that some of the most likely locations were so close to the South Australian capital that the early pioneers had probably 'dug up gold and thrown it away when they were putting in foundations for their fancy houses'.

Piet repeated this statement to Sam the following day when they were once more walking together beside the slow-moving bullock cart. It prompted Sam to ask, 'If there's gold where you say it is, why aren't you out there digging for it instead of driving a bullock cart here, in all this emptiness?'

The old man looked at Sam pityingly. 'If you think it's empty here then you must have bottle-stops instead of eyes in your head. There's more things of interest – far more – than you're ever likely to see in a place like Adelaide. There are too many people there. A man can't live life in his own way when he's surrounded by strangers. Besides, there are some days when my knees don't do what they're made to do. If I was there I'd most likely have folk fussing about me until it drove me out of my mind. When it happens out here I can take my time hitching up the bullocks, then ride on the dray until my knees start working again.'

'What happens if your knees give out one day and you find you *can't* hitch up the bullocks?'

Piet shrugged. 'When that happens I'll know my time has come. I'll die the way I've lived. In a place where I want to be, under God's sky and thinking my own thoughts.'

Sam realised that Piet van Roos was one of life's true 'loners'. A man who derived more pleasure from his own company than from that of others.

Before he could think of a reply, Piet said, 'As for this place being empty – we've had company for two days now.'

'What do you mean by "company"?' Sam asked sharply.

'A "Yura" – an Aborigine. That's the name they're

known by, up around Blinman. He's got a woman with him. A child too, I think.'

Sam looked at his companion in disbelief. 'How do you know? I've seen no one.'

'It's like I said, son. You've got bottle-stops instead of eyes. They're out there all right and not far behind us, either.'

Sam looked back apprehensively, not certain of what he might see. He saw nothing.

'If they're really there, why haven't they shown themselves to us?'

'I've seen 'em. You will too when they're good and ready.'

Sam would have pursued the matter, but at that moment Primrose called out, 'Look, there's a kangaroo! It's the closest one's ever come to us.'

They had seen many kangaroos on their journey, but when Sam looked in the direction in which the young girl was pointing, he saw one of the animals no more than twenty paces from the dray, looking at the travellers with fearless interest.

'Well done, girl,' said Piet, hurrying to the seat at the front of the dray. 'You've just found tonight's dinner.'

Taking up a gun from beneath the seat, he put it to his shoulder, took aim at the inquisitive kangaroo, and fired.

As the kangaroo dropped dead, Primrose screamed. The shot and the small girl's scream frightened the bullocks. For a moment Sam thought they would take off, dragging the heavy dray, its load and passengers with them. However, the steadiness of the older animals in the team quickly calmed the others and they came to a restless halt.

'Come and give me a hand to get the 'roo back to the dray,' Piet called out to Sam and Ira, ignoring Primrose, who was sobbing and clinging to Jean.

The kangaroo was still twitching when Sam reached it, but Piet said it was 'dead enough' and the twitching had ceased by the time it was carried back to the dray.

Jean turned Primrose's head away when the three men and their burden were close enough for her to see the hole in the animal's chest where the bullet had struck it.

Heaved into the back of the wagon and covered with a piece of tarpaulin in order to keep the flies away, the kangaroo was no longer a living thing.

On his way back to the bullocks, Piet paused alongside the dray where Jean sat with Primrose in her arms. The small girl saw him and turned away, burying her face in her mother's dress.

Seemingly oblivious to Primrose's anguish, Piet said, 'The girl's got sharp eyes. Thanks to her we'll eat well tonight.'

With this, he strode to the head of the bullock team and, cracking his whip, shouted the command for them to move off.

That evening, when the party had made camp for the night, Piet roasted the choicest portions of the kangaroo over the campfire. It was now that the Cornish party met up with the first Aborigines they had encountered.

A very small family group, composed of a man, woman and a child perhaps a little older than Primrose, they seemed to materialise from nowhere.

There was not a stitch of clothing among the three of them.

They emerged from the scrub beside the camp so silently that they startled Sam. He jumped to his feet, quickly followed by Ira.

'Sit down,' ordered Piet who had not moved. 'They're hungry and know we have food.'

Without getting up, he said something to the newcomers in a language that was quite unintelligible to the others. The Aboriginal man replied in the same language and Piet waved his hand to where he had discarded the remainder of the kangaroo, telling the others it would not keep in the heat of the outback.

Going to the spot where the unwanted kangaroo meat had been thrown, the Aboriginal man said something to his wife and the meat was gathered up. Without another word the trio then vanished back into the thick scrub – the 'bush' – whence they had come.

'Will they come back again?' Sam asked, when they had gone.

'I doubt it,' Piet replied. 'They wanted food. We've given it to them. Most of 'em are peacable enough, unless they're stirred up. All the same, make certain you sleep with your belongings close by you – and I'll sheet down the stores. There might be others around with scores to settle. If you take my advice you'll buy yourselves guns when we reach Blinman. They'll make you feel more secure.'

When Piet went off to secure the load he was carrying on the dray, Jean asked querulously, 'What sort of country have we come to where we need to carry guns to protect ourselves?'

'Don't let Piet frighten you, Jean,' Sam said. 'He

needs a gun because he travels a lot of miles through pretty wild country and, as you've seen, he uses it to get food. This may be a young and unknown country, but we'll none of us need a gun when we reach the mine at Blinman. It'll be just like St Cleer, you'll see.'

Sam's words were meant to be reassuring and to a certain extent they were. However, bedded down beneath the wagon with Primrose that night, Jean found sleep elusive. The slightest sound caused her imagination to run riot. Despite an intense dislike of firearms, she decided that having one beside her during the dark hours of an outback night would have been comforting.

She did not relax until the sun rose above the horizon the next morning and the surrounding country suddenly became less menacing.

VI

Not every night was spent camping out in the open on the journey to Blinman. The travellers would occasionally stop at one of the small pastoral communities which, although struggling for their very existence in the parched outback amidst the Flinders Ranges, made the travellers welcome.

Piet van Roos also knew of several shepherds' huts where the owners, although absent, were agreeable for Piet and his passengers to sleep there, accepting a small amount of non-perishable provisions left behind as payment.

When they vacated one such hut, Jean asked why the shepherd was not living there.

Piet gave her a pitying look. 'You've got a whole lot to learn about this country, missus. This station alone runs sheep on a piece of land about half the size of the place in England you've just come from ... Cornwall, isn't it?'

When Jean nodded, Piet continued, 'The shepherd might be as far as fifty miles from here right now, staying in another of his huts. He goes wherever there's food and water for his sheep.'

Jean was not fully aware of the dimensions of Cornwall and was unable to comprehend the size of the sheep station, but she was becoming aware of the vastness of the country they were passing through and felt awed by the sheer majesty of the Flinders Ranges.

Eighteen days after leaving Port Augusta, the creaking, dusty bullock dray reached Blinman. As they drew near, the new arrivals were pleasantly surprised by the extent of the township.

Beyond Blinman they could make out a number of buildings and tall, smoking chimneys sited on the side of a hill.

'This is more like it,' Ira said enthusiastically. 'It looks as though someone here is serious about mining!'

As they drew nearer, Sam felt a great feeling of excitement surge up inside him. They could make out the mine in more detail now – and the buildings were familiar. They and the sound of mine-engines reminded him of better days in Cornwall.

'I'll take you right up to the mine office,' Piet said. 'They'll take care of you.'

The last bundle had been set on the ground before a tall, gaunt man appeared in the doorway of the office, shielding his eyes against the glare of the sun. When he saw Sam his eyes opened wide in astonishment.

'Sam! By all that's holy . . . What are you doing here?'

Delighted and not a little relieved to find his uncle, Sam stepped forward and the two men embraced warmly.

'You're the reason I'm here, Uncle Wilf. You praised Australia so much in your letters that when things became bad in the mines on Bodmin Moor, Pa insisted I should come out and join you.'

'How is your pa . . . and your ma and the rest of the family?'

'They're all fine, and they'll be overjoyed that I've found you well too.'

'It's a pity your pa didn't come with you, Sam. There's plenty of room for Cornish farmers as well as Cornish miners out here – and there'll be more as time goes on.'

Their initial enthusiastic greetings over, Wilf Hooper looked questioningly at Jean, Ira and Primrose, and Sam introduced them.

'This is Ira. We came out on the same ship. He's a Camborne man. Like me, he was expecting to find work at Kadina, but they seem to be going through a bad time right now, so he came to Blinman with me.'

Wilf and Ira shook hands and the captain said, 'Well, I'm in charge of the mine right now because Captain Paull has gone to Adelaide for a month or two. If you know mining as well as do the other Camborne men I've got here, I'll be happy to offer you work.'

Beaming with delight, Ira surprised Sam by saying, 'I stood in for the shift captain more than once on the Wheal Mary. You won't find me lagging behind any other Camborne man when it comes to mining.'

'Good!' Captain Wilf now turned to Jean and said, 'You look familiar, are you from St Cleer?'

Replying for her, Sam said, 'This is Jean Spargo, Uncle Wilf – Jean Hodge, as was. She married Phillip Spargo, who I'm sure you remember ... ?'

The Blinman mine captain inclined his head. 'Now I know why you're familiar. I knew your mother well. You're just like her.'

'Phillip was killed in an accident at the South Caradon,' Sam explained. 'Jean had no one at home, so she's come out here to try and find her pa. She believed him to be working at Kadina, but when we were there they said he'd moved on. Probably to some goldfield, they thought.'

Captain Wilf nodded. 'I know Jeremiah. He was going to come to Blinman with me, then he met up with someone who told him of the gold that was being found way up north. He decided to go there instead. Exactly where he is now I don't know. I've spoken to men who've met up with him in at least three different camps. But what made you come here, Jean? I'm delighted to welcome anyone from St Cleer, of course, especially anyone from the Hodge family, but there's little work to be had in Blinman for a widow with a young child to support.'

'Jean's come here to be with me,' Ira said. 'We had intended marrying in Kadina, but they were suffering a serious measles epidemic. We left in a hurry fearing for the safety of Primrose. We hope to marry as soon as it's possible.'

'Congratulations. We don't have our own minister, but Reverend Maddison is due in Blinman in two weeks' time to perform two marriages. If you're serious about wanting to marry I'll make arrangements for him to marry you too.'

Ira looked eagerly to Jean for confirmation. She gave a barely discernible nod of approval and Ira beamed. 'Yes, Cap'n Hooper, we would like that very much.'

'Good! It'll also be as fine a way as any of introducing you to the folk of Blinman – although I have no doubt many will have sought you out before then. We have a great many Cornish men and women in the township who are always hungry for news from "home". Now, we'll need to find places for you all to live. I know of a nice little cottage for you and Primrose, Jean. Ira can move in with you once you're married. Until then, Ira, you can share a room in my house with Sam. But before we do anything else we'll get you and the little maid settled, Jean. I don't doubt it will be a great relief for you to be in your own place, with a roof over your head, after spending so long travelling. It's a corrugated-iron roof and the cottage is made of timber and clay, but it'll be comfortable enough, if hotter than you've been used to. You'll find many things are a bit strange at first, but I'm sure you'll enjoy Blinman. It's a good place to live. Some of the younger miners tend to get a mite out of hand on settlement night, but there's no harm in any of 'em and we have two police troopers stationed here. They're usually able to nip any trouble in the bud.'

Jean and Ira, along with two other couples, were married a fortnight later in a brief ceremony that brought almost the entire population of Blinman to the primitive chapel building to witness the multiple weddings.

Even some who lived outside the boundaries of the township attended, among them a number of women who lived in tents and makeshift huts and earned their living from prostitution.

They were shunned by the respectable women of the township. Miners, whether married or single, were careful not to catch the eye of any one of the prostitutes and be forced to acknowledge that they knew or were known by her.

Reverend Maddison was aware of their presence in the chapel and preached a sermon that drew heavily upon St Paul's Epistle to the Corinthians, making much of quotations such as 'he that committeth fornication sinneth against his own body ... know ye not that your body is the temple of the Holy Ghost ... ?' and '... it is better to marry than to burn'.

After the ceremony the three couples were given a reception at the Blinman hotel, the food paid for from mine funds. Drinks were also readily available but, miners being notoriously thirsty, those who wished to consume them were obliged to purchase their own.

The newly married couples wisely left the reception when it showed signs of rowdiness. However, the town's policemen made only three arrests that night; two were for fighting and one for causing damage to a hotel window.

There might have been a fourth and highly embarrassing arrest for drunkenness had not the minister who performed the marriage ceremonies been hastily whisked away when he fell into a drunken stupor.

Unfortunately for Reverend Maddison, he was carried away by a group of young men who possessed a wry sense of humour. They put him to bed in a hut occupied by three of the prostitutes who had attended the wedding ceremony. He would awake in the morning with a piece of card tied about his neck upon which an unusually erudite prostitute had written 'Every harlot was a virgin once – it took a man to make one of the other.'

Celebrations were still going on at the Blinman hotel when Sam made his way back to his uncle's cottage. It was a happy sound, Sam reflected, one that had been absent for too long from the mines he had left behind in Cornwall.

He and Ira had found employment on the Blinman mine with different pares. Each was working on a pitch richer in ore than they were used to. When settlement day came around, they would be paid an amount that reflected the quality and quantity of the ore they had won from the mine.

It was a state of affairs that would make any true miner happy.

Mining was a fickle occupation, subject to great fluctuations in fortunes, but Sam felt that for the first time in years he could look forward with confidence to the immediate future.

2

I

The voyage undertaken by Emily in May 1874 was very different from that experienced by Sam, Jean and their fellow travellers.

Emily, accompanied by Margaret and her two boys, booked passages on the SS *Great Britain*, and the small party occupied first-class cabins.

The *Great Britain* would have dwarfed the *Bonython* had the two ships ever met, and the steamship made the voyage to Australia in less than two-thirds the time taken by the sailing vessel. It was fitted with powerful engines to ensure a good speed would be maintained, and in addition, there were three masts, capable of carrying a fair spread of sail. When the weather was right the vessel could bowl along without the sound of engines to disturb the fare-paying passengers.

There was another difference. Despite the fact that the *Great Britain* carried more than three hundred passengers and a crew of more than a hundred, there was no feeling of overcrowding and steerage passengers were kept out of sight and hearing of the cabin passengers.

The ship carried live sheep, pigs, ducks, geese and chickens to ensure there were always fresh eggs and meat for the first-class passengers to enjoy when they dined.

Because of its huge bulk, the *Great Britain* was less affected by sea conditions than smaller vessels and Margaret and her boys thought that travelling a steamship was a marvellous experience.

The voyage terminated at Melbourne but details of Emily's arrival had been telegraphed ahead of her. When the ship berthed at her destination, a representative of the Church was waiting to escort Emily and her companions to a hotel.

Twenty-four hours later they took passage on another steamship that would carry them to the port of Wallaroo and thence to Kadina.

Emily's work would take in the three towns of the Copper Triangle, Moonta, Kadina and Wallaroo. Having been told she was free to take up residence in any of them she had chosen Kadina.

Emily had made discreet enquiries before setting out from Cornwall and had learned that the mine where she hoped she would find Sam was situated here. It should not be difficult to locate him. Hopefully, Margaret's husband would be found working somewhere in the area too.

Emily had come to South Australia on behalf of the Church of England on an open-ended mission. She was to set up prayer groups and educational centres in the area and involve herself in any activities calculated to improve the spiritual and physical well-being of the miners and their families.

Before she left England, Emily's uncle, Lord Boyce, had arranged for telegraphic messages to be sent on behalf of the British government, requesting that Emily be given every assistance during the long journey and on her arrival. As a result, when the steamer carrying her to Wallaroo called at Port Adelaide, she was greeted by a representative of the Bishop of Adelaide, who invited her to a dinner being held in the South Australian capital that evening.

The following day, back on board the ship, Emily and Margaret were taking the air on the upper deck in the late afternoon when a dapper, moustached man approached the two women.

Giving them a stiff bow, he addressed Emily. 'Good day to you, Miss Boyce. Please forgive me for approaching you in such an informal manner, but I was at the dinner yesterday evening which was graced by your presence. I am Stefan Mintoff, a councillor in the town of Kadina, which I believe is to be your destination. I felt I should introduce myself and offer to assist you in any way while you are there.'

The man had a European accent that Emily could not place.

'That is most kind of you,' she replied. 'I am afraid I do not recall seeing you at the dinner . . .' This was not true; she had seen him sitting farther along the long table at which she had been seated and was aware of the interest he was taking in her.

'I would not, of course, have expected you to notice me, but I doubt whether there was anyone present at the dinner who did not notice *you*, Miss Boyce.'

There was a strange sound from Margaret, who might have been trying to stifle a laugh. Stefan Mintoff glanced briefly at her before returning his attention to Emily.

'I was talking to the Bishop's chaplain, who informed me you are newly arrived from England with the purpose of carrying out welfare work in the copper towns. It is an admirable task you are taking on, Miss Boyce. I am quite certain you will receive the full support of all concerned. I recently allowed an institute building to be erected on land I own, next to my general store. I will ensure that all its facilities are available for your activities. I hope I may be of further service to you during what I trust will be a long and happy stay in Kadina.'

'Thank you, Mr Mintoff.' Emily was genuinely delighted that her mission had got off to such a start. Having the institute building made available to her would make her work very much easier. 'Your offer is most kind. I will certainly bear it in mind.'

Inclining her head to him in farewell, she turned to Margaret. 'Come, Margaret. I feel I would like to rest before we make ready for dinner.'

Emily moved off and Margaret followed. When they were out of earshot, Margaret commented, 'That's as smooth tongued a man as I've come across in a very long time.'

'Really? I thought he was rather charming.'

Margaret looked sharply at Emily but was unable to tell whether or not she was being serious. She felt a moment of concern. There were times when she was aware that Emily's experience with men was limited.

'He was certainly *charming*,' she agreed. 'The trouble

is that he knew it. You be careful of him when we get to Kadina.'

The relationship between Margaret and Emily had undergone a change since leaving St Cleer. It was largely at Emily's instigation. She had told Margaret that she was a 'companion' and no longer a lady's maid. They were to be on first-name terms and Margaret was not to use the prefix 'Miss' when she addressed her.

The two women had also become good friends. Emily suddenly smiled at her companion. 'You need not worry, Margaret. I have no doubt I shall have more to think about in Kadina than Stefan Mintoff.'

She did not add that one of the things she *hoped* to have on her mind in Kadina was Sam. The thought of seeing him again excited her more and more as they came closer to the South Australian copper-mining area.

II

The Church in South Australia had a very efficient system of communication. When the vessel on which Emily was travelling docked at Wallaroo, the Reverend Arnold Weeks, acting vicar of Kadina, was at the dockside to welcome her.

He apologised for the absence of the regular incumbent of the Kadina church, explaining that he was on his way to Adelaide to officiate at the wedding of his daughter.

'He had hoped to see you there,' the apologetic young priest explained. 'However, it would seem that you missed one another. But I will be happy to assist your mission in any way I can.'

'Thank you, Reverend Weeks.' Emily had taken an instant liking to the young vicar. 'Is there a serious moral problem among the miners of the area?'

Arnold Weeks looked embarrassed. 'Not on the larger mines. The mine captains are Methodists. To give them their due, they maintain a strict discipline among their men, who are largely Methodist too.'

'But there are non-Methodist miners working on the mine, surely? I know of church-going miners from my home village who have come here to work.'

Emily was thinking primarily of Sam – indeed, there had been few waking hours in recent days when she had *not* thought of him.

'They might have come to Kadina,' said the young rector. 'But such men probably took work on the smaller mines and would not have stayed long. Most men tend to move on after a while, unless they have close family with them – especially since the mines began cutting down on the number of men they employed.'

Emily felt a sense of dismay. She had not seriously considered the possibility that Sam would not be here. When a mine was working and bringing in profit, miners tended to stay in one place, especially if they had relatives working on the same mine. She had not known that the mines of South Australia were having troubles too.

Then she remembered that she was not the only one anxious to locate a Cornish miner. Turning to Margaret, she said, 'This is my companion, Margaret Minns, and these are her two sons, Albert and Thomas. She is hoping to find her husband, Charlie. He came out from Cornwall almost two years ago to find work on the mines. She has heard nothing from him since.'

The young vicar looked at Margaret sympathetically. 'It will not be easy to check on him unless he worked on one of the larger mines where they keep records. If he didn't . . .' Arnold Weeks shrugged apologetically. 'Thousands of miners have passed through the Copper Triangle in recent years.'

Margaret was crestfallen. She too had expected it to be comparatively easy to locate her husband once she and the boys arrived in Australia.

'Well, we will do what we came from England to do and find time later to enquire after them, after Charlie Minns . . . and one or two other names I have. In the meantime it is possible that Charlie will hear about our presence and realise that his wife and sons are in Australia.'

The young Kadina vicar had expected Emily to stay in the rectory with him and his wife of two years, but Emily had other ideas. She, Margaret and the boys were guests at the rectory for only two nights. By then Emily had made a tour of the area, met a number of the miners, married and single, and spoken to women who lived in the townships of Kadina, Wallaroo and Moonta. She arrived at the conclusion that nothing could be achieved by someone who lived in the rarefied atmosphere of a Church of England vicarage.

There *were* problems that needed to be tackled in the mining communities of the area and certain needs to be addressed, but in order to succeed in her aims she would need to live among those she sought to influence.

Her decision brought her into contact with Stefan Mintoff once more. Over the years he had bought up cottages vacated by those forced to move out of the area by a change in their circumstances. For the most part, the departing residents had been desperate for money and Mintoff had bought up their houses at ridiculous prices. Now all but one had been rented out by him. Some had been taken by a constantly changing tenancy of anything up to a dozen out-of-work miners. Clubbing together to pay the rent, they took whatever work was available to earn sufficient money.

The unoccupied cottage was in a highly insalubrious section of the township. Although he was anxious to see a high return from his property investments, Stefan Mintoff was horrified when Emily, accompanied by Margaret, arrived at his store and informed him that she wished to rent the cottage. The two women and the boys would like to move in at the earliest opportunity.

'I am sure I can find somewhere more suitable for you, Miss Boyce. Ewing Street, especially that particular end of the street, is not a suitable place for the niece of an English Cabinet Minister. Indeed, I would not recommend it to any lady of breeding.'

Emily looked at him coldly. 'Then perhaps you will tell me how I am to achieve the purpose of my mission to Australia? Perhaps I should sit in the Bishop's study in Adelaide and write notes to explain what has to be done?'

As Stefan Mintoff struggled for a suitable reply, Emily continued, 'When you introduced yourself on the ship, you offered your support for my mission, Mr Mintoff. If you have had second thoughts I shall seek assistance elsewhere.'

'You still have my fullest support, Miss Boyce,'

Mintoff said hastily. 'I am thinking of your comfort and safety. That particular cottage is in a part of Kadina avoided by respectable women.'

'Then it is where my work is most needed. Will you rent the cottage to me or not?'

Stefan Mintoff made a gesture of resignation. 'If I cannot persuade you to change your mind you may have it rent free, but—'

'No "buts", Mr Mintoff – and I intend paying you a fair rent. Shall we say two-and-sixpence a week?'

'The cottage is yours, Miss Boyce, and I shall donate the rent to assist your work. Now, as you can see, the cottage is furnished – after a fashion. The previous occupants could not take everything with them when they left. If there is anything else you need . . .'

'We will purchase anything else we need, Mr Mintoff,' Emily said firmly. 'I am appreciative of your generosity. Margaret and I will move our things in later today, but first the cottage needs a thorough cleaning. Margaret and I will begin work on it right away.'

After they left the store and had been walking for some time, Margaret said, 'Mr Mintoff is sweet on you, Emily. If you'd asked him he'd have had the whole cottage decorated and refurnished for us.'

'I do not flatter myself he is attracted to *me*, Margaret. Reverend Weeks told me that Mr Mintoff has ambitions of being elected to the state parliament. He quite obviously thinks I have sufficient influence to help him get there.'

'Do you?' Margaret asked.

'I doubt it,' Emily replied honestly. 'I might be able to help his nomination, but the electorate will decide whether or not he is elected – and Arnold Weeks does not seem to think our Mr Mintoff is the most popular man in these parts.'

'Nevertheless, he would seem to be a useful man to know,' said Margaret.

They had arrived at the cottage now. Margaret stopped and looked critically at the front of the home they had just rented. 'Shall we wash those curtains right away, or leave them until we can be sure of having them back up again by nightfall? I don't fancy having the people around here able to look in on us after dark . . .'

III

Because the road on which the cottage was built led nowhere but to open bush country, Emily had thought it would be quiet, at least. Unfortunately, her assumption proved quite erroneous.

There was a large grog shanty somewhere in the bush beyond the town and for some time before darkness fell men could be seen making their way along the road, heading out of town. Their numbers increased after dark when they were often accompanied by women – women with loud, raucous laughter who shouted remarks to groups of men which, while she did not fully understand their meaning, left Emily in no doubt about the class of women to which they belonged.

Soon after Emily and the others had retired to bed there was a loud banging on the door. Emily decided it would be better to ignore whoever it was, but the knocking persisted.

She rose from her bed in time to stop Margaret going

to the door. Peeping around the edge of the curtain, the two women were in time to see a roughly dressed man stagger drunkenly along the pathway to the gate and make his way out on to the street.

After discussing the incident with Margaret and telling her firmly that she was not to open the door to anyone after dark, Emily returned to bed, but found sleep difficult to come by.

Much later, in the early hours of the morning, drinkers began to return to the township and they were even noisier than before. Some of the men – and women – were singing. Others were less kindly disposed towards the world at large. There were at least two fights in the street outside the house, one accompanied by the screams of women and much shouting and swearing by both sexes.

Listening to the sounds, Emily grimaced in the darkness of her bedroom. She could hardly say she had not been warned of what she might expect by living in this particular area. Stefan Mintoff had gone as far as propriety would allow in his warning. However, there was nothing she could do about the disturbances tonight.

Turning over, she tried to ignore the sounds that the thin, corrugated-iron roof could not exclude and, before she knew it, she had fallen asleep.

Talk at breakfast time the next morning was about the noises of the night. The two boys were not unduly concerned; the sounds were not unfamiliar to them. It seemed that before their father had left to come to South Australia the family had lived close to an unlicensed grog-shop where mayhem reigned supreme on settlement nights.

'In that case,' Emily said to the boys, 'it is something we will be able to live with – for a while. I think it might be circumspect to learn a little more about Kadina and our neighbours before I try to change things *too* much. Now, I intend spending this morning visiting the Kadina mine, which I believe is the largest in the vicinity, in order to make some inquiries about your father.'

An hour later Emily and Margaret were standing in the same office visited by Sam almost two years before. They were greeted by the very same mine captain and his clerk. The boys had been left outside to take a look around the mine, which they declared enthusiastically was the largest they had ever seen.

Opening the ledger he had perused on behalf of Jean Spargo, the mine captain ran his finger down the list of 'M's and shook his head. 'I'm sorry, ma'am, it doesn't look as though there's ever been a Minns working at the Kadina mine.'

'Oh!' Margaret could not hide her disappointment. 'I didn't really expect him to still be here, but I thought you might know where he had gone. This is where he was coming to when he left Cornwall.'

'A lot of miners bound for Cornwall have a change of mind about their destination while they're on the ship. They strike up friendships with men who tell them of places where they have friends or relations and where they can earn more money. As a result we never see them once they arrive. You could make inquiries in other mines in the area. They don't all keep records but you might find someone who knows him and can tell you where he's likely to be. Who knows, you might even find him working in one of them.'

'Thank you,' said Emily. 'In the meantime would you post a notice on your board asking for anyone with information about Charlie Minns to get in touch with Margaret or me?'

'Of course, and I'll be happy to do anything else that might be of help.'

The two women had almost reached the door, when Emily stopped and turned back to the mine captain. As though it were an afterthought, she asked, 'There is something else, while I am here. Do you have a Sam Hooper working on your mine? He came from the village of St Cleer, in Cornwall.'

'Hooper is a very common name, both here and in Cornwall, Miss Boyce, but I'll have a look in the ledger. Do you know when he arrived?'

'It would be almost two years ago,' Emily replied, trying to contain her excitement.

The mine captain had begun turning the pages of the ledger when the clerk asked Emily, 'Did this Sam Hooper come to Kadina to join his uncle, Wilf Hooper?'

'He certainly came to Australia to find an uncle,' Emily agreed. 'I do not know the uncle's Christian name.'

'It sounds like the Cornishman who came here with a young widow,' the clerk said to the mine captain. 'You must remember her, she had a pretty little girl with her.'

'Was the little girl named Primrose?' Emily asked the question, her heart beating a little faster. She believed the Kadina mine captain might be able to offer her news of Sam, but was beginning to fear it would not be news she wanted to hear.

'Yes ... yes it was,' replied the mine captain. 'Her

mother was an attractive young woman too, as I recall.'

'Where is he now?' Emily asked. 'I mean, where are they all? Are they still in Kadina?'

The mine captain shook his head. 'Wilf Hooper moved on to the Blinman mine as underground captain some time before his nephew arrived here. Young Hooper went there to find him. As far as I know the young woman and her daughter went with him.'

'Thank you.' It seemed that Sam and Jean Spargo's travels together had not ended when their ship reached Australia. 'This Blinman mine . . . is it near here?'

'No, Miss Boyce,' the mine captain replied. 'It's in bush country hundreds of miles to the north – land far less hospitable than you'll find around Kadina. But Reverend Maddison is the Methodist circuit preacher in that area. His daughter lives in Kadina and he visits her whenever he can. I don't know when he'll next be here, but when he is I'll have a word with him. He may know something of this Sam Hooper. It's worth a try.'

Walking back to the cottage with Margaret, Emily thought of what the mine captain had said. She was not at all certain she should pursue the fortunes of Sam since his arrival in Australia. It was likely to bring her a heartbreak she had not anticipated when she set off from Cornwall with such high hopes for the future.

IV

Although Emily was unhappy that a swift reunion with Sam was not possible, and she was disturbed by what she had heard from the mine captain, she did not allow it to affect the work she had come to Kadina to carry out on behalf of the Church.

While Margaret and the boys tramped around the mines in the vicinity, enquiring after Charlie Minns and making arrangements for the boys to begin lessons at the local school, Emily met many people named on a list prepared for her by Reverend Arnold Weeks – and many who were not.

As a result of her own contacts, Emily had notices placed on the noticeboards of institutes and mines, calling for volunteers to form a choir. She also announced that, in addition to taking a regular Sunday school, she would start a ladies' guild.

Emily felt the latter was important in order to sound out the women of Kadina on the needs of the township. Some of the other problems encountered in the community, she was able to see for herself.

The grog-shop outside the town was still going strong and she suspected that at least two of the cottages situated on Ewing Street were being used as bawdy houses. Both were so close to her cottage that they could not be ignored.

One night, soon after moving in, Emily waited at the unlit window of the cottage's living room in order to confirm her suspicions. From here she had a clear view of one of the suspected brothels, and a rather more restricted view of the other.

She watched for two hours, during which time a number of women entered one of the cottages, accompanied by men. More significantly, during the same time no fewer than a further seventeen men also entered the house, each staying for a period of about half an hour.

This particular problem was close to home and Emily

wondered about the best means of tackling it. At the present time there was only one policeman in the town, and she realised that until he received reinforcements he would be unable to take any action about the illegal grog-shop or the bawdy house. Besides, she was also aware that if she called in the police it would alienate the very men and women she was hoping to help.

On her second Sunday in Kadina, with the problem still unresolved, Emily attended the morning service held in the church in the centre of the township.

From the outside, the church building, with its castellated tower and rough stonework, might have been lifted direct from a Cornish village. Inside, the decor was less ornate than the exterior had promised.

Emily arrived later than she had planned and took a seat towards the rear of the church. After spending a few minutes on her knees in silent prayer, she sat back and glanced at the loosely packed congregation.

Her attention was immediately drawn to a woman seated in the row of pews immediately in front of her. She had the whole row to herself. It was apparent to Emily that other members of the congregation were deliberately avoiding her.

Then, when the woman turned to glance at a couple who were taking their places to one side of her, Emily realised she had seen the woman before. She was one of those who occupied one of the bawdy houses in Ewing Street.

The woman sat on her own throughout the service. When it was time for Communion, Emily saw that other communicants were jostling for position in order that they should not take the Communion cup immediately after the woman.

Because of this, it proved an easy matter for Emily to take up her position beside the woman and smile at her when they rose from the Communion rail.

Later, as the congregation filed from the church, it was equally easy for Emily to take up a position behind the woman as they left the building.

Reverend Arnold Weeks was at the door to bid farewell to the congregation. He would have spoken at some length to Emily, but she had other plans and cut the conversation short.

She hurried after the woman she had sat behind in the church. When she caught up with her, she tried to sound casual. 'Hello, I believe we're both heading in the same direction. We might as well walk together. I am Emily Boyce. I have only recently arrived in Kadina from England.'

'I know who you are, Miss Boyce – and why you're here. I suppose I should be flattered that you've chosen to speak to me.'

Emily was genuinely puzzled. 'I'm sorry, but why should my speaking to you be anything special?'

The other woman gave Emily a quick, quizzical glance before saying, 'Well, you're a relative of a minister of the British government, friend of the Bishop of Adelaide – and of our Councillor Mintoff – and I believe you're here to make life better for everyone? In fact, it seems we lucky people in Kadina are having a visit from a female Jesus Christ.'

It was an outrageous statement to make, but Emily could not resist a smile. She realised too that in spite of the other woman's calling, she possessed both intelligence and an education.

'That's just the sort of blasphemous remark that used

to land me in trouble with my father. He was the vicar of St Cleer, in Cornwall. By the way, I do not know your name.'

The woman walking beside Emily glanced at her once more, but with increased interest. 'You *do* know how I earn my living, Miss Boyce? I sell my body to men – lots of men. I'm a prostitute.'

'No one has actually pointed you out to me, but I have both eyes and ears. We live in a noisy district and much of the din centres around your house – and another on the opposite side of the road – but I still do not know your name.'

'It's Ruth. Ruth Askew, from Wales. I'd tell you what *my* father did for a living if I knew who he was. All I can say is that he must be a fairly wealthy man. He kept my mother in as much comfort as anyone else in the Welsh village where I lived, and paid for me to go to school. Unfortunately, he never made himself known to me, not even when my mother died. She took the secret with her to the grave. Today is the anniversary of her death and I always go to church to say a prayer for her – whether I'm made welcome or not.'

There was only the faintest hint of bitterness in her voice and Emily asked, 'Is that why you came to Australia, to . . . to the life you are living now?'

'No, I came here because of a man. He worked in the smelting works close to Swansea. We walked out together for three years and had an understanding. At least, I *believed* we had an understanding. Because I believed, I let him take liberties with me – isn't that the delicate way of putting it, Miss Boyce?'

When Emily did not answer, Ruth Askew continued, 'Like many women before me the inevitable happened.

I fell pregnant. Had they known, the women in the village would have said it was "in the blood". No doubt they'd have been right. But I didn't really care. After all, more than half the women in the village I came from became mothers within six months of their wedding. David and I were going steady. We'd get married, or so I thought. I got the shock of my life when I told David of the state I was in. He said he'd got a place on an emigrant ship to Wallaroo. Said he'd been keeping it as a surprise for me. That he'd planned for me to follow on a later boat and we'd marry as soon as I reached Australia. Do you know, I *believed* him. I really did.'

Ruth gave a mirthless laugh. 'I didn't know as much about men then as I do now. If I had I'd have made him marry me right there and then, or taken him before a magistrate. Instead, I let him board the boat to come here without me. The plan was that I'd follow him as soon as I could arrange a passage. There would still have been time for us to marry before the baby was born, even if I went up the aisle waddling like a plump duck.'

The unhappy laugh was repeated. 'Oh yes, I was a very naïve young woman in those days. They wouldn't give me a free passage, so I sold everything my ma had left me to buy a passage on a boat that would get me to Wallaroo about a month before the baby was due.'

Ruth looked at Emily again, but the smile was gone now. 'We had some dreadful weather when we were only a couple of weeks away from Wallaroo. The worst he'd known in all his years at sea, the captain said. We were all being tossed about like feathers in a wind and were certain the ship would founder. I was as sick as a dog. So sick I lost the baby.'

Emily made a sympathetic sound, but Ruth said philosophically, 'It turned out to be for the best, really. When I got to Wallaroo I found David had met a girl on the ship he came out on – a Cornish girl, as it happened. They were married a month after reaching Wallaroo. He'd got her in the family way too, you see.'

'So you turned to the way of life you're leading now,' said Emily.

'There was no "turned to" about it,' Ruth said, with more bitterness than she had shown so far. 'When I left the ship at Wallaroo I was a very sick woman. Because of the *reason* I was sick none of the respectable women on board wanted anything to do with me. Oh, I can't say I blame them, they were starting new lives in a new land. The last thing they wanted was to have to take care of a "fallen woman" – and that's what I was, wasn't I? The only woman who took pity on me was Gladys. She was another Welsh girl nobody wanted to know on board the ship. At least none of the women; the crew and many of the men passengers were more enthusiastic. In fact most of them knew Gladys a great many times on the voyage. She walked down the gangway at Wallaroo with a lot more money than she'd had when she boarded the ship. Well, she was the one who took care of me, both then and later when I learned about David and his new wife.'

A brief bout of coughing interrupted Ruth's story for a few moments. Looking at her, Emily realised she was thinner and more fragile than she appeared at first glance.

'When Gladys came here and bought the house

where we're now living it seemed natural I should come with her and help with what she was doing. After all, I owed my life to her – and it wasn't as though I was some innocent young virgin, was it now?'

Instead of replying, Emily put her own question to the other woman. 'Is it what you want to be doing for the rest of your life, Ruth? You are an intelligent woman, you know such a way of life cannot last. Would you take something else if it were offered to you?'

'What do you suggest I should do, Miss Boyce? Go into domestic service, perhaps? Somewhere I'm not known? No, when it's settlement day in the mines I can earn more in twenty-four hours than a servant earns in a whole year!' Giving Emily a sidelong glance, she asked, 'Does that shock you?'

'No,' Emily lied. 'But it does sadden me. I feel you are a woman who has much more to offer the world than the life you are leading here.'

'I've never yet had a man go away dissatisfied,' Ruth retorted.

Aware that Ruth was deliberately trying to shock her, Emily said quietly, 'But they *do* all go away, Ruth.'

'That was hurtful, Miss Boyce.'

'The truth often is, Ruth, but while you are doing what you are, the men who know you will always go away. One day you will have nothing – and no one.'

Ruth shook her head vigorously. 'No! I may or may not have a man, but as soon as I've made enough money I'll leave what I'm doing – and leave Australia too. I'll go back to Wales, to a place where I'm not known, and buy myself a small inn.'

'What if the police move in and arrest you and the others, Ruth? What will you do then?'

'Are you going to go to the police and complain about us? Is that what's going to happen?'

They had reached the street where they both lived and stopped outside the small, unkempt garden in front of Ruth's brothel home.

Emily shook her head. 'I cannot condone what you are doing, Ruth. It is wrong – very wrong. But I do not condemn you. However, you and the others have offended a great many townspeople by your behaviour. Moves to have the police take action against you began long before I arrived.'

While Ruth thought about what had been said, Emily continued, 'I would like to talk to you again, Ruth. I could not help noticing in church that you have a fine voice. Why not come along to one of the choir practices I am organising? You would be a great asset—'

Ruth's laugh was genuine this time. 'Do you really think I could join your choir, Miss Boyce? You would lose all your women members immediately and they would forbid their men to attend. That would leave only the single men – and most of *them* would be frightened away for fear I might acknowledge I knew them already.'

She was still chuckling as she went up the path to the house of ill-repute.

Emily walked the few paces to her own cottage, feeling confused. Ruth was sinning against all that Emily had been brought up to believe was right and moral and was leading a patently sinful life. Yet Emily felt unable to condemn her out of hand. What was more disturbing, she actually *liked* her!

V

The two brothels in Ewing Street were raided four days later by a police sergeant and three constables. They had been sent from Adelaide for this express purpose, at the request of the town's mayor.

The whole operation had been such a well-kept secret that even Kadina's own constable had not been told. It was known that his sympathies lay with the prostitutes; they helped restrict vice and much of the miners' drunkenness to a section of the town where no one of importance lived – until Emily moved in.

Unfortunately, the operation failed because of its very secrecy. Had the township constable been consulted he would have told them that at the time they chose to carry out the raid, the 'ladies of the town' would be at the grog-shop beyond the town limits. Here they received free drinks in recognition of the trade they brought to the unlicensed and makeshift shanty.

As a result of their error of judgement the police were able to arrest only two girls when the brothels were raided. The house where Ruth lived was empty.

However, the raid provoked great anger among the men who were in the habit of frequenting the two establishments and it soon spread to others who were not.

When word of the swoop reached the illicit grog-shop the paying customers hurried back to Kadina, accompanied by the residents of the two brothels.

By the time they reached Ewing Street the police had departed, taking the two prostitutes with them.

From the cottage, Emily and Margaret watched the men and women milling about the nearest of the two houses. Emily thought they resembled a swarm of bees, with everyone hurrying around in an angry mood, achieving nothing.

Then, suddenly and alarmingly, one of the prostitutes pointed in the direction of the cottage occupied by Emily and Margaret, shouting that the new arrivals were responsible for the sudden police interest in the two brothels.

No reason was given by the woman, but none was needed. The angry mob was looking for scapegoats. Believing it had found them it switched its attention to the cottage.

Alarmed, Margaret backed away from the window and appealed to Emily. 'What are we going to do, Emily? They're angry.'

'*We* are going to do nothing. At least, *you* are not. Stay in here and keep away from the windows. I shall go outside and reason with them.'

'You can't reason with a mob like that. They've been drinking!'

'I have no intention of cowering in here while they smash our windows, or whatever else they decide to do.'

'Then I'll come with you—'

As Margaret hurried after her, Emily rounded on her. 'Stay here with the boys. If the house is attacked they will be terrified. Take care of them and leave *me* to deal with the mob outside.'

For Emily to have ventured outside would probably have been quite as foolhardy as Margaret predicted, but by the time she reached the door someone far more qualified to deal with the angry miners had intervened.

Emily heard the raised voice of Ruth Askew shouting at the mob. It seemed she was standing just the other side of the door.

'Have you all gone quite mad?!' The Welsh accent

was more pronounced than Emily remembered. 'What do you think you're doing? You, Manny, put down that stone. Put it *down*, I say!'

'You'd protect someone who's had two of your friends arrested?' called a man's voice. 'Whose side are you on, girl?'

'The side of reason,' Ruth retorted. 'I'm as upset as anyone else about the arrest of Annie and Martha, but what's it got to do with Miss Boyce?'

'Everything!' It was a woman's voice this time. 'We've never been raided before. She's a do-gooder who has no right to come and live here, among us. She belongs on the other side of the town.'

There were shouts of agreement, but Ruth ignored them. 'Where she lives is her business, not ours.'

'Not when she stops us earning a living because she doesn't like what we're doing,' called another woman. Once again there was agreement from the mob.

Ruth raised her voice, scornful now. 'Are you really looking for whoever's to blame for having Annie and Martha arrested – or are you just looking for a scapegoat, eh? Someone to have a go at, so you can walk away feeling better, whether what you've done is right or not? Mick heard what the police said when they arrested Martha. What was it, Mick?'

When there was no reply, Ruth continued, 'It seems Mick has gone, but he said he heard the sergeant tell her she was being arrested for keeping a bawdy house . . .'

There were indignant shouts from the crowd, including a woman's voice crying, 'Shame!'

Even in her present precarious situation, this particular word of protest brought a wry smile to Emily's face, but Ruth was still talking.

'That wasn't *all* Mick heard. The sergeant also said they'd had a man keeping watch on the houses for weeks.

'That's right!' Ruth cried triumphantly. 'They'd been keeping watch on our houses for *weeks*. They were watching the house before Miss Boyce moved in. How can she have had anything to do with what's happened tonight, eh? You tell me that.'

There was a great deal of angry murmuring among the mob, many of whom did not *want* to exonerate Emily, but Ruth was quick to follow up the advantage she had gained.

'If some of us girls put our minds to it I think we could come up with the names of one or two *men* who want to get us out of town. Men who were eager enough to make use of us before their wives came to Kadina to join them. Now they want us gone before someone tells on 'em.'

The shouts that greeted this statement were mixed with laughter, but Ruth had not finished with the crowd yet. 'There's another man – and we all know who I'm talking about – a man who thinks he's grown too big for Kadina. Who's grown too big for his boots, in my opinion. He's been a good customer – even though he's always used the back door . . .'

Her words brought a murmur of agreement from the men and shrieks of laughter from some of the women.

'Yes, I see you know who I'm talking about. Now he's going up in the world he wants us out of Kadina. For my money, *he's* the one who brought in the police to close us down. Think about it and you'll realise I'm making good sense.'

There was dissension from some members of the

crowd, but Ruth had succeeded in taking the heat out of their anger. As it evaporated, they slowly began moving away.

When Emily opened the front door Ruth was still standing outside.

'Thank you, Ruth, you handled that admirably. Far better than I might have done.'

'*Did* you bring in the police to have us closed down?'

The question was so unexpected it left Emily floundering for a moment. 'You *know* I didn't. The man who overheard what the police sergeant said—'

'I made that up,' Ruth said nonchalantly. '*Did* you complain about us?'

'That's not my way,' Emily replied. 'I would have come to your houses and spoken to you all first – and I fully intended that was what I was going to do.'

'That's what I thought,' said Ruth, satisfied.

At that moment one of the miners on the fringe of the mob, disappointed there had been no action, showed his displeasure by throwing a stone he had been holding. It was meant as no more than an angry gesture of frustration, but it caught Ruth on the side of her face. She staggered backwards with a cry of pain, a hand to her cheek.

'Quick, inside and let me have a look at that.' Emily took Ruth's arm and helped her inside. Slamming the door shut behind them, she led the injured woman to the kitchen where there was a lamp, turned low.

Emily led Ruth to a chair, then she turned up the wick and examined the other woman's injured face. 'It's bleeding rather badly, but I think it probably looks worse than it really is. I'll bathe it for you, then I should be able to see it more clearly.'

At that moment Margaret entered the kitchen and gasped when she saw the blood streaming down the side of Ruth's face.

'Here, let me help.' Producing a basin for Emily, she hurried to a cupboard and brought out a bottle of iodine. Handing it to Emily, she said, 'This will sting, but it will prevent any infection. At least, it works well on grazed knees.'

As the two women fussed over Ruth, Emily told Margaret of Ruth's part in preventing the mob from attacking the cottage.

'Thank heaven you were there to help us,' Margaret said. 'I was in the bedroom with the boys and the noise the crowd was making was alarming. Young Tom was quite frightened. That reminds me, I came out here to fetch a drink of water for him. Can you manage if I take one to him, Emily?'

When she had left the kitchen, Ruth said to Emily, 'Word has gone around that you're making enquiries about Charlie Minns. Is Margaret his wife?'

'Yes. She and the two boys came out with me expecting to find him straightaway, but I think we are all beginning to lose hope. He came to South Australia long ago but Margaret has heard nothing from him.'

'Charlie Minns _was_ here. He stayed in Kadina until the end of last year.'

Startled, Emily demanded, 'You knew him?'

'I knew him well,' Ruth confirmed. 'Too well. He wanted me to go away with him when he left Kadina, but I was having none of it. He'd have had me working all the hours that God made, plus a great many more added on by the Devil – just to keep him in drink and gambling money. _She_ doesn't seem too bad a person, Miss Boyce, and I like what little I've seen of the boys when they've been playing in the street; but Charlie Minns is a bad 'un, believe me.'

Upset though she was by Ruth's words, Emily remembered what Rose, wife of the St Cleer Methodist minister, had said about him. The two very different women seemed to be in agreement.

'Margaret and the boys will not give up trying to find him,' she said. 'Do you have any idea where he might be now?'

'I don't know for certain,' Ruth replied. 'When he left Kadina he said he was heading for Burra, well to the south-west of here, but I've heard he left there and went prospecting, up north. The last time I met anyone who'd seen him, he was working in bush country up in the Flinders Ranges . . . somewhere close to Blinman.'

3

I

'How do you feel about a change of scenery for a while, Sam?'

Wilf Hooper put the unexpected question to Sam one evening when uncle and nephew were seated on the porch of the captain's cottage, enjoying an evening drink together.

Almost two years had passed since Sam had arrived at Blinman with Ira and Jean. Recently, Captain Wilf had taken charge of the mine once more, the regular captain journeying to Adelaide to seek medical advice for a heart ailment.

The copper industry was facing yet another of the difficult periods that had become so much a part of the worldwide mining scene. The Blinman mine was still in profit, but had been forced to cut expenditure wherever possible.

Many miners, fearing a repetition of the bad times they had experienced in other mines, had left. Some made for the goldfields of New South Wales, others intended trying their luck mining silver, lead, or any of the other minerals to be found in Australia. They were willing to go anywhere in order to make use of the unique skills they possessed.

Although the Blinman mine was rich in good quality copper ore, it was proving necessary to go deeper for it and water had become an increasing problem in the deeper levels.

'You're not laying me off?'

Given the present uncertainty in the copper-mining industry, the seemingly frivolous question contained an element of genuine concern.

'Far from it,' Captain Wilf replied. 'I'd like you to take on a task that would normally be carried out by a captain – me, probably.'

'Tell me more.' As Sam spoke he flapped at a fly that seemed determined to share the beer in his tankard.

'There's a mine about twenty miles from here called the Nuccaleena. It started off a few years ago with a lot of promise, but folded shortly before you arrived. We've bought the engine to help with the pumping and I'm sending a team along to dismantle it and bring it back to Blinman. What I'd like you to do is go with them and survey the workings. Let me know if you think it's worth the company buying the mine as an investment for the future, should copper prices pick up once more.'

'You'd trust my judgement on something as important as that?' Sam was both delighted and apprehensive at such a prospect. He was being asked to make a decision that could lose the mining company a great deal of money if his appraisal proved to be wrong.

'Is there any reason why I shouldn't?'

'There are probably a great many reasons.' Sam grinned. 'But none come to mind right now. Thanks, Uncle, I would enjoy a few days away from Blinman. When do I leave?'

'As soon as I can organise enough bullock teams to bring the engine back. Hopefully it'll be within the week. Some of the track to Nuccaleena will have been washed away by last season's rains, so it'll take a couple of days or so for the bullock drays to get there, but you can start putting a few things together – and take a gun. The sheep stations have reported trouble from Aborigines lately.'

'I thought they were fairly friendly in this area,' Sam said, in some surprise. There had been no trouble in the area between the mining communities and native Australians during the time he had been at Blinman.

'They've been quiet until now,' Captain Wilf agreed. 'There *was* trouble some years ago, when members of a northern tribe came down to dig out ochre at Parachilna to use in a tribal ceremony, but that didn't involve the local Aborigines. Something must have happened to seriously stir them up, but until we find out what it is we're not likely to get it sorted out. I'm putting Piet van Roos in charge of the party. He knows the Aborigines better than anyone else I know.'

Sam was not unhappy to be leaving Blinman for a while. He had been working in the mine without a break since his arrival. Jean and Ira were very happy together and Sam was delighted for both of them but, in an occasional irrational moment, usually when the temperature soared to new and breathless heights and he was suffering sleepless nights, he resented their happiness. He felt it should have been his late friend, Phillip, enjoying life with Jean and Primrose.

On such days, Sam also felt deeply the knowledge that the only woman who had ever really meant anything to him was on the other side of the world. Yet, even at such moments, he realised she would have remained beyond his reach had he stayed in St Cleer.

Nevertheless, he was very disappointed that she had found no way of writing to him in response to the messages he had sent to her via the letters he had written home. He had to remind himself, guiltily, that he had been at Blinman for more than a year before sitting down to the laborious task of writing to tell his parents he had not settled at Kadina.

There was a possibility, albeit a remote one, that Emily *had* written to him and that the letter had gone to Kadina.

He felt he would be able to put such thoughts behind him for a while in the unfamiliar surroundings of Nuccaleena.

Sam was not particularly concerned about the trouble currently being experienced with hostile Aborigines. Travelling in company with forty other miners, most of whom were armed, he did not anticipate trouble.

It was a slow journey, the first night being spent at the remote sheep station of Moolooloo. The owners were delighted to have company – even in such great numbers. They killed and roasted two sheep and, in return, enjoyed a share of the beer being carried in considerable quantities by the Blinman miners.

During the course of a very pleasant evening, Sam was astounded to learn that the area grazed by the sheep station was almost the size of Cornwall! It helped him to appreciate once more the vast size of the country to which he had come.

The following morning the bonhomie of the previous evening vanished when it was discovered that more than a hundred in-lamb ewes had been speared to death during the night. The sheep had been in a pen close to the house – given the ferocity of the attack, too close for comfort.

The wagons of the miners had been secured nearby, yet no one had heard a thing.

Deeply distressed, the owners of the sheep station had difficulty coming to terms with the atrocity.

'Why would they do such a thing?' the wife lamented. 'We have always been good friends with them. In bad years we've kept them supplied with water and given them the occasional sheep. In return, they've helped find stock that have broken away from the main flock. Nothing like this has ever happened before.'

'I don't believe these "*yuras*" are from the local tribe,' said Piet van Roos. 'They're from outside the area – and they're telling us something. It's possible the Blinman miners have stirred them up in some way. If only we could catch one of 'em we might be able to find out what it is. In the meantime . . .' He shrugged. 'I suggest you stay on your guard at Moolooloo. We'll do the same.'

Halfway between the Moolooloo sheep station and Nuccaleena, Sam was walking alongside Piet when the bullock driver said in an undertone, 'Say nothing and don't look round. Just keep walking as though you suspect nothing . . .'

With this mysterious directive, the South African casually walked back along the wagon train, passing an occasional remark with some of the other men.

When he disappeared into the bush no one noticed until, ten minutes later, there was a sudden commotion to the side of one of the rear wagons. Moments later Piet reappeared, the fingers of one hand firmly locked in the short black hair of an Aborigine boy who could have been no more than twelve years of age.

As the two drew near to the South African's own wagon, Sam saw that Piet's arm was bleeding profusely.

'What's happened?' Sam asked, in concern.

'Nothing much,' replied Piet. 'I glimpsed this youngster some way back. He fancies himself as a warrior, but he's got a bit to learn first.'

'By the look of your arm he's not doing too badly,' Sam commented.

'I got careless, that's all,' Piet said. 'He's no more than a boy. The sight of my blood scared him more than it did me.'

Other miners were gathering around now and Sam asked, 'What do you want to do with him?'

'Let him go. I've managed to have a brief chat with him about what's going on. It seems he and his people are looking for someone who has deeply offended them. I've managed to convince him that none of us are involved. When we release him he'll return to his people and tell them what I've said. Hopefully, they'll then leave us alone and go off and look elsewhere for the man they want.'

In an attempt to convince the boy's people that the party meant no harm, the boy was released ten minutes later, carrying presents of food from Piet.

Watching him heading for the security of the surrounding bush, Sam felt relief. Once the Aborigines knew that the column from Blinman had nothing to do with their grievance, the miners might be able to proceed without risk of further attack.

The young Aborigine had almost reached a patch of dense bush when a shot rang out from the rear of the wagon train, startling the patient bullocks and echoing around the adjacent hills. The boy stumbled, as though he had tripped on a stone, then pitched forward on to his face, dropping the stores he had been carrying.

Sam ran forward to where the boy had fallen, Piet close behind him, but no one else from the mining column joined them.

As he turned the boy over, Sam saw blood trickling from the corner of his mouth. He knew even before he checked that there would be no pulse.

The boy was dead.

Advancing a few steps towards the wagon train, Sam demanded angrily, 'Who fired the shot?'

When no one replied, Sam said angrily, 'I suppose someone is going to return to Blinman and brag that he's a hero for shooting a young boy in the back? Well, for what it's worth, I'm saying right here and now that he's a coward. Someone who wouldn't have had the courage to fire on a twelve-year-old boy armed only with a spear had they met face to face.'

Some of the men looked resentful, others uncomfortable, but still no one spoke.

'Whoever he is, he's more than a coward,' declared Piet. 'He's also a damned fool. That boy told me his people are looking for a particular man who's wronged them – he wouldn't say how. He was going back to tell them the man they are after isn't with us. Once they'd accepted that – and they would have – they'd have gone away and left us alone. Now they won't learn the truth and they have the boy's death to avenge. Someone, probably more than one of us, is going to die because the truth didn't get back to the *yuras*. The blame will rest fairly and squarely with the fool who fired that shot.'

There was still no response from the men with the wagon train. Turning away from them in disgust, Piet said to Sam, 'Come on, boy, let's you and me go and deal with the lad.'

'What do we do?' asked Sam. 'Are we going to bury him?'

Piet shook his head. 'We'll leave that to his people. They have their own customs. I want you to take my rifle and keep your eyes skinned while I find the spear he used when he attacked me. When I've found it we lay the boy out and put the spear alongside him. It shows we respect him as a warrior. He deserves that, at least.'

The spear was quickly found and, their tribute paid to the boy, Sam and Piet walked together back to the wagon train.

'How are we going to inform the police about this?' Sam asked.

'We aren't,' Piet said curtly.

'But—'

'There's no "buts" about it,' Piet said. 'Rightly or wrongly that's the way it is. This is Australia, not some sleepy Cornish village. It's happened. Although it shouldn't have – it has. Now we forget it. All right, boy, we've done our duty, now let's get back to the job we're being paid to do.'

There was one more abortive attack on the wagons along the long and difficult track between Moolooloo and Nuccaleena, but no one was hurt. When shots were fired by the miners, the Aborigines faded away into the bush.

II

Soon after passing a remote and deserted inn, the wagons rounded a low rise and an engine house, complete with engine, came into view. It was built on the lower slopes of a round-topped hill.

Facing the mine, on the far side of a shallow creek, was a small, empty township made up of a haphazard mixture of stone cottages and shacks constructed from wood and corrugated iron.

But it was the engine house that took Sam's breath away. It was *exactly* like a hundred others to be found on Bodmin Moor.

'There's no doubting who built that, is there?' The speaker was another Cornishman named Tim, who had been at the Blinman mine only a few months longer than Sam. Proudly, the miner added, 'I don't doubt it'll still be standing here in a hundred years' time.'

'Not the way it is now,' remarked a practical Welsh engineer. 'We'll need to knock it about a bit to get the engine out. The first thing we'll have off is the roof, so we can lift out the beam.'

'Well, we'll at least have a roof over our heads while the work's being done,' Sam said. 'There are more than enough houses for all of us. What beats me is how anyone found copper here in the first place – then managed to persuade a company to build a township here!'

'It was a good mine in its day.' This from Piet. 'I've taken many a load of high-grade ore from Nuccaleena, but transport costs are high this far out – and there you have the reason why it's not working now.'

'Well, I'll start checking out its prospects in the morning,' Sam said. 'For now let's help the cook prepare something for us before it gets dark.'

The engineers began work on dismantling the Nuccaleena mine-engine the following morning. Normally, bullock drays would have been sent back to Blinman as they were loaded, but given the hostility of the Aborigines, it was decided that they should remain at Nuccaleena until all work at the site was completed and then they would all return together.

On the second day of work the men were assembling for a midday meal when the sound of a shot rang out from farther along the shallow valley.

At first it was thought some of the men had gone out shooting kangaroos, but it was quickly established that everyone in the mining party was present on the mine.

Temporarily abandoning all thoughts of eating, miners hurried away to collect their guns. They were discussing whether or not they should go into the bush to investigate the shot when two figures emerged from the bush farther along the valley. One was a white man, the other an Aborigine woman.

As the two drew nearer, the Blinman miners speculated among themselves about what they were doing out here, so far from civilisation.

The man was carrying a gun and those watching had no doubt he had been responsible for the shot.

When the couple was within hailing distance, Piet called out, 'You're a long way from anywhere, friend.'

The man waited until he was much closer before replying. 'Not far enough, it would seem,' he said ungraciously. 'There's no sense in looking for anything worthwhile in places where others have been before.'

'He's a prospector,' Piet spoke quietly to Sam.

'Isn't it dangerous for him to be out on his own at a time like this?'

Piet shrugged. 'A true prospector lives with danger every minute of the day. He prefers it to people. Most can't stand even their own company, some of the time. But this one isn't a natural loner. If he was he wouldn't have the woman with him.'

The man was closer now and Sam had no need to shout when he asked, 'Was that you who fired the shot we just heard?'

The man nodded and, matter-of-factly, replied, 'A bunch of *yuras* armed with spears came at me. After I shot one the others kept their distance.'

While Sam was left speechless at the casualness with which the newcomer had spoken of shooting and possibly killing a man, Piet said, 'We've had trouble with 'em too. You'd better come into camp. Stay out there and sooner or later they'll get you.'

Glancing at the Aborigine woman, the prospector looked back at Piet with an unspoken question.

'She'd better come in too,' Piet said reluctantly. 'Find yourselves a hut, there's more than enough to go around.'

The prospector went off without another word, the

woman trudging behind him, her glance fixed firmly on the ground. Her companion headed for an empty hut, never once looking behind him to see if she was following.

Watching them, Sam said thoughtfully, 'You know, I can't help feeling I've seen the woman somewhere before.'

Piet smiled. 'You've not seen enough *yura* women at Blinman to know one from another.'

'You could be right,' Sam conceded. 'But it doesn't matter. There's work to be done and the problems we've got at the moment aren't making it any easier. We can do without any more.'

Pointing to the prospector, one of the miners standing nearby said, 'If you really want to avoid trouble you'll send him and his woman packing right now. He's bad news. I worked with him on the Burra mine a while back. He stabbed a man in a fight there and was lucky to get away with a plea of self-defence. Some called it murder and would have taken matters into their own hands if he hadn't left in a hurry.'

'Hopefully he won't be with us for long,' said Sam. 'What's his name?'

'Minns,' came the reply. 'Charlie Minns.'

III

Assessing the future viability of the Nuccaleena mine was not as straightforward as it might have been. Sam's task was made more complicated because a series of heavy storms had swept across the Flinders Ranges, causing the lower levels of the mine to flood badly, making an accurate assessment difficult.

Sam believed there was probably copper here, but the water would need to be pumped out before it could be located – and the pump was being removed.

The upper levels proved almost as impossible to assess. The result of Sam's first cursory survey indicated that the ore had been exhausted, yet Sam was not convinced this was so. He had a gut reaction – a miner's intuition – that the copper lode had been pursued in the wrong direction.

For three days he kept returning to the mine, examining the direction of the worked-out lode before making up his mind about what needed to be done.

Most of the men sent to dismantle and remove the Nuccaleena engine were miners, predominantly Cornish. That evening, Sam discussed his problems with these men and with the engineers.

He wanted four men to help him clear a partially collapsed adit and extend it a little farther than it went at present. He believed this was where the lost copper lode might be found. Whoever had begun the tunnel was going in the right direction, but Sam felt they had given up too soon. Either that, or the man in question had been in the adit when it collapsed.

When the engineer agreed to spare the men there was no shortage of volunteers. For a true miner, any other work smacked of unskilled labour. The Blinman miners would do whatever Sam required of them – just as long as it was underground.

It took a half-day of hard work to clear the roof fall, then Sam directed the men to extend the tunnel at an angle from the course taken by the departed miners.

'Are you sure that's what you want?' A miner who

had been employed at Nuccaleena during the time it was producing copper was sceptical. 'Cap'n Morrison always reckoned the lode ran to the west, not the way you're going.'

'Captain Morrison lost the lode and the mine closed,' Sam retorted, by no means as confident as he sounded but determined to follow his instincts. 'We'll go *this* way.'

'Whatever you say,' said the dissenting miner, reluctantly. 'You're cap'n for this trip.'

Sam and his fellow miners worked until sundown without finding what Sam had hoped. As they emerged from the adit, weary and dirty and looking forward to their evening meal, a group of Aborigines broke cover. They had crept undetected through the undergrowth in the valley as far as the small creek that separated mine and township. Now, with shrieks of fury, they ran through the near-empty township, hurling spears at any miners they saw.

It all happened so quickly that the attack was over and the Aborigines were disappearing into the thick bush beyond the camp before the first of the miners was able to reach his rifle and fire a shot after the fleeing warriors.

Behind them, the Aborigines left one miner dead and three others with spear wounds.

As the wounded men were receiving attention, Sam spoke to Piet van Roos. 'That was a determined attack, Piet – and a daring one.'

The older man nodded. Speaking past the short-stemmed pipe clenched firmly between his teeth, he said, 'They're determined, all right. Something has really upset them. Rightly or wrongly, they're blaming us for whatever it is.'

'Could it now have something to do with the boy who was shot?'

Piet shook his head. 'It won't have helped, but they were stirred up before that. I wish I understood what it's about. I'm not even sure these particular *yuras* are from this area. If they're not, something has brought them up here. They won't leave until they've got what it is they're after.'

'You don't think the woman who came in with Minns might know something?'

'She might, but the only way I'm likely to get any of her time is to pay Minns for it and that's against the few principles I have.'

Sam looked at Piet in disbelief. 'You don't mean . . .'

'That Minns is a pimp? That's *exactly* what I mean. Men have been in and out of the hut she shares with Minns every night since they've been here, with Minns at the door taking the money. There's another reason we ought to speak to her. I think you were right about seeing the woman somewhere before, but I can't remember where. Perhaps she's been hanging about Blinman.'

'I don't think so,' Sam said. 'I was thinking about it today while I was working in the mine. I believe she's the woman we met when you brought me and the others to Blinman from Port Augusta.'

Removing the pipe from his mouth, Piet frowned and looked thoughtful. 'That woman had a husband – and a child.'

'I know – but I still think it's her.'

Piet remained thoughtful for a long time before speaking again. 'You might be right, Sam. If so it could be the cause of our troubles. You thought I was being generous towards that *yura* family – and so I was. The husband was a son of an influential tribal elder, as I remember. He was on his way to negotiate for the supply of a special red ochre found only up here, in the Ranges. It's used in one of the *yuras'* most sacred ceremonies. If this woman *is* his wife, then something must have happened to him. I think we'll go and have a word with her – but there'll be no money changing hands!'

Minns and the woman were not eating with the Blinman miners. Their hut was some little distance away and they were cooking on an outside fire. The skinned carcass of an animal Sam was unable to identify was cooking over the fire, the fat from it dripping down to the hot embers, producing spasmodic spurts of hissing yellow flame.

It was dusk now and Charlie Minns was seated in the shadows beside the doorway, a long-barrelled rifle leaning against the wall of the hut beside him.

Nodding in the direction of the weapon, Piet said, 'If you'd used that just now you might have scared off some of the *yuras* and a man would still be alive.'

'I didn't have the gun to hand when they attacked,' Minns replied. 'Besides, there was no sense drawing attention to ourselves.'

'I can see why you wouldn't want to attract attention from the *yuras*,' agreed Piet. Pointing to the woman, he asked, 'What tribe is she?'

'How should I know?' Minns replied aggressively.

'She's an Aborigine, that's all. Anyway, what's it to you?'

'It could be a matter of life or death for every man at Nuccaleena. The *yuras* who attacked us are going to come back again and again. I want to find out why. Do you mind if I talk to the woman?'

'Yes, I *do* mind.'

Minns stood and when the woman looked at him, Sam read fear in her expression. At a signal from Minns she lifted the meat and the spit and placed it upon a flat stone beside the fire before hurrying inside the hut, turning her head away in order not to meet the eyes of either Sam or Piet van Roos.

'I knew it would be a mistake to come into your camp,' said Minns, still aggressive. 'People just can't mind their own business.'

'That needn't bother you or anyone else who has nothing to hide. But lives are being lost for a reason none of us can understand.'

'That's nothing to do with me, so you can go now.'

'I will. But I'd like to ask you just one question before we do. What happened to your woman's husband and little girl?'

The question clearly alarmed Minns, but he recovered quickly. 'I don't know what you're talking about – and you're not going to ruin my meal. I'm taking it inside.' Picking up the hot carcass from the flat stone, he turned his back upon the two men and entered the hut.

Calling after him, Piet said, 'I'll be having a chat with the others. If there's another attack on this camp while you're here we'll all be wanting answers.'

As they walked away from the hut, Sam said to his companion, 'You got through to Minns back there. I'm more convinced than ever it's the woman we saw when you brought me, Jean and Ira to Blinman.'

'It is,' Piet agreed. 'More than that, Minns knows why the *yuras* are attacking us, but he's not going to tell and he'll prevent the woman from saying anything – if he can.'

The Aborigines launched another attack on the camp the next morning, shortly before dawn. On this occasion they did not attack the main camp but set fire to the mud and wattle hut which had been occupied the previous evening by Minns and the Aboriginal woman.

At first, the miners feared Minns and the woman were trapped inside. However, as they were attempting to dowse the fire, Minns put in an unexpected appearance.

'Where have you been?' asked Piet. 'We thought you were trapped inside.'

Minns shook his head. 'After what you said last night I feared me and the woman might be a target for the Aborigines, so I changed huts under the cover of darkness. It was just as well, by the look of things.'

'Where's the woman now?' Sam asked.

'Gone,' Minns replied. 'I thought of what van Roos said, you know, about them being after her, so I told her to go. She left during the night.'

There was something about Minns' story that did not ring true to Sam. However, unable to disprove it, he said nothing.

A couple of hours later all thoughts of Minns and his woman went from Sam's mind when he and the men extending the abandoned adit came across the lode for which he had been searching.

It was rich – as rich as any he had seen at Blinman, but Sam realised that in order to work it the mine company would still be faced with the crippling cost of transportation to Port Augusta. Nevertheless, his hunch had proved correct.

Emerging from the tunnel, Sam accepted the congratulations of the Blinmen miners.

Piet said, 'Now you've found what you were looking for and we have the engine loaded on the drays, I reckon we can make a move back to Blinman.'

'You make ready to move,' Sam said. 'I'd like to just check the depth of the water in the main shaft before we go. If prices ever rise enough to make it economical to reopen the Nuccaleena, we'll need to know how much water needs to be taken out to get at the ore that's down deeper – and I'm convinced it's down there too.'

Sam went back in to the mine accompanied by one of the miners who had been helping him. While Sam took another couple of samples from the newly discovered lode his companion attached a large rock to a rope and lowered it down the flooded shaft.

He called to Sam that the depth was some thirty fathoms. After a few minutes' silence, he called again, 'Sam, there's something floating in the water . . . it looks like a body!'

Taking his lamp from the rock shelf, Sam hurried to the flooded main shaft to add the lantern's light to that of his colleague's.

The body – and there could be no doubt about it now – was floating just beneath the surface of the water. It would probably not have been noticed had it not been disturbed by the makeshift plumb-line.

The body was only just within the range of the

lantern's light, but by throwing the stone attached to the rope over the body, the two men were able to gradually draw it closer to the edge of the shaft.

When it was nearer they could see the body more clearly. It was an Aborigine, floating face downwards.

'Help me pull it out,' Sam said, when he was able to take a grip on a thin arm.

The two men heaved the body clear of the water and realised even before turning it over that it was that of a woman.

When the body was turned over on its back, Sam was overwhelmed with a feeling of horror. It was Charlie Minns' woman.

IV

When Sam and the miner carried the body of the Aboriginal girl from the mine workings, it was Piet van Roos who voiced the question that was in the mind of every man who crowded round.

'Where's Minns?'

'I saw him going into his hut about ten minutes ago,' one of the younger miners replied. 'He's probably still there.'

'Go and fetch him,' Piet said grimly. 'We need some answers from him.'

A number of the miners set off and returned with the prospector a few minutes later.

Greeted with hostile looks from the gathered men, Minns licked his lips nervously when they moved aside and he saw the body of the woman lying on the ground.

'Sam's just found her floating in the shaft,' Piet said,

without preamble. 'Can you explain how she got there?'

'I've no idea,' Minns declared. 'I've already told you what happened. I thought of what you'd said to me about the possibility that the attack by the Aborigines might have had something to do with her, so last night I told her to go – and she did.'

'Then how do you explain her ending up in the main shaft?' Sam demanded.

'I don't know any more than you do what happened after she left the hut. She might have fallen down the shaft in the dark . . . or she could have jumped in. Come to that, she might have been thrown there by her own people when they burned down the hut we'd been staying in.'

'If it *was* them who burned down the hut,' Piet said. '*Yuras* don't carry matches with them and they wouldn't want to hang about a mining camp going through all the paraphernalia involved in making a fire.'

'Are you saying I'm lying?' Minns demanded.

'All I'm saying is that the girl has the back of her head caved in and fire's a very handy way of getting rid of any blood that might have been around.'

'I've told you what happened. If she has a head injury it probably happened when she fell down the shaft. If it wasn't, well, it could have been done by her own people, or by anyone else in the camp once she'd left the hut. If you don't believe my story then report it to the police trooper at Blinman when we get there. I'll tell him exactly the same as I've told you – and repeat it in court, if I have to.' Minns was confident no one would be able to disprove his story. Besides, there was unlikely to be too much of a fuss about the mysterious death of an Aborigine woman.

Piet knew it too. 'It'll be reported when we get to Blinman. What happens then is up to the police. More important right now is what we do with the body. The *yuras* are watching us and they'll have seen her brought out of the mine. If we just get rid of her like a dead dingo they'll remain a threat to us every step of the way to Blinman. On the other hand, if we show some respect and act as though we're sorry she's dead, we might just get the *yuras* off our backs.'

'What do we need to do?' Sam asked.

'We'll lay her out on a couple of blankets in the most prominent place we can find here in the mine and surround her with food and small presents. I want something from everyone – whatever you can spare – then we'll get on our way. It might work, or it might not, but if we don't do *something* we're going to lose more lives before we reach Blinman.'

The wagons set off for Blinman an hour later. As the dray on which Sam was riding lurched along the rough track from the mine, he looked back and felt a deep sense of sadness at the sight of the pitifully small body lying on blankets donated by Piet and himself, surrounded by an array of mostly cheap trinkets.

He wondered whether Charlie Minns felt any remorse for the lost life and looked along the line of wagons to see what he was doing.

The prospector was seated in one of the largest drays, surrounded by parts of the Nuccaleena mine-engine and looking straight ahead. Sam suspected that he cared nothing for the dead woman.

There were no attacks from the Aborigines on the return journey to Blinman. However, an incident occurred during the overnight stay at the Moolooloo sheep station to prove they had not gone away. And, for the first time, they indicated a clear target for their wrath.

The miners camped for the night in and around the wagons, as well as occupying a couple of the station outbuildings. None of the men heard anything untoward during the night, yet, when they woke in the morning, a spear was found thrust into the woodwork of the dray that had been occupied by Charlie Minns.

It was embedded in the very spot where he had been sitting.

Piet van Roos's peace offering had clearly been accepted by the Aborigines, but they had given a clear warning that the amnesty did not extend to Charlie Minns.

V

There was great relief in Blinman when the wagons returned from Nuccaleena. However, it was short-lived for the relatives of the men who had been either killed or wounded during the attacks by the Aborigines.

Nevertheless, it was considered the miners had been luckier than it had been feared. The presence of a large number of warring Aborigines from outside the Flinders Ranges had been confirmed and their presence had stirred up others from local tribes.

Most of their depredations had been against livestock, but there were unconfirmed reports from more remote areas of shepherds coming under attack.

Bullock drivers, for whom travelling through the outback without human company was one of the most enjoyable aspects of their work, now sought the company of as many others as was practical.

The men employed on wood cutting would also venture forth only when an armed escort was available to accompany them on their far-ranging journeys in search of fuel for the mine-engines.

Despite the current unrest, stagecoaches from the outside world still reached Blinman, although they now carried an additional armed guard.

The arrival of the weekly stagecoach from the south was always the subject of great interest. Not only did it bring in the mail, but it would occasionally carry passengers well-known to those who lived at Blinman.

A fortnight after the wagon train returned from Nuccaleena, the weekly stagecoach arrived at the Blinman hotel early in the evening. It was heralded by the strident notes of a horn, sounded by the scarlet-coated mail guard. Drinking miners spilled from the bar to watch the passengers alight from the vehicle.

There were three. One was an official of the company that owned the Blinman mine, arriving for a routine inspection. The second man was a farrier arriving to take up employment at the mine.

The third passenger was Ruth Askew.

Wearing a small round hat, perched at a jaunty angle, and a low-cut dress that revealed as much as it hid, she stepped from the dusty stagecoach and cast a bold glance at the miners standing outside the hotel.

All the men had worked in other mines before reaching Blinman, many in the triple-mining towns of Wallaroo, Moonta and Kadina. Some recognised Ruth and her appearance was greeted with cheers and ribald comments.

Only one man was so startled to see her that he immediately stepped back inside the hotel bar. As a result, Ruth did not see Charlie Minns.

'Hello, boys. Is no one going to offer a thirsty girl a drink? It's been a hot day and I've enough dust in my throat to lay a path.'

Half a dozen tankards containing various amounts of beer were immediately thrust towards her.

Taking one that was three-parts full, she downed its contents in one long, gulping draught. As she handed the empty tankard back to the grinning young miner who had offered it to her, Ruth wiped her mouth with the back of her hand, saying, 'Thanks, love. I owe you one.'

Reaching out she took a second tankard. When this had gone the same way as the first, she said, 'I think I'm going to enjoy it here, even if it is too damned hot! Now, which of you kind gentlemen knows the way to Lucy's house and will take me and my trunk there?'

Lucy was a prostitute and brothel keeper, known to all the miners standing outside the Blinman hotel. A number of younger miners, grinning self-consciously, stepped forward from the ranks of older men with offers of help.

'You ... and you.' She pointed to two of the men. 'You're the best looking of a poor bunch and you're young enough to learn the way to treat a poor, innocent girl.'

The statement brought the raucous response Ruth had intended. As the two young men picked up the trunk, which had been off-loaded from the stagecoach, she blew a kiss to the watching miners.

'Cheerio, boys. I look forward to seeing you all at

Lucy's place in the coming weeks. I want to find out whether what's said about Blinman men is true.'

As the men greeted her remark with ribald laughter, Charlie, still concealed inside the hotel, watched with mixed feelings as Ruth walked away with the two young miners.

Charlie made no attempt to contact Ruth for a week after her arrival. When they did finally meet, it was not in the shanty outside the township perimeter, where she now lived with four other girls who followed the same calling. It was outside the Blinman general store. Ruth had come to buy provisions for the household of women.

As she emerged from the store carrying a basket of provisions, Charlie stepped out from a space between the store and a stable.

'Hello, Ruth. I never expected to see you here.'

'There's no reason why you should,' Ruth retorted. 'But I knew I'd meet up with you again, one day. Bad pennies have a nasty habit of turning up where they're not wanted.'

'That's not a very nice thing to say to me, Ruth, especially in view of what we once were to each other.'

'All I ever meant to you was a means of making money without having to work for it.'

'That isn't true, Ruth. You and I could have made a go of it. I always believed that.'

'You mean I wouldn't have needed to worry myself about ending up floating in some flooded mine shaft? Is that what you're telling me?'

'You've been listening to idle gossip, Ruth. It's just not true, I swear it isn't.'

'Oh? Are you an authority on *truth* now? That's a new one for you, Charlie; you don't know the meaning of the word and never have.'

'That isn't so, Ruth. I've never lied to you—'

'No? I seem to remember you once asked me to go away with you to somewhere where neither of us was known. Said you'd be happy to marry me, as I remember.'

'I meant every word of it, Ruth. I still would, if you'd come with me. We could go to one of the gold-mining camps together.'

'Just you and me, Charlie? Or should we ask your wife to come along with us, just for laughs?'

'What are you talking about. I'm not married—'

'Cut out the lying, Charlie. Perhaps we could even consider taking your boys along too. I wonder what they'd think of life in a gold-mining camp with their ma and me and you. I don't think Tom would be very happy – and Albert certainly wouldn't. Margaret might have something to say about it too.'

Ruth watched in satisfaction as Charlie looked at her in disbelief. 'How do you . . . What have you heard?'

'It's not what I've *heard*, Charlie, but what I've *seen*. A wife and her two boys – two good boys. They've come to Australia looking for a husband and father who isn't worth a single minute of the heartache they've suffered by leaving everything they've ever known to travel halfway round the world hoping to find him. Now, if you'll excuse me, I've got food in here that's likely to go sour just talking to you.'

Ruth walked away but Charlie ran after her and caught hold of her arm. 'Wait, Ruth. Where have you seen them? When . . . ?'

She tried to walk away without replying, but Charlie pulled her to an abrupt halt. 'You've got to tell me, Ruth. Was it in Kadina? Yes, it must be, you've just come from there.'

'I've been to a lot of places and done a whole lot of things since you left, Charlie. Besides, I doubt if I'd be doing *them* any favours if I were to tell you where to find them. They're better off without you.'

'That isn't true, Ruth. Not any more. I've tried to get in touch with them in the past, honest I have. I wrote time after time but got no reply. I thought they must all be dead. There'd been a lot of fever in the village when I left. That's why I thought I was free to marry you. It's the truth, Ruth, I swear it.'

She knew he was lying. It was something that came naturally to him. She remained silent.

'Now I know they're alive I can do the right thing by them, Ruth. I've found a little gold here and there and I've changed some into hard cash and put it by.'

'Does that mean you can pay me back for what I gave you out of my earnings when you were out of work, or had you conveniently forgotten that?'

'I've forgotten nothing you did for me, Ruth. Here . . .' Reaching inside his shirt, he pulled out a leather drawstring bag, attached to a thong looped about his neck. Loosening the neck of the bag, he reached inside and pulled out some coins, saying, 'Here, take these.'

Looking at the coins he had thrust in her hand, Ruth said contemptuously, 'Five guineas! You'll need to do better than that, Charlie Minns. From what I've heard you probably made that much in an hour at Nuccaleena from what you were charging for that poor black woman. You can say what you like, Charlie, you haven't changed a bit.'

'Neither have you.' Charlie handed her another five gold coins. 'You'd take money from me that would be spent on those two young boys you said you cared so much about.'

'No, Charlie, I know you far too well. I'm taking money that would otherwise go on drink – or on women like me. If you want to find your kids and your wife, you'll find them living in Kadina, on Ewing Street – but don't say I was the one to tell you where they are. I don't want to be blamed for sending you back to them.'

4

I

'It has been a most enjoyable evening, Miss Boyce. You and your choir deserved a much larger audience.'

Stefan Mintoff was speaking at the conclusion of the first concert given by Emily's newly formed Kadina choir. She had performed the duties of accompanist on a piano donated by the man to whom she was talking.

'Had it not been for you the audience would have been very much smaller, Mr Mintoff. I am very grateful for the support you have given to me in this and many other matters.'

Emily was still not certain she fully trusted the Kadina councillor, but she could not deny he had shown enormous support for her and her various projects. At least half the concert audience was comprised of members of the council, local dignitaries and their family, all cajoled into attending by Stefan Mintoff.

She was aware her benefactor was not well liked, but he had the air of a man who was going places.

Because of this, many people were careful not to offend him.

'I am happy to have been of help,' he said. 'But I do wish you would call me Stefan. Mr Mintoff is so very formal. We have met on many occasions now. Enough to be friends, at least.'

It was not the first time Stefan Mintoff had suggested they should be on first-name terms. Yet Emily still drew back from becoming too familiar with the man who, more than any other, had helped her during the time she had been in South Australia.

It stemmed from her determination to find Sam. If – no, *when* she did, she wanted there to be no complications resulting from other relationships. At least not from her side.

Emily hoped Sam would have none, but she was concerned about the part Jean Spargo might be playing in his life. She wished information about his whereabouts was forthcoming.

She had put out a great many feelers about Sam, coupling them with her efforts to locate Margaret's husband, by saying he came from the same area as Charlie Minns and might have met up with him at some time.

So far there had been no definite news of either. It was certain both had been in Blinman at some time, but she and Margaret had been advised against making the long journey on the weekly coach service to the remote mining township. Especially now, when everyone was talking about the 'Aborigine problem' in the Flinders Ranges.

It seemed a number of men had been killed there. Stefan Mintoff, in particular, had insisted it was unsafe for two women to make such a journey in the present circumstances.

'I trust you are finding Ewing Street considerably quieter now those dreadful women have left?'

There was a smugness in Stefan Mintoff's voice that Emily did not find attractive. He had made much of the fact that it was *he* who had ordered the owner of the two brothels to evict his unruly and immoral tenants or face prosecution.

The houses had been vacated a week after Ruth had left Kadina, telling no one of her destination.

'The street is much quieter, Mr Mintoff, but I wish I had been given notice of their eviction. I fear most of the women will find their way to gold-mining areas where they will have no hope whatsoever of redemption. I managed to build up a rapport with a couple of the women – one in particular. It would have given me a great deal of satisfaction had I been able to persuade either one to abandon her ways.'

'You are an idealist, Miss Boyce – that is not a criticism, I hasten to add. This country needs such women, especially those like yourself who combine action with idealism, but I fear there are some things that are beyond human endeavour.'

'When I encounter such situations I remember my late father's teachings and call on the Lord. He rarely fails me, Mr Mintoff. Now, if you will excuse me I must go and thank the choir for giving us such an enjoyable evening.'

'Before you go may I ask you something, Miss Boyce? Will you do me the great honour of acting as my hostess at a dinner party I am giving in honour of the Minister of Education, who is visiting Kadina soon?

Many of the religious leaders of the area will be there
and may be persuaded to support you in your work. I
would also welcome your knowledge of such functions,
I fear I have little experience of the protocol necessary
for such an occasion.'

Emily hesitated before replying. Had it been a purely
social function she would have refused. She did not
want the people she was here to help looking upon her
as a party-going socialite. But Stefan Mintoff was right.
This was an opportunity too good for her to refuse.

'Thank you, Mr Mintoff, I will be delighted to act
as a hostess at the dinner party. Perhaps you will be
kind enough to let me have the details closer to the
time?'

'Of course.' Stefan Mintoff was quite obviously
delighted she had accepted his invitation. 'But I do wish
you would call me Stefan.'

Margaret, who was a member of the choir, had seen
Emily chatting to Stefan Mintoff. As they walked home
together later, Margaret said, 'I saw Mr "Don't-you-
think-I'm-wonderful" talking to you after the concert.
He has quite a fancy for you.'

'Quite possibly,' Emily said matter of factly. 'He's
asked me to act as hostess at a dinner party he's giving
next week for a visiting government minister.'

'You haven't accepted?' Margaret was concerned.
'He has no wife and you have no man. Folk are bound
to jump to conclusions!'

'If Mr Mintoff's guests are prepared to give their
support to my work they may jump wherever they
wish, Margaret. I will accept help from whatever source
it is sent by the Lord.'

*   *   *

It should have been an excellent dinner party for Emily. Guest dignitaries from Church and Chapel all offered her their support, especially in the schemes she had for helping the families of sick and destitute miners.

Among them was a senior churchman from Adelaide who promised that the charitable organisations in the South Australian capital would turn their attention to fund-raising in support of her work.

Not to be outdone, the government minister promised that his administration would allocate monies to help alleviate the distress of miners and their families.

In this respect the party was much more successful than Emily had dreamed possible. She even gave Stefan Mintoff a genuinely warm smile of gratitude when he introduced her to a man who had grown rich from successful speculation in the copper mines of the Yorke Peninsula. Almost sober, he wrote out a cheque for a thousand pounds there and then and handed it to her.

Then Reverend Arnold Weeks triumphantly introduced her to Ezra Maddison, the minister responsible for the spiritual well-being of all who lived and worked in a vast parish that included the whole of the northern Flinders Ranges.

'Miss Boyce's father was vicar of a mining parish at the time of his sad death,' explained Arnold Weeks, speaking loudly to the outback preacher who was obliged to cup a hand to his ear in order to catch what was being said. 'She is particularly anxious to locate a couple of miners who were last known to be at the Blinman mine.'

'Blinman?' repeated the minister. 'I know it well. Indeed, I conducted my first ever triple wedding there, it must have been about two years ago.'

Trying hard to cast aside the memory of the aftermath of the wedding celebrations, he added, 'One of the bridegrooms was newly arrived from Cornwall – as indeed was his bride.'

'Did you meet either a Charles Minns or a Sam Hooper while you were there?' Emily asked, without much hope of a positive reply.

'Samuel Hooper, you say? Yes, I think that was the name of the bridegroom. In fact I'm almost certain it was. He and the young woman had journeyed from Cornwall on the same ship. They came here first of all, as I recall. I had quite a chat with the bride afterwards. She had come to South Australia hoping to find her father, but he had moved on, probably to the goldfields. So many miners seem to rush from one mine to another in pursuit of that elusive metal. All most find are sinful and violent men and women. It is so very, very sad.'

'This bride,' Emily persisted, although she felt certain she would not want to hear the answer he was about to give her, 'was it her first marriage?'

'No . . . no, I don't think it was. I believe her husband was killed in a mine accident, back in Cornwall. She had a young daughter with a rather pretty name . . .'

'Would it be Primrose?' Emily felt as though a yawning chasm was opening beneath her feet.

'Why yes, that's it . . . Primrose. You know the young woman?'

'Yes, I know her. I know both of them. Now, you must pardon me, I see some of the guests are ready to leave and I am acting as Mr Mintoff's hostess.'

Emily hurried away before she betrayed her feelings to Reverend Weeks and his companion from the

Flinders Ranges. She felt physically sick and desperately unhappy. She had come halfway across the world in pursuit of a dream that had suddenly become a nightmare.

Coming to Australia to take up welfare work among miners and their families was an exciting adventure, but in moments of self-honesty she knew it had been the thought of a reunion with Sam that had brought her here, not a wish to serve her fellow men and women. She could have done that more effectively, perhaps, by remaining in Cornwall.

Emily somehow managed to get through the remainder of the evening. Then, declining Stefan Mintoff's entreaties that he should take her home in his light carriage, she walked home through the deserted streets of Kadina, feeling desolated, unhappy and desperately alone.

II

The morning after the party Emily was still feeling deeply unhappy about the revelations of the previous evening when there came a knock on the door of the Ewing Street cottage.

It was usual for Margaret to open the door to callers, but as Emily was passing along the passageway close to the door at the time and Margaret was working in the kitchen, she called, 'I'll answer it!'

Opening the door, she was confronted by a man in his thirties. He did not appear to have shaved for a while and his clothes had certainly known better days.

'May I help you?' Emily asked.

Belatedly, the man at the door dragged off his cap to reveal an uncombed tangle of black hair. 'I'm looking for Margaret Minns. I was told I'd find her here.'

'Yes, she is here but . . . who are you?'

Even as she asked the question Emily's intuition provided her with an answer. She thought she knew who this disreputable-looking man must be.

She hoped she was wrong. She had taken an instant but totally irrational dislike to him.

'I'm Charlie Minns, ma'am. Margaret's husband.'

'Then you had better come inside, Mr Minns.' Pointing to the living room, she said, 'Wait in there while I go and fetch Margaret. This is going to be quite a shock for her.'

Closing the door behind the errant husband, Emily hurried to the kitchen.

Margaret was making bread. It was warm work, made worse by the corrugated iron roof which considerably increased the heat inside the house. Red-cheeked and with a lock of damp hair dangling beside her face, her arms were white with flour almost to her elbows.

'Margaret, take off that apron and clean yourself up – quickly now. There's someone to see you. I have left him in the living room.'

'Someone to see me? I don't know anyone who'd come here after me. Who is it? What does he want?'

'Don't ask so many questions, Margaret. Just get tidied up as quickly as you can and go in there to see him. Here, let me do something to your hair while you wipe the flour from your hands. Hurry now, I'll clean up in here.'

As she spoke, Emily thought she might have formed a more favourable impression of Charlie Minns had he taken a little more trouble with *his* appearance before coming to the house to seek a reunion with the wife he had not seen for so long.

'You'll clean up in here while I—' Margaret's eyes opened wide suddenly. 'It's not ... You don't mean it's Charlie? He's here?'

Margaret's hand flew up to her mouth. 'Emily, come into the room with me. I ... I don't know what I'll say to him ...'

'You will think of something, I'm quite certain,' Emily smiled. 'Off you go. I'll give you a couple of minutes together before I fetch the boys from the garden.'

'Oh, Emily! I'm not sure I'm ready for this after all this time. It's so sudden, like.'

Margaret was shaking and Emily put an arm about her. 'You will be all right, Margaret. Everything is going to be all right now for you and the boys.'

Watching her quaking companion depart from the kitchen, Emily wished she felt as confident as she had tried to sound. She told herself she had been unfairly influenced by the unkempt appearance of Charlie Minns. He had probably travelled a long distance for this reunion with his wife.

However, whatever she thought was of no importance. He was Margaret's husband – and the father of Albert and Tom.

Hurrying from the kitchen to the garden where the two children were playing with a ball, she called, 'Boys, come inside and clean yourselves up. I have a wonderful surprise for you ...'

Later that day, when Charlie had gone off with the two boys to collect the few possessions he had left behind the bar at the Miners' Arms and the two women were alone, Emily said, 'Well, Margaret, you have achieved what you and the boys came to Australia to do. You have found your husband. You must be ecstatic.'

'I'm very relieved that he's alive – and delighted for the boys' sake,' said Margaret, somewhat ambiguously. 'It brought tears to my eyes to see them go off together, with little Tom holding Charlie's hand, so proud for everyone to see that he has a father. Albert is proud and happy too, of course, but I'm a little more concerned for him. He's got a strong character and has been the man of the family for so long he might well resent having someone else taking over . . . for a while, anyway.'

'That doesn't tell me how *you* feel. Has the reunion been all you hoped it would be?'

'To be perfectly honest, I'd never given very much thought to the actual moment of meeting. I was too busy thinking about trying to find him again.'

Once again Margaret had failed to give Emily a reply to her question, but she was still talking.

'He's different to how I remembered him, but I suppose we've both changed in the years we've been apart.'

Emily decided not to put her question yet again. Instead she asked, 'What do you intend doing now, Margaret?'

Uncertainly, Margaret replied, 'I . . . I just don't know. I realise I'm his wife, but we've been apart for so long we're almost like strangers. I can't go back to being a complete wife to him . . . well, not right away. I've told Charlie and he's not very happy about it, but . . . it's just the way I feel, Emily. We're going to have to get to know each other all over again. I need to learn to trust him the way I once did. It can't be any other way for me.'

'Have you given any thought to where you'll live, Margaret? Has Charlie said anything about it? No doubt you will need to live wherever he is working? Is he in work?'

'I haven't had time to think about any practical things like that, Emily. I don't think he's working right now. He said he's been prospecting and been quite lucky, so finding work isn't all that urgent at the moment. But you're right, we'll need to find somewhere to live.'

'That's no problem at all,' Emily declared. 'You'll stay right here. You, Charlie and the boys. What is more I will pay the rent for the next three months. That will be a present to you for being such a wonderful companion to me since we left Cornwall – and before that too. I'll speak to Reverend Kavanagh right away with a view to moving in with him and his wife until I find somewhere suitable.'

When Margaret began to protest, Emily said firmly, 'No, Margaret, I have made up my mind. You have found your husband. Now you both need time together with the boys in order to pick up the threads of your life. You certainly don't want me around!'

'But what will *you* do, Emily? Will you still try to find this miner friend from St Cleer – or were you only saying you wanted to find him so I'd feel better about trying to find Charlie?'

Emily had told Margaret nothing of the news she had received of Sam. She shook her head, 'I think he will have made a new life for himself here. I'll carry on

with the very many projects I have started in Kadina
– exciting projects which justify my presence in
Australia. I would just like to say I am happy for you
and the boys, Margaret. Very, very happy indeed.'

III

Emily moved out of the house on Ewing Street the
following morning.

Margaret watched her departure with mixed feelings. She would miss the company of the woman to
whom she had been successively maid, housekeeper
and companion. They had shared each other's sorrows
and enjoyed many happy moments together.

It had been Emily too who had brought about the
reunion of the Minns family, but this event had left
Margaret confused. There would need to be a great deal
of soul-searching in the months that lay ahead.

Charlie had changed since the days of their married
life in Cornwall.

Margaret had never been totally blind to her
husband's shortcomings when she had married him
against the wishes of her family and the doubts of her
employer. She was aware he had never been the hard-
est working of men and always placed his own interests before those of anyone else – including his
immediate family. Yet, despite such faults, he had been
an easy-going man who took nothing too seriously.

Since coming to Australia a change had come about
in his make-up that Margaret found disconcerting. He
was harder, both mentally and physically. She suspected
too that his selfishness had become ruthlessness and

was no longer softened by concern for his family.

She tried to tell herself it was because he had been away from her and the boys and had been forced to adapt to the harsh environment of a new and untamed country. Nevertheless, she was rapidly realising that her husband had become a stranger to her – one with whom she felt ill at ease much of the time.

'Your friend's husband is a very interesting man,' said Stefan Mintoff, one day. 'He knows a great deal about the outback – the Flinders Ranges in particular. I hope to talk to him at some length about that area of South Australia. I believe there is great mineral wealth there and I want to learn all I can about it.'

The Kadina councillor was conveying Emily and the last of her belongings from Ewing Street to the rectory, using his pony and trap.

He had been at the rectory when Emily had gone to tell Reverend Arnold Weeks of the return of Charlie Minns and to ask the rector if she might stay at the vicarage with him and his wife until she could find new accommodation.

Stefan had immediately offered to accommodate her in one of the houses he owned in the town.

Politely but firmly Emily declined the offer. It was one thing to have him perform a neighbourly act by helping her move from Ewing Street to the rectory, quite another to provide her with a home. Although she had begun to trust Stefan more than when they had first met, she did not want to be beholden to him to any greater extent.

'. . . Yes, indeed,' the councillor continued, 'there are fortunes to be made in the Flinders Ranges. Copper is there in plenty, but there are other minerals too. It is a very rich area indeed.'

'You have been there?' Emily asked.

'Sadly, no, but I take a keen interest in all parts of South Australia. It is my firm belief that the Flinders Ranges possess vast potential to benefit the whole of the colony. If you have money to invest in our country I strongly advise you to look at what the Flinders Ranges have to offer you.'

Later that evening, over a meal in the rectory, Emily asked her hosts what they knew of Stefan Mintoff.

'Very little,' confessed Arnold Weeks. 'He arrived in Kadina some years ago and began working in Tom Bray's hardware store. Two years later the two men went into partnership. Only a year after that Tom Bray died and Stefan Mintoff took over the business. It was about that time he became involved in local politics. There has been no noticeable upsurge in the hardware business, but Stefan has gone from strength to strength. He now owns a number of properties, has interests in many ventures and his sights are set firmly on the state parliament.'

'Would you say he is a shrewd businessman?' Emily asked the question remembering Stefan's suggestion that she should invest in ventures in the Flinders Ranges.

'I suppose he must be,' Arnold Weeks replied. 'He certainly isn't earning enough from the hardware store to finance his business ventures.'

'Or his life style,' said Jennifer Weeks, tight-lipped.

'Now, now!' scolded her husband. 'You should not repeat malicious gossip, my dear. Stefan Mintoff has done a great deal for Kadina since he assumed office in local government.'

Jennifer Weeks sniffed derisively. 'He's done a great deal more to benefit Stefan Mintoff.'

'Making money is not a sin, Jennifer,' her husband chided. 'He has always been most generous to the Church and our various charities.'

'Where does he come from?' Emily put the question hastily, hoping to forestall an argument between husband and wife.

'That's as much of a mystery as everything else about him,' Jennifer replied. 'No one seems to know for certain. Some say he's Greek, others that he's of Russian descent. I've even heard it said that he's from Malta.'

'It sounds as though he might come from a wealthy family,' Emily suggested.

'It is quite possible,' Arnold Weeks agreed. 'South Australia attracts men and women from many walks of life. Once here they are judged on their merits. It makes for a healthy and well-balanced society.'

'He has certainly been very kind to me,' Emily said. 'And always shown himself to be a perfect gentleman.'

Jennifer Weeks said nothing. She surmised that Emily had probably had little experience of men. However, she did not wish to argue with her about the merits of Stefan Mintoff.

'Well, we must take people as each of us finds them,' she said. 'To be perfectly honest I have had very little to do with Stefan Mintoff. Everything I know about him is no more than hearsay, and that is no way to judge anyone.'

Her husband beamed amiably at her. 'That is very true, Jennifer. Stefan Mintoff may be a stranger to our

ways but he is doing his very best to fit in – and the
whole community benefits from his generosity.'

IV

Stefan Mintoff proved to be a persistent suitor. He
attended most of Emily's charitable functions and
ensured that they received maximum publicity in and
around the three towns of the Copper Triangle.

Margaret frequently met with Emily, helping her
with various projects whenever possible, although
Charlie and the boys prevented her from devoting as
much time to them as she had during their early days
in the township.

Margaret informed Emily that Stefan Mintoff was
also a regular visitor to the Minns home in Ewing Street.
As a result both women had finally been persuaded to
call Mintoff by his first name.

Emily, curious about Mintoff's interest in the Minns
family, asked her friend about it.

Margaret shrugged. 'It's not me he comes to see, but
Charlie. The pair of them talk for hours in the sitting
room while I'm working. Then they'll go off to the
Miners' Arms together and talk some more while
they're drinking.'

'What do they talk about?' Emily asked, more curious than ever.

The two women were chatting as they washed up
plates and tea cups in the small kitchen of the Kadina
Institute after a meeting of the newly formed
'Township Benevolent Society'.

'Much of the talk seems to be about mining of one

sort or another – that and the Flinders Ranges. Stefan seems to be very interested in the mines of that area.'

'Yes, he is. He's often telling me of the money waiting to be made in that part of South Australia and, of course, Charlie has spent some time there.'

'Yes, part of it at Blinman. That reminds me, I asked Charlie if he'd ever met up with Sam Hooper, the St Cleer miner you were asking about when we first arrived here. Charlie says he's at Blinman and he's spoken to him, but he couldn't tell me any more than that. I'm sure if you wrote to him care of the Blinman mine the letter would reach him.'

'Thank you, Margaret, but I doubt if I will bother. I was really only interested in learning whether he had settled down happily in Australia, that is all.'

The lie did not come easily to her. She still frequently thought of Sam. He held a place in her affections that no one else could fill – although Stefan Mintoff was trying hard.

'Where do you think Stefan will take us for a picnic tomorrow?' Margaret put the question to Emily. The Kadina councillor had suggested that he should take Emily and the whole of the Minns family in a carriage to a picnic the next day, which was a Saturday.

'I really have no idea,' Emily replied vaguely. 'He said it was to be a surprise.'

The picnic party set off in style. A carriage called first for the Minns family and then for Emily. It came complete with driver – and with Stefan. The boys were allowed to ride on the outside seat alongside the driver, while the four adults were accommodated comfortably inside.

Stefan kept their destination a secret, even when the sea to the south of the port of Wallaroo came into view.

When the site chosen for the picnic was reached, it became evident this was no casual choice. A large tent had been erected on the edge of the sand, a short distance from the sea, and Stefan Mintoff had sent two men ahead of the carriage, one to erect the tent and start a fire, the other to organise the cooking.

In addition, there were folding chairs, a table and other luxuries not usually associated with a casual outdoor meal. There was also wine for the adults and lemonade for the two children.

'Well! This is far superior to any picnic I have been on before,' Emily was able to say, in all honesty. 'Do you have an orchestra hiding away somewhere?'

'You think I should have arranged music for you?'

Stefan looked so dismayed that Emily put a hand on his arm in a gesture of reassurance. 'I am joking, Stefan. This is truly wonderful. The setting, the food – everything. You have put so much thought into this you might have been entertaining royalty. I really am very impressed. Very impressed indeed.'

Relieved, Stefan beamed at her. 'Your company gives me far more pleasure than would royalty, Emily. But I am happy that it meets with your approval. Now, shall we have something to drink? I had Champagne brought here, packed in ice.'

Stefan could not have wished for a more perfect day for the picnic he had organised. While the boys happily paddled in the sea, or enjoyed playing with a ball on the beach, the adults sat outside the tent eating, drinking and talking on what was one of the most relaxed days Emily had spent since arriving in Australia.

However, Emily had a niggling feeling that Stefan had not organised the picnic as a purely social occasion and she was not entirely surprised when, halfway through the afternoon, he turned to her and said, 'Emily, shall we leave Margaret and Charlie entertaining their boys and take a walk along the shore?'

When Emily frowned, wondering what lay behind his suggestion, Stefan said hurriedly, 'I promise I will not take you out of sight of the others, but I would like to talk to you.'

Margaret had been unusually quiet during the day, but now Emily ignored the slight lift of her friend's eyebrows. 'I seem to have done little except eat and drink since our arrival, so a walk would be most enjoyable.'

They walked in silence for perhaps five minutes before Emily prompted her companion, 'Am I correct in assuming you asked me to walk with you for a reason, Stefan?'

'That is very perceptive of you, Emily. Yes, I do have a reason to speak to you. *Two* reasons, in fact. The first concerns Charlie – which means it will also affect Margaret, of course.'

When Emily made no reply, Stefan continued, 'You are aware, I know, of the interest I have in the Flinders Ranges. I am convinced there is a great future for mining there – once a railway links the area with the ports of South Australia – and it will be built. One of the reasons I am seeking election to the state parliament is to ensure a railway is built to serve the region's needs.'

None of what he was saying was new to Emily. Stefan Mintoff's ambitions had been the subject of local gossip for even longer than she had been in Australia.

'What has this to do with Charlie?'

'Ah, yes! Well, Charlie and I have talked long and often about the region and I am satisfied that he knows a great deal about the Flinders Ranges and its potential. I am forming a company to exploit the minerals that are to be found there. I feel so strongly about it that I am going to England in order to raise capital for my venture. Charlie intends returning to the Flinders Ranges to resume prospecting and I have asked him to act as my representative there, to keep me informed of any promising finds in order that I might register claims on them on behalf of the company.'

Emily was taken aback. 'I am ready to accept there are considerable mineral resources out there, but do you have sufficient confidence in Charlie to risk shareholders' money on his judgement?'

'I have every confidence in him,' Stefan replied. 'And he has taught me much about the region, but I will certainly check his finds against information I have already gathered over the years.'

After digesting this, Emily replied, 'Margaret has said nothing of this to me. Does she know Charlie intends going off prospecting once more?'

'That, of course, is a purely domestic matter. However, as Charlie and Margaret have only recently been reunited, she might not be terribly happy about the arrangement. I would like you to allay any fears she may have about money matters. I will ensure she has access to funds during his absence.'

'Margaret has been my friend and companion for a long time. *I* will take care of her if the need arises,' Emily declared. 'But am I correct in assuming that you wish me to persuade Margaret to raise no objection to Charlie returning to the Flinders Ranges? What of the trouble they are having there with the Aborigines?'

'That's all over,' Stefan reassured her. 'These little problems arise periodically but seldom last for more than a few weeks.'

Emily was not happy that Stefan was putting the onus of disclosing Charlie's plans to Margaret upon her, but she said, 'You mentioned there were two matters you wished to discuss with me. What is the second?'

'Ah, yes! Well, this is a more personal matter – and one to which I do not expect an immediate reply ...'

Stefan hesitated and Emily gave him a questioning look.

'You must have realised by now that I hold you in high esteem, Emily. Very high indeed. In view of this I would like you to consider becoming my wife.'

It was said in such a matter-of-fact manner that it was a moment or two before Emily realised she had just received a proposal of marriage.

When it had sunk in she looked at him in utter disbelief. 'You are asking me to marry you? It is a quite absurd suggestion, Stefan. Why ... we hardly know each other!'

'I feel we know each other very well, Emily. Indeed, I know you better than any woman I have ever met.'

'But ... the subject of marriage has never even been hinted at! I have a high regard for you, of course, but marriage should be based on far more than that.'

'Not necessarily, Emily. I *do* have a great affection for you, of course, but if we were younger and a marriage was being arranged by our families I have no doubt they would regard it as a highly satisfactory union. You are from a well-respected and aristocratic family in England. I am a successful businessman who hopes soon to be elected to the parliament of South Australia, with the prospects of high office and an eventual peerage. It is a union that would certainly receive the blessing of your uncle, Lord Boyce.'

Emily was taken aback that Stefan should choose to bring her uncle's name into the conversation, although she realised it was information the Kadina councillor knew about her. Nevertheless, she was not entirely happy that he should have done so.

'Arranged marriages are no longer acceptable in England, Stefan – however desirable they might be.'

'Yet they still take place, as they do in many other parts of the world, and the vast majority of such marriages are both happy and successful. I am not asking you to make such a marriage with me, Emily, only pointing out that our families, who are on the far side of the world, would consider such a marriage a *good* one. I am extremely fond of you and would not wish you to marry me if you did not have similar feelings for me. As I have said, I will soon be going to England on business. I wanted to express my feelings for you before leaving and to ask you to consider the prospect of marrying me. Will you do that, Emily?'

For a brief, irrational moment Emily wondered what form a proposal from *Sam* would have taken. She doubted very much whether it would have been as carefully considered as the one she had just received.

She tried in vain to dismiss such thoughts as being no longer relevant. 'I will certainly consider your proposal, Stefan, although I must admit it has taken me by surprise.'

This was not entirely true. Stefan Mintoff's attentions had been such in recent weeks that she had realised he had something more than a platonic friendship in mind. Nevertheless, she had not seriously contemplated what her reply would be.

She was grateful to him for giving her ample time to think about it, and she told him so.

'I am asking you to make one of the most important decisions you will ever need to make, Emily, and you have no family here with whom to discuss it. Please, take as much time as you wish. I will try to curb my eagerness and look forward to my return from England and being with you again.'

Taking her hand he carried it to his lips.

As he lowered his head, Emily noticed, with slight embarrassment, that he was beginning to go bald on the crown of his head.

V

'Do you think you *will* marry Stefan?'

It was the day after the picnic. The previous evening Charlie had broken the news to Margaret of his intended departure for the Flinders Ranges to resume prospecting. She had taken the news philosophically and Emily was relieved it had not been necessary for her to become involved in the discussion between husband and wife.

Both women were in the Kadina Institute, sorting through a consignment of clothing that had been sent by sea from Adelaide for distribution to the families of out-of-work miners.

They had been discussing the events of the previous day.

'I will need to give it a great deal of thought – and learn more of Stefan's background and family than I know now. But I can see no reason why we should *not* marry.'

'Do you love him?' Margaret asked.

'Not at the moment,' Emily confessed. 'But I find him attractive and the longer I know him, the more I like him – I think!'

'*Liking* a man isn't a good enough reason for *marrying* him,' declared Margaret. 'Even when you *love* a man you sometimes feel you want to send him away and live your own life again for a while. Freedom is a very precious thing, Emily. Don't give it up until you find a man you love so much that the thought of life without him is unbearable.'

Picking up on a point Margaret had made, Emily said, 'You don't seem particularly upset that Charlie will be going away again.'

Margaret looked unhappy. 'Part of me doesn't want him to go, but I think it might be a good thing. For a while, anyway.'

'Why?' Emily felt sorry for her friend. Margaret had come to Australia with such high hopes of finding Charlie and resuming a happy and settled married life with him and the boys.

'Charlie and Albert aren't getting on too well with each other. It was to be expected, I suppose. I relied on Albert a bit too much while his pa was away. He got used to being the man about the house. He's happy to have Charlie back with us, I know he is, really, but I think he resents being treated as just a kid again and having the household centred around his father.' Margaret made a helpless gesture. 'It would be easier if Charlie tried to understand the way Albert feels, but he believes that children must be taught to do as they're told without question. He's taken to cuffing Albert and he's a bit heavy-handed.'

Concerned for the small boy, Emily said, 'Albert doesn't deserve such treatment after all he's been through for you, Margaret. Have you tried explaining that to Charlie?'

'He knows I don't like it, but I daren't push it too much. It will only make him hit Albert all the harder – and he's likely to turn on me, as well.'

Emily was appalled by what Margaret was telling her, but she decided to say nothing more for the moment. She had moved into a house of her own once more and would invite Margaret there once Charlie was in the Flinders Ranges. They would then be able to discuss the problem in more detail.

Charlie and Stefan left Kadina together a few days later. They travelled in Stefan's carriage which would take them to the Wallaroo docks. From here Charlie would board a boat sailing northwards to Port Augusta. He would then journey overland to the northern Flinders Ranges.

Stefan had arranged to travel by steamer to Adelaide and there board a London-bound ship.

Emily and Margaret, together with Albert and Tom, saw them off from Stefan's house, waving to the departing coach until it passed from view.

Before leaving Kadina, Stefan and Emily had discussed the company Stefan had formed to open up the mines he intended working in the Flinders Ranges. Shares in the company would initially be valued at one pound each, but Stefan assured Emily that once they had been offered to the London Market their value would soar to at least five times this sum. He persuaded her to buy a thousand shares, telling her not to discuss the deal until his return from England. When the time was right he would sell them on for her at the new price, boosted by English investors. Stefan added that she might accept it as a wedding gift from him.

'Stefan will be gone for a long time,' said Margaret as the two women walked away from Stefan's large and impressive house.

'Six months at least,' agreed Emily. 'More if he is unable to arrange passage on steamships in both directions. Has Charlie given you any indication of how long he expects to be away?'

'No. To tell you the truth we had another argument yesterday. Once again it was about his treatment of Albert. I said a few things that would have been better left unsaid. He hasn't really spoken to me since then. I did ask him how long he thought he would be away and he told me it would be "as long as it takes". I know no more than that.'

'Why don't you and the boys come to stay with me as companions at my house while Charlie is away?' Emily suggested. 'You can keep your house on for when Charlie comes back, but it would be a change for you all and I really would appreciate your company. I will pay you the wage I gave to you when you were my companion on the voyage here.'

It was a tempting offer, but Margaret hesitated before saying, 'I don't know, Emily. The boys would enjoy the huge garden you have there, I know, and the money would be very welcome – Charlie has left me a bit short – but . . .'

'No "buts", Margaret. The arrangement will suit everyone. First thing in the morning I will have someone come to the house to collect all the things you think you and the boys might need. Oh, I am pleased! It will be just like old times!'

5

I

Charlie Minns reached Blinman three weeks after setting out from Kadina. Many of the miners who witnessed his arrival recognised him, but none proffered a welcome.

However, Charlie's unpopularity did not bother him. He had no intention of remaining in the remote mining town for any longer than was absolutely necessary.

When he had passed through Port Augusta Charlie had purchased a donkey plus the provisions he would take with him to the outback, using more money than Margaret was even aware he possessed. By buying here rather than waiting until he reached Blinman, Charlie saved himself a great deal of money.

Although the Aboriginal threat was deemed to be over, Charlie chose to travel to Blinman in the company of a number of bullock drivers, all of whom were returning to Blinman with provisions for the stores and hotels dotted along the long route.

From these men Charlie was able to confirm the

absence of trouble in the Flinders Ranges. It came as a considerable relief to him. When he set off again he would be travelling alone in areas visited by very few white men.

During the couple of days he was in Blinman, Charlie slept in a deserted and tumbledown shack on the edge of the town. Not only did it save him money, but it meant he could avoid the company of other miners.

When he decided he was ready to leave the mining town, Charlie called at the Blinman hotel to buy beer and brandy to take with him to the outback. As he was stowing them in the packs slung over the back of his donkey, tied outside the hotel, Ruth Askew came along the road and stopped beside him.

'Well, if it isn't the great prospector himself! Have you grown tired of family life already, Charlie – or has your wife come to her senses and thrown you out?'

'I've a living to earn, family or no family,' Charlie growled, continuing to load the donkey.

'And, of course, you don't need a family. You'll no doubt find some poor woman to keep you company in the outback.'

'Why don't you come with me and find out?' Charlie retorted.

'No thanks. Life may not be all that easy for me, but it's better than being found floating in a mine shaft.'

'You don't want to listen to what men tell you when they're in bed with you, Ruth. We're all liars then. You've told me so yourself, many times.'

The last bottle safely stowed away, Charlie unwound the reins from the post to which the donkey was tethered. 'I'm sorry I can't waste more time talking to you, but I want to be well clear of Blinman before dark. I'll call on you when I get back and you can amuse me with more of your stories.'

'If you do you'll find it doesn't come free for you any more, Charlie. I'll charge you, same as everyone else and I doubt you'll be able to afford me.'

'We'll see about that, Ruth. No doubt we'll be able to come to some arrangement, although you always did undervalue me and put too high a price on yourself.' With this, Charlie set off northward along the road, the donkey plodding, head down, behind him.

Ruth turned away and spotted Sam standing a few paces away. He had listened to the conversation between prostitute and prospector with interest.

'I hope you enjoyed what you heard,' she said, belligerently.

'I can think of nothing Charlie Minns has done that I've ever found enjoyable. I was the one who pulled the body of the Aboriginal woman from the mine shaft at Nuccaleena.'

'Oh! Well, I wasn't suggesting that Charlie killed her, if that's what you're thinking. He's a rat and not worth a minute of anyone's time, but I don't think even he would stoop to murder.'

Sam remembered Charlie entering the camp at Nuccaleena and the casual manner in which he had reported shooting an Aborigine. He remembered too how little emotion he had shown when the body of the woman had been found.

'I don't know him well enough to comment either way on that, but you and he seem to go back a long way.'

'Long enough,' Ruth agreed without elaborating.

'But I wouldn't lose any sleep if I never saw Charlie Minns again.'

As she walked past Sam and made her way to the store, Ruth told herself that what she had just said to Sam was the truth, but she was unable to convince herself. No matter what Charlie Minns did, or did not do, she still retained a totally illogical affection for him.

Charlie Minns was not setting out from Blinman on a journey of exploration on behalf of Stefan Mintoff. He knew exactly where he was heading.

Skirting the Moolooloo sheep station, he was careful to stay out of sight of the house and outbuildings. Had he been seen, outback hospitality demanded that he pay a call on the remote household to partake of a meal and pass on the latest news from the outside world. The owners would also have been interested in his prospecting plans and the area in which he intended carrying them out. This was not due entirely to their own curiosity, but also because, should anything untoward happen, they would know where to begin looking for him.

But Charlie Minns did not want to be found.

He made camp that night some distance from Moolooloo, but did not light a fire. The sheep station employed Aborigines who could smell woodsmoke at a greater distance than most men could see in these hills.

He made an evening meal of bread, cold beans and a beer. When it was over he carefully buried the bottle and scraps, so as to leave no trace of his camp. Then he went to sleep with a rifle cradled in his arms.

The following day he passed the site of the copper

mine at Nuccaleena, wasting only a single glance towards the spot where the Aboriginal woman had been laid out, surrounded by the gifts donated by the Blinman miners. The blankets and cheap gifts had long since disappeared. So too had the body of the woman.

His destination was still another night and day's journey away. Stefan Mintoff had suggested that Charlie should make a brief survey of sites such as Nuccaleena, but Charlie had more urgent business to attend to.

Eventually, on the evening of the third day, Charlie reached his destination. It was a deep but narrow creek; a watercourse gouged out of the earth by torrents of water pouring from the surrounding hills during the region's brief and capricious rainy season.

There had been a few days of thundery summer rain before Charlie had set out from Blinman and this suited him very well. The water rushing in torrents along the creek had long since gone, but there were places where brackish pools remained.

Taking bearings from the surrounding hills, Charlie located a heap of innocuous-looking stones. Removing them with his bare hands, he uncovered the tools he had hidden here months before. This was where he would make his camp and commence prospecting.

He began digging on a bend of the dried-up creek the following morning, carrying the sandy earth he had removed to a nearby pool of water. When he had transferred enough to work with, Charlie squatted down by the pool. Using a mortar and pestle he crushed pieces of quartz from the soil before putting earth and quartz into a pan, dipping it in the pool and swirling the whole around, gradually reducing the contents. Finally, with a grunt of satisfaction, Charlie saw what he was seeking. It was a tell-tale tail of yellow specks around the edge of the pan.

It was gold, washed down by the rains and deposited in the place where he had found it before.

Carefully extracting the fine particles of precious metal, Charlie transferred them to a pouch suspended around his neck before continuing his work.

Charlie found more gold than ever before in the creek bed. There were even one or two smallish nuggets. By the tenth day of prospecting he had accumulated a sizeable amount – yet he was beginning to feel uneasy.

He believed he was being watched. He had seen no one, but the occasional startled bird or unexpectedly disturbed kangaroo gave him warnings he could not afford to ignore.

When a magpie suddenly took off nearby with a chatter of complaint, Charlie picked up his rifle and ran swiftly along the creek bed, stooping to remain out of sight of anyone who might be near the spot where the bird had been disturbed.

When he felt he was far enough away, Charlie climbed from the creek. Taking a circuitous route and treading lightly, he approached the spot where he thought someone was hiding.

Charlie moved very carefully now. If he made a sound that was heard by the hidden observer, it could result in his death.

Suddenly, he thought he detected a movement ahead and to one side of him. He dropped to one knee immediately – and waited.

Just as he was beginning to think he might have been

mistaken, he saw another movement. A moment later
an Aborigine crept into view. The man was completely
naked – but he carried a spear.

His interest was concentrated upon the creek, at the
spot where Charlie had been working only a few
minutes before.

Seemingly puzzled by the silence, the Aborigine rose
slowly to his feet, a shoulder-high bush hiding him
from the view of anyone who might be ahead of him.
As he did so there was a commotion from the spot
where Charlie had tethered his donkey.

Charlie was alarmed to see the animal galloping off
through the scrub as though pursued by the devil.

This was when the spear-carrying Aborigine turned
and saw Charlie.

Before the man had time to recover from his surprise,
Charlie quickly raised the rifle to his shoulder, took
aim, and fired.

The Aborigine fell to the ground, but he was not
dead and he began crawling away.

Reloading as he went, Charlie approached the
wounded man but waited until he could have reached
out and touched him before firing again, the barrel of the
rifle almost touching the base of the other man's skull.

The Aborigine fell forward on his face and did not
move again.

There was a sudden sound from behind Charlie and
he whirled around in time to dodge a spear that had
been hurled from perhaps twenty paces distant.

Charlie rammed another cartridge home in the
breech of his rifle, but the man who had thrown the
spear was running away, taking a zig-zag course
through thick scrub.

Charlie fired again, but knew he had missed. Quickly reloading his rifle, he looked around him in case there were more Aborigines in the area, but he could neither see nor hear anyone.

With any luck there might have been only two men after him, but Charlie could not afford to take any chances. He had already collected more gold than he had expected to find, far more than he had collected on his previous trip to the outback. He would go in search of his donkey then make his way back to Blinman as fast as he could travel.

It would be a dangerous journey. He had killed only one of the two Aborigines who were after him, and the other would not give up – and Charlie knew why.

He believed the two men must be members of the same tribe as the woman who had died at Nuccaleena. He was not certain whether they were after him because of his treatment of her – or because they were out to avenge the death of her husband.

The reason did not matter. They had set out to kill him and the surviving Aborigine would not give up until either he or Charlie was dead.

Perversely, Charlie cursed the woman, blaming her for his misfortunes. Had they not met up his life would not be in danger now.

Charlie had met the woman and her husband when he was prospecting in the outback and they were mourning the death of their young daughter. In a rare moment of compassion, Charlie had shared his provisions with them.

Afterwards, they travelled together for a few days, until Charlie developed a fancy for the wife. She was not averse to his attentions, but the husband objected strongly. So strongly that Charlie decided to shoot him.

Unfortunately, other members of the tribe to which the two Aborigines belonged had come looking for the couple and found the body of the husband.

This is what had caused the unrest that resulted in the attack on the Blinman miners.

It seemed the Aborigines were out for revenge once more, but now they were after just one man – Charlie.

Charlie hoped there was now only one Aborigine left to deal with. Any more and his chances of reaching Blinman alive were extremely slim.

II

It took Charlie two nerve-racking hours to find and catch his frightened donkey. Twice during the search he wasted shots at startled kangaroos, mistaking them for humans.

It seemed to him that every sound of the outback had been magnified tenfold and every movement by bird or animal posed a threat to his life.

Once he had recaptured his donkey Charlie was faced with a dilemma. Should he return to the site of his digging, or abandon everything he had left there and head for Blinman immediately?

The gold he had panned was secured about his body in a belt of canvas and linen that he had made himself, but there were other items at the creek – not least food and water.

He decided he would return and approached the camp cautiously – but he was already too late.

Someone had been there before him.

The food had gone, as had the few items of spare clothing from his camp and the remaining brandy. Far more serious, his water had been poured away and the water carriers stabbed time and time again so as to render them useless.

Nevertheless, Charlie was able to rescue two of the containers which were capable of carrying about half their normal capacity. These he filled with the brackish, unpalatable water from the shallow pool in which he had been panning for gold.

Despite all that had happened, Charlie hoped one day to return to the spot and so set about removing all traces of his prospecting. Although mining experts had long been convinced that gold would be found in the Flinders Ranges, this was one of the few finds to yield a worthwhile return.

Charlie had not reported the find – and had no intention of doing so. Registering a claim would bring a swarm of gold-seekers to the area and quickly exhaust the alluvial gold in the creek.

When he was satisfied he had hidden all traces of his work, Charlie let the donkey drink its fill from the waterhole before mounting the animal and setting off in the direction of Blinman.

Charlie rode through the night, able to see his way by the light of a near-full moon. It was an anxious ride, full of exaggerated night noises, animal movements and shadows that in his imagination harboured a lurking assassin.

He would occasionally make unexpected changes of direction, carefully avoiding areas of deep shadow where someone might be waiting, hoping to take him by surprise.

At no time did Charlie doubt he was being stalked. There were too many unexplained night noises and movements. He was also satisfied by now that he was being pursued by only one man. Had there been any more it would have been relatively simple to ambush him, distracting his attention while armed warriors crept up on him.

He began to breathe more easily when dawn arrived, dispersing the shadows and taking away the advantage of his Aborigine adversary.

Turning the donkey off the trail, Charlie kneed the animal up the side of a hill, from where he could view the trail along which he had travelled and also see for a considerable distance ahead.

He carefully scoured the scrub on both sides of the trail. Although there was no one to be seen there were various places where a man could conceal himself. He wasted four more bullets, fired into patches of thick scrub where the Aborigine might be hiding. But all he succeeded in doing was to send a wedge-tailed eagle soaring into the air – and startle the donkey. Had Charlie not looped the animal's reins about his arm it would have bolted, leaving him to try to catch it once more. Given his tired state that would not have been easy, and if he had had to proceed on foot he would have been far too vulnerable. He had a better view of the surrounding countryside from the back of the donkey and could remain on guard without having to watch where he was putting his feet.

After giving the donkey most of the water he was carrying, Charlie set off once again.

Like its rider, the donkey was tired and reluctant to move off with its human burden. It took persistent rib-kicking with Charlie's booted heels before the stubborn animal was persuaded to move.

Charlie felt able to relax a little now it was daylight; the situation did not seem quite as menacing as it had during the hours of darkness. Besides, in a couple of hours he should reach the safety of the sheep station at Moolooloo.

Even so Charlie did not relax his vigilance completely until the buildings of the remote sheep station came into view – and this lapse proved his un-doing.

He could see the manager of the sheep station and his Aborigine employees working on the fence of a sheep pen and he put a hand to his forehead to shield his eyes from the low-lying sun. Suddenly, without warning, he was struck in the back by an object that knocked him off the slow-plodding donkey.

For one brief, unreal moment as he lay on the ground, Charlie thought he had been struck by a large stone, but when he tried to turn over to look behind him he was unable to do so. The haft of a spear protruded from his back, the blade embedded just beneath his left shoulder.

At the same time an agonising pain began to spread through his body – and he started to scream.

The sound that spilled from his mouth carried blood with it. Despite this, Charlie struggled to a sitting posi-tion, freeing the rifle he carried on a sling over his right shoulder.

Only a short distance away, a young Aborigine stood as though uncertain what to do now he had downed the man he had been tracking for so long.

Charlie fired and the shot spun the young man around, but it did not drop him.

The shot also alerted those at the sheep station. As a shout went up the Aborigine turned and ran, indicating that he had not been seriously hurt.

Charlie tried to stand up, but the effort proved too great. He slid sideways to the ground as his assailant disappeared from view in the scrub.

When Ben Carminow, the Moolooloo station manager, and two of his Aborigine helpers reached Charlie he was lying on his stomach, his face turned to one side, moaning in pain, blood trickling slowly from a corner of his mouth. The spear was still embedded in his back.

The two Aborigines reached him first, but they stood back to allow Carminow through.

His face distorted with pain, Charlie whispered painfully, 'Help me. Oh God! Help me.'

'The first thing we need to do is get this spear out – and hope we don't do too much harm in the process,' said Ben. 'You . . .' He pointed to one of his Aborigine workers. 'Hold him down while I pull out the spear.'

The Aborigine looked unhappy and held back.

'You heard what I said!' Carminow spoke angrily.

Still the worker held back and it was his companion who spoke in his own tongue to the station manager. Startled, the station manager replied in the same language and the Aborigine worker nodded.

'So you're the man who's stirred up all the trouble we've had around here,' said Carminow, looking down at Charlie. 'You probably deserve all you've got, but I suppose we can't leave you here to die.'

Without further thought, he placed a foot on Charlie's left shoulder and tugged at the spear, causing Charlie to scream out in agony. It took three attempts before the spear blade was pulled free, by which time the wounded man had lapsed into unconsciousness.

Turning to the two workers, Carminow said, 'I don't care what your friends out there might or might not do to you for helping their enemy. What's far more certain is what *I'll* do to you if you *don't*. Run and get a hurdle – and quickly. We'll put him on it and carry him to the house.'

III

When Charlie regained consciousness he was lying on a bed in the station manager's house on the Moolooloo sheep station – and he was in great pain.

It felt as though his chest and the upper part of his back were on fire. When he coughed, which was frequently, the extra pain caused him to cry out.

However, when Ben Carminow entered the room, Charlie's question had nothing to do with his wound. 'My belt . . .' he croaked, in a hoarse whisper, 'where is it?'

'It's hanging over the back of the bed – and the gold dust is still in it. But you have more things to worry about right now. That's why I'm not asking you whether the gold came from a registered claim.'

'I've carried it with me for months,' Charlie lied, feebly. 'It came from—'

What he intended saying was lost in another bout

of coughing, and a stream of blood trickled from his mouth.

'I said I wasn't asking,' Carminow repeated. 'And all the gold in the world isn't going to help you if we don't get you to a doctor – and damned quick. Although why I should even bother with you, I don't know. My stockmen tell me you're behind all the trouble we had around here towards the end of last year.'

'They're lying!' croaked Charlie.

Ben Carminow shook his head. 'I've had stockmen who worked harder, but these aren't liars. It seems you had something to do with the death of the son of a pretty important *yura*. When they came looking and couldn't find you they took it out on anyone else they came across. Perhaps now they've damned near killed you they'll leave the rest of us in peace.'

Charlie remembered the man he had shot dead at his camp on the creek beyond Nuccaleena. He doubted whether honour had yet been satisfied.

'I don't know what you're talking about,' he gasped.

'It doesn't matter whether you do or you don't. The *yuras* think you *do* and while you're on this station you pose a threat to me and my family, and to Mr Rounsevell's sheep.'

William Rounsevell was Carminow's employer. A Cornishman who now lived in Adelaide, Rounsevell had made a great deal of money in South Australia by his hard work and resourcefulness.

'I'm hurt too bad to be moved,' Charlie said breathlessly. 'Can't you get a doctor to come out here?'

'I've told you, none of us are safe while you're at Moolooloo. Besides, it's not at all certain there's still a doctor in Blinman. Last I heard, there wasn't, but there's likely to be someone there who can do something for you. There's no one here.'

The last thing Charlie wanted in his present state was to make the journey from Moolooloo in an unsprung farmcart along the rough track that led to Blinman, but there was nothing he could do about it. Carminow was right, he posed a threat to the sheep station and there was no one here qualified to treat his wound.

Pessimistically, Charlie thought he would probably die anyway.

Closing his eyes, he tried unsuccessfully to avert another bout of coughing. After it passed, he said weakly, 'Do what you like with me – but give me my gold before you take me anywhere.'

Charlie survived the long and painful journey to Blinman. Ben Carminow drove the cart himself, with Charlie lying upon the station manager's own feather mattress which had been placed upon a few dozen fleeces.

Despite the attempt to make him as comfortable as possible, Charlie was barely conscious when the wagon, with its two armed Aborigine outriders, entered the mining township.

As Ben Carminow had predicted, the doctor was absent from the town and no one else was willing to accept responsibility for the wounded prospector. Even the owner of Blinman's only hotel would not take him in.

A solution was found when Ruth Askew pushed her way to the front of the crowd gathered about the wagon.

Ignoring everyone else, she addressed Ben Carminow. 'How bad is he?'

The Moolooloo station manager shrugged. 'I'm no doctor, but I don't think he'll be a trouble to anyone for very long. He was speared in the back. I'd say it's pierced his lung.'

Ruth winced. Peering inside the cart she saw Charlie's pale face and the dried blood around his mouth. It took her only a moment to make up her mind. 'Bring him up to my place, I'll take care of him.'

There were murmurings from the women in the crowd and one of them, speaking louder than she had intended, said, 'They say as how like sticks with like.'

Rounding on the woman, Ruth said fiercely, 'What would you prefer for him if he was your husband? To be left by so-called Christians to die out in the open in a farmcart or be taken to a bawdy house and given a roof over his head and at least a faint chance of recovering?'

'My husband wouldn't find himself in a position where they'd be the only two options open to him,' the woman retorted piously.

'I'm sure that's what you'd like to think, you and the rest of the women here,' Ruth said angrily. 'That's no doubt what Charlie's wife thinks – yes, and the two boys who look up to him as a father.'

Seeing the woman's change of expression, Ruth continued, 'Does it surprise you? Well, I've met his wife and their two fine boys who came over from Cornwall to be with him. Charlie Minns may not be the best husband and father in the world, but he's all they've got. I'm going to do my damnedest to see they don't lose him.'

There were more murmurings and Ruth heard such remarks as 'not worth saving', and 'deserves all that's happened to him'.

Still angry, she said, 'I suggest you keep such talk to yourself. I'll be writing to Charlie's wife. From what I know of her, when she hears how seriously he's hurt she'll come to Blinman as fast as she can. When she arrives, if she hears one word from you of what you think you know about Charlie, then me and the other girls will start telling a few tales. If we do then Margaret Minns won't be the only woman in Blinman who's disillusioned with her husband!'

Satisfied she had effectively made her point, Ruth turned her attention to Ben Carminow. He had listened to her with grudging but increasing admiration as she harangued the now-silent onlookers.

'All right, there's been enough talking. Let's get Charlie up to my cottage before he's overwhelmed by the good wishes of this kind-hearted crowd.'

IV

The letter was brought to Emily's house by the young son of the Kadina postmaster late one evening.

Following the instructions given to him by his father, the young boy said, 'I'm sorry for disturbing you, Miss Boyce, but this letter came in on the stage this evening. It's for Mrs Minns and says on the envelope that it's "urgent". Although it's addressed to Ewing Street Pa knew Mrs Minns is here with you. He said I was to bring it round here right away.'

'That is very kind of you,' said Emily. 'If you go through to the kitchen one of the boys will give you a piece of cake while I fetch my purse and find a sixpence for you.'

When the boy had left the house happily clutching his unexpected reward, Emily frowned at the letter she held in her hand. So few people in South Australia knew Margaret that the letter had to be from, or about, Charlie. She feared it would not contain good news.

Margaret was at the far end of the large garden, taking advantage of the diminished heat of late evening to water some shrubs she had planted a few days before.

She smiled when Emily approached, but the smile vanished quickly when Emily failed to respond.

'Is something wrong, Emily? It's not the boys . . . ?'

'No, the boys are in the house and they are fine, but this letter has just arrived for you. It is marked "urgent". I thought it might be better if you opened it out here, away from the house.'

'A letter for me? Is it from Cornwall?'

'No, but it's not from anyone here in Kadina either. It came in on the stagecoach. Here, open it and you'll learn what it has to say.'

Margaret took the letter and turned it over two or three times before finally tearing open the envelope and extracting a single sheet of paper.

She began reading the letter and as she progressed her eyes widened in horror. When she had come to the bottom of the page, she looked up at Emily, visibly distressed. 'It's about Charlie. He's been attacked by Aborigines. He's at Blinman and is badly hurt.'

'Who is the letter from? Here, let me have a look.'

Taking the letter from her friend, Emily said, in surprise, 'It's from Ruth Askew, the woman who lived in Ewing Street. Well, in spite of her way of life, Ruth is a very capable woman. Charlie could not be in better hands. Nevertheless, it sounds as though he is badly hurt. What will you do, Margaret?'

'I'll have to go to him, but . . . the boys?'

'You need have no worries about them. They are perfectly happy with me. I will take care of them. But when was the letter written . . . ? Tuesday the twenty-third of February. That's three days ago. You must leave for Blinman as quickly as possible, Margaret.'

Margaret left Kadina the following day, but was obliged to change coaches twice en route for Blinman. As a result, the journey took five long, weary days.

When the stagecoach pulled in to the Blinman hotel, Margaret alighted from the vehicle feeling stiff and dusty. The usual crowd of miners stood around, tankards in hand, curious about who might be arriving at the remote township.

Today Margaret was the only passenger and the landlord of the hotel stepped forward to greet her. 'Welcome to Blinman, ma'am. I'm William Barnes, the hotel keeper. Do you have somewhere to stay, or will you require a room for a while?'

'I don't know,' Margaret said uncertainly. 'Before I can decide anything I need to find Ruth Askew—'

The mention of Ruth's name provoked an outburst of raucous laughter and catcalls from the listening miners and one of them said, 'If I was you I'd take up Willie's offer of a bed – for tonight, at least. You could no doubt do with some sleep after the shaking-up you'll have had in the coach – and you'll be kept too busy up at Ruth's place to get any sleep. In fact I'll pay you in advance for your first night there. All night – and I'll guarantee you don't get any sleep.'

His offer brought more laughter and crude remarks from his companions.

Margaret had spent five days travelling on three coaches along indifferent roads. She was tired and concerned for Charlie and the boys she had left behind in Emily's care. The last thing she needed was to be the butt of the ribaldry of drunken miners – Cornish miners at that, if she had identified their accents correctly.

Close to tears, she said, 'If that's the way you would speak to a respectable woman in Cornwall, then I'm sure they're all better off without you. I'm here because I've had a letter from Ruth Askew telling me my husband has been seriously hurt and she's taking care of him. Now, is someone going to tell me the way to her house?'

Her words brought an immediate halt to the hilarity of the men and the hotel keeper said, 'You'll be Mrs Minns then, ma'am. I'm sorry you had to put up with the coarse talk of men who should know better. The only excuse I can give for them is that it was settlement day last Saturday and the miners were told no more copper would be brought up until prices improved. It's an unhappy and uncertain time for them.'

'It's not exactly a happy time for me either, Mr Barnes. Will you please find someone who will show me the way to the house of Ruth Askew?'

'Of course.'

As he spoke, William Barnes was looking about him for someone sober enough to take responsibility for Charlie Minns' wife.

It happened that at that moment Sam was walking along the street, hand in hand with Primrose.

Seeing him, William Barnes called, 'Sam, will you come here, please?'

Still holding Primrose's hand, Sam looked curiously at Margaret for a moment, then said, 'Yes, Willie, what can I do for you?'

'It's not for me, but for this lady. She's Mrs Minns, wife of Charlie Minns. She's had a letter from Ruth, telling her that her husband's been hurt. She wants someone to show her to Ruth's house. As you're both Cornish I thought you might be happy to help her.'

Sam gave William Barnes a disapproving look. 'Yes, of course ... but today is Primrose's birthday and I promised to buy her some sweets ...'

Reaching into a pocket, he took out some coins and handed them to the small girl. 'Here, Primrose, take these to the shop. Tell Mr McFarlane he's to give you whatever sweets you want and then you go straight back to Mummy. Tell her I'll see her a little later.'

When Primrose ran off clutching the coins Sam had given to her, William Barnes said to Margaret, 'I'll put your things into one of my rooms, Mrs Minns. I've no doubt you'll be back later. I'll give you a quiet room at the back of the hotel and make certain you're not troubled again.'

Sam and Margaret walked in silence for a while before she said, 'You have a very pretty little girl. How old is she?'

'She's six today,' Sam replied. 'But she's not mine. She's the daughter of my best friend. He died in a mine accident in Cornwall. I travelled out here with Primrose and her mother, who's now married again. Her new husband's another Cornish miner who came out on the ship with us. He's a good man.'

There was another silence before Margaret asked, 'Do you know Charlie . . . my husband?'

'Not very well. He's a prospector and kept very much to himself. I work at the mine here.'

Sam hoped Margaret would accept what he had said and not ask any more questions about her husband. He could not tell her the truth, but lying did not come easy to him.

Much to his relief, her next question did not concern her husband. 'Do you know Ruth Askew?'

'We've met once or twice in the town and passed the time of day, but that's all.'

'I wonder why she is the one who is looking after Charlie?'

'I think I can answer that question,' Sam said. 'There's no doctor in Blinman at the moment. When Charlie was brought in Ruth was the only one around who knew anything about nursing a wounded man.' He looked at Margaret and said hesitantly, 'I don't know how much you've heard about what happened. None of us in Blinman know exactly, but Charlie's wound is serious. Very serious.'

'I gathered as much from Ruth's letter. That's why I came here straightaway.'

Margaret looked at Sam in time to catch his expression and she added, 'Ruth and . . . and some of her friends were near neighbours for a while in Kadina. She must have realised Charlie is my husband. I'm grateful to her.'

Sam believed there was much more to the relationship between Charlie and Ruth than Margaret knew about, but he would say nothing.

A few minutes later, he pointed to a rambling, rundown cottage and said, 'That's where Ruth lives.'

Margaret's pace increased and Sam let her go on ahead to the ramshackle house. As she opened the gate and hurried up the path, Ruth appeared at the door; she was in a distressed state.

'Ruth! How's Charlie? Is he any better?'

Ruth seemed to be at a loss for words for some moments and she made two attempts to reply before she finally succeeded.

'Margaret ... I'm so sorry. So very sorry. Charlie's dead. He died only about half an hour ago ...'

V

The news that Charlie was dead and that she had arrived too late was just too much for Margaret. She broke down and wept. It was not that she still loved Charlie as much as she once had, but rather it was a culmination of so many things.

She and the boys had travelled to South Australia with such hopes for the future. She was coming to be with her husband and to resume the happy albeit insecure life they had once enjoyed together. The boys would have a father to support them and impart knowledge to carry them forward into adult life.

The reunion had fallen short of all their expectations, except, perhaps, for Tom, who possessed the blindness of an infant to his father's faults. Yet Margaret had nurtured a hope that things would improve when Charlie had grown used to having his family with him again.

Now he was dead and all Margaret's hopes had died with him.

Sam and Ruth helped Margaret inside the cottage to the kitchen, where two other women sat sipping tea, their attire suggesting they had not long risen from their beds. They had not applied make-up and hurriedly departed from the room after expressing perfunctory sympathy with Margaret.

'Just sit yourself down, love, while I pour you a nice sweet cup of tea,' Ruth said. 'This must be a terrible shock to you – especially coming on top of such a long journey.'

'I . . . I'd like to see Charlie first,' Margaret replied unsteadily.

'Of course. I'll take you to him and leave you for a few minutes while I make a fresh brew.'

Ruth was away from the room for only a few minutes, during which time Sam remained in the kitchen, ill at ease at being in the notorious house.

Returning to the kitchen alone, Ruth set about making tea. 'Poor Margaret,' she said. 'To come all this way only to find her husband lying dead in a bawdy house.' Looking up at Sam, she asked, 'How is it you brought her here? Do you know each other?'

'No, I happened to be close to the hotel when she arrived. She asked to be shown the way, but it seems some of the miners gave her a hard time. Willie Barnes asked me if I'd bring her here. He's saving a room for her at the hotel.'

'I'm surprised you knew where to bring her,' Ruth commented. 'I've never seen you here.'

'No,' Sam said, without further comment. 'And, in case it's mentioned, I told Mrs Minns her husband was brought here because the doctor is away and you have a little knowledge of medicine.'

'As a matter of fact it happens to be the truth. I spent some months nursing and tended a number of injuries, but even a skilled surgeon couldn't have saved Charlie. The spear had pierced his lung and I suspect it became infected.'

'I'm sure you did your best,' Sam said. 'I'll leave you now. You can tell Mrs Minns all about it—'

'You'll stay here until she's ready to leave,' Ruth declared firmly. 'Then you can take her back to the hotel. This is no place for a respectable woman. Can I get you some tea while you're waiting?'

Sam shook his head. At that moment Margaret returned to the kitchen. She looked pale and drawn, but she was more composed than before.

'Thank you, Ruth. Charlie looks so thin and pale. There's not a scrap of colour left in his face, but he's at peace now.'

'He lost a great deal of blood,' Ruth explained. 'And he found it painful to eat – even to drink, sometimes.'

'Poor Charlie,' Margaret said, tearful now. 'He may not always have been all he should, but he didn't deserve to die in such a way.'

Sam thought otherwise, but he kept such thoughts to himself.

'I told him I'd written to you,' Ruth said, 'and before he died he asked me to give something to you if you came here. I'll fetch it for you.'

Ruth left the room briefly. When she returned she was carrying the hand-made belt that Charlie had worn about his waist. Placing it on the table in front of

Margaret, she said, 'There you are. It should see you all right for a while, at least.'

'What is it?' Margaret asked, surprised by the weight of the belt and its contents.

'I'm no expert, but I'd say it's packed with gold,' Ruth said. 'It would seem that Charlie found what hundreds of men have been seeking for years in the Flinders Ranges. Unfortunately, the secret of where he got it has died with him. Charlie would have liked that.'

Margaret picked up on Ruth's unguarded remark immediately.

'Charlie didn't die in this house just because you knew something about nursing, did he, Ruth? You and he knew each other long before he was wounded. Before I came from Cornwall, even.'

'I'd met him before,' Ruth confessed, making the admission as casual as she could. 'It was a long time ago, in Kadina, or Moonta. I can't remember exactly where. But I've met so many men, in all sorts of places. Charlie needed help and I was able to give more than anyone else in Blinman. I'd have done the same for anyone who was in trouble.'

Margaret looked at the other woman uncertainly before saying, 'Yes, Ruth, I believe you would. Thank you. Thank you for looking after him and for being so honest about this . . .' She held up the heavy, home-made belt. 'I knew nothing about it and not everyone would have given it up, as you have.'

Ruth shrugged off Margaret's praise. 'I'm not short of money, but you've got two boys to bring up.' Suddenly becoming brisk, she said, 'Now, I suggest you get back to the hotel and settle in before it gets too rowdy there.'

'There's just one thing . . .' Margaret turned to Sam for advice. 'What do I do about a funeral for Charlie?'

'Leave that to me,' Sam said. 'I'll make all the arrangements. The Blinman will pay for it out of mine funds. I know Charlie wasn't employed at the mine, but that won't be any problem.'

'Thank you, thank you both.' Margaret suddenly looked weary. 'I'd like to go to the hotel now and be by myself for a while. I have a lot of thinking to do.'

'Of course,' agreed Sam. 'I'll try to arrange the funeral for the morning. Then you'll be able to catch the afternoon coach. I doubt whether you'll want to remain in Blinman any longer than is absolutely necessary.'

Turning to Ruth, Sam said, 'I'll see that Charlie is moved out of here tonight. Do you want to be told about the funeral arrangements?'

'Of course,' Ruth replied. 'All of us in the house will be at the cemetery.' She did not feel it necessary to add that it was doubtful whether anyone else from Blinman would attend.

VI

Captain Wilf Hooper raised no objection to Sam's suggestion that Charlie's funeral be financed from mine funds. Although Charlie had been disliked by all at Blinman who knew him – and a great many who did not – there was genuine sympathy for Margaret. No one wished to make life more difficult for her.

There was another reason why Captain Hooper agreed. The coach that brought Margaret to Blinman had also carried a letter from the company that owned the mine. Captain Hooper was ordered to pay off the miners at the end of the month.

If Captain Hooper agreed, he would remain at Blinman, on a reduced salary, together with just enough men to keep the pumps running and effect essential maintenance.

Such drastic measures had been brought about by the world price of copper, which had dropped to a new low, making the Blinman mine no longer viable.

There were small amounts of money left in various welfare funds and it was the captain's task to disburse it as he felt fit.

Charlie Minns was buried on a gentle slope at the edge of the cemetery just outside Blinman. Around him were the graves of many fellow Cornish men, women – and even more of their children. The hard Blinman environment had claimed a great many lives during the few years the mine had been in existence.

The graveside service was given by a Methodist lay preacher, his accent that of Cornwall. There were also a few miners and their wives who had shown grudging Christian forgiveness to the late Charlie Minns, out of sympathy for Margaret.

They stood apart from Ruth and three fellow prostitutes, with Sam, Margaret, Jean and Ira standing between the two parties.

Jean had gone to the hotel the previous evening, at Sam's request, to invite Margaret to come home with her for a meal. Margaret had pleaded extreme weariness, adding that she wanted to try to get a good night's sleep before boarding a coach for the return journey to Kadina soon after the funeral.

The gravedigger, called from his bed at dawn to dig the grave that would hold the body of Charlie, was nearby, leaning on his long-handled Cornish shovel. Impatiently, he waited for the service to come to an end so that he might shovel earth back in the narrow grave and hurry off to the hotel bar to spend the money he had earned digging a grave in the rock-hard earth.

The brief and impersonal ceremony over, Margaret thanked those who had attended before walking back to the hotel, accompanied by Sam, Jean and Ira.

Margaret was far more composed than she had been on the previous day and Sam felt emboldened to ask her whether she had made any plans for the future.

'I haven't thought about it in any detail,' Margaret replied. 'I shall certainly stay in Kadina with Emily until she's married. Then I will probably take the boys back to Cornwall.'

'Emily?' Sam asked. 'Is she a relative?'

'No, she's doing work for the Church in Kadina. I came out from England as her companion. You might know her, she was the daughter of the vicar of a mining village – St Cleer.'

Sam stopped walking abruptly and caught hold of Margaret's arm, staring at her in disbelief. 'Emily? You're not talking of Emily Boyce? Are you telling me she's here . . . in South Australia? When did she arrive?'

Startled by his excitement, Margaret said, 'We've been in Kadina for some months . . .' Suddenly, everything fell into place. '*Sam* . . . of course! You must be Sam Hooper! Whenever we went to a mine to enquire after Charlie, Emily would ask after you.'

Margaret's words gave Sam more of a lift than she

would ever know, but she had mentioned something else that had disheartened him. 'You said Emily was to be married. Who is she marrying?'

'Stefan Mintoff. He's a councillor and store owner in Kadina. He's also expecting to be elected to the South Australian parliament soon. I think he and Emily will be married when he gets back from England. He's gone there to raise money for a mining company he intends setting up. He's particularly interested in the Flinders Ranges. He and Charlie would talk a lot about mining and the prospects for making money here. I think Charlie was doing some work for him in this area.'

'I wonder how much, if anything, that had to do with Charlie finding gold somewhere in the ranges,' mused Sam. 'It's very interesting indeed – but I want to know more about Emily. How is she? I mean, is she happy?'

'I think so. She's certainly a whole lot happier than when she was in St Cleer looking after her father, with that old battleaxe of a housekeper watching everything she did.'

'This man she's going to marry ... Mintoff. I think I met him when I passed through Kadina. Nobody seemed to like him, as I remember, but if Emily is to marry him ... What's he really like?'

'Between you and me, I don't like him. He's far too "smarmy", but then I'm not the one who's marrying him.'

'No, Emily is,' Sam said unhappily. 'I wish I'd known she was coming out here. I'd have gone to wherever she landed, to meet her.'

'She'd have liked that,' Margaret replied. 'As I said, she tried to find out where you were when we first arrived. She was still trying, right up until the time things got serious between her and Stefan Mintoff.'

They had arrived at the Blinman hotel now and Margaret said, 'Thank you for all you've done for me, Sam. I really don't know how I could have coped without you.'

'I'm glad I was able to help.'

Sam meant it. Margaret was a very pleasant woman. However, he was deeply unhappy at the news of Emily she had divulged. If only he had known she was in South Australia!

In fact it was probably his own fault they had not met. He had taken so long to write to his parents after arriving at Blinman that by the time the letter arrived Emily had probably already left St Cleer.

Had he written sooner his father could have told her where he was and they might have met before she found the Kadina councillor.

Even as these thoughts were going through his mind, Sam had to admit to himself that he could not have hoped to compete with the man Emily was to marry. It was a deeply depressing thought.

In an attempt not to think about it right now, Sam asked, 'Are you all packed and ready to catch the stage when it arrives?'

'Yes. I'll be pleased to be back with my boys. Emily's looking after them for me and I know they're happy with her, but I miss them.' Suddenly morose, Margaret added, 'I've got a lot to discuss with them, too. With Albert, anyway. He's old enough to have a sensible opinion about the future, now there's no Charlie around.'

'I wish you well, whatever you decide,' Sam said.

'And take good care of that gold belt, it's worth a lot of money. Make sure you find an honest man to buy the gold from you; it could help you decide what you want to do.'

'Thank you again, Sam. Will I be seeing you before I leave?'

'Yes, I'll see you safely on to the stage – and there's something I'd like you to take to Emily . . .'

6

I

Margaret returned to Kadina exhausted, both mentally and physically. She dreaded the thought of having to tell Albert and Tom that their father was dead.

The ordeal was postponed for a while, at least. Arriving home, she learned the boys had been allowed to go to the Wallaroo mine with friends to watch an exhibition of Cornish wrestling.

Emily took one look at the strained face of her friend and realised something was seriously wrong.

'I wasn't expecting you back in Kadina for at least another week, Margaret. What happened?'

'I got to Blinman too late,' Margaret replied wearily. 'Charlie died half an hour before I got there. He died in a bawdy house.'

'Oh, Margaret! I am so sorry. It must have been absolutely horrible for you. Here, sit down, I will make you some tea ... No, you need something a little stronger. I have a bottle of French brandy put away.

Stefan gave it to me before he left for London. I will open that. There is also a nice hot tub prepared in the kitchen. I was about to take advantage of the boys' absence to relax in a bath for a while. But your need is far greater than my own. Take the drink in there with you, soak yourself and relax. When you have finished and put on clean clothes you'll feel very much better. If the boys come home before you are out I'll keep them entertained.'

'Thank you, Emily, it will give me time to get it clear in my head what I'm going to tell them. To be honest it's something I'm dreading. All the way back here I've been trying to think of the best way to break the news to them. Some way of lessening the blow. Albert will probably be all right, he's a stoic, but it will hit Tom hard. He thought his pa was the most wonderful person in the world.'

'I am quite sure you will not disillusion him, Margaret.' Pouring an extremely large brandy into a glass, she said, 'Collect your clean clothes and take them to the kitchen. I'll take the brandy there and make certain the back door is locked and the curtains drawn. Stay there until you feel ready to face the world.'

Margaret had been in the bath for half an hour when the boys returned, enthusing about the wrestling they had just seen. The sight of Margaret's bag in the hallway excited them even more.

'Our ma's back!' Albert exclaimed in delight.

'She is,' agreed Emily. 'And she's very tired. She is having a bath in the kitchen right now, ridding herself of the dust of the road. She'll be out to see you both in a few minutes.'

'Is our pa with her?' Tom asked eagerly.

'Don't be silly,' Albert said scornfully. 'He wouldn't be with Ma when she's having a bath.'

'I meant, is he all right and has he come home with her,' explained Tom. 'You *knew* what I meant.'

'Your mother will tell you all about it when she has freshened up,' Emily said. 'Now, I brought some cakes from the larder, in case you returned home before your mother was ready for you. They have sugar icing on them; who would like one?'

Tom accepted a cake eagerly, but Albert was aware that Emily had avoided giving a reply to his younger brother's questions. He guessed what the reason for such evasion might be.

Tears sprang to his eyes, but he said nothing. Taking a cake he made no attempt to eat it.

When Margaret came from the kitchen a few minutes later she looked much less travel weary and more in command of herself.

Tom ran to her straightaway. Flinging his arms about her, he asked, 'Where's our pa, Ma? When is he coming home?'

Albert said nothing and, with one arm about Tom, Margaret held out her other hand to her eldest son. 'Come here, Albert.'

When he came forward and grasped her hand, Margaret turned to Emily. 'I'll take them to their room and stay with them there. I'll see you in the morning. Thank you for the bath, it gave me the opportunity I needed to sort myself out.'

Desperately sorry for Margaret and aware of the heartbreaking task that lay ahead of her, Emily could only nod her head. Then she went in search of the part-time gardener who would empty the galvanised iron bath and stow it away in the shed at the end of the garden.

Margaret came into the kitchen the following morning when Emily was making herself a pre-breakfast cup of tea. She had quite obviously been crying during the night and, as a result, she was puffy-eyed and seemed drained of energy.

Emily poured an extra cup of tea without asking her friend whether she wanted one and Margaret took it from her gratefully.

'How did the boys take the news?' Emily asked eventually.

'Much as I expected they would,' Margaret replied. 'Tom cried himself to sleep. Albert said nothing at the time, but when I put their lamp out and kissed him goodnight he clung to me and I had to cuddle him for the best part of an hour before he let go and allowed me to tuck him in.'

'He is a very sensitive boy,' Emily said. 'I am very fond of him. Indeed, I am fond of both of them. I hope that if I one day have sons they might turn out just like them.'

'That day shouldn't be too far away,' Margaret said. 'No doubt you and Stefan won't want to wait too long to be married once he returns from England.'

'I have not given him a definite "yes", just yet. I have told him only that I will give his proposal very serious consideration.'

'That reminds me,' Margaret said. 'When I was in Blinman I met someone who knew you. It's the man you were hoping to find when I was seeking Charlie, Sam Hooper. He was very, very kind to me. I told him you were getting married to Stefan and he told me to say he wished you every happiness. Oh yes, he gave me something for you. It's in an envelope in my luggage. I'll go and fetch it.'

Trying to control her emotions at the knowledge that Margaret had actually met with Sam, Emily felt a thrill of excitement when Margaret returned and handed the envelope to her. She opened it eagerly. There was a brief note inside – and something else.

Emptying the contents of the envelope into the palm of her hand, Emily looked down at the crucifix she had given to Sam as a farewell present. Ridiculously, tears sprang to her eyes and, half turning away from Margaret she took out the note. Blinking away the tears, she read:

Dear Emily,
I have thought of you often during the time I have been in Australia. I did not know you were here or I would have tried to see you. Margaret says you are to be married, so I feel you would like to have this back. I have carried it with me always and feel it has kept me safe. I trust it will always do the same for you and that you will be very happy in your new life with your husband.
Yours, Sam.

Emily felt so choked she would not trust herself to speak. She swept past the surprised Margaret and hurried off to her bedroom, leaving her friend standing staring after her open-mouthed.

It was twenty minutes before Emily returned to the kitchen, appearing composed once more. About her neck she wore the crucifix Margaret had seen drop from the envelope.

'That's a beautiful cross you're wearing,' Margaret said. 'Is it the one Sam sent to you?'

'Yes, it once belonged to my mother.'

Margaret had no need to ask how it had come into Sam's possession. As she observed Emily's reaction to having it returned a great many things fell into place, in particular the frequent innuendoes by the St Cleer vicarage housekeeper about Emily's 'fondness for Cornish miners'.

'How was Sam looking?' Emily asked suddenly. 'Was he well?'

'He looked fit and tanned,' Margaret replied. 'But things aren't going too well with the Blinman mine. The talk among the men travelling on the stage with me was of the possibility of the mine closing.'

'Yes, Stefan mentioned the troubles of the mines in the Flinders Ranges. He says it is due to the high cost of transporting ore. His first priority when he is elected to parliament – *if* he is elected, of course – will be to bring the railway to the mines.'

'Even if he does, it's not going to happen for some years.' Margaret was relieved to be talking about something other than the death of Charlie. 'It won't help Blinman though, there's not much up there apart from copper. It might be different if they found a lot of gold. Charlie found some – I have it in my room right now – but Sam said it was alluvial and didn't mean there was a rich goldfield up in the Flinders.'

'It sounds as though you talked to Sam quite a lot,' Emily said somewhat wistfully.

'I did. More than to anyone else. I found him very kind.'

'Did you meet with Jean and Primrose too?'

'Yes. Jean is expecting another baby and Primrose was with Sam when I first met him. It was her birthday and he was taking her to buy some sweets.'

'She was a small girl of about three years old when I first saw her,' Emily reminisced. 'It was at the South Caradon mine on the day her father was killed. I took care of her after Jean learned of the death of her husband. She was heavily pregnant then, but she lost the baby.'

'Poor woman,' Margaret said. 'But I think she's happy enough now.'

'I am very pleased to hear it,' Emily replied, trying hard to convince herself she really meant it. 'Things should work out well for her, she and Sam have known each other from childhood and Primrose is the daughter of the man who was Sam's best friend. He will love her as his own. The new baby will no doubt bring them even closer together.'

Margaret looked puzzled. 'Why should Jean's baby bring her and Sam closer together?'

Now it was Emily's turn to be puzzled. 'Why ... ? Because it will be theirs, hers and Sam's, and no matter how much he might love Primrose—'

'But Jean isn't married to Sam. Her husband's name is Ira.'

'You must be mistaken, Margaret. I met Reverend Maddison soon after we arrived in Kadina. He told me he had married Sam and Jean in a triple wedding service in Blinman.'

Margaret made a derisive sound. 'I've met Ezra Maddison too! He's so confused I'm surprised he can get an ordinary wedding right. With three couples standing in front of him, they're lucky they aren't all wedded to the wrong partners.'

'But . . . he would not get something like that wrong, surely?' Emily was thoroughly dismayed. 'He told me he remembered the wedding – and Sam.'

'He might have met Sam there and remembered the wedding, but it wasn't Sam he married to Jean. Her husband's name is Ira. He's very pleasant too. He came to Charlie's funeral – with Jean.'

'Then . . . who *is* Sam married to?'

'He's not married to anyone – and isn't likely to be while he's at Blinman. I certainly didn't see any eligible young women during the short time I was there.'

Emily felt a sudden need to sit down. The whole pattern of her life in recent months had been dictated by the belief that Sam was married to Jean. Had she *not* believed it matters might have taken a very different course. It was certain that Stefan Mintoff would not have figured so largely in her life. She would have travelled to Blinman . . . to find Sam.

Unconsciously fingering the crucifix about her neck, she said agonisingly, 'How could Reverend Maddison have told me something so untrue? How *could* he?'

'Does Sam mean so much to you, Emily?' Margaret asked gently.

Looking up at her friend in bewilderment, Emily said, 'I don't think I realised quite how much, Margaret – until now.'

II

'What shall I do, Margaret? Do I carry on with my life as though Sam went out of it for ever when he left St Cleer, or do I try to contact him and give up all I have here in Australia?' Emily voiced aloud the question that had kept her awake for much of the night. Usually a decisive and positive young woman, she was not used to such uncertainty.

It was twenty-four hours since Margaret had told her of Sam's unmarried state, but Emily was no closer to a solution to her dilemma.

'By "all" I suppose you mean Stefan Mintoff?' said Margaret.

'Well . . . yes – that and everything else I have worked for in Kadina.'

Margaret shrugged. 'I'm sorry, Emily, I would help you if I could, but this is a decision that only you can make.'

'I realise that, Margaret, but what would *you* do in my place?'

'I would never be in your place, Emily. I find Sam very attractive and someone I am comfortable talking to; Stefan Mintoff is a different man altogether.'

'That is perfectly true, they are both *very* different.'

'There is one thing you could do to help make up your mind, Emily. You could go to Blinman and see Sam again. In fact, you *must* if you're to reach the right decision.'

'No, Margaret, I go weak at the knees just thinking about the chance of meeting up with Sam once more.'

'Do you feel the same way when you think of Stefan returning to Kadina?'

'No,' Emily admitted. 'I feel apprehensive.'

'You've answered your own question about what to do, Emily. If you don't meet with Sam and go ahead with a marriage to Stefan, you'll spend the rest of your life wondering about what might have been.'

'But I feel it would not be fair to Stefan if I went off to see Sam while he is so far away.'

'It will be even more unfair to him if you don't get this settled before he gets back. As I've said, unless you see Sam quickly you'll always have a doubt in your mind about whether you married the right man. I never had any doubts about Charlie, even though I knew early on that a lot of the things folk said about him were true. If I had my time over again I would still marry him. The only thing I'd do different would be to come out here with him when he came to Australia. Charlie changed during the time we were apart from one another. He changed so much he just wasn't the same any more. I can't help blaming myself for that. I should have come out here with him . . .' Suddenly and unexpectedly, Margaret's feelings about Charlie poured out.

Emily put a consolatory arm about her. 'I am sorry, Margaret, I am so wrapped up in my own affairs that I keep forgetting you have problems of your own that far outweigh mine. You have the future of your two boys to consider. Have you reached a decision about what you might do?'

'We haven't agreed on anything definite yet. I think we might eventually go back to Cornwall, but I'll take the boys to Blinman first, to show them where their pa is buried. I'll even consider having a headstone set up on his grave. It depends how much I am able to get for the gold he's left for us.'

'Let me pay for the headstone, Margaret. It would please me greatly to be able to do it for you and the boys.'

'Thank you, Emily, that would be a very generous gesture—' A sudden idea occurred to Margaret and she said excitedly, 'Why don't we *all* go to Blinman? While the boys and I do what needs doing you could meet up with Sam again without making it a major drama and feeling guilty about it. The meeting would be a much more casual affair. Do it this way and you will get a much better idea of how you really feel about him, Emily. You know how much *I* like him, but you and he come from very different backgrounds. You might decide you just aren't suited for each other.' Giving Emily a speculative look, she added, 'At least you'll know then who it is you really want. Of course, if you *were* to decide it's Sam and not Stefan you want . . . But that's a bridge to cross if, and when, you get there. What do you say?'

Emily, Margaret and the boys set off for Blinman in late April. It had been six weeks since Margaret had returned to Kadina. Emily had been unable to get away any earlier due to her various commitments.

Emily set off not fully convinced she was doing the right thing, yet feeling more excited than at any time she could remember.

The first half of the journey was far more leisurely than it had been for Margaret when she was travelling alone. It was completed on a steamer as far as Port Augusta, where they boarded a stagecoach for a two-day journey to Blinman.

The stage halted for the night at a small hotel in Hawker. Stepping from the coach, Emily looked apprehensively towards the ranges. A heavy blanket of cloud had been building up during the day, hiding the ragged peaks.

'That looks ominous,' she commented to the coach driver as he handed her down from the vehicle.

'Don't you worry yourself about the weather up there, ma'am. It sometimes hangs around the peaks for days, then it disappears as suddenly as it arrived.'

Emily was not reassured. She was even more concerned when she caught the coach driver talking to the hotel keeper a few minutes later. Both men had their gazes firmly fixed on the cloud-capped mountain ranges.

The night that followed was not the most restful Emily had experienced. The temperature was exceptionally high for the time of year and the mosquitoes were intent upon making the most of the extended season. Unusually gregarious, they attacked every inch of exposed skin they could find.

As a result, Emily appeared for breakfast the following morning puffy-eyed and irritable. It did not help her mood when she peered from the hotel balcony and saw the storm clouds were still thick on the mountains. If anything they now extended farther down the slopes.

It seemed the hotel keeper had been keeping watch on the weather too. Appearing at the breakfast table, hands caressing each other in soapless ablution, he said, 'Ladies, boys, I trust you have enjoyed a good night's sleep?'

When confirmation was not forthcoming, he said, 'The weather to the north is somewhat uncertain . . . indeed, it causes me some concern. Should you wish to remain here until it improves you would be most welcome guests and I would be happy to offer you a substantial reduction in an already very competitive tariff.'

'Thank you, landlord,' Emily said. 'But what are the views of the coach driver?'

'Ah yes, the coach driver,' the hotel owner said unhappily. 'Well, of course, the coach carries the mail and the driver is penalised if he fails to deliver it to its destination on time. He will press on without regard for the safety of his passengers.'

'Does he believe he is able to deliver the mail on time to Blinman?'

'That is his belief, ma'am, but—'

'I will listen to no "buts", landlord. If the driver believes he can safely convey the mail to Blinman, then I have no doubt our safety is assured.'

'I hope your faith in the coachman will not prove to be misplaced, ma'am,' said the offended hotel keeper.

'So, too, do I,' Emily said. 'We have rather more to lose than you. Now, if you will prepare a bill, you may tell the coach driver we will be ready to board as soon as the coach is ready.'

III

When the stagecoach set off from Hawker, the four travellers from Kadina were its only passengers. There should have been one other, a carpet-bagger of Middle Eastern origins, who had been persuaded by the hotel keeper to spend a few days in Hawker until the weather improved in the mountains of the Flinders Ranges.

As the coach bumped and jolted along the road from Hawker and she viewed the heavily laden clouds through the windows, Emily wondered whether she should have followed her earlier instincts about the weather and not put her faith in the coach driver's forecast. She pushed aside any thought that her decision to go on might possibly have been influenced by her eagerness to meet up with Sam once more.

For a while, it seemed her misgivings were misplaced. The heavy dark clouds remained where they had been the previous day, touching only the tallest peaks of the serrated mountain range to the right of the dirt road.

Then, after they had made a final change of horses, the cloud began to lower alarmingly and the sky darkened as though night was imminent.

The wind increased too. Soon it was buffeting the coach in an uncomfortable fashion. Then a brief but fierce flurry of rain swept over the coach, beating against the windows on one side of the vehicle with the rapidity of a drummer's call to action on a man-o'-war.

When the shower had passed on, lightning began rending the dark clouds in its wake, frightening Tom. Suddenly, the coach came to an unexpected halt.

Opening a window on the more sheltered side of the coach, Emily leaned out and saw the driver donning a voluminous waterproof coat.

'Shouldn't we be seeking shelter somewhere until the storm passes over?' she called.

'I'm sorry, ma'am, but I've got mail on board. I'm subject to a stiff penalty if I get in late. Besides, there's nowhere to shelter a coach and horses between here and Blinman.'

'How long will it be before we arrive?' Emily queried.

'About an hour and a half, as long as none of the road has been washed away. Now, if you'll close the window and seat yourself, we'll get under way again.'

Moments later the coach jolted into motion and it seemed to Emily the driver was attempting to reach Blinman before the eye of the storm that was raging on the mountains swept down upon them.

If it *was* his intention to outrun the storm, his efforts were unsuccessful. They had been travelling for perhaps another half an hour, with the storm moving ever closer, when, preceded by a fierce wind, the rain returned – and suddenly the storm was raging all about them.

Tom cried out in fear as the coach driver fought to control his four terrified horses.

When the coachman had won his battle, he drove on, but they were travelling much slower now. A few minutes later the coach slowed to a crawl and began to tilt forward, as though negotiating a steep slope.

Suddenly it came to a halt and the occupants of the coach heard a new sound, this time it was of fiercely rushing water.

The coach door opened on the sheltered side of the vehicle and the driver leaned inside. He had lost his hat, his hair was plastered down against his head and face, and water poured off his sodden waterproof coat.

Shouting to make himself heard above the sounds of wind, rain and rushing water, he informed the passengers that they had just reached a creek that bisected the road on which they were travelling.

'It's usually dry,' he shouted. 'But it's carrying water from the mountains right now. It's not impossible to cross – yet, but it will be if we don't get across pretty quickly. You may have some water come inside the carriage. Just keep your feet up and you'll be all right.'

Before either woman had time to question the driver's wisdom in attempting to cross the flooded creek, the door was slammed shut.

A few minutes later the coach jerked into motion and the hazardous crossing commenced. The coach slewed sideways almost immediately and began shaking alarmingly, but it was not the wind causing the movement now, it was rushing water, the sound blending with the considerable noise of the storm raging all about them.

Suddenly the coach tilted to one side, throwing everyone off balance, before coming to an abrupt halt.

Above the noise of the elements, those inside the coach could hear the shouts of the coachman and the sharp crack of his whip.

The coach still shook alarmingly, but there was no forward movement now – then Emily became aware that water was covering the floor of the vehicle.

No sooner had she made this observation than the door was flung open. Above the noise of storm and rushing water, the driver shouted, 'Quick! Get out and make your way to the far bank! The stage is stuck and the creek is rising. A few more minutes and it's likely to be washed away.'

'We have two young boys with us—' Emily began, but the driver cut short her protest.

'Don't argue!' he bellowed. 'Get out of the creek, or you'll all drown ... Here, give me the younger boy.'

Reaching inside the carriage, the coach driver snatched Tom from Margaret. Without waiting to see if the others were following, he set out for the far bank of the creek, fighting his way through waist-high water.

After only a momentary hesitation, Emily caught

hold of Albert's hand. 'Take hold of your mother and follow me into the water.'

She stepped down from the coach, stumbled and would have been swept away had not Albert gripped her hand, holding on with all his strength. Moments later the young boy was also in the water, followed by his mother. They began fighting their way through water that threatened to carry them away with every step they took.

Twice Emily stumbled and on the second occasion was totally submerged, then the coach driver was hauling them from the raging water while they still clung tightly to each other's hands.

Water was streaming down from the road to the creek, but it no longer threatened to take them with it.

Pointing along the barely discernible road ahead, the coach driver shouted, 'Up there a little way . . . old shepherds' hut . . . falling down, but will give some shelter.'

'What about you?' Emily shouted back.

The coach driver pointed to the creek. 'My coach . . . the horses . . . the mail . . .'

Before Emily could argue that his intentions were suicidal, he had plunged back into the flooded creek and was floundering ponderously towards the stranded stagecoach. The storm had turned day into night and following his progress was difficult. In addition, the rain was falling with such force that it was painful.

Although concerned for the driver, Emily realised there were others to be considered. Margaret was holding Tom to her and, grasping Albert's hand, Emily shouted, 'We must try to find the shepherds' hut. Keep hold of me in case I get lost, Albert.'

As they were about to set off, Tom glanced back

towards the creek and cried, 'Look – the coach.'

His shout was barely audible above the noise of the storm. Looking back and shielding her eyes against the force of the rain, Emily was horrified to see the coach being swept away down the creek by the ever-rising waters.

'Oh, my God! What do we do now?' Quite as wet and bedraggled as Emily, although she had not been totally immersed in the waters of the creek, Margaret put the anguished question.

Calling on all her reserves of mental and physical strength, Emily said, 'We must get well away from here, before the water rises still more and reaches us. When we find the shepherds' hut – we pray. For ourselves, and for the driver.'

The coach driver had probably been trying to boost the spirits of his four passengers when he told them the shepherds' hut was 'up there a little way'.

Buffeted by wind and rain, they were staggering through the storm for more than half an hour before Albert squeezed her hand and shouted, 'What's that – over there?'

The storm had marginally eased and visibility had improved accordingly. Had it not done so it was doubtful they would have seen the hut. Set back from the road, it was almost hidden among a small copse of gum trees.

'Well done, Albert. You are more alert than any of us.'

Upon closer inspection, the hut was not at all prepossessing. The door was missing, the window was no more than a hole in the wall and a corner of the wood-shingle roof had broken away. However, when the four travellers from Kadina staggered inside the hut they were instantly sheltered from wind and rain.

Emily felt close to exhaustion. Thankfully, she sank to the dirt floor and Margaret followed her example, Tom immediately cuddling up to his mother.

It was now possible to talk without shouting above the noise of the storm and Margaret asked, 'What do we do now, Emily?'

'We sit out the storm, then set off for Blinman,' Emily declared, hoping her words conveyed more assurance than she felt.

'How far *is* it?' Margaret asked.

'I don't know,' Emily confessed. 'But we know it's somewhere along this road. If we carry on for long enough we will find it.'

IV

The storm raged for another two hours before the rains moved on, leaving behind thunder, rumbling away in the distance, and a dark, uncertain ceiling of cloud that hid the uneven heights of the Flinders Ranges.

As the two women stood outside the derelict shepherds' hut, with heavy drops of rain dripping from the trees about them, Margaret said, 'If we try to go now it's likely to be dark before we reach Blinman.'

'If we sit it out here all night we could experience another storm tomorrow. When we tried to move on then we would be colder, hungrier and more tired than we are now. I think we should set out and trust that we reach either Blinman or some other place before nightfall.'

'What if we don't?'

'Then we walk on through the night,' Emily said firmly. 'Do you agree, boys?'

'What about the coach – and the driver?' Albert asked.

'We will send men back to look for them,' Emily declared, not wishing to dwell upon the matter. 'Now, does anyone know a hymn that will set us marching along the road like soldiers? No? Then I will teach you one. It is called, "Onward, Christian Soldiers" and if you keep in step with the tune we will all be in Blinman before we know it . . .'

The four weary travellers were found by a rescue party comprised of five horsemen and a light cart – thoughtfully provided should there be corpses to be conveyed to Blinman. By this time 'Onward, Christian Soldiers' was indelibly imprinted upon the minds of the two boys and they had lost count of the number of times they had sung the chorus lines.

The light cart was immediately turned around to convey the four survivors to Blinman, preceded by a galloping horseman to alert the remote community of the fate that had befallen the mail-carrying stagecoach.

Meanwhile, the four remaining horsemen set off for the creek crossing, where the coach and horses had been swept away.

As a result of the advance warning carried by the horseman, the hotel keeper of the Blinman hotel and his staff were waiting with blankets and an assortment of clothing, donated by the sympathetic residents of the mining town.

As they were being helped down from the cart, one

of the first people Emily saw was a heavily pregnant Jean, standing with Ira and Primrose.

'Jean!' Ignoring her own dishevelled state, Emily called out to the woman she had helped years before when she was in a similar state of pregnancy as today.

Jean did not recognise her immediately. Even when she did, she believed she must be mistaken. 'It's not . . . Miss Boyce?'

'Of course it is.' Suddenly aware of the state she was in, Emily added wryly, 'I am not exactly as neat and tidy as one might expect the daughter of the late vicar of St Cleer to be, Jean, but we've been at the mercy of the elements. We are all very fortunate to be alive.'

'It *is* you, Miss Boyce. You poor woman – and Margaret, you too! What are you – no, this is not the time for questions. Let me help you inside – and find you something to wear. We knew two women and two boys were on the way here and in sore need of clothing, but we had no idea what sizes you were. If there is nothing suitable here I'll find some clothes for you from home.'

'Thank you,' Emily was touched by Jean's obvious concern. 'I would appreciate a hairbrush and some soap. When I feel like a woman again I would like to meet with Sam. I believe you and he are still great friends?'

'Sam? You mean Sam Hooper? He's not here any longer. When the mines shut down, Captain Wilf – Sam's uncle – offered to keep him on, but Sam persuaded the captain to take on my Ira in his place, him being a married man and me being pregnant. Sam left Blinman about three weeks ago.'

'Left?' Emily was stunned by the news and she looked at Jean, her expression a mixture of dismay and disbelief. 'Where has he gone?'

'I don't know exactly,' Jean said. 'He told Ira he'd had enough of copper mining. He said he was going to try his luck with gold. I believe he's gone to the gold-fields in the hills somewhere outside Adelaide.'

Later that night, in the privacy of her hotel room, Emily gave way to a rare bout of tears. The deep disappointment at hearing that Sam was no longer in Blinman, coming on top of the tragic and terrifying ordeal she and the others had suffered at the flooded creek, was just too much for her.

Jean had stayed with her for a while, and Emily believed she alone had realised just how upset she was that Sam had moved on from Blinman. Remembering the gift Emily had given to Sam on his departure from St Cleer, Jean had tried to cheer Emily by telling her how often Sam had spoken of home – and of Emily in particular.

Despite her unhappiness, exhaustion brought about by the events of the day meant that Emily swiftly dropped off into a deep sleep once she was in bed.

She was awakened soon after dawn the next morning by an insistent hammering on the door of her room. It took her some moments to realise where she was. Then she became aware of a voice calling her name.

'Miss Boyce! Miss Boyce – are you awake?'

'Yes . . . yes, I am awake. What is it?'

'Come outside, there's something you should see.'

'Come out? I am in bed!'

'Put something on quickly. You'll not want to miss this!'

Wondering what could be so important that it should

demand her urgent attention at this time of the morning, Emily took down a man's dressing-gown from a hook behind the door. The hotel keeper had placed it there the night before, explaining it had been left at the hotel by a gentleman guest who had come to Blinman to celebrate the marriage of his daughter to the then-manager of Moolooloo sheep station. It seemed he had arrived intoxicated and left Blinman in the same state, five days later.

The dressing-gown reached to the ground and Emily's hands failed to protrude from the sleeves, but it effectively hid all she wore beneath it.

Slipping on her shoes, which had not yet dried out from the soaking they had received the previous day, she went to the door and opened it to the excited hotel keeper.

'What is it?' she demanded.

'Come outside and see for yourself – quickly.'

Emily followed him outside and found Margaret and the two boys already on the porch.

Seeing her coming through the door, Margaret said, excitedly, 'Look, Emily. Look who's coming into Blinman.'

Following the direction of her pointing finger, Emily was astonished to see the stagecoach she had last seen floating away along the flooded creek. Perched on the driving seat was their coach driver, accompanied by one of the Blinman men who had gone out expecting to find his body.

Seeing the women and the boys, the driver gave them a cheery wave.

When he stopped the stage outside the hotel and climbed down from his high seat, Emily hurried

forward and gave him a warm hug and Margaret
followed suit.

'How did you escape from the flood?' Emily
demanded as the embarrassed coach driver gave Albert
and Tom a cheery smile. 'When we last saw the coach
it was being swept away. There was no sign of you!'

'I was clinging to the luggage rack, at the back of
the coach,' the driver explained. 'I'm not surprised you
never saw me, though. I was under water more often
than I was above it. We seemed to be swept down the
creek for miles before the coach grounded on a shallow stretch of floodwater. I was able to get to the horses
and led them and the coach clear of the creek. I found
a piece of higher ground and the water gradually went
down. That's all there was to it.'

'Not quite all,' said the Blinman man who had been
on the seat beside the driver. 'The place where Harry
here got the coach and the horses out was the only bit
of high ground for miles around. The flood waters
turned it into an island. We found him in the early
hours, but it wasn't until first light that the waters went
down far enough for us to risk bringing the coach back
to the road.'

'The horses were far too tired to do anything before
then,' said the coach driver. 'That reminds me, they've
earned their feed this trip. I'll unload your trunks,
ladies, then get the horses into the stables. I'll also need
to have the coach checked for any damage before it sets
off anywhere again.'

'We knew an hour or two ago that Harry and the
stage had been found safe and well,' explained the hotel
keeper. 'I didn't want to wake you then, but I thought
you'd want to be on hand to see him drive into Blinman.'

Indicating the dressing-gown that enveloped Emily from neck to feet, he added mischievously, 'You'll no doubt be relieved to have your own clothes to wear once more, but you're quite welcome to keep the dressing-gown. It will serve as a reminder of your eventful trip to Blinman.'

V

The headstone set upon Charlie's grave proclaimed to the world at large that it was in memory of 'Charles Wesley Minns, a loved husband and father'. It satisfied the Minns family that due respect had been paid to his memory.

While she was in Blinman, Emily was able to speak at some length with Captain Wilf Hooper, who remembered her as a small child in St Cleer, before he left Cornwall for South Australia.

The mine captain told her that Sam had spoken of her often and greatly valued the crucifix she had given to him as a farewell gift, commenting that it was very similar to the one she was wearing at that time.

He was obviously not aware the gift had been returned to her. It saddened Emily that Sam had felt it necessary to give the gift back to her. At the same time she was moved that others should be aware how much he had valued it.

The mine captain confirmed that Sam had left Blinman with the intention of trying his luck in the goldfields in the hills close to Adelaide.

'He could have stayed in Blinman and worked with me on mine maintenance,' Captain Wilf added, 'but it's not much of a life for a young man, especially when he sees everyone else leaving. It would have given him a living, but not much more. Besides, Sam became very restless during the last few weeks here, almost as though something had happened to unsettle him. Strange, really, it wasn't like Sam to let anything get to him in such a way.'

Emily did not flatter herself that Sam had changed his way of life because Margaret had told him she was to marry someone else, but it might have contributed to his feeling of restlessness. Just as news that he was *not* married had unsettled her.

Walking back from the mine, Emily decided she would pay a call on Ruth Askew at the bawdy house, which Margaret had pointed out to her on their visit to the cemetery the previous day.

Here, too, changes were in the air. Emily found Ruth and her companions packing their belongings in a somewhat lackadaisical manner.

Ruth greeted Emily enthusiastically, introducing her to the three prostitutes with whom she shared the cottage as 'the rich lady who was my neighbour in Kadina, the one I've told you about'.

Emily was successful in hiding her distaste for the untidy state of the cottage. Instead, referring to the trunks in the passageway inside the door, she said, 'It looks as though someone is leaving.'

'We all are,' Ruth replied, adding, 'The mine has shut down. With no miners left in Blinman there'll be no business for us. Before long the only men left here will be those with families who can't afford to move on, and them in the cemetery.'

'Where will you go?' Emily asked.

'To Adelaide.' The reply came from one of the other women. 'We won't need to rely on mining to earn a living there.'

Trying hard not to dwell upon the nature of the women's means of earning a living, Emily asked, 'Are you all going to Adelaide?'

'That's right,' came the reply. 'It won't be the same as working in a mining town, but we've got to go where the business is.'

When the speaker and her companions left the room, Emily asked Ruth, 'Why not give up this life, Ruth? Come back to Kadina with Margaret and I.'

'To do what?' Ruth queried bitterly. 'I can't see anyone falling over themselves to offer me respectable work, can you?'

'I would find something for you to do, Ruth. Work that would help you regain your self-respect.'

'Self-respect and money rarely go hand in hand for a woman like me, certainly not enough to live on,' Ruth retorted.

'You could give it a try,' Emily said. 'With my help you could succeed, I am certain of it.' When her plea brought no immediate response, Emily added, 'What is the alternative for you, Ruth? What happens when you lose your looks and you can no longer attract men?'

Meeting Emily's look, Ruth said defiantly, 'Then I'll move out to the goldfields. It's the end of the road for a "working woman" and conditions are as tough as anywhere in the world, but there's money to be made there. Big money – and gold-miners are not so particular as many other men.'

At that moment one of the women returned to the room and Emily said, 'You'll find me in Kadina if ever you need me, Ruth. You can contact me there at any time. What's more, if you run into any trouble while you are in Adelaide, contact the Bishop's chaplain. I will write to him as soon as I return to Kadina and ask him to give you whatever help he can if you go to him.'

Emily stood up and began to walk from the house, but suddenly turned back. 'Do you know a miner named Sam Hooper who was in Blinman until recently?'

Surprised at the question, Ruth replied, 'Yes, he's Captain Wilf's nephew – and the one who brought Margaret to the house when she arrived in Blinman looking for Charlie. Why do you ask?'

'I knew him in Cornwall,' Emily replied. 'We lived in the same village. I was hoping to meet up with him here, but I am told he has gone to the goldfields near Adelaide. If you happen to meet him, perhaps you will tell him I was asking after him.'

Ruth gave Emily a quizzical look. 'Sam Hooper and I don't frequent the same places, Miss Boyce. To the best of my knowledge, the only time he ever came to this house it was to bring Margaret here to see her husband.'

Uncomfortably aware that she was blushing, Emily said, 'I am not suggesting—'

'I know what you're *not* suggesting,' Ruth said. More kindly, she added, 'Sam Hooper was respected in Blinman. Folk looked up to him. I hope you find him. If I hear anything of him in or around Adelaide I'll get word to him that you've been asking after him.'

VI

When Emily, Margaret and the boys arrived back in Kadina it was mid-afternoon and Emily's deep disappointment that Sam had not been at Blinman had to be put to one side immediately as she found herself caught up in a matter that was both puzzling and disturbing.

A matter that involved Stefan Mintoff.

Three years before, by a monumental feat of ingenuity and endurance, a telegraph line linking Britain and the north of Australia had been extended from Darwin to Adelaide, a distance of three thousand, two hundred kilometres, across some of the most inhospitable country in the world.

Before long, many other towns had been linked to the system, Kadina being one of them.

Emily returned to find two telegraphed messages from London awaiting her. Both were from her uncle, Lord Boyce.

The first, dated the day she had left Kadina for Blinman, congratulated Emily on her betrothal to Stefan Mintoff, but added, somewhat ominously, 'What is known of your fiancé's background?'

The second telegraph, sent only three days after the first, was longer, but less congratulatory and its tone reflected alarm.

It read:

Mintoff raising money in the City for an unknown mining company, making much of Boyce connection and investment and own political future. Nothing known here of company, or political

prospects. Most urgent you confirm veracity of Mintoff's claims.
Percy Boyce.

The telegraph messages posed questions that needed to be answered as a matter of urgency. Her uncle had asked about Stefan Mintoff's background, but in truth Emily knew nothing of his life before Kadina. Neither, it seemed, did anyone else.

As Emily prepared to leave the house, Margaret came from the bedroom, where she had been putting away some of the clothes.

'You're not going out again now, Emily? I thought I would make something for us all to eat and drink as we haven't eaten since breakfast.'

'Something important has come up, Margaret ...' After only a moment's hesitation, she showed Margaret the two telegraph messages.

Reading them, Margaret looked up at Emily in bewilderment. 'What do they mean, Emily? What is happening?'

'I wish I knew. I am going to Stefan's store, to have a word with Andrew Stewart, his manager.'

Margaret shook her head in disbelief at what the messages implied. 'I have never liked Stefan, Emily, you know that, but I have never doubted his honesty, have you?'

'I gave him a thousand pounds to invest in his company, Margaret. It sounds as though he might be using that fact to convince others to do the same – but that's pure conjecture. I shall go to the store to see how much Andrew knows about him. He has been managing things for Stefan for a long time, he probably knows more about him than anyone else.'

Margaret was unhappy. 'I hope everything is as it should be, Emily. If it isn't I shall feel I'm largely to blame. Those telegraph messages have been here for almost two weeks. If we hadn't gone to Blinman you would have been able to reply to them straightaway.'

When Emily reached the store owned by Stefan, she found it closed and there did not appear to be anyone on the premises. Even more ominous, a handwritten sign on the door informed would-be customers that the store was closed 'until further notice'.

Now Emily was very concerned indeed. She needed to speak to Andrew Stewart, but had no idea where he lived. She decided to call at the rectory and have a chat with Arnold Weeks.

Here too she was frustrated. The incumbent was not at home. His wife, Jennifer, explained that he had been called to visit a dying parishioner in nearby Wallaroo.

The two women had always got along well and Jennifer invited Emily inside for a cup of tea, adding, 'I am sure Arnold will be sorry to have missed you. Did you want to see him about anything in particular? Perhaps I might be able to help.'

'Yes, Jennifer, it is possible you can. I returned from Blinman only today, to find I had two unexpected telegraph messages from my uncle in London. He asked a number of questions about Stefan – Stefan Mintoff. They are questions to which I should already know the answers, but I don't. I called at Stefan's store a short while ago with the intention of speaking with his manager, but found the store closed. Do you know what's happening, and where I might find Andrew Stewart?'

'Of course, you have been away from Kadina for a while. Oh dear! A great deal has happened, Emily – but before I say more, is it true that you and Stefan Mintoff are to be married when he returns from England?'

'He has asked me to marry him, but I have said neither "yes" nor "no", although it seems he has told my uncle and others that we are engaged to be married. I am very angry about it – and not a little concerned.'

Jennifer Weeks had been uncertain whether she should tell Emily all that had happened, and what was being rumoured about Stefan Mintoff. Now, hearing of Emily's concern, she decided she could not keep matters to herself.

'The reason the store closed in the first place was because the suppliers are owed a great deal of money and the bank refused to honour the cheques left with Andrew Stewart by Mintoff. They wouldn't even advance enough to pay the salaries of those who worked at the store. It seems the bank is owed a great deal of money too.'

Emily was appalled by what she had heard – puzzled too. 'But Stefan has such a grand house – and his lifestyle is hardly that of a man with money problems.'

'It seems the house is heavily mortgaged. As for his lifestyle . . . Mintoff is not the first man to live beyond his means.'

'What of his companies . . . his mining interests – and his political plans?'

Jennifer Weeks shook her head. 'I know nothing of them, Emily. Perhaps Arnold can tell you something about them, but I'm not expecting him back until late tonight. Would you like me to ask him to call on you tomorrow morning?'

Emily thought about it for a moment before saying, 'No, if you don't mind I will call here. We can talk with more privacy.'

'Of course, come as early as you like. I'll make certain Arnold doesn't go out before you call.'

'Oh, there is one more thing. Can you tell me where Andrew Stewart lives? I would like to speak to him, to see if he knows anything about Stefan's life before he came to Kadina.'

Jennifer had hoped Emily would not ask questions about Andrew Stewart. She would much rather it had been left to her husband to break the news, but she could not avoid the issue now.

'I'm afraid there is nothing to be learned from Andrew Stewart, Emily. The poor man hung himself at the back of the store the day after the bank refused to honour Stefan Mintoff's cheques. He's dead.'

VII

Emily was extremely upset to hear of the tragic death of Andrew Stewart, especially when she learned from Jennifer that the shop manager had a wife and young child.

Her distress was increased when she learned that on the strength of his employment as manager of Stefan Mintoff's store, Andrew Stewart had taken out a bank loan in order to purchase his home and some land adjacent to it. In addition, he had been persuaded by his employer to invest his life's savings in Mintoff's

company, with the expectation of a high return when
Mintoff returned with the money he claimed would be
invested by the London bankers.

Emily wanted to call at Stewart's home to offer her
condolences and more practical help to his widow, but
Jennifer advised her strongly against such a course of
action. She explained that feelings against Stefan
Mintoff were running very high at the moment – and
Emily was believed to be closely associated with him.

Reverend Arnold Weeks explained the feelings of the
residents of Kadina in more detail when Emily called
on him the following morning.

Speaking to her in the rectory study, across the width
of a desk that brought back uncomfortable memories
of the many distressing interviews she had had with
her father back in the St Cleer vicarage, Arnold Weeks
said, 'For some reason Stefan has never been popular
with the residents of Kadina. I don't know why.
Although he has always been most generous with his
time and money and supported projects beneficial to
the Church, he has never succeeded in winning the
support of the community.'

'Yet he was elected to be a Kadina councillor,' Emily
pointed out. 'People must have trusted him enough to
vote him into office.'

'Regrettably, the only emotion engendered by a local
election is apathy. By ensuring that votes were forthcoming from those who owed their living to him, Stefan
was assured of election. Now even they are coming out
against him. Indeed, since the tragic suicide of poor
Andrew Stewart there is not a single man or woman
in Kadina who has a good word to say for him.'

Increasingly ill at ease, the acting rector of Kadina fidgeted uncomfortably for a few moments before saying, 'Because of the present strength of feeling, everyone is anxious to distance themselves from any hint of sympathy for, or association with, Stefan Mintoff. I regret, my dear, that you are regarded as one of his closest friends.'

Emily said bitterly, 'I have lost a great deal more than most of the people here in Kadina. I entrusted Stefan with a thousand pounds of my money. I doubt very much whether I will ever see a single penny of it again.'

'I fully understand your position, Emily, and you have my full support. I am merely pointing out the beliefs of the public at large. Your name is inextricably linked with that of Stefan Mintoff. I have already heard from a number of prominent citizens who feel unable to support our various charitable programmes if you remain involved with them.'

Emily was both hurt and confused. 'But ... I don't understand. Why should I be held responsible for anything that Stefan has done? I have been more gullible than most of his victims. I gave him money for a company that probably does not even exist. He has made use of the name and high office of my uncle, Lord Boyce, in order to sell shares in the same bogus company. What is more, I have given serious consideration to his offer of marriage. Only the family of poor Andrew Stewart has suffered more!'

'Believe me, I am fully aware of all this, Emily. The people of Kadina will be too, in due course, but for now feelings against Stefan Mintoff are running so high that I fear some of the anger is likely to spill over and engulf you. Once started there would be no stopping it and all that has been gained for the community by your hard work would be irretrievably lost.'

Deeply unhappy, Emily asked, 'What do you suggest I should do?'

'I feel it would be better for everyone – you, me, the Church and the community – if you were to leave Kadina until this unfortunate affair runs its course and the truth becomes acceptable to all reasonable people.'

Emily shook her head unhappily. 'I came to South Australia to work among Cornish miners and their families. Men and women I understand. If I leave my work now I will have failed in my mission.'

'That is not so, Emily.' Arnold Weeks leaned forward across the desk. 'You have laid a strong foundation here for many societies and charitable organisations. Jennifer and I will ensure the work you have begun is carried on. Unfortunately, were you to remain in Kadina in the present atmosphere of anger against Stefan Mintoff, the societies would be boycotted and much of your hard work undone.'

When Emily began to protest, Arnold Weeks added quickly, 'I realise it is most unfair, Emily, but I assure you that things will return to normal once the anger has died down.'

'What do you propose I should do until that happens?'

'I think we may have found an alternative that you will find acceptable, Emily.'

'We? Are you talking of you and Jennifer?'

'No, Emily, someone rather more exalted. When things came to a head with the suicide of poor Andrew Stewart and the anger of the Kadina community showed itself, I realised you would be subjected to a great deal of unpleasantness, if not actual physical abuse. I wrote to acquaint Bishop Short with the situation. I made it quite clear that Mintoff had taken in the whole community – myself included – but, because they feel foolish, they are seeking someone to blame for their gullibility. The mood will pass, as such things do, but until it does it would prove to be very unpleasant for you if you were to remain here.'

'I can see sense in what you are saying,' Emily conceded. 'But what can I do until the anger dies down?'

'That question has been answered by Bishop Short himself.' Arnold Weeks picked up an envelope lying on the desk in front of him and opened it. 'This is his reply to my letter. He suggests you go to work for the Church in Adelaide. Indeed, he is eager to have you there. He says the city is experiencing a problem with "fallen women". He would like to encourage them to return to respectability and, perhaps, have the Church set up a home to help them. He feels you are just the person he is looking for to put his ideas into practice. How would you feel about it, Emily?'

Emily was still smarting at the thought of being forced to leave Kadina, but the idea did appeal to her. She had regretted not being able to do more to entice Ruth away from the life she was leading. Ruth was now in Adelaide, or on her way there. It could be another opportunity to help her – and the many others like her.

There was another consideration, which Emily tried not to allow to influence her decision.

Sam was somewhere in Adelaide . . .

'I think Bishop Short has offered me a very exciting challenge.'

7

I

Sam took a leisurely route to Adelaide, travelling first to Port Augusta with Piet van Roos. Along the way the South African reminisced about his own gold prospecting days in the hills outside Adelaide and lamented that he was not young enough to return there.

Sam left him with the advice that he should head for the Echunga goldfield and an area known as Jupiter Creek ringing in his ears. This, said the bullock driver, was where there was far more gold than had yet been dug from the ground.

From Port Augusta, Sam boarded the steamer *Pride of Wallaroo* for the journey to Adelaide, a city he had never visited.

Upon his arrival, Sam was immediately impressed by the sheer size and incredible bustle of South Australia's capital. It was like nothing he had seen before, even in Plymouth, the only place of comparable size he had ever visited.

Yet, despite the activity, there was a remarkable sense of order about Adelaide, the streets being laid out in a regular and orderly pattern.

Sam took lodgings at a small hotel in Flinders Street, an establishment recommended by Piet van Roos.

Quite apart from the name of the street – which would have appealed to anyone from Blinman – the hotel was frequented by miners and prospectors. According to Piet it was a suitable setting-off point for anyone wishing to mine in the hills around Adelaide.

Sam was made to feel at home as soon as he entered the hotel and was greeted by the desk clerk. The clerk had emigrated to Adelaide from Redruth in Cornwall. He booked Sam into a room with a balcony, from where he said it was possible to 'watch the whole of Adelaide pass by'.

Having ascertained that this was Sam's first visit to the capital city, the clerk suggested he take a walk along Hindley and Rundle Streets in order to see the shops and experience the busy streets illuminated by gaslight.

His clothes stowed safely in his room, Sam enjoyed an evening meal that made up in substance for what it lacked in presentation. By the time he had finished the meal, darkness had fallen over the city and Sam decided to act upon the clerk's suggestion that he view Adelaide's shopping area by night.

Obtaining simple directions from the clerk, he set off from the hotel, heading for Rundle Street. Arriving there he found himself in a new and fascinating world. There were more shops than he had ever seen before, stocked with everything that man, woman or child could conceivably desire, and it seemed to Sam that the entire population of Adelaide must be here in the thronged streets.

He was impressed too by the gaslights, their hissing blue flames adding greatly to the magic of the scene.

Sam spent well over an hour walking along the busy thoroughfare and gazing in awe at the amazing array of goods offered for sale.

Eventually, the effects of the long journey he had completed only that day began to tell on him, and he decided to return to his hotel.

He had almost arrived at his destination when he heard what sounded like a violent scuffle in a narrow alleyway alongside the building.

Stopping, Sam called out, 'What's going on? Are you all right?'

There was a momentary lull in the sound from the alleyway, then a man's voice called, 'Mind your own business and go on your way—'

He was interrupted by another voice, this time that of an older man. 'They're trying to rob me—'

The scuffling began again and, without further hesitation, Sam dived into the alleyway. The only light here came from the curtained windows of the hotel, but it was sufficient for him to see two men struggling with an ageing, grey-bearded man, who was desperately fighting to retain possession of a heavy bag.

As Sam reached the scene one of the younger men knocked the older man to the ground and snatched the bag.

'Stop him!' cried the old man. 'Get my swag!'

The young man carrying the bag tried to rush past Sam, who stuck out an arm, catching the thief across the throat. Thrown off balance, the thief crashed heavily to the ground.

The bag dropped from his hands and the old man promptly fell upon it, covering it with his body. Fists flew for a few more moments, but Sam's blows were landing with more effect than his opponents'. When he knocked down one of the assailants, the man scrambled to his feet and ran from the alleyway, closely followed by his companion.

'Are you all right?' Sam put the question as he helped the older man to his feet.

'I am, thanks to you. And do I detect a Cornish accent?'

'You do,' Sam said. 'Sam Hooper, from St Cleer. And you?'

'Abraham Gundry, originally from Redruth. My friends call me Abe.'

Suddenly the old man chuckled. 'We certainly showed them two larrikins what Cornishmen are made of.'

Sam did not argue the accuracy of the other man's account of the incident. Instead, he asked, 'Are you staying near here?'

Pointing to the hotel where Sam had a room, Abe said, 'I'll be staying right here. And you?'

'I've got a room here too. I arrived today from Blinman.'

'I'm on my way in from the Lofty Ranges to the east of Adelaide,' said Abe Gundry. 'I suspect these two have been following me for much of the day.'

'Why?' Sam asked. 'Why were they following you?'

'They thought an old man would be an easy target for 'em, but they picked on the wrong man. Long before

I'd reached their age I'd reckon it to be a poor day if I hadn't shot half a dozen better men than them before breakfast.' The old man caught the look Sam gave him and he added, 'No, I'm not mad, boy. I'm talking of the days in Texas when I was fighting for Sam Houston against old Santa Anna.'

'Sam Houston . . . ? Santa Anna . . . ?'

'In America . . . but it was before your time, boy. I went mining to Mexico when I was fifteen. But where are my manners? Come in to the hotel with me.'

Raising the bag to his shoulder, Abe said, 'When I've booked in and had what's in here put away in the hotel safe I'll buy you a drink or two. I reckon I owe you that.'

Once inside the hotel reception area, Sam was able to see that Abe Gundry was hardly dressed for the city. He looked as though he had come straight off a mining shift, having hand-brushed away any excess mud that might have been on his clothing.

The hotel was small and informal, but Sam doubted whether the desk clerk would give the old man a room.

To his surprise, the clerk greeted Abe effusively. 'Mr Gundry! Good to see you again, sir. Your usual room is free at the rear of the hotel. Do you have something for the safe? You have? I am pleased to know things are still going well for you.'

Abe Gundry produced a small but heavy sack that had been carefully stitched up in order to efficiently seal its contents. 'Weigh it before you put it away,' he said.

'Of course.'

Placing the sack on a set of scales sitting on the desk counter, the clerk added and subtracted weights until he was satisfied. 'There you are, thirty-three ounces. You *have* done well, sir.'

The clerk's admiration was genuine. Moments later he put the bag in the safe behind the desk and wrote out a receipt, which he handed to Abe Gundry.

Slinging his bag on to the counter, Abe said, 'Look after this for me, Clarence. I'm taking this young man for a drink. He stepped in when two young larrikins bundled me into the alleyway beside the hotel and tried to rob me.'

'What a *dreadful* thing to happen – and so close to the hotel! I should think you *do* owe Mr Hooper a couple of drinks. I shall report the matter to the manager. I have no doubt he will send a bottle of something special to Mr Hooper's room. We don't expect this sort of thing to happen to our guests – especially to our regulars like yourself, Mr Gundry.'

On the way to the hotel bar, Sam said to his companion, 'I take it that was gold you had put in the safe?'

'That's right. Gold enough to kill for – and I've seen men die for a whole lot less.'

When they reached the bar Abe ordered two cold beers. As the two men carried them to an empty table, he asked, 'Are you a mining man, Sam?'

When Sam confirmed that he was, Abe asked, 'Gold mining?'

'Just copper, so far – both here and in Cornwall. I've left Blinman because the mine there has stopped working.'

'Why come to Adelaide? There's no copper mining around here to speak of right now.'

'I've been bringing copper to grass since I was eleven and don't have a whole lot to show for it. I thought it was time I had a change. To see if I could make myself rich and not someone else.'

'You mean you want to go looking for gold? I'd have thought you'd be heading for Victoria. That's where most go who want to get rich quick.'

'I might go on there one day,' Sam said. 'But I was friendly with a bullock driver up at Blinman, a man named Piet van Roos. He said he'd made his money in the hills near here, so I thought I'd give it a try.'

'You know Piet van Roos? I thought he must have died years ago. Him and me were partners for a while and did a bit of prospecting together. He should have stayed with me. He wouldn't need to be tramping halfway across Australia beside a bullock cart if he had.'

'He enjoys the life,' Sam replied. 'He once told me that if he died in the outback on his own he'd leave this life a happy man.'

'I don't doubt he would,' said Abe. 'Hey, your pot's empty, I'll get another couple of beers.'

'No, I'll get these in,' Sam said. 'You've said "Thank you", now we'll drink together because we're two Cornishmen who have met on the far side of the world.'

While Sam was at the bar, waiting to be served, Abe watched him speculatively. When he returned to the table and both men had taken a swig from their newly replenished tankards, Abe asked, 'If you were to find enough gold to give you a decent stake, what would you do with it?'

'I've been thinking about that a lot just lately,' Sam replied. 'I suppose it would depend on how much I made. I'd like to send something to my family in St Cleer. My pa's a farmer and things are no better for Cornish farmers than they are for Cornish miners. It would be good to think he could take things a bit easier.'

'That's taken care of your family. What about yourself? Isn't there something you want to do? Someone you'd like to impress?'

Sam grimaced. 'There was a time when I had ideas way above my station in life, but that's behind me now. I used to enjoy working on the farm, back home. I quite like the idea of farming here – if ever I find land anything like that in Cornwall.'

'Have you been up in the Adelaide Hills yet and seen the country out towards Scott's Creek?'

'I've never been this way before. Why do you ask?'

'Some years ago I bought a piece of land out that way. A few hundred acres. I'm no farmer, but there *are* farms around there and they seem to be doing well. I'll be going back through there in a few days' time on my way to my claim. Come with me for a while. You can see at first hand what gold mining's all about and on the way I'll show you land that's like nothing you'll have seen around Blinman.'

II

'This is beautiful! It's wonderful!' Sam said excitedly. 'I haven't seen anything to match this since I left Cornwall – and there weren't too many places there that had better soil. A man could grow anything he wanted here.'

Abe had stayed in the Adelaide hotel for a full week. When he left, heading for the Lofty Ranges, he took Sam with him.

While Sam was extolling the breathtaking beauty of

the hill country, Abe's fingers had been linked together on the top of a gatepost. Now he rested his bearded chin upon them briefly before saying, 'Your father would be proud of you, Sam. You're a farmer at heart.' Pausing to look along the valley, from left to right, he added, 'Perhaps all Cornishmen are. I knew as soon as I saw this place that I wanted to own it.'

'You own this land? This is the place you brought me out to see?'

'The whole valley is mine, Sam, from the trees at the far end, to the creek below us – and up the hills on either side to beyond both ridges. Just about everything you can see belongs to me – and I paid cash for it.'

'You have an eye for scenery, as well as good land, Abe, but why are you still grubbing for gold when you could build yourself a grand house and live here in style, enjoying what you've earned?'

Scratching his grey, unkempt beard, Abe said, 'You know, I sometimes ask myself the very same question, but I haven't yet come up with an answer I can believe. I guess the truth is that I'm a bit like a mole. I've been prospecting for so long that I'd probably shrivel up and die if I had to spend all my life above ground. Now, we'll cook ourselves something to eat, spend the night here, then tomorrow go on to Jupiter Creek and I'll let you help me dig out some more gold.'

Jupiter Creek had been the scene of a gold rush some years before. When gold was discovered hundreds of men had descended upon the area and the slopes of the denuded hills all around were pitted with the results of their inexpert and largely fruitless labours.

The successful finds had been of alluvial gold,

washed down to the creek by countless centuries of rain. In a bid to find the source of the riches, men with little or no knowledge of gold-mining had spread over a vast area, scratching out shallow holes in a frenzy of activity, in the vain hope of discovering the source of the elusive mineral and making themselves an instant fortune.

Very few succeeded in finding anything worthwhile, but each minuscule success would send the hopeful prospectors scurrying to a new area to repeat the largely futile process all over again.

Gold *had* been found in workable quantities, but usually only by men with knowledge and patience. Eventually, as the finds became smaller and less frequent, the disappointed prospectors moved on, in pursuit of an elusive dream. When they had gone, nature took over once more, gradually hiding the scars they had left behind.

It was now that Abe Gundry appeared on the scene, but first he spent a great deal of time in the mining and assaying offices in Adelaide. After carefully checking their records he set out for Jupiter Creek, armed with a detailed map.

Studying the land and his map with great care, he began fossicking for the gold he was certain others had missed.

Within a week he had found what he was seeking. This was alluvial gold too, but it had been deposited many years before that found by others. It was deeper than the other prospectors had gone, richer too – much richer.

It was from this find that Abe had been making his money, quietly and unobtrusively, for more than a year.

Yet the prospector was still not fully satisfied. He believed the main source of the alluvial gold was not too far away. He was already making a great deal of money from his present workings, but it had become a matter of pride with him to find a lode that might profitably be mined on a grand scale.

Sam and Abe toiled through the scrub, following the course of what was once a deep creek but was now barely discernible. Suddenly they both heard the sound of spades striking rock.

'I thought you said you were the only one working here,' Sam said.

'That's right,' Abe replied. 'And I will be again very soon. Unless I'm mistaken that's *my* claim that's being worked – and without my say so.'

Abe turned off along another shallow depression until they came to an area where recent excavation had gone far deeper than most of the workings they had passed.

This was where the sound was coming from. Three men were digging with long-handled spades, while a fourth was operating a gold 'cradle', using water from a pool dug out of the creek bed with which to wash the gold-bearing gravel through a primitive separation system.

'What the hell do you think you're doing?' Confronting the diggers, Abe put the question to them angrily as he dumped his heavy bag on the ground.

The four men stopped work and looked at each other before one replied. 'We're digging for gold. What's it to you, old man?'

'You're working on my claim, that's what it is to me. If you want to dig for gold around here, that's fine, but you can do it somewhere else And before you go you can hand over any gold you've already taken out.'

Again there was an exchange of glances and the same spokesman said, 'No, old man, it's you who can find somewhere else to dig for gold. We're here and we're staying.'

'Then we'll make it a case for the police trooper over at Echunga,' Abe said. 'I'm sure he'll be interested in you. You'll no doubt be from one of the prison colonies. Did you serve out your time – or are you escapees?'

The odds were four to two, with one of the two being an old man, and Sam believed the four men were probably quite as tough as they appeared to be. 'Come on, Abe, let's go and find a trooper. We'll let him sort this out.'

'Wait! If you have a licence to work this claim, show it to me.' It was more of a command than a request from the spokesman for the illegal prospectors.

'Do you think I'm foolish enough to let you get your thieving hands on it? I'll show it to the trooper and to no one else.'

'First you have to get to Echunga. That might not be so easy, old man. It's a very long way. I think you should find the licence for me – and quickly.'

The spokesman gave his companions a brief nod. Downing their spades two of the men closed in on Abe, the others, led by the man who had been operating the cradle, moved towards Sam.

'Now, just wait a minute . . .' Sam made a half-hearted attempt to reason with the two men advancing on him, knowing full well it would be fruitless. He was ready when the first of them rushed at him. Slipping easily beneath the man's outstretched arm,

Sam dived towards a long-handled shovel that had been resting against the cradle.

He straightened up with the shovel in his hand in time to strike the second man a resounding blow across the face with the flat of the spade blade, knocking him backwards into the creek.

Swinging the spade back again in a pendulum motion, he struck his first assailant on the head as he was about to rise to his feet.

The other two men temporarily turned their attention from Abe. Picking up the spades they had dropped before taking on the old man, they rushed at Sam.

He succeeded in parrying the blow from the first assailant and almost did the same with the second, but the spade bounced up and caught him on the side of his face.

It was fortunate it was the flat of the spade that hit Sam, or it would have sliced his face open. As it was, it caused an explosion of light in his head. He dropped to one knee, the spade he was holding falling from his grasp.

The man raised his spade to strike what would undoubtedly have been a mortal blow when the loud sound of a shot caused Sam's assailant to stop in his tracks.

Gathering his senses, Sam saw Abe sitting beside his open swag, smoke gently trickling from the barrel of a handgun in his hand.

'Hit him!' The self-appointed spokesman for the illegal prospectors shouted at his colleague. 'The gun's been fired now—'

Before he could say any more Abe fired again and the speaker was knocked backwards. The smoking barrel of the revolver now pointed towards the man with the raised spade and Abe said, 'Throw it to the ground. Now!'

The frightened man immediately did as he was told. Abe then used the gun he was holding to motion the man towards the other two prospectors, who stood with their hands held shoulder-high.

Abe patted the gun and said to Sam, 'It's a six-shot Army Colt. I fought in the American civil war, as well as in Texas. First time I've needed to use it since then, but I don't seem to have lost my touch. Are you all right?'

Sam worked his jaw from side to side. It hurt, but he doubted whether anything was broken. 'I'll live.' Nodding towards the wounded man, who lay in the mud of the creek bottom, moaning, he added, 'I'm not so sure about him.'

Abe climbed to his feet and walked over to the man he had shot, keeping the revolver pointed in the direction of the other three men.

Looking down at his victim, he said, 'He's lost a bit of blood, but he'll probably be all right. I aimed to shoot him in the shoulder. It's a bit lower than I intended, but I've seen men pull through when they've been hurt a whole lot more.'

To the three men who still stood with their hands held in the air, he said, 'Take him away. Well away. If I ever see any of you near Jupiter Creek again I'll shoot you dead, is that understood?'

'What do we do with him?' One of the men lowered a hand long enough to point towards their wounded companion. 'He needs a doctor.'

'Then find one for him,' Abe said callously. 'But make

it a long way from here. When you've gone we'll be heading to Echunga to tell the troopers what's happened. No doubt they'll come looking for you. Whether or not you want them to find you is up to you. Now, take him away – but leave everything else.'

One of the men seemed inclined to argue, but a slight shift in the aim of the revolver effectively silenced him. Making for their wounded companion, the three men lifted him to his feet. Ignoring his screams of pain they dragged him away, along the creek.

When they had passed out of sight, Abe said to Sam, 'You're a sight quicker than me. Climb to the top of the hill there. Make sure they keep going without stopping. Don't let 'em see you but don't come down until you're certain they're not likely to turn back.'

'Will we go to Echunga and tell the police then?'

Abe shook his head. 'No need. We've sorted out our troubles in our own way. That's the way things are done out here. It's easier for everyone concerned, including those four. They're no doubt all wanted men. Hurry up now, go and make sure they're not likely to come back.'

When Sam returned from the hilltop to report that the four would-be claim-jumpers had seemed in an almighty hurry to get as far from the Jupiter Creek gold diggings as they could, he found Abe calmly brewing tea on a wood fire as though nothing untoward had taken place.

'How's that face?' Abe asked. 'You're going to have a nasty bruise. Sit yourself down and I'll pour you a mug of tea.' Nodding towards the few belongings the four men had left behind, he said, 'There's a few ounces of gold among that lot that should help ease the pain a little.'

'Are we going to share it?' Sam asked. They had not discussed how any gold they found would be apportioned. They had not even talked of Sam helping Abe work his claim.

'Of course we are, that's the way partners usually work.'

When Sam stared at him, wondering if he had heard him correctly, Abe said matter of factly, 'Oh, didn't I tell you? It must have slipped my mind. When I was in Adelaide I called in to the Gold Commissioner's office. Had your name added to the licences I took out on the claim. We're legal partners now.'

III

Sam had very little sleep that night.

It was not entirely due to the possibility that the three able claim-jumpers might return and try to retrieve the gold Abe had forced them to leave behind. His mind was also filled with the implications of what becoming the partner of a successful gold prospector would mean to him.

It had already made him considerably richer. The work of the claim-jumpers had yielded at least four ounces of gold. Abe believed they had hit upon a rich pocket, with more gold to be taken out.

Abe also told him that in addition to having him made an official partner on the claim licence he had taken out licences on a whole section of the creek they would be working.

The reason for this was that one of the assayers in Adelaide had warned him that a large mining company had been to the Assay Office to carry out a similar search to the one Abe had made prior to taking out a licence on the successful Jupiter Creek claim.

'We don't want no big company coming in and benefiting from the work we've already done,' declared Abe. 'I thought we'd best get in ahead of 'em and stake a claim for ourselves, just to keep 'em out.'

Sam was already aware that Abe was not only a very successful prospector, but a shrewd businessman as well. If they were able to enjoy a few trouble-free months working on their claim, Sam's dream of owning land in the Adelaide Hills could become a reality.

He marvelled at how much his life had changed in little more than a week – and all because two young men had tried to rob an old man in an Adelaide alleyway.

'What's the matter, boy, you having trouble sleeping?'

Sam had not thought he was being particularly restless, but it seemed he had succeeded in disturbing Abe, who was wrapped up in a blanket on the far side of the dying campfire.

'What is it? You worried them claim-jumpers might come back? Would you rather my revolver was tucked in your belt instead of mine?'

Sam grinned in the darkness. 'No, Abe, you can handle it a sight better than me. Anyway, I don't think they'll be back. They've learned it's not a good idea to try to rob helpless old prospectors like you.'

'Then if it's not them, what *is* coming between you and sleep?'

'I started thinking how well I was doing out of the misdeeds of others. The two in the alley in Adelaide got me a partner, now the four we've met up with today have given me enough to buy the first few acres of a piece of land like yours.'

'Is that what you're going to do with the money you make from the claim?' Abe asked.

'That's right – and send enough home so that my pa can come out here if he wants to and see what really good land looks like. Perhaps by then I might have a house built there, one large enough for the whole family. Do you have any idea what sort of house you'll build on your land one day, Abe?'

'I've known from the first time I set eyes on the land,' Abe replied, speaking more quietly than was usual for him. 'It'll be just like the house once owned by my wife's family in California.'

In the darkness, Sam sat up, intuitively aware that Abe's revelation was not one he was in the habit of sharing with others.

'You're married, Abe?'

'I was, for all too short a time. I had a child too. A daughter.'

'What happened to them?'

'It's a long story, boy, and I don't intend spending the night telling all the details, but when I was a whole lot younger than you are now, I went out from Cornwall with some others to work in the silver mines in Mexico. I was quick to learn the language and grew to like the people, although I wasn't very taken with the men who governed them. Things eventually became so bad I left the mines and made my way to Texas.

'I arrived there just as Santa Anna, the Mexican president, and Sam Houston met head on. Seeing as I was there, I felt I should join in, so I became part of Houston's army.

'We won the war, but one government's as bad as another, so I headed out west and ended up in California. That's where I first started prospecting. I met a girl there too.'

Once started it seemed that Abe *wanted* to speak of his earlier days. It was more than Sam had ever heard him say at one time.

'California belonged to Mexico in those days and she was the daughter of a Mexican landowner,' Abe continued. 'He didn't think much of me at first, but Rosalia and me were married anyway. Little over a year later we had a daughter and life was pretty good.

'Then another war came along. I didn't get too involved in this one, but Rosalia's pa did and by the time the war was over he'd lost everything. We hung on to a small piece of his land for a couple of years, then there was a gold find not too far away and I was one of the first to join in the rush to have a share of it.'

Quieter now, he said, 'I found gold all right – but I lost just about everything else.'

Abe was silent for so long that Sam had to prompt him. 'What happened?'

'I got back home and found that Rosalia and the little 'un had died. An epidemic that took off more than half the Mexicans in that part of California. Funny, though, it didn't touch any of the Americans who'd moved into the area.

'I didn't care very much about things after that. I went back up in the hills prospecting for a while, found more gold – and managed to lose it all again, one way or another. Then, as there weren't enough Mexicans left for them to fight in the United States, the Americans decided to fight each other.

'I met up with a general who'd fought alongside me in Houston's army and before I knew it I was an officer in the army of the North. Because I'd been a miner and knew something of explosives and shoring up tunnels, I spent most of the war either blowing things up or putting them together again – although I did get involved in a bit of shooting now and then.

'When the war ended I thought I'd head back to Cornwall, but I found one of us had changed too much during the time I'd been away. We didn't suit each other any more so, like you, I came out here to South Australia, first to Wallaroo, then to the Flinders Ranges. The trouble was I'd got out of the habit of working for others, so I turned to prospecting again – and here I am.'

Sam had listened, enthralled, to the abbreviated story of Abe's life. However, he was aware the older man had left out far more than he had revealed.

'You've led a very adventurous life, Abe – and had more than your share of bad luck.'

'I wouldn't argue with that, boy, but I've known good times too. More than most men I've met with. Because of that I take issue with something you said to me in the bar of the hotel back in Adelaide when we'd just met. You said there'd been a time in your life when you'd had ideas "above your station". There's no such thing as having a "station" in life. I've worked with men who've been thought of as being so low that folk would cross the street rather than have to walk close to 'em, yet they've been men as fine as any I've ever met. Then there've been presidents like the Mexican Santa Anna. I was with him for nigh on a month when we took him prisoner and I wouldn't trust him any more than I would those four we saw off today. A good man is a good man, and a bad man is – just bad.'

Part of the fire collapsed inwards and for a few seconds a flame rose high enough for Sam to see Abe's bearded face above the blanket he had wrapped around himself. Then the old man was talking once more.

'When a man talks about having "ideas above his station", it usually means there's a woman involved in his thinking. Well, I had designs on a woman whose family had high-faluting titles in Spain going back hundreds of years. We got married and our years together were the happiest of my life – of both our lives. If there's someone you feel strongly enough about then you should go ahead and tell her. Let *her* make up her mind about it. Most women with anything about 'em can tell the worth of a man – whatever his so-called station in life.'

The flame had died now and in the darkness Sam heard Abe turn over. With his face turned away now, the old prospector said, 'There, I've finished telling you a bedtime story now, so just get off to sleep. We've got work to do tomorrow if you want to dig out enough gold to buy your land and build a house and a future on it.'

IV

The promise of Sam's first few days on the Jupiter Creek diggings with Abe were not entirely fulfilled. Nevertheless, by the end of three weeks they had gathered sufficient gold to make a trip to Adelaide advisable and this was a routine they maintained for four months. They would work for three weeks, then take the gold they had unearthed to Adelaide, remaining there for about a week.

Sam was delighted with the amount of money accumulating for him in the Adelaide Bank. It was more than he had ever dreamed of possessing.

He was happy to be working with Abe as his partner and learned a great deal from the older man about the art of prospecting. Sam had also grown very fond of the old man. He was tough without being aggressive and the toughness belied a streak of gentleness that occasionally showed in his dealings with the various animals that found their way to the remote camp.

The two men had one brief worrying occasion when prospectors from the Southern Goldmining Company arrived at the diggings. This was the company Abe had been warned about by the assayor in Adelaide.

Fortunately, it turned out to be a reputable company. Although extremely interested in what Abe and Sam were doing, the visitors acknowledged the men's prior claim to the area around their diggings and did not interfere with their work. Instead, they invited the two men to share a meal with them at their camp and left them with some welcome provisions when they moved on.

Nevertheless, Abe was unsettled by the visit. 'The fact that they were here at all means word has got around that we're doing well. The company will try to keep it quiet, of course. They won't want men swarming all over the place taking out licences for land they hope to work, but sooner or later we're going to be overrun with folk hoping to make their fortunes in just a few days – and many of 'em won't be fussy about the way they do it.'

'But we've got a legal claim to this whole stretch of the creek. Surely it won't affect us that much?'

'You haven't seen men – hundreds, perhaps *thousands* of men – when gold fever's got into 'em. I've seen fights to the death over whether a strip of earth no wider than a young girl's ribbon belongs to this claim or that one. Although this is our claim, we can't guard it twenty-four hours a day, every day of the week. They'll all know we're taking out gold – and gold is what they want.'

'What are you saying, that we should pack up and go if they move in?'

'No, boy, I've never been a quitter, but I think we should make our plans. I suggest we work ourselves fit to bust for as long as we can, then offer to sell out to this Southern Goldmining Company. The more gold we can take out between now and then, the more we can ask from them.'

'Then what will we do, Abe, you and me?'

Abe did not allow Sam to see how pleased he was that the younger man had not suggested they would go their separate ways if they were forced to leave the Jupiter Creek diggings.

'Let's cross that bridge when we come to it. In the meantime, let's see what we find if we extend our digging out to the north a little. I have a hunch it'll be a move in the right direction.'

On their next trip to Adelaide, Sam and Abe were carrying almost double the amount of gold they usually took to the city, as a result of working even longer hours than before.

On the way they called at Abe's landholding,

adjoining Scott's Creek. It was not the best of days to view land, although Sam still thought it incredibly beautiful.

There was an impressive build-up of storm clouds over the whole area and they had decided they would not remain in the valley for too long.

As they stood looking at Abe's property, Sam asked, 'Where will you build your house when the time comes, Abe?'

Without hesitation, the older man replied, 'Over there, to the right of those blue-gums, halfway up the slope. There's a natural level platform that's an ideal site for a house. It's protected from the winds, yet makes the most of the view. Where would you put a house, if you was me?'

'In exactly the same place,' Sam said honestly. 'The spot has everything. But I think we should be moving on now. Judging by the look of those clouds there's a whole lot of rain up there and it's not going to be long in coming.'

'I reckon you're right, boy. It'll be on us long before we reach Adelaide.'

Abe's forecast was uncomfortably accurate. The two men had been walking from Abe's valley for no more than twenty minutes when the deluge began. It was accompanied by thunder and lightning, making it too dangerous to take shelter beneath a tree.

For perhaps fifteen minutes they battled on through the downpour, buffeted by rain and wind and unable to see more than a few paces ahead. Then, fortuitously, Sam made out the outline of a building ahead of them. It was a smithy, standing beside a flooded crossroads.

Pulling open the door, both men stumbled inside and found at least fifteen men already in there, also sheltering from the storm.

Most had sought shelter before the storm broke and there were murmurs of sympathy for the two sodden newcomers.

'Here, there's room by the forge for the pair of you,' said the blacksmith. 'But keep away from my tools. There's enough water coming off you to turn them rusty.'

Space was made for the two newcomers beside the forge and as their clothes began to steam, Sam said, 'Shouldn't you change out of those wet things, Abe? It can't be healthy having them dry on you like they are.'

Abe grinned at him. 'The clothes in my swag are just as wet as these I'm wearing. What do you suggest I do, stand here with nothing on while they dry?'

Pipe in mouth, Abe was contentedly breathing out smoke to mingle with the steam. 'I've been as wet as this before, boy, and had nowhere warm like this to dry me off. There have been times when I stayed wet for days on end. By the time we set off again today I'll be near enough dry right through.'

'Wouldn't it be just as well to stay here for the night?' Sam suggested.

Abe took the pipe from his mouth and shook his head. 'I've got my heart set on a whisky or two, followed by a night in a comfortable bed. Besides, if we waited until morning it would most probably be raining again.'

Knocking out his pipe in the forge, he added, 'As a matter of fact it looks as though the storm is moving on. A few more minutes and we'll make a move.'

Soon most of the men inside the smithy began leaving. Darkness was falling and they wanted to reach their destinations while it was still light enough to negotiate flooded creeks. It was not long before Sam and Abe followed their example.

It took them three and a half hours to reach the Adelaide hotel. By the time they arrived the temperature had plummeted to depths Sam had not experienced before in South Australia.

Although his outer clothing had dried off to a great extent, that against his skin was still wet. When they stood in the hotel entrance hall he was so cold he could barely return the reception clerk's friendly greeting.

Sam saw that, despite his earlier bravado, Abe was shivering too, and he was concerned for him. He was relieved when Abe declared his intention of taking a bottle of whisky to his room, getting out of his damp clothes and enjoying a drink in the warmth of the hotel bed.

By the following morning Sam felt better, especially when a maid came to his room with his clothes, which had been dried for him overnight. However, he became concerned for his friend when Abe did not appear for breakfast.

As soon as he had eaten, Sam made his way to the room occupied by his partner. He found Abe sitting in a chair, still not fully dressed. The old prospector appeared older and more frail than Sam had ever seen him.

Thoroughly alarmed, Sam asked, 'Are you not feeling well, Abe? Is there something I can get for you?'

'No, I'm all right, boy,' Abe lied. 'A bit stiff after all

the walking we did yesterday, that's all.'

He had hardly finished talking when he began coughing, giving the lie to his statement. It was a cough that had him fighting for breath for a few minutes.

Sam was extremely anxious, but Abe waved his fears aside. 'Don't fuss over me, boy. Go off and take our gold down to the Assay Office. By the time you get back I'll be as right as rain.'

The Assay Office was only a short distance away and Sam was waiting for the staff when they arrived to open up. His business completed, Sam stopped off on his way back to the hotel to buy some of Abe's favourite tobacco for the old man.

However, when he went to Abe's room, Sam was concerned to find that his partner had not improved and was coughing more than before. His breathing too was increasingly laboured and Sam insisted, 'I'm not happy with the way you are, Abe. I'm going to get a doctor to come and take a look at you.'

'I don't want no doctor touching me!' Abe's outburst brought on another bout of painful coughing. When it had passed, he said, with less vehemence, 'The only time in my life I've ever seen a doctor was in Texas. He'd have taken off my arm if I'd let him, just because it had a bullet lodged in it. I had a horse-doctor dig it out for me and a week or two later I'd forgotten all about it.'

'Well, if I can't find the right man for you I'll fetch a horse-doctor instead,' Sam said. 'But I'm going to get one or the other in to listen to that chest.'

Wheezing painfully, Abe conceded defeat. 'All right, boy, I'll go along with you because I know you mean well, but if I don't like what he says I'll likely throw

him right out of the room. You make sure he understands that.'

The doctor's surgery was close to the hotel, but by the
time a doctor arrived to examine Abe, the old man was
in no condition to throw anyone from his room. The
pain in his chest was worse and his breathing was
increasingly laboured.

Only a cursory examination was necessary in order
for the doctor to make a rapid diagnosis.

'He's got pneumonia,' he told Sam, removing the
stethoscope from his ears. 'And he's got it bad. I'd say
it's certainly as a result of the soaking you said he got
yesterday. He needs to go into hospital immediately.'

'I don't want to go into no hospital,' Abe protested
breathlessly.

Sam looked at the doctor questioningly and the
medical man shrugged. The doctor walked to the door,
followed closely by Sam, and confided in a low voice,
'I don't guarantee that we can save him, even if he goes
to hospital, but *unless* he does there is no hope for him
at all.'

Sam needed to consider the doctor's words for only
a moment. 'All right, doctor, you make arrangements
to have him taken in right away. I'll make sure he's
ready.'

Abe was on his way to hospital less than half an hour
later. Sam accompanied him in the ambulance carriage
and realised by the swift manner in which the sick man
was dealt with once they arrived that he *was* seriously
ill.

Despite his protestations, Abe realised it too. When

Sam made a return visit to the hospital that afternoon, Abe handed him an envelope.

'What's this?' Sam asked.

'It's my will, boy, all signed up and witnessed by two of the doctors. It's not that I intend dying, because I don't, but as I told them, I thought I'd better get it done because I don't trust them not to make mistakes.'

Because of the will he carried, unopened, in his pocket and the poor condition of his friend and partner, Sam was feeling very depressed when he left the hospital; he was lost in thought and not looking at anyone he passed along the way. It therefore came as a great surprise to him when a voice suddenly called his name.

'Sam! Sam Hooper! It is you, isn't it?'

Coming to a halt, Sam turned to face the speaker. It was Margaret Minns.

8

I

When Emily was obliged to leave Kadina, Margaret decided she and the boys would go with her.

Emily protested that it was not necessary for the small family to disrupt their lives because of her problems, but Margaret reminded Emily that they had already decided they would most probably return to Cornwall and the passage home would be easier to arrange from Adelaide. The family was finding it difficult to settle in Kadina because of the uncertainty in the copper-mining industry, and it would be even more difficult now Charlie was dead.

In addition, although Margaret would never say so to Emily, because of their close relationship with her, the boys were already being targeted by malicious neighbours.

The party arrived at Port Adelaide by steamship, then travelled to South Australia's capital city on a train that was more sophisticated than the one that connected Wallaroo with Kadina.

Once in Adelaide, Emily and her companions went first to the bishop's office. It was here Emily received the first intimation that she could no longer expect the welcome previously extended to her as the niece of a minister of the Crown.

Because of the possibility that she might become involved in a scandal, all those who held a position of authority were most anxious not to be considered closely associated with her. The bishop himself was 'not available', and it seemed most of the senior cathedral clergy had pressing engagements they were unable to break. It was left to a comparatively junior clergyman to welcome her to Adelaide and escort her to a house that had been rented on her behalf.

Although the house was in an area somewhat superior to that where Emily had first lived in Kadina, it was a considerable distance from the bishop's palace and the homes occupied by the scions of Adelaide society.

If Emily was aware of the downgrading of her social status, she certainly did not allow it to show.

'What a delightful house!' she exclaimed to the distinctly embarrassed clergyman. 'We will be very comfortable here, will we not, Margaret?'

The house was small and because it had only two bedrooms, one of the living rooms would need to be adapted to accommodate the two boys.

Aware of the house's shortcomings, the young clergyman said, 'I don't think His Grace expected you to be accompanied by a companion ... and two children.'

'Had His Grace enquired about my requirements, I would have been happy to acquaint him with them,'

Emily replied, smiling sweetly at the young churchman. 'Now, where are Adelaide's bawdy houses?'

Her question was so unexpected it left the young clergyman speechless for some moments. When he had recovered sufficiently to reply, he stammered, 'I ... I am sure I don't know, Miss Boyce.'

'Come now,' said Emily, 'I was asked here to take on the task of saving "fallen women". Surely His Grace is not the only man in the Church who knows the whereabouts of Adelaide's bawdy houses? I would hate to cause him embarrassment by having to put such a question to him.'

'I think ... I have heard that Knox Street has a certain reputation – as have the taverns in Hindley Street,' said the red-faced clergyman. 'But I wouldn't know for certain. Our duties rarely take us there.'

'Then they should,' Emily said firmly. 'The women – and the men too – in such areas are those most in need of the Church's help and guidance. You must accompany me there some time.'

When he felt the two women and Albert and Tom were sufficiently settled, the young clergyman said a relieved farewell and hurried away.

'You gave him a hard time,' Margaret chided Emily. 'I don't suppose he has ever met a woman quite like you before.'

'That matters very little,' Emily declared. 'What is so sad is that he has apparently never met any women of the sort I am here to help. It isn't the type of priest I expected to find in a young, vibrant country like this.'

'Well, *you're* here now,' declared Margaret. 'I have no doubt you'll soon sort things out.'

* * *

Emily set about 'sorting things out' the very next day. Her first call was to the police headquarters to inform a slightly bemused police commissioner that she would be working among the prostitutes of the city in a bid to save their souls – and their bodies too, if these were not beyond redemption.

Over the next weeks Emily found the prostitutes to be almost as bemused as the police chief by her presence among them.

Initially Emily faced resentment from some of the older women when they realised she was trying to persuade them to give up their way of life. Consequently they went out of their way to shock her. However, they soon discovered that Emily did not shock easily.

Gradually they learned to accept her and soon discovered she was someone they were able to talk to, someone outside of their immediate and necessarily narrow circle of friends with whom they could discuss their problems in the knowledge that whatever was said would remain confidential.

Emily was soon able to claim that the rapport she had built up with the prostitutes had borne fruit. One of the older women actually came to Emily's home to tell her about a young girl who had arrived in Knox Street only the previous day.

'I spoke to her last night,' said the woman. 'She's run away from home with an older man. He wants her to go on the streets to earn money for them both. I doubt if she's more than sixteen. She's so confused about what's happening in her life that before she knows it she'll be one of us – except that she'll be keeping a ponce as well as herself.'

'The only way I can do anything for this girl is to have her and her "ponce", as you call him, arrested,' said Emily, after giving the matter some thought. 'She's probably so infatuated with him that if I try to persuade her to leave him and go home they'll both run off somewhere else. I'll have a word with the police first and after the arrest do my best to persuade this girl to go home. Do you think she might?'

Now it was the prostitute's turn to be thoughtful. Eventually, she said, 'I think she will, once you've got her away from his influence.'

'Good.' Emily was grateful for her information, but she wondered what had prompted this woman, whom she recognised as one of the oldest and most hardened of the prostitutes, to come to her.

When she asked the question, the woman was at first reluctant to explain. When Emily persisted, she said, 'I have a daughter of my own. I had her before I took to the streets. I wasn't married and it brought such shame on my family that I ran away, leaving my baby behind. I know she will have been properly looked after, but I often think of her. She'd be about the same age as that young girl.'

After a meeting with a senior policeman at the main Adelaide police station, a raid was carried out on the house where the girl and the man were staying.

The man remained in custody while the girl stayed with Emily and Margaret for two nights, during which time both women had many talks with her.

Emily then accompanied the girl to her farmhouse home, a few hours' journey from Adelaide. Here she met the girl's parents, who were so relieved to have their daughter back that they would have forgiven her anything.

It was possible that Emily had other successes too. At least three of the younger women with whom she spoke at length left the Knox Street area without telling anyone where they were going and Emily liked to think her talk with them had persuaded them to leave Adelaide and return to a respectable life.

Some of the prostitutes had children and Emily claimed another small victory when she persuaded the women to allow their offspring to attend Sunday school classes. She realised it was too much to ask that they attend a church for the lessons, so they took place in an empty house in the street.

Some of her other efforts were less successful. Her attempts to organise various social events to interest the women were well intentioned but failed dismally.

Nevertheless, Emily persisted with her efforts to help the city's 'fallen women' in any way she could and gradually their confidence in and respect for her grew. She still had the support of Margaret, who was not yet certain that she really wanted to return to Cornwall.

One Sunday, after Emily had been in Adelaide for some months, she had dismissed the children from the afternoon school and was locking the front door of the empty house, when she was approached by a young woman whom she recognised but she could not remember from where.

The woman was the first to speak and it was immediately apparent that she knew Emily.

'Hello, Miss Boyce, may I speak to you?'

'Of course, but do I not know you from somewhere?'

'We met at Blinman where I shared a house with Ruth. You called in to see her when we were getting ready to move.'

'I knew we had met before. Are you still with Ruth? How is she? I was rather surprised not to have found her here when I arrived in Adelaide.'

'We decided we would go to Port Adelaide, close to the docks. Ruth is there right now, but she's very sick, that's why I've come here to find you, to see if you can help her.'

'What is wrong with her?' Emily's tone was urgent.

The prostitute hesitated for a few moments before saying, 'Most of the men we meet at Port Adelaide are seamen, from all over the world. Some of them can be a bit rough after they've been drinking. Ruth, me and some of the other girls were in one of the beerhouses close to the docks a couple of nights ago when we picked up with a few of the seamen off a foreign ship. The blokes me and the other girls were with were happy enough to drink half the night away, but Ruth's man went back with her to our house early on. By the time I got back there it must have been after midnight. The house was in darkness, but as I went to my room with my man I thought I heard someone groaning. I didn't take any notice then, but I wish I had.'

The woman showed signs of distress, but she continued. 'The next day – that's yesterday morning – I got up a bit earlier than usual and went to the kitchen to make myself a cup of tea. That's when I heard this groaning again, coming from Ruth's room. I knocked at her door but got no reply, so I went in. Poor Ruth was lying on the floor and there was a lot of blood around. She'd been badly knocked about.'

Aghast, Emily demanded, 'Is she seriously hurt? Did you call in a doctor?'

'I got one to come round to the house, but he wasn't a lot of help. He kept saying, "If you live this sort of life then you've got to expect to have violence like this occur." He wouldn't even examine her properly. He made me pay him right away and promised to come back later in the day, but he didn't. Last night I tried to get her to take some soup, but she didn't want anything. This morning she was in a whole lot of pain and I didn't know what to do. Then I thought of you. We'd heard you were in Adelaide and had been told of what you were doing. Ruth always said that if any of us were in trouble we couldn't do better than to come to you for help.' Looking at Emily, she finished lamely, 'So here I am.'

Emily was touched that Ruth should have such faith in her, but she felt Ruth probably needed more help than she could give to her.

'How far is it to the house where you live?'

'If we were lucky enough to catch a train right away we could be there in half an hour or so.'

'Then we'll set off right away. I will tell Margaret where we are going.'

When the two women arrived at Ruth's home, Emily realised the prostitute had not been exaggerating about Ruth's condition. She was in great pain and kept drifting off into delirium. One moment she was expressing gratitude to Emily for coming to see her, the next she was babbling incoherently.

'She needs to be seen by a doctor – a *good* doctor – immediately.' Emily was extremely concerned by

Ruth's condition. 'Are there any doctors other than the one who has already seen her in Port Adelaide?'

'I don't think so – but there's a big immigrant ship alongside in the port. There's bound to be a doctor on board.'

'Come along and show me where it is. We must go there right away.'

At the busy Port Adelaide docks, Emily had a great stroke of luck. Not only was there a doctor on board the immigrant ship, but he was being visited by his brother, who was the senior surgeon at the Adelaide hospital.

At first the two doctors were reluctant to involve themselves with the problems of a dockland prostitute. However, they realised Emily was a woman of some education and breeding and when she told them of the work she was carrying out on behalf of the Bishop of Adelaide, they agreed to accompany her and Ruth's friend to the prostitutes' house.

Their examination of the injured woman was swift but thorough. After a brief consultation with his brother, the Adelaide surgeon agreed with Emily that there was cause for concern.

'That she has been the victim of a vicious attack is quite apparent from the number of cuts and bruises that are to be seen,' he said, 'but I am far more concerned with the injuries that *cannot* be seen. She has a possible fracture of the skull, but – and I believe this to be far more serious – I fear she has sustained damage to one of her kidneys, possibly as the result of a kick. She needs to be taken into hospital. I suggest my own hospital in Adelaide is best equipped to carry out the necessary tests and give her the care she needs at present.' Looking at Emily from beneath bushy eyebrows, he added, 'Unfortunately, such treatment is not free, nor is it cheap.'

'I will pay for all the costs incurred,' Emily declared. 'Now, how do we get her to the hospital in Adelaide?'

'The harbour authorities have an ambulance,' said the ship's doctor. 'We used it for two of the immigrants who were ill upon arrival. I'll hurry to the docks and make arrangements for it to be sent here immediately.'

'Good!' said his brother. 'Come here with the ambulance, Charles. We will both travel to Adelaide with the patient and you can spend a few days with me there.' Smiling reassuringly at Emily, he said, 'You can be certain this unfortunate young woman will be well cared for on the journey to Adelaide and will be given my personal attention once she is there.'

'Thank you. Thank you both for your kindness,' Emily said gratefully. 'I will return to Adelaide by train and come to the hospital tomorrow to visit Ruth and discover what is likely to happen to her.'

II

'What are you doing here?'

Sam and Margaret both asked the question in unison and Margaret laughed, explaining, 'You remember Ruth – Ruth Askew from Blinman? She left there some time ago to come to Port Adelaide. Unfortunately, she hasn't changed her ways and has been badly beaten by a foreign seaman. She's here in the hospital and we've just been to see her. But why are you here?'

'My prospecting partner is in here seriously ill. We

were caught out in a storm a couple of days ago. He has pneumonia. But you said "we"?'

'That's right, me and Emily.'

It was a deliberately blunt statement on Margaret's part, in order to gauge Sam's reaction.

Sam jumped as if a firecracker had exploded behind him. His mouth opened and closed several times, as though he would speak, but no sound came.

Acting as if she had noticed nothing out of the ordinary in his reaction, Margaret said, 'We were on our way out when Emily remembered she hadn't asked the nurses what she could bring in for Ruth to eat or drink. The doctors suspect she's got a damaged kidney and they're being careful what she is given. Emily will be out in a minute, she'll be absolutely delighted to see you—'

'No – I won't stop. Wish her well for me.' Sam turned with the intention of hurrying away, but Margaret grabbed his arm and brought him to a halt.

'Don't go, Sam. Emily will be very upset if she misses you again—'

Sam tried to free his arm, but Margaret said hurriedly, 'She travelled all the way to Blinman hoping to find you there, but you had left a couple of weeks earlier.'

He stopped pulling against her. 'She went to Blinman to see *me*? Why? What did the man she is to marry think about that? Or is she married already?'

'She's not married and there will be no wedding.' Suitably contrite, Margaret added, 'I had my facts wrong, Sam. Stefan Mintoff *had* asked Emily to marry him, but she had neither accepted nor turned him down. Since then a whole lot has happened. Mintoff went to

England to raise money for a bogus mining company. I think he's made a great deal of money by telling everyone he was to marry into Emily's family. He even persuaded her to put a thousand pounds into the company. She's lost that money and there's no question of her marrying him now. Besides, long before he came on the scene she was trying to find you. Indeed – and I may be telling you far more than she would wish me to – I believe that the real reason she came to Australia was because she hoped to meet up with you again.'

Sam was more in control of himself now, but he found it impossible to fully take in the implications of all that Margaret had told him.

'I . . . I'm not sure I'm ready to meet her right now.'

'Of course you are,' Margaret said confidently. 'Look, you go and sit down over there, by the window. You'll see Emily when she returns. I'll break the news that you're here and you gauge her reaction for yourself. Go on, Sam – and remember, she'll be just as nervous as you when she knows you're here.'

It was all too much for Sam to take in immediately. Emily was close at hand. He would soon see her – and she was *not* about to be married to someone else!

He sat down heavily upon a chair on the far side of the hospital reception area and began looking apprehensively at every woman who emerged from the wards, wondering with an increasing degree of panic whether she was a much-changed Emily.

Suddenly Sam's attention was distracted by a woman leaving the wards hand in hand with a seriously disturbed child of about twelve. Sam watched as the woman showed great patience in coaxing the child to the exit door.

When the pair had passed out of the building, Sam returned his gaze to the corridor that led from the wards – and there he saw Emily.

Seeing her made him wonder how he might ever have imagined that any of the other women could possibly have been her. She was perhaps thinner than before and she had matured since their last meeting, but she was everything he remembered – and he realised immediately that his feelings for her had not changed. He still experienced the same thrill at seeing her that he recalled from his church days at St Cleer.

He wanted to jump up and call out her name, but he dared not. He had promised Margaret he would let her speak to Emily first.

Getting to his feet, he waited quietly.

'It seems there is very little we are permitted to bring in for poor Ruth . . .'

Emily continued talking as she walked towards the hospital exit, expecting Margaret to fall in beside her. When her friend did not move, Emily stopped and turned back, clearly puzzled.

'Is something wrong, Margaret? I thought you were in a hurry to get home and prepare tea for the boys?'

'I am, but something unexpected has happened, Emily. I've just seen someone I think you've been anxious to find.'

Startled, Emily said, 'You are not trying to tell me that Stefan Mintoff has had the gall to return to South Australia?'

Margaret smiled at Emily's indignation. 'No, I think this will be a far more pleasant surprise for you.'

Emily was momentarily puzzled. Then, aware that

Margaret was more than ordinarily pleased with herself, her eyes widened and she reached out to grasp the arm of her friend. 'You don't mean . . . ? Not *Sam*? Where, Margaret? Where was he?'

'He was standing right here and we talked about you. Now he's over there, by the window, waiting to meet you again.'

Emily spun around and looked towards the window. The hotel reception area was extremely busy, but she saw Sam immediately. Tall and suntanned, he was nervously screwing up the brim of the soft hat he held in his hands.

As blood rushed to Emily's face, she thought she might faint. Margaret thought so too and she held out a hand to support her friend.

It was doubtful whether Emily felt it. Leaving Margaret behind, she hurried across the hospital foyer with eyes for only one person.

'Sam! How wonderful to see you again . . . and you are looking so well!' She wanted to hug him, but contented herself with kissing him warmly on the cheek.

Now it was his turn to blush as he murmured, 'It's good to see you too, Emily. You haven't changed a bit . . . well, not much.'

Aware of the crucifix dangling on a chain about her neck and the reason he had returned it to her, he added feebly, 'I . . . I thought you were to be married.'

'No, Sam . . . but it is a very long story and we have so many much more pleasant things to talk about. How is your family – do you hear from them regularly? And what are you doing in Adelaide – and here, at the hospital?' Suddenly, overcome by emotion, she reached out and touched his arm. 'Oh, it really *is* wonderful to meet up with you again, Sam, truly it is.'

Sam felt at a complete loss for words, but fortunately his expression spoke for him.

Watching them from across the reception area, Margaret felt a pang of envy. Turning away, she left the hospital to make her way home. She realised that Emily and Sam had a great deal to talk about and would prefer to be alone.

III

Margaret's departure did not go unnoticed, but neither Emily nor Sam made any attempt to stop her. Leaving the hospital soon afterwards they walked slowly to a small park situated nearby, talking all the while.

In the park they found a seat and sat down and talked some more.

Sam gave an outline of all that had happened to him since leaving St Cleer and Emily related the story of her own life and why she was now in Adelaide.

'So you're still a very important person, even here in Australia,' Sam said despondently. He realised he had allowed the euphoria of their reunion to obscure the differences in their backgrounds and ways of life.

Aware of what he was thinking, Emily said firmly, 'No, Sam, I am what I have always been, deep down. My *own* person. It's what no one would ever allow me to be back in Cornwall. I was told how I must behave, how I should talk, who I was allowed to talk to. I always had to live up to someone else's expectations: my father's, sister's, titled uncle's – even Maude, the housekeeper's. I came out to South Australia because I intended being myself at last. To live my life the way I choose – and that is what I intend doing. As for being important, thanks to Stefan Mintoff I have become an *embarrassment* to anyone who considers themselves to be in any way "important". He has turned out to be thoroughly dishonest. As a result people look at me and wonder how much I was involved in his schemes.'

'Surely no one thinks you had anything to do with his dishonest dealings. It's quite ridiculous!'

Resting a hand on his arm, Emily said, 'Thank you, Sam. No one has actually *said* they believe me to be involved in any way, but they are all keeping me at arm's length, just in case. It doesn't worry me because it means I can get on with my work with no social distractions, but it sometimes hurts when I see churchmen turning their backs on those they believe to be sinners. It is contrary to fundamental Christian principles.'

'No one can accuse you of doing that,' Sam said. 'How *is* Ruth?'

'Hopefully she will recover. But what of your partner?'

Sam shook his head unhappily. 'The doctor says there is very little hope for him. They say his heart is affected. I've promised to go in and see him again this evening.'

'I am so sorry,' Emily expressed genuine sympathy. 'I can tell by the way you've spoken of him that you are very fond of him.'

'He's a very special friend who's lived through a great many adventures during his lifetime. It's ironic that he should die as a result of getting wet in a rainstorm.'

'Do you think he would mind if I came with you when you visit him this evening?' Emily asked.

'It would give him a great deal of pleasure,' Sam said delightedly. 'I'd like it too.'

'Good! I was about to ask what we should do until it's time to visit, but I just heard a clock strike six o'clock. Would you like to go and visit him now?'

'That sounds a good idea, I don't want to leave it too late.'

On the way back to the hospital, Emily asked, 'Where are you staying while you are in Adelaide?'

'At a small hotel on Flinders Street. Abe and I always stay there. They've known him for a long time and he trusts them to look after our gold when they have it in their safe.'

'You mean you have actually *found* gold? Enough to make your prospecting worthwhile?'

'Very much so. I probably have enough right now to buy a nice piece of land, up in the hills. That's what Abe has done. It's really beautiful up there.'

'Perhaps you will take me to see it some time,' Emily suggested. 'I haven't been outside the city since I arrived in Adelaide.'

They chattered on happily until they arrived at the hospital. Here, their mood became more sombre.

Abe was in a ward with more than a dozen men, occupying the first bed inside the door, close to the ward sister's desk. He appeared to be asleep, but as the young couple stood by the bedside, uncertainly, he opened his eyes and managed a weak smile for Sam before his glance shifted to Emily, who had been brought a chair by a ward orderly.

'Abe, I'd like you to meet Emily. We knew each other

in Cornwall. Her pa was vicar of St Cleer. I knew she was in South Australia, but didn't know she was in Adelaide until we met up this afternoon, just after I left you. She said she'd like to meet you, so here we are.'

'Sam has been telling me so much about you I felt I just had to meet you. Abe . . . is that short for Abraham, the father of the Hebrew nation?'

'It is, miss.' Abe's voice was little more than a weak whisper. 'I think Sam has told me of you too, but he never put a name to you.'

Emily looked up at Sam questioningly, but realised an explanation would need to await the right occasion.

'Sam was telling me of the land you own in the hills outside the city. He says it is really beautiful.'

Showing an unexpected knowledge of biblical history, Abe said, 'Like my namesake, the Lord showed me the promised land and gave it to me . . . but I'm afraid I've left it too late to reap any benefit from it.'

'Nonsense!' Emily lied. 'Sam is convinced you can overcome *anything*. You certainly won't allow a setback like this get the better of you. He says you never acknowledge defeat. You will win this battle too.'

Glancing towards Sam, Abe whispered wearily, 'He's a good boy, but he needs someone to take care of him and teach him the things that are important in life.'

'I will see what I can do,' Emily promised. Suddenly and unexpectedly, she leaned over and kissed him on the forehead. 'God bless you, Abe.'

Her gesture delighted the old man and he said, 'He's never been mean with his blessings to me, Emily. Mind you, the devil's been in there running against him at times, but I reckon the Lord left him far behind.'

Abe was looking very tired now. Sam said, 'We'll

leave you in peace now, partner. I'll be here to see you first thing in the morning. I hope you'll be feeling a whole lot stronger then.'

As Sam moved forward to clasp his hand in farewell, Abe pulled him down towards him and whispered, 'She's a fine girl, Sam. Don't let her get away from you again. Remember what I told you, you're as fine a man as any she's ever likely to meet, and you'll be able to give her more than most – whatever their station in life.'

IV

Sam walked Emily from the hospital to her modest home and accepted her offer to have his evening meal with the household. Margaret made a big fuss of him and when she told the boys that he was a 'gold prospector' his acceptance was assured.

'Our pa was a prospector,' said Tom. 'He found gold too.'

'I know he did,' Sam agreed. 'And he found it near Blinman, where no one else had.'

'Did you know our pa?' asked Albert.

'Not very well,' Sam replied guardedly. He did not want to be drawn into a conversation where he might be questioned on his views of the character of Charlie Minns. 'But I did meet him at the Nuccaleena mine on one occasion, and travelled back to Blinman with him and a whole lot of other miners.'

Emily changed the subject at that moment, telling the boys that Sam came from St Cleer. After this much of the conversation was of Cornwall, people and places they all knew.

They spoke of what Margaret and the boys were likely to find different when, or if, they went back. Margaret would not consider returning until she had seen Emily settled and out of the shadow that Stefan Mintoff had cast over her life.

The evening passed all too quickly for Sam, even though he did not leave the house until long after the boys had gone to bed.

Emily came out to the front verandah to see him off. As they stood in the shadows, she said softly, 'I really am glad to have found you, Sam. I never gave up hope that I would, one day.'

'I'm glad too, Emily. I thought of you often after I arrived in South Australia, but I couldn't see how we could possibly meet again. It would have been a lot easier had I been able to write direct to you. As it was I could only send messages through the family. I was never sure whether they would reach you.'

'They did not, I'm afraid, but I think that was due largely to the influence of my father.'

'Probably,' Sam agreed. 'Then, when I learned you'd been out here some time and were due to be married to this Mintoff man, I despaired of us ever meeting.'

'That was when you sent back my crucifix?'

'Yes, and left Blinman shortly afterwards. I thought that if you were to be married it might embarrass you to remember you'd given such a valuable and treasured present to . . . to a miner.'

'I gave it to you because I wanted you to have it, Sam. I still want you to have it.'

'Thank you, but I believe the proper place for it is around your neck.'

At that moment a crowd of some seven or eight

young men came around the corner and walked along the street towards the house, talking loudly. As they neared, Sam and Emily edged farther back into the shadows close to the door.

When the young men made their way past, Sam became aware that he and Emily were standing very close.

'Do you remember that last night, in the church porch, when we heard someone coming?' she asked.

'There have been very few days when I *haven't* remembered it,' he replied. 'I sometimes wonder what might have happened had those miners not passed by, going on shift.'

'I suppose you could always find out by kissing me goodnight now, Sam Hooper. That is if you want to, of course.'

If he wanted to! There were many replies he might have made, but he tried not to allow his desire to run away with him.

'I'm not going away this time, Emily.'

'And I don't have to hurry home for fear of what a spiteful housekeeper might tell my father.'

When he still hesitated, she said quietly, 'Don't you *want* to kiss me, Sam?'

He stepped forward then and, taking hold of her, kissed her with a pent-up passion that left them both breathless.

Then the voice of Albert, in the room alongside them, called, 'Ma! Ma! I feel sick. Can I have a drink of water?'

Pulling back from Sam, Emily was confused and not a little frightened by the emotions that Sam had stirred up. She had never felt like this before. 'I think I had better go inside now, Sam.'

'Yes ... I think you should.' Sam, too, was shaken by the sheer intensity of their embrace. 'But ... can I see you again?'

'Of course, Sam. Shall we go to the hospital together tomorrow afternoon? I have to see the cathedral treasurer in the morning about a scheme I wish the Church to finance. Shall we say two o'clock? I should be free by then.'

'That will be fine.'

Sam was greatly relieved. He had half believed Emily to be joking when she suggested he might want to kiss her, that she was perhaps teasing him about that night in the St Cleer church porch when he had been slow to take up her shamelessly bold offer. He had feared she might have taken offence at what he had just done.

'I will probably call in to see Abe early in the morning though,' he said. 'I was very worried about him today.'

'Of course. Tell him I shall come with you again in the afternoon and hope to see him looking much better.'

They remained standing close without saying anything for a few minutes before he said, 'I really am glad we've found each other.'

'And so am I, Sam. Until tomorrow then ...'

She kissed him again. A kiss as perfunctory as the last kiss she had bestowed upon him in the St Cleer church porch but this time they parted with a feeling not of despair but of anticipation.

V

Sam arrived at the hospital early the next morning. Making his way to the ward where Abe was being treated, he walked through the door – and came to an abrupt halt.

Abe's bed was empty.

As he stood there, thoroughly confused, a nurse came hurrying towards him from farther along the ward. He had not met with her on the ward before and she said, 'May I help you?'

'I'm here to see Abe ... Mr Gundry, but his bed is empty ...'

'Are you a relative?'

'I'm his partner and the closest thing to a relative that Abe has.'

The nurse hesitated, but for only a moment. 'I am very sorry, but I am afraid Mr Gundry passed away during the night.'

Observing the shock and disbelief on Sam's face, she added gently, 'He died very peacefully at about three o'clock this morning and his body has been taken to the chapel. Will you wait here while I go and find the sister in charge of the ward? I believe there are some formalities to be completed and one or two items of personal property to be handed over ...'

Sam left the hospital in a very upset state later that morning, having made the necessary arrangements for Abe's funeral.

He wished Emily had not been at a meeting; he would have liked to talk with her. She would understand how he was feeling.

Returning to the hotel, he was thankful the desk clerk was busy and so did not ask after Abe.

Once in his room, Sam sat down heavily and considered for the first time what Abe's death would mean.

He was not at all certain he was capable of working the Jupiter Creek claim on his own. Indeed, he was not at all sure he *wanted* to work it without Abe.

Suddenly, he remembered the envelope Abe had given to him, saying it contained his will. Sam had told the hospital authorities that the old prospector had no living relations; it was possible the will might prove him wrong.

He opened the drawer where he had thrown the envelope the previous evening, after returning to the hotel from Emily's house. He had a moment of panic when he thought it was no longer there, but then he discovered it had slid to the back of the drawer.

Tearing open the envelope, Sam unfolded the two sheets of paper it contained and read the last will and testament of Abraham Wesley Gundry.

When Sam called upon Emily that afternoon, she was saddened at the news of Abe's death, yet she was as supportive as Sam had known she would be.

'I'm so sorry, Sam,' she said. 'But at least he did not die a lonely old man, with no one to care about him. He cherished your friendship and I am convinced both your lives were enriched by knowing each other. What would you like to do now? You probably won't want to accompany me to the hospital. I could ask Margaret to go in my place, she'll understand.'

'No, you go to see Ruth. I won't come with you, there are a great many of Abe's affairs that will need to be sorted out – but I would like to see you later in the day, if I may?'

'Of course. Come to the house for dinner.'

* * *

The funeral of Abe took place on a wet and dreary day in the cemetery to the south-west of the city. The only mourners were Sam, Emily, Margaret and a desk clerk from the hotel where he had always stayed.

There was no gathering of mourners afterwards, but Sam declared all was much as Abe would have wished it to be.

That evening, Sam arrived at Emily's house carrying a cylindrical leather case which, at first glance, appeared to be a container for a telescope. Inside were plans for the house Abe had hoped one day to build on his land, as a reminder of his young wife's family home in California.

On the dining-room table, Sam laid out the plan for the main house, using two candleholders, a vase and a heavy, leather-bound dictionary to weigh down the corners of the document and prevent it from curling up.

'What do you make of it?' Sam put the question to Emily as she studied the detailed plan.

'It's magnificent!' Emily enthused. 'Who would imagine that a prospector would carry a dream like this around with him for so long?'

'Abe was no ordinary prospector,' Sam said sadly.

'I must agree,' Emily said. 'I do wish I had been able to know him better . . . Look at these.'

She held up a number of excellent sketches, apparently drawn by Abe, and which had been used by the architect to produce a professional sketch of how the house would appear from front, side and rear aspects.

'It is sad to think he died with his dream unfulfilled. I wonder what will happen to his land now?'

Aware of the impact his words were going to have,

Sam was unable to make them sound as casual as he would have wished. 'I haven't made up my mind yet. You see, Abe has left it to me. I thought we might all go out to look at it tomorrow.'

There was a squeak of delighted surprise from Margaret, and Emily looked at Sam accusingly. 'Sam! How could you keep something like this a secret from us until now. How large is this piece of land?'

'*Very* large,' Sam replied. 'You'll be able to see for yourselves tomorrow. The boys must come along too. With any luck they'll see a koala or two. Abe and I have seen them there.'

Margaret looked slightly puzzled and Sam explained, 'The koala looks like a small, cuddly bear. They live in the trees up in the hills.'

The following morning Sam arrived at Emily's house with a one-horse buggy he had hired for the day.

The boys were very excited to be riding in the vehicle and along the way Sam allowed each of them to clamber into the front seat beside him and take the reins for short distances. Then, as they reached the winding road that led into the hills, he took the reins once more.

It was not long before they topped a rise and, as they rounded a bend, a valley opened up, extending away to their left.

'This is quite breathtaking!' Emily exclaimed. 'Just look at that marvellous view along the valley.'

'You wait until you see it from the far slope,' Sam said. 'You can see even farther, with views of higher peaks in the distance.'

The pride in his voice caused Emily to look at him

quickly. 'Is this the valley, Sam? It is! How much of it belongs to you?'

'It's marked on the map I brought with me,' Sam replied. 'Roughly speaking, it's everything you can see.'

Emily was incredulous. 'Truly, Sam? All this valley is yours?'

'That's right. My reaction was the same as yours when I first saw it. Abe's must have been, too. He saw it, fell in love with it – and bought it.'

'What a wonderful thing to do. But tell me, where did he intend building his house?'

'We'll drive into the valley so you can see it properly, then you can say where *you'd* put it and I'll tell you how close you are. It's a game we can all play.'

'What's the prize for the winner?' Tom asked cheekily.

'Whoever wins can have first choice from the picnic basket Emily has brought along for us,' Sam declared.

When they arrived at a suitable spot in what Sam still thought of as 'Abe's valley', he set the brake on the buggy, gave the horse a nosebag and they all set off to choose the spot where they thought a house should be built.

After half an hour they all met back at the buggy and told Sam where they would like their own home to be.

Emily was the undisputed winner, choosing the exact spot where Abe and Sam had both agreed a house should be built.

Margaret and Albert preferred a spot a short distance away, hidden in the fold of a hill from the winning site.

Tom said he would prefer to live on the valley floor, so that he would not need to tire himself out coming back to the house when he was out playing and his mother called him in.

They all enjoyed a wonderful day in Abe's Valley. The crowning pleasure came when Albert spotted not one koala but *two*, perched in a eucalyptus tree, close to the water-filled creek which encroached on a section of the valley floor.

It was a very happy group that drove back to Adelaide, although Emily seemed unusually silent.

Later that evening when the boys had gone to bed, Margaret, Emily and Sam sat out on the front verandah of the small house discussing Abe's Valley.

'You are from a farming family, Sam,' Emily said, after a while. 'What do you think might be grown there?'

'The soil is so rich that I can't think of anything that *wouldn't* grow. What I'd really like to do is have a huge apple orchard. Apples for cooking and eating. There could even be cider apples. With a press on the farm I could make cider and sell it. I'd also run cattle and, while I was waiting for the trees to establish themselves, I'd probably grow wheat. From what I've heard it's been grown very successfully elsewhere in the area.'

'Is that what you *will* do, Sam, or what you would *like* to do?'

'I haven't quite made up my mind yet,' Sam said cautiously. 'I still haven't got used to the idea that the valley now belongs to me.'

At that moment, Margaret decided she would go into the house and make drinks for them all. When she had gone, Emily said, 'This farming venture, Sam . . . if it's a question of money, I would be very happy to let you have an interest-free loan. You would not need to begin paying me back until you started making a profit.'

Deeply touched by her generous offer, Sam reached across the space between their chairs and found her hand. Squeezing it affectionately, he said, 'Thank you, Emily, I appreciate the offer. But I have one or two decisions to make before I start planning my future in earnest. Not least of them is what to do with the mining leases Abe took out on the land around our claims. I need to go along to the Mines Department tomorrow and sort out just what we have.'

Retaining a hold on his hand, Emily hoped Sam might decide to give up mining, accept her offer and begin farming in his newly acquired valley. That way she was certain of seeing far more of him.

It might even be that he would not need to repay the loan at all ...

It was as well that she could not look into the very near future.

VI

A week after her visit to the Adelaide Hills with Sam, Emily received an unexpected visit from the Reverend Gordon Glover, chaplain to the Bishop of Adelaide.

She had been in Adelaide for more than three months, during which time she had spoken no more than a few words to the chaplain – and none at all to the bishop.

She was therefore taken aback when the chaplain greeted her with a warm smile and said, 'How are you, Miss Boyce? His Grace asked me to call on you to make certain you are receiving all the co-operation you need from the Church and other official bodies in Adelaide. We have received a number of reports on the success of your mission. He regrets he has been remiss in not acknowledging your progress before now. But he is, of course, a very busy man. This is a fast-growing colony and the Church must keep pace with its growth.'

'Of course,' Emily said, smiling sweetly at her visitor. 'We must try to regain some of the ground we have lost to the non-conformist faiths. I fear it will not be easy.'

For a few moments the chaplain's smile appeared somewhat forced.

While they were speaking, Emily had been leading him through the house. She now invited him to sit down in the kitchen, explaining that this was the only room in the house that was not in use as a bedroom.

Looking about him, he said, 'Dear me, I had no idea you were living in such cramped conditions, Miss Boyce. Something will need to be done about it right away.'

He had still not given her a hint of why she had seemingly been re-admitted to the fold of the Established Church and Emily was curious.

At that moment Ruth entered the kitchen, wearing night attire, over which she was wearing an unfastened and somewhat shabby dressing-gown, which Margaret had somehow managed to acquire for her.

The chaplain stood up hurriedly and Ruth said, 'Oh! I'm sorry, Miss Boyce, I didn't realise you had company. I see the kettle is boiling, I'll make myself a quick cup of coffee and get out of your way.'

The chaplain was looking at Ruth's bruised and battered face with great concern and Emily explained,

'We are looking after Ruth for a while. She only left hospital yesterday after being brutally attacked.'

When the chaplain murmured a few meaningless words of sympathy, Ruth said cheerfully, 'The doctor at the hospital told me that if Miss Boyce hadn't got me to him when she did I'd have died for sure. I've very good reason to be grateful to her.'

When Ruth had wandered out of the kitchen with her cup of coffee, the chaplain asked, in a strangled voice, 'Is that . . . is she one of the women you are trying to redeem?'

'That's right. I first met her when she was in a bawdy house in Kadina. We met again in Blinman. A few days ago a friend of Ruth's came to ask for my help when Ruth was attacked by one of the seamen she took to her home in Port Adelaide.'

'But you . . . you should not have such a woman wandering about your home!' The chaplain was aghast.

'It was either that or send her back to the bawdy house in Port Adelaide,' Emily said bluntly. 'Had I done that she would have been back to her bad old ways within days. As it is, I feel there is a very good chance that Ruth will change and, hopefully, be able to persuade others to do the same.'

'But . . . to have her living in your home, in such close proximity. My dear Miss Boyce, we must take immediate steps to move you to more suitable premises. To a house where you can have your own private quarters – and servants to help with such women!'

'When I first came to Adelaide I sent a number of letters to the bishop suggesting that if we were to wean some of these unfortunate women from their ways we would need properly supervised accommodation for them. My letters were not answered.'

The chaplain appeared uncomfortable. 'His Grace *has* been extremely busy, but I feel certain he would have acted upon your request had he seen the letters. Unfortunately, his secretary was replaced very recently, for inefficiency. Your letters must have been mislaid during the period of uncertainty we have suffered. However, things are running more smoothly now – as I believe they are for you. You are no doubt relieved that your unfortunate problems with Mr Mintoff are at an end, Miss Boyce.'

'At an end? I am afraid I don't know what you are talking about, Reverend Glover.'

'Really? I thought you would have been informed by your uncle, Lord Boyce. He is widely quoted in the London newspapers that have recently arrived from England. It seems his lordship was able to prevent a great many influential men in the City from investing in Mintoff's fraudulent companies and so losing large sums of money. His lordship gives credit to you for telegraphing him in time to thwart Mintoff's schemes. Well done, Miss Boyce. Well done indeed.'

Rising to his feet, the chaplain said, 'I feel it is time I returned to my office. Be assured I will treat the question of more suitable accommodation for you with the utmost urgency.'

The Reverend Glover was as good as his word, and only four days later Emily was invited to look over a house in the prosperous and growing suburb of Walkerville, to the north-east of Adelaide.

A solidly built two-storey house, it had been erected by one of the township's earliest residents, who had recently died and bequeathed the property to the Church.

Emily was told she could live in the house, rent free, and continue the work she had begun so successfully. The chaplain felt it was ideal for her purposes. Surrounded by large and attractive gardens, it enjoyed considerable privacy.

The messenger also brought her an invitation to a reception being held at the bishop's palace in a few weeks' time.

Emily despatched a note to the chaplain confirming her acceptance of the house and expressing a wish to take immediate possession. As a result, Emily, Margaret, the two boys – and Ruth – moved to the rather grand new house only two days later, assisted by Sam.

Albert and Tom thought it a marvellous new home. Not only did they share an upstairs room but it possessed a balcony. Once they had settled who would occupy which bed, they set off together to explore the extensive gardens.

Margaret would occupy a room next to the boys, while Ruth was allocated one of the four spare bedrooms in which Emily intended housing any other women she could tempt away from a similar lifestyle.

With Sam present to help and share with her each idea she had for utilising the facilities offered by the vastly superior accommodation, it was a very happy day.

Unfortunately, the happiness lasted only until late that evening when the bishop's chaplain arrived to see how they were settling in. With him he brought some mail for Emily that had arrived from England the day before and been delivered to her former address.

When the chaplain had left, Emily opened the first of the letters while she chatted to Sam in the lounge. Meanwhile, Ruth and Margaret were in the kitchen preparing an evening meal.

Emily glanced down at the letter, then she looked again and suddenly stopped talking in order to concentrate on the contents of the letter, her expression one of increasing consternation.

'Is something wrong?' Sam asked.

Continuing to read without replying for a few more moments, Emily eventually looked up, more shaken than Sam had ever seen her. 'It's from my uncle Percy. It seems that Stefan Mintoff has been forging my signature on banker's drafts and cheques. My uncle says he has been able to draw a great deal of my money. Because of his standing in the City, Uncle Percy has been able to persuade the banks not to honour any further demands for money bearing my signature, but I need to return to England in order to sort out the mess. Oh! Why did I ever get involved with a man like Stefan Mintoff?'

'It sounds extremely serious,' Sam said. 'But is there no way to deal with it other than going to England?' He was deeply concerned that once there she might never return. 'Can't you at least leave making a decision until you have had time to think about it?'

'No, Sam. I have probably already lost a great deal of money. More than I can afford. I wish I did *not* have to go, but Uncle Percy would not have said I was needed if he could possibly deal with it himself. I will go into town tomorrow, find out when the next steamship is due to leave, then telegraph my uncle.'

She looked at Sam and, suddenly and unexpectedly, tears welled up in her eyes and she said, 'It would have to happen now, just when everything seemed to be working out.'

Sam was not sure whether she was referring to *their* relationship or to the fact that she had just moved into a new house and was once more in favour with the Church.

He moved to comfort her, but at that moment the two boys burst into the house, shouting that they had just seen an unidentified animal run up one of the garden trees.

Ruth and Margaret were both upset that Emily was going to have to return to England. Margaret wondered whether it might be a good time to return with her, but she did not need a great deal of persuading to stay in Adelaide and continue the work Emily had begun.

Later that night when the boys were in bed and Sam and Emily had been left alone on the spacious verandah of the new house, Sam asked, 'You *will* come back to Australia, Emily?'

'Of course. Everything I want is here, Sam. *Everything.*'

'Then it will all still be here for you when you return. But if you decided you didn't want to travel all that way I'm sure we could work something out here.'

'If you mean what I think you do, I would rather it remained unsaid until my return, Sam. Unless . . .' She looked at him excitedly as an idea took shape in her mind. 'Unless you come to England with me! I would pay your fare.'

Sam thought of what she was offering him. It was

tempting, but ... He shook his head. 'No, Emily.'

'Why not?' she asked eagerly. 'It would be a wonderful opportunity for us to really get to know each other. To make up for all the time we have lost.'

He dared not allow her to realise how much the idea appealed to him. 'I have a great many things to attend to here, Emily. There's my land ... and I must make plans for the future. Besides ...' He faltered and fell silent.

'Besides?' she prompted.

Sam knew that what he was about to say to her might change things between them for ever, but it had to be said and there would never be a better opportunity than now.

'Emily ... before I left St Cleer I had grown far fonder of you than I should have. Your father saw it. That's why he had me sent out here – and I don't think there's any doubt that he *did*. While I was here and you were back in Cornwall I thought of you constantly and I had your crucifix to remind me I had meant something to you too. Then, when I learned you were here and was told you were getting married to someone important, I felt I'd been fooling myself all along, that our backgrounds are so far apart that I was reaching for the moon. I told myself I had to forget you, though I knew it wasn't going to be easy. Then we met again and somehow I seem to have moved towards you, and you to me. Our ways of life are not quite so far apart now. Even if they were, it doesn't seem to matter quite so much here, in Australia. I've come to feel I'm as good as anyone else. I like things this way, Emily. I believe that if we both stay here, we ... well, things could be different to the way they were in St

Cleer. But if I came back with you to England, once we arrived there you'd be mixing with your uncle and his friends. Peers and government ministers. I don't think I'd show up very well in their company . . .'

For a moment it looked as though Emily would protest, but Sam had more to say.

'I don't think I'd show up well in their company, any more than they would be at their best tramping through the outback or working a claim. I could offer you a good life here, Emily. I have my land and it's good land, but I don't think we could be happy together in England.'

Very quietly, Emily said, 'You know, Sam Hooper, if I was an impressionable young girl I might think you *almost* proposed to me then.'

'I couldn't do that, Emily, not when I know you're returning to England and will be going back to the life you used to lead before coming out here. I'd rather you thought of what I've said as an explanation of the way I feel. The way I've always felt, and always will. I don't *want* to hold you to anything until you've been back to England and had a chance to make up your mind about the life you want, so you won't ever regret whatever you decide is right for you.'

Embarrassed at having made a longer speech than he could ever remember, he shrugged awkwardly. 'I suppose that, really, the decision is whether you want Australia and a different way of life here – or whether you want England and all that means.'

Emily remained silent for some time before saying, 'No, Sam, the choice is far more important to me than that. It's a choice of whether I want you or whether I don't – and you are a very special man to me, Sam Hooper.'

VII

Emily left Adelaide three days after receiving the letter from her uncle. She travelled first to Melbourne, from where she would take passage in one of the fast steamships that now made the voyage between Australia and England in slightly less than two months. Even so, it meant she would most probably be away for at least five months.

Sam travelled with Emily to Melbourne and saw her safely on board the ship. As they were about to part at the top of the ship's gangway, Sam self-consciously pulled a small, velvet-covered box from his pocket.

Handing it to her, he said, 'I'd like you to have this to take with you, Emily.'

Surprised, Emily took the box from him. Opening it, she gasped with delight. Inside was a gold ring, mounted with a large, expertly cut precious opal that captured light and set it free again in myriad colours.

Speechless, Emily looked to Sam for an explanation.

'The gold is from the claim,' he said. 'I dug it myself and had a jeweller make it into a ring. The opal was dug out by Abe, years before he met me. It was among his things when he died. I know he would have liked you to have it.'

'It's an absolutely wonderful gift, Sam. It will be my most treasured possession for as long as I live – but won't you put it on my finger for me?'

She handed the ring back to him, then held out her left hand.

Sam hesitated, uncertainly, 'Where . . . ?'

By way of reply, Emily folded back three fingers, leaving only the third finger of the hand she had extended.

It was a somewhat tight fit, but eventually the ring slipped over the knuckle joint and Emily held it up, delighted. 'There! You may be keeping your proposal until I return, Sam, but you have just staked your claim.'

The call went up for all visitors to go ashore and for a moment Emily looked alone and very vulnerable. Then she said, 'I love you, Sam. I love you very much.'

'I love you too, Emily.'

They had time for only the briefest of embraces before a crew member said, 'Time for you to go ashore if you're not travelling, sir.'

'Take care, Emily – and hurry back.' Sam released her reluctantly.

'You take care too, Sam. I will let you know by telegraph as soon as I know when I will be leaving England. And the name of the ship.'

Sam made his way down the ship's gangway, past sailors who were impatient to have the gangway lifted ashore in order that they might begin their long voyage home to England.

He stood on the quayside, waving, until the vessel moved off and was lost in the gathering dusk.

For five months, Margaret carried on the work that had been started by Emily. For all this time she was ably assisted by Ruth, who seemed determined to put the life she had been living behind her.

Early in November, Sam received a telegraph message from Emily telling him she was taking passage on the SS *Great Britain*, on what would probably be the great liner's farewell voyage to Australia.

Emily made no mention of whether or not her stay

in England had been successful, but as the telegraph charge was a pound for each word sent, Sam had not expected a long message. She would tell him all when she arrived. It was sufficient for now that she had decided to return to Australia – and to him.

He contacted the harbourmaster in Melbourne and made arrangements to be informed by telegraph when the *Great Britain* docked.

Meanwhile, Ruth would take on an ever-increasing role in the day-to-day running of the Walkerville house. She was having some success among her former colleagues, having enticed two young prostitutes away from the city's bawdy houses. Even Chaplain Gordon Glover was forced to concede that she was fully justifying Emily's faith in her. He was finding it far less embarrassing to hold conversations with Ruth now and had even developed a sneaking regard for her.

Sam had hoped, somewhat optimistically, that Emily might manage to return to the colony for Christmas. However, her telegraph stated that her ship was departing from Liverpool on the 17th November. It meant she would not arrive in Australia until mid-January of 1876, at the earliest.

Sam, too, was away from Adelaide for long periods of time. But in January he let Margaret into the secret of his activities, and took her and the boys away from the house for a few days, leaving a curious Ruth behind in sole charge of the home for 'fallen women'.

On 19th January, Sam received the message for which he had been waiting. The SS *Great Britain* had docked at Melbourne. Emily could be expected home within the next couple of days.

Anxious to learn what she had achieved in London

and, of even more importance to him, how she viewed her future in Australia, Sam called at the Walkerville house three times a day, hoping to find her there.

On the afternoon of the third day, when he was considering telegraphing his misgivings to the Melbourne harbourmaster, Sam knocked at the door of the house – and it was opened to him by Emily herself.

For a moment they looked at each other uncertainly, then Emily flung herself at him and amidst a mixture of laughter and tears he was able to ascertain that she had missed him, was deliriously happy to be back in Adelaide, and that she never intended leaving him again.

Later that evening, after a scorchingly hot day, Ruth and Margaret discreetly retired to the kitchen, leaving Emily and Sam sitting close to each other on the verandah, in the shadows cast by a full, midsummer moon and taking advantage of a slight breeze.

'I'm glad your trip proved successful,' Sam said. 'But it's galling that Mintoff should have got away with so much of your money. Does anyone know where he's gone?'

'Opinion has it that he is probably in hiding somewhere in eastern Europe. Unfortunately, although Uncle Percy ensured that City financiers did not lose their money, he was unable to help a great many smaller investors. Even so, I believe I lost more than anyone else. Perhaps that is as it should be. I was certainly the most gullible.'

'I prefer to see you as the most trusting,' Sam said gallantly. 'But I doubt whether Mintoff will enjoy his ill-gotten gains. He'll be forever looking over his shoulder, expecting someone to catch up with him.'

'Well, he may have defrauded me of a great deal of my money,' Emily said philosophically, 'but, thanks to Uncle Percy, he was stopped before my losses became disastrous. There is enough left to finance your farming venture, if that is what you still want to do?'

'Shall we talk about that tomorrow?' Sam suggested. 'You've had a very tiring time. You should have an early night and a good rest. I know! Why don't we ride out to Abe's Valley tomorrow? You have riding clothes?'

When Emily affirmed that she had, he said, 'Good! I've been doing quite a bit of riding myself recently. I'll hire two horses and pick you up here at about nine o'clock. We'll ride out to the valley and you can tell me more about your visit to England and who you met there.'

When Sam had gone, Emily was left with a sense of frustration and deep disappointment. She still wore Sam's ring on her engagement finger. Indeed, she had worn it throughout her time in England. Although it had aroused a great deal of curiosity among friends and family, she had said nothing to anyone about its significance.

On the voyage back to Australia she had felt a growing excitement at the thought of meeting with Sam once more, wondering whether he would propose to her immediately, or wait until they were alone – as they had been for almost an hour on the verandah.

Instead, he had made no mention of his intentions towards her. Indeed, when Emily had tried to guide the conversation in that direction he had carefully sidestepped the issue.

It had been the same when she asked about his future and what he intended doing now. He had also ignored her offer of money to finance a farming venture on the land he now owned.

Emily went to bed bitterly disappointed with Sam's apparent lack of enthusiasm. She wondered whether there might be something on his mind. Perhaps some difficulties he had not been willing to disclose to her.

Such thoughts kept sleep at bay for much of the night.

VIII

Emily rose from bed the next morning determined to voice her fears to Sam as soon as they met. However, he seemed so happy at the prospect of riding to Abe's Valley with her that she decided she would put it off until a suitable opportunity arose, possibly later in the day.

It was a very pleasant ride out to the valley. On the way Sam pointed out a couple of cottages that had been built since they last made the journey together.

Soon, the beauty of the countryside through which they were passing mellowed Emily's mood, especially as Sam was being as attentive to her as she could have wished.

Then, when they were almost at the brow of the hill that marked a boundary of Sam's land, he pulled his horse to a halt. Uncertainly, she did the same.

'I am going to blindfold you now,' he said unexpectedly.

'You are going to do *what*?' she said, taken aback.

'Blindfold you,' he repeated, as though such a thing should have been commonplace in her life. 'When you last came here it was winter. Now it's summer and every-thing has changed. I want all the summer colours and flowers to come as a surprise to you.'

'Can't I simply close my eyes?'

'No, I couldn't trust you to keep them closed.'

She made no further protest, but Sam could sense her deep indignation as he secured a folded necker-chief about her eyes.

'Don't worry, I'll lead your horse and make sure we stay on level ground.' He was glad she could not see his smile.

'This is *silly*!' Emily declared as they moved off and she grabbed at the pommel of her saddle in order to retain her balance. 'I have already seen the different colours of the trees and bushes as we rode along – the flowers too.'

'Ah, but this is special. When I take off your blind-fold you'll gasp in admiration, I promise you.'

Despite his reassuring words, Emily grumbled in a good-natured manner as the horse left the dirt road and trod the soft grass of the valley floor.

When Sam brought the two horses to a stop, Emily said quickly, 'Can I remove my blindfold now?'

'Not for a minute. Let me lift you down from your horse first.'

He helped her down, then guided her a few paces from the animals before saying, 'Right, now you may remove it.'

Untying the neckerchief, she squinted against the strong sunlight. As her eyes became used to the light, she frowned. 'I can't see anything different in the trees and bushes here. They are all very much the same as those we have seen along the way.'

'That's because you're facing the wrong way. Why don't you turn around?'

Emily did so and gasped in utter disbelief. 'Sam! You've tricked me! You've built a house . . . Abe's house. The one he had drawn up plans for. But . . . how? How have you managed it so quickly? It's quite impossible!'

'No, Emily, I found a wonderful builder who told me that nothing is impossible – if the money is there. We must have had every skilled man in Adelaide working on the house.'

'But where did the money come from?' she asked anxiously. 'You haven't put yourself in serious debt with a bank? I can help you with money, but not as much as I would have wished.'

Sam shook his head. Taking her hand he said, 'Let's go up to the house. I'll tell you all about it on the way.'

Once they began walking, he said, 'Abe didn't only leave me the land, Emily. Because he had no living relatives he left me everything he owned – and I discovered he was a very wealthy man. So wealthy that I doubt whether *he* knew just how much money he had. What's more, I don't think he cared. He enjoyed what he was doing too much. It's taken me a long time to sort out his affairs, but it's done now. There's money in the bank – a great deal of money – and I don't owe a penny to anyone. What's more, the day before you arrived back I sold the leases Abe and I had on Jupiter Creek to a mining company. They paid me six thousand pounds, together with enough company shares to ensure a good income for the foreseeable future.'

'Sam! You have done wonderfully well! I am so proud of you I could cry!'

Tears had sprung to her eyes as she was speaking

but she brushed them away with an embarrassed laugh.

'There are still one or two important matters to be cleared up,' Sam said. 'But let me show you around the house before we talk about them.'

The interior fulfilled all the promise of the exterior, even though there were very few furnishings just yet. Standing on a balcony with breathtaking views over the valley and the surrounding country, Emily said honestly, 'I don't think I have ever seen a lovelier house, Sam. Certainly not one with a view like this. When do you plan to move in?'

'Well now, that depends entirely upon you. When you left for England we left a lot of things unspoken between us. I wanted you to experience the life you had led before – and could lead again – in order to make up your mind. I wouldn't want you to regret giving up your society friends without thinking seriously about it. I can give you a good life here in Abe's Valley, in this house, and I promise you will never want for anything, but I can't give you the prestige you could enjoy, if that's what you want.'

'I have never wanted any of that, Sam. *Never*. I always hated being told how I must behave; how I must talk – and to whom – and all because my uncle is a peer of the realm and my father was a vicar. All I have ever wanted is the chance to live my life in my own way, doing the things I want to do, with those I want to be with.'

'Do you really mean that, Emily? Are you absolutely sure?'

Close to tears, Emily said, 'I have never been more certain of anything in my life, Sam.'

'That's the way I feel about you, Emily. I am absolutely certain too. So . . . will you marry me?'

'I was beginning to think you would never ask! Of course I will – and it's not just because you'll be bringing me to the most wonderful house in the whole world. I would marry you if all you had to offer was a cave at some remote diggings. I love you, Sam – and I think I always have. I believe you know that . . .'

They clung to each other for a very long time before Emily suddenly said, 'But what of Margaret . . . and the boys . . . and Ruth?'

Sam smiled. 'Just around the corner from here, in the place where Margaret and Albert said they would live if they had a chance, the builders are putting the finishing touches to their new home. Margaret has agreed to stay in Australia and run this house for you, in whatever way suits you best. The boys will work on the farm as soon as Margaret thinks they're ready. As for Ruth . . . I had a word with the bishop's chaplain a couple of weeks ago. He's extremely impressed with her – in spite of his earlier misgivings. He's quite happy for her to continue the work you started, remaining in the house where you all live now. I think he feels you've stolen a march on the other churches. He wants to keep it that way.'

'Well!' Emily looked at Sam with a new respect. 'You *have* been busy, Sam Hooper. But you took a great deal for granted!'

'Was I wrong, Emily?'

'No, Sam. You have made me even more proud of you than I was already . . . but you don't seem to have left anything for me to do.'

Hugging her happily, Sam said, 'I can't imagine you ever being idle, Emily – and there's plenty to do here. First there's the house to be furnished and a wedding to organise. There'll be a whole estate to plan too, because I have ideas about expanding into the next valley. That will need workers. Then there are my mining interests and I'll need your help to manage the money Abe has left me . . .'

Sam's voice trailed away but he had said enough to excite Emily. She gazed towards the valley where he intended expanding and in her mind's eye envisaged a whole new community of those who, like herself and Sam, had come to a new land, seeking a fresh beginning.

There would be houses . . . a school . . . a church too, perhaps.

Turning to Sam she said, 'Yes, Sam. I know we're going to be very happy here . . .'

Winds of Fortune

To John St Aubyn, DSC, DL, 4th Baron St Levan, for allowing artistic licence in my depiction of his ancestors. Susan, Lady St Levan, for her warm hospitality on my visits to St Michael's Mount.

The Hon Piers St Aubyn, MC, for his encouragement and enthusiasm.

Prologue

Summer 1812

John Humphrey St Aubyn was standing on the stone-flagged terrace of the fortified house which occupied the summit of St Michael's Mount, talking to his father, Sir John, when the sound was first heard.

It came from the direction of the English Channel, somewhere beyond the extent of the bay which took its name from the Mount. It sounded like a peal of distant thunder but, although a slight haze hid the horizon, there was not a cloud to be seen in the late evening sky.

'What do you think that was?' Known as Humphrey, to avoid any confusion with his father, the speaker was an intense young man of twenty-two, and he put the question anxiously to Sir John.

'I know *what* it was. It was a broadside, fired from a man-o'-war, but I'm damned if I know who is responsible. There have been no answering shots, so there can't be a battle taking place.'

Not very tall, but elegant and still handsome, Sir John looked much younger than his fifty-four years, despite his well-groomed grey hair.

While the two men were still pondering the source of the sound, it was repeated.

Humphrey gave his father a quizzical glance and the older man shook his head. 'That was from the same ship. At a guess, I'd say it's most likely a French privateer, harassing the fishing fleet – but he's a bold man to risk coming so close to our coast, although he's no doubt depending on using the cover of darkness to escape from any pursuit.'

Both men looked out across the bay, frustrated by the haze that prevented them from seeing the farthest point of the Lizard, the thick thumb of Cornwall, which protruded out into the Channel.

On a clear day the occupants of the castle on St Michael's Mount had an unequalled view of the Lizard coast. The Mount itself was unique. A high, rocky island for much of the time, it became linked to the mainland by a glistening stone causeway at low tide.

The castle, perched on the summit of this part-time island, had been in turn a church, priory, fortress and private house during its centuries-old history. Today, it was an architectural blend of all four and, when not simply called 'the Mount', was referred to as 'the castle'.

When the sound of a cannonade was heard yet again, Sir John strode to the battlement, looking out over one of the gun emplacements sited there as defence against the threat of a French invasion.

Since Admiral Lord Nelson's great victory over the French and Spanish navies, more than six years before, such a risk had become virtually non-existent. However, history had taught the inhabitants of this part of England not to underestimate the determination of the French to carry the war to their traditional enemy.

'That was closer, Humphrey. The ship would appear to be heading this way. Run and fetch my telescope. You'll find it on the windowsill in my study.'

About to carry out his father's instructions, Humphrey hesitated. 'What of Juliana? Will she mind . . . ?'

'Mind? You're my son, dammit! Why should she *mind*, eh?'

Humphrey inclined his head and hurried away without replying. Hopefully he would not meet up with Juliana, the mistress who had taken the place of his own mother in his father's affections.

He could think of many reasons why she would object to his presence on the Mount. One in particular was that she was pregnant, yet again. Another was that he was Sir John's son by his *first* mistress, Martha Nicholls. Juliana had never fully accepted that one of Humphrey's brothers, and not her own eldest son, would one day inherit the Mount and much of the St Aubyns' extensive land-holdings.

In truth, the situation was difficult for everyone. Sir John was a genial and generous man, attracted to women. The attraction was invariably reciprocated, but he seemed to have an aversion to matrimony.

Humphrey's mother had been Sir John's mistress

for many years, bearing him three sons and two daughters. Then his fancy had been taken by Juliana Vinicombe, daughter of a local farmer.

Not that Sir John had abandoned Humphrey's mother entirely. Given a generous allowance of three hundred pounds a year, she had been settled in a village, inland from the Mount, when Juliana moved in with the baronet.

That had been some years ago. Since then, Juliana had presented Sir John with a further five sons and three daughters – and was now expecting her ninth child.

The amorous Sir John was also believed to have a daughter, born to him by an Italian woman he had met in France. It was rumoured, there were also a number of unacknowledged children born to tenants on the island, and some on the mainland, too . . .

Clattering down the stone staircase that led from the terrace to the living quarters, Humphrey put all such thoughts to one side. His father had been good to him. Indeed, he had been generous to *all* the children of his long-term mistresses.

Humphrey and his brothers had attended university. Humphrey himself was a student at Jesus College, in Oxford, and both their sisters had made good marriages.

The children had also been encouraged to adopt their natural father's name and he had most generously settled ten thousand pounds on each of them – money he could ill-afford.

Humphrey was in a long corridor inside the castle

when, turning a corner, he came face-to-face with Juliana.

Normally a vivacious, attractive woman, she was not at her best during pregnancy. She tended to put on weight and her skin became somewhat blotchy. Her state also tended to make her short-tempered.

'What are you doing here, in this part of the castle? You have your own quarters.'

'I was under the impression the *whole* castle belongs to my father.' Humphrey showed considerable restraint. He resented this woman who had taken the place of his mother in Sir John's affections, but knew it was wise not to offend her. She wielded considerable influence over his father.

Although she was careful to conceal her feelings from the baronet, Juliana was jealous of the money and affection lavished upon the children who Sir John had fathered by Humphrey's mother.

'I'm in this part of the house because my father sent me to fetch a telescope from his study. It's likely a French warship is offshore, firing at something or another.'

Juliana's resentment was immediately forgotten. 'A French warship? Is it coming this way? Catherine and Richard have been spending the day riding at my father's farm. They will be coming back from the mainland at any time now. What if the French ship sees them and fires upon them?'

Catherine and Richard were Juliana's two youngest children. Despite the bitterness Humphrey felt towards Juliana, he was genuinely fond of both of them.

'The course of the French boat – if indeed it *is* a French vessel – is not certain. But after I've taken the telescope to my father, I'll run and tell one of the boatmen to go to the mainland. He can make certain Catherine and Richard remain there until it's clear what is happening. The causeway will be passable before night falls. They can be brought back to the Mount then.'

'Thank you . . . Thank you, Humphrey.' Juliana was a highly emotional woman and tears suddenly filled her eyes. For a moment it seemed she would say more to him. Instead, she turned and hurried away, heading in the direction of her own room.

As Humphrey emerged on the terrace carrying the leather-bound, brass telescope, he heard the sound of yet another broadside. It was still some distance away, yet he realised it was closer than before.

Sir John greeted him impatiently. 'The damned French ship could have been upon us and away again by now!' Unabashed by such a gross exaggeration, he demanded, 'What kept you so long?'

When Humphrey repeated his conversation with Juliana, Sir John's attitude underwent an immediate change and he became thoroughly alarmed.

'Go and tell Abel to take a boat to Marazion right away. He's to find somewhere safe for the children until any danger has passed. Tell him I shall hold him personally responsible for their well-being . . . And Humphrey!' As Humphrey turned to hurry away, Sir John brought him to a halt, '. . . I'm very pleased indeed to see you showing such concern for the two children.'

Clearing his throat noisily, he added, 'I know it can't be easy for you, but Juliana's children really do think the world of you, you know. Young Richard in particular . . .' He mentioned his youngest son, one of his favourites. 'He's a lot like you. A thoroughly good lad.'

As though embarrassed by such a declaration of affection, Sir John turned away, at the same time putting the telescope to his eye. 'Now, let's see if I can get a sight of the Frenchman – if that's what it is.'

With his back to Humphrey, he added, 'Once you've given Abel his instructions, go to the inn. You'll no doubt find most of the Mount's gunners there. Order them to muster here. Tell them I am waiting and will give them the key to the powder room when they arrive. I only want *sober* men, but God help any man who is too drunk to carry out his duty to his King – and to me.'

Humphrey located Abel Carter in the St Aubyn Arms with a number of other St Aubyn men. He was tall, taller than Humphrey, and there was something about his eyes that always uncomfortably reminded Humphrey of his father.

Ten years older than Humphrey, Abel had been destined for a promising career in the Royal Marines Artillery. Unfortunately, he had received a serious leg wound fighting against Napoleon's army, some years before, and had been discharged.

When he recovered he spent some time at sea

before returning to the Mount as the St Aubyns' senior boatman.

Abel was the son of a Mount woman who, as a young girl, had been employed at the great house as a housemaid. She had fallen pregnant when just sixteen.

It was strongly rumoured that she had been the first of Sir John's fruitful mistresses. However, no one had dared voice such thoughts aloud at the time and she was married off to Isaac Carter, a rather simple woodsman who worked on one of the St Aubyn estates.

She never lived to reveal the secret of her son's parentage, dying while giving birth to a still-born child when Abel was three years old.

Abel had been brought up by his grandparents on the Mount until he joined the Regiment of Marines at the age of sixteen. Now he lived in the village situated at the foot of the Mount, with his widowed grandmother.

It was probable that she knew the identity of his true father, but both grandparents came from generations of loyal St Aubyn retainers. They told him nothing.

Nevertheless, there were others whose love of gossip was stronger than the loyalty they owed to the family they served. Abel was left in no doubt that he had as much of a claim to the St Aubyn bounty as Humphrey and the children of Sir John's two acknowledged mistresses.

The inn frequented by the St Aubyn employees was the end building of a terrace of cottages facing the harbour, at the foot of the Mount. It was crowded and noisy, but the men inside fell silent when Humphrey ducked through the low doorway.

Abel had been drinking, but he seemed comparatively sober. The other St Aubyn employees appeared to be in a similar 'in-between' state.

They broke their silence and set up a rousing cheer when Humphrey told them they were to man the guns on the Mount, with the possibility of action against a French warship before darkness fell.

Abel would have led them from the inn, had Humphrey not put out a hand to detain him. 'Wait. Sir John has a special task for you.'

As the others rushed past him from the inn, Abel protested. 'But . . . I'm a trained gunner. The only one of them with any real experience!'

'Nevertheless, Sir John has said you are to take a boat to the mainland. Catherine and Richard are due back from the Vinicombe Farm at any time now. They'll be looking for a boat to bring them off to the Mount.'

As Humphrey was speaking, he and Abel had followed the other men from the inn. Once outside the sound of cannon-fire reached them. It was more of a ragged volley than a broadside on this occasion, but it was certainly closer than when Humphrey had heard it before.

'You hear that? It's the French ship. I'd lay a bet it's cruising close inshore, shooting at anything that presents itself. If it comes this far the Mount will be an obvious target, together with any boat in the vicinity. You're to make quite certain that isn't one carrying the

children. Keep them onshore and out of range of the
French guns. If all is clear, bring them over the cause-
way after dark, when the tide has fallen. Remember,
Abel, you're to take no chances with them.'

Abel gave Humphrey what his grandmother would
have referred to as 'one of his looks'.

Humphrey shrugged. 'Those are Sir John's orders,
not mine.'

'You know as well as I do that I'd be far more
usefully employed up at the house, aiming the
cannon.'

Humphrey's lips tightened. 'Sir John named *you*
as the one to fetch the boys. Should you not be on
your way?'

Abel remained looking at Humphrey for some
moments. Then, shrugging his shoulders, he turned
away without another word and strode off, heading
in the direction of the harbour.

On his way up the steep hill leading to the fortified
house, Humphrey looked back and saw Abel making
for the harbour entrance, rowing in a small boat.
When he reached the mainland there would be men
to pull the boat up on to the beach and secure it until
it was needed again.

As Humphrey watched, the boat cleared the harbour and began to plunge and rise with the motion
of the open waters of the bay. It would pose no
problem for Abel. He was a very capable man and
thoroughly reliable. But Humphrey always wondered whether Abel had resentment bottled up inside
him that would one day come out into the open.

All the same, he could not help feeling sorry for

the man. Aware of Abel's story, Humphrey was sufficiently observant to see the St Aubyn likeness for himself. He wondered how *he* might have felt had his father chosen to acknowledge only Juliana's children and not Humphrey and his brothers and sisters . . . ?

Another ragged cannonade broke into his thoughts. He hurried through the house and made his way to the open gun platform.

'There she is, Humphrey. It's a French ship right enough, not a privateer, but a man-o'-war – and heading this way.' Pointing out across the battlements, an excited Sir John handed the telescope to his son, but it was hardly necessary to use it.

The French ship had emerged from the haze and was now no more than two or three miles distant. An outsize tricolour, almost as large as a top-sail, billowed from a masthead.

All around, on the terrace, men were hurrying to-and-fro, carrying cannonballs, cartridges of gunpowder, rammers and wads for the thirty-two-pounder guns positioned at embrasures around the gun platform.

This was only one of a number of such platforms sited on and around the Mount, but the baronet considered it to be the most effective site if the French ship continued on its present course.

'Load the guns – but keep them back out of sight until it's time to use them,' ordered Sir John. 'We don't want to frighten the Frenchmen away. You! Isaac! Throw that pipe away. Are you mad, man? There's gunpowder all around and you're smoking a pipe! No! Don't knock it out against the wall. That's even more dangerous. Throw it away, over the wall. I'll deal with you later.'

Turning to Humphrey, Sir John demanded angrily, 'Has he been drinking?'

'Most of the men were at the inn when I called them out,' replied his son.

'Heaven help us! They are poor enough gunners at the best of times. I should have kept Abel on the Mount. He's the only man capable of sending a cannonball where it's intended to go – but I've sent him to fetch the children.'

'He said as much himself,' agreed Humphrey, 'but it's too late now. I saw him heading out of the harbour as I entered the house.'

'Then we'll just have to do the best we can without him.'

The French ship opened fire once more and Humphrey counted at least eight shots.

'What are they firing at?' Sir John demanded.

'The cottages beyond Perranuthnoe.' Humphrey named a small fishing community less than two miles from the Mount. 'They don't appear to have hit anything – but one thing is certain. They *are* heading this way.'

'Then we must make quite certain we're fully prepared for them.' Turning to the men loading the guns, he shouted, 'Hurry and have those guns ready – and bring up more powder and shot. The French will be within range before we've a single gun loaded if you don't move yourselves.'

The Mount men redoubled their efforts and Humphrey watched as the French ship drew nearer.

It was not a huge man-o'-war, no more than a thirty-two-gun frigate, and its shooting did not appear to be particularly accurate. But the castle on the Mount was a large target. Not all the French shots would miss.

Humphrey was not alone in such thoughts. Sir John was watching the approaching vessel anxiously. Suddenly he said, 'Humphrey, go down and tell Juliana to remove the children and servants to the north side of the house. We don't want to run the risk of anyone in the household being injured.'

At that moment, much to the surprise of both men, Abel ran up the steps to the terrace, showing little trace of the leg wound which had ended his career as a Royal Marine gunner. He was breathing heavily as a result of the speed at which he had hurried up the steep approach to the gun platform.

'What are you doing here?' demanded the baronet. 'Where are Catherine and Richard?'

'Inside the house. The boat bringing them home was already two-thirds of the way here. It was quicker to bring them to the house than turn around and return to the mainland.'

For a moment or two it seemed Sir John would dispute Abel's assessment of the situation he had encountered. Another salvo from the French ship, this time clearly aimed in the general direction of the Mount, changed his mind.

'Humphrey, hurry down and clear the seaward side of the house . . . Abel, you're the best gun captain we have. See if you can sight the guns so that some shots, at least, are not lost in the sea.'

Relieved that he had escaped the wrath of Sir John,

Abel hurried away to lay the guns on the rapidly closing target.

Humphrey found Juliana and the remainder of her children excitedly watching the approaching French ship from a window in the blue drawing-room, probably one of the most dangerously exposed positions in the castle.

Her initial response was resentment at being obliged to obey an order given to her by Humphrey. However, when he pointed out that the Mount was already the target of the enemy ship, she hurried from the room, ushering the protesting children before her.

By the time he returned to the south-facing gun platform, the sun was already dipping into the ribbon of haze that hid the horizon. The duel between ship and shore would be short-lived. If the French ship was to clear the dangerous Cornish coast before darkness closed in, it would have time to fire no more than a couple of salvoes before turning into the onshore wind and tacking away into the Channel.

There could be little doubt the captain had scanned the Mount through his own telescope, but he could not have seen the guns. As a result he was coming recklessly close to his intended target.

It seemed that his intention was to turn at the last moment and fire a broadside or two at the imposing granite castle.

'Run out the guns . . . now!'

Abel's shouted command startled Humphrey, who had been watching the sailors busying themselves about the guns on board the French ship.

Anticipating the French ship's imminent manoeuvre, Abel hurriedly inspected the elevation of the cannons. He had made chalk marks on the stones of the terrace, indicating the tracks that the wheels of the gun carriages should follow. There were further marks where they were to stop.

As the heavy guns were trundled into position, Abel exhorted the men to even greater efforts. The French warship had almost reached the position upon which he had laid his guns. He was anxious to hit the French vessel before its gunners fired upon the Mount. An unexpected salvo should effectively throw the French aim off balance.

Abel's plan was more successful than anyone could have dared to hope, his timing perfect. An officer on board the French warship saw white smoke belch from the embrasures on the south-facing terrace and shouted a warning, but it came too late.

A number of the heavy cannonballs splashed harmlessly into the sea around the vessel, but as many more succeeded in striking their target – and with considerable effect.

One carved a path through the packed ranks of a gun crew on the open deck. Two more tore away sails and rigging. The most telling shot of all was one of which any gunner would have been proud. It struck the mainmast at one-third of its height from the deck, bringing it crashing down, tearing sails and severing rigging as it fell.

The French gunnery officer made a call upon his men to return the fire. They did so, but, as Abel had intended, the volley from the Mount had thrown the

ship off course. Not one of the French cannonballs
struck its large, immobile target.

Meanwhile, on the Mount, Abel was exhorting his
jubilant gunners to swab out the barrels of their
cannons and reload, in order to open fire once more.

While they carried out his orders, he hurried
among them, depressing the elevation of the guns
slightly.

It was unnecessary to change the direction in which
they would fire. A stiff onshore wind was bringing the
French vessel ever closer to the shore. Still broadside
on to the Mount, the vessel pursued an almost straight
line from the spot where she had been hit by the
Mount's salvo.

The men on the Mount could clearly see the panic
on board the French ship, as officers and crew sought
to hack away the broken mast and rigging in a desperate attempt to regain at least some control of
the vessel.

But the French captain's arrogant recklessness had
already sealed the fate of his ship.

'Fire!'

Another volley thundered from the guns on the
terrace of the Mount. Once again many of the cannonballs struck home on their target. The skills gained
by Abel during his service with the Royal Marines
Artillery had not been forgotten. The French ship was
doomed.

The only uncertainty now was the exact spot where
the French vessel would come ashore.

Sir John ordered the St Michael's Mount cannons to

cease firing when it became apparent that the French crew could do nothing to save their ship.

The gunfire directed by Abel had brought down a second mast and spars. Rigging and tattered sails lay in a tangled mess on the main deck and spilled over the side of the ship, blanketing the gun ports.

By now darkness had closed in on the scene of the one-sided battle. Although it hid the confusion on board the French ship, the excited voices issuing and countermanding orders could clearly be heard.

All thoughts of hostile action were forgotten now. The only aim of those on board was survival. The stiff onshore breeze was accompanied by a heavy swell. Born in the depths of the Atlantic Ocean, the rollers died a noisy death on the rocks around the Mount and they were bringing the ship ever closer to destruction.

'Where do you think the ship will come ashore? It looks almost as though it might be driven past us and on to the mainland.'

Humphrey put the question to his father, but it was Abel who replied. 'It will strike below the old warren.'

The spot he mentioned was at the foot of one of the steepest parts of the Mount. Pointing in the direction of the causeway, he added, 'They know where it's coming aground.'

A great many shadowy figures were hurrying along the barely visible causeway and making their way around the shoreline of the Mount, heading for the spot where Abel had predicted the ship would be driven ashore. Some carried dim lanterns and these cast an eerie yellow light on others about them.

Now, those on the gun platform became aware of excited voices as men and women scrambled over the rocks on the foreshore.

'The causeway is barely open,' exclaimed Sir John. 'But whole families are coming from the mainland, hoping to salvage something from the wreck.'

'They'll be out for blood too,' said Abel. 'The French have taken many Cornish fishermen who'll never be seen again – and this particular ship has just been bombarding villages along the coast. There'll not be many prisoners taken tonight.'

Humphrey possessed a gentle nature that would one day lead him to become a member of the clergy and he was appalled by the statement of the Mount boatman. 'But . . . that's murder! Can't we put someone at this end of the causeway to turn the mainlanders back from the Mount?'

Sir John looked at his son pityingly. 'You've never seen your fellow-men when there are spoils to be taken from a wreck, Humphrey. I have. All the constables in the county couldn't stop them. All we can do is go down there when the ship strikes and try to save as many Frenchmen as we can.'

Calling to the men who had manned the cannons, Sir John said, 'I want you men down there too – saving lives. You can pass the word that if I see any Mount men doing harm to the French sailors, they'll have neither work nor a home tomorrow. Abel, you've got more about you than most. Hurry to the inn. Tell the landlord to prepare to receive French prisoners – and arrange for a guard to be placed on them. They'll be held there until we can hand them over to the Admiralty.' The Admiralty was the authority responsible for prisoners-of-war.

The men who had only a short while before been intent on reducing the French warship to an unmanageable hulk were unhappy at not being allowed to take part in plundering the vessel when it came ashore. There was some subdued grumbling among them, but they knew better than to express their dissatisfaction openly in the presence of the baronet who employed them.

Aware of their feelings, Sir John called after them, 'You did well this evening, men. I'll see you're rewarded for your efforts. You especially, Abel. I was impressed by your gunnery skills. Very impressed indeed.'

If Abel was pleased by Sir John's praise, he did not allow it to show. Following the other men from the terrace, he made no reply.

'Did you hear that there Humphrey when he thought it likely there might be blood-letting when the French ship comes ashore? He wasn't so particular when we was shooting at 'em and couldn't see any blood. I reckon the time he's spent at that university has softened him up.'

One of the Mount men made the comment as the St Aubyn gunners made their way down the steep path from the castle. They were not dawdling and would be on hand to see the vessel come ashore. However, with no chance of acquiring any plunder, there was little sense of urgency among them.

'Shooting at men in battle is one thing. Killing them

when they're beaten and defenceless is something different,' said Abel scathingly.

'Tell that to *them*,' retorted the man who had made the derogatory remark about Humphrey St Aubyn. He pointed to the crowds gathering on the rocks ahead of them. 'I wouldn't try to stop them doing what they've come here for, if I were you. In the darkness they won't be fussy whether they're killing a Frenchman or a St Aubyn man.'

They had rounded a corner of the path which brought the causeway into view. The tide had receded enough to make the rock and shingle path passable between Mount and mainland, but the swell was still occasionally sending water swirling over it. However, by the light of the many lanterns being carried, it was possible to see a great many people – men, women and children – heading towards them.

'Good God! It looks as though the whole of Marazion is heading this way,' said Abel.

'They'll be from all along the coast and the Frenchmen have only themselves to blame,' said one of his companions. 'Their cannonading has stirred up the fishermen and their women. Besides, they have many old scores to settle. It'll be the Devil and not Sir John who'll be calling the tune tonight.'

At the last minute it seemed as if the French warship might cheat those waiting eagerly on the rocky foreshore of the Mount in the hope of plundering something of value from the stricken vessel and wreaking revenge on its crew, and a howl of frustration went up.

Then, just as it seemed that the ship would drift past the rocks of the Mount and into the bay, a capricious wind swung it back towards the waiting Cornish men and women. An obliging swell immediately lifted it and carried it over the outermost rocks.

The listening mob heard the screech of tortured timbers as the stricken ship was battered mercilessly by a combination of rocks and a restless sea. Panic-stricken, the unfortunate crew-members began jumping overboard in a bid to save their lives.

This was the signal for the waiting horde to swarm down upon them. Scrambling over rocks and splashing dangerously through the heaving water, they sought to intercept the Frenchmen.

The ensuing scene was one that would never be forgotten by those from the Mount who witnessed it. The mainland Cornish men and women were armed with a wide variety of makeshift weapons. Staves, spades, pitchforks, pieces of timber, axes and more conventional weapons were all used to batter those survivors who made it to the shore – and many who were still in the sea.

When a French seaman was felled, he was immediately surrounded by a swarm of men and women. Robbed of everything of value, even the clothes he was wearing, he could consider himself fortunate if he escaped with his life.

Soon the whole foreshore was a heaving mass of screaming, shouting and fighting humanity and Abel felt unable to stand back from it any longer.

Calling on the Mount men to follow him, he did not wait to see if they were obeying his call. Scrambling

down to the rocks, he plunged among the mob, trying
to pull his fellow-countrymen from those who were
being attacked.

He was aware of others with him. Whether it was
Mount men, or mainlanders with a conscience, he did
not know – and no longer cared.

Coming upon a seaman crawling painfully from
the sea, Abel put his shoulder to a man intent upon
bludgeoning the bedraggled and exhausted survivor.
As he did so, the distressed man cried out, 'For
God's sake save us! There's almost a hundred English
prisoners on board – most are Cornish men . . .'

A wave rose from the sea, threatening to drag the
man back out with it, but Abel reached forward and
held him firmly until he was able to pull him to safety.

Others had heard the man's words and a shout
went up – 'There are Cornish men on board . . . save
the Cornish men.'

The cry was taken up and the mood of many
plunderers changed immediately. It was one thing
to kill Frenchmen who had been bombarding homes
in the vicinity, quite another to attack their own kind,
unfortunate enough to be taken prisoner.

Hands began to drag men from the sea and pass
them back to others behind them.

Not all the plunderers were ready to give up a
chance to enrich themselves. They showed no mercy
to survivors from the ship, whatever their nationality.
Others ignored the floundering men altogether, as
they pulled from the sea any item that floated free
of the doomed vessel.

Not far from Abel, the lantern held up by a woman

from the mainland showed a young lad desperately trying to secure a grip on a smooth, glistening rock in order to pull himself clear of the sea.

As Abel scrambled over the rocks to go to his assistance, one of the mainlanders, armed with a stout, pointed pole, struck at the desperate young man, knocking him backwards. When the sea sucked the helpless survivor back on to rocks, the pole was used in an attempt to pull him closer and rob him.

So angry was Abel that when he reached the rock, he wrenched the pole from the man's grasp. Knocking its owner into the sea, he pulled the young survivor close enough to heave him clear of the swirling water.

The young man was of slight build and much younger than Abel had at first thought. It took little effort to pull him clear of the water.

Ignoring the cries of the man he had knocked off the rock into the sea, Abel carried his unconscious burden to safety, leaping from rock to rock until he reached dry land.

He was pulled up a slope clear of the chaos of the foreshore by Humphrey St Aubyn.

'I saw what you did, Abel. Had I been closer I would have helped you. That man was an animal. He deserves to drown . . . But the boy? Is he badly hurt?'

'I don't know. He's certainly unconscious. Can you find someone with a lantern?'

The young boy was laid on the ground and a lantern brought to the scene. In its pale yellow light, he appeared pathetically young and possessed skin that Abel thought had never yet felt the touch of a razor.

'He's still breathing, at least,' said Humphrey.

'Yes, but he's been hurt. There's blood showing through his shirt.'

The boy was wearing no coat, only a light shirt of finer material than that worn by most seamen. If he was French, Abel thought he was probably a young gentleman, perhaps training to become a ship's officer.

'The wound would have been caused by the sharp stave,' said Abel. 'We'd better check and see how badly he's hurt.' As he spoke, he pulled the shirt clear of the boy's trousers and lifted it.

He frowned. There was a wide band of cloth wrapped about the boy's chest. It looked as though it might have been placed there earlier, perhaps to serve as a bandage. If so, it was possible the blood that could be seen came from an earlier wound. It must have reopened when he was being thrown about in the sea.

The source of the blood appeared to be beneath one of the boy's armpits. Abel called, 'Does anyone have a sharp knife? I'll need to cut this bandage away.'

One of the Mount men handed him a knife. Inserting the blade beneath the wide cloth bandage, he sliced through it before gently peeling it away from the boy's body, hoping that by doing so he was not going to open the wound further.

Suddenly, a gasp went up from the men standing about them. Abel, too, rocked back on his heels. He had found the wound. Slicing through the skin between two ribs, it was not particularly serious.

But it was not the wound that had caused the gasp from the watching men. The cloth bound about the young survivor's chest had not been a bandage to hide any injury. It had been worn to flatten the breasts of the young survivor. It was not a boy whom Abel had pulled from the sea – but a young *woman*!

Book One

1

Summer 1810

'Thomasina! THOMASINA!'

Standing in the doorway of a small cottage on the hill above the fishing village of Mevagissey, Mary Rowe called her niece yet again, her impatience increasing.

Turning, she called into the cottage, 'Dolly, did Thomasina say anything to you about where she might be going?'

Dolly shrugged her indifference. 'Nothing at all, Ma, but you know her as well I do. She's probably somewhere along the cliff, day-dreaming – or off with a boy.'

Mary Rowe expelled her breath in a sound that combined anger and frustration. 'I really don't know what's the matter with that girl. However unhappy she may be about starting work as a live-in maid, you'd think she'd show some gratitude to me for getting it for her. It's a job most girls would give their eye-teeth to have. Yet she goes missing just when she should be getting ready to set off to Trebene. I despair of that girl, I really do.'

Adding a couple of stitches to the hem she was letting down on one of her frocks, Dolly spoke without looking up, 'She really hates the thought of going to work as a servant, Ma.'

'What she thinks of it is neither here nor there,' snapped her mother. 'She has far too many ideas above her station in life, that one. We all have to do things we don't want to do and it's about time she realised it. I didn't want to be widowed, or have a young girl who isn't my own to look after – but it happened, and I've had to get on with it. I don't know what her mother would have said, had she known how Thomasina would turn out. The girl might have been born to my own sister, but she's like no other girl I've ever known. Anyway, she's going to work at Trebene House, whether she likes it or not. They'll be paying her six pounds a year, all found, and half of that is coming to me. It's little enough return for what I've spent on her all these past years – but it's better than the nothing I'm getting from her right now. By now most girls of her age have gone off and found themselves husbands – but not our Thomasina, oh no! She thinks she's too good for any of the village lads. I'm expecting better things from you, my girl, and don't you forget it, but at least your sewing brings a few coppers into the house. Now, put that dress down for a while and go off and find her. When you do, tell her I want her back here – *this instant.*'

*   *   *

Huddled in the shelter of a free-stone field wall, Thomasina Varcoe hugged her legs tightly and rested her chin on her knees. In front of her the field ended in a sheer cliff, beyond which were the grey waters of the English Channel.

Thomasina was not a typical Cornish girl. Her fair hair set her apart from her dark-haired contemporaries. Nor was she 'pretty' in the conventional sense. Her mouth was too large, her nose too proud and her firm jaw set a little too determinedly. Yet most people who glanced at her, whether they were men or women, usually looked again.

She had heard her aunt calling and knew why she was wanted, but she had no intention of returning to the cottage just yet. Trebene House would not fall to the ground because she was not there to begin work when they were expecting her.

She gazed out to sea, to where a formation of eight men-o'-war, in line ahead, ploughed through the choppy water, leaning away from the wind. The ships had put out from the nearby naval port of Plymouth and were bound for the open waters of the Atlantic, doubtless to seek out the ships of Emperor Napoleon's navy.

Resentfully, Thomasina thought that if only she had been a boy, *that* was where she would be. A sailor on a man-o'-war. She probably already had as much experience of the sea as many of those on board. More, certainly, than most who had been impressed into the King's navy.

Thomasina's father had been master of a modest sailing vessel, trading between Bristol and the smaller English Channel ports.

It had not been a grand vessel – indeed, it was scarcely larger than a fishing boat – but Thomasina had thought it the finest boat that had ever sailed from Mevagissey harbour.

After her mother died Thomasina had gone to live with Mary Rowe, her mother's sister, but she was happiest when accompanying her father on his coastal voyages, allowed to help work the boat.

Then, four years ago, when Thomasina was fifteen, her father and his boat had failed to return from what should have been no more than a short voyage between Falmouth and Portsmouth.

The weather had been fair along the coast at the time, but no trace of his vessel was ever found.

It was believed it must have been sunk by a French warship, or perhaps a privateer. Had it been taken as a prize, word would have been received from France long before now. Many such tragedies had been visited upon the families of seafaring men during the long struggle with France for supremacy of the sea.

His loss had devastated Thomasina, but she had received scant sympathy from her aunt, who seemed far more concerned about the loss of income than about the fate of her widowed brother-in-law.

This had done more to turn Thomasina against Mary than anything else she did, or would do, but she would not allow her dislike to show. It was then that Thomasina had learned to control many other emotions, too. She often came to the spot where she was now and for more than an hour cried as though she would never stop. But eventually she *did* stop and, by the time she returned to Mary Rowe's home some hours later, she had succeeded in putting an almost impenetrable shutter between herself and the rest of the world.

Since that time, Thomasina had not settled at anything for very long. For a while she had repaired fishing-nets in Mevagissey, then she tried her hand as a dairy-maid. This had been followed by general work on an inland farm, housework for an elderly widow crippled with arthritis and, more recently, preparing fish in a Mevagissey fish-cellar.

She particularly hated working in the fish-cellar. No matter how many times she bathed, she could never rid herself of the smell of fish.

Now Mary had found work for her at Trebene House, the manor home of the Vincent family, who owned much of the land in the Roseland area, a few miles away, opposite the busy sea port of Falmouth.

No doubt such employment would have delighted many young girls of her acquaintance. It offered security, regular food and the possibility of marriage to a fellow-household employee, who had the added attraction of enjoying a job for life.

However, Thomasina had long been aware that she did not share the aims and ambitions of other girls of her acquaintance. For most, the acquisition of a sweetheart and the prospect of an early marriage dominated their whole outlook on life.

Thomasina *had* a sweetheart, but he was frowned upon by Mary – and by the mothers of most of the girls in the area, too. Considered a ne'er-do-well, Jeffery constituted the only chink in the defences she had put up against the world. He alone had been kind and understanding at the time she had lost her father – and Thomasina loved him for it.

Jeffery scorned the aims and ambitions of his contemporaries, believing there were easier ways for a man to earn a living than by working his way into an early grave. He was fond of pointing out that while men, women and children in the countryside spent their lives in poverty and drudgery, those who lived in the great houses grew rich from their labours. He vowed he was not going to break his back in order to keep such people in idle luxury.

Thomasina fiercely defended Jeffery in the face of his critics, chief among whom was Mary Rowe. But this attitude led to him being shunned by those who were content to accept their lot in life. Because of her loyalty to him, Thomasina too was excluded from their company.

During these past few years Jeffery had spent an increasing amount of time away from his home village. Left behind, Thomasina had become more and more of a 'loner', refusing to conform to the ways of her aunt and the friends whom the older woman had gathered about her.

Not that Thomasina minded. Unlike many of the other girls, she had learned to read, and she read well. She was quite happy to lose herself within the pages of a book – one of an unclaimed consignment acquired by her father, many years before. Engrossed in the pages of a book, she was able to exclude the world about her.

When she was not reading, Thomasina would often come here, close to the cliff, and sit gazing out to sea. At first it had been in the vain hope that one day she would see the ship captained by her father sailing home, its increasingly long absence miraculously explained away.

The hope, although never entirely abandoned, had gradually receded. Sometimes, if Jeffery was home, he would come here with her, unbeknown to the disapproving Mary.

More recently, Thomasina would sit and watch the large ships with envy, wishing she were sailing with them to parts of the world she could otherwise only learn about through the pages of the books she read.

'Our ma's been calling you till she's gone blue in the face.'

Dolly's words broke in upon Thomasina's thoughts. The feet of the younger girl had made no sound on the soft grass as she approached the wall that sheltered her cousin.

'I heard her.'

Thomasina spoke truculently, resentful at Dolly's intrusion on what were probably the last moments she would ever spend here, in the spot she had come to regard as a personal sanctuary from the world about her.

'Then why didn't you come? You'll only make Ma mad by staying out here, pretending you haven't heard her.'

'Well, she's not going to have to put up with me for very much longer, is she? After today there'll only be you to grumble at.'

'Ma isn't that bad, Thomasina,' said Dolly unhappily. 'She'll miss you, really . . . I will, too.'

Thomasina looked up at the young girl who was five years her junior and her expression softened. 'Don't take any notice of me, Dolly. I'm just miserable at the thought of going off somewhere I don't want to be, to live and work. I'll miss you too – and your ma,' she added grudgingly. 'Life can't have been easy for her since my pa . . . since he didn't come back. I don't suppose I've helped very much, have I? I should have looked out for some farmer's son and trapped him into marriage. That way, you and your ma would never have been short of something to eat, at least.'

'You could still do that if you wanted to.' There was a hint of mischief in Dolly's expression as she spoke. She was very fond of Thomasina and wanted desperately to cheer her up. 'Billy Kivell's still single and his pa's got a nice-sized farm.'

Billy Kivell was a middle-aged simpleton who possessed the mind of a six-year-old. Desperate to find someone to care for Billy before he and his wife became too old, the farmer had let it be known that whoever married Billy would one day inherit the farm along with him. So far there had been no takers.

Thomasina smiled. 'That's something *you* can think about when you're a year or two older, young lady. But don't be in too much of a hurry to marry. I won't be able to save much for a wedding gift from the money I'll be earning for working at Trebene.'

Dolly looked at Thomasina sympathetically. 'I know you hate the thought of going there to work, but I'm sure it won't be as bad as you think. You'll eat well, have a nice uniform to wear and be able to come home to see Ma and me for one day a month, at least.'

'Yes, you're right, Dolly, but will you do something for me?'

'That depends on what it is,' replied Dolly guardedly.

'It's nothing much, really. If Jeffery comes looking for me, will you tell him where I am?'

'All right – but I won't be able to do it if Ma's around. She won't let me talk to him.'

'You'll find a way. Tell him I'll be free on Sundays, after the family have been to church – and I'll be back here on the first Sunday of each month, after I've been paid.'

'I don't know whether I'll be able to remember all that.'

'Of course you will,' said Thomasina sharply.

'What if he doesn't come around asking for you?' Dolly asked mischievously.

'He will.'

Thomasina spoke with more confidence than she felt. Jeffery had promised he would return to her, but she believed he had gone to London. There would be a great many temptations for him in the capital city of England.

Putting such thoughts to the back of her mind, she rose to her feet. 'Come on, Dolly. Let's get back to the house and put your ma out of her misery.'

2

Thomasina approached Trebene House carrying a
bundle containing the few personal items she was
being allowed to take with her to the great house.

She had been told she did not need very much.
The Vincents would be providing her with uniform,
toiletries and bedding, but she carried a neat outfit to
wear on the one day of the week when she would be
allowed to leave the house.

She also had a few items of simple jewellery,
acquired during her young lifetime. Among these
was a bangle given to her as a birthday present
from Dolly, a crucifix that had been a gift from her
father, and a few ribbons she had bought herself
from the pedlars who would occasionally call at the
Mevagissey cottage.

There was also a leather-bound Bible which had
belonged to her mother, given to her by her own

father, on the day she was married.

Thomasina walked alone to Trebene, following a route which took her along many miles of narrow country lanes. There was a quicker route which would have reduced the distance by almost one-third, but it would have taken her across fields and through a muddy, wooded valley.

Mary Rowe had warned her niece against taking this route. It would not do, she said, for Thomasina to arrive at Trebene with mud clinging to her shoes and staining the hem of her dress.

When she eventually turned into the open entrance gate of Trebene House and passed by the Lodge, Thomasina pondered irritably about the merits of the advice she had been given by her aunt. It was a hot day. She wondered whether arriving with a little mud attached to her might not have been preferable to presenting herself as she was now: hot, cross and bathed in perspiration.

The driveway to the house was long and it curved away through well-wooded parkland. Not until she was quite close to her destination did the house itself come into view.

It commanded a view over Carrick Roads, one of England's safest and busiest anchorages, but it was the house that took her attention. Seeing it at close quarters for the first time, Thomasina found it quite awesome.

A very large, square-built building, Trebene was bigger than any house she had ever seen. There seemed to be innumerable windows and Thomasina became uncharacteristically self-conscious as she drew closer. She felt her approach was being observed from every one of them.

As she paused, looking at the house uncertainly, she heard the sound of a horse coming along the driveway behind her at a fast trot.

Moving to one side, she peered up beneath the wide peak of her bonnet to see a horse and rider coming towards the house. They formed a contrast of colours. The horse was white, but its rider was dressed in black from his top boots to his tricorne hat. The only relief in his dark ensemble was a white cravat worn high at his throat.

The rider gave only a brief glance at Thomasina as he passed by – then he glanced again, longer this time.

Pulling his horse to a halt, he asked, 'Who are you, girl? What are you doing here?'

From the manner of his speech, Thomasina realised at once that he had been drinking heavily.

'I've come to work in the house . . . sir.' The respectful word was expected, she knew, but servility did not come easily to her.

'Have you, now?'

Swaying in the saddle, the rider took in Thomasina's body, from head to foot, in a manner that angered her more than she dared show. She bristled with defiance, but avoided meeting his gaze.

The moment was brought to a halt by his mount. Restless at being pulled up only minutes from water and a hay bag, it tried to move on.

Before the horse was brought under control it had made a full turn and moved farther away from Thomasina.

'It's high time Aunt Harriet brought some young blood into the house. What are your duties to be?'

'In the house . . . sir. A maid.'

'Then we shall certainly see more of each other in the future, young lady.'

As the horseman was about to dig his heels into his horse, Thomasina asked hesitantly, 'May I ask who you are, sir?'

The young man raised an eyebrow at her boldness, but he gave her an answer.

'Sir Charles Hearle, nephew of Mrs Vincent, your new employer. You'll find she demands much of you, but don't let her break your spirit. I like women who have a boldness about them.'

'You just keep clear of Sir Charles, he's a wrong 'un, and no mistake.'

The warning came from Lily, a big-boned, ungainly maid in her early fifties. She and Thomasina were working together, making up the bed in the room of Henry Vincent, owner of Trebene House.

Much to her disgust, Thomasina was now known as 'Ethel' within the Vincent household. On her first full day at the house she had been taken before Harriet Vincent, a tall, stern-faced woman whose opening words to her had been, 'Thomasina? *Thomasina?* What sort of a name is that for a servant girl. I'll not have a maid in my household called Thomasina. Do you have a second name, girl?'

When Thomasina admitted she had not, the mistress of the household said, 'Then you shall be called "Ethel". It's a name far more in keeping with

your position. Off you go, Ethel. Be sure you put
in a full day's work for the money you are being
paid.'

Lily had been given the task of familiarising
Thomasina with the layout and routine of the big
house and acquainting her with the duties she would
be required to perform.

'I've known Sir Charles since soon after he was
born,' continued the senior housemaid, warming
to the subject of the Vincents' titled nephew as
she expertly folded and tucked in a corner of the
bed-cover. 'There's not been a housemaid in Trebene
safe since Sir Charles was old enough to know what
it was all about. He's caused more grief here than
Napoleon, that one. Master Henry should have had
him put in the army, when he was persuading other
men from hereabouts to go off and fight for King and
country. I doubt if Sir Charles would make much of a
fighting-man, but it'd have saved many a young girl a
whole lot of sorrow.'

Lily spoke with such bitterness that, somewhat
unkindly, Thomasina wondered whether she was
genuinely angry about the downfall of the girls of
whom she spoke, or aggrieved because Sir Charles
Hearle had not included plain and ageing servants
among those to whom he made his overtures.

'Do Master Henry and the mistress have any children of their own?' Thomasina had seen no one about
the house who seemed to belong, and no one had
mentioned any offspring.

'Yes, Master Francis. He's off at university right now,
so you won't be seeing much of him for a while. Different

as chalk and cheese, him and Master Charles are. They can't abide one another, neither.'

Smoothing out imaginary creases in the silk coverlet with her hand, Lily said, 'There, that's the bedrooms finished in this part of the house. We'll go and see if Mrs Mudge has anything more for us to do before we check out the linen cupboards. When we've done that I'll pass you over to Mr Pengelly. He'll show you what goes on in the dining-room before the family come in for their meals. There's a sight more to it than sitting down with a pasty in your hand, I can tell you that.'

Cyril Pengelly was the family's butler. A tall, somewhat rotund figure with a pompous manner, he was the true ruler of the servants' domain – although it was a claim that would have been hotly contested by Eliza Mudge, the Trebene housekeeper.

The professional feud between the two was exploited to the full by the household servants, although none would dare openly offend either of them.

Thomasina had learned the names of the more important members of the staff, but had not yet been able to ascertain the full extent of their duties. Equally confusing was the routine of the house, as explained to her by Lily.

The only thing that had been made quite clear to her by the other servants was that she was very much an outsider. At Trebene, servants were usually taken on because he, or she, was related to another member of staff.

Thomasina had been employed on the recommendation of the local rector. A man who had been friendly with Thomasina's missing father, the cleric had become concerned about the worsening state of Mary Rowe's finances.

Thomasina was made aware that many of the other servants had relatives waiting for a vacancy to occur in the great house. As a result of her own appointment outside the established procedure, she was resented by the others.

Although she tried to shrug off the unfriendly attitude of the other servants, it did not make settling in easy for her. She felt that even Lily resented having to teach simple household duties to a complete stranger.

Although Thomasina was finding it difficult to fit into the household routine and had made no friends, she did not believe she had actually made any enemies. Then, one day, Mistress Vincent took Thomasina to task for not checking and emptying the wash-basins in each of the bedrooms when the members of the family came downstairs to breakfast.

It was a task she had not realised was hers. When she complained to the middle-aged maid responsible for the omission, the maid shrugged, disinterestedly.

'I've got my own work to do. I can't go around teaching you every little thing you ought to know. If you want to blame anyone, then blame the mistress for taking you on in the first place. It should have been quite obvious to her that you don't know the first thing about working in a big house.'

'No, I don't,' admitted Thomasina, 'but I'm doing my best to learn. I don't suppose *you* knew everything when you first came to work here.'

The maid sniffed her indifference. 'It was different for us. We all have mothers, aunts and grandmothers who've worked in the house. What goes on here comes natural to us. Trebene House has always been part of our lives and we're part of Trebene. We all know it – and the house knows it, too. You'll not see your time out here, young lady, you mark my words.'

Angrily Thomasina retorted, 'If you're an example of what the house does to people, I'm sure I don't want to live my life out here anyway.'

She glared at the other woman until she turned and went on her way without another word.

Thomasina felt she had got the better of the exchange, but it had disturbed her and left her feeling unsettled. It had been an uncomfortable insight into what the other servants felt about her.

Although she had now been working at the house for some weeks, she had come no closer to being accepted by the others. She wondered if she ever would.

Thomasina told herself it did not matter. She had already decided she had no intention of spending the rest of her life pandering to every whim of the Vincent family.

The big problem was what else she could do to ensure that regular money went to her Aunt Mary and to Dolly.

3

Thomasina had hoped that matters at the house would improve with the passing of time. That the other servants would gradually accept her as one of their number.

They did not.

The maid with whom she had argued spread the word that Thomasina regarded her employment at Trebene as purely a temporary expediency. This immediately set her farther apart from the others.

For each of the servants working in and about the house, Trebene was at the very heart of their being. A servant who did not hold such a view, especially a *female* servant, was regarded as a heretic. Soon even Lily, who was comparatively easy-going and simple-minded, began to avoid her.

Another thing that upset Thomasina was the name

given to her by Harriet Vincent. The other servants quickly realised how much she disliked it and made use of the name far more often than they might otherwise have done.

Then, one Saturday evening, an event occurred which temporarily drove all thoughts of domestic quarrels from the minds of the servants. Henry Vincent, travelling in his carriage with two elderly women neighbours, was held up by a highwayman outside the gates of Trebene.

The women, on their way to a dinner party at the house, were wearing a considerable amount of jewellery. By the time the highwayman disappeared into the night, the two near-hysterical ladies had been relieved of all such inessential accoutrements and a feebly protesting Henry Vincent had handed over a heavy purse.

Before dinner at the house could be contemplated, the two swooning ladies had to be plied with an amount of brandy that in any other circumstances would have raised eyebrows.

By now, Henry Vincent had recovered from his fright and was beside himself with blustering fury.

'The sheer impudence of the fellow!' he declared to the assembled family guests. 'Had the ladies not been with me, I'd have tackled the blackguard, pistol or no pistol. As it was, of course, I dared not take the risk of having the ladies involved. A rogue who's bold enough to hold up a gentleman's carriage within sight of his own house would not think twice about shooting at women.'

'Then it was fortuitous you had them with you,

dear,' said his wife placatingly. 'Had you been alone and tried to resist, you might not be here to tell the tale now.'

There were murmurs of agreement from the sympathetic guests. One said, 'Should you not inform the constable, Henry? After all, if there's an armed highwayman at large, he might well strike again.'

'The constable wouldn't risk his own skin by turning out after dark,' declared Henry Vincent derisively. 'No, I armed two of the grooms and sent them off to find Magistrate Williams. He'll organise a search party. Hopefully we'll have our man by morning.'

'I sincerely hope they *do* catch him,' said one of the more timid of the ladies. 'I shall be a bundle of nerves by the time I arrive home tonight. Indeed, I shall be praying that I reach my home safely.'

'There is no need for anyone to be alarmed,' declared Henry Vincent with pompous reassurance. 'Anyone who wishes to stay at Trebene overnight is quite welcome to do so. For those who feel they must return home, I will provide an escort – an *armed* escort. Now, we've done all that can be done. Let us forget about highwaymen for a while and try to enjoy the remainder of our evening together.'

There were servants in the room during the exchanges about the highwayman and the conversation was repeated with the addition of a few imaginative embellishments in the servants' dining-room, later that evening.

'Heaven help any honest stranger who's travelling the lanes of Cornwall tonight,' commented one of the footmen. 'If the gentry are in the same mood as

Master Henry, he'll be shot before he's able to explain his business.'

Thomasina was in the room with the other servants. Although she took no part in the conversation, she was concerned about a highwayman being at large in the countryside. The following day she would be walking along the lanes to pay a visit to her Aunt Mary and Dolly – and in her pocket she would have her month's pay. Half to hand over to her aunt and the other half to be 'put by' on her own behalf.

She comforted herself with the thought that a highwayman who held up carriages, and stole jewellery and the purses of rich men, would hardly be likely to want to rob a young servant girl.

The Sunday church service seemed to go on for an exceptionally long time, the elderly rector being carried away by the message of his sermon.

He preached on the subject of the eighth Commandment, 'Thou shalt not steal'. The text pleased Henry Vincent, but Thomasina grew increasingly impatient, knowing she had a long return journey to make once the service was over.

As soon as the service had finished and the servants had waited respectfully for the Vincent family to end their conversations with the rector, Thomasina set off.

She had been hoping, unrealistically, that she might arrive at her aunt's cottage in time to join them in their Sunday lunch. Taken in mid-afternoon, it was the highlight of the small family's culinary week.

Thomasina knew that she had no hope of making it now. She would be lucky to arrive in time to gulp

down a cup of tea before making her way back to
Trebene.

As she hurried along the church pathway she was
pursued by the voice of Eliza Mudge, the Vincents'
housekeeper, warning her to return to Trebene before
nightfall, in order to ensure she was not waylaid by the
highwayman.

Thomasina had no intention of obeying the housekeeper's instruction. She would pretend she had not
yet grown accustomed to the name of 'Ethel' and so
did not realise the housekeeper was talking to her.

4

Thomasina had only just left the last house of the village behind when she saw a horse and rider standing in the road ahead of her.

Even at this distance, Thomasina could see that his clothes were those of a gentleman. The fact that he was making no attempt to move out of her way vaguely disturbed her, but she cast her eyes down, with the intention of passing by without acknowledging the presence of horse and rider.

The horseman had other ideas.

'Has working at Trebene made you so high-and-mighty that you no longer recognise your friends, Tom?'

Startled, Thomasina looked up at the smiling rider.

'Jeffery!' As the horseman swung from the saddle, Thomasina ran to him with a cry of delight. Still holding the rein of his horse, he hugged her to him with his free arm.

Suddenly, she pulled back. 'But . . . what are you doing dressed like a gentleman – and riding a horse?'

'Is there a law in England which says I can't ride a horse – or give a lift home to my sweetheart – if that's what you still are and are on your way home?'

'The answer is yes – to your last question. I promised Aunt Mary I'd come to see her once a month and give her half my earnings – but you still haven't answered *my* questions.'

Instead of replying, Jeffery climbed back in the saddle. Steadying the restless horse, he extended a hand to Thomasina. 'I'll tell you on the way to Mevagissey. Come on.'

Holding her hand, he paused in the act of pulling her up behind him, 'What is your aunt's share of your month's pay?'

'A half – four shillings and ninepence. It should have been five shillings, but I was clumsy and broke a saucer. Mistress Vincent deducted sixpence from my pay.'

Releasing her hand and feeling inside a waistcoat pocket, he pulled out a number of coins and said, 'Here, share these with her, too.'

Glancing down at the money he had given to her, Thomasina saw that she was holding four dull, golden coins. She looked up at him in astonishment.

'You've given me four guineas!'

'That's right, two for you and two for your aunt.'

'But where did you get them – and your clothes, and the horse?'

'You ask too many questions, Tom – but you always did. For now, just let's say I didn't get it by touching my cap to the sort of people you're working for. Now, do you want a ride home, or not?'

After tucking the coins away safely, Thomasina took his hand again, this time a little uncertainly, and he pulled her up to sit behind him on the horse.

When she was about to resume her questioning, Jeffery put the horse into a canter and she encircled his body with her arms in order to maintain her balance.

He smiled back at her over his shoulder. 'Do you have to go straight home, or shall we stop somewhere along the way? I know a barn with plenty of fresh hay in it. We wouldn't be disturbed. The farmer's a lay preacher. He'll be out praying around the countryside all day today.'

With her face pressed against his back, Thomasina said firmly, 'We'll go straight home to Aunt Mary's, Jeffery Kent. You may have given me four guineas, but you haven't bought *that*.'

After a few moments she added, 'Besides, it's not decent to do it in the daytime. It might be a different story if you were to bring me back to Trebene again tonight, when it's getting dark. That's if you've told me by then where your money's coming from.'

He grinned back at her once more and kneed the horse to greater speed.

The change of gait caused Thomasina to grip him tighter than before. As her arms slid down to his waist, she felt a bulge beneath his coat.

Curious, she slid a hand between two of his coat buttons. What she felt there caused her to pull back from him so suddenly that she almost fell from the horse. He brought the animal to a halt immediately.

'Jeffery! You have a pistol tucked inside your belt!'

Seemingly unconcerned, he put the horse to a walk, 'You're *almost* right. In fact, there are *two* pistols.'

'What for . . . ?'

Suddenly, things dropped into place. His clothes, the horse, the money he had so casually given to her – and the incident involving her employer the previous evening.

With a thrill of excitement that was mixed with a degree of fear, she said, 'You . . . ! You've become a highwayman. It was you who held up Mr Vincent and his guests last night.'

'So *that's* who it was? I wish I'd known at the time. As it was, he was so scared he practically begged me to take his purse. The ladies were a bit more reluctant, but they coughed up in the end and presented me with some very nice baubles. They'll fetch a guinea or two when I go back to London.'

Jeffery spoke in an almost jocular vein, but Thomasina could feel a tenseness in him that had not been there before.

When she said nothing, he said, 'So now you know how I get the money to buy the fine clothes I'm wearing. What are you going to do about it, Thomasina?'

'I . . . Nothing . . . but it's come as a shock.' She had no intention of telling him of the excitement she felt. Of the contrast between the lives they were both leading.

'Will you tell your Mr Vincent who it was who held him up last night?'

'Of course not,' she replied sharply. 'But what will happen to you if they ever catch you?'

'They'll hang me. You know that as well as I do – but they're going to have to catch me first.'

Thomasina made no reply and they rode on in silence for a while. Then Jeffery said, 'It beats working, Thomasina. I've got things now I could never have bought if I'd worked all my life.'

'But . . . it's not honest.'

'Isn't it, Thomasina? Perhaps you can tell me what honesty is? Do you know how that Mr Vincent of yours can afford a fine house, lots of servants and all the other things he has?'

When she said nothing, he continued, 'I'll tell you. He's got shares in half the mines down Camborne way. He takes a huge profit from them, although he won't spend a penny on safety measures. A month or two back there was an accident at one of the mines. Five men were killed. Your Mr Vincent parted with twenty-five pounds for the widows. Five pounds for each man's life. Five men dead, and twenty-five pounds is all it takes to wipe his conscience clear. Afterwards he probably went home and spent more than that on the drink he and his friends enjoyed while he boasted about his generosity in looking after the families of the "poor dead miners". No doubt he added that their deaths were caused by their own carelessness.'

As he spoke, he jerked angrily on the reins and the horse threw up its head uncertainly.

When he had brought it under control once more, Jeffery said, 'I take money from the rich, Thomasina. Vincent and his kind take fathers, husbands and bread-winners from their families. Tell me, which of us is the robber?'

Thomasina said little for the remainder of the ride home, but Jeffery was aware of her side-turned head resting against the expensive cloth of his coat back, and of her arms encircling his body. He knew she was thinking deeply about what he had said to her.

5

'So you still enjoy letting me love you then, Thomasina, even though you know how I earn a living?'

In the darkness of the barn, Jeffery straightened his clothing and brushed unseen wisps of hay from his hat before replacing it on his head.

'Don't flatter yourself that it's love, Jeffery Kent. You don't need to be anything special to do what you've just done. There's not a man or boy over fifteen around here who can't do the same.'

'True, but not with you, Thomasina. I know that.'

'Like I just said, you think too much of yourself for your own good.'

Despite her words, Thomasina reached out and her fingers found his cheek.

'Perhaps I do, Thomasina, but I think even more of you.' Reaching up, he moved her hand from his cheek to his lips. 'Why not come away with me – tonight?

Don't go back to Trebene. You're not happy there. You never will be.'

Thomasina knew she dare not let him know how genuinely tempted she was to take up his offer. How much she wanted to be with him and never see Trebene again.

She *hated* working for the Vincents and living among their spiteful servants. She would dislike it even more now, thinking of Jeffery and the dangerous, yet exciting life he was leading.

Nevertheless, she said, 'There can be no future in going off with you, Jeffery, as well you know. One day you're going to be caught. You'll either hang or be transported. What would I do then?'

'By the time that happened you'd have enough money put by to set yourself up in a little business – or perhaps a grog shop, whatever suited you best.'

'If I went off with you it would be because I wanted *you*, not your money.'

He grinned in the darkness. 'Come away with me and you can have me *and* my money.'

'Only until they catch up with you – and they will, one day.'

'There'd be less chance of being caught if you were working with me, Thomasina. Think about it. If after I'd held someone up, you were hiding nearby with a change of clothes and another horse, we could ride off together and no one would even think of stopping us. They'd be looking for a highwayman, not a respectable couple of travellers.'

'If they ever caught up with us then we'd *both* hang. That doesn't bother you, I suppose?'

'I wouldn't let them catch you, Thomasina, even if it cost me my own life. I promise you that.'

She shuddered. 'I'd rather we didn't talk about it – and I'd better be on my way now. I'll be in trouble as it is from Eliza Mudge. She told me to be back at the house by nightfall. It's been dark for almost an hour now.'

She was aware that Jeffery was disappointed because she would not go off with him, but she thought it a stupid idea – albeit an exciting one.

As they approached Trebene House, Thomasina said she would walk the remainder of the way, just in case they met up with one of the family. She would need to make some awkward explanations if she was seen sharing a horse with an apparent 'gentleman'.

Jeffery did not dismount. Standing beside his horse, she looked up and said, 'Will I see you again soon?'

'Do you want to?'

'Of course I do! Will you still be in Cornwall next Sunday?'

'I might be.'

She realised he was sulking because she had not seriously considered the suggestion that she should go away with him. She dared not let him know just how tempted she was by the idea.

'If you are, I'll be free for the remainder of the day after the morning church service. I could walk along the Tregony road and you could be waiting for me somewhere along the way.'

'If I'm around I might be there.'

'You will,' she said confidently, laying her head against his leg. 'You want to see me as much as I want to see you. Take care, Jeffery – and don't do anything foolish.'

Turning to walk away, she suddenly stopped. Calling back softly, she asked, 'If I want you for any reason before then, where can I find you?'

'If I'm still in Cornwall you'll find me at the Heron Inn at Malpas, close to Truro. It's a comfortable, out-of-the-way inn where a man can come and go without any questions being asked of him. Do you think you're likely to come looking for me, Thomasina?'

'Who knows? It wouldn't be difficult to fall out with the Vincents. There's no telling what I might do then.'

6

Asking Jeffery where he was staying had been
prompted by no more than curiosity on Thomasina's
part, but the events of the next few days would make
her thankful she had asked the question of him.

On the Wednesday after Thomasina's visit to her
former home, the servants at Trebene were called
together by the housekeeper before they sat down
to their breakfast. This was to be a very special day
in the Vincent household. One for which plans had
been laid for many months. It was the ruby wedding
of Henry and Harriet Vincent and to celebrate it there
was to be a grand ball at Trebene.

It was an exciting occasion for the family – and also
for the servants, especially the young, unmarried girls.
The carriages of the gentry would be arriving all day,
bringing friends and acquaintances of the Vincents.

With them would be coachmen, grooms and perhaps

one or two footmen. There was speculation, too, among the men-servants about the numbers of ladies' maids who would accompany their mistresses, to ensure they looked their best for the evening ball.

Such occasions served as 'marriage markets' for all strata of rural society. It also provided an opportunity for those who did not have marriage in mind to flirt with members of the opposite sex.

At the gathering of household staff, called by Eliza Mudge, the servants were warned about the possible consequences of forming hasty liaisons with the servants of guests. It was one thing to fall pregnant by one of the Trebene men-servants. Many marriages had begun in such a fashion. It was quite another to bring a man to the altar when he lived many miles away and would probably deny responsibility for the condition of a girl he had met only once.

The Trebene servants were also reminded that the esteem in which the Vincent family was held in Cornwwall would suffer if they – each and every one of them – did not work hard to ensure that the ball was hailed by the country's gentry as a great success.

When Eliza Mudge was certain each servant had been made aware of the pitfalls of the day, she allocated them their duties.

Thomasina was given the lowly task of ensuring the fires in the bedrooms along each side of a long corridor were kept alight, coal-scuttles replenished and hearths kept clean. She was also to ensure that wash-basins were emptied and cleaned and water jugs kept filled at all times.

Such heavy carrying was usually delegated to a footman but, as Eliza Mudge explained, all the footmen would be employed on ground-floor duties beyond the capabilities of an inexperienced housemaid.

Thomasina's duties meant she would see little of the splendour of the ball. Nor would she meet any of the men-servants from the other country houses.

Neither omission bothered her too much, but the smirks on the faces of the other servants when her duties were given to her showed that they, at least, thought it would.

The evening was particularly busy for Thomasina. She hurried hither and thither fetching hot and cold water for guests as they prepared themselves for the evening's celebrations.

Most would be returning to their own homes when the ball ended, but some would remain at the house until the following day.

Although large, Trebene did not possess unlimited resources and many of the unmarried young guests were required to share a room with others. This put an additional burden on Thomasina and the other housemaids.

Two of the men sharing a room along Thomasina's corridor were Sir Charles Hearle and Francis Vincent, who was home from university for his parents' wedding anniversary.

Despite their reputed dislike for each other, both had given up their own, larger rooms in order that more guests might be accommodated on this special occasion.

When Thomasina went into their room to make up

the fire, only Sir Charles was there. He said nothing to her, but she was aware he was watching her movements closely. It gave her an uncomfortable feeling. She was glad that other guests were constantly passing along the corridor outside.

Once the ball began and the guests had left their rooms, her duties became far less onerous. There were still fires to be made up, water jugs to be filled and rooms to be tidied, but she could take her time now. The ball would not end until the early hours of the next morning.

She even had time to snatch something to eat from the kitchen, despite the frenzy of activity there.

By midnight Thomasina was feeling the effects of the long working day. There was little to do now except occasionally check the rooms and clean up any cinders from the grate.

Making one of her routine checks, she entered the room occupied by Francis Vincent and his titled cousin. She was startled to find Sir Charles Hearle there. He was standing in front of the fire wearing a dressing-gown. A pair of pantaloons lay crumpled on the floor close by the fire.

Backing away towards the door, Thomasina said, 'I'm sorry, sir. I didn't realise you were in here. I'll come back later.'

'No, you won't, I need you.'

His speech was slurred, as it had been on their first meeting, and Thomasina realised he had been drinking heavily during the evening.

Bending down, he picked up his crumpled pantaloons. As he straightened up he temporarily lost his balance and took a shaky half-pace forward. Recovering, he said, 'Some damned fool of a young woman spilled half a jug of cold water over my pantaloons. Look . . . they're soaked!'

Although she tried to appear suitably sympathetic, Thomasina wondered whether it might have been a deliberate act, but Sir Charles was still speaking. 'This isn't my usual room and I have no other pantaloons here. It's inconvenient, to say the least.'

Thrusting the offending item of clothing at her, he said, 'Iron these for me, then bring them back here – and be damned quick about it, you hear?'

Taking the pantaloons, Thomasina backed away from him. 'I'll be as quick as I can, sir, but it'll take a little while to find an iron and heat it. Everyone's busy and there's too much going on in the kitchen to have an iron anywhere near the fire there.'

'I don't want to hear any stupid excuses, girl.' Suddenly lunging across the room, he took back the pantaloons from her. 'Go off and find an iron and bring it back here. You can use this fire to heat the iron. While you're gone I'll stir some life into it.'

As Thomasina had anticipated, she could find no one in the kitchen with time to tell her what she should do. It was left to the Vincents' cook, the busiest servant there, to say, 'You'll find what you want in the ironing-room, girl. Next to the laundry – it's back there.'

She pointed to a door which led to the many utility rooms at the back of the house.

Thomasina had not known there was a separate

ironing-room at Trebene, but she did have an idea where the laundry was situated.

The ironing-room had shelves on one wall, on which was a confusing array of flat-irons. There was a special fireplace here too, with hobs to hold the irons while they were being heated, but it seemed that this was the one room in the whole of the house where a fire was *not* burning.

Choosing a middle-weight iron, Thomasina hurried back upstairs. She found Sir Charles Hearle pacing the bedroom impatiently.

'You've taken your time,' he grumbled, unreasonably. 'Get the iron heated and press these pantaloons dry – and quickly.'

Thomasina placed the iron on the small hob fitted to the fire. While it was heating, she put the damp pantaloons over the back of a chair, moving it close to the fire. She then laid a towel on the marble top of the wash-table. She would iron the pantaloons here.

As she hurried back and forth between fire and wash-table, she was aware that Sir Charles was watching her every movement. It made her increasingly uneasy.

The iron did not take long to heat and she set about the unexpected task. She was quite used to ironing, but never anything as fine as Sir Charles Hearle's pantaloons.

At last she put the iron to one side and handed the garment to him. She was greatly relieved she had not scorched them.

'What's your name, girl?' Charles Hearle put the question to Thomasina as she prepared to leave the room.

'Ethel, sir.'

'Ethel, eh? I don't care for the name. It's not the name for a pretty girl – and you are a damned pretty girl, Ethel, but I'm sure you've been told that many times before, eh?'

Thomasina had reached the door and was about to open it when Sir Charles hurried across the room and leaned against it. 'Don't go just yet, girl. Stay and talk to me a while. No, better still, have a drink with me. It's the least I can do. I appreciate a servant girl who's prepared to go beyond the call of duty to please those for whom she works.'

Sir Charles Hearle's drunken leer left Thomasina in no doubt about what he meant by going 'beyond the call of duty'. She had other ideas. She had already seen the half-empty bottle of brandy on a bedside table. Harriet Vincent's nephew was amorously drunk.

'I must get back to work, sir. Mrs Mudge will be here soon to make certain I'm working.'

'Nonsense, girl! She's far too busy downstairs to worry herself about anything that's happening anywhere else in the house. Besides, everyone is enjoying themselves, so why shouldn't you have a little fun too, eh? You and me.'

Putting an arm about her shoulders, he began leading her across the room towards the bottle – and the bed. 'Come along, Ethel, you'll feel more relaxed when you've had a drink.'

'All right, thank you, sir.' Thomasina knew she could not match his strength, so she decided to resort to subterfuge.

'Good girl! I knew I hadn't misjudged you. Shall we now . . . ? Or would you like a drink first?'

'Yes, please. A large one.'

'That's my girl!' Releasing his hold on her, Sir Charles picked up the bottle. Clumsily he began to remove the cork.

This was the opportunity Thomasina had anticipated. She ran for the door. Yet again, Sir Charles Hearle foiled her. Moving surprisingly swiftly, he forced the door shut once more, before she could escape from the room.

'I thought you changed your tune a little too quickly. It was a good try, girl, and I do like a woman with some spirit. We're going to get on well, you and I. Come on, over to the bed.'

He had an arm about her again, while his other hand gripped her forearm. She began to struggle now, but he gripped her even harder.

Wriggling in his grasp, Thomasina suddenly found the side of his face against hers. Turning her head sharply, she gripped his ear between her teeth and bit him – hard.

She tasted blood on her tongue as he shrieked in pain. Releasing her, he reached up to her face to push her away, at the same time crying, 'You little bitch! You'll pay for this . . .'

Thomasina turned to run for the door, but Sir Charles recovered far more quickly than she had anticipated. He hit her on the back of her head with his clenched fist, causing her to stumble and fall to her knees.

Before she could rise, he dropped on her and twisted

one of her arms, forcing her down to the floor, on her back.

He continued twisting and she cried out in pain. Then, as he lay on top of her, she tried to bite him once more, but in the struggle his head came down sharply, striking her on the forehead with considerable force.

Afterwards, Thomasina was not certain whether or not she had been knocked unconscious for a while. She was certainly dazed and it was long enough for the drunken baronet to achieve his aim.

She felt him force his way inside her and opened her mouth to scream, but the sound was cut off by his free hand. She tried to throw him off her, but, quickly realising that the movement of her body only excited him further, she attempted to prevent her body from responding to what he was doing to her – and hated Sir Charles Hearle all the more because of it.

The ordeal lasted no more than a few minutes, although it seemed much longer.

It ended almost as violently as it had begun. Then he sagged, a dead weight on top of her, and now she was able to push him from her without any resistence on his part.

This time she made it to the door and fled along the long corridor, heading for the servants' quarter.

She returned to work later that night, but did not go near Sir Charles Hearle's room again and had no idea if he ever returned to the ball.

A fierce hatred for the baronet burned inside her with an all-consuming intensity, but, as with the loss of her father, she succeeded in pulling down a shutter that set it apart from reality.

She would never forget what he had done – and certainly never, ever forgive him. But life would go on.

7

It was a decidedly jaded Charles Hearle who tackled his aunt the morning after the grand ball. It did not help that Harriet Vincent, who could not have had more than a couple of hours' sleep, appeared to be her usual immaculate self.

Looking at him critically as he entered the breakfast-room, she said, 'Well! If I thought all my guests were going to look like you this morning, I would cancel breakfast. You look absolutely *awful*!' Leaning forward to peer at him more closely, she asked, 'What have you done to your ear? You have a very nasty wound there.'

Sir Charles put a hand up to his ear, guiltily. 'I went out in the garden in the dark last night and became entangled in one of those climbing roses of yours.'

'It looks painful. You should have Mrs Mudge put something on it for you.'

'I'll think about that later. I have come down early to speak to you about something of rather more importance than a scratched ear, Aunt Harriet. I very much fear that one of the maids is a thief.'

Harriet Vincent looked at her nephew sharply. 'That is a very serious accusation to make, Charles. I think you had better tell me about it. Who is the girl in question?'

'I can't remember her name – to be quite honest I can't even recall her face, but she was working in my room last night.'

Frowning, Harriet Vincent tried to remember the arrangements that had been made for the ball.

'I think it might have been Ethel. A new girl – and not local. She was recommended to me by Parson Trist, and had some ridiculous name when she came to me. Quite unsuitable for a servant. I said that she was to be called Ethel. She has not proved entirely satisfactory, but are you saying she's dishonest? What do you think she has stolen?'

'Two guineas, Aunt. I had an accident at the ball last night. Water was spilled over my pantaloons. I went up to my room, found this maid there and asked her to iron the pantaloons dry. She did so, but when she'd gone and I went to return the items I had taken from my pockets, two guineas were missing.'

'Are you absolutely certain, Charles? This is an extremely serious matter for such a young girl.'

'I am quite certain, Aunt Harriet. I took the two guineas from my pocket, but when I went to return them, they had gone.'

Walking to the bell-pull in a corner of the room,

Harriet Vincent gave it a tug. 'I think we should speak to Mrs Mudge about this.'

When the housekeeper came into the room, Harriet Vincent had her nephew repeat his accusation.

Eliza Mudge looked sceptical. 'The girl doesn't really fit in with the other servants, ma'am, but I've never had cause to call her honesty into question. Shall I send for her now and see what she has to say?'

'Not yet. Take one of the senior maids with you and search her room. If you find nothing, you will search the girl's person. If you still find nothing, we will discuss the matter again and decide what to do next.'

The search was brief. Less than five minutes after leaving the morning-room, Eliza Mudge returned, grim-faced, holding something clenched in her hand. When she opened it out to show her employer, two guinea coins were nestling in her palm.

'I found these in a drawer in her room, ma'am. No attempt had been made to hide them. Shall I have one of the footmen go and fetch the constable?'

'No!'

Sir Charles spoke more loudly than he had intended. When both women turned towards him he said, pale-faced, 'What will happen to this girl if she is taken before a court and found guilty? What will they do to her?'

'That need concern none of us. She's a thief and the law will deal with her as she deserves.'

'If she is found guilty the court will sentence her to hang, Aunt Harriet. You know the girl, she's been working here, in your house. Would you have her put to death for a mere two guineas?'

'Her fate is of her own making,' said his aunt unfeelingly. 'The girl is dishonest. I have no doubt she is fully aware of the consequences of her act.'

Eliza Mudge was looking at Sir Charles Hearle with a quizzical expression on her face. It was out of character for him to have any regard for others. Fully aware of his reputation with the female staff, she felt there was more to his concern than the fate of a dishonest housemaid.

'I'm damned if I'll see a young girl hanged for two guineas. I have my money back, I'll lodge no complaint with a magistrate.'

Harriet Vincent looked at him contemptuously. 'You disappoint me, Charles. I had thought you favoured my side of the family, but it seems you have inherited the feebleness of your father. Well, whatever action *you* take, the girl will not remain in my house for another hour. Mrs Mudge, bring her here, if you please.'

'Yes, ma'am. Right away.' With a final speculative glance at Sir Charles, Eliza Mudge hurried from the room.

The housekeeper was badly shaken. She did not particularly like Thomasina and felt that Harriet Vincent should have consulted her before taking on a new housemaid. Nevertheless, knowing how close Thomasina had come to a hangman's rope horrified her. It was too dreadful to contemplate. She felt more strongly than ever that Sir Charles had not told the full story of all that had happened in his room the previous evening.

*   *   *

Thomasina was that morning cleaning and tidying the rooms for which she was responsible in the normal household routine. She was making up the bed just vacated by two house guests who had left the room to go in search of breakfast.

She was still in a state of considerable shock as a result of what had happened to her the previous night. She felt sickened and dirty, and doubted whether she would ever feel clean again. Nevertheless, she automatically speeded up her work when Eliza Mudge entered the room.

'You can stop that and come with me.'

The tone of the housekeeper's voice made it clear to Thomasina that this was more than a temporary change of duties.

'What is it, Mrs Mudge? Is there something I've forgotten to do?'

'Yes. To keep your hands off other folk's property, it would seem.'

The housekeeper adopted an expression of thin-lipped disapproval. 'Come with me. Mrs Vincent wants a word with you – although why she should want to waste her breath on the likes of you, I don't know.'

As they hurried along the passageway from the room, Eliza Mudge went on, 'You're lucky you're not being taken straight before the magistrate, young girl – but perhaps there's something you'd like to tell me about what's been happening? Something that might have happened last evening?'

Thomasina's stomach contracted in sudden fear, but she said nothing and the housekeeper continued,

'We've never had a thief in this house, not in all the thirty-odd years I've lived and worked here.'

Hurrying to keep up with the older woman, a bewildered and frightened Thomasina asked, 'But . . . what am I supposed to have stolen?'

'There's nothing "supposed" about it,' snapped the housekeeper grimly. 'I found the proof myself. Proof enough to have you hanged, had Sir Charles decided to press charges against you.'

While she was speaking, Eliza was looking at Thomasina to gauge her reaction. What she saw confirmed her earlier suspicions even before Thomasina spoke again.

'The only thing I took from Sir Charles was a little blood from his ear when he attacked me last night, in his room.' Bitterly she added, 'Had there been a knife to hand, it would have been more than his ear.'

It was as Eliza had thought. However, there was still the matter of the money she had found in Thomasina's room and she had a word of caution for her.

'You'd do well to be careful what you say about Sir Charles – especially to the mistress. If she was to persuade him to change his mind and have you arrested, you'd hang, for certain.'

Thomasina looked aghast at the housekeeper. She did not doubt that this whole incident had to do with what had occurred in Sir Charles Hearle's room the previous evening. But she had stolen nothing. This must be his way of getting rid of her. She should, perhaps, be grateful that he had stopped short of having her hanged – but gratitude was not an emotion that immediately sprang to mind.

By now they had reached the morning-room. When they entered, Harriet Vincent was alone, Sir Charles having refused to remain in the room until Thomasina arrived.

The mistress of Trebene came straight to the point. 'My nephew tells me you stole money from his room last night . . .' She held out the two dull-gold sovereigns. 'These were found in your room. Can you tell me where you obtained them?'

'They're mine . . .' Even as she spoke, Thomasina was remembering who had given them to her and how he had come by them. '. . . they were given to me.'

Harriet Vincent raised an eyebrow. 'Can you tell me the name of the person who gave them to you?'

When Thomasina remained silent, the mistress of Trebene said scornfully, 'Of course you can't. You are not only a thief, Ethel, you are a liar too. If I had my way, you would be taken before a magistrate and suffer the fate you deserve. However, my nephew feels he cannot have your execution upon his conscience. Needless to say, I do not agree with him. I feel that you should be punished as you deserve. Be that as it may, I want you out of this house immediately. You will gather your belongings and be gone by the time breakfast is over. Do you understand?'

'Yes, but . . .' Thomasina was trying to put on a brave front for this woman, but was finding it difficult, '. . . the two guineas – they're mine.'

'Such impertinence! You will leave this house immediately, or I will ignore my nephew's wishes and have you charged. Mrs Mudge, take her away –

and do not leave her side until she is out of this house. We do not want anything else to be stolen.'

Breakfast for the Vincent family and their guests was a somewhat subdued affair until Francis Vincent entered the breakfast-room.

Unaware of the atmosphere that prevailed, he made for the end of the table where Sir Charles was picking at his food next to his stern-faced aunt.

Taking a seat, he said cheerfully, 'You must have had a very good night at the ball, Charles.'

'Why do you say that?' Sir Charles reacted guiltily.

'Well, you'd obviously been throwing your money around. I knew you'd had more than enough to drink when you had to return to the room to change your pantaloons. Then, when I went to bed, I found two sovereigns beside my slippers. You must have dropped them when you changed, but you were nowhere to be found, so I kept them for you until this morning . . .'

Suddenly aware of the looks that both his aunt and Sir Charles were giving him, he said, 'What's the matter? Have I said something . . . ?'

8

The small bundle that Thomasina carried away with her from Trebene House contained all her worldly possessions and was no larger than the one she had taken to the house only a few weeks before.

The only extra thing she now possessed was a smouldering resentment against the Vincent family in general – and a burning hatred for Sir Charles Hearle.

There was no doubt in her mind that he had deliberately engineered her dismissal, either because he felt guilty or, more probably, because he wanted her out of the way in case she said anything about what had occurred.

She was also angry with Harriet Vincent for taking her two guineas. Then she managed a wry smile as she realised just how unreasonable her anger was over this particular aspect of her dismissal. The money given to her by Jeffery had been stolen from Henry Vincent and the two guests travelling with him.

Thomasina was forced to admit to herself that there was a certain wry justice in the whole affair. However, it did not lessen the very deep bitterness she felt towards Sir Charles Hearle for what he had done to her.

Then she began to wonder what life held in store for her now. She could not return to her old home. The revelation that she had been dismissed for dishonesty would shock Aunt Mary beyond belief. She would take the shame of it upon herself, but would never allow her niece to forget that she was the cause of it.

There was a moment of conscience when Thomasina thought that her aunt would already mentally have spent the money she should have earned at Trebene House. Then she consoled herself with the knowledge that the half of Jeffery's gift she had already given to Aunt Mary represented eight months of the wages she would have received from Harriet Vincent.

Thomasina was now heading for Truro, in the hope that Jeffery was still at the Heron Inn at Malpas. He might be able to help her. If he was not there, she did not know what she would do. She had only two shillings in her possession – all that was left over from her previous month's wages.

She had been owed more than a week's wages by Harriet Vincent, but in the circumstances she had felt it would not have been prudent to ask for it!

It was a long walk to Truro, but not unpleasant. The day was fine and time passed more quickly when she fell in with an itinerant fiddle-player. He called himself Ulysses Smith, although he admitted to her along the way that Ulysses was not his true name, adding, 'My real name is Joe, but tavern keepers wouldn't give work to a fiddle-player named Joe Smith. It sounds too much like a gipsy name. I've had much more work since I began calling myself Ulysses.'

In answer to Thomasina's question, 'Ulysses' replied that he had taken the name from a play put on by a troupe of actors he had once travelled with. He also informed her that he was now on his way to earn some money in the Truro taverns.

He was not much older than Thomasina, but she doubted whether he would enjoy his new-found success for very long. Slightly built and bowed over as he walked, Ulysses had a cough that suggested he was suffering from a serious lung complaint.

However, the fiddler was an amusing companion and the long walk to Truro passed more quickly than it might otherwise have done. When they arrived at Truro town and parted company, Thomasina felt she had said goodbye to a friend.

The lane to Malpas ran alongside the Truro river. It was normally a very busy waterway, but the tide was low. Only a narrow channel remained, winding its tortuous way through a wide expanse of glistening, evil-smelling black mud.

A number of ships were settled in the mud on both sides of the river and cargoes were being unloaded, or carried on board. A number of seamen were taking advantage of the low tide to paint the sides of their vessels. Suspended on cradles, they were able to reach parts of the ship normally underwater.

Farther downriver the lane began to rise above the river bank. It was more wooded here too. Then, turning a bend in the lane, Thomasina saw the Heron Inn.

It was an ideal spot for a highwayman. She doubted very much whether any constable from Truro would put himself at risk by coming out here. It seemed too that most of the inn's business took place later in the day.

Thomasina had left Trebene House very early. It was now mid-morning, but there was little sign of life in and around the inn.

Ducking in through a low doorway, she found herself in a public room, the stone floor of which was being swabbed by an elderly pot-man who saw no urgency in the task he was performing, spending a great deal of time leaning upon the mop. Through a nearby open doorway Thomasina could hear the clatter of pots in what she took to be a kitchen.

When she asked about Jeffery, the pot-man said that he knew the names of none of the guests staying at the inn, preferring to mind his own business. The landlord was in the cellar, but would be up in a few minutes. She would need to speak to him.

The 'few minutes' stretched to twenty and when the heavily bearded landlord eventually entered the public room, he smelled very strongly of ale, much of it on his breath.

When she asked after Jeffery, the landlord shook his head. 'There's no one of that name staying here, Missie.

As far as I can recall, we've *never* had anyone of that name at the Heron Inn.'

Belatedly, Thomasina realised she had probably committed a serious error of judgement. Jeffery would not want his real name known here. She immediately tried to put things right.

'I must have got the story wrong. It's probably his friend who is staying here. I can't remember his name, but . . . She proceeded to give the landlord a full description of Jeffery and his dress, as she had last seen him.

Stroking his beard thoughtfully, the landlord said, 'That sounds like young Mr King. He's waiting here for his father's ship to come in from the West Indies, or somewhere out that way. But I haven't seen any friend with him – at least, not a *man*-friend.'

Choosing to ignore the implications of the landlord's statement, Thomasina said, 'No doubt he'll know where Jeffery can be found. Is Mr King in right now? Can I go up to his room?'

The landlord cast an eye over Thomasina. She looked highly respectable, dressed as might a maidservant on her day off. Not at all the type of young woman who usually frequented the Heron Inn.

'I expect he's in, but he hasn't been down yet. I'll send Albert upstairs to see if he's decent and tell him you're here. Who shall I say is wanting to see him?'

'Tell him it's Thomasina – I think he'll remember me,' she added, as an afterthought.

It transpired that Albert was the lethargic pot-man. After grumbling about not being left in peace to get on with his work, he could be heard stomping heavily up the wooden stairs which led to the first floor from the passageway outside.

'Can I get you something to drink while you're waiting?' asked the landlord.

Thomasina hesitated. She was hot and thirsty after her long walk from Trebene, but she was also remembering the state of her purse.

'I'll wait until Mr King comes down. If he has a drink, I'll have one with him – but for now I would be grateful for some water.'

The landlord grunted disapprovingly. 'It's a good job everyone else who comes to the inn drinks more than water. If they didn't, I'd soon go out of business.'

Pointing to an alcove, he said, 'Take a seat in there while you're waiting. I'll have water sent in to you.'

Gratefully Thomasina sank down into a wooden-armed chair in the alcove. Some minutes later she heard Albert coming heavily down the stairs and could follow the progress of his metal-studded boots on the flagstones of the passageway.

Entering the room, he looked about him, frowning, before he saw her. When he did, he said irritably, 'He'll be down in a few minutes – that's if he's got the strength left in him to climb out of bed.'

Making no attempt to explain his remark, Albert retrieved his mop and bucket and resumed his task.

Shortly afterwards a serving girl came from the kitchen carrying a jug of water and a mug. As she reached the alcove, Thomasina heard someone running down the stairs to the passageway outside.

Thinking it might be Jeffery, she rose to her feet, only

to sit down again, almost immediately. The footsteps were too light to be Jeffery's.

As the serving maid put the water down upon the table in front of Thomasina, a young girl hurried into the room. She too was dressed like a serving girl and was probably quite pretty.

However, at this moment she looked as though she had just woken up and dressed in a great hurry. Not all her buttons were fastened and her hair was dishevelled, her eyes bloodshot and the lids puffy.

The girl who had brought water for Thomasina rounded on the new arrival sharply. 'Where have you been? You should have started work an hour ago, helping me get the dining-room ready.'

'I overslept,' said the girl briefly. Belatedly she pulled the drawstring at the neck of her dress, tying it in a bid to hide at least some of her bosom.

The girl who had brought water to Thomasina made a sound that indicated disbelief. 'If you had more sleep and less of the other, you'd probably be able to get out of bed – whosoever's bed it might be – and get to work on time. I suggest you put a brush through your hair before you go and say you're here, but don't be long about it. There's already talk of taking someone else on in your place.'

The tardy serving girl disappeared through the kitchen door, making a futile attempt to smooth her hair with a hand. A few minutes later Thomasina heard heavier footsteps clattering down the stairs outside.

When Jeffery entered the room it was apparent to Thomasina that he had taken more care with his toilet than the girl who had no doubt been sharing a bed with him.

'Tom! What are you doing here?'

Aware that Albert was within hearing, she replied, 'I came here to see if you had any news of Jeffery. I'm sorry, I don't remember your first name from when we last met.'

For a moment, Jeffery was taken aback, but when her glance shifted meaningfully to Albert, he recovered quickly and followed the lead she had given him.

'My name is Jeremy, Jeremy King – but you're enquiring after Jeffery, you say? I've heard nothing from him for a while. But where are my manners? Would you care to have a drink with me?'

'Thank you, but I've just had a drink of water. As it's a fine day, why don't we take a walk along the river bank. You can tell me about the last time you saw Jeffery, and what you think his plans might be . . .'

9

As Thomasina and Jeffery walked together by the river bank, she told of her meeting with the landlord of the Heron Inn and the realisation that Jeffery had taken on a new identity.

'That was very astute of you,' said Jeffery approvingly. 'But then you were always brighter than most of the other Mevagissey girls.'

'Bright enough to realise that my coming here is likely to cause you some embarrassment, certainly,' commented Thomasina acidly. 'Perhaps you'd like to tell me about the girl who was in your bed when Albert came to tell you I was at the inn asking for you?'

Jeffery's immediate instinct was to disclaim all knowledge of the girl Thomasina had seen. He had actually opened his mouth to voice a protest when he saw the expression on her face. He realised that denial would be a waste of time.

'She doesn't mean anything to me, Tom, I promise you.'

'I didn't ask what she means to you. I want to know who she is.'

'Her name is Hebe. She's one of the serving girls at the inn. Yesterday was her birthday. The customers gave her a birthday celebration.'

'It seems that some gave her more than others,' retorted Thomasina. 'Or are you saying she slept with all the customers?'

'I'm saying only that it was her birthday and we all had more to drink than was good for us. She means nothing to me, Tom. You do – but you still haven't told me what you're doing here. Why aren't you at Trebene?'

Jeffery had not fully explained his involvement with Hebe to Thomasina's satisfaction, but she let the subject drop – for now. She had decided she would not tell him what Sir Charles had actually done to her, only that he had tried and that he had trumped up theft charges against her in revenge for the bite she had given him.

Jeffery was incensed. 'The money he took – was it what I had given to you?'

'Yes. I was very cross about it at first, but then I saw the funny side of it. I wonder what Mrs Vincent would have said, had she known it was stolen from her husband in the first place!'

'But she didn't know, although her nephew must have known it wasn't *his* money. He could very easily have had you hanged for something you hadn't done.'

'Doesn't it worry you that *you'll* probably end up

on the end of a hangman's rope?' Thomasina asked, grateful for an opportunity to move the conversation away from the reason for her dismissal from Trebene House.

Jeffery gave a nonchalant shrug. 'My pa spent his short life slaving his guts out catching fish. That's what he was doing when he died. During his working life, if the weather was kind for a week or two, he'd earn just about enough money for us to have food in our bellies, but there was nothing left for luxuries. If the weather was bad for more than a few days, we'd go hungry. Then there was my grandpa. He'd worked in the fields all his life, going out in all weathers. By the time he was forty he was crippled with rheumatism and couldn't work any more. He was in constant pain all the time I knew him, and what hurt him even more was knowing he was a liability to his family.'

It was an emotive subject for Jeffery. When he stopped talking he came to a halt, looking out over the river, away from her.

For a few minutes they stood together in silence, watching a mist-grey, stoop-backed heron, standing long-legged and motionless at the river's edge.

Aware that it was being watched, the bird eventually became unnerved and took off on long wings in ungainly flight, legs trailing as it flew downriver to find a more secluded spot in which to fish.

'The sort of life my pa led isn't for me, Tom,' Jeffery spoke again, more quietly now. 'One day I may have to dance the Tyburn jig for what I'm doing now, but before I do, I'll have enjoyed life as I never could if I'd stayed in Mevagissey.'

'I've no doubt there are plenty of girls like Hebe who are happy to help you spend your money and enjoy life,' commented Thomasina.

Jeffery looked only mildly embarrassed. 'Hebe's fun – but no more than that. I know it, and so does she.' Turning to her, he continued, 'You're the only one I've ever really cared about, Tom. I think you know that.'

'I thought I did. That's why I came here when I lost my job. Now I'm not so certain.'

'You *can* rely on me, Tom, I promise you, but now you're here we need to decide what we're going to do with you. Do you have anything in mind?'

'That depends.'

When she did not attempt to clarify her brief statement, he asked hesitantly, 'Depends on what, Thomasina?'

'On you and this . . . Hebe.'

'I've already told you, she means absolutely nothing to me. Nothing at all.'

'So you say – but does she know this?' Thomasina was not ready to offer him absolution just yet.

'It's never been more than a bit of fun. She knows that . . .' Jeffery was now suffering agonies of remorse. 'I really am sorry, Tom, but I thought – I thought you had given yourself up to a career as housemaid in the Vincent household. That you wouldn't want to be mixed up with someone like me.'

'You, of all people, should know me better than that, Jeffery. I couldn't spend the rest of my life curtseying and saying "Yes, sir" and "No, madam" every time they spoke to me. You and I have talked often enough about that sort of thing.'

'True, but lots of people say one thing yet do something different when it's time to act.'

'Do they? Is that why I've come here, when I know how it is you get your money?'

'I'm sorry, Tom,' said Jeffery dejectedly. 'But now you're here, what can I do to help you?'

'More to the point, what can I do to help *you*?'

Thomasina's question took Jeffery aback. 'What do you mean? You know what I am. There's no permanent place for a woman in the sort of life I'm leading.'

'Why not? I've been thinking about it while I was on my way here. When you rob someone you need to be far away before they report it to a constable or a magistrate – and that isn't always easy. You said so yourself, the last time we met.'

'Yes . . . but there's nothing that can be done about that. A highwayman needs to be miles away, before a "hue and cry" is raised. Anything else would be too risky – whatever I said to you before.'

'Not necessarily. In fact, it means you can usually rob only those who are miles away from their homes. For that very reason they'll not be carrying anything of real value. What if we were to hold up those who are in towns, or so close to their homes that they don't even consider the possibility that they might be robbed?'

'It wouldn't work, Thomasina. They'd be able to set up an immediate hue and cry. I'd most likely be arrested before I could get clear of the area.'

'Not if I was helping you. Waiting somewhere nearby? You could rob someone, then come to where I was hiding. We'd swap horses, then ride off together as though we were a gent and a lady. You've said yourself it would work – and it *would*. They'd be looking for a *man* on a particular type of horse. They wouldn't think of looking at the horse *I* was riding. I could even help you in a hold-up, sometimes. Dressed as a man. My pa taught me to shoot when we were out on the boat. I'm better than most men with a gun. We could leave the horses hidden somewhere, carry out the robbery on foot, then go back to the horses. I'd change clothes and suddenly we'd be a respectable couple. While we rode off they'd be looking for two men.'

Jeffery was doubtful. 'I don't know, Thomasina. I know I suggested it, but I can't think of anything like it having been done before.'

'Exactly! That's why it would work. Nobody's done it before, so they wouldn't be expecting it.'

Jeffery was still uncertain. 'I'll need to think about it . . .'

'Oh? And what will I do while you're making up your mind?'

'Why, stay at the Heron, of course. Alf, the landlord, will be only too glad to find you a room. He provides clean linen, good food and stands for no nonsense. Mind you, it gets a bit rowdy when a smugglers' boat comes in – and that seems to have been most nights, just lately.'

'I can think of two snags with that idea. One, I've no money to pay for a room. Two, I have no intention of having a dispute with a certain Hebe about who's sleeping where.'

Jeffery looked embarrassed. 'I keep telling you, Thomasina, Hebe means nothing to me.'

'As I said before, are you quite certain *she* knows that?'

'Of course. You'll see, she's as friendly with everyone who comes to the Heron.'

'You mean . . . she's a whore?' said Thomasina scathingly. 'Perhaps I've made a mistake in suggesting we should work together. A highwayman who spends his time with whores isn't going to last very long. Whores talk to whoever they go to bed with, be they highwaymen, smugglers, revenue men – or constables. I'm not prepared to risk my neck with such a man. I was probably wrong to come here in the first place. Perhaps I should go back to Aunt Mary, say I'm sorry and find work in Mevagissey. Yes, that's what I'll do.'

'Now, don't be hasty, Thomasina. I've told you that Hebe means nothing to me – what more do you want? Besides, if you're staying at the Heron, I'll have no need to look at anyone else, will I now?'

'No,' agreed Thomasina, 'but will that stop you? It never has in the past.'

'Thomasina, you're worth more than all the girls I've ever known put together. Stay here with me and I promise I'll never, ever look at another girl.'

'And you'll put my idea to the test?' Thomasina asked. 'We'll work together?'

Jeffery hesitated, but when he saw her expression harden, he said hastily, 'All right. We'll give it a try – after I've thought about it – but if it doesn't work we'll talk about it again. Is that a deal?'

Thomasina nodded, 'All right, it's a deal.'

'That's wonderful!' Jeffery could hardly hide his

relief. 'Now, let's go back to the Heron. We'll book you into a room, then I'll buy you a lunch that will be like nothing you've ever had before. You'll not regret coming to Malpas to find me, Tom. I promise you . . .'

10

The first robbery carried out by Thomasina and Jeffery together took place on a road just outside Truro. While she waited in a nearby copse, her heart beating at an alarming rate, Jeffery held up a light carriage belonging to Rector Wheeler, whose church was at nearby Ladock.

The reverend gentleman protested indignantly about a man of the cloth being held up in such a fashion, promising eternal damnation for Jeffery's soul. There was a markedly more secular tone to his protest when Jeffery forced him to hand over his heavy purse.

The rector was returning from market, where he had that day sold a number of milking cows, grown fat on the pasture acquired from a local farmer who had defaulted on his tithe payments.

Chiding the rector for his unclerical language, Jeffery gave the victim's horse a resounding whack on the rump and stood back as horse, carriage and angry rector disappeared into the night.

The amount taken that evening was the largest purse Jeffery had ever stolen. It remained so even when he had passed on half the takings to Thomasina.

Declaring that Thomasina had brought him renewed luck, Jeffery forecast a happy and profitable partnership for their illegal venture.

The next purse was also a heavy one. This time it was taken from a drunken farmer, also returning from market. However, on this occasion Jeffery had to discharge a pistol before his victim was persuaded to part with his money.

The shot attracted the attention of a party of militiamen returning from a duty parade. Had Thomasina not been waiting in a nearby copse and able to join Jeffery before the arrival of the part-time soldiers, he would most likely have been taken.

As it was, they were clear of the shouting farmer before the militiamen arrived on the scene. Not suspected of any involvement in the robbery, they were able to take a leisurely ride to the Heron Inn and, once there, were safe from any pursuit.

Thomasina's first impression of the Heron Inn had been that of a tranquil rural tavern, tucked away at the end of a quiet country lane. The reality was very different.

When darkness fell men flocked to the Heron Inn, for all the world like bats emerging from caves at sunset and congregating at a feeding ground. The inn was then a busy, lively place until well into the early hours of the morning.

Thomasina had taken a room next to that occupied by Jeffery, paid for by him. It was an open secret among the inn staff that she rarely used it, choosing instead to share the bed of 'Jeremy King'. It mattered little to anyone at the inn – except, perhaps, Hebe, the serving girl.

Despite Jeffery's assertion that she had never meant anything to him, Thomasina was aware of the other girl's smouldering resentment towards her whenever the two girls met. Nevertheless, Thomasina was a paying guest and Hebe a servant girl whose own conduct made her employment at the inn less than secure, so she caused no serious trouble. Besides, Hebe did not lack suitors among the inn's late-night customers.

Many of the men who came to the Heron Inn after dark were smugglers; others were their customers. Evading the Customs men downriver at Falmouth, the smugglers' boats would ride the tide to Malpas. If there was insufficient tide left for them to arrive at the inn before daylight, or if the Customs men were active on the river, they would hide their boats. There were a great many remote creeks to provide hiding places or, if the boat was not too large, it could be safely tucked beneath the overhanging branches of one of the many trees bordering the river.

Much money changed hands at the inn, but such traders and smugglers remained safe from the night-time activities of Jeffery and Thomasina. The Heron Inn was an invaluable refuge. They would not put it at risk when there were rich pickings to be had elsewhere.

*　　*　　*

After their close brush with the militia, Jeffery and Thomasina lay low for some days. Then they both felt the time was ripe for Thomasina's first active involvement in highway robbery.

Although they had been lucky with their victims, so far, Jeffery felt it might be safer – and more profitable – if they could select their intended victim *before* the event.

With this in mind, when another market day came around Jeffery took Thomasina to dine at one of the most popular hostelries in Truro.

At first, she was anxious lest she meet up with friends of her late employers, but Jeffery persuaded her that she had no cause for concern. Even if she *were* to be seen by anyone who had met her at Trebene House, it was doubtful whether they would recognise her now.

The proceeds of Jeffery's two most recent robberies had provided Thomasina with sufficient money to purchase clothes that would not have disgraced a young woman of considerable means.

Jeffery had chosen this particular hostelry because it was frequented by gentlemen farmers and others who had been to the market that day. He and Thomasina intended enjoying a meal surrounded by such men, listening to their conversations and choosing a prospective victim.

The choice was made surprisingly easy for them. Seated at a table not too far away was a red-faced, heavily perspiring farmer whose voice became progressively louder as more and more drink was consumed by him and his friends.

Careful to give no sign that they were listening with great interest, Jeffery and Thomasina learned that the farmer intended retiring and was in the process of selling up his farm. With this in mind, his men had brought a herd of milking cows to market. Their sale had fetched more than two hundred guineas for him.

'That's a handsome sum indeed,' said one of his companions, suitably impressed. 'Your banker will have been pleased to see you today.'

'Bankers!' The farmer spat out the word, disdainfully. 'I've got no time for such men.' Patting a bulging pocket in the waistcoat distended across his ample belly, he added, 'I like to know where my money is. I'll not put it in the hands of them as takes other men's money, only to spread their hands wide one day and say it's all gone – claiming they don't for the life of 'em know where to.'

A local bank had recently gone into bankruptcy and the men about the farmer's table nodded their agreement with his sentiments.

'All the same, you be careful on your way home, Howard,' warned another of them. 'There's word that a highwayman's been at work around Truro in recent weeks.'

'That don't bother me none,' said the farmer, boastfully. 'Truro men have always been parted from their money a sight easier than us folks from Probus. A highwayman wouldn't find me such easy pickings. Besides, one of my men is coming to pick me up in my chaise soon. Come on, gentlemen, let's have another drink. Now my cows have gone, I don't have to get up early tomorrow to make certain the milking's being done properly . . .'

'I think we've found our man,' said Jeffery, the softness of his voice hiding the excitement he was feeling.

'What about the man who's coming to fetch him?' Thomasina voiced her misgivings equally quietly.

'It evens things up, but we'll be more than a match for them. You finish off your meal while I settle the bill. We know which way they'll be heading – but you'll need to be a man by the time they take to the road.'

There was a full set of men's clothing in the saddle bag of Thomasina's horse, which had been left saddled in the stables behind the hostelry. There were also four loaded pistols in the same bag. Two for Jeffery and two for herself.

The saddle itself was Jeffery's own brainchild. Made by a saddler who worked in a village ten miles from the Cornish capital, it was ostensibly a normal saddle for a male rider. However, by detaching the right stirrup and screwing in a specially adapted, padded leather attachment – the work of no more than a minute – it was converted to a temporary, albeit somewhat uncomfortable and insecure, side-saddle.

When the bill was settled, the two made their way to the rear of the building. On the way Jeffery outlined a decidedly sketchy 'plan' of action. They would retrieve the horses and make their way to the edge of town. There, in the darkness, Thomasina would change into the clothing of a man. They would then return to town once more and wait in the shadows within sight of the hotel for the money-laden farmer to leave.

Thanks to the farmer's indiscreet boasting, they knew where he lived. Once he came out of the hotel they would hurry off and waylay him on the Probus road.

When the robbery had taken place, Thomasina would once more change into women's clothing and they would ride back into Truro together and make their way to the sanctuary of the Heron Inn.

The farmer was in no hurry to break off his celebrations and make his way home. A light chaise with a farm labourer holding the reins was standing outside the hostelry door when Thomasina and Jeffery returned to the town, but it was a full hour before the farmer left, supported by two of his friends.

Helped upon the vehicle, the farmer sat slumped in his seat while the farmhand climbed up beside him and flicked the reins to set the horse in motion.

Thomasina and Jeffery were waiting beneath a wide-spreading oak tree on the edge of town when the chaise left the houses behind and trundled along the Probus road. It was not travelling fast, the farmworker fearing that his employer might fall from the vehicle if they dropped into a pothole at any speed.

Frustratingly for the two would-be robbers, a farmer mounted on a cart-horse left town at the same time as the chaise and kept pace with it for almost a mile. Not until the unknown farmer had turned off along a farm track did Jeffery and Thomasina canter past the chaise.

The road led downhill to a narrow bridge. Here it levelled off – and this was where they decided they would waylay the farmer.

With Thomasina a shadowy figure in the background, Jeffery kneed his horse to the centre of the bridge and called upon the driver to bring the chaise to a halt. The farmworker obeyed the command immediately, the suddenness of the stop causing his drunken employer to fall forward.

Saved only by a light rail from tumbling to the ground, the farmer began cursing his worker. Then he saw Jeffery.

'What d'you think you're doing, stopping us like that? You might have caused an accident. Get out of the way.' He spoke belligerently, unaware that Jeffery had deliberately brought the chaise to a halt.

'My friend and I will be on our way when you've handed over your purse, sir. Be kind enough to oblige without causing us any trouble.'

Struggling to gather his wits about him, the farmer said, 'I'm damned if I will! That's money for my retirement. I'll not give it to any thieving rogue.'

Raising his pistol, Jeffery said, 'Then I'll have to take it, sir, and I fear your retirement will be short-lived.'

Thomasina sucked in her breath, but the chaise driver said, 'Give him your purse, Mr Dainty. It's not worth dying for, no matter how much is in it.'

'It's not your money, so you can shut up . . .'

While the farmer was remonstrating drunkenly and foolishly with his employee, Jeffery brought his horse in close. Leaning forward now, he raised his heavy pistol and brought it down hard on the side of the farmer's head.

The farmer slipped off the seat and lay half-hanging out of the chaise.

'There were no need for that,' said the farmworker. 'I'd have got him to give it to you, without you needing to hit him.'

'Shut up and find his purse for me – and hurry, I'm getting angry and that causes my finger to twitch on the trigger of my pistol.'

The farmworker was concerned for his employer – but even more concerned for his own life. He knew where the farmer kept his purse and less than a minute later had found it and thrown it to Jeffery.

Unfortunately, the man was nervous. The purse fell short and dropped to the road with a heavy thud. Cursing the clumsy farmworker, Jeffery swung down from the saddle and felt around on the ground for the purse.

He did not find it immediately and, while he was searching, Thomasina saw the farmworker lean over his employer once more. At first she thought he was merely checking on his well-being. Then, with a shock of horror, she saw him straighten up – and he had a pistol in his hand.

Afterwards, she realised the pistol would not have been cocked and it was doubtful whether the farmworker knew how to fire it, but her first thought was for her companion.

'Look out! He's got a pistol.'

Jeffery's pistol was cocked and ready for use. Before the other man had even pointed the pistol in his direction, he had fired.

She could not see where the farmworker had been shot, but he was knocked backwards off the chaise, the pistol falling from his hand.

Thomasina was not certain whether or not she screamed. Jeffery neither noticed nor cared. He continued groping on the ground until he said triumphantly, 'Got it! Come on, let's get far away from here as quickly as we can.'

'But the driver . . . He might be badly hurt!'

'What do you suggest we do, bind his wound and take him to a doctor? Come on. We've got what we were after. Now let's get out of here in case someone heard the shot and comes to see what it was all about.'

11

The farmworker shot by Jeffery survived. His employer did not. News circulated the following day that he had died from a fracture of the skull, the injury having been inflicted by a highwayman.

Local residents were incensed by this latest incident of highway robbery. A reward of a hundred pounds was posted for the arrest of the two men responsible for the farmer's death.

Thomasina was contrite about the death of their victim, but Jeffery professed indifference.

'The risk of hurting, or even killing, someone has to be accepted when you take up this life, Tom. It's certainly not a one-sided affair. If you hadn't called out when you did, I too might be lying dead somewhere today.'

Thomasina shuddered at the thought of it. 'Is it worth such a risk, Jeffery?'

'What sort of a question is that? Think about it. You've already made more money than you'd have earned in a lifetime of working for Mrs Vincent. We only need to make a little more and you'll be able to go somewhere you're not known and open a little shop – if that's what you want from life.'

'I don't think I'd find it any easier to settle down to that sort of life than you would,' replied Thomasina, adding, 'well . . . not yet, anyway.'

'Good. Then we'll carry on with what we're doing – but not around here. There will be far too many people out looking for us now, all eager to earn the reward.'

'Won't it seem suspicious if we move on and the robberies cease right away?'

Jeffery laughed. 'You're assuming we're important enough to be noticed, Tom. We're not. People come and go all the time from inns and taverns without it being commented upon – especially from the Heron. Even if we *were* suspected, there's nobody from here would tell on us. Anyway, the magistrates are looking for two men, not a man and a woman.'

'Where will we go?' Thomasina asked the question uncertainly, not sure whether Jeffery intended that they should go off somewhere *together*.

He shrugged, 'We could go to London, I suppose, but the constables and Bow Street Runners are making things pretty hot there for strangers these days. I know, why don't we give Bristol a try?'

Happy that Jeffery intended taking her with him, Thomasina nodded. She had been to Bristol on two occasions with her father. It was a sprawling, bustling city, with a very busy docks area and many impressive houses. 'Yes . . . I wouldn't mind going to Bristol – but you need to know a place well in order to succeed in what we're going there for.'

'I know it as well as any other city,' replied Jeffery, surprisingly. 'In fact, that's where I started doing what we're doing now. I met up with another Cornish man there. Yes, Jack and I did quite well . . . for a while.'

When Jeffery fell silent, Thomasina prompted, 'Why didn't you carry on working with him? What went wrong?'

'He fell out with his woman and she turned him in for a reward. He was hanged.'

Thomasina shuddered, 'Are you sure you want to go back there? What if this woman sees you? She could tell on you too.'

Jeffery shook his head. 'Jack had many friends. She was warned that if she stayed in Bristol she'd be found floating in the docks one morning. She left in a hurry. We'll be all right there. Anyway, I think it's time we left the Heron Inn.'

Something in the way he spoke made Thomasina ask, 'Why are you so positive about that?'

Looking mildly embarrassed, he replied, 'I don't entirely trust Hebe any more. She always used to ask me too many questions about myself. I've been told she's started asking others about me now.'

Alarmed, Thomasina said, 'Then we ought to have left before this. What if she finds out the truth about you?'

'She won't – but she might pass on any suspicions she has. The way things are at the moment that could be enough to have me arrested.'

'Then we must leave right away.'

'We'll go first thing tomorrow morning. I'll tell the landlord I feel I've waited long enough for my father to return. That I'm returning home, just in case he's put in to another port. I'll leave a false address for him to send on any information he might get.'

'What excuse will we give for me leaving at the same time?'

'You'll say you don't want to stay on here on your own and that you believe the man you're waiting for is probably on the same ship as my father.'

The stories sounded convincing enough for Thomasina and she nodded her agreement.

Thomasina and Jeffery left the Heron Inn the following day. They would be leaving their horses at a stable in Truro, having sold them to Alf, the Heron innkeeper, but Thomasina's 'special' saddle would be travelling with them.

'Did the landlord believe your story?' asked Thomasina as the inn passed from view.

'I think so, although he did say that you hadn't seemed too unhappy that the man you were waiting for hadn't showed up.'

'I don't believe he missed very much that was going on,' commented Thomasina. 'We're not leaving the inn before time.'

In Truro the couple caught a coach to Penzance, uncomfortably aware that a constable was closely scrutinising the passengers boarding the vehicle. But he took little notice of the young couple and soon the coach was bouncing along the potholed road from Truro, heading westwards.

From Penzance they would board a boat that would take them around Land's End and on to Bristol.

Thomasina enjoyed the sea voyage immensely. It reminded her of better days when she would go to sea with her father. Jeffery did not share her pleasure. A bad sailor, he was very sick for much of the time they were on board.

He did not improve until they arrived at the upper reaches of the Bristol Channel. They were on deck together for the final part of the journey, which took them between the high cliffs on either side of the River Avon.

When they stepped from the boat to the quay at Welsh Back, in the busy port of Bristol, Thomasina was immediately caught up in the bustle, noise and pace of life in the great West Country port.

On the quayside a gang of young lads, some with two-wheeled handcarts, others with nothing, jostled each other in a bid to take charge of the luggage of the disembarking passengers.

Brushing them aside as best he could, Jeffery hailed a waiting hire-carriage. Well used to dealing with the persistent young boys, the coachman dispersed them by the simple expediency of vigorously cuffing a few ears.

Observing Thomasina's expression of concern, he said gruffly, 'You need to watch those young lads, Miss. Eight or nine of them will be clamouring around, then they'll suddenly disappear – along with you luggage. I don't doubt that half of 'em will end up dangling on the end of a hangman's rope one day. If it's sooner, rather than later, then the property of honest folks like yourselves will be a whole lot safer.'

Neither Thomasina nor Jeffery dared look at each other until they were both safely inside the vehicle, out of the coachman's view.

In Bristol, they stayed at an inn near Temple church. It was close enough to the busy city centre for their comings and goings at odd times not to excite comment, and it was within easy reach of the cattle market. It was a similar situation to that which they had found to be profitable in Truro.

Their luck held here, too. Farmers from outlying districts who attended the market would make for the nearest inn at the end of a successful day. Here, as in Truro, they were inclined to boast to each other about how much money they had made.

Another factor in Thomasina's and Jeffery's favour was the almost universal mistrust that farmers had of banking institutions. They believed it safer to take their money home with them – until Jeffery and Thomasina came on the scene.

Thomasina took a more active part in the robberies in Bristol. She possessed a naturally deep voice and it took little effort on her behalf to sound like a young man, once she had learned to control the excitement she felt each time she drew a pistol and spurred her horse forward.

She perfected a speedy means of changing her clothing. Within minutes of a successful robbery, the two highwaymen had disappeared. In their place was a pleasant young couple riding together on the King's highway, shocked at having passed so close to the scene of a robbery.

The couple remained in Bristol for a full two months. During this time they made more money than Thomasina had ever dreamed of possessing.

However, although the thrill of a successful hold-up did not wane, she was always aware that the day would come when their activities would need to be brought to an end. Nevertheless, as the weeks of successful highway robbery slipped by, thoughts of arrest and its inevitable consequences became more remote to both of them.

As a result, it came as a shock to Thomasina when, as she and Jeffery sat together at a table in the dining-room of their inn, Jeffery suddenly lowered his voice and spoke urgently to her.

'Say nothing, Thomasina. Just smile at me as though all is well – but get up, go to our room and stay there until I join you.'

Startled, Thomasina asked, 'Why . . . do you have something planned? Have you seen someone interesting?'

It was market day and the room contained a number of farmers making their way home after selling stock and produce.

'Just do as I say. Go . . . *now!*'

Thomasina had come to know Jeffery very well during the weeks they had spent together. He was not a man to overreact to any situation. Her heart beating rapidly, and wondering what was happening, she succeeded in smiling sweetly at Jeffery before rising to her feet and making her way from the dining-room.

Most of the men in the room followed her progress with admiring glances. She had always been an eye-catching young woman and the clothes she was now able to afford had transformed her into a fetching beauty.

Once in the room she shared with Jeffery, she awaited his arrival with increasing apprehension until she heard his hurried footsteps in the passage-way outside.

When he entered the room, she demanded, 'What's happened? Why did you send me up here so hurriedly? Has someone recognised us?'

She knew this was highly unlikely. The wide, black felt masks they wore when carrying out a robbery hid too much of their faces for recognition to be possible.

'I think someone has realised that all the men we've robbed these past few weeks dined here shortly beforehand.'

Thomasina breathed a sigh of relief. The authorities were not close to them yet. Jeffery did not share her relief.

'One of the local constables seems to be smarter than most. He's brought two of the farmers we've robbed to the dining-room to see if they could identify anyone who was in the room on the night they were robbed. If both men identified us, we'd become prime suspects.'

Her relief gone, Thomasina asked anxiously, 'Do you think they recognised us?'

Giving her a wry smile, Jeffery replied, 'They were

all far too interested in watching you leaving the room – as a woman, that is, not as a suspected highwayman. But now the constable has his suspicions about this place, I think we'd better leave Bristol – and right away.'

'You don't think he'll check on who's been staying here and try to trace us?'

'He might, but we'll be long gone by then. On the other hand, if we stayed and they became suspicious, they'd search this room and find the money and other things we've taken. We've got no alternative, Tom. We have to go.'

'Where to this time?'

'To London first of all, to lay a false scent. Even if they got on to us, they could search there for years and never find where we were and we'd have moved on again long before they got on our trail.'

When she made no reply, wrapped up in her own thoughts, Jeffery said, 'I think perhaps it's time to go home, Tom. Back to Cornwall.'

It was a matter they had discussed on a number of occasions. Cornwall had become something it had never been for either of them in reality . . . an idyllic place where they would both be happy.

'We've made a lot of money, Tom,' Jeffery continued enthusiastically. 'Enough to buy a small farm.'

Thomasina made no comment, but Jeffery was warming to the subject. 'It would be a nice little place, Tom. We'd have sheep, cows and a pig or two. There could even be a couple of dogs – and a cat.'

'I thought you didn't like farm work? That's what you always told me when we were in Cornwall.'

'I don't like working for someone else. This would be different.'

'Am I included in these plans of yours? The farm . . . and all that?'

Jeffery looked at her in surprise, 'Of course! We'll get married and be just as respectable as any other married couple.'

'I'm glad you want me to be your wife, Jeffery.' Thomasina meant it. 'But won't people want to know where our money's come from?'

'No one who knows us will find out where we are. At least, not for a long time, because we wouldn't go back to Mevagissey right away. We'll find a farm somewhere in the far west, where we'll be strangers. If anyone becomes curious, I'll think up a story – tell them that an aunt died and left me the money, perhaps. Something like that. Well, what do you say?'

'I say it's a wonderful idea, Jeffery. Not least because you've said you want us to be married. You've never said so before.'

She was close to tears and Jeffery held out his arms to her. Standing pressed close to him, Thomasina tried hard not to give way to a fit of trembling.

She had an incredible feeling of relief. Until today she had not realised how much of a strain the life they were leading had become.

Now it was all over. Now they could go home. Together.

12

Jeffery and Thomasina spent a week in London, during which time they visited a great many of the capital city's attractions and Thomasina was left awestruck by the sheer size and beauty of London's buildings.

Jeffery took the opportunity to dispose of the jewellery, watches and other valuables they had acquired during their nefarious activities in Cornwall and Bristol.

When he returned to the hotel where they were staying he complained that the pawnbroker to whom he had sold the items was a more accomplished robber than he or Thomasina had ever been. Nevertheless, they now had a great deal of money to share between them.

Only one incident happened to mar their stay. One day, when riding in a hired carriage through the streets close to Newgate, they were brought to a halt by a great crowd. When Jeffery asked the reason for the delay, the carriage driver said that there was to be a public hanging outside the prison, a short distance ahead.

He added that he had friends living nearby, with rooms overlooking the scaffold. For a few pounds he could guarantee them an unimpeded view of the proceedings.

Thomasina shook her head, but Jeffery asked who was being hanged. He was told it was Will Cullen, a notorious highwayman. For many months he had terrorised every man and woman of wealth who had occasion to venture across Hampstead Heath, by day or by night.

Thomasina insisted that the carriage be turned about and a new route taken. She would not even allow Jeffery to mention the execution at Newgate.

It was this incident, as much as anything else, that hastened their decision to leave London. Thomasina declared she had tired of city life. She wanted to return to the fields and shores of Cornwall, where the air was sweet and untainted.

Jeffery raised no objection. However, remembering their voyage from Cornwall to Bristol, he insisted they travel by road and not sea.

They journeyed in a leisurely fashion, travelling only by day. Their nights were spent at coaching inns along the way – and Jeffery did not stint on the food and wine they bought there.

This was the most relaxed time they had ever spent together. It was with almost a sense of regret that Thomasina acknowledged the coachman's call that they were crossing the bridge spanning the River Tamar, near Launceston.

Moments later they were in Cornwall.

That night was spent at the Jamaica Inn, on Bodmin Moor, where the landlady, Widow Elizabeth Broad, impressed by their apparent wealth, suggested that they might like to aid the digestion of their food with fine wines and brandy, brought in from France.

When Jeffery expressed his surprise that such luxuries were available, when Britain and France had been at war for many years, the innkeeper retorted that war was fought by soldiers, on behalf of politicians. The Cornish had never allowed such considerations to stand in the way of trade with those who had been their friends for generations.

Widow Broad's words were brought home to Thomasina later that same night. Awakened by sounds in the early hours of the morning, she peered from behind the bedroom curtain and saw a number of pack-laden donkeys being hurriedly unloaded in the cobbled yard outside the inn. She knew immediately what was happening, having spent much of her life in a coastal community.

The men unloading the donkeys were smugglers. The Jamaica Inn was about as far from the sea as it was possible to be in Cornwall, but it was ideally situated as a well-established outlet for smuggled merchandise.

She released the curtain and went back to bed when one of the men turned his face up to her window.

The following morning, when Thomasina and Jeffery went down to breakfast, she found a delicate silk scarf folded beside her plate. When she questioned the serving maid, she was told that the scarf was by way of being an apology from one of the gentlemen who had disturbed her during the night.

It was a warm welcome back to the Cornwall she had always known.

Jeffery and Thomasina had decided that their destination in Cornwall would be somewhere beyond Falmouth. This should prove far enough away from both Mevagissey and Truro to serve as a suitable base while they sought a farm somewhere to the west of the region.

They had thought of returning to the Heron Inn for a while, but decided against it. In view of the stories they had told during their previous stay, suspicion would inevitably be aroused. It was highly unlikely the landlord would comment upon their new and open relationship, but there were others on his staff who were less discreet.

An additional reason was that Jeffery intended purchasing a farm in his real name. That would pose problems if they were staying at the Malpas riverside inn.

They eventually chose to stay at an establishment known as the Norway Inn, close to the river on the Falmouth road and some few miles from Truro. From here Jeffery set about the task of finding a suitable farm for sale.

It did not take long. Within a week he had located a delightful property some twelve miles farther west of where they were staying.

When he took Thomasina to see it, she fell in love with the farm immediately. Small enough not to require an excessive number of farmhands to work the land, it was sufficiently large to ensure they could enjoy a comfortable lifestyle.

However, they encountered a problem immediately. The asking price was higher than they had anticipated. Although Jeffery possessed enough money to purchase the farm, there would not be enough left over to buy livestock and keep the farm running until it began to pay its way.

Talking about it during the evening, after they had both looked at the farm, it was apparent to Thomasina that Jeffery was bitterly disappointed. She did her best to console him.

'Never mind. We'll find another farm that's just as nice – but perhaps a little bit smaller.'

'I doubt if I'll ever find one that appeals to me quite as much as this one, Tom. It's *exactly* what I want. You feel the same way about it, too. I know you do.'

It was true, but she shrugged, 'We haven't been looking for very long. There must be dozens of others out there that I'll like just as much. Besides, if we haven't got enough money to stock and run it, then we'll just have to look for somewhere else.'

Giving her a calculating look, Jeffery said, 'There's nothing to stop us going out to get more money, is there?'

'*No*, Jeffery!' Thomasina looked at him aghast. 'You promised we'd finished with that sort of thing, once and for all.'

'I thought we had – I *hoped* we had, but if it's going to

make the difference between getting the farm we want and settling for second best, then I'm ready to go out once more. On my own, if need be.'

Although his words made her desperately unhappy, Thomasina shook her head. 'If that's what needs to be done, we'll do it together – but I'd much rather we kept to our decision to lead an honest life now we're back in Cornwall. We stirred up the magistrates here once before. We got away with it then. We might not be so lucky the next time.'

'It will be all right, Tom, I promise you.'

Reaching across, he took her hand and gripped it tightly. 'I'll tell the agent that we'll have the farm, but he'll need to give me a few weeks to raise the money. We'll try to get it all at once.'

He smiled at her, 'We'll do it, Tom. We're a great team, you and I.'

'I'm not happy with the idea, but if you're determined to go ahead . . .' She shrugged. 'How are we going to go about it? I don't fancy going back to looking over farmers on market day. I believe our luck has run out using that ploy.'

'We won't need to do anything like that again – and the one job should be all we'll need do.' Suddenly enthusiastic, he continued, 'It's the Duchy Ball this weekend. It's attended by all the richest men and women in the county. They go there wearing their finest clothes and most expensive jewellery. There'll be riches for the taking. Enough to purchase the throne of England, if we wanted it.'

While Thomasina was digesting his words, he leaned towards her and added, 'We'll only need to hold up one coach as it's on the way home, then we'll have all the money we need. I know a pawnbroker in Plymouth who pays top money for good jewellery. I've never used him before because it's a bit too close to home, but as it's going to be just this once . . .'

'I still wish we weren't going to do another robbery, Jeffery.' Thomasina spoke unhappily. 'I have a bad feeling about it. Very bad . . .'

13

It was not the best of nights on which to wait to waylay a coach. Autumn was being rapidly superseded by winter, there was a heavy drizzle and the wind was steadily increasing in strength.

Jeffery had decided on the eastern outskirts of Truro as a suitable spot to hold up a coach that was homeward bound from the Duchy Ball.

He chose a spot where the road narrowed before climbing uphill from the town. They could shelter from the rain beneath leafy trees lining the road.

They had been waiting for almost an hour, and as Thomasina grew colder, Jeffery became increasingly impatient.

'The ball should have come to an end at least half an hour ago,' he complained. 'There should have been some movement along the road by now.'

'Shh! Listen.' Thomasina silenced him in a low voice.

Jeffery stopped talking immediately. After a few moments they both heard the sound of a coach and horses coming from the town. Then the lights of a carriage came into view.

'This is it, Tom. I'll stop the coach. You stay here ready to back me up, if I need you.'

It took a while for the labouring horses to reach them, but suddenly Jeffery was kneeing his horse into motion. Riding out in front of the carriage brandishing one of the two pistols he carried, he shouted, 'Halt! Stop there, coachman – or I'll shoot you dead.'

The driver of the carriage was not a man given to heroics. Hauling back on the reins, he brought the horses and vehicle to an immediate stop.

There was a small lantern suspended from the roof of the carriage illuminating the interior. It was this that alerted Thomasina to the fact that the occupants of the carriage were not as craven as their coachman.

As Jeffery approached the offside of the coach, she saw the sudden glint of glass from the *nearside* door, as it swung open silently.

'Look out! The other side of the coach.'

She remembered only just in time to adopt the gruff voice of a man, at the same time jabbing her heels into the flanks of her horse and driving it forward.

Her warning came too late. Jeffery swung his pistol to aim at the far side of the coach and pulled the trigger – but nothing happened. Rain had seeped inside the pan of the pistol, causing it to misfire.

At the same moment came the flash and report from a pistol on the nearside of the carriage. Thomasina heard a grunt of pain or surprise – or both – from Jeffery.

Pointing her own pistol in the direction of the unseen marksman, she pulled the trigger.

The pistol leaped in her hand and there was a cry of pain from the man who had shot Jeffery. A pistol dropped from his hand and bounced off the carriage step.

'Are you all right?' She brought her horse alongside that of Jeffery and put the question to him anxiously.

'No, I'm not,' Jeffery spoke to her through clenched teeth. 'Get me out of here, Tom.'

In the faint light from the interior of the carriage Thomasina could see him slumped in the saddle. Alarmed, she reached out to take hold of his reins.

The coachman, suddenly rediscovering his courage, seized the opportunity to slap the reins across the back of his horses and startle them into motion.

As the coach moved away, Thomasina caught a glimpse of its occupants. Incredulously, she saw that Harriet Vincent was one of the passengers. She was in the act of pulling back the coat sleeve from Sir Charles Hearle, revealing a bloody shirt sleeve. Then the coach passed on into the night and was gone, leaving Thomasina alone with the wounded Jeffery.

'I'm sorry, Tom . . . but I won't be able to make it as far as the Norway Inn.'

Jeffery's words were in response to Thomasina's attempt to urge the horses to a trot in order to take them clear of the scene of the abortive hold-up as quickly as possible.

Slowing the horses once more, a distraught

Thomasina said, 'There's nowhere else to go? We've got to get away from here – and quickly. The Vincents will waste no time in sending a search party out to look for us.'

'Take me to the Heron, Tom. That's close by. I'll be safe there.'

'Are you sure . . . ?' Thomasina was uncertain. She remembered they had felt it advisable to leave the waterside inn on the previous occasion they had both been staying there, and that Jeffery had not wanted to stay there more recently.

'Yes . . .' The pain he was in was causing him to speak through clenched teeth. 'Hurry! If I fall from my horse before we get there, I'll be found and be as good as dead. You know that.'

Twenty minutes later they were approaching the Heron Inn. By now Thomasina was riding alongside Jeffery, supporting him in the saddle. But he was conscious enough to realise where they were.

'Leave me here, Tom. Go on back to the Norway Inn and make up some story to account for my absence. You'll think of something.'

'I can't just leave you. You can hardly stay in the saddle without me holding you.'

'Do as I say,' he spoke angrily and painfully. 'I'll make it as far as the inn door. The landlord will get me inside and send for a doctor. One who can be trusted.'

Thomasina began to argue that she wanted to remain with him, but he cut her short. 'You've *got* to go back to the Norway. All our money is hidden in the room. If the landlord gets concerned that we might have run off without paying him, he'll search the room and find it. Then all this will have been wasted. Go . . . but change your clothes before you ride through Truro. The constables might already be out.'

Thomasina had no time to put forward any further arguments. Jeffery urged his horse into motion and headed for the inn.

She waited in the shadows as he halted outside the door and called out to those inside. A few minutes later he was being helped through the door by the landlord and his cellarman, leaving Thomasina to ride off alone, desperately worried about Jeffery and filled with renewed hatred for the man who had twice changed the course of her life.

It was as well that Thomasina heeded Jeffery's warning and changed her clothes before riding through Truro. The Vincents had already managed to get word back to Truro of the attempted robbery. Constables, accompanied by a great many sworn men, were out on the streets in force.

One of the latter stopped her to warn her of the dangers of riding unaccompanied at such a late hour. He informed her that 'desperate villains' were at large. He also passed on the information that one of them had shot a young gentleman 'well nigh to death'.

Thomasina told the sworn man that the reason she was out so late was that she had been to visit a sick relative and had left much later than she had intended. In spite of her protests, the man insisted upon accompanying her to the Norway Inn – and it was a most uncomfortable ride for Thomasina. The improvised side-saddle was never intended to be used over any distance.

Fortunately, he was flattered by her apparent interest in him and neither noticed her constant changing of position, nor questioned her too closely. Instead, he was content to do much of the talking himself, before turning his horse about and returning to Truro when they were only a short distance from the Norway Inn.

A grumbling inn servant, awakened from slumber to perform the duties for which he was employed, opened the door to her. She told him the same story she had given to the sworn man who had ridden with her to the inn. She added that Jeffery had stayed with the sick relative and intended accompanying him to a renowned doctor in London, so he would undoubtedly be away for some time. In a day or two she would be settling the bill and travelling to join him.

Thomasina had already decided that if she had received no word from Jeffery in a couple of days, she would go to the Heron Inn and join him there whatever the consequences.

Despite her intentions, Thomasina remained at the Norway Inn for a week, fully expecting that the following day would be the one when she would receive a message from Jeffery. Then, desperately worried by the total absence of news from him, Thomasina made the decision to leave the Norway Inn and go to Malpas to find out what was happening.

The landlord was sorry to see her depart. Business was decidedly slack at the moment. He was also concerned that she would be travelling alone. However, as she was about to depart, he commented, 'Mind, you'll be a lot safer now that the desperate highwayman who has caused so much trouble in the past has been taken.'

Thomasina swung around so quickly that she startled the landlord. 'What highwayman? Where did they find him?'

'I don't suppose you know anything about it. A coach was held up on the outskirts of Truro the other night. One of the passengers was shot and has been left with a crippled arm. The men who did it are believed to be responsible for a number of robberies around the town a while back. Their luck certainly ran out this time. One of the highwaymen got himself shot too. Hopefully he'll die of his wounds. He'll only hang if he lives, so it would save everyone a lot of time and money.'

Trying desperately hard not to show the distress she was feeling, Thomasina asked, 'You say there is more than one . . . ?'

'There *was* a second highwayman, but if he has any sense, he'll have put a great many miles between himself and Truro by now.'

This, at least, provided Thomasina with a grain of comfort. They suspected Jeffrey's accomplice was another *man*. Nevertheless, news of his arrest came as a great shock. He had been convinced that he would find safety at the Heron Inn. It was a place usually avoided by the magistrates' men. What could have gone wrong?

She decided someone must have told the constables of his whereabouts. She went cold when she realised that she had come within a hair's-breadth of sharing the same fate as Jeffery.

Had she gone to the Heron Inn with him – or even called there to check on his well-being – she too would probably have been arrested.

The problem now was what she should do? Truro would be too dangerous a place in which to make enquiries about where Jeffery was being held. There was even a remote possibility that she might be recognised as having been associated with him.

A similar problem arose about visiting the Heron Inn. If someone there had betrayed Jeffery, they would probably know of her association with him.

The landlord of the Norway Inn unwittingly provided the answer to her dilemma.

'The trial will be held in Bodmin – that's where the highwayman is being held. I know one of the court ushers there. If you're going to be around that way, just mention my name and he'll see that you have a place in court for the trial. You might like to stay there for the hanging, too. A fair comes to town and people come from miles around to enjoy the festivities and have a grand time.'

His words sickened Thomasina. She tried not to think of the part Jeffery would play in the 'festivities'. But at least she now knew where he was being held.

She would travel to Bodmin and find some way of visiting him in prison.

14

Arriving in Bodmin town on a coach, Thomasina
put up at the Royal Hotel, just out of sight of the
grim, grey-walled prison where Jeffery was being held
prisoner.

The coach had passed close by the prison on its
way into Bodmin. It was a forbidding place, and she
was greatly distressed at the thought of the wounded
Jeffery being held within its high walls.

He would be enjoying scant comfort in such a
place, and it was this thought that made her decide
to throw caution to the wind and visit him as soon
as possible.

She found it surprisingly easy to obtain information
about the prison and the occupant she had come to
Bodmin to see. The young servant girl who arrived to
tidy her room the following morning actually volunteered information about the 'desperate highwayman'

locked up inside the gaol, without Thomasina finding it necessary to broach the subject.

The servant girl informed her that he was known to be wounded, but would be well enough to stand trial when the judge arrived in town to conduct the Assizes in a couple of weeks' time.

The garrulous servant also volunteered information that the gaoler was a certain Herbert Carminow who, according to town gossip, enjoyed his comfort and drink a little too much. Because of this, it was said that he made little real effort to provide any unnecessary comforts for those prisoners placed in his care – especially if it was going to cost him money.

Armed with this information and wearing some of her finest clothes, Thomasina called upon the gaoler that evening.

Her looks and appearance gained her immediate entry to the gaoler's office. However, when she expressed a wish to see 'Jeremy King', the name by which Jeffery had been known at the Heron Inn, the gaoler was taken aback.

'The highwayman? I'm amazed that anyone would want to see *him*. Besides, he told me he knows no one in these parts.'

'He probably doesn't,' agreed Thomasina easily, 'but news travels fast and far in Cornwall, as you must know. I once knew someone named Jeremy King. When I heard that a highwayman of that name had been arrested, I thought I must come at once and see if it was the same man.'

Smiling sadly at the gaoler, she explained, 'If it *is* him, then his poor mother would have been deeply distresed, were she still alive. She was once very kind to me. This would be an opportunity to repay that kindness in a manner of which she would have approved.'

'Such thoughtfulness!' said the gaoler ingratiatingly, sensing that a profitable transaction might be in the offing. 'I doubt if the young rogue will appreciate it, but then, even the worst of men is some poor mother's son. Besides, he only has a few weeks left in this world. Come the Assizes, he'll be tried, convicted and hanged.'

Doing her very best to blot out the picture that his words conjured up, Thomasina asked, 'May I be permitted to see him right away?'

The gaoler shook his head doubtfully. 'It would be extremely dangerous, Miss. He's being held with men who have no respect for decent young ladies like yourself. I don't think I dare take such a risk.'

'Wouldn't it be possible for him to be moved to a cell on his own? I could visit him safely then.'

The gaoler appeared to be thinking, 'Well . . . it's not out of the question, Miss, but such a move would cost money. You see, there's extra work involved in guarding a prisoner who's on his own. Then there's the business of cleaning out his cell, taking his food in separately . . .'

'How much would this involve?' Thomasina interrupted him, well aware that the gaoler was out to get as much money as he could from her.

'At least two pounds a week, Miss. At the very least.'

Thomasina thought of the work she had carried out

at Trebene for the Vincent family for a grand total of less than two shillings and sixpence a week.

'I'll give you five guineas for accommodation and special food for the remainder of the time he's in your care. If he's here for longer than a month, I'll make it more – but only if he's moved immediately and I'm permitted to see him right away.'

The gaoler's wife would be cooking the 'special' meals for the prisoner and the cell cleaning would be carried out by one of the older prisoners, in return for the promise of a more relaxed routine. Consequently, the gaoler knew he was assured of a handsome profit, but he agreed with apparent reluctance.

'You strike a hard bargain, young lady, but as you're doing this as an act of charity, why then, I can't refuse. You wait here and I'll have this young rogue moved to a cell that's as comfortable as any in the prison. Once he's there, you can go in and speak to him.'

Just before the gaoler left the office, he added, 'It might take me a little while. The prisoner was shot by one of the men he tried to rob and still needs help to get around. It's fortunate he's a fit young man, or no doubt he'd have died. As it is, he'll be fit enough to be put on trial when the time comes – and I've no doubt he'll stand straight enough for the hangman to place a noose about his neck.'

Once again Thomasina needed to shake off the horror she felt at the gaoler's callous words.

It was twenty minutes before the gaoler returned to his office. Beaming obsequiously at her, he announced,

'The young man who is benefiting from your generosity has been moved to a single cell. It's as comfortable a room as you'll find in any prison. It could almost be an inn room. Indeed, if you add another guinea to what you are going to give me, I'll see that he has all the ale or spirits he wants while he's here.'

'Can I see him now?' Thomasina asked eagerly.

'Of course . . . You have the money with you?'

Thomasina took six guineas and a half-guinea from her purse and handed the coins to the avaricious gaoler. 'That's half-a-guinea more than we've agreed. Make absolutely certain that he lacks for nothing and you'll be thanked generously when he . . . When he passes out of your care.'

In the gaoler's experience, when a prisoner had suffered the fate meted out to him by a judge, the generosity of his friends died with him. However, this young woman had already given him more than the agreed sum. It was just possible she might keep her promise.

'As I said to you before, Miss, he doesn't deserve to have such a friend. Come, I'll take you to him.'

Inside the prison, following in the wake of the gaoler and a turnkey, Thomasina found the stench overpowering. She did her best to ignore the lewd shouts and general clamour of the prisoners who sat or lay upon the straw strewn upon the floors of the communal cells.

Eventually the small party arrived at a single cell that was by no means palatial. However, it did have a wooden bunk upon which Jeffery was lying beneath an old blanket, his eyes closed.

His face looked gaunt and he had an unhealthy pallor. Thomasina had to resist the urge to drop to her knees beside him and hold him close.

'There, you see, he even has a window in here.' The gaoler pointed to a tiny barred aperture, high up in one of the walls, through which a shaft of feeble, dusty sunlight lit up a small square on the opposite, whitewashed wall.

Jeffery had opened his eyes at the sound of the gaoler's voice and was now looking up at Thomasina in disbelief.

'Thank you, sir. Can you leave us alone for a while now?'

'Well . . . I shouldn't, but seeing as how *you're* performing an act of kindness, I'll do the same. But I can give you no more than ten or fifteen minutes – and I'll need to lock you in.'

As the footsteps of the gaoler and turnkey receded along the corridor outside the cell, Jeffery pushed back the blanket and held his arms out to her. At last, she was able to cuddle him to her.

When she released him, he said, 'What are you doing here, Tom? You shouldn't have come, it's far too dangerous for you.'

'Nonsense. I told them your mother had once been kind to me and I owed her a debt. They suspect nothing. More to the point, what are *you* doing in here? How were you caught? I thought you would be safe at the Heron Inn.'

'I should have been, but the Truro magistrates put out a reward for me – a very large one. More than they've ever offered for anyone before, I believe.' He spoke of it with something very like pride in his voice. 'The temptation was too great.'

'Too great for whom? Who actually led the magistrates' men to you?'

'Hebe.'

'That bitch!' Thomasina spoke angrily. 'I knew she wasn't to be trusted. I ought to lie in wait and shoot her.'

Jeffery managed a weak, tired smile. 'I'm glad to know you still care for me, Tom, but don't even think of doing anything like that. You shouldn't come to see me again, either. It's far too risky. You might be recognised by someone. You've done more than enough by having me taken out of that stinking hole I shared with the others. I'm beholden to you. If you can arrange for me to be brought some decent food, I'll be even more grateful. For the rest . . . I knew the risk I was taking when I set out to do what I did. I'll pay the price. It's been a good and exciting life. It was even better when you joined me.'

Thomasina would have liked to be able to give him some words of comfort and hope, but the lies would not come. Instead, she said defiantly, 'I'll come as often as I like, Jeffery. I've already given the gaoler enough money to make sure you're well looked after in here, but here's another twenty guineas. Use it to buy any extras you need. If you find a turnkey who'll help you to escape, then offer him all the money we've made – your share and mine – and get word to me. If we need even more, than I'll get it for you, you can be quite certain of that.'

He smiled at her once more, a watery smile this

time. 'Thanks, Tom. I couldn't have wished for a better partner – in anything that we've done together, but it's the parting of the ways. You know that, and so do I. Use the money we've made wisely. Make certain you'll never need to rely on anyone else for the rest of your life. If you promise me that, I'll die happy and know that all I've done has been worthwhile.'

15

A few days after Jeffery had been transferred to the single cell, Thomasina called on him again and found him in an agitated state.

No sooner had the turnkey left them, locking the cell door behind him, than Jeffery said, 'You've got to go, Tom – and you mustn't come back here again to see me.'

Taken aback by his words, Thomasina demanded, 'Why? What's happened to change things?'

'Half a dozen smugglers were taken and brought here during the night. They're from Mevagissey!'

This was alarming news for both of them. Mevagissey was a small, close-knit community. Any man from the fishing village would be likely to recognise both Jeffery and Thomasina.

Yet, desperate to find a way to continue to visit Jeffery, Thomasina said, 'But you're in a cell by yourself – and wounded. There's no need for them ever to see you. To see either of us.'

Jeffery shook his head. 'I'm able to go out to the exercise yard now, Tom. To get there I'm taken past the cell where they're being held. No one's recognised me yet, probably because of this . . .' he stroked the stubbly beard that had grown during his imprisonment, '. . . but if they were to catch a glimpse of you, it wouldn't be long before we'd both be identified. The magistrates' men would realise what's been going on and you'd be arrested, too. We can't take a chance on that happening.'

Jeffery managed to communicate to Thomasina the fear he felt. She had passed a number of communal cells on the way to visit him and it was not inconceivable that some of the men who had called out to her were Mevagissey men and had already recognised her.

'What should I do, Jeffery?' Thomasina was more scared than she could ever remember.

'Leave Bodmin right away. Go to Falmouth, to the inn close to the ferry, where we once thought of staying when we were looking for a farm, remember? I think it's called the Ship Inn. Don't try to get in touch with me again until after the trial. The newspapers will publish details of when the Assizes are due to begin. The Mevagissey men assaulted the Customs men who arrested them, so they'll probably be sentenced to transportation and sent off to a hulk right away. I'll get a message to you when it's safe to come and see me again. I have money enough to get it brought to you by a horseman.'

'I don't like to think of you here, with no one to care about you and with your trial coming up soon . . .' Thomasina found herself close to tears.

'I'll be happier knowing you're somewhere safe, Tom. You've done all you can for me, and I'm more grateful than I can say. Take care now and remember: don't come back to Bodmin until it's safe to do so.'

'I wish there was some way to get you out of here, Jeffery.' The tears were uncontrollable now.

Giving her the wry semblance of a smile, he said, 'So do I, Tom – but there isn't.'

He wiped away her tears with the heel of his hand and then he was holding her. He held her for perhaps five minutes before saying gently, 'You must go now, Tom. Remember to turn your head away when you're passing the men in the main cells on the way out. Fortunately, the light isn't very good along there, and the gaoler is too careful with his money to have candles burning at this time of day.'

As she pulled away from him, he said, 'I meant what I've already said to you, Tom. I couldn't have wished for a better partner, but it's the parting of the ways now. It has to be. You know it and so do I.'

When Thomasina made no reply, he went on, 'Make good use of the money we've made, Tom – for my sake. Do that and nothing that happens will have been in vain.'

As Thomasina walked away from the prison, she thought of all he had said to her. She realised that Jeffery had not only accepted that he would be found 'guilty' by the judge, but had spoken as though he did not expect to see her again.

* * *

Thomasina conceded that it would be unsafe for her to remain at the Royal Hotel until the trial. Many relatives of the Mevagissey smugglers would be visiting their menfolk in the prison. Some would no doubt find their way to the town's inns and taverns. It was always possible that she would meet up with some of them. The unnecessary complications so caused would help neither herself nor Jeffery.

She decided she would do as Jeffery had suggested and go to Falmouth, to the Ship Inn – but she intended returning to Bodmin as soon as was prudent.

16

Thomasina returned to the Royal Hotel in Bodmin on the first day of the trial, but remained in her room for the whole of the first couple of days.

To have attended Jeffery's trial would have proved far too dangerous. The families of the Mevagissey fishermen would have been there in support of their men.

Not only would Thomasina have been recognised, but her presence would have aroused considerable speculation, and suspicion might have fallen on her.

Jeffery's arrest and forthcoming trial had already excited much interest in the newspapers. All the reports had mentioned *two* highwaymen being involved in the robberies and had declared that Jeffery's accomplice was still actively being sought.

No one had suggested that the accomplice might be a woman, but it was not beyond the intelligence of an astute constable or magistrate to arrive at an accurate conclusion. It would be even more likely if the apparently wealthy woman taking an interest in the highwayman was recognised as one Thomasina Varcoe, a poor, orphaned servant girl from Mevagissey who had been dismissed from Trebene House for dishonesty.

It was also possible that Hebe, the servant girl from the Heron Inn, would be called to give evidence. Quite apart from the danger that posed to her, Thomasina did not feel she could trust herself if she came face-to-face with the woman who had betrayed Jeffery to the authorities.

At the hotel, the trials being held at the Assize Court were the main subject of conversation, both among servants and customers.

From the maid who brought food to her room, Thomasina learned that, of the six Mevagissey fishermen, three had opted to be pressed into service with the Royal Navy rather than take their chances in a trial. The others had been found 'guilty' by the judge. As expected, they had been sentenced to transportation, two for fourteen years, the other for seven.

The outcome of their trial meant that seeing Jeffery again would now be less dangerous than before. Nevertheless, Thomasina decided it would be better to wait until his trial had been over for a day or two before attempting to visit him again.

Sir Charles Hearle and the Vincents would no doubt be called upon to give evidence against him. A confrontation with them would be even more dangerous than meeting the families of the Mevagissey fishermen.

However, Thomasina's plans were thrown into confusion late on the very day of Jeffery's trial.

Feeling it still unsafe to eat in the hotel's dining-room, she once more arranged for a meal to be brought to her room. When the servant girl entered bearing a tray, Thomasina's first question to her was whether or not the trial of the highwayman had been concluded.

'Yes, indeed,' affirmed the girl, evidently eager to share her knowledge. 'He pleaded "guilty" and was tried, convicted and sentenced in less than half an hour.' She sounded disappointed.

As Thomasina composed herself to ask a question about the inevitable sentence, the servant girl asked cheerfully, 'Will you be going to the hanging?'

'Hanging?' Thomasina repeated, stupidly. 'When?'

'They're going to hang the highwayman in the morning. The judge said there was no sense in prolonging the life of such a rogue for a single minute more than was absolutely necessary. He's to be hanged at eight o'clock. There'll be a great crowd to see it, I can tell you. I don't know how news gets around so quick, but folk'll be coming overnight from miles around to watch him get his just desserts. If you'd like to watch, there's a young stable lad who'll be happy to keep a good place for you . . .'

Thomasina did not know how she managed to keep control of her voice when she informed the girl that she had no intention of watching a man die . . . watching *Jeffery* die.

Not until the girl had left the room did Thomasina discover she was shaking. There was no question of attempting to eat the meal that had been brought to the room. It would have choked her.

It took her many minutes to pull herself together. Even when she had succeeded in calming herself, she was incapable of logical reasoning. The one thought dominating all others was that she must go and see Jeffery right away.

Leaving the untouched meal on the table where the servant girl had placed it, Thomasina put on her outside clothes and hurried from the hotel.

At the prison, the turnkey answered her insistent knocking and called the gaoler when she insisted she wanted to see Jeffery.

The gaoler shook his head. 'I'm afraid that's not allowed, Miss. Not when a prisoner is due to die the next morning. Besides, the vicar of Bodmin is due to come and spend time with him. Even a villain the likes of him must be given an opportunity to make his peace with God.'

'I'll go as soon as the vicar arrives,' promised Thomasina. 'But I *must* see him.'

When it became evident to her that the gaoler was about to refuse once more, Thomasina said, in desperation, 'I'll give you ten guineas if you'll allow me in.'

The offer brought an immediate change in the gaoler's attitude, but greed and long experience in such matters caused him to hold out for a little longer.

'Well . . . I'd be willing to oblige, of course, but it's not just me as is involved. There's the turnkey . . .'

'I'll give you fifteen guineas to share with the turn-key as you see fit. It's all the money I have on me.'

'Then I've no doubt we can come to some satisfactory arrangement, Miss. Do you have the money to hand?'

Ten minutes later Thomasina was let into Jeffery's cell.

He was seated on the edge of the wooden bunk. Both hands had been pressed to his head when he heard the footsteps of Thomasina and the gaoler.

Now, pale-faced, he looked up at her, but made no move to rise to his feet as the gaoler left the cell and closed and locked the door behind him.

Hurrying to the prison from the inn, Thomasina had mentally rehearsed a dozen different versions of the words she would say to Jeffery. Now that she was here, all were forgotten.

Dropping to a seat beside him on the hard wooden bench, Thomasina threw her arms about him and cried, 'Jeffery! My poor darling. What have we done?'

For a few moments he said nothing, but she could feel him trembling in her arms. Then, pulling himself together, he said gruffly, 'I knew what I was doing, Tom – and was carrying out robberies before you joined me. There was always the risk of being caught. We both knew that.'

'But it's so unfair,' declared Thomasina fiercely. 'To have this happen after we'd given up that life.'

'Do you think we'd ever have given it up altogether?' Jeffery asked philosophically. 'We went back to highway robbery this time because we needed some extra money. Don't you think we'd have turned to it again and again when times were bad, or when we needed money for stock, or feed – or a hundred and one other things?'

'No! We wouldn't have, Jeffery. We'd have married, had a family and settled down to make a success of our own farm.'

'It's a wonderful picture, Thomasina. One I shall take with me to the scaffold tomorrow. I'd have gone through with it, too – for your sake. But I don't really think I would have made a successful farmer. The only thing I've ever *really* enjoyed is carrying out highway robbery. The excitement . . . the sense of power when someone trembles before you because you're pointing a pistol at him. I've enjoyed the money I've got from it, too. So have you. We've made more money than either of us ever dreamed we'd have when we were kids together in Mevagissey. That reminds me . . .'

Feeling inside his sock, he pulled out the small bag of coins she had given him on her earlier visit. 'Here's the money you gave me when you had the gaoler move me to this cell. I won't have need of it now.'

Thomasina hesitated – taking the money from him seemed somehow disloyal. An acceptance of his fate. 'Is there nothing we can do to save you, Jeffery? Perhaps have the sentence commuted to transportation?'

Pushing the small bag of money into her hand, he shook his head. 'I couldn't spend the rest of my life as a convict. I've had a full and exciting life, Tom. Having you share it with me for these past months has been best of all. Leaving you alone is the only thing I'll regret, but I'll die happy in the knowledge that I've made you a rich woman.'

For some time Thomasina clung to him, too choked with unhappiness to talk. Then they both heard the jangling of keys and the sound of voices approaching along the corridor outside.

'That'll be the parson,' said Jeffery. 'Goodbye, Tom. Will you . . . will you be outside tomorrow?'

She shook her head, seeing him only dimly through her tears. 'I couldn't bear it. But I'll be thinking of you. Praying for you.'

As a key turned in the lock, Jeffery said huskily, 'There'll be a whole lot of praying for me between now and the morning. Goodbye, Tom. Think of me sometimes – but think of the happy times . . .'

His voice broke as the door swung open.

The vicar's expression indicated deep disapproval, but Thomasina pushed past him without a word. The door was closed behind her, then the gaoler was leading her along the dark, evil-smelling corridors towards the prison entrance.

17

The cheer that rose from the thousands who witnessed Jeffery's plunge through the wooden trapdoor to eternity reached Thomasina as she rode out of Bodmin town.

Fully aware of the event they were applauding, she urged her horse on. She should have been crying, but yet again she had brought down the shutter on reality and emotion and felt only a dull numbness.

She had purchased a horse and tack the night before from the stableman at the inn. She wanted to travel to Falmouth on her own, unwilling to face anyone just yet.

She was returning to Falmouth only because she had left her belongings at the Ship Inn. She had no real plans for the future. She would not pursue the purchase of a farm, as she and Jeffery had planned.

She could not manage such a venture on her own and did not know enough about farming to make a success of it using hired help.

Besides, an idea she had always kept at the back of her mind had come to the fore, even before Jeffery met his fate. It was the germ of a dream she had always entertained, although it was not one she could ever have shared with him.

The Falmouth inn would prove ideal for what she had in mind, and when another week had passed she put her newly formed plans into action.

The inn was frequented by masters, owners and brokers of merchant vessels based in Falmouth. Thomasina listened in to their conversations as they ate at the tables around her and was able to decide that the most honest of the town's solicitors was a company called Bennett and Pengelly.

It was to their offices that she made her way one morning, ten days after Jeffery's execution.

Seated across the desk from one of the firm's partners, Zachariah Bennett, she exaggerated the status of her late father as a ship-owner and master.

She informed the solicitor that she had recently inherited some money, as a result of his death. While it was not sufficient to enable her to buy a deep-sea vessel outright, she believed it would be sufficient to purchase a half-share in a vessel where a co-owner had the qualifications, like her late father, to take the vessel to sea as its master.

The solicitor declared that he knew of a number of such men who were seeking a partner to invest in their vessels. He promised to submit details of their ships to her, together with the amount of investment required, accounts of their recent voyages and plans for future ventures.

When these had been passed to her, Thomasina said she would interview those owners she felt most likely to suit her and decide whether to invest her money in one of them.

It was perhaps not the most usual means of carrying out such a business, as Thomasina was aware, but the continuing war with France was making life extremely difficult for many ship-owners. Some were desperate to attract additional capital. The solicitor felt that few owners would refuse to cooperate.

Forty-eight hours later details of no fewer than twenty-three desperate ship-owning masters were delivered to Thomasina.

By the following morning she had whittled down the number in which she was particularly interested to four. Wasting no time, she began interviewing them that same afternoon.

By early evening she had ruled out three of the men and was feeling increasingly despondent. Then Captain Malachi Wesley Ellis arrived at the Ship Inn.

Captain Malachi was a Scillonian whose family had been island fishermen for countless generations. Malachi had been the first of the Ellis men to break with family tradition. At the age of thirteen, he had persuaded his reluctant father to allow him to enter the Royal Navy as a midshipman, serving on a ship commanded by a naval officer who had married Malachi's aunt.

With his uncle, the young Scillonian had sailed

the world. Before long, his intuitive skills of sea-manship had earned him grudging promotion in a service dominated by patronage, titles and family connections.

Eventually, given command of a frigate in the West Indies, Malachi set a record for the amount of prize money won by a ship of such size. Then came the fateful day when Malachi's ship encountered a French fleet in the Caribbean.

Under normal circumstances, the unwritten rules of naval warfare said that the French would fire a war-ning shot or two and allow the smaller vessel to go on its way, without further molestation. However, such was the reputation of this particular British frigate and its captain that the enemy made a determined attempt to send them both to the bottom of the ocean.

Malachi's superb seamanship enabled him to escape from the French fleet under the cover of darkness, but not before the frigate had received a number of hits. Malachi himself suffered a severe wound. When the ship reached Kingston, in Jamaica, it was necessary for a surgeon to amputate his right leg, below the knee.

It marked the end of Malachi's naval career, but not the cessation of his seagoing days. With his prize money he purchased a merchantman, the *Melanie Jane*.

Sailing this ship, Malachi traded to and from the Mediterranean, making a satisfactory living. He even purchased a second vessel – and this was his undoing. It was taken by a French privateer off the coast of Africa and Malachi learned that the master had failed to insure the latest cargo.

Now Malachi had secured a valuable cargo, with

profit virtually assured, but all the money he had was tied up in property and investments. He needed ready cash to purchase the cargo – and he needed it quickly. This was why he was seeking a partner to purchase a half-share in the *Melanie Jane*.

As he spoke with modesty to Thomasina of his past achievements and of the ambitions he had for the future, she observed him with increasing interest.

A man of perhaps sixty years of age, Malachi was tall, broad-shouldered and bearded. Despite his age and disability, his blue eyes twinkled in a manner that proved he had lost none of his zest for living – which for him meant sailing.

When he had ended his narrative, Thomasina asked, 'Have you never married, Captain Ellis?'

The eyes twinkled once more as he replied, 'I never have, Miss Varcoe – 'though I've come almighty close to it once or twice. But I reckon my way of life put 'em off, when it came down to it. The sea is a demanding mistress.'

'An orphan-maker too,' said Thomasina, with a trace of bitterness in her voice. 'That's how I lost my father.'

'It happens,' commented the sea captain philosophically.

Thomasina had already decided she liked this man, but now she wondered how he would react to the proposition she intended putting to him. There was only one way to find out.

'I like the ideas you have for your ship, Captain Ellis, and I'm very impressed by your own record. I'm prepared to buy a half-share in the *Melanie Jane*, but I have a condition which you may not feel able to accept.'

Malachi shrugged. He liked this young woman, too. He felt she knew what she wanted, but would not prove to be too difficult as a partner. 'Try me, Miss Varcoe. I'm not an unreasonable man. If I can remain master of the *Melanie Jane* and continue to make decisions about where we trade, I'll go along with most things. The ship will be safer in my hands than under the command of anyone else. What's more, I'll return a handsome profit for both of us.'

'I don't doubt it, Captain Ellis. That's why I'd like to have you as my partner, after interviewing three other masters and rejecting a score more.' Looking straight into the blue, bright eyes, she continued, 'I'm prepared to go into partnership with you, Captain Ellis, but only on condition that you take me with you on your voyages.'

Malachi's eyebrows rose in unison and he stared at her for a few incredulous moments before shaking his head reluctantly. 'I'm very sorry, Miss Varcoe, but the *Melanie Jane* has no facilities for women passengers. Besides, seamen are a superstitious bunch. Many consider it unlucky to carry women on a working ship.'

'I'm not talking of travelling as a passenger, Captain, and if we do it my way they won't even know there's a woman on board the *Melanie Jane*.'

Frowning, the sea captain said, 'I think you'd better explain what it is that you're suggesting, Miss Varcoe.'

'I'm suggesting that I join your ship as a boy and learn to become a seaman.'

Malachi looked at her as though she had just suggested she could fly. 'It would never work. They'd realise in no time that you were a girl. Even if they didn't, you couldn't keep up the pretence for long, not living in such close proximity. No, it wouldn't work.' He shook his head emphatically.

'I needn't live in close proximity with them,' Thomasina persisted, 'I could go on board as a relative of yours. You could fix up a place for me to sleep, close to your own cabin.'

She nodded in the direction of the wooden stump that served as the lower part of his right leg. 'You could say the leg is beginning to trouble you and you need someone to help you out – as a servant, perhaps. I could help with a seaman's duties when I wasn't working for you.'

'It still wouldn't work,' declared Malachi, shaking his head emphatically. 'Someone would see through your disguise the moment you stepped on board.'

Thomasina stared at him and for a while it seemed she would argue further. Then, abruptly, she said, 'Perhaps you're right – but I've been interviewing all afternoon and have a few things I must do right now. Look, return to the taproom here at nine o'clock tonight and send word to me that you've arrived. I'll come down as soon as I can and we'll go to a private room and talk about this some more. See if we can work something out. But, remember, I *do* want to go into partnership with you.'

Before Malachi could either agree or disagree, she had risen to her feet and swept from the room, leaving him shaking his head in disappointment.

He would keep the appointment, but he felt they would never find a way to enter into a partnership. Not on Thomasina's terms.

* * *

The taproom of the Ship Inn was not a place where Captain Malachi Ellis would have chosen to meet a lady. It was a drinking room favoured by seamen of various nations and was both noisy and boisterous.

One of the rowdiest groups was in a corner of the room. Choosing a table farthest away from the noisy drinkers, Malachi ordered an ale and asked the serving girl to send someone to the room occupied by Thomasina to inform her that he had arrived.

He had consumed half of his ale and was becoming impatient at being kept waiting when a figure detached itself from the group he was avoiding.

A young man walked with a swagger across the room towards him. Malachi was aware that he was heading in his direction, but took little notice. He did not know the lad and his thoughts were of Thomasina.

He wondered whether she knew the type of clientele that a taproom attracted in a busy port such as Falmouth. She might even have looked in and decided not to enter. He would finish his drink and see whether she was waiting for him outside.

'Are you deliberately avoiding me, Captain Ellis? We agreed to meet here, remember?' The speaker was the figure who had crossed the room towards him.

The voice was that of a young lad, not fully a man, but with childhood left behind. It was hardly deeper than the voice he had heard earlier in the day, yet the subtle change made all the difference. The 'lad' was Thomasina.

As he leaned back against the wall behind him, Malachi's disbelief changed to delight and he bellowed with laughter. Looking up at her, he shook his head in amused acknowledgement of her deception. 'Had I not seen this with my own eyes I would never have believed it possible – and if you can fool me, you can fool anyone!'

'So, what are you going to do . . . *Uncle* Malachi?'

'First of all, you'd better tell me what I should call you . . . Nephew.'

'Tom. My name is Tom.'

Malachi reached up to brush away a laughter tear before reaching out his hand. 'Put it there, Tom. I think I'm going to enjoy sailing with a partner. Especially one as lively as you.'

Book Two

1

'Come on in, Tom. You'll never have swum in water like this around Cornwall. You could almost boil an egg in it!'

The Cornish accent sounded strangely out of place in the small, palm-fringed bay, warmed by a breeze from the inland desert.

The *Melanie Jane* was anchored close inshore, off a seemingly deserted stretch of the North African coastline. The vessel had taken a cargo of salted pilchards from Cornwall to Sicily. Here Malachi had loaded a cargo of wine and a quantity of polished marble, for delivery to the West Indies. On the third leg of its voyage the *Melanie Jane* would return to England with a highly profitable cargo of sugar and, possibly, rum.

'I can't swim.' Thomasina's reply to the man who had called her was a lie. She was an excellent swimmer, her father having taught her by the time she was three. However, in view of her subterfuge, it would have been impossible to join the other crew members, especially as they were all swimming in a state of utter nudity.

Patting the long-barrelled musket lying across her knees, she added, 'Besides, someone's got to stand guard.'

This, at least, was the truth. The North coast of Africa was home to the infamous Barbary corsairs. All appeared peaceful about them now, but a single pirate ship could change the picture immediately.

Posing as Captain Malachi Ellis's young nephew, Thomasina had settled in to seaboard life and been fully accepted by the men. In spite of the confined conditions of life on board ship, none of the seamen appeared to entertain the slightest suspicion that 'Tom' was, in fact, a young woman. The deception was made possible by the fact that she had her own tiny cabin and did not share their cramped quarters.

Scarcely more than bunk's width, the 'cabin' was adjacent to Malachi's own cabin and had been converted from a small store room where the captain had previously kept a number of old trunks and chests.

The crew had also accepted that such accommodation had been made available not solely due to the fact that 'Tom' was supposed to be Malachi's nephew, but because the main reason he was on board was to help take care of the ageing, one-legged captain.

However, Thomasina had never intended to be merely a passenger on board the *Melanie Jane*. In addition to learning navigation and sailing skills from Malachi, she enjoyed taking on many of the crew's duties when the opportunity arose.

She particularly enjoyed working in the rigging, helping to furl and shake out the sails, whatever the state of the weather.

They had recently been hit by a storm that Malachi declared was the worst he had ever encountered in the Mediterranean, a sea not normally given to such excesses. The suddenness and sheer violence of it had taken Malachi by surprise. Before all the sails could be furled, some of them had been torn asunder. Malachi had anchored in the North African bay to repair or replace them.

The storm had long since passed and the repairs having been effected satisfactorily, Malachi was allowing his hard-working crew to enjoy the rare pleasure of a swim, before they resumed their voyage.

'Can you really not swim, Tom?'

Seated in the shade of a spare sail, stretched above a section of the deck, at the stern of the *Melanie Jane*, Malachi sat enjoying a pipe of tobacco.

The hot weather did not suit him. He found it difficult to ignore the perspiration which stood out on his forehead and irritated his neck, beneath the bushy grey beard.

'I can swim like a pilchard,' replied Thomasina, 'but can you imagine the sensation it would cause if I were to strip off and go swimming with the men?'

Malachi chuckled. 'They'd be too busy trying to hide their own embarrassment at having you see *them* naked, I reckon.'

Puffing on his pipe, Malachi looked at Thomasina

admiringly. He had gained an increasing affection and respect for her during the months she had been accompanying him on his voyages. 'You're quite a remarkable young woman, Tom. One day I'll sit you down and have you tell me the story of your life. I've learned little enough about you in the time we've been together.'

Thomasina shrugged. 'You wouldn't want to hear it, Malachi . . . and I have no intention of telling. We enjoy a very satisfactory arrangement right now. One that's making a handsome profit for both of us. Let's keep things that way.'

'It suits me, girl. Having you on board has added a bit of sparkle to life. At times it's had me wishing I was a younger man with two good legs.'

'Had you been any different from the way you are now, we wouldn't be sailing together,' retorted Thomasina. Suddenly relaxing and smiling at him, she added, 'But I do enjoy sailing with you. The *Melanie Jane* is a very happy ship.'

It was true and the two got on very well. She had in many ways become the 'son' he had never had. In turn, Malachi reminded Thomasina of the father she had lost.

Malachi had never questioned the story of how she had come by the money with which she had purchased a partnership with him, but he was shrewd enough to realise there was a great deal more to her background than being orphaned. However, he never tried to probe too deeply into her past. She was a cheerful presence on board his ship and the remainder of the crew all liked the young cabin 'boy'.

Suddenly, Thomasina stood up, only just succeeding in grabbing the musket before it slipped to the deck.

'What's that, Malachi?'

She pointed to where a ship was rounding the finger of land to the east of the bay. Carrying a sail that was quite unlike their own, it had been hidden until this moment by the scimitar of palms around the shoreline.

'It's a corsair ship! Get the men out the water – quick, Tom. I'll prime the guns. We're going to need them.'

As Thomasina shouted to the men to clear the water and get back on board, Malachi stomped off as fast as he could to the gun mounted on the bow of the *Melanie Jane*.

2

The bay was not very large. By the time the last
member of the *Melanie Jane*'s crew cleared the water
and was clambering up the rope ladder hanging over
the ship's side, the corsairs' ship was within cannon
range – and they opened fire.

Fortunately, only the bow gun could be brought to
bear and the corsairs' aim was woefully poor. The shot
fell far short of its target and well to one side of the
Melanie Jane. Nevertheless, it added urgency to the
already feverish activity on board.

Even as the last of the crew scrambled back on the
ship, the *Melanie Jane* was under way.

Such was the danger they were in that few of the
crew wasted precious seconds pulling on their clothes.
They carried out their duties in the state in which they
had emerged from the sea. Naked.

Thomasina hardly noticed. The merchantman did

not carry a large crew, and therefore she, the ship's cook and a sick seaman were busily loading the ship's two cannons, which had been manhandled to the starboard side of the ship.

This was the side from which the Barbary vessel would need to try to board, if it could get close enough in time.

The sails of the *Melanie Jane* were raised and set for all possible speed, but the corsairs were now frighteningly close. Their excited shouts sent shockwaves of horror through Thomasina.

They were hurling unmistakeable, though unintelligible threats across the water, confident that the *Melanie Jane* and its crew would soon be theirs.

English ships fetched a good price on the Barbary coast. English sailors were equally prized – and not only for their seamanship, or their endurance when chained to the oars of corsair ships. When castrated, they were much sought-after as guards in the harems of wealthy men.

But on this occasion the corsairs had reckoned without the determination and skill of Malachi.

'Crowd on every bit of canvas we've got,' he bellowed at the men hoisting the sails. 'We've got the wind in our favour. They expected to surprise us at anchor and will need to turn in order to chase us.'

'Will we be able to outsail them?' Thomasina asked anxiously.

'We'll soon find out,' said Malachi grimly. Then, recognising her concern, he added, 'The *Melanie Jane* is Fowey-built for the smuggling trade. There's many a time she's outstripped a Customs cutter.

We'll not be caught by a Barbary ship.'

At first, it seemed that Malachi's faith in his ship would be justified. The Cornish vessel was heading out of the bay before the corsair ship had completed its turn.

Malachi ordered the coxwain to steer out to sea, away from the coast. They would head for the Straits of Gibraltar. There they would be certain of finding a British man-o'-war to deal effectively with the pursuing Barbary-coast vessel – if it was still with them by then.

It was soon apparent that they were not, however, going to lose the other vessel as easily as Malachi had hoped. Indeed, the corsairs were actually gaining on them. For the first time Malachi showed some concern.

'What's happening?' Thomasina asked him. 'I thought we would have left the corsairs behind by now.'

'We should have.' Malachi frowned. 'The trouble is, there's quite a strong current close inshore – and it's running in their favour. The ship that's closest to the shore has an advantage.'

'Then why don't *we* move closer inshore?' Thomasina asked.

'I don't know this coast, but the corsairs do. It's their hunting ground. The best thing we can do is stay out here and try to keep out of range of their guns. They seem to be poor gunners, but that ship is carrying almost as many cannon as a British man-o'-war. If we allow them to come close enough to give us a broadside, not all their shots will miss. But there's one more thing we can try.'

'What's that?' Thomasina asked eagerly.

'We can pray. Pray as we've never done before.'

It had been mid-morning when the chase began and Malachi had hoped to shake off the pursuers within a couple of hours. Instead, four hours later, the Barbary-coast ship was about two miles away, on a parallel course with the *Melanie Jane* – and beginning to pull ahead. The crew of the British ship were watching the other vessel anxiously.

'What do you think they're doing, Malachi? Why don't they attack us?' Thomasina was finding the puzzling tactics of the corsairs unnerving.

'They want to make certain we don't escape again. I'll wager they'll begin edging towards us before too long. When they come within range, they'll open fire. But they can see we're fully laden, so they won't want to risk sinking us. They'll need to come close enough to use chain shot, or something similar, to try to bring down the rigging.'

Malachi was talking half to himself now, thinking things out as he went along. 'Yes, they'll need to come *really* close.'

Appearing to reach a decision, he turned to the man at the ship's wheel. 'Stay on this course, Harry – but let me know if the corsairs do anything new . . . You come with me, Tom.'

Thomasina followed the one-legged captain to the rear hatch and down the ladder to where their cabins were situated. Entering his own cabin, Malachi took a bunch of keys from his belt and inserted one of them into a stout cabinet, bolted to a bulkhead.

When the cupboard door swung open, Thomasina saw half a dozen long-barrelled muskets, together with powder and shot.

Lifting some of the muskets out, Malachi said, 'Help me carry these on deck. If the corsairs try to board us, we'll give them something to think about.'

As they carried the muskets to the upper deck, the coxwain called, 'You're just in time, Malachi, the corsairs are edging in this direction. I think they're about to try for us again.'

'What will you do?' An anxious Thomasina put the question to Malachi.

'We'll let them come as close to us as I dare, then I'll need all hands to help with the sails so we can fall astern of the corsair – but still remain close. They've got tiller steering. If we can shoot the men manning the tiller, they'll turn and lose way. Before they are able to bring her under control again we'll be so far ahead they'll never catch us, not now we're both on equal terms away from the shore.'

'Do you have any men who are expert shots?'

'They'll manage as well as any other seamen, I reckon.'

'We don't have to manage,' Thomasina said excitedly. 'Let me do the shooting.'

'*You?* Have you fired a gun before?' Malachi expressed incredulity.

'My pa taught me to shoot – and shoot well,' Thomasina said. 'Besides, you're going to need every man in the crew to work the sails and make sure we get well away from the corsairs.'

'Firing a gun is one thing,' Malachi said doubtfully.

'Do you think you can shoot a man?'

Thomasina recalled the last time she had fired a gun, but it was not an example she could give to Malachi.

'With what's at stake for all of us, I have no doubts at all. I'll load the muskets and carry them up to the bows now.'

While she loaded the guns, Thomasina heard some of the crewmen talking in low tones to Malachi. They were unhappy about a young man taking on such a responsibility, pointing out that all their lives depended upon its success.

'You heard what Tom said,' was Malachi's reply. 'I'd say he's done more shooting than the rest of us put together.'

'Aye, but it's one thing to shoot at rabbits, or gulls, but quite another when you're looking to kill a man.'

'Right,' Malachi said to the man who seemed to be the most concerned. 'As it *is* of such vital importance, I'll tell you what I'll do. You can go up on the fo'c'sle with Tom and reload for him as he shoots. If he hits no one with the first three shots, you can have the next three. If he downs any of the men on the tiller, you'll load twice as fast so that he can shoot some more. Is that a fair enough compromise?'

The seaman agreed with Malachi that it was, although a few minutes later Thomasina heard him telling one of his fellow-crewmen that it should have been *he* who fired the first shots.

The tactics of the Barbary-coast corsairs were exactly what Malachi had predicted they would be.

Maintaining their course, they gradually edged

their vessel towards the *Melanie Jane*, until the two ships were sailing side-by-side.

When they were so close that the English sailors could see the eager grins of anticipation on the faces of the North African seamen, a cannon was fired at the merchantman.

Again, Malachi had guessed correctly. The shot consisted of two balls linked by a chain. Fortunately for the sailors on the British merchantman, it was woefully off target and dropped in the sea behind the *Melanie Jane*.

But Malachi was taking no chances of future shots being equally ineffective. *'Now!'* he bellowed and the seamen standing by immediately began taking in two of the largest sails.

It seemed to Thomasina that it was hardly more than a minute before Malachi was ordering the men to let the sails out once more – but it proved to be long enough.

The *Melanie Jane* was now tucked in behind the Barbary-coast ship, safe from the corsairs' guns – and it was time for Thomasina to carry out her part of Malachi's plan.

The distance between the two ships was much less than she had thought it would be. Nevertheless, her first shot went wide and there were anxious mutterings from those of the crew able to see what was happening.

Picking up another musket, she took careful aim and fired again. This time one of the corsairs steadying the tiller abandoned his duties and staggered away across the deck, one hand desperately clawing at his back.

When Thomasina fired a third time a corsair dropped to the deck of the other vessel. The fourth shot produced a loud scream, although she could not see where she had hit the man at whom she had aimed. But it was enough for the other corsairs about him. With four men out of action, it was already proving difficult – and dangerous – to hold their vessel on course. The remaining men abandoned their now exposed post.

Out of control and with sails flapping unmanageably, their boat veered off course and the *Melanie Jane* surged past.

Thomasina managed to get off one further shot, aiming for a man she thought might have been the corsairs' captain. She could not tell whether or not she hit him, but it no longer mattered. The pursuit was over. The crew of the other vessel ran around the deck in apparent panic, seeming not to know what they should do to bring their boat back under control.

On the *Melanie Jane* the crew cheered Thomasina until they were hoarse. The loudest of them was the man who had questioned her ability to carry out the task for which she had volunteered.

She valued Malachi's praise most of all. When she helped him to carry the muskets back to his cabin, he said, 'Well done, Tom. Your actions today saved my ship – *our* ship – and you were as cool in action as any seaman I've ever sailed with.'

3

The voyages of the *Melanie Jane* under the co-ownership of Malachi and Thomasina continued to be highly profitable. The sea captain told Thomasina she had brought him luck and gave her advice on banking the money she was making as his partner.

He also convinced her that the purchase of houses in and around Falmouth was a sound investment and she followed his advice. The purchase and subsequent renting particulars were negotiated through an agent – again recommended by Malachi.

In addition, when he ascertained that Thomasina had no one with whom she wished to spend time during the brief periods spent ashore between voyages, he insisted that she should stay with him, in his home.

It was a large house, which he had shared with his sister until her death, a few years before. He gave Thomasina the whole of the top storey, declaring dishonestly that his infirmity prevented him from using it, even had he wanted to.

The top floor of the house contained far too many rooms for Thomasina's needs, but the arrangement suited her very well. She was able to enter the house as a young man and leave it as a young woman, if she wished, although she found she felt increasingly vulnerable when she faced the world as a woman.

She and Malachi had agreed that should any of the *Melanie Jane*'s crew suspect anything, they would say that 'Tom' had a twin sister who bore a remarkable resemblance to 'him'.

As it happened, it was unnecessary to put the lie to the test. Malachi's house was situated high on a steep hill beyond the harbour. None of the crew found their way there.

Besides, Thomasina did not venture out very often and the *Melanie Jane* spent little time in harbour. When it did, Thomasina was quite content to remain at Malachi's house, cooking for him and enjoying his company during the evenings.

He was very much a father figure for her by now. She saw in him many of the fine qualities she remembered – or thought she did – being possessed by her father.

For his part, Malachi told Thomasina that he saw in her the qualities of the son – or daughter – he had never been fortunate enough to have for himself.

Yet, although he never tried to pry, Malachi could not help feeling curious about her past. All he really knew was that her father, like himself, had been master of a vessel, but she had never given him any details.

One evening, when the *Melanie Jane* was laden and

ready to sail on the night tide, Malachi taxed her with this in his own quiet way. They were seated in the kitchen of his house, the remains of one of Thomasina's meals on the table between them.

'I enjoy your company as much as I do your cooking, Tom, but, unlike me, you're still young. Are there no relatives you'd like to visit on your last evening ashore – or a young man, perhaps?'

During the meal Thomasina had shared a quantity of wine with Malachi. It made her relaxed, but caution had become instinctive to her.

'I have an aunt and a cousin in Cornwall, Malachi. I send them money regularly, but I have no wish to see them again. We – my aunt and I, at any rate – were never very close. I'll probably go back and see my cousin one day, but not just yet.'

'What about young men? You're an attractive young woman, Tom.' He smiled. 'At least, when you're not being an important part of *Melanie Jane*'s crew.'

'There was someone – but I lost him. If you don't mind, it's something I'd rather not talk about.'

Thomasina had thought less about Jeffery recently, but when she did it still hurt just as much. She gained a degree of comfort from the certain knowledge that he would have been proud of the use to which she had put the money they had made together.

'You can't mourn for ever, Tom, or you'll end up like me, bemoaning all the things that have passed you by.'

'I doubt I'll do that, Malachi, any more than you do. You're happy in the knowledge that you're one of the most respected captains sailing out of Falmouth. I'm doing what *I've* always wanted to do. Now, isn't it time we shut up the house and went to the ship? We need to make a move if we're to set sail on the tide.' Smiling at him, she added, 'I'm getting just like you, Malachi. I get restless when I've been ashore for too long.'

'Heaven help me, Tom, you're becoming something of a slave driver. I never thought when I took on a partner that I'd be taking on a master as well. *I'm* the one to decide when the *Melanie Jane* is going to sail, and don't you forget it.'

Despite Malachi's grumbling, Thomasina knew it was all good-natured and that she had distracted him from his gentle prying. While he went about the house ensuring it was safely locked and secured, she cleared the table and washed up the dishes they had used.

Thomasina was aware that Malachi was even more restless than herself when he was on dry land. Here, he was an ageing, one-legged man with very few friends. On the *Melanie Jane* he was the ship's captain – a highly respected seafarer, in command of all those who crewed the ship and thoroughly at ease with his chosen environment.

They had already taken their goods to the ship for what should prove to be a very interesting voyage. They had loaded salted pilchards for the West Indies, for sale to the sugar planters as food for their slaves.

From the West Indies there was a variety of cargoes they could take on board. Their destination would depend very much on what they had to sell and they would take it wherever it was wanted.

This was one of the great advantages of being an owner/master. They were free to take on board any cargo they wished and deliver it to wherever it would command the best price.

4

The problems of the Cornish people, brought about by a dire countrywide shortage of wheat, were brought forcibly home to Malachi and Thomasina that very same evening.

They were walking to the ship, Malachi having refused Thomasina's offer to arrange for a carriage to take them there. She had not argued with him. Malachi made a habit of proving he could do anything that could be done by a man with two legs.

The *Melanie Jane*'s captain succeeded in covering the distance between house and dock, but by the time they arrived he was perspiring with the effort of walking a distance that might well have taxed the stamina of a man his age in possession of two good legs.

As a result, he was not in the best of moods when they reached the quayside and found it occupied by a mob of noisy, angry men and boys. Many were

wearing the hard hats favoured by Cornish tin miners
and with them were a number of equally vociferous
women.

'What's going on?' Thomasina put the question to
a young man, one of many bystanders observing the
angry tinners and their followers.

'It's miners from up Camborne and Redruth way,'
the young man replied. 'They say their families are
starving for want of wheat and barley and they've
heard a rumour that one of the ships here is loading
barley for an up-country port where it'll fetch more
money. One of the miners I've just spoken to said
they'll stop the ship sailing, even if it means sending
it to the bottom of the harbour. A magistrate was here
a few minutes ago, reading out the Riot Act, but the
miners booed him down.'

'They're fools,' Malachi declared. 'All they'll succeed in doing is having the army called out against
them and getting themselves arrested. A man brought
before a magistrate for rioting will either be hanged
or transported. That'll not help his family buy food.
But it's none of our problem, Tom, we've got a ship
to get ready. Let me take the lead. There's nothing
like a peg-leg brought down hard on a man's toes to
persuade him to move out of the way.'

Using a combination of stamping and pushing,
Malachi forced a way through the noisy, but largely
well-behaved crowd. Soon, he and Thomasina reached
a line of uniformed and nervous militiamen, keeping
the crowd back from the water's edge.

It seemed that the ship suspected of carrying grain
was moored alongside the quay, immediately astern

of the *Melanie Jane*. The militiamen were reluctant to allow Malachi and Thomasina to pass through their extended line.

'I'm sorry, sir,' said one of the harassed militiamen, 'Captain Hearle's orders are that *no one* should be allowed close to the ships.'

At the mention of his name Thomasina went cold. Then she told herself she was being foolish. The man who had twice been responsible for changing the course of her life was not the only man in Cornwall to possess the surname 'Hearle'.

'You can tell Captain Hearle to go off and play his foolish soldiers' games somewhere else. I've a ship to take to sea. Come along, Tom.'

Brushing aside the protesting militiaman, Malachi stomped towards the *Melanie Jane*, closely followed by a somewhat nervous Thomasina, who expected them to be fired upon at any moment.

The miners who had heard the exchange between the sea captain and the militiamen set up a cheer. It was taken up by others, even though they had no idea *why* they were cheering.

The sound only served to heighten the nervousness of the militiamen. Moments later a uniformed officer came running along the quayside towards Malachi and Thomasina, calling out to them, 'Halt!'

The officer's right arm swung uselessly at his side and, to Thomasina's utter dismay, she saw that the officer *was* the same Sir Charles Hearle who had been responsible for Jeffery's death and for her own ordeal at his hands in Trebene House.

She was wearing a colourful stocking-cap she had

purchased in the Mediterranean some months before. It had a long, tasselled end, which she now swung around to fall in front of her body, covering part of her face.

There was little chance that he could possibly remember her, but she felt her heart rate increase, either from fear, her hatred of the man or a combination of the two.

Sir Charles Hearle reached them, angry and out of breath. Placing himself squarely in front of Malachi, he demanded, 'Were you not told you must not pass through my line of militiamen?'

In command of a company of the Second Roseland Militia, Hearle and his men had been carrying out drill in the area when called upon by the magistrate to contain the miners. It was a situation with which he had never before been faced and he was both nervous and uncertain.

'I was told something of the sort by a damned fool with a musket who should have had something better to do,' Malachi growled.

'He was acting upon my orders,' Sir Charles said. 'You had no right to disobey him.'

He hardly glanced at Thomasina, who was trying to keep Malachi between them.

'I had every right,' Malachi declared. 'I'm the owner and captain of the *Melanie Jane*. We're putting to sea on tonight's tide. You're supposed to be here to ensure law-abiding folk can go about their business, not stopping them from doing so.'

Falmouth was a wealthy port. Ship-owners here were often influential men. Sir Charles Hearle had a number of minor business interests in the town and was not a man knowingly to upset anyone with influence.

'That's very true, Captain. Once I had ascertained your business, you would have been allowed to board your ship. Unfortunately, I have few men I can trust to use their discretion, so I need to give them hard-and-fast orders. Please accept my apologies for inconveniencing you.' He shrugged. 'As you can see, I have an ugly mob to control.'

'It's a pity someone can't control the prices charged by farmers and land-owners for their corn,' retorted Malachi. 'If they did, there would be none of this trouble.'

As they talked they had begun walking towards the *Melanie Jane*, passing a number of lanterns hung upon poles at the water's edge. As though noticing Sir Charles Hearle's useless arm for the first time, Malachi said, 'I can see that, like me, you perform your duties with a disability. Is it a war wound?'

'One serves one's country as best one can,' Sir Charles Hearle replied, ambiguously, '. . . and yours?'

Malachi nodded, saying nothing.

'Then I salute you, sir, and wish you a safe voyage. Now I must return to my duties.'

When Sir Charles Hearle hurried away, Thomasina needed to fight an irrational urge to tell Malachi about the militiaman's 'war-wounded' arm. She restricted herself to saying, 'Pompous little man. I can't see him as a wounded hero.'

To her surprise, Malachi chuckled. 'You're a good judge of character, Tom. I've come across Sir Charles

Hearle on more than once occasion, although I very much doubt if he remembers me. He's a young ne'er-do-well. Since he inherited a title and nothing else, he's devoted his life to spending the money of those rich relatives who'll have anything to do with him. The closest he's come to action is shooting a highwaymen from the cover of darkness. He wasn't even bright enough to realise there were *two* highwaymen. The second one shattered his arm.'

Her heart beating faster as memories of that tragic night came back to her, Thomasina said, 'Why did you ask him if it was a battle wound if you already knew it wasn't?'

'I was being sarcastic, only Sir Charles is too stupid to realise it. You'll have noticed he wasn't anxious to give me the true story.'

'You're a crafty and devious old man, Malachi,' Thomasina smiled at him affectionately, but the un-expected meeting with Sir Charles Hearle had disturbed her greatly.

5

A single lantern hanging from a pole illuminated the gangway that linked the *Melanie Jane* with the quayside. By its light Thomasina could see a number of the ship's crew on deck, watching what was going on ashore.

From somewhere in the darkness farther along the dockside, she heard the sound of iron-shod hooves clattering on cobblestones. There was an immediate upsurge of noise from the miners, who began shouting angrily.

Suddenly there was the sound of a shot. It was immediately followed by two more.

Until this moment the mob had been contained opposite the ship astern of the *Melanie Jane*. Now the crowd began to move, spreading out in all directions.

Only the faint-hearted were fleeing. Others, roused

to anger, began prising up cobblestones to use as
missiles. Their target was a troop of mounted regular soldiers, summoned from the nearby fortress of
Pendennis.

It was these soldiers who had fired the shots. By so
doing they stirred the noisy, but previously peaceful,
demonstrators into action.

'Quick! Get on board while I douse this lamp.' The
order came from Malachi.

Thomasina obeyed him without question. Moments
later, after extinguishing the lamp on the shore end of
the gangway, he joined her and the remainder of the
crew on the deck of the *Melanie Jane*.

Spasmodic firing from the shore continued, accompanied now by shrieks of pain, clearly discernible
above the shouting of those in the crowd.

Men, and women too, were running past the ship,
fleeing from soldiers who now seemed to be firing upon
them indiscriminately.

During a brief lull in the firing those on board the
Melanie Jane could just make out two figures pursuing
an erratic course along the dockside, heading in their
direction. The larger of them seemed to be leaning
heavily upon the smaller and every so often they both
appeared to stumble.

When they reached the foot of the gangway, the
groans of one of the two became increasingly audible,
while a young voice could be heard imploring his
companion, 'Hold on for just a while longer, Pa.'

'Who's that out there?' Malachi called out the question when the taller of the two stumbled and fell to the
ground.

The young voice came back in reply, 'It's my pa. He's been shot by the militiamen.'

There was despair in the voice and Thomasina said immediately, 'I'm going ashore. Some of you come and help me get them on board.'

'We can't afford to get involved, Tom. The *Melanie Jane*'s sailing in little more than an hour's time. Leave well alone and let things sort themselves out.'

The words of advice came from Malachi, but they were already being ignored. Thomasina was on the gangway. Calling back, she declared, 'I'm not going to leave a boy and his father to the mercy of Sir Charles Hearle and his militiamen, Malachi. But I'll need help to get them on board.'

The crewmen were less reluctant than Malachi to take a part in what was happening. After a brief glance in the direction of their captain, some of them ran down the gangway to assist Thomasina.

Hurriedly they helped the wounded man and his thoroughly frightened young son on board. Abandoning his stance of non-involvement, Malachi said, 'Get them below to my cabin – quickly. There are soldiers coming along the quayside.'

The seamen hurried the man and boy below, leaving Thomasina uncertain whether to follow them or remain on deck.

She decided upon the latter course for the moment and was at the head of the gangway when the militiamen arrived alongside the ship. One was carrying a lantern.

Thomasina recognised the man who had unsuccessfully attempted to keep them from the ship. Then

Sir Charles Hearle pushed his way to the front of his men. Calling up to those on the ship, he said, 'We're searching for rioters. Some of them were seen heading this way.'

'A lot of people have been running past,' Malachi replied. 'I've no way of knowing whether they were miners or militiamen.'

'Some might have slipped on board without you noticing?' suggested Sir Charles. 'Do you mind if we come on board and carry out a search?'

'Yes, we do mind!' Thomasina stated angrily, before Malachi could reply. Stepping on to the darkened gangway, she glared down at the militia officer.

'I was talking to the captain, not to his cabin boy.'

Sir Charles started up the gangway, but now Malachi pushed past Thomasina to confront him.

'It doesn't matter who you're talking to, the answer is the same. I'm not having clumsy, heavy-booted militiamen tramping over my ship when I'm getting ready to put to sea. Our lives depend upon everything being exactly the way it should be when we leave harbour. I've already told you, there's no one on board this ship who shouldn't be. There have been at least two men guarding the gangway since this trouble began. We intend removing the gangway now, so I'll be obliged if you and your men will stand clear.'

The light from the lantern held aloft by the militiaman just touched upon Thomasina and it was to her that Sir Charles now spoke.

'Your face seems familiar, lad. Don't I know you from somewhere?'

'You're likely to get to know me well if you step on

board this ship. You'll be sailing with us – and we're bound for the West Indies.'

'That's right, Captain,' confirmed Malachi. 'Either you go on your way, or you sail with us. I don't mind. I could do with another hand or two – but you'll do a full day's work, the same as everyone else. What's it to be?'

There were sounds of amusement from the seamen standing on the deck of the ship. Mustering as much dignity as was possible, Sir Charles Hearle said haughtily, 'I'll not waste your time, or mine, by arguing with you, Captain, but the attitude of you and your crew is less than helpful to a man who is only carrying out his duty.' Turning away, he said, 'Come along, men. Spread out and search as you go along the dockside.'

When the militiamen had resumed their search along the quayside, Thomasina breathed a sigh of relief. Despite her disguise, had Sir Charles come on board and taken a good look at her, he might have recognised her as his aunt's one-time maidservant.

She expected Malachi to say something about her confrontation with the militiaman. Instead, he said, 'You'd better go down and see what's happening to the boy and his father. We'll need to get them off the ship before we sail. Hopefully, Hearle and the army will go about their business once they've searched the dockside. Off you go. I'll stay up here and make certain we're ready for the tide.'

Below, in Malachi's cabin, Thomasina found the boy in tears. He crouched beside his father, who was lying on Malachi's bunk, his pale face screwed up in pain.

One of the crew members who had helped him to

the cabin was still with him and it was to him that
Thomasina spoke.

'How is he?'

Looking up at her, the seaman said, 'He's lost a fair
amount of blood and is in quite a bit of pain, but
he'll live. A musket ball hit him in the fleshy part of
his thigh. Fortunately, it seems to have passed right
through without breaking any bones along the way.
The worst thing was the bleeding, but I think I've
stopped most of that – for a while, at least.'

When Thomasina expressed surprise at the crewman's
apparent knowledge of medicine, the sailor replied,
'Many years ago I served with the King's navy and
served as a "loblolly boy" – a surgeon's assistant –
during the war in America. I learned enough to know
whether or not a man was going to live or die. This
one will live, but he'll need someone to help him get
around for a day or two.'

The relief of the young boy was so transparent that
Thomasina had to resist an unmasculine urge to hug
him. Instead, she asked, 'Is there anyone in Falmouth
who can help you with your pa? We're sailing within
the hour. He'll need to be off the ship by then.'

The boy's relieved expression was obvious. 'One of
my uncles lives here, in Falmouth . . . But what about
the militia? If they take Pa, he'll go to prison.'

Thomasina knew that what the boy said was true. If
he was arrested and found to have a wound caused by
a musket ball, it would be sufficient proof that he had
been in the forefront of the rioters. The boy's father
would face the same fate as Jeffery.

She kept such thoughts to herself. 'The militia have

probably left the docks by now. Go and find this uncle. Tell him to get help and come here quickly to fetch your pa. Hurry now. We'll look after him.'

The boy was gone for almost a full hour, during which time Malachi became increasingly concerned that they would be forced to sail with the wounded man still on board.

Much to everyone's relief, the boy returned with two men, his uncle and a friend. Wasting no time in unnecessary introductions and brushing aside the thanks of the boy's uncle, Malachi hustled the injured man and his helpers ashore. Then he gave orders for the *Melanie Jane* to cast off and put to sea.

In the early hours of the following morning, with all sails set and the comforting beam of the Lizard Point lighthouse falling away on the starboard quarter, Malachi sent all non-essential crewmen below.

Taking the wheel himself, he ordered his coxwain to go to the galley and make hot drinks for Thomasina and himself. He delighted in taking the wheel whenever it was possible, especially during the night hours.

At such times as this Thomasina enjoyed being on deck with him, especially when they had just left port. This was when Malachi was most content with his chosen life – but tonight he had other matters on his mind.

In the darkness he spoke softly to Thomasina. 'Back there in Falmouth . . . Sir Charles Hearle thought he'd seen you somewhere before. Had he?'

'It's possible,' Thomasina gave him a guarded reply. 'I've been to a lot of places and met many people.'

'Is it likely to cause any problems to you if he *does* remember?'

Thomasina looked at her companion sharply, but it was impossible to see Malachi's expression in the darkness. 'Why should it?'

'No reason I can think of offhand, Tom – but I like to think we've become more than just business partners. If there *is* any way Hearle could cause trouble for you, I'd like to know. I'm on your side, Tom, come what may, but I have a very strong feeling that your distaste for the man goes far beyond anything that happened last night. I dislike him too. I'm not a man for prying, so please don't think that's what I'm doing now, but if there's anything I can do to help, whatever it might be, I'm always here.'

'Thanks, Malachi, I appreciate your support, but there's really nothing to worry about.'

Thomasina was moved by Malachi's words. However, she had no intention of putting his loyalty to the test by telling him the true story of her life.

Nevertheless, she had an uneasy feeling that Captain Malachi Ellis was not convinced she had told him all he should know about his partner. Thomasina hoped he would never learn the truth.

6

Lush green slopes of long-extinct volcanic mountains hove into view above the horizon long before the crew of the *Melanie Jane* sighted the frond-topped canopies of palm trees that fringed the sun-bleached beaches of Jamaica.

'Have you thought any more of the cargo we'll be taking back to England with us?' Thomasina put the question to Malachi as they stood on the deck together, watching the island ahead of them show up in more detail as they drew closer.

'No, but I'm not particularly concerned. We'll have plenty to choose from.'

'I don't doubt it, but I have a suggestion. I'd like to know what you think about it . . .'

Thomasina hesitated. Since leaving Falmouth she and Malachi had not discussed the events of their last evening there. She was not sure she was wise to risk broaching the subject again now.

'If you don't tell me what's in your head, I can't say whether or not I think it's a good idea.'

Malachi's words broke into Thomasina's thoughtful silence and she made up her mind.

'I was thinking about the miners and their families, starving because they can't afford the price asked for corn. What if we took on a cargo of, say, sugar or rum, in Jamaica, but instead of carrying it back to England, took it to America, sold it there and loaded corn, or flour, for Falmouth?'

Malachi looked at Thomasina in silence for a while. When he eventually spoke he said, 'Would you be looking to sell it again at corn merchants' prices – or at the price the miners were demanding?'

Back in Cornwall there had been much discussion about the fact that, at the height of their unrest, the miners had forced a number of farmers to sign an undertaking to sell wheat and barley at pre-shortage prices.

'Would it mean taking a loss if we sold it direct to the miners?'

'We'd make a small profit, but it would be a mere fraction of what such a cargo would fetch if we landed it up-country.'

'Does that mean you don't agree with the idea?'

Their partnership agreement was that Malachi should have overriding control of all matters appertaining to the type and destination of the cargoes carried by the *Melanie Jane.*

'Not necessarily. In fact this is one decision I'll let you make, Tom. I'm an old man. I already have more than enough money to keep me comfortable for the remainder of my life. You're the one with a future to consider.'

'So you'll do it? You'll take American corn back to Falmouth?' Thomasina could not hide her delight.

Malachi smiled. 'The idea has crossed my own mind, once or twice, but I felt it would be unfair to put it to you. I'm glad you thought of it for yourself. I'm proud of you, Tom.' To hide such unaccustomed feelings, Malachi suddenly became brusque. 'Now, let's prepare the ship for entering harbour.'

Kingston's deep-water harbour was the scene of much activity. In addition to merchantmen and local Caribbean vessels, there was a fleet of British men-o'-war anchored in the harbour.

More excited than Thomasina had ever seen him, Malachi pointed out that the flag flying from one of the impressive seventy-four-gun warships was that of Admiral Lord Cochrane, adding, 'He's one of the few naval officers to have earned more prize money than me!'

In among the tall-masted seagoing vessels, small boats of every description plied between ship-and-ship and ship-and-shore, in a seemingly haphazard fashion on the teeming waters.

The overcrowded harbour presented far too many hazards for a ship to berth without help. The *Melanie Jane* was taken in tow by a multi-oared boat manned by slaves, their black skin glistening with perspiration as they obeyed the orders of the English harbour official in charge of the boat.

The berth allotted to the *Melanie Jane* obliged the merchantman to pass by all the men-o'-war. Thomasina was impressed by the general air of neatness and cleanliness of each ship.

The *Melanie Jane* had two men on the wheel following the course of the towing boat. By the time they reached their allotted berth both men were perspiring as freely as the slaves.

The heat was quite oppressive here and Thomasina was feeling it too, but as the crewmen were throwing mooring ropes ashore to the waiting men, it was not the heat that bothered her.

Sniffing the air, she puckered her nose in an expression of disgust. 'Ugh! What's that horrible stench, Malachi?'

'If you haven't come across it before you can consider yourself lucky.' Taking the pipe he was smoking from his mouth and using it as a pointer, Malachi said, 'There's your answer. It's a slaver, direct from Africa. I swear the smell from some of 'em is so bad you know you're getting close to one at sea even before they come over the horizon. The trade was officially banned a couple of years back, but no one's tried to enforce the law here yet.'

The ship Malachi had pointed out was moored at a jetty protruding at right angles towards their berth from the other side of the dock.

It was not berthed tight against the wall of the dock, as was the *Melanie Jane*, but was being held off by a number of timbers, leaving an expanse of water between ship and shore. A number of men stood on the shore side, many armed with long-handled brushes.

There was a great deal of activity about the boat and, as Thomasina watched, she was horrified to see a number of naked African men, all linked together by heavy chains, pushed into the water from the ship.

As the unfortunate slaves struggled to reach the shore, they were pushed back into the water by those on land, who then used the brushes on them with considerable vigour.

Suddenly, Thomasina realised that not all the slaves were men. A number were in fact young women – and one was desperately clutching a baby to her, despite the fact that by doing so she ran a very real risk of drowning!

'What are they doing?' Thomasina asked in alarm.

'They're bathing the slaves. No one will be over-keen to buy them until the stench of the slave ship's been scrubbed away.'

'But . . . some will drown!'

Malachi shook his head. 'They're worth too much money for the master of the slaver to allow that to happen. They'll be well scrubbed, then pulled ashore . . . see.'

He pointed to where a group of shackled slaves huddled on the jetty, their numbers growing as newly clean slaves were hauled roughly from the waters of the harbour.

'It's barbaric!' Thomasina found it difficult to express the disgust she felt at what was happening on the other side of the dock.

She also experienced a growing sense of disbelief at the astonishing number of slaves being unloaded from a ship that was no larger than the *Melanie Jane*.

'There would have been many more when they left Africa.' Malachi's matter-of-fact tone of voice did not quite hide his own feelings. 'A quarter will have died on the voyage here and been heaved over the side. You can always tell a slaver when you're at sea, even if you're upwind of her. She'll have sharks around her like hounds around a fox.'

Thomasina shuddered as she watched yet another batch of newly scrubbed slaves being dragged ashore to join their terrified and confused countrymen.

'What will happen to them now?'

'They'll be taken to the market and auctioned off. You can go along and see it for yourself, if you like.'

Thomasina shook her head vigorously. 'I can't think of anything I'd like less. People shouldn't be bought and sold like sheep, or pigs, or cattle.'

Even as she spoke the words, Thomasina was thinking back to the days when she worked at Trebene. Although the terms of their employment stopped short of slavery, there had been a feeling among the servants in the great house that they were *owned* by the Vincent family.

She dreaded to think what her fate might have been had she actually been owned by the Vincents. She would certainly never have dared to fight back against Sir Charles Hearle.

'I don't want to see the auction, Malachi, but I would like to go ashore to stretch my legs. It feels as though we've been at sea for months. I'll come with you when you go off to find a buyer for our cargo.'

7

As well as being a seaport, Kingston was also the capital of Jamaica, yet Thomasina found its buildings less than impressive.

'There's two reasons for that,' Malachi explained as he and Thomasina walked together through the town. 'A serious earthquake only a few years ago destroyed most of the older buildings. When they set about rebuilding it, the money wasn't forthcoming from the planters. They prefer to spend their earnings on their own homes and estates. Some of those are truly magnificent.'

Their destination was the office of a merchant with whom Malachi had traded for many years. Having spent so long on board the *Melanie Jane*, Thomasina's legs were aching by the time they arrived.

Malachi introduced her to the merchant as his young nephew. After shaking hands, she was grateful to sit down in a chair while the two men got down to some hard bargaining. Whilst this was going on a bottle of rum was placed upon the table between them, the level of its contents dropping steadily as they talked.

When they began haggling over a matter of mere pence per hogshead of fish, Thomasina lost interest. Rising from her chair, she walked to the window of the office, which overlooked a square where a crowd was gathering.

Then, from the direction of the docks, a large number of the slaves she had seen earlier were led to the centre of the square. Men, women and children, they were indiscriminately linked together by chains. Now Thomasina remembered what Malachi had said to her earlier. This was where the slaves were to be auctioned.

She turned away from the window so abruptly that both men looked up at her in surprise.

'What's the matter, Tom?' Malachi put the question to her.

'It's the slaves we saw at the docks. They're bringing them into the square to be sold.'

'Are they, by God?' exclaimed the merchant, rising to his feet abruptly. 'Either they're early, or you've kept me here for longer than I intended. Get your ship unloaded, Malachi. We'll talk more of this tomorrow. I need to be out there when they start bidding if I'm to buy prime stock.'

It took a moment for his meaning to sink in. Then Thomasina asked, 'You mean . . . you're going out there to buy slaves? To buy men and women?'

'And a few children, if I can get them for the right

price,' the merchant replied cheerfully. 'They sell particularly well because they're quick to train and have a good working life ahead of them. But I buy adults, too. A good buck will make a fine profit once he's got over the voyage and put a bit of meat on his bones.'

Winking at Malachi, he added, 'You ought to make a trip or two from Africa carrying slaves, Malachi, while it's still possible. Bring a few young African girls back with you. This young man will have learned all he needs to know about life by the time you reach Jamaica.'

The merchant hurried from the office chuckling, mistaking the red anger shining in Thomasina's cheeks for embarrassment.

Turning to Malachi, Thomasina asked fiercely, 'Do we need to do business with *him*?'

Malachi nodded, 'You won't find anyone more honest in the whole of Jamaica – and no one here will look at things any differently. Come on, Tom, let's get back to the *Melanie Jane*. I need to work on the figures I've been given.'

Thomasina walked silently beside Malachi as they crossed the square, skirting the huge and excited crowd gathered around the newly arrived slaves.

Looking across to where the raised platform was sited in the centre of the square, she saw two young African women standing there shackled together. Naked from the waist up, each was dressed in a 'garment' consisting of a strip of sacking. Tied about the waist, it extended to just below the knee. Both girls stood silently looking down at the boards beneath their feet.

As she watched, the auctioneer placed his hand beneath the chin of one of the girls and lifted her head, in order that prospective buyers might see her face more clearly.

It could have hardly been more degrading for the girl. Thomasina managed to keep a tight hold on her feelings, but she did not fool Malachi.

'It won't be too long before slavery is abolished altogether,' he said. 'At least, as far as England is concerned. I doubt if it will ever end here – or in the Americas.'

'The whole thing is an absolute disgrace,' fumed Thomasina, with a depth of feeling she would have found difficult to explain. 'First they scrubbed them raw with brooms and now they're selling them off like pigs in a market.'

'They're worth considerably more than animals,' said Malachi. 'For that reason alone a good owner will look after his slaves. Unfortunately, all owners aren't reasonable men – and some have too much money to concern themselves with the welfare of their slaves. Try not to think about it too much, Tom. You can't change the ways of the world, much as you might like to. Let's get back to the ship and see about having the cargo unloaded. Then we'll give the crew some of their pay and let them have a night ashore. It's been a good trip, but a long one. They deserve a break.' He shook his head and grimaced. 'Not that any of their wives or sweethearts would agree. Kingston offers more temptations to a sailor than any other town on this earth.'

8

Thomasina felt a great sense of relief when the *Melanie Jane* had been towed clear of Kingston harbour and she could turn her back on the dockland area and the slave ship. It had given her a glimpse of suffering and degradation which would remain with her for a very long time.

When the ship turned into the open sea and the sails bellied out, filled by a following wind, she felt she had returned to a cleaner, more wholesome world.

'Still thinking of the slaves you saw back there, Tom?'

Malachi had been watching her before he put the question.

Thomasina nodded. 'I doubt if I'll ever be able to forget them.'

'You'll need to hold your feelings in check for a while longer,' Malachi said. 'There are more slaves in

the port where we'll be taking on wheat. Upset anyone
there and we'll find the price of wheat will rise very
suddenly.'

'Can't we buy it somewhere else?'

Malachi shook his head. 'Norfolk is the place suggested by the merchant we've been dealing with here.
He's given me a letter of introduction and the cargo
we're taking there is his idea. He says coffee always
fetches good money. We're in business, Tom. Whatever our thoughts, we mustn't lose sight of that.'

'I'll do my best to keep my feelings to myself,
Malachi – but I'm not promising anything.'

'You start talking like that and I'll begin to wish we
were heading straight back to Falmouth with a cargo
from Jamaica,' Malachi admonished her. 'After what
we saw back there, half the crew would gladly take up
a crusade against slavery if I gave them time to think
about it.'

Before Thomasina could reply, Malachi continued,
'Don't think I'm disagreeing with you, Tom. It's high
time slavery came to an end, but we're already heading off on one crusade, right now. Buying wheat
for hungry Cornish men, women and children. As
I've said, upset the Americans in Norfolk – *really*
upset them – and we'll be forced to leave with an
empty ship.'

Waiting a few minutes for his words to sink in, he
said thoughtfully, 'I remember a tapestry I used to see
on the wall of a preacher's house, back home. It was a
prayer of some sort. It read, "God grant me the serenity
to accept the things I cannot change, courage to change
the things that should be changed, and the wisdom to

know the difference." They're the words of a wise man, Tom. Think about them. They've saved me a whole lot of grief during my lifetime. They might do the same for you.'

Thomasina could not entirely agree with Malachi's advice, but she knew he was right. There was nothing she could do about what she had seen.

Malachi had never before sailed into Norfolk's deep-water harbour and he took on board a pilot to guide him to a suitable berth. The pilot, a man born and raised in Virginia, was able to tell Malachi that wheat was readily available in the port, brought downriver from established wheat fields away from the coast.

He also confirmed that coffee was a commodity in great demand. He proved it by making an offer to a surprised Malachi to purchase half the *Melanie Jane*'s cargo on his own behalf.

There was a far more relaxed atmosphere in the harbour here than there had been in Kingston. The houses too, those that could be seen from the water, had an air of tranquillity and solidity that had been lacking in Jamaica.

One thing that was distressingly similar for Thomasina was the employment on the dockside of a great many slaves. There was little to distinguish those who came on board to unload the *Melanie Jane* from the slaves she had observed at Kingston.

They were working under the supervision of an American overseer who walked among them wielding a heavy riding crop. He was not slow to use it on any slave who, in his opinion, was not working hard enough.

One slave in particular appeared to be the target of the overseer's whip. Yet, as far as Thomasina could judge, he was as hard-working as any of his companions.

Malachi was about to go ashore to negotiate the purchase of a cargo of wheat and flour when he saw Thomasina watching the slaves.

Placing a cautionary hand on her shoulder, he said, 'Remember our little chat, Tom. Go below – or look over the other side of the ship and see what's going on in the harbour. Better still, come ashore with me.'

Thomasina shook her head. The *Melanie Jane* had encountered a couple of days' bad weather on the voyage from Jamaica. During this time one of the yards had cracked, requiring temporary repairs to be carried out. It had been an exhausting and dangerous task. Malachi hoped to be able to renew the yard here, in Norfolk. Before that, when the day's work was over, the men would want to go ashore and find relaxation in one of the many waterfront taverns.

It was what the sailors usually did when they reached harbour, but Thomasina rarely joined them. She preferred to remain on board, enjoying the peace of a near-deserted ship.

An opportunity to be alone was one of the few things she missed on board the *Melanie Jane*. This apart, she thoroughly enjoyed life at sea.

Malachi had left the ship only a matter of minutes when Thomasina heard shouting on the dockside. She ran to the side of the ship and immediately saw the cause of the commotion.

At the foot of the gangway a split sack of coffee beans lay on the ground. Crouching beside it was the slave who had earlier been singled out for the overseer's attention – and he was receiving it once more.

The overseer was raining blows on the slave's bare back with the riding crop and appeared almost beside himself with rage.

'Stop that! What do you think you're doing?' Malachi's cautionary warning forgotten, Thomasina hurried down the gangway to where the slave was being beaten.

'Keep out of this, son. It's none of your business.'

Whilst talking to Thomasina, the overseer ceased his assault on the defenceless man long enough to enable the slave to scramble out of reach of the riding crop.

'It's my business when you're causing him to bleed all over the cargo we've just brought in – unless you're ready to pay for it out of your own pocket?'

The slave had sustained a bad gash upon his right upper arm. He had probably struck it on the iron corner-piece of the gangway when he slipped and fell with a heavy sack of coffee on his bent back.

The overseer was taken aback by the suggestion that he should pay restitution for the split sack and its contents. Thomasina took advantage of his uncertainty.

'I'll take him on board and bind something around that cut to stop him bleeding over everything in sight, then you can have him back.'

Giving the overseer no time to argue, she took the slave by the shoulder. As he rose to his feet she propelled him up the gangway.

'Make sure you don't let him out of sight for as much as a second,' the overseer called after her. 'If he runs off, *I'll* be the one looking for cash from *you* – and slaves don't come cheap.'

Ignoring the man, Thomasina led the slave to the stern of the ship and sat him down beside the ship's wheel. The *Melanie Jane* was riding on a high tide and the overseer could not see them from his place on the quayside.

Some of the crew who remained on board had seen the incident between the slave and the overseer. They stood around now, murmuring sympathetically.

'It was him and his whip who caused what happened,' explained one of the crewmen, jerking his head shorewards. 'He made this one slip and fall. Had it been his head, and not his arm that struck the gangway, he'd have had a dead slave on his hands.'

'Better he kill me,' said the slave bitterly. 'They don't hand out no beatings in heaven.'

'That's quite enough of such talk,' said Thomasina sharply. Looking up at the watching crewmen, she continued, 'One of you go down to Malachi's cabin and fetch the medicine box. Another go to the galley and find a drink and something to eat – but be quick about it. If we take too long, we'll have the overseer up here ordering him back to work.'

Thomasina was the youngest member of the crew, but in addition to her special relationship with Malachi, she had gained the respect of the other crew members by her presence of mind in an emergency. They hurried to do her bidding without question.

Inspecting the slave's wound, Thomasina asked, 'What's your name?'

'Shadrack.'

He seemed disinclined to talk. Thomasina thought he was probably uncertain why she and the other members of the crew should want to help him.

'My name's Tom. We'll only have a few minutes, but in that time I'll bandage your arm and you'll have something to eat and drink.'

Giving her a puzzled, searching look, Shadrack asked, 'Why?'

'What sort of a question is that? Because you've hurt yourself and need help, that's why. We all need help at some time or another.'

The crew member returned carrying the medicine box. Shortly afterwards a tankard of beer and some bread and cheese arrived.

Shadrack ate and drank hurriedly, using one hand, while Thomasina cleaned and bandaged his arm. As she did so, she asked, 'Why does the overseer pick on you in particular, Shadrack? You seemed to be working just as hard as any of the others – probably harder, knowing he's watching you all the time.'

When he made no reply, she looked up and was startled to see that tears had filled his eyes.

'What's the matter?'

At that moment one of the crewmen called urgently, 'The overseer's coming up the gangway . . .'

In a matter of seconds the food and drink had been whisked away and Thomasina concentrated on securing the bandage she had wound around Shadrack's arm.

'You're taking your time!' The overseer glared at Thomasina.

'Perhaps things appear by themselves in America,' retorted Thomasina. 'They don't on board the *Melanie Jane* – they have to be fetched. I've done it as quickly as I could.'

'Well, you've finished now,' said the overseer ungraciously. 'He can get back to work, and quick.' Shaking his riding crop at Shadrack, who had climbed to his feet, he went on, 'I expect to see you working twice as hard as everyone else to make up for the time you've lost. Now, get back to it, if you don't want to feel this across your lazy back again.'

As the overseer went off, driving Shadrack ahead of him, the slave cast a swift glance over his shoulder towards Thomasina, but she was unable to read his expression.

'That bully boy will make full use of his riding crop, no matter how hard the poor soul works,' said one of the crew sympathetically. 'There's not a single one of the slaves who hasn't got the scars of a whipping on his back.'

'True,' agreed Thomasina, 'but he seems to have it in for Shadrack in particular, for some reason. I wish I knew what it is all about.'

9

The *Melanie Jane* remained in Norfolk, Virginia, for nine days. It was longer than Malachi had anticipated. The cargo had been unloaded and the hold packed with a mixed cargo of corn and flour, but Malachi was unable to find a yard to satisfactorily replace the broken one.

Eventually, he settled for what he complained was a second-rate one, but was far from satisfied with his purchase.

'It will hold as long as the weather does,' he grumbled to Thomasina, 'but I wouldn't trust it in a storm like the one we ran into on the way here.'

'What's wrong with it?' Thomasina asked. 'They make ships here, don't they? They should know what they're doing.'

'Oh, they know all right,' Malachi moaned. 'But they think I don't. The wood they used to make this yard was too green. It needs a whole lot more seasoning. Unfortunately, right now Englishmen aren't too popular among American shipping men. It seems our navy's been stopping their ships – from this port in particular – and impressing a great many of their seamen, claiming they're British, whether they are or not. Talk is that, if it doesn't stop, we'll not only be fighting the French, but at war with America again, too – and soon. I'm not sorry to be leaving.'

'Do the Americans have a navy?' Thomasina asked, in some surprise.

'Not a very large one,' Malachi explained, 'but they're building ships – good ships – in a hurry. I'm convinced that's where all the decent wood is going.'

'I won't be sorry to leave here, either,' Thomasina said, 'war or no war. The sight of *them* upsets me.'

She pointed to where a line of slaves was being escorted from the dockside. Almost dusk now, it was the end of their long working day.

Thomasina was unable to see whether Shadrack was one of their number, but he had been working on the dockside during the time that the *Melanie Jane* had been in harbour. On the first occasion she recognised him she had waved. She believed he had seen her, but he did not acknowledge her greeting.

Unfortunately, the overseer had also seen her gesture. It brought Shadrack immediate unwelcome attention from the omnipresent riding crop.

Malachi planned to sail shortly before midnight, striking out immediately across the vast breadth of the

Atlantic Ocean, bound for Falmouth – and home.

Less than an hour before their departure time, Thomasina and the crew working on deck heard the sound of iron-shod hooves on the stone-paved dockside. A party of about twenty horsemen cantered into view. Upon reaching the ship, they brought their mounts to a halt at the foot of the gangway which provided the link between ship and shore.

The lanterns on the quayside cast their yellow light upon the grim faces of the horsemen – and upon the guns carried by them.

As they milled around the foot of the gangway, Malachi called out, 'What's going on? Are you wanting something?'

'Yes, sir, we're after a runaway slave.'

'What makes you think he might be down this way?'

'There's nowhere else for him to go. Runaways get short shrift inland, so most try to get on a ship. Besides, this slave's been working here. He knows the docks.'

'There's nowhere for him to hide on my ship,' Malachi said. 'And all my hands have been on deck getting ready for sea. No one could have slipped on board unnoticed.'

'Thank you, Captain. We'll find him down here somewhere, I'm sure of that. The murdering son-of-a-bitch will dance at the end of a rope before the night's out.'

'He's murdered someone?'

'Didn't I say? He stabbed Mick Kellerman to death. You might have known Mick, he was in charge of a labour-gang here, on the dock, and he knew how to treat 'em. They wouldn't dare try anything when he was around.'

Thomasina had listened with growing apprehension to the conversation between Malachi and the horsemen. She had never heard mention of the name of the overseer who had supervised the unloading of the *Melanie Jane*, but it would not have surprised her to hear that *he* had been killed by one of the slaves – and there was probably no one with greater justification for turning on the bully than Shadrack.

'You thinking the same as me, Tom?' Malachi came to stand beside her as the armed men rode along the dockside to the next ship.

'I expect so, but we're probably both wrong. There must be a lot of overseers working on the docks. Even more slaves. We don't even know the name of the overseer we had on board the *Melanie Jane*.'

'I do,' said Malachi quietly. 'He introduced himself to me when he first came on board. It was Kellerman. Mick Kellerman. I think the sooner we leave Norfolk and its problems, the better.'

The *Melanie Jane* slipped quietly out of the American harbour half an hour later, but Malachi's hopes that they were leaving the problems of Norfolk behind would receive a severe blow.

When Thomasina woke and went on deck the following morning for some fresh air, she found three of the crew there, talking together in low voices.

When they saw her they reacted in a manner that made Thomasina immediately curious, especially when she realised that none had duties on deck at this time of the day.

'What's the matter with you, can't you sleep? Or are you excited because we're heading for home?'

The three men did not smile or come back with a jocular response, as she had expected. They put her in mind of three young boys who shared a guilty secret.

Frowning, Thomasina asked, 'What's the matter? Is something wrong?'

The men exchanged glances, as though each was hoping one of the others would be the first to speak.

Impatiently, Thomasina said, 'Is no one going to say anything? You, Ned. What's troubling you?'

Ned shuffled his feet nervously before saying, 'There's something Captain Malachi should know about, Tom, but it would be better coming from you than from us.'

'What you mean is that it's something you're too scared to tell him about, so you want me to do your dirty work for you. All right, tell me about it.'

'It's that slave, Tom. The one the Americans were after last night. He's here.'

'On board the *Melanie Jane*? When did you find him? Where is he now?'

The men appeared even more ill-at-ease. 'We didn't find him, Tom. He came on board last night, about an hour before the men came looking for him. We took him down to the mess-room. He's there now.'

Thomasina was aghast. 'Do you know what would have happened, had they found him on board? There'd have been hell to pay! I'm certainly not on their side, but he's wanted for murder, for Christ's sake!'

Then, feeling sorry for the three downcast men, she said, more normally, 'It *is* Shadrack we're talking about, I presume?'

The three men all nodded. One who had said nothing so far now spoke, 'That's right, it's Shadrack – but before you tell Malachi, I reckon you should come below decks and hear his story.'

'There's no need for that. We all saw how the overseer treated him.'

'There's more to it than that, Tom. Far more. You ought to hear it for yourself before you speak to Malachi.'

In the low-beamed mess-deck where the crew lived, ate and slept, Shadrack was seated hunched on a stool in a corner. When he saw Thomasina, he greeted her eagerly. 'Master Tom . . . ! You've spoken to the captain? He won't take me back to Norfolk?'

'I don't think there's any fear of that, Shadrack, but he'll need to decide exactly what we are to do with you. The first thing he'll want to know is whether or not it's true that you killed Kellerman.'

Shadrack's chin came up in a momentary expression of defiance, then he bowed his head, before replying. 'Yes, Master Tom, I killed him.'

Thomasina remained silent for a few moments, then said, 'I'm not saying the way he treated you was right, Shadrack. It certainly *wasn't* – but neither is murder.'

'That isn't why he murdered the bastard.' One of

the crew standing nearby spoke with great feeling. 'Tell him, Shadrack. Tell Tom about this Kellerman – and your wife. Tell him what he did to both of you.'

Thomasina looked from Shadrack to the seaman who had spoken, then back again to the slave. 'I think you'd better tell me, Shadrack. Tell me everything.'

Hesitantly at first, but with increasing emotion, Shadrack told the story of the events that had led to the murder of the bullying overseer.

He spoke softly in the dimly lit mess-room, surrounded by grim-faced and silent seamen. The only other sounds were the creaks and groans of the wooden ship and the regular slap of the sea against the bow, as the *Melanie Jane* dipped into the waves.

It was a story that Thomasina listened to in growing horror.

Shadrack had been born on a cotton plantation far to the south of Norfolk – in Georgia. He had been happy there, working for an easy-going planter and his wife.

When he was twenty years old, Shadrack had married an attractive young girl named Millie. She was a slave, like himself, although it was generally accepted that her grandfather had been a white plantation owner.

Millie was, according to Shadrack, 'the prettiest girl on any of the plantations for miles around'.

For a year they led a very happy life, occupying a small, one-roomed cabin on the plantation. Then an epidemic swept through their region of Georgia, laying low slave and owner alike.

Millie and Shadrack survived, but many others

fell victim. Among their number were the elderly plantation owner and his wife.

As a result of their deaths the plantation was broken up and the land divided among local land-owners. The slaves too went to new owners.

To the great relief of Shadrack and Millie, they were shipped off together to a relative of their late employer, who lived in Norfolk, Virginia. Here their good luck came to an abrupt and brutal end.

Shadrack was sent to work on the docks, in a gang supervised by Mick Kellerman. Millie was put to work as a servant in the house occupied by the bachelor overseer.

It was not long before she caught his eye. One night he ordered her from the slaves' quarters to his bedroom, where he violently raped her. From that night on she became his unwilling mistress.

Despite this, Shadrack still contrived to meet her occasionally, but when Kellerman caught them talking, he had Shadrack publicly whipped. It was this that had caused the extensive scarring Thomasina had witnessed on his back during the time he was working on board the *Melanie Jane*.

When the beating was over, Kellerman had warned Shadrack that if he tried to see Millie again, his punishment would be even more severe. But Shadrack had no intention of obeying the unreasonable order. He continued to meet his wife whenever he could steal a few moments.

Inevitably, Kellerman caught them together again.

It was now, for the first time, that Shadrack faltered in his narrative.

'Go on, Shadrack. Did he whip you again?' Thomasina prompted gently.

'No, Master Tom.' The fugitive slave turned his face up to her and there were tears streaming down his face. 'He had Millie whipped and forced me to watch. Then . . .'

Shadrack needed to compose himself before continuing. 'Some of Boss Kellerman's friends held me down on the ground while Kellerman stamped on me, saying that by the time he'd finished I'd never want to so much as look at any other woman. I don't know which hurt worse, Master Tom, what Boss Kellerman did to me, or hearing Millie crying when they let go of me. I ain't a man no more, Master Tom. No good for my Millie, or for any other woman.'

Feeling physically sick, Thomasina said fiercely, 'He deserved to die, Shadrack. A man like that didn't deserve to be given life in the first place.'

There were angry murmurs of agreement from the listening crew, but Shadrack said, 'I wished him dead for that, Master Tom. Many nights I would go down on my knees and pray he would die, but I wouldn't have killed him. Then one day I met my Millie again. She told me that Boss Kellerman was hitting her and doing bad things. She said she didn't want to live no more. She begged me to kill her and put her out of her misery. I wouldn't do that, Master Tom, I couldn't have done anything to hurt her.'

The tears were streaming down Shadrack's cheeks now, but he had not ended his tragic story.

'Yesterday, after I finished working, I was told that Millie was dead. She'd hanged herself from a tree in

Boss Kellerman's garden. That's when I went to his house and killed him, Master Tom. I didn't do it for me, but for Millie. For my wife.'

10

In Malachi's cabin an emotional Thomasina repeated the story related to her by Shadrack. When it came to an end, Malachi reached out and took her hand, squeezing it comfortingly before releasing it.

'It's not a story you should have had to listen to, Tom, but the men weren't to know that.'

'I'll get over it soon enough – but I doubt if Shadrack ever will. What are we going to do with him, Malachi?'

'What do you suggest?' Malachi countered her question with one of his own. 'Do you have any ideas?'

'None, beyond taking him to England with us – and hoping he'll learn something of seamanship along the way,' Thomasina admitted.

Malachi shrugged. 'I can't think of any other course of action, so that's what we'll do.'

'You're not angry with the men for hiding him on board?'

'I'd be happier had they felt able to tell me what they were doing – but no, I'm not angry.' Malachi shrugged once more. 'I probably wouldn't have behaved any differently, had I been one of them.'

'You're a good man, Malachi,' Thomasina gave him a watery smile. 'I'll go and tell the men. They'll be greatly relieved.'

Shadrack settled down to shipboard life well. Impeccably clean and willing to tackle any task, he quickly won the respect of the Cornish seamen.

He was also quick to learn. By the time they had been at sea for five days he could be relied upon to tackle most of the routine duties of shipboard life.

On the sixth day out from Norfolk the weather deteriorated alarmingly and Malachi's fears about the suspect yard on the mainmast were realised. As the wind touched gale force, it suddenly snapped.

Cursing the integrity of the Norfolk boat-builders, Malachi supervised the crew as they fought to remove the broken yard, hampered by the severe weather. When this was done, they needed to clear and unravel a mess of tangled rigging.

The task completed to his satisfaction, Malachi said, 'I'm not happy with things as they are, Tom. I'm not going to risk pressing on without a new yard.'

'Will we need to return to Norfolk?' Thomasina expressed the apprehension already showing on the face of Shadrack. Helping the coxwain on the wheel, he had been listening to the conversation with increasing alarm.

'No, Bermuda's little more than a day's sailing to

the south. There are boat-builders there. They are also gathering stores, with a view to opening a naval-supply depot. Hopefully we'll find what we need there.'

Malachi had seen Shadrack's concern. For his benefit, he added, 'Bermuda belongs to Britain, Shadrack. You'll be safe enough there as one of the *Melanie Jane*'s crew.'

The fugitive slave had come to have great respect for Malachi. He accepted what the captain said without question.

Unlike Jamaica, the island of Bermuda, although hilly, had no tall mountains to guide a mariner to its shores. At first sight it seemed to Thomasina that it might have been floating upon the surface of the ocean.

As they approached, Malachi issued a string of orders, gradually reducing sail and speed until the *Melanie Jane* was hardly moving through the water.

They were close to land now. Without shifting his gaze from the sea ahead of them, Malachi spoke to Thomasina. 'I've only ever been here once before. That was many years ago. I seem to remember it's a difficult approach to the harbour and the town of St George. We'll anchor and hope another ship comes in. Then we'll follow it through the channel. I don't want to lose my ship for the sake of a broken yard.'

Malachi had to wait for twenty-four hours before he was able to put his plan into operation. Then it was not a single ship that guided him into the St George harbour, but six. They were British men-o'-war, the largest a seventy-four-gun warship, flying a commodore's flag.

By the time the last of the warships had passed through the narrow channel to the harbour, the *Melanie Jane* was under way. Inside the harbour she anchored clear of the Royal Navy vessels and Malachi ordered the ship's boat to be lowered.

Thomasina had already told Malachi she would like to go ashore, and Shadrack was delighted when he was chosen to be one of the boat's crew, having informed Malachi that he had occasionally crewed a boat in Norfolk.

'Thank you, boss,' he said to Malachi. 'It will be the first time I've been anywhere as a free man.' Suddenly his expression clouded and he asked, hesitantly, 'I *am* a free man now?'

'I don't have slaves crewing on my boat, Shadrack. You're as free as any other man on board, as far as I'm concerned.'

'You've made him a very happy man,' Thomasina commented, as the ex-slave hurried away to help the men lower the boat.

'It wasn't a hard thing to do,' Malachi replied. 'I only wish everyone else on board was as easily satisfied.'

A few members of the *Melanie Jane*'s crew, anxious to be home, had grumbled that they could have sailed on without repairing the broken yard. In their opinion it had not been necessary to sail so many miles off course to Bermuda.

'Before we go ashore let's go down below and make sure we have enough English money left to buy a new yard. It won't come cheap this far from home.'

11

The boat from the *Melanie Jane* set off for the Bermudan capital, St George, less than half an hour after the ship had anchored, yet already boats from the British men-o'-war were busily plying back and forth between their ships and the shore.

'It's as well we've not called in for provisions,' Malachi commented. 'It looks to me as though the navy intends buying up everything they can lay their hands on.'

Shadrack and three seamen were at the oars of the *Melanie Jane*'s boat, with Malachi and Thomasina sitting in the stern. Malachi called out an occasional order when he thought the boat was straying off course, and soon it bumped gently against a dock where stores for the British squadron were piled up ready to be loaded.

Significantly Thomasina observed that the bulk of

the stores consisted of gunpowder and cannonballs. It seemed the British squadron had either been recently involved in a sea battle or expected to meet with an enemy very soon.

Once ashore the seamen, Shadrack with them, headed for the nearest tavern. Malachi said he would visit the boat-builders along the waterfront but warned the crewmen to be back on the quay in an hour's time.

Thomasina decided to have a walk around the town by herself.

It was quite small, as was the island on which it stood. Indeed, the sea on the other side of the island was within easy walking distance of the harbourside. The buildings of the little town were a mixture of impressive, stone-built buildings belonging to the island administrators, shanties and waterfront taverns. The last had no pretence of permanency about them. They had been thrown up to meet the increase in business brought about by the war with France and the ever-increasing possibility of further conflict with America.

Not wishing to visit any of the taverns, Thomasina slowly made her way back to the quay. The hour given to the crew by Malachi was almost up, yet there was no sign of them. Malachi was not to be seen, either. Thomasina knew the crew would remain in the tavern drinking for as long as they were able, periodically sending a member of the party outside to check whether the captain was in sight.

She hoped they were taking care of Shadrack. He would not be used to strong drink.

Contrary to her expectations, she had seen many slaves on Bermuda, but they appeared to enjoy far greater freedom of movement than their fellows in either Jamaica or Virginia. The reason was undoubtedly because this was a very small island. There would be nowhere for them to hide if they absconded.

While she stood on the quayside Thomasina observed a boat coming in from the direction of the British naval squadron, but she took little notice of it. Boats from the men-o'-war were flitting across the waters of the harbour like so many water beetles.

There was a midshipman seated in the stern of this particular boat. Another man, whom she took to be a petty officer, was seated beside him. Thomasina also noticed in passing that the crew seemed small for the size of the boat. She assumed, with very little real interest, that they were leaving as much room as possible for the stores they would be taking back to their ship.

As the boat bumped alongside the stone wall of the quay, Thomasina turned away, impatient that the crew members from the *Melanie Jane* had not yet put in an appearance.

To her relief, she saw Malachi making his way towards her. Something in the way he was walking told her immediately that his quest for a new yard had not been successful.

She was about to set off to meet him when a voice from behind her called, 'We'll make this our first . . . Take him.'

She turned to see what was happening and was

shocked to see the midshipman from the newly
arrived boat pointing at her.

The midshipman led a Royal Navy press-gang!

It was too late to escape. Before she could make a
move, a sailor had taken hold of one of her arms, then
the other was seized by a second.

Trying in vain to shake them off, Thomasina
demanded, 'What do you think you're doing? Let
go of me.'

'Now, don't go causing any trouble, lad. You're
needed to serve on board HMS *Victorious*. She's a good
ship. Agree to join us as a volunteer, and you'll be
given a very generous bounty. Refuse, and you'll get
nothing – but still be impressed into His Majesty's
service. Be sensible about it now, lad. What would you
rather do? Serve His Majesty and have money in your
pocket, or serve him just the same and have nothing?'

'I'll do neither. Let me go.' Once again Thomasina
tried desperately to break free, but to no avail. The
grip of the two sailors was too strong for her. 'Let me
go, do you hear? I'm needed on my own ship.'

Ignoring her plea, the midshipman said, 'All right,
put him in the boat. We'll go off and see how many
more we can find.'

Thomasina continued to struggle, but she was not
very heavy. It took little effort on the part of her
captors to propel her towards the waiting boat.

'WAIT! What the devil do you think you're doing?'
Malachi bellowed for all the world like an angry bull
as he hurried awkwardly towards them, his peg-leg
tapping out an erratic rhythm on the stone-paved quayside.

His authoritative voice was sufficient to bring the seamen holding Thomasina to a halt, but before Malachi reached them, the midshipman stepped into his path.

'This young man is being impressed into the Royal Navy. I advise you not to interfere.'

For a few moments Thomasina thought Malachi would knock the junior naval rating from his path. Instead, the *Melanie Jane*'s captain seemed to swell to twice his normal size.

Fixing the other man with a shrivelling glare, he said, 'Don't you tell me what to do, you young whipper-snapper. I was having midshipmen "kiss the gunner's daughter" when you were still on your hands and knees in the nursery – even though you're older than any midshipman worth his salt ought to be.'

Through his reference to 'kissing the gunner's daughter' – a naval term used to describe being stretched over the barrel of a cannon and flogged – the midshipman was aware that Malachi had once been a naval man. Probably one who had held a senior rank. Nevertheless, he stood his ground.

'I don't doubt you were . . . sir, but as an ex-naval officer, you will appreciate that I have a duty to perform . . .'

'I don't give a damn for your "duty", mister. I've served my country in a manner you will never achieve. By the time I was your age I had command of my own ship and had lost a leg proving my patriotism. I'm on my way to England now with food for my starving countrymen – your countrymen, too. I have a broken yard that I can't replace and need every one of my crew if I'm to get there safely. Tom here, especially. He's the

one who helps me do all the things I can't do for myself
since I lost my leg. You'll let him go and find someone
else to press into service.'

'I'm sorry, sir,' declared the midshipman doggedly. 'I
have my orders . . .'

'Orders be damned!' snapped Malachi. 'If Admiral
Nelson – yes, and me too – if we'd stuck blindly to
orders, the French would have swept us from the sea
years ago. Have you never wondered why you're still a
midshipman when most men of your age are commanding their own ships? I'll tell you, mister. It's because you
follow orders so blindly that you've lost the ability to
think for yourself. Do you want to become another Billy
Culmer?'

The man to whom Malachi referred had gained noto-
riety in the Royal Navy by serving as a midshipman for
thirty-five years before being promoted to lieutenant at
the age of fifty-seven.

Malachi knew he would need to bully the unimagi-
native officer in charge of the press-gang if he was to
persuade him to release Thomasina – and he *had* to
succeed. Her sex would be discovered very quickly in
the between-decks confines of a man-o'-war.

'I carry out my duties as I see them, sir.' The midshipman was aware that the members of his press-gang were
enjoying this one-sided exchange. He wished now they
had never chanced upon this lad. But they had. He could
not back down now.

To the men holding Thomasina, he snapped, 'I told
you to take him to the boat. What are you waiting for?'

As the seamen turned to do his bidding, Malachi
suddenly called, 'Not so fast.'

When they turned to look at him, Malachi was pointing a double-barrelled pistol at the midshipman. He was not in the habit of carrying a pistol, but he had brought a lot of money ashore with him in the hope of purchasing a new yard. Knowing very little about crime on the island of Bermuda, he had thought it wise to go armed.

'I suggest you order the release of my lad now. If they try to take him, I'll shoot you dead. I doubt if the navy will consider a ship's boy fair exchange for the life of a midshipman.'

'Don't do anything stupid, Malachi.' Although dismayed at being taken by the press-gang, Thomasina was thoroughly alarmed at this turn of events. 'They won't keep me on a man-o'-war. You know that.'

Thomasina hoped the captain of the *Melanie Jane* would take the hidden meaning in her words. Once on board the warship, she had only to disclose her sex and they would send her back to her own ship. It would mean she would never again be able to sail on the *Melanie Jane* as a crew member, but it was preferable to seeing Malachi die for murdering the midshipman.

'He's right.' The midshipman was trying unsuccessfully not to appear frightened. He did not doubt Malachi would do as he said. 'You might murder me – and possibly another of my men, but you'd be taken and hanged.'

Malachi shook his head. 'I've already said you were lacking in imagination. I wouldn't shoot you. My shot would go there . . .' He waved the pistol in the direction of a stack of small barrels only a few paces away. Each was stencilled with a single word. GUNPOWDER. 'A single shot should be sufficient to blow us all to eternity, but I have a second, if it's needed.'

The midshipman looked at him in disbelief and Malachi said evenly, 'I've lived a full life and done all the things I've ever wanted to do. As for Tom . . . I know him too well to think he'd settle to life on board a man-o'-war. He'd be better off dead – but if he dies, he'll travel to heaven with an escort of good, honest sailors – and you too.'

For the first time, Thomasina became aware that the boat's crew from the *Melanie Jane* had left the tavern. They realised immediately what the duties of the sailors from the man-o'-war were. They were prepared to run if they were targeted, but they remained within hearing and their expressions revealed their horror at Malachi's words. They were in no doubt that he meant every word.

Neither was the midshipman. He was caught between death and humiliation.

Succour came from a welcome but unexpected quarter. All those involved in the drama had been so engrossed in what was going on that they had not noticed the arrival of a boat bringing the commodore of the squadron ashore.

Commodore Sir Benjamin Andrews was a fine commander, well used to rapidly assessing difficult situations. It did not take him long to grasp this one.

'What's going on here?' With apparent casualness, Commodore Andrews walked between Malachi and the naval party.

Malachi was the first to speak. 'Your midshipman wants to impress my cabin boy. I consider my need is the greater. I must have a full crew if I'm to get a ship with a broken mainmast yard back to England.'

Looking at Thomasina, the commodore said disparagingly, 'He's not much of a lad for such a big fuss to be made about him.'

'That's as may be,' replied Malachi, 'but I've lost a leg in the service of the King – and the war has cost this lad his father. Let the midshipman find his men elsewhere.'

The commodore had been looking thoughtfully at Malachi as he had been speaking. Now he said, 'Haven't we met before? What's your name, sir?'

'Ellis. Captain Malachi Ellis.' Malachi eyed the commodore warily, in case he was trying to put him off guard.

'I knew it! We met many years ago, when every man in the service knew of Commander Ellis of the *Pickle*.' Turning his attention to the midshipman, he said, 'Mister, you have the privilege of having met one of the most famous frigate commanders ever to have served in the Royal Navy. A frigate commander who made as much prize-money as my Lord Cochrane. You'd never have found him press-ganging men. Seamen would fall over themselves to serve on board his ship.'

Holding out a hand to Malachi, he said, 'It's a great pleasure to meet you again, Captain Ellis. Will you do me the honour of dining with me on board my flagship tonight? The governor will be there, together with many of the island officials.'

'Thank you for the invitation, Commodore, but I have my ship to repair as best I can – and a load of flour and corn to get back to Cornwall.'

'You say you've lost a yard from your mainmast?'

'That's right.'

'We've got a number of spares among the various ships of my squadron. Midshipman! Take the details from Captain Ellis of what's required. If we have nothing of the exact size, have one adapted.'

Returning his attention to Malachi, the commodore said, 'The yard will be a gift from a grateful navy, Captain Ellis – but it is conditional upon you accepting my invitation to dinner. You're a legend among senior officers. An inspiration to young, would-be frigate commanders. Your presence would be a social coup for me.'

'What of young Tom? Do I get him back?'

'Of course. He should never have been taken. The place to find new recruits is from the ships we stop at sea. Taking men here will only antagonise the local residents. We can ill afford to do that at a time when it looks as though we're likely to go to war with America before the month is out. If that happens, Bermuda will be a most important naval base. We'll try to recruit men here, of course, but they will need to be volunteers, not pressed men.'

'In that case I shall consider it an honour to be your guest tonight, Commodore – and I'm most grateful to you for your offer of a yard. I thought I would need to sail without one, and it's the wrong time of year to take such a chance. Come on, Tom. Let's take the crew back to the ship. We've had quite enough excitement for one day.'

It was not quite the end of the day's events. Shadrack was very quiet for much of the remainder of that day, before speaking privately with Malachi that evening.

When Malachi went to dine with Commodore Andrews, Shadrack went to the flagship with him. He had been highly interested in what the commodore had said about war between Britain and America being in the offing. If it happened, he wanted to be part of it – fighting against the Americans.

With Malachi's recommendation, Shadrack went aboard the flagship as a recruit for the British navy. A free man.

12

In the summer of 1812 the *Melanie Jane* slipped her moorings at Plymouth, setting off on a voyage that was like many others the vessel had made.

Loaded with a general cargo, the ship was bound for Gibraltar, the British-occupied stronghold that guarded the entrance to the Mediterranean Sea. Malachi hoped to return with a cargo of fruit, port wine and lace goods, taken on board at Lisbon.

It was a fine, warm day with nothing to indicate that this would be the last voyage which the ship, master and crew would make together.

Yet, no more than three hours out from Plymouth, events were set in motion that would take the lives of all but one of the crew and change the future of the sole survivor for ever.

A French frigate, daringly disregarding the fact that it was almost within sight of one of the busiest naval ports in the country, intercepted the Cornish merchantman.

Malachi had seen the vessel⋅ approaching them from an oblique angle and was fully aware it was a man-o'-war. However, being so close to a major naval port, he thought it must be a British warship.

Not until it closed to within range and opened fire with a powerful salvo did the *Melanie Jane*'s captain realise his mistake.

Malachi immediately ordered the man on the wheel to put the helm hard over and steer towards the Cornish coast, still clearly visible on the horizon. But his attempt to evade the French man-o'-war was already too late. The French vessel was under full sail and steering a steady course, parallel with the *Melanie Jane*.

Drawing level with their intended victim, the French gunners let loose a second devastating broadside that brought down the *Melanie Jane*'s foremast and swept two seamen into the sea.

It might have been better had Malachi surrendered his ship now. However, during his illustrious naval career he had never once struck his colours to an enemy. It was a habit he found hard to break.

Maintaining course as best he could, Malachi shouted, 'Hack the rigging clear. Hurry, or they'll be upon us . . . !'

The French captain was hoping for prizes, but if it was not possible to take this laden English merchantman, then he was determined it would not escape him. He would sink it first.

The French seamen were experienced gunners. The

next salvo struck the *Melanie Jane* along the water-line, the merchantman shuddering under its impact.

At the same time, French sharpshooters began firing at the men on deck as they struggled to free the mast and rigging and heave them over the ship's side.

Two more members of the *Melanie Jane*'s crew fell dead as a result of this volley. The helmsman was wounded and momentarily knocked clear of the wheel.

He had been hard put to maintain the course of the damaged ship for some minutes. Now, free from his restraint, the wheel spun madly and the ship veered off course, sails flapping wildly in the breeze. Splintered timbers were now below the water-line and the *Melanie Jane* began settling in the water as the sea flooded its hold.

Malachi knew his beloved ship was doomed. Had it been possible, he would have had the ship's boat lowered and struck for the shore with the surviving crew members, leaving the *Melanie Jane* to its fate.

Unfortunately, the boat had been an early casualty of the French cannonade, its splintered woodwork strewn across the deck.

'Leave what you're doing, gather up as many personal belongings as you can carry and muster on deck,' Malachi shouted the order to the crew. 'The Frenchmen will probably come alongside and take us off. If they don't, we'll clear the rest of the rigging and try to run the *Melanie Jane* ashore.'

The men ran to do as he ordered, but Thomasina remained on deck with Malachi. 'Is there anything you want, Malachi? I'll go and fetch it for you.'

'There are many things, Tom.' Malachi spoke carefully and deliberately, trying to hide his deep emotion. 'Possessions collected over a lifetime spent travelling the world, but the Frenchmen will steal anything of real value that we take on board their ship. I'd rather it went down with the *Melanie Jane*. To be honest with you, I'd prefer to go down with her, too. She's been a great ship, Tom, one of the best. A part of me. It'll be a sight more painful than losing a leg. But you go below for anything you might want to rescue. If it's not of too much value, then the French will likely let you keep it.'

'I've a bag of gold sovereigns in my cabin. I'll fetch them and hand them out among the crew. Between us we might be able to hold on to a few. They'll no doubt come in handy.'

'You'd better hurry. The French ship is coming alongside now. When they take us on board, stay close to me. Keeping your secret will be more important than ever when we're taken prisoner and you'll need all the help you can get.'

The French frigate swiftly drew alongside the sinking *Melanie Jane* and it was a very dejected crew who transferred to the enemy warship.

Thomasina helped Malachi from one ship to the other as they rose and fell unevenly alongside each other. Other men helped two wounded seamen board the French warship. One had a serious leg injury which would need immediate attention.

With the other survivors, Malachi and Tom were herded down a ladder to a lower deck. Here they found a couple of dozen more British seamen, many of them Cornish men who had been taken prisoner during the course of the previous twenty-four hours.

The prisoners were sharing their accommodation with a number of live pigs, which they had managed to pen in a corner, making use of a number of wooden stools lashed together.

From the conversations which were immediately struck up, it was learned that the French frigate had been cruising back and forth along the coastline of Devon and Cornwall for the past twenty-four hours, preying on English shipping.

Many of the captives were fishermen. There were also the crews of two coastal trading vessels. Both ships had been captured intact and sent to France, crewed by French sailors.

The *Melanie Jane* was the French captain's largest prize, to date. However, although the French sailors made a hasty attempt to loot their latest prize, they would not be able to sail her to France. The *Melanie Jane* was sinking and would never leave Cornish waters.

From the conversation of the French sailors, one of the captured English seamen who understood their language gathered that the *Melanie Jane* was expected to be the final victim of the daring French captain. The man-o'-war now intended cruising westwards, staying close to the Cornish coast and bombarding a number of coastal villages before returning across the Channel to France.

Shut in below decks, with very little fresh air entering the crowded accommodation, the odour of the pigs was almost unbearable. It was so bad that one of the *Melanie Jane*'s sailors suggested they should slaughter the animals, dismember them and drop them, joint-by-joint, through the tiny single porthole that was all the compartment possessed.

However, as no one had yet been able to open the tiny, brass-ringed aperture, the suggestion was not acted upon.

Not long after the *Melanie Jane* had been abandoned, the French ship got under way once more and commenced firing at targets onshore as they presented themselves. Speculation among the imprisoned men immediately switched to which of the Cornish coastal communities was coming under attack from the French raider.

All the prisoners were in agreement that, although the French captain was a naval man, his reckless behaviour was that of a privateer. He seemed contemptuous of the fact that the gunfire might be heard by any of the English men-o'-war en route to, or from, Plymouth.

For many hours the Englishmen incarcerated with the pigs were forced to listen to the bombardment of the fishing villages where many of them had their homes.

Then, suddenly and unexpectedly, came the sound of splintering wood and the unmistakeable thud of cannonballs bouncing across the deck above them. The sounds were accompanied by excited shouting from the French sailors.

'What's happening?' Alarmed, Thomasina put the question to Malachi.

'I'd say someone's decided to shoot back!'

Malachi's elation was tinged with anxiety. They were locked in, with no means of escape. If the ship were to be holed and sunk . . .

'Do you think we've met up with a British man-o'-war?' Thomasina asked.

'I doubt it. If we had, there would have been a great many changes of course to put the ship in the most advantageous position. It's probably one of the fortresses along the Cornish coast. St Mawes, or Pendennis, perhaps. It might even be St Michael's Mount.'

'I didn't know the Mount had any guns.' This from one of the *Melanie Jane*'s crew.

'The Mount has a great many guns,' confirmed Malachi. 'They've used them in the past when other guns in Cornwall have remained silent . . .'

He was interrupted by another volley from the unknown battery, and the French ship shuddered under the weight of the cannonade.

'Whoever is firing on us, their gunners have got the range of this ship. They've caused damage too, by the sound of things. Listen to that . . .'

From the deck above the imprisoned men, they could hear the frantic shouts of the crew. Something serious must have happened to cause such consternation among the Frenchmen.

Suddenly, the hatch above their heads was thrown open. A heavily accented voice called down, 'Up on deck, all of you. The ship is running on to rocks. Save your lives – if you can.'

In the ensuing dash for the ladders, Malachi hung back, not wishing to slow down the others. After initial uncertainty, Thomasina and the surviving crew members of the *Melanie Jane* stayed with him.

When the ladder was clear, Malachi was helped from the small hold. As he climbed awkwardly to the upper deck, he glanced shorewards. It was dusk now, but there was no mistaking the triangular shape of the island that rose from the sea between ship and shore.

'It's the Mount right enough,' he said. 'But those waiting there are not *all* from the Mount.'

They were clear of the hatch now and he pointed to where a vast number of men and women could be made out crowding the foreshore beneath the castle that occupied the summit of the small island.

'They're wreckers. The French are going to find them even more dangerous than the rocks.'

'How will they know who are French and who are Cornish men?' Thomasina asked.

'They won't,' Malachi replied grimly. 'Even if they did, there'll be those among them who wouldn't care. We're in trouble, Tom. Very real trouble.'

The French man-o'-war was so close to the rocky foreshore that the sailors had given up all attempts to save the ship. Their one thought now was how best to save themselves. It would not be easy.

Waves were breaking against the menacing, water-blackened rocks, hurling spray over the mob, which was noisily anticipating the spoils that the sea was about to bring them.

Suddenly the stricken ship rose on a swell that accelerated its progress towards the shore. It seemed to Thomasina they were travelling at breakneck speed.

Onshore, the mob thought so too and howled in primitive approval.

Sailors began leaping from the French vessel now, hoping to save themselves before it struck. Many more remained, reluctant to leave the ship which had carried them safely to all parts of the world and had been the only home they had known for many years.

Just short of the shore, the ship struck a number of underwater rocks and came to a violent and unexpected halt. The force of the impact knocked those on deck off balance and many were catapulted into the sea. They immediately struck out in a desperate attempt to reach the shore.

The howling of the mob was now blood-curdlingly close and Thomasina asked, 'What shall we do, Malachi?'

'There's nothing I can do for you, Tom – or you for me. We're on our own in this. Good luck to you. I couldn't have wished for a finer nephew . . .'

As he spoke, another wave lifted and turned the ship, spilling more of its occupants into the sea, Thomasina among them.

She tried to see what was happening to Malachi, but the cold salt water closed about her, sucking her down, and all else was forgotten as she fought her way back to the surface.

When her head emerged above water, she gulped in air gratefully, then instinctively she struck out for the shore, only to be lifted and thrown against a rock that stood proud of the water. She attempted to cling to it, but the sea prised her free, pulling her back down.

Another swell lifted her, threw her over the rock

and carried her on, battering her against other rocks closer to the shore. Suddenly she found herself floundering in a pool of comparatively calm and shallow water.

As she attempted to secure a grip on a wet rock, four or five of those onshore – two of them women – made for her. One man lunged at her with a weapon that might have been a pike, or perhaps a pitchfork.

She felt a sudden pain as it struck one of her ribs and slid away again. It caused her to lose her grip on the rock and she fell backwards.

Caught by another wave, she was carried back towards the sea by the swirling water. She heard a sound that might have been water rushing through a narrow gap between the rocks, or it could have been the cries of the mob.

Then, as she struggled in vain against the pull of the sea, her head came into hard contact with a rock . . . and she knew no more.

Book Three

BookThree

1

Thomasina regained consciousness painfully slowly. With her eyes still closed, she tried to recall what had happened to her. Her mind was in a state of utter confusion. Feeling cautiously about her, she made the discovery that she was lying in a bed. A large bed with a luxuriantly soft mattress.

Opening her eyes slowly and apprehensively, she thought it must be night. Then, gradually, she made out a window at which there were closed curtains. There was light showing around the curtain edges and she realised it must be daylight outside.

In the faint gloom she could see that the walls of her room were of unplastered stone. It reminded her of the cell in which she had last seen Jeffery. For a moment she thought she too must be in a prison. Then fragmented memories began to return.

When she moved her head she suffered blinding

pain. She recalled feeling a similar pain when her head had struck against a rock after the French warship had been driven ashore.

Recalling more details of the shipwreck, she started up in sudden anguish. This time the pain in her head proved so acute that she cried out. Dropping her head back on the pillow once more, she lay still and allowed the pieces of the jigsaw to fall into place.

She relived the moment when she was washed from the deck of the French ship and attacked by a Cornish mob . . . Here the recollection came to an abrupt end.

How had she escaped – and where was Malachi? Had he been responsible for bringing her here – and where was *here*? If it had been him, where was he now?

Suddenly she realised she was wearing a nightdress: women's clothing! Whoever was responsible for her rescue must have realised she was a woman. How had they found out?

When she tried to change her position in the bed, the answer to this question dropped another piece of the confusing jigsaw into place. A sharp pain at the side of her ribcage reminded her that she had been attacked with a pike, or something similar. Whoever had treated the wound must have discovered her secret.

That would surely not have been Malachi? But if not him, then whom?

As she thought about the events of that dramatic evening, the unanswered questions multiplied in her mind.

Thomasina must have been pondering the situation for about twenty minutes before the door opened and she heard someone enter the room.

Any movement of her head still pained her, but Thomasina turned it slowly and saw that a woman of about forty had entered the room. Dark-haired and attractive, she was also heavily pregnant.

'So you have returned to the land of the living? We were becoming anxious for you.'

Thomasina could detect neither pleasure nor regret in the woman's voice.

'Can you understand me? What's your name? Are you English, or French?'

As she spoke, the woman drew back the curtains. The light was like a hammer striking at Thomasina's brain. Closing her eyes, she turned her head away, although this too caused her pain.

The question was repeated, this time in French.

'I'm English, my name is Thomasina.' She found speech difficult and slurred her words alarmingly. 'Where am I? Where are the others from the *Melanie Jane*?'

'You are in the castle on St Michael's Mount. I am Juliana, but I am afraid I know nothing of the *Melanie Jane* . . . I presume you are talking of a ship? You were rescued from the wreck of a French man-o'-war, dressed in a man's clothing. No doubt there were good reasons. I can think of some myself. However, because you are a woman, it meant you could not be treated in the same way as the others who were rescued. We brought you here and sent for a physician. He said you have suffered concussion and possibly a cracked skull. He also looked at the wound in your side. You have a fractured rib, but he says the injury should heal well. No doubt you will wish to inform your family of your well-being and return to them as soon as you are able.'

Juliana was brusque and matter-of-fact. As soon as she heard Thomasina talk, she realised she was Cornish and from a working background. When the doctor said she was fit to be moved, Juliana would have her transferred to the house of one of the tenants. She could remain there until she was fit enough to return to her own home.

This was neither callousness nor snobbishness on her part, but self-preservation. She was the mistress of Sir John St Aubyn. The baronet was devoted to her, of this she was certain – for most of the time – but she was heavily pregnant and feeling particularly insecure. Sir John's head was easily turned by a young girl – and this one had a strangely attractive quality about her.

Juliana's was also a far from regular situation. She could be excused for being neurotic about having Thomasina in the house, particularly in view of the unusual and rather romantic manner in which she had arrived on St Michael's Mount.

'I have no family – unless Malachi survived the shipwreck?'

It was a forlorn half-question. Conditions on the evening of the wreck had been such that even the fittest of men would have considered himself lucky to escape with his life.

'I know nothing about survivors, my dear, except

that Sir John said there were pitifully few. The sea and the wreckers between them took a heavy toll – but you'll not want to be talking about that right now. I believe Humphrey – Sir John's son – has a list of survivors and the names of . . . others. I'll send him along to see you, if I can have him found. He'll be relieved you've regained consciousness. He's looked in on you at least three or four times a day while you've been here.'

'How long *have* I been here?'

'This is the fourth day, dear, but by the look of you you're not fit to be moved just yet.' Observing Thomasina's squint, she asked, 'Is the light hurting your eyes?'

'Yes.'

'Then I'll draw the curtains again, leaving just a small gap to allow a little light in.'

'What time is it?' Taken aback by the duration of her unconsciousness, Thomasina tried to gain a grip on reality.

'Late afternoon. Do you fancy something to eat?' Without waiting for a reply, Juliana said, 'I'll have a maid bring some broth up to the room. You really should have some food inside you.'

Thomasina did not feel she would be able to eat anything, but she was thirsty and said so.

'I'll have some milk and water sent up for you, too. We'll talk again later, when you are a little stronger. In the meantime I'll send word to the doctor that you've regained consciousness. He'll be relieved, I've no doubt. I don't think he was terribly confident of your survival.'

* * *

When Juliana left the room, Thomasina lay in the comfortable bed and tried not to think of Malachi and the others. It was not easy, but she knew that if she were to dwell upon their possible fate in her present weakened state, she would dissolve in tears and thoroughly exhaust herself.

Besides, thinking of what had occurred would achieve nothing. She urgently needed to think of the future, and what she was to do with her life, if she was on her own once more.

If there was no Malachi to lean upon.

Despite her resolution, Thomasina could not stem the tears that sprang to her eyes at the thought of what must have happened to Malachi. She had been sailing with him for two years. During that time he had taken the place of the father she had lost years before.

She tried to exclude such thoughts and concentrate on practicalities, but no matter how hard she tried *not* to think about him, every thought led her back to Malachi.

If he was no longer alive there would be a great many loose ends to tie up in connection with their partnership. She had accumulated a number of possessions at the Falmouth house she had shared with him. She would need to collect them before the house was sold, as she felt certain it would be if Malachi had not survived the wreck.

She wondered whether the *Melanie Jane* and its cargo had been insured. It was not something she and Malachi had ever discussed. As soon as it was possible, she would need to speak to the solicitor who had drawn up the partnership agreement and who had managed Malachi's affairs. He would be able to answer many of her more pressing questions.

Not until then would she be able to make a reasoned appraisal of her future.

All these things were passing through her mind when she heard the door to her room open once more.

Opening her eyes, she saw a man looking at her uncertainly. No more than a year or two older than herself, he appeared hesitant to cross the room to the bed. Curious, Thomasina asked, 'Who are you?'

Approaching the bed, he said eagerly, 'I'm Humphrey. Humphrey St Aubyn. It's John, really. Humphrey's my second name, but they call me that so that I'm not confused with my father. I'm glad to see you with your eyes open. When Abel and I pulled you from the sea I thought at first you were dead.'

Seemingly embarrassed by being alone in the room with her, he gave a short, nervous laugh and with words tumbling over themselves, he added, 'But then I thought you were a young boy – I was wrong about that too.'

'You're the one who pulled me from the sea?'

'Yes . . . well, that's not *strictly* true. It was actually Abel who rescued you from those *creatures*, who would have killed you, but I helped bring you ashore on that dreadful night. It was Mount guns that sank the French ship, you know. There was such a frightful and unnecessary loss of life – and a great many of those who died were our own people. It was *awful*.'

'I owe you my life,' said Thomasina, '. . . you and

the others. Thank you. But I'm very concerned for the members of the *Melanie Jane*'s crew. Especially Malachi . . . Captain Ellis. Juliana said you would know about them.'

'You've already spoken to Juliana?'

'She was in here a short while ago. Why?'

'Well, she knows I've been anxious about you, but she doesn't really approve of me wandering about the house.' Hesitatingly he added, 'It's a long and somewhat complicated story but, although Sir John is my father, Juliana is not my mother. She lives at Ludgvan, across on the mainland. I live there too for most of the time, although I like to spend time on the Mount when I'm not at university. Mind you, Juliana and Sir John don't spend much time here, either. They are usually in London, or at Clowance.'

The story sounded too complicated for Thomasina in her present state. Although she was mildly intrigued, she could not cope with matters of a complex nature just yet. Besides, there were more immediate issues to be settled.

'Do you know anything of the crew of the *Melanie Jane*?' she asked.

'Only what the Frenchmen were able to tell me.'

'I'm sorry . . . I don't understand. Juliana said you have a list of the survivors.'

Humphrey nodded unhappily. 'That's right – but there were none from a ship called *Melanie Jane*, although the French survivors told me they had sunk a ship and taken prisoners on the day they were wrecked on the Mount. Would that ship have been the *Melanie Jane*?'

It took a few moments for Humphrey's words to sink in. 'You mean . . . there were no survivors at all from the *Melanie Jane*?'

'Only you – if that was the name of your ship.'

Thomasina winced, but the expression had nothing to do with the pain in her head, even though that had begun to throb unmercifully. Nevertheless, there was a further question that needed to be asked.

'Among those who died . . . Was there a man who had lost the lower half of a leg, his left leg?'

'Yes. One of the Cornish fishermen said he was the captain of the last ship that the French had sunk, but he could not remember the name of either the captain or his ship.'

Aware that his news had distressed Thomasina, Humphrey asked unhappily, 'Was he someone particularly close to you?'

Not trusting herself to speak, Thomasina gave a slight nod of her throbbing head, saying nothing.

'Was it *his* idea that you should dress as a boy? So the French would not know they had captured a woman?'

Thomasina's grief went deep and the pain in her head made logical thought difficult. Yet she realised that the assumption made by Humphrey St Aubyn would simplify a great many of the problems she would have to face in the future. Especially if there were no survivors from the *Melanie Jane* to contradict such a story.

'Yes . . . Yes, that's why Malachi made me dress as a boy. He thought it would be for the best.'

Thomasina turned her head away from Humphrey

St Aubyn now and allowed the tears to flow
freely.

After standing by her bedside in embarrassed
silence for a few minutes, Humphrey tiptoed from
the room. At the doorway he paused to look back at
her, his expression one of sympathy and concern.

Then he left the room, closing the door silently
behind him.

2

In spite of Juliana's initial reservations about her unexpected guest, she found herself increasingly drawn to Thomasina as the days passed and her health improved.

There were a number of reasons for this. One was that Thomasina displayed no hint of disapproval in respect of Juliana's own unusual situation.

Juliana thought this was because, from what little Thomasina had chosen to reveal about herself, she too had enjoyed an unusual and interesting lifestyle. Travelling around the world with her 'uncle' on his ship, Thomasina would have experienced more real-life adventures than most girls – or young men – could even imagine.

In Thomasina, Juliana thought she recognised a kindred, non-conformist spirit, albeit one whose non-conformity had taken a different direction from her own.

Her more relaxed attitude was also helped by the fact that Sir John, who held a local parliamentary seat, had gone to London, accompanied by James, his eldest son.

Had it not been for her heavily pregnant condition Juliana would have gone too, taking the younger children. In truth, she was not looking forward to this confinement and was pleased to have Thomasina staying at the Mount to keep her company.

In her turn, Thomasina enjoyed Juliana's company and got on well with the children. She also found an unexpected relief in not having to maintain the pretence of being a young man.

The ancient castle on St Michael's Mount had been built many hundreds of years before as a monastery. Extensive modifications had been made in later years to fortify it against attack, with scant regard for comfort. Only in its more recent history had it become a home, but practical considerations had not yet caught up with intent. It would be many years before the castle became a comfortable home.

Juliana was quite old to be carrying a child. This would pose additional dangers during the actual childbirth. Summoning a doctor from the mainland was dependent upon the vagaries of weather and tide.

Fortunately, the baby was not due for more than a month. When the time for her confinement drew closer, Juliana would probably move to Clowance, the St Aubyn home on the mainland, although builders were in the house, carrying out extensive alterations.

A regular visitor to Thomasina's room was Humphrey St Aubyn, Sir John's third son and namesake by his first mistress.

Although Juliana had never attempted to hide her antipathy towards the offspring of the baronet's earlier liaison, she tolerated Humphrey's attendance upon Thomasina. His visits gave Thomasina someone new to talk to and it amused Juliana to see how besotted he was with the young castaway.

Eventually the doctor decided Thomasina was well enough to leave her room to go outside and take advantage of the current spell of fine weather. It was Humphrey who insisted upon helping her to the terrace and fussing over her there.

'Humphrey is terribly smitten with you, Thomasina,' Juliana commented as the young man in question hurried off to find drinks for them all.

'He's a very nice young man,' Thomasina commented, non-committally.

Juliana did her best to hide a smile at Thomasina's description of someone who could be no more than a year or two older than herself. However, she felt that although Humphrey had received a university education and was soon to take up a career in the Church, he lacked the worldly maturity of Thomasina.

'I hope I'm not giving him the wrong idea by letting him do things for me. There's no place for a man in my life just yet,' Thomasina said to her hostess. 'I've got things to do before I think about taking a husband.'

'What sort of things?' Juliana never missed an opportunity to learn more about her guest.

'For a start, I need to visit Falmouth to settle my

uncle's affairs. I'm his only relative and am not even certain his solicitor knows he's dead.'

Even now, Thomasina found it difficult to talk about Malachi without a keen sense of loss. She felt tears well up in her eyes.

Realising that Thomasina was upset and aware of the reason, Juliana said gently, 'If he was master of his own ship and you're his only relative, you could learn you are quite a wealthy young woman.'

Thomasina nodded. 'It's always possible, I suppose, but I'd much rather have Malachi back with me.'

'Life doesn't always take our wishes into account, my dear. As for Humphrey . . . you could do a great deal worse. His father intends to settle ten thousand pounds on him. With that, and your own money, you could be very comfortably off. Very comfortable indeed.'

There was a degree of resentment in Juliana's statement. Sir John was an extremely generous man, especially where his children – all his *acknowledged* children – were concerned. Juliana often thought his generosity stemmed from a need to compensate for the many things his unorthodox domestic circumstances deprived them of. For instance, his eldest son would not be able to inherit his baronetcy, and many of the St Aubyn lands and estates would be lost to his illegitimate offspring.

Nevertheless, Sir John was giving them money he could ill afford. No one was more aware of this than Juliana. Sir John was inclined to juggle with his debts. There had been one occasion when he had been obliged to hide inside a wide, but extremely sooty chimney in order to evade a deputation of determined tradesmen to whom he owed money.

Further talk on the subject was brought to a halt by the return of Humphrey, carrying a tray upon which were drinks for them all.

When the two women fell silent upon his approach, Humphrey asked perceptively, 'Have I interrupted an important conversation, or were you talking about me?'

'You're as conceited as your father!' declared Juliana. 'If you must know, Thomasina was saying she needs to go to Falmouth as soon as possible.'

'To stay?' Humphrey's expression was one of dismay. 'Do you intend leaving the Mount soon, Thomasina?'

'I sincerely hope not.' Juliana had arrived at a surprising decision. 'I would like you to remain here for as long as you possibly can, Thomasina. Preferably until the baby arrives, or until Sir John returns. I know there are many things you must attend to, but you have said you have no relatives to go to. Why not stay while you consider your future? I very much enjoy your company. I know the children do, too.'

Juliana had not mentioned Humphrey, but she knew he was as eager as she was herself that Thomasina should act upon her suggestion.

'That's very kind of you.' Thomasina meant it. She was not yet ready to face an uncertain future on her own. 'I would like that – for a while, at least, but I must go to Falmouth as soon as I'm able. I have a great many things to do there. I'm not sure how long they will take. It could be a day or two.'

'That's splendid!' Juliana was genuinely delighted. 'But when do you think you will feel fit enough to make the journey to Falmouth?'

'It depends very much on how I travel. If I were to go by sea, I'm fit enough to go at any time. By road . . . ?' She shrugged. 'In three or four days' time, I suppose.'

'Shouldn't you check with the doctor first?' Humphrey asked hurriedly. 'He might not agree with you. After all, you were hurt quite badly. You don't want to hurry things.'

His concern was so transparent that Juliana was amused. Before leaving for London, Sir John had said he would be discussing his son's future with the Church authorities there. Humphrey expected to be called to London for an interview any day now. He was concerned lest he should be called away during Thomasina's absence from the Mount.

Unaware of the reason for his concern, Thomasina replied, 'The doctor has already told me I'm fit enough to do anything I feel up to.'

'Then, if you are agreeable, I'll have Abel, our senior boatman, take you to Falmouth tomorrow,' said Juliana. 'It isn't a terribly large boat, so I hope your recent dreadful experience won't make you nervous of sailing in it for such a distance.'

Despite her earlier confident assertion that she was fit enough to travel by sea, Thomasina felt a brief twinge of fear at the thought of setting out on a voyage from the place where so many of her former companions had died.

Putting such thoughts behind her, she asked, 'Isn't Abel the man who pulled me from the sea?'

'Yes,' Juliana replied. 'I was forgetting you have not met him yet. That is very remiss of me. From all I have heard, he put his own life at risk in order to rescue you from the combined efforts of mob and sea. Never mind, that can be put right tomorrow. Now . . . would it be inconvenient for you to remain in Falmouth for three nights, Thomasina?'

Thomasina felt it would suit her very well. She said so, adding that probably she could not complete her business in less time.

'Good! It is high time I got off the Mount for a while, and I will need new clothes to wear once the baby is born. I don't want to leave the children overnight without me, but even the shortest sea journey makes me sick. I'll travel in the coach to Falmouth on Friday and return the same day.' Juliana became suddenly enthusiastic, 'We can meet up at some point during the day, do some shopping together, then return late in the evening. How are the tides on Friday, Humphrey?'

Somewhat sulkily, because Juliana had suggested that Thomasina should stay away for three nights, he replied, 'You'll be fine if you leave early in the morning – but you'll need to return by seven-thirty in the evening, at the latest.'

'That is earlier than I had intended, but it should create no real problem. Splendid! Now, where shall we meet in Falmouth, Thomasina? How well do you know the town?'

3

Juliana had referred to the boat which was to convey Thomasina to Falmouth as being 'not very large'. Much to Thomasina's relief, she found it to be of sufficient size to require a crew of three to sail the vessel comfortably.

Abel Carter was in charge of the boat and Thomasina was introduced to him by Humphrey, who had taken it upon himself to rise early in order to accompany Thomasina to St Michael's Mount's small, sheltered harbour.

'I'm delighted to meet you at last,' Thomasina said to Abel. 'Everyone tells me I owe my life to you and that you rescued me at no small risk to yourself. I am very, very grateful.'

She found the St Michael's Mount boatman disturbingly attractive. Indeed, he was the only man to have seriously caught her attention since Jeffery.

The thought of her one-time lover provoked a stab of conscience within her. It was the first time Jeffery had come to mind for some time.

'You were unconscious for so long that it was rumoured you weren't going to pull through. I'm glad the rumours have proved to be unfounded.'

Listening to the exchange between Thomasina and the boatman, Humphrey felt a need to stamp his authority on the conversation.

'You be sure to carry Miss Thomasina safely to Falmouth, Abel. Take no chances with her. She is still not strong.'

'I am quite sure she's strong enough to tell me if she thinks I'm not handling the boat the way it should be done,' countered Abel. 'From what I've heard, she's sailed more miles than most sailors ever will.'

For a moment Thomasina was startled by his statement. Surely Juliana would not have gossiped about her to this man? Then she remembered she had talked of sailing the world to the maid who cleaned her room. She must have passed the details of the conversation on to Abel.

The maid had been a comely young Cornish girl. Thomasina wondered about the relationship between her and Abel.

'Are you certain you're going to be warm enough, Thomasina?' asked Humphrey anxiously. 'There's a stiff breeze blowing.'

'I'll be fine, Humphrey. The breeze means we'll get there more quickly.'

'How long will the voyage take?' Humphrey put the question to Abel.

'No longer than three hours – once we get under way,' Abel added pointedly.

'Then let's not waste any more of the day,' Thomasina said. 'I have a great deal to do once we arrive.'

Turning from the boatman, she said, 'Thank you for seeing me safely to the boat, Humphrey. It was very kind of you. I hope to see you again when I return on Friday.'

'You will, if I'm not called to London before then,' Humphrey replied unhappily.

'If you are, then I wish you good luck with your interview,' Thomasina spoke firmly, but kindly. 'May we go now, Abel?'

Without replying, Abel nodded to his crewmen. The boat was quickly cast off and the two men used oars to clear the harbour. Once beyond the break-water, sails were raised and the boat began slicing through the choppy water, quickly leaving the small harbour and a still-waving Humphrey behind them.

'The motion of the boat doesn't trouble you?' Abel put the question to Thomasina as the boat left the shelter of the Mount.

'It comes as naturally to me as walking,' Thomasina replied honestly. She found the wind on her face clean and fresh and the movement of the boat exhilarating.

'Then I think we might crowd on a little more sail and gain a knot or two.' Abel said.

'Would Humphrey approve of that?' Thomasina put the question to him with an air of mock concern.

Abel countered the question with one of his own. 'Is his approval important to you?'

It was an impertinent question. One that Abel

would not normally have put to a guest of Sir John St Aubyn and Juliana. However, he was aware that Thomasina did not belong to the aristocracy. Nor did he believe that she had a similar background to Juliana. Indeed, his observations, based upon a very brief acquaintanceship with her, tended to confirm the rumours spread by the servants who worked on the Mount.

Thomasina was a working-class girl.

Had it not been for the dramatic circumstances associated with her arrival on the Mount, she would never have seen the inside of the castle.

'His approval – or disapproval – matters neither way,' Thomasina replied. 'But I'm grateful for the kindness he and Juliana have both shown me.'

As an afterthought, she added, 'I'll always be grateful to you, too. I realise I owe you my life.'

Embarrassed by her words, Abel said, 'Had the tide been higher and the Mount cut off from the mainland, we'd have been able to save a whole lot more lives. I'm convinced the mainlanders killed as many as did the sea.'

Thomasina gave a brief shudder. 'Do you know how Captain Malachi Ellis – the one-legged sea captain – died?'

She asked the question, although she was not certain she wanted to know the answer.

'I'd say it was the sea. I found him the next morning when we went out to look for bodies.' Watching her as he spoke, he asked, 'Was he close to you?'

Thomasina nodded and repeated the story she had

told everyone else. 'He was my uncle – and a wonderful man.'

'Do you have any other relatives in Cornwall?'

'No one close enough for me to care if I ever see them again. I'm on my way to Falmouth now to speak to Malachi's solicitor, in the hope that I can settle his affairs.'

'Then you might need to call on me, to say what I know about finding his body. The solicitor will be able to confirm the details of my story with the coroner. He took a full description of all the victims who couldn't be named. I'll stay in Falmouth for a couple of hours, just in case.'

'Thank you.'

There was a silence between them for some minutes, each of them lost in their own thoughts. Then Thomasina asked, 'Are you related to the St Aubyns? You look a lot like Humphrey.'

One of the two crewmen who heard the question made a strangled sound deep in his throat, which might or might not have been a stifled laugh.

Abel glanced briefly at the man before replying, 'In all honesty, I'm not sure exactly who I'm related to – except for my grandmother. I live in her home, on the Mount. Mind you, some folk think they know more than I do. The truth is, I never knew the name of my father. My ma died without telling me, and if my grandmother knows she's never told me.'

'Oh! I'm sorry.' Thomasina realised her question had been both rude and tactless. Hastily she went on, 'I don't know whether it's best never to have known your father, or to lose him when you know and love him. My father was lost at sea some years ago. He set off in his own boat one day and was never seen again.'

Abel looked duly sympathetic. 'So the sea is pretty much in your blood?'

'Very much so. In fact, the last couple of years spent sailing with Malachi were the happiest of my life . . . but now he's gone.'

'What will you do when you've settled your uncle's affairs?'

'I don't know. Juliana has asked me to stay on at the Mount, at least until the baby is born.'

'You're honoured,' Abel said. 'She doesn't take readily to many people.'

'I can understand that, for she's in a very difficult situation.'

'Why?' asked Abel, unexpectedly sharply. 'She has a fine home – more than one, in fact – and wants for nothing. Although Sir John hasn't married her, she's known as M'Lady and her children have taken the St Aubyn name – as have the children by his earlier mistress, come to that. What's more, every one of the sons has been given a gentleman's education.'

There was an element of bitterness in his voice now. Thomasina thought it surprising that it was not more evident. She had no doubt there was St Aubyn blood in his veins. From the expressions on the faces of the other men in the boat, it seemed others thought so, too. It must have been a bitter pill for Abel to swallow when the other illegitimate children of Sir John were given the recognition of their father and a place in life that had been denied to him.

'Have you always been a boatman?'

She asked the question as a means of changing the subject. Most of the St Aubyn retainers seemed to have been employed on the Mount since childhood. She thought Abel was probably the same.

His reply surprised her.

'No, I served in the Royal Marines as an artilleryman, until I was wounded. Then, after spending some time at sea, I came back to look after my grandmother, and Sir John took me on as his senior boatman.'

Interested now, Thomasina asked, 'I know very little about the Marines, what did you do?'

'I was a gunner – a sergeant gunner – serving both on ships and on land. I was considered an expert gunlayer. I was the one who was in charge of the guns which sank the French ship that was carrying you as a prisoner.'

'Oh!'

Abel was quite obviously proud of the vital part he had played in sinking the French ship, but Thomasina's thoughts dwelled on the fact that it was Abel who was responsible for the death of Malachi.

Her silence lasted until they came within sight of Falmouth town.

4

Malachi's solicitor, Zachariah Bennett, who also represented Thomasina, listened to all that Abel had to tell him, shaking his head sadly when the St Michael's Mount boatman told of the conduct of those who waited to plunder and murder the survivors as they struggled desperately to save themselves from the doomed French ship.

'Sadly, there have always been those around our coasts who seek to benefit by such tragedies. Of course, this *was* a French warship, which had been bombarding the coastal communities in the vicinity. It could be argued there was some justification for taking revenge upon those believed responsible for such an unnecessary act of war.'

Pushing his spectacles higher on his thin nose, the diminutive solicitor added, 'I am very grateful to you for coming to see me and acquainting me with the sad fate of Captain Ellis, Mr Carter. I had already learned of the sinking of the *Melanie Jane*. The incident was witnessed by a number of fishing vessels in the area. However, when nothing was subsequently heard of the crew, it was assumed they had been taken to France, possibly in another French vessel.'

'Miss Varcoe is the only survivor from the ship – and has only very recently recovered from her experiences,' Abel said.

'Thank you again, Mr Carter. Perhaps you will be kind enough to come with me and make a signed declaration to my clerk in the outer office. I will make arrangements to obtain a report from the coroner in order to satisfy the legal requirements in this sad matter. If you will kindly remain here, Miss Varcoe, we have a few business matters to discuss . . .'

With a glance at Thomasina, Abel stood up to follow the solicitor from the room. As he reached the door, she called out, 'If you are finished before I am, will you wait for me, please, Abel? There are a few things I'd like you to take back to the Mount for me.'

A few minutes later Zachariah Bennett returned to the office. Seating himself behind his desk once more, he examined her over the top of his spectacles in a manner which had become familiar to her.

'Reading between the lines of that young man's story, I feel you probably owe your life to him.'

'I do,' Thomasina replied. 'He put his own life at risk to save me.'

'You will soon have the means to reward him, if you so wish, Miss Varcoe.'

'From the insurance money, you mean?'

'That will, of course, be quite substantial, but the investments you so wisely made on Captain Ellis's recommendation have also paid handsomely.'

'I owe Malachi such a lot,' Thomasina spoke emotionally.

'Far more than you know . . .' Zachariah Bennett hesitated for a moment. 'I shouldn't really be telling you this until all the legal requirements have been complied with, Miss Varcoe, but you will soon have rather more money than you anticipate. You see, when Captain Ellis was last in this office he made a will, naming you as his sole beneficiary.'

'What exactly does that mean?' Thomasina looked at him uncertainly.

'It means that you will soon be a wealthy young woman, Miss Varcoe. Indeed, a *very* wealthy young woman. Captain Ellis left everything he owned to you.'

'That's typical of Malachi's kindness,' Thomasina said emotionally, 'but I'd happily forgo all the money to have Malachi and the crew alive and the *Melanie Jane* still afloat.'

'Captain Ellis was a fine man. A *splendid* man. He will be sadly missed. He was also far more organised than most sea captains. There will be a number of claims to be settled with owners of the cargo, but all his affairs have been left in good order. He has also kept the *Melanie Jane*'s insurance at a level commensurate with the increasing value of the vessel.'

Leaning back in his chair, Zachariah Bennett looked at her in silence for some minutes, before adding, 'I have a complete list of Captain Ellis's assets and will give them to you in the fullness of time. Meanwhile, I will keep you informed of my progress. You have no immediate marriage plans, I take it?'

The question took Thomasina by surprise. She shook her head vigorously, 'None whatsoever.'

'Good. A husband tends to complicate things when a young woman inherits such a large sum of money. There are also a number of unscrupulous men of breeding eager to marry wealthy women, whatever their age – tempting them with social status, or perhaps even a minor title. Should such a man appear in your life, Miss Varcoe, I will be happy to have enquiries made into his background, on your behalf.'

Despite the sadness she felt at the reason for being in the solicitor's office, Thomasina smiled. 'Thank you very much for your concern, Mr Bennett. I will remember it, should an offer of marriage come my way.'

'Then it only remains for me to bid you good day, Miss Varcoe. I trust you will allow me to extend to you the service I like to feel we always gave to Captain Ellis. Should you have need of money for an urgent major project, before the estate is settled, I am quite certain we can be of assistance.'

'Thank you again, Mr Bennett. Malachi always spoke well of you and I trusted his judgement implicitly. I am most grateful to you.'

'Will you be staying in Falmouth for a while?' Zachariah Bennett put the question to her as they walked from his office.

'Only for a couple of days, at Captain Malachi's

house, then I'll be returning to the Mount as a companion for Miss Juliana. At least until her next child is born. You can send any letters for me either to the Mount or to Malachi's house . . . I'll have to get used to calling it *my* house now, I suppose. I shall call in there from time to time, until I've decided what I'm going to do. But I'm glad you've reminded me. Do you have a key to the house? I lost mine when the *Melanie Jane* was abandoned.'

'Of course. My clerk will give it to you.'

When she had the key, and while they waited for Abel to complete his statement to the clerk, the solicitor said quietly, 'Sad though this occasion is – and I realise it is a most unhappy time for you – I trust you will think about the opportunity that Captain Ellis has given to you. It is one rarely given to any young woman. The chance to prove you can succeed in commerce, should you so wish. I feel you will, having already proven that you can compete in what is ostensibly a man's world.'

'I will need to give it a great deal of thought,' Thomasina said. 'I no longer have Malachi to advise me.'

Peering over his spectacles, the solicitor said, 'You were indeed fortunate to have the advice and guidance of Captain Ellis, Miss Varcoe, but he considered you a quite exceptional young woman. I have every confidence that you will make the most of the opportunity you have been given – for Captain Ellis's sake, if for no other reason. Now, it would appear that Mr Carter has completed his declaration.'

Holding out his hand, he said, 'I look forward to our

next meeting – and to hearing of any plans you might
have made by then.'

5

When Thomasina and Abel left the solicitor's offices, she was still thinking of all that Zachariah Bennett had told her. Abel broke into her thoughts to remind her that she had said there were things she wanted taken back to the Mount.

'Yes, that's right. At the moment I'm wearing clothes that Juliana has found for me. If you have the time to come to Malachi's house and take a few clothes back to the Mount for me, I'd be very grateful.'

If Abel was surprised that Thomasina's clothes should be in Malachi's home, he made no comment on the fact. 'I've got all the time in the world. Miss Juliana has put the boat and its crew at your disposal for the day.'

Soon they were walking together along Falmouth's narrow streets, climbing the hill away from the busy harbour. For a while the steepness of the incline made the conservation of breath more important than communication.

When they turned to follow a street along the side of the hill, Abel asked, 'Were you able to get all your business completed, back there at the solicitor's?'

'Only some of it,' Thomasina replied. 'I'll need to call in to see Mr Bennett again before I leave Falmouth. It's also going to be necessary for me to come back here once or twice in the next month or so. It would probably be more sensible to remain here, but I've promised Juliana I'll stay with her until after the baby's born.'

'You can always travel by sea when you think you need to come back here,' Abel pointed out. 'As long as wind and weather are right, there's no reason why you shouldn't be able to leave the Mount in the early morning, spend six or seven hours in Falmouth and be back in time for dinner.'

'With you in charge of the boat, of course?' said Thomasina, glancing at him.

'Of course! I couldn't guarantee anyone else getting you to Falmouth and back in the same time.'

Thomasina smiled, but for all his apparent boastfulness, she conceded that he was probably right. Abel was a natural seaman. He had handled the boat with considerable skill on the way from the Mount that morning. She felt his talents were wasted as a St Aubyn boatman.

They chatted quite happily as they continued on their way to the house of the late sea captain. Not until they reached it did Thomasina's mood undergo a change.

Hesitating as she was about to insert the key in the lock, she said unhappily, 'It's going to be strange not to have Malachi call out to me as I go upstairs.'

'Does no one else live in the house?' Abel asked.

'No. Malachi employed an elderly woman to come in and clean twice a week while we were at sea and every day when we were here. Her husband looked after the garden. I don't know whether she'll want to carry on, now Malachi's no longer alive. I suppose I'll gradually take over the whole house, instead of using only the first floor. But I'll stay up there for a while, at least.'

Her words answered a question that Abel had been curious about, but would have left unasked. Thomasina lived in a separate part of the house.

He had another question. 'Is the house yours now?'

'Malachi's will hasn't been read yet,' Thomasina's reply was cautious, 'but Mr Bennett says I can stay here.' Squaring her shoulders she said, 'Let's go in.'

Turning the key in the lock, she pushed open the heavy door. Stepping through the doorway, she immediately stopped, her nostrils assailed by the heavy aroma of Malachi's tobacco smoke. It was stale, but unmistakable.

She remained motionless for so long that Abel, standing behind her, asked anxiously, 'Are you all right?'

'I will be. Memories of Malachi came flooding back when I walked through the doorway, that's all. I . . . I half-expected Malachi to call out to me, as he always did when he heard me coming in.'

Turning to look at him apologetically, she managed the semblance of a smile. 'I'm all right now.'

Leading the way to the stairs, which rose from the hallway, she resisted an urge to look in through the doorway to the study where Malachi would sit surrounded by charts and mementoes from his many voyages.

'Apart from the *Melanie Jane*, this is the only home I've known for the last couple of years. I wouldn't have had even this, had it not been for Malachi's kindness.'

Walking up the stairs behind her, Abel said sympathetically, 'You were very fond of him, weren't you?'

'He was a great sailor and a wonderful man.' Thomasina spoke feelingly. 'He's probably had a greater influence on my life than any other person – more, even, than my father.'

Consciously shaking off the melancholy that threatened to overwhelm her, she pointed to a small trunk on the landing. 'If I put some clothes in that, do you think you'd be able to carry it back to the boat?'

'Easily.'

There were a great many questions Abel would have liked to ask Thomasina about the life she had led with Captain Malachi Ellis, but this was not the right moment. If she thought him presumptuous it could destroy any chance he might have of getting to know her better – and he had already decided that was what he wanted to do.

*   *   *

Thomasina and Abel remained in the house together for almost an hour. When the clothes she wanted to wear at the Mount had been placed in the trunk, she made a pot of tea for them.

As they sat drinking in the kitchen, Abel felt an unaccustomed sense of cosiness. It bordered on a domestic situation that was strange to him and tended to make him somewhat shy. As a result, it was left to Thomasina to ask questions in order to keep the conversation from flagging.

She learned a great deal about Abel and his background. Far more, perhaps, than he realised he was telling her.

He had obviously enjoyed serving with the Marines – the 'Royal' being added to their title in the year 1802, whilst Abel was serving with them.

After service at Aboukir at the turn of the century, he had transferred to the Royal Marines Artillery in 1804, seeing fierce action, first in South America and, later, in the Dardenelles.

Then, when his battery was sent to Spain, Abel received a wound which resulted in his discharge from the Royal Marines. Although he quickly recovered, he would always walk with a slight limp, but this did not prevent him from going to sea for a few years before returning to the Mount.

'Are you fully recovered from the wound now?' Thomasina asked solicitously.

Abel grinned. 'I can forget it for much of the time, but it forecasts bad weather far more accurately than a piece of seaweed.'

Suddenly embarrassed at having chattered about

himself for so long, he said, 'I'd better be getting your things to the boat, before the others fear I've run off somewhere and leave for home without me.'

'Not to mention a certain young maid who will be anxious if you haven't returned by the time you're expected.'

Thomasina was aware that she was being obvious in her attempt to establish the relationship that existed between Abel and the Mount housemaid who often talked to her about him.

Aware of this too, Abel was delighted. 'You must mean Carrie? Yes, she'll start worrying if we don't return on time – but it won't be me she's concerned about, even though she's my cousin. Young Perran is one of my crewmen and she is due to marry him later this year. As we both have the same grandmother, she's often at the house. That's how I hear much of what goes on up at the castle. She's a great one for gossip – so be warned!'

Far more pleased than she ought to have been at the discovery that there was nothing between Abel and the pretty young housemaid, Thomasina said, 'She'll find little enough to gossip about as far as I'm concerned. I've been far too ill to provide anyone with any scandal.'

'Don't you believe it!' Abel declared. 'The very manner of your arrival caused more excitement than the Mount folk have had for many years. Then, of course, there's Master Humphrey. They do say he's taken quite a shine to you.'

'You mean, *Carrie* says so,' Thomasina retorted. 'You've already said she's a gossip.'

'Perhaps, but it's well known that Humphrey is an incurable romantic – and he's a good catch for any girl.'

'You're the second person to describe him to me as "a good catch",' declared Thomasina. 'Well, as far as I'm concerned "good catches" are for fishermen. I'm not on the look-out for a husband!'

Grinning at her, Abel said, 'I've heard that making such a positive statement is tempting fate. However, it's time I set off back to the Mount.'

Reaching down, he lifted the small trunk and swung it up on to a shoulder. Shrugging it to a comfortable position, he said, 'Enjoy your stay in Falmouth. I hope we'll meet up again when you return to the Mount.'

Watching from a window as Abel walked down the hill from the house carrying the trunk on his shoulder, Thomasina decided that if fate was going to tempt her with anyone, it might do worse than put Abel her way.

6

Although Thomasina had told Abel that the elderly cleaner came to the house during the absence at sea of Malachi and herself, in fact she cleaned only the part of the house occupied by Malachi.

She had been told to leave the first floor. Nevertheless, Thomasina had locked her clothes cupboards and hidden the keys, just in case the cleaner decided to be nosey. The discovery of men's and women's clothes in the flat would have been certain to arouse her curiosity.

As a result of this ruling, Thomasina's rooms had gathered a great deal of dust. There were also one or two items that needed washing. She spent the remainder of that day attending to the chores, but went to bed early, aware that she had not yet fully recovered from the wrecking of the French man-o'-war.

The following day was fine, so she spent a couple of hours in the garden, weeding and generally tidying up. Later she went downstairs to Malachi's rooms to sort through his possessions and clothes and decide what should be done with them.

Reminders of Malachi were everywhere. They ranged from the rack containing some of his tobacco pipes to a spare peg-leg propped against the wall in a corner of his study.

Thomasina was able to cope with these items, but then she entered his bedroom. After glancing in his wardrobe, she turned to see Malachi staring down at her, with his familiar quiet smile.

It was an oil-painting for which she had persuaded him to sit and which had been her Christmas present to him, only months before.

The portrait was such a remarkable likeness that it completely unnerved her. Fleeing from the room, she ran back upstairs. When she came to a halt in her own sitting-room, she was trembling.

Thomasina told herself she was behaving in a ridiculous fashion, yet she knew that she would not be able to return to Malachi's rooms again that evening. She did not even feel comfortable remaining in the house alone.

As night descended upon the town, bringing with it a cool, damp mist, she decided she would go to the Falmouth waterfront, dressed once more as a young man. There she would seek the noise and warmth of a harbour-front tavern.

Dressed in male clothing, Thomasina felt somehow more certain of herself. Less vulnerable. Looking in the long, hallway mirror, she was satisfied that she would once more be accepted as a young man.

Letting herself out of the house, Thomasina made her way down the hill, heading for the Ship Inn, the tavern where she had first met Malachi. Although usually busy, it had a reputation for being less rowdy than many other inns and taverns in the town.

Entering the crowded taproom, it seemed to her that the Ship Inn was in danger of losing its reputation. Crowded with men, mainly seamen, there was an inexplicable air of anticipation in the room.

Two serving girls were having to force their way through the crowd to carry out their duties. Perspiring visibly, they warded off the attentions of the seamen, who made the most of the opportunity afforded by the crowded conditions to take liberties with the hard-working women.

Thomasina decided it would be quicker to obtain her own beer. This she did, purchasing a tankard of small beer from the leather-aproned landlord drawing drinks to order from a selection of barrels. He and the barrels were separated from the customers by a fold-down counter, upon which he placed the overflowing tankards.

When she had been served, Thomasina located a space at a table occupied by a number of men whose dress identified them as sea captains, or perhaps senior mates. Carrying her beer with difficulty through the crowd, she made her way to their table.

'Do you mind if I sit here?'

Thomasina put the question to a bearded, pipe-smoking seafarer seated at the end of a long bench stool, where she thought there was room for one more.

Without replying, he moved along the bench to give her a little more space, others on the stool doing the same.

'I've never known it so busy in here,' she commented as she settled herself.

'Then you'll not be here hoping to find a berth on Hearle's ship then?'

At the mention of the name Thomasina started involuntarily, going cold for a moment and spilling some of her beer on the table. 'Hearle? You're not talking of Sir Charles Hearle?'

She thought the glances exchanged by some of the mariners at the sound of his name contained a hint of contempt.

'That's the man. He's interviewing prospective crewmen in a private room. You know him?'

'I know *of* him.' Thomasina's reply was cautious, unsure of her company. 'But I've never thought of him as a sailing man.'

'Neither has anyone else,' said another of the men at the table. 'Until now he's contented himself with playing at soldiering with his militiamen – and he's made a mess of that, whenever he's been called upon to carry out more than an hour or two's drilling.'

'He'll be no better as a ship-owner, you mark my words,' declared another of the seafaring men. 'Why, a ship's cat knows more about sailing than Sir Charles Hearle.'

His companions chuckled. Satisfied that the men at the table regarded Sir Charles no more highly than she did herself, she asked, 'Then why has he bought a ship – and where has the money come from? The last I heard, he'd drunk or gambled all his money away and was being supported by an aunt.'

'That's about right,' said the man seated beside her. 'The aunt was Harriet Vincent, of Trebene. She died some months ago, only weeks after her husband. The house and lands have gone to their son, Francis, but Sir Charles was left enough money for him to prove just how foolish he is. Someone has managed to convince him there's a fortune to be made in the shipping business. He's bought a ship that's been laid up in the Fal for nigh on two years. The packet service to Corunna has just been resumed and, thanks to another relative in the Postal Service, he's hoping to secure a contract with 'em.'

'He'll not get it,' said another of the men at the table. 'Even if he did, he wouldn't keep it. He'll not have his ship for long, either, especially if he takes on some of the men I've seen in here today. I wouldn't have them on board a ship of mine if they were kept in chains.'

The others at the table nodded in agreement. Thomasina frowned. The course taken by Sir Charles Hearle was something she had considered doing with some of the money she had at her disposal. 'There's money to be made carrying cargoes, surely, especially between here and Spain? Napoleon's had the country closed to us for so long that they'll be eager to trade with us.'

'Of course they will,' agreed the bearded seaman. 'But Spain has a merchant fleet as big as our own and they've spent recent years blockaded by the Royal

Navy. They'll be falling over themselves to carry cargoes once more. As a result their prices will be keener than ours, you can safely wager on that.' He looked at Thomasina with increased interest. 'But what would a young lad like you know about such things?'

'I sailed with Captain Malachi Ellis,' said Thomasina proudly. 'I learned more from him in two years than most seagoing men learn in a lifetime . . .'

Thomasina broke off, aware she suddenly had the full attention of her companions.

'You've sailed with Malachi? Then you'll be worth two of any other seamen to a good captain,' said one of them, removing a pipe from his mouth. 'But we won't be seeing him around for a while. I heard his ship was sunk by a French man-o'-war. He'll be a prisoner in France right now.'

The last thing Thomasina wanted was to talk about Malachi, fearing that she might break down, but she felt she had to put these men right.

'The French ship that took him prisoner was crippled by gunners at St Michael's Mount. It came ashore on the rocks. Malachi was among those who died. The man who took his body from the sea was in Falmouth today making a statement to his solicitor.'

The seafarers about the table looked shocked. 'Are you sure of this, boy? This man – the one who claims to have taken Malachi from the sea – could he have been mistaken?'

Thomasina shook her head. 'I'm afraid not. No one would be happier than me, were it otherwise.'

She hoped they would soon stop talking about

Malachi – and at that moment came an unexpected diversion. The inn door was flung open and someone shouted, 'Quick! The press-gang . . . !'

The cry created pandemonium inside the crowded taproom. All thoughts of being taken on as a crewman for Sir Charles Hearle were forgotten as men sought to evade the very different recruiting techniques of His Majesty's navy.

'Quick, lad – under the table. Get tight up against the wall. We'll bunch up and hide you. The press-gang won't trouble us, and they won't see you in this light . . .'

Thomasina dived beneath the table and scrambled to the wall, crouching as close to it as she could. A moment later her tankard was passed down to her.

All she could see from her hiding-place was a mêlée of feet and legs beyond the table under which she was hiding. The patrons of the Ship Inn seemed to be running this way and that in a bid to escape from the press-gang. However, for all but the boldest and most determined, their attempts to escape were in vain.

The press-gang was unusually large, made up of sailors and marines from a holding ship moored off the town. They were familiar with Falmouth and much of what went on here. They knew that seamen were being recruited at the Ship Inn – and experienced sailors were what they were looking for. They had placed a strong guard on all the inn's exit doors before entering the building.

Some of those inside *did* succeed in making good their escape, but only by showing great resourcefulness. They ran upstairs, through rooms occupied by startled residents, and dropped out of any window they believed to be some distance from the well-guarded doors.

It was some time before things quietened down inside the inn. Just as she felt she might come out from beneath the table, Thomasina found herself staring at the white hose and buckled shoes of a naval officer, visible between the legs of two of the seafaring men who had remained seated at the table throughout the fracas. She froze instantly.

'Good evening, gentlemen. I trust I and my men have not disturbed your drinking too much?'

'It would take more than a press-gang to do that,' came the reply from the man who had been seated beside Thomasina. 'Most of us here have served in the King's navy and we're all too old to be taken now.'

'I have no doubt you served His Majesty well,' said the officer. 'Kindly allow me to buy you all drinks – for past services. Landlord, drinks here, if you please. This coin should take care of it . . .'

Thomasina heard the coin thrown on to the wooden counter in front of the barrels. Then the naval officer said, 'Goodbye, gentlemen. We have taken more than our quota of men for tonight. We won't be troubling you again.'

She listened as the footsteps crossed the flagstone floor to the door. A few seconds later the bearded seafarer who had suggested her hiding place smiled down at her. 'It's all right, lad, you can come out now.'

Crawling clear of the table, Thomasina returned the smile and the seafarer called, 'Landlord, bring another for the lad. He's got something to celebrate. He came within a hair's-breadth of being carried off to serve His Majesty. The lieutenant's money will stand another beer, I don't doubt.'

'It's not going to make up for all the custom I've lost as a result of his press-gang, that's certain,' grumbled the landlord. Nevertheless, he topped up another pewter tankard and the two serving girls carried them to the table.

'The last person to save me from a press-gang was Malachi, in Bermuda . . .' Thomasina said.

She was telling the seafarers of the incident in question when two men entered the taproom from another room.

One was Sir Charles Hearle – and he was angry. For a moment Thomasina froze, but he was not looking in her direction.

'Damn the navy,' he was saying to his companion. 'How am I supposed to know whether or not I have a crew? They might all have been carried off, for all I know.'

'We'll manage,' replied the other man. 'I'll be able to make up the numbers when we're taking cargo on board. There are always seamen hanging about the docks looking for a berth.'

'Aye, and most would cut their best friend's throat for a shilling or two.'

The opinion was voiced by one of the men at the table with Thomasina. He spoke quietly so that only his companions might hear. 'Only a captain like Silas Carberry would even think of taking on such men as crew.'

'He and Hearle deserve each other,' said another of the seafarers, equally quietly. 'I gave Carberry his marching orders when he served with me as a second mate. He's a drunkard and a bully. Those he signed on, who've been taken by the press-gang instead, can consider themselves lucky. They'll enjoy a better life on a man-o'-war than on a ship with Carberry as captain. They'll be a sight safer, too – war or no war.'

The table at which the seafarers and Thomasina were seated was the only one in the room fully occupied. Few had more than two or three men at them, all too old to have run from the press-gang, even had they needed to.

Around the room the two serving girls were picking up overturned stools, benches and chairs and replacing them at empty tables.

When she first saw Sir Charles Hearle, Thomasina experienced the same chill of fear and hatred she had known at all their previous meetings. The fear increased when he stopped talking to his companion and made his way to the table at which she was seated.

He stood for a few moments, looking from one man to another, and Thomasina realised that his flushed face was not due entirely to anger.

'I'm looking for experienced men to crew my ship . . .' he began.

'Then it's no use talking to us.' Sir Charles Hearle was interrupted by one of the seafarers. 'Not unless you want a crew made up of captains, some of whom should have retired years ago.'

The amusement which greeted the words caused Sir

Charles to flush even more deeply than before. 'I'm not suggesting you sign on personally. I ask only that if you know of any young seamen looking for a ship, you tell them I'm paying top wages for the right men.'

'There are some things more important to a man than money,' responded the seagoing man who had just spoken. 'You ask Mr Carberry. I told him what they were many years ago – when I threw him off my ship for ignoring them.'

Sir Charles Hearle's befuddled state became apparent when he looked from the man who had spoken to Silas Carberry. Deciding not to pursue the matter, he now turned his attention to Thomasina.

'You, lad. Have you ever been to sea?'

'Indeed I have, sir – have you?'

Thomasina's confidence had returned when it became evident that in the dim light of the inn room Sir Charles Hearle had not recognised her.

Unable to decide if Thomasina was being impertinent, the new ship-owner said, 'Whether or not I've been to sea doesn't matter. Do you want to be taken on?'

'Would I be paid as a full deckhand, or as a boy?'

Thomasina was beginning to enjoy herself.

'You'll be paid what you're worth,' Silas Carberry said, aware – as Sir Charles was not – that Thomasina was being deliberately insolent.

'I doubt it,' said Thomasina. 'When I sailed with Captain Malachi Ellis, he would tell me I was worth my weight in gold.'

The seafarers around the table chuckled and Carberry scowled. To Sir Charles he said, 'Come along. We're wasting our time here. We'll not find a crew among old men who should have been paid off years ago, and a boy with more lip than a wash-jug.'

Silas Carberry turned to go, but Sir Charles was peering drunkenly at Thomasina, a frown on his face. 'We've met before . . . where was it?'

Trying hard to hide her alarm and fearing that she might have gone too far with her insolence, Thomasina said, 'Right here in Falmouth. You were chasing miners who were trying to prevent corn being taken from Cornwall. Your men wanted to stop me and Captain Malachi getting to our ship. You didn't succeed.'

Sir Charles was not convinced of the accuracy of her explanation, but he had been drinking too much to argue with it. Turning away, he followed the captain of his vessel from the Ship Inn.

Later that night, on the way back to the house, Thomasina thought over the incidents of the evening. The confrontation with Sir Charles Hearle worried her. If he ever recognised her as 'Ethel', the housemaid he had raped when she worked for his aunt, a great many awkward questions might be asked about the manner in which she had acquired the money with which she had bought a partnership with Malachi.

She found some small consolation in the knowledge that each of the captains who had been her drinking partners at the Ship Inn had told her there would always be a place on their ships, should she choose to go back to sea once more.

7

Thomasina was waiting outside the Packet Inn when the St Aubyn carriage arrived in Falmouth. Juliana climbed stiffly and heavily from the carriage. She showed no signs of the enthusiasm she had evinced for the shopping expedition when it had first been proposed at the Mount.

Her first words to Thomasina were, 'I wish I had your sea-legs, Thomasina. Travelling here by carriage has left me black and blue. The coachman assures me he followed the roads, but I swear it would have been a more comfortable journey had we travelled in a straight line, across country.'

'Would you like to take some tea before we go shopping?' Thomasina felt concerned for Juliana. Heavily pregnant, she was supporting her bulging stomach as though fearing that the baby was likely to drop into the world at any moment.

'Yes. Yes, I would – perhaps something a little stronger, too. Where shall we go? Inside the inn?'

Thomasina had already peeped inside the building and decided it was perfectly respectable. She said so now.

'Good, then let's go inside. The coachman can find something for the horses and wait for us here. God! I really do need something to revive me – and quickly.'

Juliana linked her arm through Thomasina's and the two women entered the inn. The landlord had seen the carriage arrive and recognised the crest painted on its door. Hurrying to meet them, he escorted them to an alcove at the side of the dining area. Here, fortified by a large brandy, cake and a pot of tea, Juliana gradually regained her balance and composure. It was not long before she declared herself ready to face the shopkeepers of Falmouth.

They had not been shopping for long when Thomasina began to wonder whether the shopkeepers were ready for the mistress of St Michael's Mount. She found Juliana's method of shopping quite amazing.

Although Juliana had already given birth to eight children and must have amassed a mountain of baby clothes, it seemed to Thomasina that she was intent on buying a new outfit for every day of the unborn child's life!

She also purchased a great many items of clothing for herself, in anticipation of the day when her figure would have returned to normal.

She paid cash for very few of her purchases. In

the vast majority of shops Juliana told them to bill
Sir John St Aubyn, directing that her purchases be
taken to the Packet Inn and placed on the St Aubyn
carriage.

Such was the esteem in which the St Aubyn name
was held that not once did a shopkeeper question the
arrangement.

Eventually Thomasina found Juliana's enthusiasm
for shopping contagious. She bought more clothes
than at any time in her life. She too delighted in
having them delivered to the St Aubyn carriage,
although in her case she was required to pay cash
for her purchases.

If Juliana was surprised that Thomasina had such
sums of money readily available, she made no comment.

After they had both bought what Thomasina considered to be a phenomenal quantity of goods, the
two women returned to the Packet Inn for a late
lunch. Here Juliana ensured that the St Aubyn's
coachman had safely locked away their purchases
in the secure box situated beneath his carriage seat.

In the dining-room they occupied the same alcove
as before. They were settling themselves when
Thomasina was startled to see Sir Charles Hearle and
Captain Silas Carberry passing through the dining-
room, heading for the door.

She and Juliana were wearing hats, which helped
hide their faces to a greater or lesser degree. Juliana's
was a wide-brimmed hat of silk and lace, which
she had told Thomasina was currently the height of
fashion in London.

Thomasina wore a more traditional poke-bonnet, which had lace and ribbon trimmings – and a short veil. It had been purchased only that day. She had found it so appealing that she insisted upon wearing it there and then.

She was grateful for the veil when Sir Charles Hearle looked up from the conversation he was holding with Captain Carberry and caught sight of Juliana. He immediately changed direction. Leaving his companion behind, he headed towards the two women.

Stopping just short of the alcove, he bowed to Juliana. After only a moment's hesitation, he inclined his head briefly to Thomasina, too. Returning his full attention to the mistress of St Michael's Mount, he said, 'Good day to you, ma'am, I am delighted and surprised to find you here, in Falmouth. I trust you are well?'

'Very well, thank you, Sir Charles.'

Thomasina had the impression that Juliana was saying no more than courtesy demanded from her.

'Sir John, and your family – they are well too?'

'All well, thank you.'

Now Thomasina knew for certain that Juliana was merely being polite.

'I trust Sir John will look kindly upon my request, in due course.'

'Sir John was absent from the Mount when your letter was delivered, Sir Charles. He is still away. It will receive his attention when he returns.'

'Of course.' Sir Charles switched his glance to Thomasina, but could see no more than a vague outline of her face beneath the veil of the bonnet.

He returned his attention to Juliana. 'If I may be of any service to you while you are in Falmouth, pray consider me your willing servant, ma'am.'

'Thank you, Sir Charles. Good day to you.'

'Good day to you, ma'am . . . Miss.'

Giving the two women a half-bow, Sir Charles Hearle turned away and made his way across the room to rejoin Captain Carberry. After an exchange of words, the latter glanced across the room to the two women, then both men left the inn together.

'I make no apology for not introducing you to Sir Charles,' said Juliana, when the two men had gone. 'I can't stand the man. He's a notorious roué of the worst possible type. A cousin of mine found herself alone with him some time ago and, had she pursued charges, Sir Charles would have been transported. Fortunately for him, she felt that the shame of having others know what had happened to her would have been a worse experience than letting him get away with what he did – or tried to do.'

'Malachi warned me about him,' said Thomasina, wishing she could tell Juliana of her own ordeal at the hands of Sir Charles. 'He had nothing but contempt for Sir Charles Hearle – and I valued Malachi's opinion more highly than that of any man I've ever known.'

'He seems to have been a good judge of character,' Juliana agreed. 'Sir Charles has applied to Sir John for permission to use the harbour at the Mount to load and discharge cargoes. I've suggested that permission is refused, but he probably won't take any notice of my wishes. Sir John is a very understanding man in many ways, but he believes that personal opinion should have no part in business. He will probably allow Sir Charles to use the harbour at the Mount, although if I have my way he will charge higher dues than he takes from the other ship-owners. However, I have not come to Falmouth to waste time talking of Sir Charles Hearle. We will order lunch, then might have time for a little more shopping before we need to set off to return to the Mount.'

Her words took Thomasina by surprise. 'Shouldn't we leave straight away for the Mount? Abel said . . .'

'Abel is boatman to the St Aubyn family, not its guardian.'

Juliana spoke so sharply that Thomasina looked at her in surprise.

Aware that her reply had been sharper than she had intended, Juliana explained, 'Abel occasionally tends to take too much upon himself. He means well, I have no doubt, but it can be annoying.'

Thomasina said nothing. Juliana's resentment of Abel was quite unreasonable. It was possible that she, too, was aware of the rumours about his parentage.

'Now, what shall we eat? When I arrived in Falmouth this morning I felt quite certain I would not be able to look at food for days, but all our shopping has given me quite an appetite . . .'

8

By the time the two women ended their lunch even Juliana was forced to admit that more shopping was out of the question. It was now almost four o'clock in the afternoon. The St Aubyn coachman had twice looked in through the doorway of the dining-room at the two women, his anxiety plain to see.

'I suppose we should start back,' said Juliana, looking unusually petulant. 'Being an island for much of the day is one of the Mount's major drawbacks. Never mind, Thomasina, once the baby is born and life returns to normal, you and I must go on a *real* shopping spree. Have you ever been to London . . . ?'

When the carriage set off, the coachman drove at breakneck speed, soundly cursing any waggoner who did not move to one side quickly enough to allow the carriage to pass. Inside, the two women were bounced about alarmingly until, risking injury by putting her head outside the window, Juliana ordered the coachman not to drive the horses so hard.

'We need to make up time, if you don't want to take a boat across to the Mount in the dark, ma'am. We're running late.'

'The child that I'm expecting will be running early if you don't do as you're told and slow down.'

Thomasina remembered what Humphrey had said about the need to be back on the Mount before seven-thirty, but she remained quiet. Although she felt sympathy for Juliana's state of extreme discomfort, she was concerned about the crossing from Marazion to what would probably be an island by the time they arrived.

It was dusk when they reached Marazion and the carriage came to a halt at the water's edge. The castle atop the Mount was a dark, irregular shape, silhouetted against a cloud-patterned sky, tinged by the embers of the sun that had sunk beneath the horizon.

The colours of the sky were reflected in the water that stretched between land and island.

'There we are, ma'am,' said the coachman, trying not to sound smug. 'I knew we wouldn't make it in time. Shall I go off and find a boat?'

'No!' replied Juliana. Her reply was made firmer by the knowledge that it was her fault they had arrived at Marazion later than had been intended. 'The causeway can only have been covered for a short while. Surely you can get to the Mount? It will take only a few minutes.'

Thoroughly alarmed, Thomasina protested. 'Surely that would be very dangerous – especially now, in this light.'

'Sir John would dismiss me on the spot if he knew I had taken such a chance, ma'am. I might risk it in daylight, but now . . . ! I'll go and look for a boat, if you like, but if you don't want to make use of it I suggest it would be better for you to remain in Marazion for the night.'

'I'm not asking for your suggestions,' Juliana retorted angrily. 'Only your expertise – such as it is. I feel ill enough as it is after enduring the abominable ride here. I have no intention of making things worse by crossing to the Mount in a boat. As for remaining here . . . I have children in the castle who will be waiting for me. If you won't drive me, then I will take the reins myself and *you* can spend the night here. If I have to take such measures you needn't bother coming to work in the morning.'

She had placed the coachman in an impossible situation. He turned to Thomasina in near-despair. 'I've tried my best, you'll bear witness to that, Miss.'

'He's right, Juliana, it *is* far too dangerous.'

'Then you can stay in Marazion, too. *I*'ll take the carriage myself . . .'

'That won't be necessary,' said the coachman unhappily. 'I'll attempt the crossing – but only to prevent you from trying to do it yourself.'

'Are you coming?' The question was put very stiffly to Thomasina and she remembered Humphrey telling her that Juliana could be impossibly stubborn on occasions. Even more so if opposed.

'Of course I am – but I still believe the coachman is right.'

Juliana ignored her. Instead, she snapped at the coachman, 'Well, what are you waiting for? The longer you wait, the deeper the water will be.'

Making no reply, the coachman shook the reins and the coach swayed from the road, down the slope that led to the sea-covered causeway.

The horses were as reluctant as the coachman to attempt the crossing. He needed to bring his whip into play before they could be coaxed to step into the featureless sea.

The coachman had crossed the causeway by day and night on many occasions. He knew the route, guided by the lights of certain cottages situated around the harbour. He also knew there was a particularly dangerous spot where the causeway narrowed, just short of the harbour wall. It was this that was to prove the undoing of the coach and those it carried.

Juliana had been right about one thing. The water was not particularly deep, although the causeway dipped slightly as they neared its narrowest point. Here the water was axle-deep. There was also a slight swell running. This, coupled with the meeting of two currents at the spot, meant that the actual depth of the water was unpredictable.

The two horses were actually on the narrow section of causeway when the two currents came together, accompanied by a swell. Suddenly the horses were chest-deep and the coach was lifted by the water and swung to one side.

The coachman tried desperately to keep the horses on a safe course, but the floating carriage pulled them askew. Then one of the horses slipped from the causeway.

Frantically attempting to regain its footing, the horse pulled the carriage farther off course. When the swell subsided once more, only two wheels on one side of the vehicle were still on the causeway. Suddenly the carriage tipped over, causing the two passengers to slide helplessly along the bench seats inside – and throwing the coachman into the water.

Juliana screamed and the coachman shouted in terror before he disappeared beneath the waves. At that moment both horses regained their footing on the causeway and began pulling in the right direction once more. The whole of the carriage was off the causeway now and, as water poured inside, it tilted over even farther.

It was impossible to open either of the doors. Fortunately, the windows were open. As the water rose inside the carriage, it righted itself temporarily and Thomasina was able to climb out through the window, pulling Juliana after her.

'Can you swim?'

Thomasina put the question to Juliana as they both clung to the carriage, which was now almost totally submerged. It seemed to be resting on the sea-bed at the moment. The horses, unable to shift the water-filled vehicle, struggled to keep their footing. By so doing they prevented the carriage from drifting into deeper water.

Of the coachman there was no sign.

'Not very well,' gasped Juliana in answer to Thomasina's question, the sudden coldness of the water robbing her of breath.

'Then hold on tight to the rail on the carriage roof. I'll try to keep the horses on the causeway.'

Making her way hand-over-hand along the edge of the carriage roof, Thomasina took advantage of another rising swell to swim to where the horses were struggling to retain their footing on the causeway.

When she reached the horses' heads, she found she could just maintain her own footing. The horses were also holding their ground for the moment, but pulling the water-filled carriage back to the causeway was an impossibility.

With the tide rising steadily, women and animals were in a particularly precarious situation. Then Thomasina heard a shout. Turning her head, she saw a boat heading towards the stricken carriage from the direction of the harbour, the blades of oars churning up white foam as the oarsmen strained to their task.

'We're here . . . hurry!' Thomasina called out to the boat's crew, before shouting the good news to Juliana. 'Hold on, Juliana, a boat's almost here.'

The St Aubyn boat reached them in a couple of minutes, although it seemed an age as Thomasina fought to keep the horses steady.

The oarsmen stopped rowing and, as the boat glided towards her, Thomasina called, 'Get Juliana. She's clinging to the carriage. Hurry!'

A voice she recognised as belonging to Abel called an order and the boat passed her by and collided heavily with the almost submerged vehicle. Then she heard the men shouting to each other as Juliana was unceremoniously hauled on board the boat from the Mount.

Moments later the boat was alongside her. As Thomasina was pulled on board to join Juliana, Abel gave orders to the men to cut the horses free in order that they might make their own way to the Mount.

As this was being done, Abel asked, 'Where's Harry . . . the coachman?'

'I don't know. He was thrown from the coach. I heard him shout before he went under. I haven't seen him since then.'

'I doubt if you will,' said one of the oarsmen. 'He can't swim.'

'We'll stay out and search for him,' said Abel. 'Not that Sir John will thank us for saving him. He must have been mad to attempt crossing after dark, with the causeway covered – and on a rising tide, too.'

Thomasina said nothing, waiting for Juliana to accept the blame for what had happened. But Sir John St Aubyn's mistress had other matters on her mind.

'Get me back to the Mount and send other boats out looking for the coachman,' she said in some distress.

'We'll call them out if we can't find him ourselves,' said Abel, 'but as we're here . . .'

'Get me back,' a hard-breathing Juliana demanded. 'Once we're ashore you can send out as many boats as you like – but if you don't hurry . . .' She paused in obvious pain. 'Quickly . . . the baby's on its way.'

9

By the time the boat bumped alongside the jetty at the foot of the Mount, Juliana was writhing in agony. Deeply concerned, Abel tried to comfort her by saying, 'It'll be all right, we'll have you up at the castle in no time.'

'Don't be a fool, Abel,' she snapped at him. 'The baby would arrive before we were halfway there. What's more, if we don't get me somewhere quickly, it's likely to be born right here in this boat.'

Alarmed, the boatmen who were preparing to help Juliana from the boat turned to Abel for guidance.

He looked at the sodden, bedraggled mistress of Sir John St Aubyn. Oblivious to his uncertainty, she doubled over with a cry of pain, clutching her stomach as yet another spasm took control of her body.

Her time was very close. It was now apparent to

him that she would not be able to contain the child within her body until they reached the castle atop the Mount.

Making a hasty decision, he said, 'Take her to the house of my grandmother.'

The anxious boatmen had been waiting for him to take the initiative and give them a clear directive. They obeyed with alacrity.

Helped ashore, Juliana was supported to the house of Verity Trannack by a couple of the boat's crew. Every minute or so they were obliged to call a halt when labour pains forced Juliana to double over in agony.

By the time the party reached the small, terraced cottage occupied by Abel's grandmother, Juliana was in very real distress and hardly able to walk.

One of the boat's crew had hurried ahead of the slow-moving party, but when Thomasina and Juliana arrived, Verity Trannack had still not recovered from the shock of being told that the mistress of St Michael's Mount was on her way to her home to give birth to Sir John St Aubyn's child.

After settling Juliana on her own bed, Verity said querulously, 'I don't know who we can get to help bring the child into the world. Mother Sennett is the one who takes charge of births on the Mount, but she's over to Marazion, helping to deliver the first of her great-grandchildren. I doubt if we can have her back here much before dawn.'

'By then I'll have either presented Sir John with another child or he'll need to go into mourning for me,' gasped the distressed Juliana. 'Thomasina, you'll have to take care of me – and of Sir John's child. There's no one else I can trust.'

'Don't worry, you'll be all right, I'll look after you.' Reaching out, Thomasina grasped Juliana's hand as yet another spasm racked her body.

'I know you will,' said the other woman, between gritted teeth. As the spasm passed she added, 'I've known you only a short time, Thomasina, yet I already trust you more than anyone else I know.'

'I'll do what I can,' Thomasina promised, 'but I've never helped at a birth before.'

'I've gone through it enough times to know what to expect,' said Juliana. 'I wish I could say it's going to come easier because of that, but it never does. Each time I say it will be the last – but this time it's going to be, Thomasina, I swear it . . .'

Her head went back on the feather-filled pillow and her body arched as yet another pain knifed through her. As it subsided, Abel entered the room carrying a bowl of steaming-hot water. His grandmother walked behind him bearing a number of towels, most borrowed from neighbours.

The sight of Abel aroused Juliana to fury. 'What are you doing here? Have you no sense of decency? Get out, do you hear me? GET OUT! All of you get out . . . No, not you Thomasina. You stay with me – but *only* you.'

As the others hurried from the room to escape Juliana's wrath, Thomasina said, 'They were only trying to help, Juliana. I'm sure Abel's grandmother knows far more about childbirth than I do.'

'We don't need her. I don't want strangers fussing

about me at a time like this. I'll tell you what has to
be done. Now they've gone, you can pull my clothes
up – right up around my body . . . that's right. Now,
I'm going to raise my knees and spread my legs apart.
When I do, you'll realise why I didn't want anyone else
around. Giving birth is the most inelegant situation any
woman can ever find herself in . . .'

Despite all the pain that occurred before Juliana's child
entered the world, the birth itself was surprisingly easy
– much to Thomasina's relief.

No more than forty minutes after entering the Trannack
home, Juliana held her latest son in her arms. Meanwhile, Thomasina bundled up the bloody towels. When
things were tidy she would call in the rightful occupiers
of the tiny cottage.

'Isn't he a delight, Thomasina?'

Now the birth was over, Juliana was as relaxed as
though she had never been close to drowning and
had suffered the pains of childbirth immediately afterwards.

Satisfied she had done all she could with the room,
Thomasina looked to where Juliana held the baby.
Wrapped in a towel, only a shock of black hair and
his blotchy-skinned face were visible, although he had
a strong voice. She felt vague, maternal stirrings within
her, and yet, if she were brutally honest, she thought
that only a mother could love such a wrinkled, noisy
little object.

'What will you call him?' she asked Juliana.

'Why, there's only one name for him. I shall name
him after you. He shall be Thomas St Aubyn. Thomas

John St Aubyn – John being a family name. You don't mind, Thomasina?'

'I'm flattered. I hope he grows up to be a great blessing to you. May I allow Abel's grandmother in now?'

'Of course. Was I very horrible to her?'

'Yes, and to Abel too,' Thomasina replied with complete honesty.

'I'll find some way to make it up to both of them,' said Juliana contritely. 'Go and find them, and tell Verity Trannack I want her to be the first to see young Thomas. That will please her. Oh, and ask if there is any news of the coachman. I feel dreadful about him . . .'

10

When Thomasina left the room in which Juliana was holding her new-born son, she found Verity Trannack waiting uncertainly outside. The older woman had heard the first, healthy cries of the baby, but, afraid of incurring the wrath of Sir John's mistress, had not dared enter the room to check whether all was well.

Suddenly Thomasina felt desperately tired. It had been a very eventful day. She felt now as though all the energy in her body had seeped away.

Handing over the blood-stained towels, she managed to give the other woman a weary smile. 'Juliana says she would like you to go in and see the baby.'

'Mistress Vinicombe . . . is . . . She's all right?'

'She's fine, as far as I can tell. She tells me the birth was an easy one, but it certainly frightened the wits out of me.'

'I'll put these towels in to soak, then I'll go in and see her and the babe.'

'Where's Abel? Perhaps he might like to see the baby, too?'

'He'll not want to see it,' Verity said quickly – too quickly. Recovering herself, she added, 'He went to the harbour. All the village men are taking boats out to look for poor Harry Miller, the coachman. His young wife is in some state about him. They've only been married for two months and she's expecting her first in the next month or so.'

'I'm sorry.' Thomasina was genuinely upset. She felt she should have tried harder to dissuade Juliana from insisting that they should attempt to cross the causeway, but she said nothing to the other woman of her thoughts.

'Is there any chance that Abel and the others will find him alive?'

Verity shook her head, 'Harry never learned to swim and there's a strong tide running to the east of the causeway. His wife knows he won't be coming back to her. She's started her mourning already.'

When Verity went in to see Juliana and the new-born baby, Thomasina left the small cottage and made her way slowly towards the steep path which climbed the Mount to the castle.

She had promised Juliana she would make certain the servants at the castle were fully aware of what was happening. Thomasina would then remain with the children. In the morning Juliana and baby Thomas would be carried to the castle in the ancient sedan chair used for the conveyance of elderly or infirm visitors to St Michael's Mount.

Walking along the paved quay beside the harbour,

Thomasina could see lanterns twinkling from many boats on the stretch of water separating St Michael's Mount from the mainland. They danced on the restless waves of the bay as though carried by ballet dancers on a giant, darkened stage.

The imagery belied the macabre mission of those who scoured the waters of St Michael's Bay for the body of Harry Miller.

'Hello, Miss Thomasina.'

Stepping out from the shadows at the end of the row of harbourside cottages, Abel momentarily startled her.

'Abel! What are you doing here? I thought you'd be out in a boat with the others, searching for the poor coachman.'

'If there was the slightest possibility of finding him alive, I *would* be at sea, but Harry couldn't swim. That means they're searching for a body. They don't need my help for that.'

Changing the subject, Abel said, 'As you're on your way up to the castle, I presume Juliana has had her baby?'

'Yes, it's a boy. She's naming it Thomas. I'm on my way to the castle to make certain the other children are all right and to let the servants know what's happening.'

'They'll know already. There's little that goes on in the village that they don't learn about right away. In fact, I wouldn't be surprised if they already knew the baby's name and all.'

'How do they learn things so quickly?'

By the light of the last cottage in the village she

saw him shrug. 'I don't know, but it's always been that way.'

Leaving the village behind now, they were on the path that led up the Mount to the castle. Here Abel stopped, intending to allow Thomasina to proceed on her own.

Quickly she asked, 'Will you come up to the castle with me, Abel? The only time I've ever walked along the path was when I came down to the village to take the boat with you to Falmouth. It seemed very steep in places.'

'It's downright dangerous, especially if you don't know it well. I'll take you up to the castle door.'

'Can I take hold of your arm? I think I'll feel safer if I do.'

She took his silence to be assent and linked her arm through his.

They walked on in silence for a short distance before he asked, 'Was there much belonging to you being carried in the carriage?'

'A whole lot – although Juliana had even more. Some was clothing I'd brought from Malachi's house, but most was new, bought in Falmouth only today. I suppose it's all lost now, like poor Harry Miller?'

'Not necessarily. We tied a small buoy to the carriage when we rescued you and Mistress Vinicombe. Unless we have any bad weather during the night – which I doubt – we'll be able to recover the carriage tomorrow.'

'That at least is good news! None of the clothes will ever be as they were when we bought them, but

Juliana and I will certainly be able to do something with them. Was the buoy your idea, Abel?'

She sensed, rather than saw, the nod of his head.

'That was very clever of you, but then you seem to keep your head, whatever the emergency. If you didn't, I doubt if I'd be here now.' She squeezed his arm almost unconsciously and felt him stiffen. It was an instinctive reaction, but she went on, 'I'm sorry, would you rather I let go of your arm?'

'No.'

They both realised his reply had come too quickly. Breaking the silence that followed, Abel added jocularly, 'Having saved your life once or twice, it wouldn't do for me to lose you off the edge of the path now, would it?'

She gave a light laugh, quite content to continue to hold his arm. After a while she asked, 'What brought you back to the Mount after you'd spent years travelling the world as a marine, Abel?'

She felt him shrug, 'I've always looked upon it as being home, I suppose.'

'There wasn't anyone in particular to bring you back here?'

'Only my grandmother.' After a few moments' hesitation, he corrected the brief statement. 'No, that isn't strictly true. There *was* someone I came back hoping to see, but she had got married and moved away by the time I returned. I went off to sea for a few years then, working for a time as mate on a coaster out of Bristol. I stood in as master on another ship belonging to the same company and planned to make it my life. Then I got word that my grandfather had died and my grandmother wanted me, so I came back here to be close to her, and Sir John offered me work as his head boatman for the time I was here. I never left – and here I am!'

Thomasina thought that working as head boatman for Sir John St Aubyn was a considerable come-down for a man who had once had command of a deep-sea vessel. She said as much to Abel.

Once again he shrugged. 'Perhaps it is. I've never thought about it too much, for I enjoy living on the Mount. Although that's not to say I wouldn't move on if anything special came along. My grandmother has recovered from the loss of my grandfather and could manage well enough without me now. But I'm not looking for anything. There are worse things than being a St Aubyn boatman.'

'I suppose so, even though the situation up at the castle isn't exactly a normal one.'

'It doesn't seem to worry Sir John too much – nor anyone else, come to that. He's greatly respected by everyone in Cornwall – and farther afield, too.'

'All the same . . .'

Thomasina broke off what she was saying as they both heard the sound of someone breathing heavily, labouring up the steep pathway behind them.

Afraid that something might have gone wrong with Juliana and that whoever was on the path behind them was seeking her, Thomasina pulled Abel to a halt.

'Who's that? Are you coming after me?'

'Thomasina? Thank the Lord. I was at home in Ludgvan when I heard about the accident with the carriage. I thought something might have happened to you.'

It was Humphrey St Aubyn.

11

'Thank God you're safe, Thomasina! I was told that the carriage carrying you and Juliana from Falmouth had been washed from the causeway and I hurried here straight away. When I saw the boats in the bay, obviously searching for something, I feared the worst. You don't know what a relief it is for me to find you here.'

'As you can see, I am perfectly safe. The boats are out searching for one of the Mount coachmen. He was washed away when our carriage went off the causeway. But I'm touched by your concern, Humphrey. Perhaps you would also like to know about Juliana and your new half-brother.'

Before Humphrey could reply, Abel coughed discreetly in the background darkness.

'Who's that?'

'It's me, Master Humphrey. Abel.'

'Abel? What are you doing here with Miss Thomasina?'

Thomasina wondered whether Humphrey's indignation was because his effusive expression of relief that she was safe had been overheard by Abel, or outrage that he had found the two of them together in the darkness.

'I asked Abel to guide me along the path to the castle. I have only walked it once, and never in the dark.'

'I would have thought you would have been out in a boat searching for the coachman, Abel.' Humphrey was not mollified by Thomasina's explanation.

'If they find anything at all, it will be a body,' said Abel. 'They don't need me for that.'

'Had it not been for Abel, they would have been searching for me and for Juliana, too,' explained Thomasina. 'He came out in a boat in the darkness and rescued us.'

'He seems to make a habit of rescuing you,' said Humphrey peevishly. 'It must be very satisfying for him.'

'What an incredible thing to say!' declared Thomasina. 'I owe my life to him. I've no doubt your father will be grateful to him for rescuing Juliana, too.'

'No doubt,' said Humphrey, almost grudgingly. 'I'm grateful too – that he was able to save both you and Juliana. The St Aubyns are fortunate to have a boatman with such skill and initiative.'

Despite the jealousy which had overwhelmed him when he discovered that Abel was with Thomasina in the darkness, Humphrey meant it. He was not a mean-minded young man.

'I'll make certain my father rewards you generously when he returns, Abel. Thank you for escorting Miss Thomasina to the castle, too, but I'm here now. You may go back to the village and see if there is anything you can do to help in the search for the coachman.'

'You can *both* escort me to the castle,' Thomasina declared. 'I shall consider myself fortunate indeed to have two such gallant men attendant upon me.'

'No,' Abel said, 'Master Humphrey is right. I should be down at the harbour, seeing if there is anything I can do to help in the search. I'll have word sent to you tomorrow, when we recover the carriage. It shouldn't be too difficult at low tide.'

Trying to hide her disappointment, Thomasina said, 'Well, all right then. I'm sure the poor coachman's widow would feel much more at peace with herself if his body could be recovered. Thank you again, Abel – although mere thanks seem totally inadequate to someone who has saved my life not once, but twice.'

'I am glad I was there on both occasions. Good night to you both.'

When Abel had left them, Thomasina resumed her walk to the castle with Humphrey. They walked with Humphrey between her and the sheer drop to the right. But although they walked close together, Thomasina did not take his arm.

'Abel is a sound and reliable man,' Thomasina said conversationally. 'He seems to have had an interesting life, too. Your family is fortunate to have him working for you.'

'Yes.'

'Life can't have been easy for him. I mean, not knowing who his father is – or was.'

'No.'

Alone in the darkness with Thomasina, the last thing Humphrey wanted to do was spend the time talking about Abel. But she was not deterred by his lack of enthusiasm.

'Does anyone have any idea who his father might be?'

They were both aware it was a sensitive question. Much to Thomasina's surprise, Humphrey did not try to side-step it.

'There have always been a great many rumours. Some say he has St Aubyn blood in his veins. I have to admit there *is* some resemblance to the family, but no one has ever come forward to make any claims about it. Besides, whatever other faults they may have, the St Aubyns have never evaded their responsibilities. Had he been a St Aubyn, I feel certain he would have been acknowledged as such. Has he ever said anything to you about the matter?'

'It's nothing we've ever discussed,' she lied. 'But I admire your open-minded attitude on the subject. I think Abel might, too.'

'To be perfectly honest, I rather admire the man,' said Humphrey. 'He's already done far more with his life than I ever will.'

'But I thought you were going into the Church? That will make you one of the most important and respected men in the parish to which you are appointed.'

'That's what my mother is always telling me,' agreed Humphrey unhappily. 'I suppose she's right. It isn't what I *really* want to do, but my brother Robert is a curate, so I suppose I'll have to become a cleric, too – because that's what my father expects of us. I sometimes wonder whether putting us all in the Church is a way of atoning for his own life.'

'If you really feel so strongly about becoming a parson, you could always go off and do something else.'

'If I did, Father would cut me off without a penny. He's said as much. No, Thomasina, I'll do as he wishes, but I'll never be anything more than a very comfortably off, but rather mediocre country parson.'

Thomasina thought there were a great many men who would be perfectly happy to settle for such a state of affairs, but she said nothing.

'Of course, things might be very different if I were to be blessed in marriage with the right woman. One who would give me her full support as the wife of a parson; who took an interest in what I was doing. Who knows, I might then go on to become a dean – or a bishop, even.'

Thomasina thought the idea of Humphrey becoming a bishop far removed from his statement of only a few minutes before. Nevertheless, she hoped he would prove to be a successful servant of the Church.

With no object in mind but to humour her companion, Thomasina said, 'There are lots of women who would be proud to be the wife of a churchman, Humphrey. I'm sure you'll find one and go on to great things.'

'I think I already have found the woman I want to help me through life, Thomasina. I haven't said anything to her about my intentions, yet. But if she will have me, I have no doubt that all you say might come about.'

His statement took Thomasina by surprise. Early marriages were by no means uncommon among the society from which she came, but the sons of gentlemen – especially *titled* gentlemen – tended to marry later in life.

'What will Sir John say about you making an early marriage? I presume he knows nothing about it yet.'

'Nobody knows – except you. That's the way it should be, really. You see, I believe *you* are exactly the wife I have always dreamed of having, Thomasina. You are courageous, determined . . . Oh, everything that a man like me could ever want. This might come as a great surprise to you, Thomasina, but I am making you an offer of marriage. Please say "yes".'

12

'You saw me for the first time only a couple of weeks ago. We've had hardly any time together since then. Why, you know nothing at all about me, Humphrey!'

Thomasina and Humphrey stood outside the main entrance to the castle on St Michael's Mount. After recovering from the initial shock of his remarkable offer of marriage, she had tried to pass it off as a bizarre joke. However, Humphrey had assured her that he was in deadly earnest. As a result, Thomasina had spent the remainder of the walk up the steep path to the castle telling him how preposterous such a proposal was.

'Time has nothing to do with one's emotions, Thomasina. Once in a lifetime someone will come along and you know immediately that he, or she, is the only one you will ever love. *Really* love, that is.'

'I don't believe that, Humphrey. You need to know

someone for a long time before you can be sure you love them. To know how they behave in different situations. Whether you can trust them. Rely upon them.'

'I don't doubt that is what parents would have us believe, Thomasina. They are more concerned with the practicalities of marriage than with the romance of two people falling in love. The poet, Byron, looks at things very differently . . .'

'Humphrey! You have just asked me to marry you! Marriage is about making a life together and accepting responsibilities. Children. Matters of substance, not . . . poetry! I've no doubt Sir John would tell you the same, if you were to tell him you wanted to marry.'

'I don't think he is in a position to tell me anything of the sort, Thomasina. He could hardly have a more unconventional lifestyle – and all in the name of "love".'

'Very well, since you consider "love" to be all-important, I don't love you, Humphrey. I have grown fond of you, in the short time we have known each other, and have great respect for you as a person. I am also deeply grateful to you for the part you played in rescuing me after the shipwreck, but that's not a strong enough basis for marriage.'

'You would grow to love me, Thomasina, I am quite certain of it. No one could love you as I do and not be loved in return.'

'Life doesn't work that way, Humphrey. Wanting something very badly doesn't mean that you will one day get it.'

'Promise me you'll at least *think* about my proposal, Thomasina. Please don't dismiss it out of hand.' Desperate at her refusal, Humphrey tried to find a vestige of hope to which he could cling.

'Of course I'll think about it.'

Aware how desperately unhappy he was at this moment, Thomasina tried to restore some of his wounded pride. 'I doubt if I will be able to think of very much else for many days. But, just for now, let's not talk of it again. I would like us to get to know each other a little better before we do – and please don't mention this to anyone else. If word of your proposal were to reach the ears of Sir John, it would be very difficult for me to remain at the Mount.'

'As long as I know you are considering my proposal, I will not say a word to another soul. It will remain our secret. But in all your deliberations please remember that I *do* truly love you, Thomasina.'

Sir John St Aubyn returned to the Mount nine days later. He had left London post-haste when news reached him of the birth of his fifteenth acknowledged child, and his sixth son by Juliana. Given sketchy details of the circumstances leading up to the birth, he was anxious to learn the full story of the accident which had occurred on the submerged causeway.

The baronet entered Thomasina's room, after no more than a cursory knock at the door, while she was working on the financial details of Malachi's legacy.

Abel had taken a boat to Falmouth the day before, carrying with him a letter from Thomasina to her

solicitor. He had returned with details of the monies
and assets willed to her by Malachi.

'I do hope I am not disturbing you, Thomasina,'
said Sir John. 'I felt I had to take the earliest opportunity of thanking you for all you have done for
Juliana and our latest son. I heartily endorse Juliana's
decision to name him Thomas in your honour. Indeed,
as a result of her foolishness in insisting upon crossing
the causeway on a rising tide, I doubt if *either* of them
would be here today had it not been for your courage
and resourcefulness. We owe you a debt which can
never be repaid.'

'I've already been amply repaid by the kindness I
have been shown since my rescue from the French
man-o'-war. If anyone is to be thanked for what happened on the causeway, it should be Abel. Without
him none of us would be here. He's the true hero.'

'Yes . . . of course.' Sir John St Aubyn was not a
man who was easily embarrassed, but he appeared
discomfited now. 'I have arranged for him to be given
a hundred pounds. No amount of money could repay
anyone for saving Juliana – and yourself, of course
– but it will give him an indication of my deep
gratitude.'

'I'm sure it would be even more appreciated, were
you to present it to him yourself, Sir John. Abel has
a very high regard for you.'

Sir John seemed even more ill-at-ease than before.
'Unfortunately, I am unable to remain at the Mount
for very long. This is the most fleeting of visits. There
are urgent Parliamentary affairs that must be dealt
with personally in London. Before that I need to visit

Helston and Penryn to discuss forthcoming elections. However, I felt my first priority was to thank you for your part in saving Juliana. She tells me you have remained on the Mount at her request. I trust you will stay for a while longer? Indeed, there will *always* be a room at the Mount for you – and at Clowance too, if the builders ever complete the work they are carrying out there. In the meantime, I hope you will regard the Mount as your home, for as long as you wish to make use of it.'

'Thank you, Sir John. I am sorry to hear you will be absent from the Mount again so soon. Juliana misses you. Humphrey and your other children do, too.'

'Humphrey? Well, he will soon have other matters to think about. He will be leaving for London tomorrow morning. I have made arrangements for him to stay with a friend, a bishop, who will take him under his wing and introduce him to a few ecclesiastical friends. Hopefully, they will prove useful to him in the future.'

Suddenly thoughtful, he looked at her speculatively. 'You are aware, of course, that Humphrey is destined for a career in the Church? That he has a number of years of study ahead of him in order to fulfil that goal?'

'Of course. He's spoken of it on many occasions. He'll make an excellent parson, one day. You must be very proud of him?'

Partly relieved, but still uncertain that Thomasina's interest in Humphrey was purely platonic, Sir John said, 'Yes . . . yes, I am indeed. I am proud of all my children. I hope young Thomas, too, will grow up

to justify all you did to ensure the survival of him
and his mother. You are a remarkable young woman,
Thomasina. Juliana and I are eternally gratefully
to you.'

When Sir John had gone, Thomasina thought of all
he had said. His offer of a permanent welcome on
the Mount fitted in with her own plans very well.
An idea for a business venture based largely on the
Mount was already forming in her mind.

Sadly for Humphrey, he was not included in her
plans and the knowledge that he would be going to
London so soon came as a considerable relief. He had
once more broached the subject of marriage, and his
absence in London would be welcome to her.

She felt her immediate future was tied up with the
Mount, but there were a great many things to be done
before any of her ideas could move forward and take
substance.

13

It was a very unhappy Humphrey who set sail from the St Michael's Mount harbour the following morning, en route for London.

Thomasina knew that much of his misery was caused by the knowledge that he was leaving her behind and would probably not see her again for many months. She was also aware there was a much deeper reason for his unhappiness. Humphrey was not convinced that his future lay with the Church.

However, there was little she could do about this. As she had told Humphrey, it was a matter that must be settled between him and his father.

Thomasina went to see Humphrey begin his journey from the small harbour at the Mount, taking two of Juliana's children with her.

Nine-year-old Catherine and five-year-old Richard were both eager to wave their older half-brother off on his voyage and Thomasina felt that, with both children present, Humphrey was unlikely to become over-emotional.

Because of this, she even allowed Humphrey to give her a farewell kiss before he boarded the London-bound ship.

It was no more than a friendly gesture, but one she might not have been so ready to permit had she noticed Abel coming towards them along the quayside.

When she realised he must have observed the kiss, she coloured up and greeted him with unreasonable belligerence.

'Have you taken to spying on me now?'

Raising his eyebrows, Abel retorted, 'Why should I wish to do that? What you, or the gentlemen of the castle, get up to is none of my business, Miss Thomasina. I'm interested only in getting Master Humphrey's ship out of the harbour to make room for the *Celestine*. It's hove to in the bay at the moment. It will be the largest ship to enter the harbour for as long as I can remember. No doubt the children would like to stay and see it arrive.'

Her anger forgotten, Thomasina expressed her interest. 'Why should such a large ship be coming in here? What load will it be taking out?'

'Copper ore, bound for a Swansea smelting-house. There have been cartloads of ore arriving at the pens for days now. However, unless I am sadly lacking in my judgement of Sir Charles Hearle, the profit on a single cargo of ore is unlikely to keep him happy.'

Thomasina started at mention of the baronet's

name. Now she asked, 'What has Sir Charles Hearle got to do with the *Celestine*?'

'It's the ship he bought with the money left to him by his aunt. He'll no doubt get a return on his investment, but I doubt if it will be enough to satisfy his spending habits.' Aware that he might have said more than was circumspect, he asked, 'Is Sir Charles Hearle a friend of yours?'

'Far from it, and from what little I know of him I'd say you're right about his attitude towards small profits. But with the Spanish merchant fleet returning to sea in increasing numbers and eager for any cargo that's going, he's not likely to make a fortune with a ship in the short term. Even smuggling is out until the French war is over.'

'War has never stopped the smuggling trade – and it never will,' Abel replied. 'It might have stopped Cornish boats trading direct with France, but there's enough undutied spirits hidden away in the cellars of Jersey and Guernsey to satisfy demand for the next ten or fifteen years.'

'You seem to know a great deal about such things,' observed Thomasina. 'Far more than might be expected of a boatman who earns his daily bread ferrying between the Mount and Marazion.'

'I'd have to be deaf and blind not to know something of what's going on,' Abel retorted. 'Besides, I doubt if there's a clergyman, magistrate or country gentleman in the whole of Cornwall whose cellar isn't stocked with wine and brandy that wasn't even a flower on the vine when this war started.'

'Would you involve yourself in smuggling if you

were master of your own ship?' Thomasina hoped it sounded a perfectly innocent question.

'Not if men like Sir Charles Hearle were night-trading in the same area,' Abel replied. 'A successful smuggler needs a good ship, a reliable crew – and a close mouth. Sir Charles has none of these . . . But here's the *Celestine* coming in to harbour now – and carrying far too much sail.'

Almost as Abel said the words, the sails of the large sailing ship were hurriedly furled. While this was taking place seamen could be seen scurrying about the deck belatedly preparing to make things ready to berth the large vessel.

Despite Abel's misgivings, the *Celestine* came alongside the quay without mishap. Thomasina watched with considerable interest as he and the other Mount men secured the large vessel and busied themselves about it.

'Isn't she one of the most beautiful sights you have ever seen?'

Startled by the question, Thomasina swung around to find the subject of her recent conversation with Abel standing behind her. She suddenly felt as though the breath had been squeezed from her body.

She had not observed Sir Charles cross the gangway from his ship and walk to where she was standing with the two children.

She was wearing a hat known as a 'Dolly Varden', which tilted down almost to the tip of her nose, hiding much of her face and making recognition difficult – even if Sir Charles had been aware they had met before.

The hat in question was extremely popular and had been much copied by working girls. Her own hat was of the more expensive variety, purchased in Falmouth, but immersion in sea water in the St Aubyn carriage had destroyed its original pristine condition.

And her hair had been allowed to grow. Gathered behind her head, it was secured with an elaborately worked silver hairpin, a present from Juliana. It was highly unlikely that Sir Charles would recognise her – from anywhere – but she still felt uneasy in his presence.

'It's a very fine ship,' said Richard, trying to act grown-up. 'I hope my father will allow me to look over it sometime.'

'Your father?'

Richard's manner of speech and air of confidence alerted Sir Charles to his family ties. It was hardly necessary for Richard to provide confirmation.

'My father is Sir John St Aubyn. He owns this harbour, you know?'

'Indeed I do. I have brought my ship here with his express permission. But we have no need to wait until he comes visiting. Please allow me to show you and your sister over the *Celestine* right now.' Shifting his attention to Thomasina for a moment, he continued, 'You too. You'll not have an opportunity to see such a ship again.'

Thomasina realised Sir Charles had made the assumption that she was the children's nursemaid. She had personal experience of his behaviour towards female servants, but she would not allow the children to be taken on board the *Celestine* without her.

'I'd love to come, but would you mind if Sir John's senior boatman came too? He's very interested in ships and was telling us about yours when it was on the way in.'

She indicated Abel, who was standing with his back to them, looking up at the ship's tall masts. He was not close enough to have overheard the conversation.

After a brief hesitation Sir Charles said, 'Of course not. One of the crew will show him around. Shall we go, children?'

His momentary lack of enthusiasm at the thought of having Abel join them was enough to alert Thomasina. Sir Charles had not changed his ways. She suspected that his response to the children's interest in his ship had little to do with a desire to satisfy their curiosity.

Calling out to Abel, she said, 'You were telling me what a wonderful ship the *Celestine* is, Abel. Sir Charles has kindly invited you to look over it with us.'

'Do come with us, Abel,' said Richard excitedly. 'You've often told us about the ships on which you've served. Come on board and tell us what you think of this one.'

Abel had correctly guessed the reason why Thomasina had suggested he should go on board too, but he said, 'I would love to look over such a beautiful ship, but Sir John has just sent for me, Master Richard. I'll ask one of the boatmen to go with you instead.'

14

The *Celestine* was a large vessel, but it did not exude the same air of efficiency that Thomasina had come to accept on board the *Melanie Jane*.

Unfurled ropes snaked across the deck and there was an indefinable air of slackness among the crew, who either stood around talking or were going about their tasks in a lacklustre manner.

Nevertheless, Thomasina found the same thrill of excitement she had felt when she stood on the deck of the ship that she and Malachi had owned. She would have enjoyed it even more, had Abel come on board with her.

Richard was fascinated by all he saw and, as they went around, the various crew members pointed out to him the features of the ship most likely to appeal to a five-year-old.

Determined not to be completely overawed by the

sheer size of the vessel, Catherine dutifully followed her brother, Thomasina and Sir Charles around, saying very little.

When they had been on board the *Celestine* for about fifteen minutes Thomasina said, 'I think we should go now. We only came down to the harbour to see the children's half-brother off to London. Everyone at the castle will be wondering where we are.'

Sir Charles had always been an opportunist where women were concerned and he had no intention of allowing Thomasina to escape so easily. 'Nonsense, there is still a great deal of the ship to see . . .' Awkwardly scooping Richard up in his arms, he continued, 'We haven't visited the galley yet, have we, young man? We must go down and see if the cook has anything nice for you.'

When Sir Charles hurried off towards a hatch at the stern of the vessel, Thomasina's suspicions were immediately aroused. The galley on most ships of this size was situated towards the bows. But he was carrying Richard, with Catherine close on his heels. She could do nothing else but follow.

Thomasina's suspicions increased as they descended the ladders and were faced with a couple of cabin doors.

A third door was set in another bulkhead. She decided this probably gave access to a cargo hold.

'I thought you were taking the children to the galley for something to eat,' Thomasina said accusingly to Sir Charles.

'I am, but I remembered something of interest

that they might enjoy seeing first. It's here, in my cabin.'

Putting Richard to the deck and throwing open the door, he startled a seaman who was tidying the cabin. 'There, have you ever seen a more magnificent room anywhere?'

Although she remained wary of the baronet, Thomasina had to agree it was indeed a splendid cabin, far superior to the one Malachi had occupied on board the *Melanie Jane*. Panelled in fine mahogany, it was furnished in the manner of the study of Henry Vincent, at Trebene.

Sir Charles's next words explained this. 'Much of the furniture came from the home of my late uncle. I was allowed to choose a few bits and pieces from his home when he died. I picked them with just such a cabin in mind. The panelling is very special indeed. It came from the admiral's cabin on board a French ship-of-the-line. The ship was captured after a fierce battle and was too badly damaged to be commissioned into our own navy. I saw it in Plymouth when we took the *Celestine* there to have some work carried out. I bought the panelling and had it fitted there and then . . . But here you are, children, this is what I brought you to see. Have you ever seen a fish that flies? Well, now you have. This was also in the French admiral's cabin. See those long wings?'

The flying fish was in a glass case on a desk. As the children looked at it more closely, Thomasina asked the baronet, 'Do you intend using this cabin and sailing in the *Celestine* yourself?'

Flattered by her interest, Sir Charles replied, 'Occasionally. However, when the war with France is over – and I don't think that day is very far off – trade with Europe will recommence. The *Celestine* will begin trading with France. I will be able to offer a luxury cabin to anyone who wishes to travel to the Continent in comfort.'

'Do you think you will be able to find such passengers prepared to travel from St Michael's Mount harbour?'

Thomasina believed Sir Charles was being unrealistic. She felt that most prospective passengers in the area would prefer the facilities offered by ships from the nearby ports of Falmouth, Penzance or other large towns.

Impressed that Thomasina should have asked such a pertinent question, Sir Charles replied, 'Sir John St Aubyn has told me he is looking forward to the day when it is possible to travel to France once more. No doubt his many sons will want to visit that country, too – and where the St Aubyns go, others in the area will certainly follow. But enough of such talk. We can't have the children becoming bored, can we?'

Turning to the seaman who had been tidying the room when they entered, he said, 'Symonds, take the children to the galley. Have Cook make them something special.'

With a knowing smirk in Thomasina's direction, the seaman said, 'Certainly, Sir Charles. The cook has children of his own, he'll know what boys and girls enjoy.'

'I'll go with them,' Thomasina said hurriedly.

'Nonsense! They'll be delighted to escape from your authority for a few minutes. You'll enjoy a brief time away from them too, I don't doubt. While they are away you can help me make lemonade for them.'

Jerking his head at the seaman, in what he believed to be a surreptitious signal for him to depart with the children, Sir Charles continued, 'I purchased a whole bag of lemons only yesterday. They were brought to Falmouth on a ship newly returned from Spain. I also have water and sugar here. Sadly, I lack experience in catering for the young. I believe their tastes differ from my own.'

Sir Charles had placed himself between Thomasina and the others as he was speaking. It would be impossible now for Thomasina to escape from the cabin without creating a scene that might upset the children. Increasingly concerned, she was taken back to a similar situation at Trebene House, some two years before. Had he not been so drunk at the time, she felt that Sir Charles might have remembered it, too.

When the door closed behind the children and their escort, Sir Charles beamed at Thomasina in what he clearly hoped was a reassuring expression. 'Now, where did I put those lemons? I know they are here somewhere. While I try to recall their whereabouts, why don't we have a drink ourselves? What can I offer you? I have brandy, sack, whisky, gin – and some excellent port. It was brought back from Lisbon by my cousin.'

'Thank you, but it's far too early in the day for me to begin drinking.'

'It's never too early in the day to enjoy a drink, girl. Here, I'll pour two glasses.'

He poured two large glasses of port. When she declined to take one from him, he set it down on a small nearby table.

'I thought we were going to make lemonade for the children,' Thomasina reminded him.

'There's lots of time for that. They'll be kept amused in the galley by the crew. Sailors love having children on board ship.'

'I'd like to make it now, if you don't mind,' Thomasina declared stubbornly.

'Please yourself.' Sir Charles shrugged. Then, belying his earlier statement, he said, 'You'll find lemons in the cupboard over there, in the corner. Sugar too – and plenty of water in the jug on the table.'

While she crouched down, removing lemons and sugar from the floor-level cupboard, Sir Charles sipped his port and watched her, observing with increasing arousal how her dress tautened over her buttocks as she crouched in front of the cupboard.

Putting his drink down, he strode across the cabin to her. 'Here, allow me to help.'

Leaning over her, he reached out to take the sugar from her, at the same time staring down inside the front of her dress as she leaned forward to reach inside the cupboard.

'I can manage, thank you,' she said firmly.

'Don't be so damned independent, girl. You should learn to relax a little more. Life is far too short to allow a sense of dignity to stand in the way of enjoyment.'

'What you mean is that *my* dignity is standing

in the way of *your* enjoyment,' Thomasina retorted. Standing up suddenly with some of the ingredients for the lemonade in her hands, she almost knocked the lecherous baronet off balance. 'Perhaps you'll bring a couple more lemons to the table.'

Sir Charles successfully contained the anger which flared up at what he considered to be Thomasina's impertinence. She might be no more than a nursemaid, but she was a *damned* handsome woman. One who would doubtless prove worthy of a little patience. However, time would not allow his patience to be stretched too far.

Putting down his glass, he picked up three of the lemons, recovering one when his crippled arm caused it to drop to the cabin floor.

'Here you are, young lady. Now I insist that you take a glass of port with me.'

He brought the glass to her, but she ignored it, busying herself with mixing the ingredients for the lemonade.

After standing holding the glass out towards her for a while, Sir Charles frowned, set the glass down on the table beside the items with which she was working, then crossed the room to refill his own glass.

He had refilled it once more before Thomasina finished her task. Looking at him boldly, she asked, 'Shall we take it to the children, or will you send someone to fetch them back here?'

'Symonds will bring them back when they have had something to eat,' he replied. 'You haven't touched *your* drink yet.'

'I told you, it's too early for me, and I must be getting the children back to the castle. I'll go and find them now.'

She reached the door just ahead of him, but as she lifted the latch on the door, his good arm came over her shoulder and held it closed. 'Just a minute . . . please?'

She swung around to face him and he staggered back with a cry of pain. The glass he had been holding dropped to the carpet and his hand went up to his neck. When he took it away and looked at it, there was a smear of blood on his finger.'

'I'm terribly sorry, I completely forgot I had this in my hand.' She was looking down at the silver hairpin from Juliana, as though she had forgotten she had been holding it. 'I thought I had put it back in my hair.'

'You might have killed me!' Sir Charles looked at her in disbelief.

In truth there had been a brief moment when Thomasina had been sorely tempted to plunge the long pin deep into his throat.

'Yes, indeed I might have. That would have been very careless of me. Never mind, it's really only a scratch. In a day or two you'll have forgotten all about it.'

Still holding the hairpin, she smiled sardonically at him. 'I think I should go and fetch the children now, don't you?'

'You are treating the fact that you might have killed me as some kind of joke. Go and fetch the damned children, but don't bring them back here. I'll have the lemonade brought up to the main deck. I must put something on my neck to stop it bleeding.'

He hurried to a small cabinet fixed to the bulkhead of his cabin. With a fleeting smile, Thomasina left the room. Once outside, she replaced the hairpin in her hair, then went off in search of the two children.

15

Halfway up the steep pathway leading to the castle, Thomasina and the two children met up with Abel, who was returning to the harbour.

Greeting them all, he asked, 'Have you had a good time on board the *Celestine*? I think it must be the largest ship you've ever seen here.'

'I don't think there's anything special about it,' said Catherine, with a determined lack of enthusiasm.

'Sir Charles showed us a fish that had wings,' Richard told Abel animatedly. 'Sir Charles said it could fly out of the water, just like a bird.'

'That was exciting,' said Abel.

'It was,' agreed Richard.

'No, it wasn't.' Catherine contradicted him with all the superiority that came with being four years older than her brother. 'Our Uncle George, who lives in London, has one. His is much larger than the one Sir Charles showed us.'

'We had some nice lemonade,' said Richard, doggedly determined to prove that they had enjoyed themselves, '. . . and I had a piece of maggoty pie.'

Abel looked puzzled and Thomasina laughed. 'I think Richard must mean "muggety" pie. It's made from a sheep's insides. It's about as cheap a meat dish as you're likely to get anywhere.'

'Ugh!' exclaimed Catherine in a grimace that left no one in any doubt about the disgust she felt at Thomasina's explanation. 'No wonder I didn't like it.'

Abel gave the nine-year-old girl a sympathetic smile. 'It doesn't sound as though you enjoyed your visit to Sir Charles Hearle's wonderful new ship.'

'I didn't,' she agreed emphatically. 'I don't like Sir Charles very much, either.'

'Now, Catherine, that's very uncharitable of you. After all, he did invite us on board his ship.' Thomasina gently chided the young girl.

'It was *you* he really wanted to go on his ship,' Catherine said perceptively. 'As soon as we got there he wanted to get rid of Richard and me, so he could be with you.'

'Catherine! You shouldn't say things like that,' said Thomasina, but once again it was a very gentle admonition.

'Well, that's what the sailor who took us to the galley said to the cook. Anyway, you didn't like him very much either, did you?'

'Now how can you possibly know that, Catherine? You mustn't make up such stories.'

'I'm not making it up,' Catherine said indignantly. 'When the sailor said Sir Charles had sent him with us to get us out of the way, because he had you in his cabin, the cook said in that case he'd probably have us for the whole of the morning. The sailor said he wasn't so sure about that. He said you seemed like someone who wouldn't take any of Sir Charles's "old buck". What does "old buck" mean?'

'That doesn't matter. He shouldn't have been talking like that in front of you.'

Ignoring Thomasina's admonition, Catherine continued with her recital of the sailor's conversation. 'He said that if you wouldn't take any of Sir Charles's "old buck", we'd be off the ship quicker than . . .' Catherine was about to repeat the sailor's swear word, but thought better of it, '. . . quicker than you could say anything. So he told the cook he'd better hurry up and dish something up for us. Richard had only just finished eating his pie when you came for us.'

Less aggressively she added, 'I was glad you *were* so quick, though. It meant I didn't have to eat my pie – and I think "maggoty" is a better name for it than "muggety".'

'Well, *I* liked it,' declared Richard sulkily. 'I don't care if it *was* maggots.'

Abel's glance had shifted to Thomasina while Catherine was talking. Now he asked, 'Are you all right? You had no trouble from Sir Charles Hearle?'

'Nothing I couldn't handle.'

'So he *did* try something?' Abel's anger flared. 'No

woman has ever been safe anywhere near him. It's high time something was done about that man.'

'Nothing happened, Abel.' Thomasina was secretly delighted by his reaction, but she felt obliged to ensure that he did nothing foolish. 'I made it very clear I would welcome neither the drink he offered to me nor his advances. He accepted it without question.'

Thomasina was not entirely certain Abel believed her, but she gave him no opportunity to dwell upon the matter.

'He told me his ship will be carrying copper ore to Swansea, but his cabin is much too grand for an ore vessel and I doubt if he'll find many passengers wanting to go to Swansea from the Mount.'

'True. He'll not make many trips carrying ore, either. There are too many small boats, with a crew of three or four, ready to carry a cargo of ore for little more than a living wage. He'll need to look farther afield if he wants to take on profitable cargoes, but I doubt if the *Celestine* is capable of deep-sea trade without a lot of work being carried out on it. The ship's getting old and was laid up without attention for far too long. The signs are there for anyone with a seaman's eye to see. Everything above deck should be checked, and much of it needs replacing. What the ship is like below the water-line is anyone's guess. I certainly wouldn't want to take her to sea – even if the master's cabin was fitted out in pure gold.'

'Sir Charles told me the war with France will soon be over. When it is he expects to open trade with the French ports, carrying passengers in the cabin.'

Abel snorted derisively. 'Napoleon won't acknowledge he's beaten until Paris itself is threatened. That's not likely to happen for at least another couple of years.'

'So what will Sir Charles do if the markets he's hoping for aren't open to him? Do you think he might take to smuggling, through Guernsey?'

'It's possible. Something like that is certainly more in keeping with his character than legitimate trading. But to be successful he should have chosen a different ship. The *Celestine* is too large, too old and much too slow – and neither Sir Charles nor his captain are the right men for moonlight trading.'

'What sort of man is right for smuggling, Abel? Most Cornish sailors try it when times are bad.'

Abel gave her a crooked smile. 'That's quite true. Given the right boat and an owner I could trust, I would do whatever was needed to turn in a profit, too. But I'm no longer a deep-sea man. I'm Sir John St Aubyn's boatman and I'll give him my loyalty for as long as he pays my wages.'

'Can we go up to the castle now? I'm cold.' Catherine was not having a happy day. She was bored with standing waiting on the path while Thomasina and Abel talked and there was a cool breeze blowing across the slope of the Mount from the west.

'Come on then, we'll have a race to the castle door. Hopefully we'll be home before Sir John sets out for Helston.'

'He's not going today after all,' said Abel. 'After checking on the tides, he's decided to put off his journey until tomorrow, or even the day after. He too saw Sir Charles's ship enter harbour. He said he'll likely go down to pay a call on him. Probably later this morning.'

16

Thomasina and Juliana were seated on the castle terrace enjoying a pre-lunch drink when Sir John returned from his visit to the *Celestine*. Baby Thomas was sleeping in a canopied cradle nearby.

They were sheltered from the cool westerly breeze here and although rain clouds were building up on the horizon, the Mount was bathed in warm sunshine.

Unlike Thomasina, earlier in the day, Sir John had not declined Sir Charles's invitation to drink with him. As a result, he was in a jovial mood.

After peeping beneath the lace canopy at his newest son, Sir John beamed at the two women. Sitting down heavily upon an empty chair, he said, 'You know, Juliana, I really think Sir Charles Hearle has turned over a new leaf, at long last.'

'Really, dear?' Juliana recognised that Sir John had

drunk enough to feel at peace with the whole world. 'What makes you say that?'

'This ship of his. He seems to have taken on a new sense of responsibility now that he's bought it. Full of enthusiasm. Lots of plans for the future, that sort of thing. He's fitted the ship out rather well, too. We'd be proud to have a room in the castle that was furnished half as well as the cabin he occupies on board.'

'I hope he's saved enough money to spend on the rest of the ship.' Thomasina repeated what Abel had said to her without disclosing they were not her own views. 'There's a whole lot of rigging needs replacing. The masts and spars should be checked out, too. The *Celestine* was laid up for a long time without any work being carried out on it. A ship needs constant attention if it's to remain fully seaworthy.'

'I was forgetting you come from a family which has produced a number of sea captains and have yourself spent a great deal of time at sea, Thomasina. You'll have an opportunity tonight to tell Sir Charles what you think he should do with his ship. I've invited him to the castle for dinner.'

'I really can't, Juliana. I don't think I could bear to spend the whole of a meal with that man. Try as I might, I just don't like him. I couldn't wait to get away from him this morning.'

'That seems to be the feeling of every woman in the castle,' commented Juliana. 'I can't stand the man, either – and Catherine told me when she came back from the ship that *she* thinks he's sly. For someone who has the reputation of being a "lady's man", he seems to have failed miserably to impress anyone here.'

'What excuse can I possibly make?' repeated Thomasina. 'I don't want to offend Sir John, but I really don't want to share the same table as Sir Charles Hearle.'

'I'm sorry, Thomasina. In any other circumstances you would have my full support. Unfortunately, if you fail to join us for dinner, it means I will need to entertain Sir Charles without you. I doubt if I would be able to carry it off successfully. We'll go to dinner together, put on a brave front and provide support for one another. Who knows, with each of us being aware how the other feels about our unwanted guest, it might turn out to be an amusing, if *not* an interesting evening.'

Thomasina had doubts about the potential for amusement in the forthcoming evening. Furthermore, should details of any of her previous meetings with Sir Charles be recalled, it would prove disastrous.

Sir Charles was not in the best of moods when he arrived at the castle. The wind had increased from the west, bringing with it the rain that had threatened for much of the day.

The breeze had snatched at the umbrella he carried, turning it inside out, and rain had made his bicorne hat soggy, leaving his carefully curled hair wet and bedraggled. Much of his clothing had been kept dry by a waterproof coat which had a fitted cape, but the

lower half of his pantaloons were wet and his shoes
had lost all their shine.

He was grateful to Sir John for hurrying him off to
a guest room in order to tidy and dry himself as best
he could before joining the two women for pre-dinner
drinks.

Despite this brief respite, it was not possible to
entirely eradicate the effects of wind and rain. As
a result, Sir Charles was aware that he was not
at his debonair best when he was escorted to the
sitting-room by a servant.

Standing in the doorway, he was welcomed by Sir
John, who stood between him and the two women.
'Ah! Here you are at last, Charles! I trust you have
managed to dry off. I am sorry we couldn't arrange
better weather for your visit, but a glass or two of
good brandy will put some cheer back in you – but
is that blood I see on your neck? Have you hurt
yourself, old chap?'

'No.' Sir Charles put a hand up to his throat,
self-consciously. 'I nicked myself shaving, that's all.
I must have set it off bleeding again when I dried
myself. It's nothing.'

Sir Charles stepped inside the room, bowed to
Juliana, then turned to Thomasina, who had been
hidden from view by the castle's owner until this
moment. He started to bow to her too – then suddenly
recognised her from the morning. Jerking upright, he
turned to Sir John, seeking an explanation for her
presence.

Instructing a servant on the drinks he was to
pour, Sir John did not observe Sir Charles's shocked

expression. Juliana did and she was quick to react.

'You've met Thomasina, of course, Charles. She and the children were kindly shown over your boat this morning. You have met her before too, when she and I were shopping together in Falmouth. She is a great friend and has been a wonderful companion during my recent confinement.'

'Thomasina has been absolutely marvellous,' enthused Sir John, breaking into the conversation. 'Saved Juliana's life when their carriage was washed off the causeway, you know?'

'. . . And brought baby Thomas into the world,' Juliana added. 'In fact, we named him after her.'

She was intrigued by Sir Charles's reaction to Thomasina. She looked forward to having Thomasina on her own in order to learn what lay behind it.

'I . . . I'm sorry,' said Sir Charles, finding a voice that did not sound like his own. 'As I remember, Thomasina wore a veil when we met in Falmouth, and this morning . . .'

He faltered and Thomasina said, 'This morning Sir Charles thought I was nursemaid to Catherine and Richard. I failed to enlighten him, I'm afraid. It was very naughty of me.'

'Nursemaid, indeed!' Sir John chortled. 'There has been a sight more to Thomasina's life than looking after young children, Charles. A damned sight more! She was a prisoner on that French ship we drove ashore on the Mount. Brought ashore unconscious by my son Humphrey and one of the boatmen. They all thought it was a young lad until they went to dress a wound inflicted by one of the mainlanders.

They soon discovered their mistake! It caused quite a stir at the time. At least, it did among our people. Quite a tale to tell, has Thomasina – and I suspect we haven't heard a fraction of it yet.'

Recovering some of his composure, Sir Charles said, 'I am intrigued, Sir John. Perhaps Thomasina will tell us something of her life over dinner? I, for one, would love to hear her story.'

'I'm sure there are far more interesting things to talk about, Sir Charles. You, for instance, and how you came about the injury to your arm. A war wound, is it?'

'Well, no, not exactly . . .'

The two women exchanged brief glances that contained a hidden meaning. Without going into any details, Thomasina had told Juliana how she and Malachi had met Sir Charles on the quayside at Falmouth, when he claimed his arm had been crippled as a result of enemy action.

'Charles is being modest,' said Sir John, unaware of the women's thoughts. 'He tackled two desperate highwaymen who tried to rob the carriage in which he was travelling with his uncle and aunt. Despite being wounded, he shot both of the villains. One was later captured, convicted and hanged. The other escaped, but Charles is convinced he badly wounded him, so he probably died too. Charles was the toast of the county at the time.'

'Nevertheless, I cannot ever forgive them,' declared Sir Charles. 'The injury prevented me from fulfilling my dearest wish, that of obtaining a commission in a cavalry regiment and serving with the Duke of

Wellington on his glorious campaign in the Spanish peninsula. Instead, I have had to be content with command of a militia company.'

'You are serving King and country as best you can,' Sir John declared. 'No man can do more.'

Thomasina had gone cold at the mention of the abortive hold-up in which Jeffery had been seriously wounded. This gave way to anger at Sir John's inaccurate description of what had happened on that fateful night.

Gaining control of herself, she said, with apparent sympathy, 'Such an injury must make it very difficult to carry out a great many everyday activities, Sir Charles. It's hardly surprising you cut yourself shaving. You were fortunate it was nothing worse.'

An expression of acute embarrassment momentarily crossed Sir Charles's face. It made Juliana more determined than ever to question Thomasina at great length about what had taken place that morning on board the *Celestine* in the St Michael's Mount harbour.

The small dinner party was hardly an unqualified success. Sir John's blatant efforts to pair Thomasina off with Sir Charles failed miserably and she blocked every attempt by Sir John's guest to learn more about her background. Any details that did emerge came from Sir John and were largely inaccurate.

The only information Sir Charles Hearle was able to glean with any certainty was that Thomasina was an unexpectedly wealthy young woman.

This alone was sufficient reason for him to take more than a passing interest in her.

The evening was drawing to a close when five-year-old Richard, dressed in a night-gown, put in an unexpected appearance in the sitting-room to which the four diners had adjourned.

Sleepily the young boy complained that he had been woken by the crying of his baby brother.

'That must be where the servant girl is who should have been taking care of Richard,' said Juliana. 'I'll take him back to bed and settle him down. It should not take more than a few minutes.'

Juliana had hardly left the room before Sir John made an excuse to hurry after her. His hope was that Thomasina and Sir Charles might get on better with each other if left alone.

When the others had gone, Sir Charles said, 'May I take this opportunity to say how terribly sorry I am for my unforgivable behaviour this morning?'

Thomasina said nothing.

'I really do not know what got into me. It is not the way I would normally behave, I can assure you.'

Thomasina would have enjoyed telling him that she *knew* differently, but once more she remained silent.

'I can fully understand your attitude towards me, Thomasina – indeed, I deserve nothing less – but may I be permitted to call on you?'

'I am only a guest in this house, Sir Charles. I can't invite anyone to come calling. Nor do I have any control over who does, or does not, visit the house.'

'Of course. I am aware of your difficulty, but should I pay a call, would I be welcome?'

'As I said before, this is not my home. I would not

abuse Sir John's hospitality by being rude to anyone who is a welcome guest in his house.'

'In that case I will leave here tonight happy in the knowledge that we will certainly meet again. I hope you will allow me an opportunity to prove that your first impression of me is not an accurate one.'

Thomasina had no wish to point out the inaccuracies in Sir Charles's statement, but she *did* wish to talk with him again. However, she would prefer it to be in the company of others.

She had heard a great deal that evening about his plans for the *Celestine*, but wanted to know more. With this in mind, Thomasina would put on an act of civility towards Sir Charles. Nevertheless, inside she carried a smouldering hatred of the man. When it eventually flared into life, she hoped it would prove powerful enough to consume him.

17

Thomasina saw Sir Charles Hearle only once more before the *Celestine* sailed for the Swansea smelters with her cargo of copper ore.

The baronet did not go with his ship. Instead, he returned to his home near St Mawes, a short ferry trip away from Falmouth town.

Before he left, he paid a further courtesy call on Sir John St Aubyn, at the castle. It was a fine day and Sir John, Sir Charles, Juliana and Thomasina stood on the terrace admiring a squadron of ten ships-of-the-line.

Sheltering in the Mount's bay overnight, the ships had just weighed anchor and were tacking to westward, heading for the open waters of the Atlantic Ocean.

'That's where the *Celestine* will be heading in a few months' time,' said Sir Charles, 'out to the open sea.' As he spoke he passed to Thomasina the telescope being shared by the viewers.

'Then you must intend taking ore farther afield than Swansea,' Thomasina said.

'There's very little profit to be made in shipping ore anywhere,' replied the baronet, confirming the observation that had been made to Thomasina by Abel, some days before. 'Too many ship-owners involved in the trade are willing to carry ore for next to nothing. No, Thomasina, I have been told of a much more lucrative market.'

'Can you share this exciting news with us?' asked Thomasina, 'or are you going to keep us guessing?'

Pleased at her unexpected interest, Sir Charles said, 'I can tell this company, but it is important that it should go no further. Hubert Fox, probably the most important shipping agent in Falmouth, visited the fish cellars on the Mount yesterday. He was here to check on the quantity of pilchards caught and how many are likely to be cured. He has received word that the Italians will allow pilchards to be taken into Leghorn – but it is an unofficial concession and must not be generally made known.'

'I don't doubt it's "unofficial",' Thomasina said scornfully. 'But I'm sure Napoleon will have something to say about an English ship trading with a country he controls.'

'A "say" is probably all he will be able to have about it right at this moment,' said Sir John. 'Napoleon has over-extended himself in his Russian campaign. As a result, many of the countries he has occupied are taking advantage of his weakness. Besides, there is little chance of Charles's ship being taken by the French. They hardly dare put to sea these days.'

'That's quite right,' agreed Sir Charles. 'And Mr Fox says that in Italy a ship-owner with nerve and initiative can make at least eight times the price that pilchards are fetching anywhere else in the world. The Italians have always been particularly partial to Cornish pilchards, but they have not been available for many years. The first boat to land them there will make a killing.'

'Hubert Fox has proved himself a keen business-man in the past,' commented Sir John. 'And he has a near-monopoly on the product in question in these parts. He'll no doubt be asking a high price for them?'

'Higher than anyone would dream of paying for the home market,' admitted Sir Charles. 'But with the money they will fetch in Italy, it is well worth paying.'

'When will you send off your ship?' Sir John put the question.

'Hubert Fox says he should have a good cargo ready for me by late October, or early November.'

'I envy your crew the voyage, at least,' Sir John said. 'It is a good time of the year to get away and enjoy the Mediterranean sunshine.'

Thomasina nodded in agreement, but her thoughts were not of sunshine. She had heard Malachi speak of Hubert Fox, but she had known of him long before that. Many years ago he had fallen out with the fishermen of Mevagissey. As a result, they refused to sell their catches to him. As far as she knew, their

ban on trading with him still stood. This might be
the very opportunity for which she had been waiting
in order to strike a momentous blow at Sir Charles
Hearle.

The following day Juliana announced to Thomasina
that Sir John wanted her to accompany him to London
to finalise arrangements he had made for their children. The older boys would be going to Westminster
School while the girls were to stay with an aunt, who
would ensure they learned all the skills demanded of
young women of breeding.

They would also be formally introduced to the
society in which they would one day meet young
men considered suitable husbands for wealthy young
women.

'How long will you be away?' Thomasina asked.

'We will probably stay in London for the whole
of the winter,' Juliana replied. 'We rarely spend any
time in the castle during the cold months and leave
only the minimum of staff here. Unfortunately it is
such a cold and dreary place then. But if you wish
to remain here . . .'

'I wouldn't dream of it,' replied Thomasina,
'although I would like to stay on the Mount for
a while longer, if it's at all possible. I am very happy
here. Do you think I might move into the new house
that's been built and furnished for the steward? I
understand he prefers to remain in Marazion for the
time being. Perhaps I could rent it for a while?'

Aware that Thomasina owned property in Falmouth,
Juliana was taken aback by her request. 'I am quite

certain it will be no problem,' she said, 'but I thought you would want to move to Falmouth? You will meet far more people there.'

Thomasina shook her head. 'I don't need people – or the memories that are there. No doubt I will go to Falmouth occasionally – quite soon, in fact – but I really would prefer to live here.'

'Then Sir John and I would be very happy for you to move into the steward's house. If ever the steward decides to live on the Mount you will need to vacate it, of course, but I don't doubt we will be able to find you somewhere else. But you will need to take on some staff . . .'

'I've thought of that,' said Thomasina, delighted to be remaining on the Mount. 'I decided that, if you agreed I could live in the house, I would ask Abel's grandmother to act as my housekeeper.'

'You could do a lot worse than to take on Verity Trannack,' said Juliana thoughtfully. 'She's a well-respected woman. You would have Abel on your side, too. That would pose no problem to you, I am sure. But how do you think Sir Charles will behave when he learns you are living on your own in the steward's house? He might try to take advantage of the situation.'

Thomasina had told Juliana, in confidence, of what had occurred when she and the younger children had visited the *Celestine* on the ship's first arrival in the St Michael's Mount harbour.

'That's why I want Verity Trannack for my housekeeper. It would ensure that Abel was more likely to be around whenever Sir Charles was on the Mount.'

*   *   *

On the day that Sir John St Aubyn, Juliana and
the children left the Mount, bound for London,
Thomasina moved into the newly built steward's
house. Situated at the foot of the Mount itself, it was
on the edge of the village. Although sandwiched
between two fishing cellars, it was a large and
impressive building.

The house had been furnished by the St Aubyns and
Thomasina's few possessions were carried down from
the castle by Abel, at her request, the move being
supervised by Verity Trannack, who was taking her
new duties very seriously.

'You are going to be very comfortable here,' commented Abel, depositing a chest of clothes in the
bedroom Thomasina had chosen for her own. It was
the same chest he had once carried from Malachi's
house in Falmouth to the St Aubyn boat. 'You have
a fine view of the harbour, too.' Unexpectedly he
added, 'Does Sir Charles Hearle know you're moving
in here?'

It seemed to be a fairly innocuous question, but
Thomasina felt it contained an unspoken query.

'He doesn't know yet, but he'll no doubt learn
about it when he next visits the Mount. That's partly
the reason why I've asked your grandmother to act as
my housekeeper. One of her tasks is to ensure she's
always in the house with me whenever Sir Charles is
on the island – and to call you if I'm in need of help.'

A brief raising of Abel's eyebrows represented a
possible expression of disbelief. 'Then it would seem
the village gossips have it wrong.'

'Have what wrong?' Thomasina demanded.

'They're saying you've set your cap at Sir Charles Hearle,' replied Abel, his expression telling her nothing of his own thoughts. 'Opinion is fairly evenly divided on whether or not you'll catch him.'

'If they're taking money on it, you'll be safe betting against it – whatever the odds. I have nothing but contempt for Sir Charles Hearle. As for "catching" him . . . I'd rather catch smallpox.'

Abel smiled then, a genuine, open smile that she had rarely seen. 'I'll take you at your word and see if I can't persuade someone to take a wager on the outcome.'

Returning his smile, she said, 'You've worked hard for me today, Abel. Toiling up and down to the castle must have been warm work. I'll ask your grandma to make some tea for us – and I do appreciate your help in moving in here.'

He shrugged. 'The causeway's open and there's not much for any of the boatmen to do while Sir John and the family are away.'

'That reminds me,' Thomasina spoke as though she had only that moment thought of what she was about to say, 'do you need to take a boat to Falmouth in the near future? I have some business there.'

'I've nothing specific to go there for, but Mistress Juliana said I was to take orders from you as though you were one of the family. Tell me when you want to go and I'll sail you there.'

18

'Is there anything you need me to help you with while you're in Falmouth?'

Abel put the question to Thomasina as he took the St Aubyn boat between Pendennis Point and Black Rock. They would soon be entering Falmouth's busy harbour. There would be little opportunity for conversation while he was guiding the boat between the vessels of all sizes that always crowded the Cornish sea port.

They had made good time from St Michael's Mount. It was Thomasina's hope that she would be able to explain her business proposition to the solicitor, Zachariah Bennett, leave him with sufficient details to enable him to carry out some enquiries on her behalf, and be free to return to St Michael's Mount early in the afternoon.

'I don't want to stay in Falmouth for too long, Abel.

I should have finished my business soon after midday. Why don't you join me for a meal somewhere?'

Abel and Thomasina had come to know each other a little better since her decision to move into the unoccupied house that had been built for the St Aubyn steward. The previous evening, he, Thomasina and his grandmother had shared a meal in the kitchen of the house.

Despite this, the invitation to join her for lunch in Falmouth came as a surprise.

'I can't go to the type of inn you're used to, looking like this.' He made a gesture that took in his clothes. 'I'm dressed for work, not for dining out – and certainly not with a friend of the family who employs me.'

The two crewmen were out of hearing in the bow of the boat, sorting out mooring ropes, so Thomasina said quietly, 'I'm a friend of Juliana's because fate had me shipwrecked on St Michael's Mount. I might just as easily have been cast away on an island among cave-dwellers. When fate doesn't take a hand, I like to choose my own friends. If those friends prefer to eat at a sailors' inn so as not to feel out of place, then I'm perfectly happy with that. Besides, I shall be hungry and I don't enjoy eating alone. Where shall we eat?'

Abel was constantly being reminded that Thomasina neither thought nor behaved like any other woman he had ever known. Yet her suggestion that they should eat together in public had taken him by surprise.

'Are you quite sure . . . ?'

'Of course I'm sure! Where do you suggest we go?'

He tried to think of an inn suitable for her. He was not only concerned about the clothes he was wearing. The choice was limited by the small amount of money he carried in his pocket.

Thomasina was shrewd enough to realise that his hesitation was not entirely due to the manner in which he was dressed. 'One other thing. As it's my idea, I'll be paying the bill.'

Putting the tiller hard over in order to clear the path of an outgoing merchant vessel, which had unexpectedly altered course to catch the wind, Abel said, 'I suggest we make it the British Marine, on the harbourfront. The food is good and I served in the Marines with the landlord. He runs a respectable inn.'

'That sounds fine. I'll meet you there at one o'clock.'

Solicitor Zachariah Bennett greeted Thomasina effusively, expressing genuine delight at seeing her. Showing her to his inner office, he instructed a junior clerk to make tea and bring it to them.

When he had drawn up a chair for her, he scurried around to the far side of his huge, highly polished desk and beamed at her.

'Your visit is most timely, Miss Varcoe,' he declared. 'The insurance company has made a settlement for the loss of the *Melanie Jane* and its cargo. It is a most generous settlement, if I may say so. I have also discovered two more houses that were owned by Captain Ellis. He purchased them prior to putting his affairs into my hands. They were brought to my attention as a result of a notice I placed in a newspaper in connection with his death. It adds a substantial sum to your wealth, my dear. Would you like me to suggest some investments that I consider to be both safe and wise?'

'We can discuss that at a later date,' Thomasina replied. 'I'm here today because I have an idea of my own. I want to buy a ship, Mr Bennett. A large deep-sea ship of at least two hundred tons – and I want it to be a fast ship. Indeed, speed is essential if I am to carry out the plans I have for such a vessel.'

Zachariah looked at Thomasina sharply. 'Do you intend using the vessel for smuggling? I must warn you, Miss Varcoe, that since the navy has assumed anti-smuggling duties, it has become an extremely hazardous business.'

Thomasina smiled disarmingly at the solicitor. 'Buying a ship for smuggling is not in my plans, Mr Bennett. I want it to be speedy in order to beat other ship-owners to markets that I see opening up in countries where Napoleon's grip is weakening. I believe a great deal of money is to be made in such trade – especially for those who are among the first to take advantage of the situation.'

Relieved, but not yet fully convinced, Zachariah said, 'I don't doubt you are correct in your assessment of the trading situation, Miss Varcoe. Indeed, I can recall the late Captain Ellis sitting in that very chair and telling me that your business acumen was at least equal – if not superior – to his own. But bearing in mind your requirements, would you want a ship built to your own specifications?'

'That would take far too long. I want a ship as

soon as it can be found. Certainly within a month or so.'

'That might prove difficult,' Zachariah said dubiously. 'Even if you were able to purchase the boat you are looking for, there is still the question of a captain and crew . . .'

'I already have a captain in mind,' Thomasina said. 'He would find his own crew . . . But I have a further requirement. The purchase must be made by a third party. I don't want it known that *I* am the buyer. It is to be kept a closely guarded secret shared only by you and me. Not even the captain is to know.'

Zachariah peered at Thomasina over the top of his spectacles for some seconds. 'Is there a reason for such extraordinary secrecy, Miss Varcoe?'

'Yes, but you don't need to know what it is, Mr Bennett – at least, not right away.'

'Hm!' The elderly and somewhat staid solicitor was perplexed, and it showed in his expression. 'Are you quite certain you have nothing illegal in mind? If you have, there is my reputation to consider . . .'

'You have my solemn word, Mr Bennett. Furthermore, the man I have in mind to command the ship is as honest a man as you'll find anywhere.'

'Very well, Miss Varcoe, but if we are to keep such a transaction secret, I will need to bring in the third party. A shipbroker.'

'Do you know of one you can trust?'

Zachariah nodded, 'Yes, my brother-in-law, Claude Coumbe. I believe he was the shipbroker used by Captain Ellis on a number of occasions.'

'That's right, he was – but you must swear him to secrecy about my identity.'

'If that is your wish. He will no doubt be as full of curiosity as I am at such unprecedented secrecy, but he will accept my word that you are a bona-fide customer.'

Now that he had agreed to do as she wished, Zachariah seemed more relaxed. Leaning back in his chair, he said, 'You never fail to intrigue me, Miss Varcoe. I hope you will one day feel able to confide in me the need for such secrecy in this particular transaction?'

'I hope so too, Mr Bennett. Now, when will you be able to speak to your brother-in-law about the possibility of buying such a ship as I have in mind?'

'I have some business to attend to this morning, my dear, but I could call on him this afternoon. If you care to call in to see me later in the day, I will be able to tell you what he has said and perhaps provide you with details of any ships on offer that meet with your requirements.'

19

Abel was waiting for Thomasina outside the British Marine when she arrived at the inn. Much to her surprise, he was no longer wearing his boatman's jersey. Instead, he had on a clean, white linen shirt.

When she commented upon the change, he appeared mildly embarrassed. 'I thought about it and decided you shouldn't be seen with me in my old working clothes, so I borrowed this from Jim, the landlord here. I told him about you and said you had offered to buy me dinner, but I wasn't dressed to sit down at table with a friend of my employer. He agreed and loaned me a shirt. At my request he has also set a table for us in a private room. I hope you don't think that was presumptuous of me, but he gets a lot of seamen in here. The language they use shouldn't be overheard by a woman. I didn't think you would feel comfortable walking into a crowded inn by yourself, either. That's why I decided to wait out here for you.'

Thomasina smiled at him. She doubted whether the patrons of the British Marine would talk about anything she had not heard discussed on the *Melanie Jane*, or in any one of the many bars she had frequented when disguised as a boy. However, she was touched by Abel's consideration for her.

Taking his arm, she said, 'I appreciate your thoughtfulness, Abel, but why are we standing out here talking? I'm hungry.

Abel had apparently impressed the landlord of the British Marine with his story of Thomasina's social standing. He hurried to meet them when they entered the inn, personally escorting them to a small private room where a single table had been elaborately laid for lunch.

The first drinks came with the compliments of the landlord, then they were served with a meal that Thomasina enjoyed as much as any she could remember.

As they ate, she told Abel that her business in Falmouth town was going to take longer than she had anticipated. Because of this, she would not be returning to the Mount, as planned.

When he expressed disappointment, she suggested that he might return for her the following day.

'Unfortunately, tomorrow is probably the only day when I can't come to Falmouth,' he said apologetically. 'Polly Miller, the widow of the coachman, is moving from the Mount to Penzance. Sir John said I'm to help her. It's been arranged for tomorrow, but will probably take two days.'

'The poor woman.' Thomasina was genuinely sympathetic. 'Of course you must do all you can to help her. Is there a Falmouth boatman you could recommend to take me back to the Mount?'

'Not one,' said Abel emphatically. 'You'd be better taking the Penzance coach and leaving it at Marazion – unless you'd prefer to stay in Falmouth until I can come back for you in a couple of days' time?'

Thomasina thought about his suggestion, but dismissed it almost immediately. She did not relish the thought of spending long hours in the house that had once been Malachi's.

The only way she might go out after dark would be to disguise herself as a young man once more. Somehow, she had lost all enthusiasm for such an adventure.

She had money and was hoping to buy a ship, which would bring her a handsome profit and at the same time achieve her aim of ruining Sir Charles Hearle. That was sufficient excitement for the moment . . .

Bringing her thoughts back to the present, she said, 'I don't want to spend any more time than I need to in Falmouth town. I'll catch the coach back to Marazion as soon as I can. Either that, or I'll buy a horse and ride back. That will get me there more quickly and it might be useful to have a horse available whenever I have need of one.'

Abel looked doubtful, but he already knew better than to question a decision made by Thomasina once she had made up her mind about something.

Thomasina's meal with Abel lasted for more than two hours. At the end of this time she walked back with him to the St Aubyn boat. When they reached it she was aware, as was Abel, of the nudges given by one crewman to the other, and of the sly looks they both gave Abel when he stepped on board. The boatmen carefully avoided looking in Thomasina's direction.

She remained on the quay, watching the boat until it was well clear of the harbourside, then she made her way to the offices of Zachariah Bennett.

The solicitor had not yet returned to his office and it was another half an hour before he put in an appearance.

It was immediately apparent to Thomasina that Zachariah and his brother-in-law had enjoyed a lunch that would not have met with the approval of the town's Temperance Society, which was holding a meeting on the quay only a short distance from the solicitor's office.

However, Zachariah's animated manner was not entirely due to the amount of alcohol he had consumed. Ushering her to the inner office and carefully shutting the door behind them, he said, 'My dear, I do apologise most profusely for keeping you waiting, but when I tell you my news I am certain you will forgive me. I think I have found a vessel that meets with your every requirement. It is certainly fast – very fast indeed, I am told. It is almost new and may, hopefully, be purchased for a very reasonable sum of money.'

'If it's such a wonderful ship, why hasn't it been

snapped up already?' asked Thomasina sceptically.

'Because it's a prize. A captured American schooner, due to come up at auction next week. It was taken in a Swedish harbour by a privateer. I am told that, had the two ships met on the high seas, the American would have disappeared over the horizon before the privateer had time to make a positive identification!'

Thomasina knew that the Americans had built some very fast ships. She had seen some of them in American waters. They were capable of far greater speeds than could ever be coaxed from the ill-fated *Melanie Jane*.

A number of American sea captains had been taken by surprise by the United States's declaration of war against Britain in June of that year. The result had been that they proved easy prey for the British navy and the predatory privateers that sallied forth from many British ports.

Thomasina remembered something else about these fast American vessels.

'Don't the American schooners have a different sail conformation to most British ships?'

'I believe my brother-in-law did say something of the sort – but there are seamen in Falmouth who have sailed on such vessels. It could work very much in your favour, my dear. Cornish seamen are a conservative breed. The fact that the vessel is slightly different from those we are used to seeing here will undoubtedly affect bidding at the auction. You could possibly acquire the vessel for a bargain price.'

Thomasina thought about it for some moments, then said, 'When can I look at this ship?'

'Right away, if you wish. My brother employs a boatman who will take us all there. Should he be inclined to talk indiscreetly, we will make it clear that my brother-in-law is taking us to the American ship purely as a social exercise.'

Thomasina fell in love with the American vessel at first sight. It was anchored a short way up the Penryn River, close to the little village port of Flushing. Ironically, the port had carried out a flourishing trade with America until the present war brought such business to an end.

As they approached, Thomasina could see the name *Henry Mallory* painted on the stern. Claude Coumbe said that whoever bought the ship would need to rename and register the vessel in an English port.

A watchman was kept on board the ship. He had a strong aroma of alcohol about him and grumbled incessantly at having his afternoon nap disturbed, but he helped the trio on board before disappearing inside the crew's quarters, leaving them free to wander over the ship at will.

'It's a beautiful ship,' declared Thomasina, when the watchman had gone. 'I don't think I've ever seen better.'

'Nor will you,' replied Claude Coumbe, enthusiastically. 'I believe such ships are known as "Baltimore Clippers". The *Henry Mallory* is certainly Baltimore-built and, with this particular sail configuration, requires a smaller crew than an English ship of comparable size. As for its speed under full sail

. . . I doubt if there's a ship in the world could outpace it.'

Thomasina and the two men spent almost an hour on board, during which time she examined the *Henry Mallory* from stem to stern. Not only was it of an outstanding design and construction, but it had been lovingly and carefully maintained, in a manner of which she thought Malachi himself would have wholeheartedly approved.

It was without doubt the finest ship she had ever seen. She grew more and more enthusiastic with everything she saw and had already decided that she had to own the vessel, yet she managed to contain the excitement she felt.

'You have made no comment about the ship,' said Claude Coumbe despondently. 'No doubt you feel, as others have before you, that the ship's design is somewhat revolutionary for British waters. I can fully understand your reservations, but, I assure you, you have just inspected a very fine vessel indeed.'

'I wouldn't argue with you, Mr Coumbe. She *is* a fine ship. If I seem preocupied, it's simply that I am deciding what I will call her when she is mine – and she *will* be mine, whatever the cost.'

Turning from the astonished shipbroker to the solicitor, she said, 'Mr Bennett, I trust I can leave the financial details in your hands? If Mr Coumbe is right, we might purchase the vessel for a bargain price, but I will leave the bidding in Mr Coumbe's hands. You know how much I can afford to spend in order to purchase the ship, but do not lose it because you feel the price is going too high. I want the *Henry*

Mallory, although my name is not to be revealed. Is this fully understood?'

Both men agreed that her wishes would be respected. It was a very happy trio who returned to Falmouth town that evening.

20

In the office of Claude Coumbe the shipbroker drew up an outline contract for Thomasina to sign. It would give him the necessary authority to purchase the *Henry Mallory* on her behalf.

'I will need to register the vessel in another name,' he said. 'Would you like time to consider what you might call the ship?'

Thomasina shook her head. 'No, the ship will be called the *Edward V.'*

Jeffery had provided the money that had enabled her to become a co-ship-owner in the first place and she would have liked to have called the ship the *Jeffery and Malachi*, but that might have alerted a number of people to the new ownership of the American-built vessel.

Both men were curious about the reason why she was giving that particular name to the ship but neither put the question to her and she did not explain that it was named in honour of her father, Edward Varcoe.

'I believe you have a captain in mind?' said Claude Coumbe. 'May I be permitted to know his name?'

'Of course,' agreed Thomasina, 'but my ownership must be kept a secret from him, too. If he knew, he would probably refuse to accept command of the ship, even though he is the right man.'

'All this is most irregular.' Claude Coumbe shook his head disapprovingly. 'I wish you could tell me the reason for such unprecedented secrecy. Should there be anything involved that is in any way illegal . . .'

'I have already convinced Mr Bennett that I have nothing illegal in mind,' Thomasina declared firmly. 'I'll give you the same assurance, Mr Coumbe. I *do* have very good reasons for not revealing my ownership of the *Henry* . . . the *Edward V*, but they are of a personal nature.'

'Very well.' The shipbroker sighed, not entirely convinced. 'If that is your wish, I will honour it – but who is this captain you have in mind?'

'His name is Abel Carter – you have met him, Mr Bennett. He came to your office to give you a statement about finding poor Malachi, after the shipwreck. At the moment he is head boatman for Sir John St Aubyn, at St Michael's Mount. Before that he spent some years in the Royal Marines, seeing a great deal of action, I believe. He has also been mate on a deep-sea merchantman and has occasionally carried out duties as master. He's the man I want.'

Zachariah Bennett and Claude Coumbe exchanged

concerned glances, but it was the solicitor who spoke. 'Do you think he has sufficient experience to take command of a ship such as this, my dear? It would pose a challenge to a seaman of considerably more experience than this "boatman" appears to possess.'

'I feel fully confident that Abel will rise to any challenge,' Thomasina said. 'So confident that he is the *only* man I am prepared to take on as master of the *Edward V*. I might add that, if it were not for Abel, I would not be discussing the purchase of a ship at all. Abel is the man who pulled me from the sea when the French ship was driven on to the rocks at the Mount. He risked his own life to do so.'

The two men relaxed visibly at her words. They felt they now had a logical answer to at least one of their many doubts about her actions.

Their relief showed and Thomasina thought she would give them another crumb of comfort. 'Abel is a very proud man. If he knew the offer of captaincy of the *Edward V* came from me, he would think it had been made out of gratitude and not from recognition of his ability. As a result, he would refuse to accept it. He must *not* know and you must think of a good story to explain why he is being asked to take the ship.'

Now the two men had been given a reason for Thomasina's actions that they were able to accept, Claude Coumbe promised to do his best to persuade Abel to take the post of master of the *Edward V*.

'There is one other thing,' said Thomasina. 'Once Abel has his crew and they are thoroughly familiar with the ship, I have their first voyage planned. In order for it to be a success you will need to travel to Mevagissey, Mr Coumbe. I want you to purchase all the cured pilchards that the *Edward V* is capable of carrying. Her first voyage will be to Leghorn, in Italy. I know it's still under Napoleon's control, but my information suggests that the *Edward V* will be allowed to land her catch – and to negotiate a price that might well fetch eight times what it would in this country. But – and this is vitally important – the *Edward V* must be loaded and on its way by the end of September. Any later and it will be beaten to Leghorn. In that event the cargo's value would drop by an unacceptable amount.'

As she spoke, Claude Coumbe had been making rapid pencilled notes. Putting down his pencil, he looked up at Thomasina admiringly. 'I apologise for doubting you earlier, Miss Varcoe. You have a keen business mind – as Zachariah told me when he first spoke of you. I very much look forward to acting as your shipbroker. I feel it will prove to be highly profitable for all concerned.'

The next morning, while Thomasina was eating a late breakfast, there came a heavy knocking on the front door of the house.

It was unusual to have callers come to the house at any time. For someone to arrive at this hour of the day was unheard of. Frowning, she rose from the breakfast table and made her way to the front of the house.

On the way, she thought it might be the woman who came to the house to check that all was well. Today was not one of the days when she would normally come to the house, and she had a key, but there was only one way to find out about the mysterious caller.

Opening the door, Thomasina was astonished to see Abel standing outside.

'Abel! What are you doing here? Is something wrong at the Mount?'

'Nothing at all,' Abel assured her. 'But when I spoke to Polly Miller last night, she said she wasn't quite ready to make her move to Penzance. She asked if we could put it off for a few days. That left me free today. I knew you would prefer to return to the Mount by sea – so here I am!'

'That's very thoughtful of you, Abel, and you're quite right. Travelling by coach is a nightmare and hours spent riding side-saddle would be almost as bad. But why are we standing talking at the door? I was just having some breakfast. Come and join me.'

As he stepped inside the hall of the house, Thomasina closed the door behind him. Leading the way to the kitchen, she said, 'I'm sure you're ready for something to eat. What time did you leave the Mount in order to get here at this time of day?'

'We saw the sun-up at sea,' Abel confessed. 'I was worried that if we didn't arrive early enough, you might already be on your way back to the Mount.'

'I'd intended going out to buy a horse and tack this morning,' Thomasina confessed. 'But I wasn't looking forward to it. Now, let me pour you a cup of tea. While you drink it I'll finish my own breakfast. When I've done I'll cook something for you.'

Thomasina enjoyed cooking breakfast for Abel. As

she said to him, 'It's far better than either wasting good food or leaving it for a cleaner who may, or may not, come in to work while it's still edible.'

Abel sat down to porridge, followed by eggs, bacon, fried bread and some cold beef, left over from the joint she had bought at a cooked-meat shop the previous evening.

Cooking, eating and sitting together at the breakfast table seemed a very intimate and cosy thing to be doing. It was a feeling of which they were both very much aware.

Thomasina wished she could have told Abel about the *Edward V* and how he was to be an essential part of the plans she had for the ship, but she was convinced it would be a dreadful mistake.

Their intimacy would need to extend far beyond having breakfast together before she felt able to confide her plans to him. Besides, she was not entirely certain that she herself fully understood the reason she had decided he was the only man she wanted to become master of the American-built ship.

One thing of which she was far more sure: she was going to miss Abel when he was at sea on board the *Edward V.*

21

The wind direction had changed during Abel's absence from the Mount. When he set off it had been blowing from the south west. However, during his stay at Falmouth the wind had shifted around to the east.

It made leaving harbour difficult, but sailing became easier when the boat reached the open sea beyond the two fingers of land protecting the deep-water anchorage for which Falmouth was famous. Once they rounded the Lizard the wind would be astern of them and they would make good time to the Mount.

Shipping was always busy on the approaches to Falmouth and Thomasina found dodging among the varied craft exciting. In addition to the many boats operating from the Cornish fishing communities, there were coastal and deep-sea traders, packet

ships which worked from Falmouth and a couple of
warships patrolling farther offshore.

As the harbour dropped away behind them, the
volume of shipping gradually decreased, but there
was still much to occupy Thomasina's attention.

Soon they were steering south-eastwards, hugging
the coast of the land mass known as the Lizard.
Suddenly Thomasina noticed a ship that was tacking
on an opposite course to the St Aubyn boat.

'That ship's finding it hard work making Falmouth.'

The vessel was steering a zigzag course between
coast and open sea in a bid to make headway against
the unfavourable wind.

'It's a big ship,' Abel commented. 'Far too big to
be sailing so close to shore. A vessel that size needs
plenty of room to turn. Whoever's in charge isn't
giving himself enough sea space.'

Thomasina could see that the decks of the ship
in question were crowded with women, men and
children. When she pointed this out, one of the boat
crew said, 'It's a troop transport on its way back
from Spain, I'd say. It'll have wounded men, wives,
widows and children on board.'

'Then they deserve a safe homecoming,' Abel commented. 'But if that damned fool of a master isn't
careful, he'll put them on the Manacles.'

The Manacles constituted a group of half-submerged
rocks off the Lizard coast, feared by every sailor who
sailed the south Cornish seas. Over the years they had
claimed a vast number of victims.

'Look! He's taking her around again!'

The cumbersome transport ship had appeared to

be heading for the safety of the open sea, but now the vessel slowly came about once more, wallowing with flapping canvas for a few minutes before the sails caught the wind and billowed out, taking the ship in towards the coast.

The captain appeared oblivious of the white foam that swirled around the rocks of the Manacles, between sea and shore.

'She's going to strike!' The youngest member of the St Aubyn boat's crew cried out in horror.

'They must surely have posted a look-out?' Thomasina expressed disbelief at the drama taking place in front of their eyes.

'If they have, then he's fallen asleep,' Abel said grimly. 'There's no way they can sail clear of the Manacles now. We'd better get across there. They're going to need all the help they can get.'

Glancing away from the doomed ship for a moment, Thomasina saw that other boatmen were also aware of the impending disaster. As the notorious reef prepared to claim yet another victim, boatmen and fishermen abandoned what they were doing and headed for the rocks.

When the transport struck the Manacles, it seemed to Thomasina that everything happened in slow motion. The captain made no attempt to steer clear of the hazard. Indeed, it was quite apparent that he did not realise the rocks were there, maintaining his suicidal course to the very end.

Rising with the swell, the bow of the ship hung in the air for a few long moments, before beginning to fall. Suddenly it struck the rocks and the ship came to an immediate, grinding stop, sending passengers on the upper deck sprawling in tangled heaps, screaming with alarm.

This first impact tore a great hole in the transport below the water-line. As water poured inside the doomed ship, the panic-stricken passengers fought each other for a place on the ladders leading to the upper deck.

Some failed to make it even this far. The transport was carrying wounded and sick soldiers, many too weak or too badly maimed to rise from their cots and hammocks.

Unable to escape from the reef upon which it was impaled, the vessel seemed to Thomasina to be writhing in agonising death-throes as the motion of the sea pounded the ship's hull to splinters on the relentless rocks.

A number of fishing boats were on the scene ahead of the St Aubyn boat. By this time some of the more courageous passengers were already leaping into the sea from the stern of the transport, which was still clear of the rocks. Once in the water, they struck out desperately towards their would-be rescuers.

Only the strongest of them made it to safety. Others, caught by the swell and a treacherous current, were carried back to the very rocks that had proved the undoing of the transport ship.

Despite the very real dangers posed by sea and rocks, it was evident that those still on board would soon have to follow the example of those who had already abandoned the ship. The transport was breaking up. Before long it would slide from the reef and disappear beneath the water to join many other wrecks littering the seabed around the Manacles, taking with it those who remained on board.

Terrified passengers, many of whom could not swim, sought anything that would float and support them. Wooden deck lockers, broken spars, hatch covers, even items of cabin furniture were somehow hauled up from below decks. All were utilised.

When a passenger took possession of such an item, he, or she, would throw it overboard immediately to prevent it being stolen by other fear-stricken passengers, then leap into the sea after it.

The St Aubyn boat was among the wreckage and the survivors now, and those on board began reaching over the side to drag half-drowned survivors into the vessel.

Other boats were doing the same. A Royal Navy man-o'-war, outward bound from Falmouth, had dropped anchor and lowered all its available boats to help pluck luckless men, women and children from the sea.

Despite all the efforts to save them, it seemed to Thomasina that, for every person rescued, there were two or three more screaming out for help.

Before long the St Aubyn boat had twenty-five survivors on board, far more than she could safely carry. Then Thomasina heard someone screaming just over the side from where she stood, soaking wet as a result of helping to pull others into the vessel.

Looking over the side, Thomasina was horrified to see a young woman desperately trying to keep a child of perhaps two years of age above the water. She was largely successful, although her own head was below the surface of the water more often than above it.

As the woman and child bumped against the boat, Thomasina reached down and managed to take a hold of the child's clothing. Pulling the child screaming and coughing into the boat, she dumped it unceremoniously into the arms of a uniformed soldier before turning back with the intention of pulling the child's rescuer to safety.

To Thomasina's dismay, the woman had disappeared!

Pushing aside the retching, crying survivors, Thomasina fought her way to the boat's stern, where Abel was fighting to keep the heavily overladen boat clear of the Manacles. She peered into the water, hoping to see the woman surface, but there was nothing. The woman who had succeeded in saving the young child had disappeared.

'Are you all right?' Abel called the question to a distraught Thomasina as she stood at the stern of the boat staring down into the sea, wondering what she could do next.

'No! I just pulled a young child on board. Its mother, if that's who it was, has disappeared.'

'A great many women have disappeared, Thomasina. So have their children. Men, too. We must be thankful for those we've been able to save and pray that God will take care of those we haven't.'

Thomasina made her way back to the place where she had left the child. Greatly relieved, the soldier passed the terrified and crying infant back to her.

Now she was able to see for the first time that the

child was dressed in a girl's dress and, after the terror of her ordeal, was shaking with cold.

Hurriedly stripping off the child's wet clothing, Thomasina pulled off her own flannel petticoat, which had remained comparatively dry beneath her dress, and wrapped it around the sobbing child.

'We've got as many on board as we can safely take, Abel. Probably more, in fact.' The concern of the older of the two St Aubyn boatmen was fully justified. The boat was packed with wet and shivering men, women and children, many of whom were weeping. Others were calling out to those they recognised, who were still in the water.

'But . . . there are still so many left,' cried Thomasina. 'We can't just leave them here.'

'All those we've already rescued will be back in the water if we try to take any more on board,' said Abel grimly. 'But, like you, I can't bear the thought of leaving so many of them behind . . .'

Having a sudden idea, he called to the two boatmen. 'Tie a rope to the two oars – make sure it's secure, then throw the oars over the stern. We'll tow them behind us and hope that some of those still in the water will have the strength to hold on until we reach shore.'

'Are we taking them back to Falmouth?' asked Thomasina.

'No, we need to use the wind and make the nearest landfall. We'll put into Coverack. It will be a smoother run there than to anywhere else.'

22

A small knot of villagers was waiting when the St Aubyn boat bumped against the quay in Coverack village. Most were women and children, with only a sprinkling of old men. The remaining men were either among the fishermen who had been at sea and gone to the aid of the troop transport, or had put to sea to help save lives – or see what might be retrieved, depending upon their particular inclination.

The boat's mooring ropes were secured by two small boys. Then a number of old men, assisted by women, pulled in the survivors who were still clinging to the rope and oars towed behind the boat.

Village women, who in other circumstances might have been as eager as the Mount's Bay villagers to profit from a wreck near at hand, were touched by the sight of the injured, bedraggled survivors.

Crowding close to the boat, they helped soldiers

and their women and children to the shore, then hurried them off to the shelter of their homes to offer dry clothes and 'a little drop of something to put life back into you, my poor soul!'

As the last of the survivors stepped from the boat, Abel turned to see Thomasina still holding the small girl she had plucked from the sea.

'What are you going to do about the poor little maid?' he asked.

'What *can* I do with her, Abel? Who is she? Who does she belong to?'

'*I* don't know – but somebody must.'

'Then let's ask among those we've just landed. We might get a name, at least. Unless we do, we can't just dump her on a stranger and say, "I think her mother has drowned. I don't want her, you have her"!'

As she spoke, Thomasina jigged the small girl up and down in her arms, in a bid to put a stop to the body-racking sobs that still escaped from her.

Abel admitted that the girl posed a problem, but added, 'What will you do if no one knows anything of her?'

Thomasina had no answer to the question. She shrugged. 'I don't know . . . I suppose I'll have to spread the word that I have her and wait until someone comes forward to lay claim to her. There's nothing else I can do for her, poor little scrap.'

Abel had deep reservations that this would provide an answer to the identity and ownership of the young survivor, but all he said was, 'Then I suppose we had better set to and see what we can find out.'

Between them, Abel and Thomasina spoke to most

of the survivors they had landed at Coverack. The result was very much what Abel had anticipated. Most had no recollection at all of the young girl before today.

A few claimed to have a vague recollection of seeing her on board, but were unable to agree about her identity. Some thought she was the child of a wounded soldier. Others that she had been in the care of a nursemaid accompanying the widow of an officer killed in the fierce battle which had caused so many of the casualties on board the transport – the battle to take the city of Salamanca.

When the last of the survivors had been questioned, Abel said to Thomasina, 'We're no further forward than we were when we started speaking to everyone. What do we do now?'

'Take her back with us to the Mount,' said Thomasina firmly. 'I've spoken to the local vicar. He'll pass on the word that if anyone has lost a small girl, I have her, at the Mount.'

The rescued child in question, exhausted by her ordeal, was now asleep in Thomasina's arms as she sat in the stern of the boat, talking to Abel.

Looking down at her, Thomasina's expression softened. 'In the meantime I'll take care of her and try to help her forget all she's been through today.'

For lack of a name to which the rescued child would respond – and Thomasina had exhausted all those she knew – she decided she would call her 'Emma'.

By the time Emma had been with Thomasina for a week, two survivors from the wrecked transport had come to the Mount in the hope that she was their missing child. On both occasions Thomasina had been forced to endure their harrowing anguish when they confirmed she was not the child in question.

When two letters were delivered to the Mount, one for her and the other for Abel, Thomasina thought, with a sinking heart, that hers would contain news from the St Keverne vicar that more desperately hopeful women would be calling on her.

She opened it with mixed feelings, not entirely due to the thought of witnessing the raw grief of mothers who had lost a child. Although she felt that Emma should be returned to her parents – if they were still alive – Thomasina had grown extremely fond of the little girl during the time she had been taking care of her. She would miss Emma greatly if she were claimed.

In fact, the letter proved to be from Zachariah Bennett. Claude Coumbe had successfully bid for the American ship at auction. The *Henry Mallory* was now hers.

As Coumbe had anticipated, the ship had not proved popular with the Cornish ship-owners. He had purchased it for even less money than had been forecast. He had already taken steps to have the ship renamed the *Edward V* and had told his brother-in-law to inform Thomasina she had obtained a wonderful bargain.

Abel's letter was from Claude Coumbe himself. It said that through his offices an American schooner, taken as a prize, had been purchased by one of his clients and that the name of Abel had been put forward as a possible master of the vessel. Coumbe said that if Abel were interested, would he please present himself at the shipbroker's Falmouth office as soon as possible. He would then have an opportunity to be taken over the ship, which was to be known as the *Edward V*. Should he agree to become the ship's master, terms of employment would be discussed. Coumbe added that he felt quite certain Abel would find his salary an extremely generous one.

Abel was utterly bewildered when he brought the letter to the steward's house to show to both his grandmother and Thomasina that same afternoon.

'I can't understand it,' he said, for at least the third time during the ten minutes he had been in the house. 'Why *me*? It's been such a long time since I was at sea in a deep-sea vessel. There must be any number of masters they could have chosen.'

'The letter says it's an American-built ship schooner,' said Thomasina. 'Didn't you once tell me about such a ship? There must be many others who are aware of your experience. Your friend, the landlord of the Falmouth inn, for instance.'

Abel nodded. 'Yes, he knows all about me – and he's a great one for gossiping with anyone with time to talk. This offer has probably come about as a result of something he's said to someone.'

'More to the point,' said Thomasina, 'do you intend taking up the offer?'

'Of course he doesn't,' snapped Verity. 'He's got a perfectly good job right here on the Mount. Why would he choose to go gallivanting off all over the world? He's already done that once.'

'There's nothing wrong with working here for Sir John,' Thomasina agreed, 'but any one of a hundred men could be a boatman and none of them will ever make a fortune doing it. On the other hand, taking over as master of a deep-sea ship, especially one such as this, Abel could become a rich man. I saw some of these schooners when I was in the Americas. They're probably the fastest ships sailing the oceans. I'd *love* to sail in one. I can't think of anything more exciting. You can't possibly turn such an offer down, Abel!'

'What about Sir John?' asked Verity, tight-lipped. 'What do you think he'd say about it, after him going over the heads of many others to make Abel his head boatman?'

'He'd say the same as me,' declared Thomasina. 'It's a wonderful offer.'

'Grandma has a point, though,' said Abel uncertainly.

He was torn between a sense of loyalty to both Sir John and his grandmother and the unexpected opportunity to return to a way of life he had loved, and had given up only because he felt Verity had needed him when his grandfather died.

She had now recovered from the grief she had felt and was well able to cope with her daily life. She would certainly be more comfortably off if he were to take the opportunity that was being offered to him. Abel would be able to give her enough money to make her fully independent.

'Sir John would urge you to take it, I know he would,' said Thomasina. 'If you like, when I next write to Juliana I'll tell her all about it and of your reluctance to leave the Mount. I'll say it was me who insisted that you take it. You saved her life, too, remember? She'll wish you well.' Thomasina shrugged. 'Of course, you might not want to go to sea again, even as the master of such a wonderful ship . . .'

'No man in his right mind would *not* want such an opportunity,' said Abel. He looked at his grandmother, who was registering stern disapproval, then looked away again, his mind made up.

Speaking to Thomasina, he said, 'You're right. Only a fool would turn down such an offer. Thank you. I'll write to Sir John myself and tell him *why* I'm leaving, but I'd be grateful if you'd write to Mistress Juliana at the same time and explain things to her, too.'

'It seems I have no say any more in what's best for my own grandson!' Chin in air, Verity added, 'I'll leave you to arrange his plans with him, Mistress Varcoe. I know my place – and I have work to do.'

With this parting shot, Verity turned and walked out of the room.

'I'll not be happy going away from the Mount if Grandma is going to be so upset,' said Abel uncertainly. 'After all, I'm the only family she has.'

'She'll be all right, believe me, Abel. She doesn't like the thought of you going away, but she'll get used to it in no time. You gave up everything for her sake once, don't do it again.'

Thomasina could not tell Abel that she herself would probably miss him quite as much as his grandmother. But at least she had Emma now. 'When you

bring your ship into St Michael's Mount harbour – as
I have no doubt you will – your grandmother will
be the proudest woman on the island. You just wait
and see.'

23

Abel left the Mount for Falmouth the day after receiving the letter from Claude Coumbe. Three days later another woman arrived at Thomasina's door, clutching a letter from the vicar of St Keverne. It stated that she was a survivor who had lost a child when the transport foundered on the Manacles.

She believed that Emma might be hers.

Thomasina took an instant and quite unreasonable dislike to the woman from the moment Verity showed her into the sitting-room. Although Verity had still not forgiven Thomasina for the part she had played in persuading Abel to leave the Mount, she did little to hide her own disapproval of the visitor.

Introducing herself as Jean Toms, the woman had a thin, pock-marked face and eyes that seemed incapable of focusing on anything, or anyone, for longer than a second or two at a time. In addition, her nose would twitch when she sniffed, which occurred every minute or two.

The woman's clothing was shabby and none too clean, but Thomasina, trying to be generous, reminded herself that the visitor had survived a shipwreck and had lost her every possession – and lost her child, too.

Waiting while Thomasina read the St Keverne vicar's note, Jean Toms said, 'The reverend gentleman told me how you'd saved Sophie from the sea and said I was to come here and fetch her.'

'That's not *exactly* what is written here,' said Thomasina, 'but suppose you begin by telling me something about the child?'

'What is there to tell?' asked the woman, her glance shifting from one place to another around the room, but not touching upon Thomasina. 'She's my little girl, my Sophie, that's all.'

'No, it's *not* all,' retorted Thomasina. 'How old is she? Where and when was she born – and what was she wearing when you lost her?'

'Like I told you, her name's Sophie,' said Jean Toms. 'Named after me late, dear husband's mother. As for when she was born . . . No one worries about dates and such things when an army's on the march, and that's where Sophie was born. On the march. It might have been Spain, or it could have been Portugal.'

When the woman fell silent, Thomasina prompted her, 'What about the colour of her eyes? What would you say they were?'

'Why . . . I can't say I've ever thought about it

too much, but they're like mine, I suppose. Sort of a greyish-brown.'

'They're bright blue,' Thomasina replied.

'Of course,' Jean Toms said hurriedly. 'The same as her father's were. To tell you the truth, I've never been able to tell one colour from another, not properly, I haven't.'

'What about the clothes she was wearing when the ship went on the rocks?'

'Now how do you expect me to remember that?' Jean Toms asked indignantly, her glance pausing just long enough to meet Thomasina's eyes for a fleeting moment. 'There were so many clothes I might have dressed her in. Fresh ones for every hour of the day, if she wanted 'em. I just dressed her that day, that's all. I didn't know the ship was going to go down and that I'd have to remember every little thing I did before it sank.'

'The future of a small girl is no "little" thing,' Thomasina said. 'And what future is she likely to have with you?'

'I'll have you know that she wants for nothing,' Jean Toms declared indignantly. 'Her poor late father's family have money. He used to tell me about the market stall they own in Petticoat Lane, up in London. He used to say that if anything happened to him, I was to take young Sophie there to find 'em and they'd look after us. Never want for anything for as long as we lived, that's what he used to say.'

Thomasina refused to believe that this shifty, untidy woman was Emma's mother, but until this moment she had been unable to think of a reason why Toms should want to claim Emma as her own. Now she thought she knew.

'So you've never actually met your late husband's family?'

'No. Me and Jed were married in Spain, when I was widowed for the first time.'

Thomasina was slightly taken aback and Jean Toms explained defensively, 'It happens when you're married to a soldier who's fighting in a war. Some of the women who follow the army have been married four, five or even six times. Mind you, I never married outside the regiment. All me husbands were Buffs. The best regiment in the army, that is.' She spoke proudly. 'Wellington himself used to come and talk to us whenever he had the chance. Spoke to *me* once, he did.'

'We're talking of a young child's future,' Thomasina said curtly. 'Not of your life with the army. I'll be perfectly honest with you, I don't believe she belongs to you.'

Again Jean Toms's glance met Thomasina's, but it contained anger now. 'How can you tell? I haven't even seen her yet.'

Instead of replying, Thomasina went to the door and called Verity. The housekeeper was so close to the door that Thomasina felt she had probably been eavesdropping on the conversation taking place inside the room.

'Verity, will you please go upstairs and fetch Emma down. I know she's awake, I heard her just a few minutes ago.'

'Are you sure that's what you want to do, Miss

Thomasina? If you ask me, I think you should send this "baggage" packing. She's no better than she ought to be. As for being Emma's mother . . . !' She made an expressive sound through her nose before adding, 'Them two are no more related to each other than a pilchard is to a chicken.'

'I'm inclined to agree with you, Verity, but we need to put it beyond any doubt. Bring her down to the room just as she is. Don't change her clothes.'

Returning to the sitting-room, Thomasina spoke briefly to Jean Toms. 'She'll be down in a few minutes.'

'I can't wait to see her again,' the other woman gushed. 'I'll know her right away, you'll see.'

Thomasina said nothing.

When Verity entered the room, Emma was in her arms and half-asleep. She had been laid in her bed wearing her daytime clothes. Only her shoes had been removed.

As she entered the room, Jean Toms said immediately, 'It *is* my Sophie, I'd know her anywhere. Come to Mummy, my lovely.'

Emma looked at her just once, uncertainty on her face, then hurriedly turned away. As she did so she caught sight of Thomasina. Her arms went out to her immediately.

Taking her from Verity, Thomasina said, 'I think Emma has given us the answer we were all looking for. She doesn't know you.'

'Of course she does,' Jean Toms said. 'She's been through such a bad time that she's confused, that's all. Why, I even recognise the clothes she's wearing. I bought them myself, in Badajoz. Spent a whole week of her father's pay on them, I did.'

Thomasina and Verity exchanged triumphant glances. 'I think you've just settled the matter once and for all, Mrs Toms – if that's your real name. The clothes Emma is wearing today were bought for the children of Sir John St Aubyn. They were borrowed from the castle when Emma came here, because she had only the clothes she was wearing.'

Aware that she had been caught out, Jean Toms began to bluster that after all she had suffered it was easy to make a mistake, but Thomasina cut her protestations short.

Handing Emma back to the housekeeper, she said, 'Take Emma to the kitchen, Verity. Give her whatever she wants. Mrs Toms and I have some things to talk about.'

Kissing Emma, she passed her over to the housekeeper once more.

When they had left the room, Thomasina rounded upon the woman who had claimed Emma for her own. 'You have some explaining to do and I want the truth from you. Either you tell me what this is all about, or you can explain it to a magistrate.'

'I *did* have a daughter. One just like Emma, but now she's gone. Dead . . .' She began to cry noisily, but Thomasina was convinced it had more to do with the likelihood that she might meet up with a magistrate than with any bereavement she might have suffered.

Following her instinct, Thomasina said, 'You may

very well have lost a child – but it had nothing to do with the shipwreck, did it?'

Jean Toms looked up at Thomasina and for a moment it seemed she would challenge her statement. Then she dropped her glance to the floor. 'No, my Sophie died soon after I lost Corporal Willis, my third husband. Not that we were properly married. You see, Sophie wasn't his daughter, either. Like I said, Sergeant Toms, my second and proper husband – and the best of 'em all – was her father. Almost a gentleman, he was.'

When Thomasina felt she had a grasp of Jean Toms's tangled matrimonial affairs, she believed she knew why the woman had tried to claim Emma for her own.

'This Sergeant Toms . . . is it his family who has the stall in Petticoat Lane?'

Jean Toms nodded.

'. . . And they know about him having a daughter, but don't know she's dead. Am I right?'

Once again the woman nodded without speaking.

'So in order to deceive them you would have claimed Emma as your own, even though you would always know she wasn't. It wouldn't matter to you that she would might never know who her real parents were?'

'I'd have taken good care of her,' Jean Toms replied defensively. 'I'd have treated her as though she *was* my own – and she'd have had Jed Toms's family to love her. If they were the same as him, she'd have wanted for nothing.'

She began crying once more. This time Thomasina believed the tears were genuine.

'I *would* have looked after her well, just as I did Sophie. When we were retreating from the French, some of us got parted from the main army. That's when Sophie died. There was rain and mud and we had practically no food. When men and women fell – and they were doing it all the time – they just got trampled into the mud. I had nothing to eat for nigh on five days – but I made sure Sophie never wanted for anything. If there was no shelter when we lay down at night, I stayed awake to cover her up with myself, best I could. Then she caught the fever that had already carried off half the children. In twenty-four hours she was dead. I couldn't believe it at first and carried her with me for another day and night before the sergeant-major had her buried. If I could have died in her place I would have done, believe me.'

The sobbing became noisier and Thomasina said sharply, 'That's enough of that.'

'I . . . I'm sorry.' Giving Thomasina another of her rare direct looks, she said, 'Can I go now? I won't trouble you again, honest.'

Moved, despite herself, by the woman's story of the ordeal she had undergone, Thomasina nodded. Then, as Jean Toms turned to leave the room, she called, 'Just a minute.'

Going to a small bureau standing beneath a window, she opened a drawer. Taking a small box from it, she picked out a number of gold coins and held them out to the woman.

'Here, these will help you on the way to wherever it is you're going.'

For a few moments the woman looked down at the ten guineas she held in the palm of her hands. Then, reaching down the front of her dress, she pulled out a small bag attached to a cord worn around her neck. Pulling open the drawstring, she poured the coins inside.

Instead of saying 'Thank you', as Thomasina was expecting, she asked, 'Do you have the clothes the girl was wearing when she was taken from the sea?'

It was such an unexpected question that Thomasina replied, 'Yes . . . why?'

'I was a dressmaker before I married a soldier and went off to follow the drum. I'm not good at remembering faces, but I've an eye for clothes. If I was to see those she was wearing, I might be able to tell you something about the child.'

Thomasina looked at the woman uncertainly, then, satisfied she was telling the truth, hurried to the door. Opening it, she called, 'Verity, will you bring the clothes Emma was wearing when she was pulled from the sea?'

A few minutes later Verity entered the room with the clothes over her arm.

Jean Toms pounced upon the dress immediately. 'This is one I've seen before. I'd know it anywhere. I saw it on board more than once. It must have been worn by the child you've got.'

'You know her? Who is she?' Thomasina's heart was thumping, 'Can you give me a name?'

Jean Toms shook her head. 'No – but I can tell you

about her parents. Both of them were on board. He
was an officer who'd been wounded in the leg. A
Guards officer – Foot Guards. The only one of his
regiment on board. His wife was pregnant and they
had a nursemaid. I spoke to her once, a Spanish girl
she was, name of Mary. Spoke good English, too. Yes
. . . I remember now, she told me she was going with
the family to their home, just outside Newhaven. I'm
sure about that, because that's where the battalion
sailed from when I was married to me first husband.
A something "Hall", it was. Very proud about it,
was the young Spanish girl. Thought she was going
to live the life of a lady there, she did.' Handing
back the small dress, Jean Toms said, 'That's all I
can tell you.'

Going to the bureau once more, Thomasina gave
the delighted woman another five guineas.

Once Jean Toms had left the house, Thomasina sat
down to gather her thoughts. Although she now had
a lead which could take her to Emma's family, she
was suddenly not certain it was what she wanted.

She had come to love Emma as though she were
her own.

24

Thomasina had not made up her mind what she should do to follow up Jean Toms's story, when the *Edward V* sailed into St Michael's Mount harbour, three days later.

As word went around that this was Abel Carter's ship, the Mount villagers turned out to watch it berth. In the village school, lessons were suspended in order that the children might witness the arrival of the American-built clipper ship.

Standing beside Verity, with Emma in her arms, Thomasina could almost feel the pride emanating from Abel's grandmother, despite her opposition to his decision to leave the Mount.

When the ship was safely berthed, Abel, smiling happily, threw the vessel open for the inspection and approval of his former neighbours.

When Thomasina, Verity and Emma went on

board, Abel greeted them warmly. 'Let me show you around,' he said enthusiastically. 'She's the best ship I've ever set foot on – and to think I'm the master! I wake up every morning convinced it must all be a dream!'

'It's certainly a lovely ship,' Thomasina agreed, adding, 'You've had no problem finding a crew?'

'None at all. I was amazed at how many seamen in Falmouth had sailed on ships such as this – and they're as keen to sail on board her as I am. The mate I've taken on gave up a good berth on a packet ship to join the *Edward V*. He's a first-class man, too, quite capable of having his own command, if that was what he wanted.'

'What are you doing in St Michael's Mount harbour?' asked Verity.

'The shipbroker has given me a fortnight to get myself and the crew familiar with the ship. This is our first trip and our first experience of entering harbour. I don't think I need fear doing it again. The ship handles beautifully, and the crew know exactly what they're doing. I'm a very lucky man.'

Thomasina wished she could tell Abel how pleased she was to have made the right decision about appointing him as captain of *her* ship, but the time was not yet right.

'What do you think, Grandma?' he asked Verity. 'Is the *Edward V* a good ship, or is it not?'

Determined not to sound too enthusiastic, Verity replied, 'A ship's just a ship to me. It's no better, nor no worse, than any other that's come in here – but I doubt whether you'll have a job for life, as you would have had if you'd stayed with Sir John. Who's the owner of this wonderful ship of yours, by the way?'

Abel frowned. 'I can't tell you – not because I don't want to, but because I don't know. The shipbroker says he doesn't want his name known. It's not unusual. The *Edward V* was taken as a prize. If the person who bought it has other ships and this stupid war with America comes to an end, he might find all his ships boycotted in America. Better to keep his name quiet and stay in the background.'

'That's all very well, if you ask me . . .' said Verity, '. . . but then, no one *is* asking me, so I can only wish you luck. You certainly won't accept anything else from me.'

Abel met Thomasina's glance and they both smiled.

'It's a beautiful ship, Able. I envy you sailing in her. Where will you go when you leave the Mount?'

'I thought I'd sail eastwards, along the Channel. There should be enough British men-o'-war to frighten off the French. If we do meet up with a privateer, we have the speed to lose them.'

Thomasina was thoughtful for some time, then she said, 'Would you consider taking on board a couple of passengers and putting into Newhaven, Abel?'

'It depends very much on who the passengers are,' replied Abel cautiously.

'I'm thinking of me and Emma.'

When Abel expressed his surprise, Thomasina gave him brief details of the visit of Jean Toms and told him of all she had said.

'Do you believe her?' Abel asked.

'She had no reason to lie to me, Abel. At least, not by then.'

'You haven't got a great deal to go on when you get there,' said Abel doubtfully.

'Don't try to stop me going, Abel,' said Thomasina. 'I wouldn't need a lot of persuading to forget all about trying to find any family Emma might have, and keeping her for myself. But it wouldn't be fair to her, to me or . . .' Thomasina made a gesture that indicated resignation. 'It just wouldn't be fair to anyone.'

Making a determined effort not to appear too emotional, she added, 'Anyway, if we don't find her family then, it will still be a wonderful experience to sail with you in the *Edward V*. She's a truly beautiful ship, Abel.'

Fully aware of how much Emma had come to mean to Thomasina, Abel thought that Thomasina's decision to make such a determined effort to locate the child's family did her great credit, but he said nothing of his thoughts. Instead, he said, 'I keep forgetting that you're almost as experienced a sailor as I am. You'll enjoy the voyage, at least, I can promise you that. Would first thing tomorrow suit you?'

'That will be be perfect. Now I must take Emma home and let her have a few hours' sleep. Come to the house for dinner tonight, Abel. Verity will be delighted to cook for you. Over our meal we'll discuss what else we're going to do.'

Dinner that evening was a happy affair, with Verity apparently having forgiven her grandson for leaving the Mount, and Thomasina doing her best not to think that Emma might be taken from her in the next few days.

Instead, she got Able to tell her all about the *Edward V*. Verity understood very little about ships and was more interested in speculation on the identity of the mysterous ship-owner – and the reason for keeping his identity such a close secret.

Thomasina tried to keep the conversation away from the subject, but it was Abel who gave Verity an explanation that she accepted – albeit reluctantly.

'You see, it's not entirely uncommon for a ship-owner to be in competition with friends. Rather than lose their friendship, he keeps his identity secret. He might put them out of business, but he doesn't want to lose their friendship!'

'That's immoral,' Verity exclaimed indignantly.

'And so it might be,' agreed Abel. 'It's also business. Now, if we're all to make an early start in the morning I suggest you and I go home, Grandma. Miss Thomasina will need to get some sleep and the hour is getting late.'

'I have some clearing up to do before I've finished for the night,' said Verity.

'Leave it until tomorrow morning,' Thomasina suggested. 'Abel is right, I must get some sleep. Emma will be awake at the crack of dawn. If you're working it will only keep me awake.'

As Verity and Abel walked to his grandmother's home, Abel said, 'I don't know whether to hope we find Emma's family or that we don't. Thomasina will be very unhappy if she has to part with the little girl.'

'How she feels is none of your business,' Verity said sharply, 'and you'd do well not to forget it. She's neither fish nor fowl, that one. She may be living on the Mount, as a guest of Sir John, and have that Sir Charles Hearle dancing attendance on her, but she's not one of *them* and never will be. She's not one of us, neither. She's got money – more than any of us will ever see in our lifetime – but no one's heard the truth of how she came by it. Nor shall we, if I'm any judge of character.'

'That's hardly fair, Grandma. I don't think she's being particularly secretive. She's just keeping herself to herself, that's all. Some of the money came from the insurance on her father's boat, when he was lost. The rest was left to her by the uncle who died on board the ship I helped to sink.'

'So she says,' said Verity uncharitably. 'But has anyone been able to check on her father – or this uncle? There's no doubting that she's Cornish, but where exactly does she come from? That's what I'd like to know.'

'Well, when I first took her to Falmouth, I made a statement to a solicitor there about the death of her uncle, so I know that's the truth, at any rate. Anyway, what are you doing working for her if you dislike her so much?'

'I haven't said I dislike her,' said his grandmother. 'She's got more spirit than most of the girls around here. But she's doing neither herself nor Emma any good by lavishing all the love she does on the child.

She doesn't belong to her and, sooner or later, someone will claim her.'

'Well, you should soon have your mind put at rest, Grandma. If we find her family at Newhaven, we'll be coming back to the Mount without Emma.'

'I've grown fond of the child, too, so I hope you do. Emma needs her own family – and so does Mistress Thomasina. The sooner she finds a husband and raises a family, the better it will be for her. She's likely to do well for herself, too. They're saying up at the castle that Sir John's son Humphrey is besotted with her. There's also a very strong rumour that Sir Charles Hearle would give up his bachelorhood – if not his bachelor ways – and make her *Lady* Thomasina. That's not bad for a girl who came to the Mount out of nowhere.'

Abel said nothing. He too had day-dreamed about a future with Thomasina – with more hope than before, now that he had achieved a certain status. But he had nothing to offer her that could compete with either Humphrey St Aubyn or Sir Charles Hearle.

He decided he would need to lavish his affections upon his new ship, the *Edward V*.

25

Early the following morning, Thomasina arrived at
the harbour with a still-sleepy Emma in her arms. A
number of crewmen spoke to the young child, but
she would not respond, turning away and hiding her
face in Thomasina's shoulder.

As a result, she was declared to be 'a shy little
maid'.

The *Edward V* set sail from the Mount at eight
o'clock that morning. Abel estimated that, with a
lightish south-westerly wind, their sailing time to
Newhaven would probably be in the region of thirty-
six hours. It would be the longest voyage undertaken
by him and his crew since taking over the ship.

Abel had given his cabin to Thomasina and Emma.
He would be sharing a much smaller cabin with
the mate.

As the ship left the harbour behind, more sail was

crowded on and the schooner began slicing through the water, at the same time rising and falling with the powerful motion of the sea's swell. It was a motion that brought back many happy memories for Thomasina and she began to enjoy it immediately.

Not so Emma. Whether it was because she had less happy memories of the sea, or because she was in unfamiliar surroundings, she clung to Thomasina even more than usual.

Eventually, having prepared the cabin for their brief time on board the *Edward V*, Thomasina carried the small girl to the upper deck. Here, aware of Emma's recent tragic experience, the sailors tried to put her at ease by offering to let her hold the wheel and 'steer the ship'.

When this failed to work, they drew her attention to the large flag, billowing from the mast in the breeze, but Emma refused to allow herself to be seduced from the shelter of her shyness.

Standing beside the helmsman, feet wide apart on the deck to maintain his balance against the movement of the ship, Abel smiled at Thomasina.

'What do you think of the *Edward V*? How does it compare with the ship you sailed in with your Captain Malachi?'

Mention of Malachi's name gave Thomasina a brief moment of pain. When it passed, she said, 'If you can command the same loyalty from your crew as Malachi had, then the *Edward V* will be the happiest ship afloat. I believe that it's probably already the speediest.'

'You're witnessing the birth of a legend.' The

helmsman unexpectedly broke into their conversation. 'Once in a lifetime, if a sailor's very lucky, he'll find himself crewing on a ship like no other he's known before, or will ever know again. I believe the *Edward V* is just such a ship. The rest of the crew feel the same, too. We're all excited about being on board her.'

Addressing Thomasina, he said, 'I knew your Captain Malachi Ellis and actually sailed with him for one voyage, many years ago. It's my opinion that he'd feel the same about the *Edward V* as we do.'

Moved by the man's words, Thomasina observed, 'If that's what you truly feel, then Abel is a very lucky man.'

Aware of the depth of Thomasina's feelings about Malachi, Abel said, 'I *am* a very lucky man – and I have you to thank for it, Miss Thomasina.'

Startled, Thomasina looked at him in alarm, wondering whether he had discovered the truth about his appointment as captain of *her* ship. His next words reassured her.

'If you hadn't been so persuasive, I might never have had the courage to accept the offer to become master of the *Edward V*. Had I turned it down, I would have missed the greatest experience of my life.'

They made good time that day. When Thomasina sat down in her cabin for a meal, they had passed Start Point and would be out of sight of land for the whole of the night hours. Abel said that they should be passing south of the Isle of Wight at about eight o'clock the next morning, with perhaps another twelve hours of sailing before they arrived at their destination.

With Emma asleep in a hanging cot in the cabin, Thomasina sat down at the table with Abel and the mate. Jamie Stocking was a young but experienced sailor who was proud of the fact that his home was Burnham Thorpe, in Norfolk, birthplace of Admiral Lord Nelson. As a small child, Jamie had met that most famous admiral on more than one occasion.

A great deal of the conversation at the table was about Nelson, until they turned to the reason for their voyage to Newhaven. Jamie asked if they had any definite plan in mind to find the family of the couple who might, or might not, have been the parents of Emma.

When Thomasina confessed that she had been unable to come up with anything that guaranteed success, Jamie offered an idea of his own.

It was one that Abel wryly suggested would no doubt have great appeal for those crew members chosen to take part.

It had already been decided that the ship should be anchored offshore. Jamie's suggestion was that half the crew, including Abel, should remain on board. That would leave enough crewmen to take the ship to sea should an emergency arise.

The remainder of the men, led by himself, would go ashore. Once there they would disperse and seek out the inns and taverns of Newhaven. In each establishment they would make enquiries about an officer in the Foot Guards who lived locally and was known to have taken his wife to the war in the Spanish peninsula.

It was possible that news that he was a casualty would have reached England long before he took passage in the ill-fated transport.

By the time the two men left the cabin, it had been agreed Jamie's plan should be given a trial. Indeed, it was the only one they had.

Checking on the small child before she herself went to bed in the captain's bunk, Thomasina gazed at Emma for a very long time. She secretly hoped the plan would not succeed.

If the search to find the girl's family was unsuccessful, Thomasina felt she would be able one day to tell Emma in all honesty that she had done all she could to locate them and learn her true identity.

26

Thomasina found sleep elusive that night. She was still awake when the sailors who had been onshore returned to the *Edward V*.

She wondered whether they had learned anything and did not have to wait too long in order to find out. Minutes after their return there was a light tap on the door of her cabin.

Swinging herself out of the bunk, she put on a robe and answered the door. One of the crew stood outside and said, 'Sorry to disturb you, ma'am, but Captain Carter thought you might like to come up on deck. The mate has some information for you.'

When Thomasina climbed the ladder to the upper deck, she found Abel and Jamie waiting there for her.

'I hope we didn't wake you, Miss Thomasina,' said Abel, 'but Jamie has found out something about the family we were seeking . . . But I'll let Jamie tell you himself.'

Trying hard to conceal his excitement, Jamie said, 'We all went around the town and one of the men and I went to the Paris Inn. I spoke to the landlord and explained why we were there. He called for silence, told everyone of our quest and asked if anyone knew anything that might help us. We struck lucky. One of the men in there said that Lord Pardoe has a son who is in the army. He was recently returning home after being wounded in Spain and his ship was wrecked on the coast somewhere off Cornwall. The man wasn't sure, but he thought he'd lost a child, too.'

'Where does this Lord Pardoe live?' asked Thomasina, not at all certain she wanted to know.

'In Walkden Hall, in a village of the same name. It's about five miles from Newhaven.'

Thomasina thanked him for his information, but was by no means sure now that she wanted to follow up the information he had obtained.

When Jamie had gone below, Thomasina remained on deck, thinking about all she had been told. If the information was accurate, she might lose Emma the next day.

'Miss Thomasina . . . ?'

Abel broke into her thoughts and Thomasina said irritably, 'I do wish you wouldn't call me *Miss* Thomasina, Abel. I *hate* it. It smacks too much of master and servant. I am just plain "Thomasina". Will you call me that, please?'

'Thank you,' said Abel understandingly. 'Look, I

know you're unhappy about this. If you like, we can forget all about this family, which may, or may not, belong to Emma. We can go back to the Mount and carry on as before.'

'No, Abel, I can't do that. I would wonder every time I looked at Emma just how much better off she might have been had we found her own family – especially if they're titled.'

Abel was not entirely convinced, but he agreed to accompany Thomasina the next morning when she called at Walkden Hall.

The following morning, Thomasina, Abel and Emma went ashore and Thomasina hired a carriage in which they would travel to Walkden. She also persuaded the daughter of the carriage owner to come, too. Thomasina had decided she would not take Emma into the house immediately, but would assess the situation first, while Emma remained in the carriage in the care of the young girl.

By the time they entered the drive of Walkden Hall and came within sight of the house, Thomasina was trembling. She was so nervous that Abel reached out and took her hand to comfort her.

Walkden Hall was a very grand house indeed. It had extensive lawns, formal flower-gardens and a great many gardeners in evidence. From the rear of the garden, grooms were taking a number of pedigree horses out for exercise. It was apparent to both Thomasina and Abel that this was the home of a very rich man.

Thomasina suddenly felt uncertain of what she was

doing. What if Emma was nothing to do with the Pardoe family and they thought she was trying to make money from a family tragedy?

'It's all right, Thomasina,' Abel tried to reassure her. 'Either Emma belongs to this family, or she doesn't. If she belongs to them, you've made everyone happy. If she doesn't . . . Well, you've tried your best for her – and she's still yours.'

Giving him a wan smile, Thomasina turned to Emma. 'Stay with the lady for a few minutes, darling. I'll be back directly.'

Emma started to protest, but the carriage owner's daughter had a great deal of experience with children, having several brothers and sisters of her own. Producing a peg doll, which had a brightly painted face and was dressed in cleverly home-made clothing, she began to hold a conversation with it, telling the doll about Emma.

Satisfied she was leaving the small girl in good hands, Thomasina left the carriage and set off for the front entrance of Walkden Hall, with Abel at her side.

The entrance was as impressive as the great house itself. Overawed by the grandeur of the building, Thomasina thought that if this was indeed where Emma belonged, she had nothing to offer the young girl that could take its place.

Reaching the door, Thomasina hesitated for a moment before tugging at the bell-pull. In that brief time the door was opened by the imposing figure of a uniformed butler.

'May I help you?' he asked, politely enough.

'Yes,' Thomasina said. 'We'd like to speak to Captain Pardoe.'

'I am afraid that is not possible, Miss. The captain is in London. At the War Office, I believe.'

'Oh!' The word expressed both Thomasina's disappointment and relief. She found it difficult to forget she had once been a servant in a house considerably less grand than this one.

'Do you know when he'll be back?'

'I do not, Miss. I am not kept informed of such matters.'

Aware that the butler had begun to talk down to her, Thomasina said sharply, 'Then perhaps I should speak to someone who *does* know.'

The butler was uncertain how he should deal with this young woman and her companion. Her manner of speech betrayed her country origins, yet she was expensively dressed and displayed a disturbing air of confidence.

'May I ask your name, Miss?'

'It's Thomasina Varcoe – and this is Captain Carter, master of the schooner, the *Edward V*, moored off Newhaven. Neither name would mean anything to Captain Pardoe, but I am here on a matter of some importance.'

Slightly reassured now that he knew one of the two callers was a sea captain, but still uncertain of Thomasina, the butler said, 'I am quite certain Mrs Pardoe is aware of the captain's plans, but the staff have been given strict instructions she is not to be disturbed. She recently suffered the loss of a child . . .'

Startled, Thomasina looked at Abel excitedly, then

asked, 'This Mrs Pardoe . . . she survived the wreck
of the transport?'

'Yes, both she and Captain Pardoe, but . . .'

'Then it's more important than ever that I see and
speak to her. Very important indeed.'

Convinced at last by the urgency in her voice, the
butler said, 'If you care to come into the hall and take
a seat, I will speak to Lady Pardoe, Captain Pardoe's
mother.'

The hallway was in itself as large as most houses
– and considerably loftier. From it, a magnificent
staircase curved away to the upper storeys of the
grand building.

Seated in two padded chairs beside the staircase,
neither Thomasina nor Abel spoke. Both were overawed by their surroundings, although Thomasina's
excitement almost overrode such a consideration.

It was a few minutes before the butler returned,
walking a few paces behind Lady Pardoe.

Thomasina had expected the mistress of such a
grand house to be tall, elegant – and perhaps somewhat formidable. In fact, Lady Pardoe was short,
plump and had a kindly manner.

Before the butler could introduce the visitors, Lady
Pardoe said, 'Good morning . . . Miss Varcoe and
Captain Carter, is it? I understand you have expressed
the wish to speak with my daughter-in-law, Lavinia. I
am afraid she is far too ill to receive visitors. Perhaps
I may be able to help you?'

'Yes. Yes, you probably can.' Thomasina decided
she would explain her mission to this woman. 'It's
about the child she's lost. Her little girl . . .'

'Little *girl*. No, I am afraid there must be some mistake, my dear. The child she lost was a son. It would have been my first grandson.'

'Oh, I'm sorry!' Thomasina was devastated. 'We've been wasting your time. I thought . . .'

She was interrupted by Abel, who said, 'We *are* talking of a child who was lost when the transport bringing them back from Spain was wrecked off the Cornish coast?'

Startled, Lady Pardoe said, 'No, but the baby she was carrying was lost as a result of the shipwreck . . .'

Belatedly she realised the implication of Abel's words and her eyes widened in an expression of dismay, 'You don't mean . . . you must be talking of Maria, the daughter born to Lavinia and my son in Spain. Oh dear! Has the . . . Have you recovered the child's body? Oh, dear, dear! This will be too much for poor Lavinia. I cannot tell her. I cannot . . . Although the body of the child's nursemaid was identified by my son, Lavinia has always hoped . . .'

Interrupting the increasingly distraught viscountess, Thomasina produced a child's dress that had been tucked inside her coat. 'Lady Pardoe, would you please show this to your daughter-in-law? It's very important.'

When the other woman hesitated, Abel said, 'Please do as Thomasina asks, Lady Pardoe. If we are given the answer we are hoping for, I promise you your daughter-in-law will not be upset.'

After looking at both their faces for some moments, Lady Pardoe took the dress and hurried away up the curving staircase without saying another word.

She was away for some minutes, then both Thomasina and Abel heard the sound of running feet. A moment later a young, pale-faced woman appeared at the top of the stairs. In her hand she held the dress Thomasina had given to Lady Pardoe.

Hurrying down the stairs, she held out the dress to Thomasina and cried, 'This dress, it's Maria's. I bought it for her in Madrid. She was wearing it when the ship struck the rocks. You . . . you've found her body.'

Lavinia Pardoe was trembling and Thomasina reached out and clasped both her hands in her own. 'No . . . no, there is no body. We have Maria. We've brought her here with us. Abel . . .'

She did not need to explain. Abel was already hurrying from the house. Minutes later he returned with the child Thomasina had called 'Emma'.

There was no need to ask whether she belonged here. Her mother screamed Maria's name and, after only a moment's hesitation, the small girl cried out 'Momma' and there was a reunion that no one who witnessed it would ever forget.

'Emma' had been reunited with her mother and the family she might never have known, had it not been for Thomasina's tenacity and selflessness.

27

The *Edward V* weighed anchor later that same afternoon, but Thomasina did not leave her cabin until the sun had disappeared beyond the western horizon of the English Channel.

She had broken down and wept in the carriage on the return journey to Newhaven. Abel had done his best to comfort her, but she did not regain full control of herself until the carriage reached the first houses in the port.

Now, in the darkness, Thomasina made her way to the upper deck, where a number of seamen were still working to ensure that the ship sailed safely through the night hours.

Abel was standing beside the helmsman, but in the light of a quarter-moon he saw her emerge from the hatchway that led to the cabins and came to meet her.

Solicitously he asked, 'Are you feeling better now?
Would you like me to send someone for something to
eat? Cook told me you'd eaten nothing. He is worried
about you. In fact, the whole crew are.'

'I'm sorry I've caused you all concern. I'm all right
now, but don't feel like eating. Thank you for asking,
though. Thank you for everything. I'm glad I had you
with me. Very glad. Without you I couldn't have got
through the day.'

Aware of her conflicting emotions about parting
with the girl she had learned to love as 'Emma', he
said, 'It's probably no consolation, but you did the
right thing, you know? Not only for Emma . . . sorry,
I mean Maria. She's now where she should be. With
a mother who was breaking her heart over the loss
of two children, and with a family who can give her
everything she'll ever want.'

'I'd have given her everything, too,' declared
Thomasina unhappily. 'She'd have wanted for nothing.'

'Except her own family and rightful name,' Abel
pointed out. 'One day her father will take *his* father's
title and she will become "The Honourable Maria
Pardoe".'

'She'll be no happier for that,' Thomasina said
fiercely. She apologised immediately. 'I'm sorry,
Abel. It's just . . . I didn't realise I would miss her
quite as much as I do.'

She was gripping the rail which ran around the
stern section of the ship. Abel put his hand over
hers and squeezed it sympathetically. For a moment
she leaned against him, then the ship bounced on a

wave and they were both obliged to move in order to maintain their balance.

'When do you expect to reach the Mount?' Thomasina asked. The question was as much to fill the silence that had fallen upon them after a moment in which each had been acutely aware of the closeness of the other.

'The day after tomorrow,' Abel replied. 'But I have a cargo of pilchards to take on board from Mevagissey some time soon. I thought of calling in there to see if they are ready yet.'

The thought of putting in to Mevagissey, where she would undoubtedly be recognised, alarmed Thomasina, but she succeeded in sounding calm as she said, 'If it's all right with you, I would prefer to go straight back to the Mount. There are a number of things I want to do that were put off while Emma – "Maria" – was with me.'

'Fine, then we'll go straight to the Mount. I can come back to Mevagissey later in the week. There's no urgency.'

Abel's statement about the lack of urgency involved in his proposed visit to Mevagissey had to be revised when the *Edward V* reached St Michael's Mount harbour.

Sir Charles Hearle's ship, the *Celestine*, was there loading a cargo of pilchards.

The sight of the other ship taking on its cargo troubled Abel almost as much as it alarmed Thomasina. If the *Celestine* reached Leghorn before the *Edward V*, then all her plans would come to nothing. But she could not allow her feelings to show.

'I wonder where the *Celestine* is finding a market for pilchards?' mused Abel. 'I doubt if it will be a home port.'

'I can give you the answer to that,' replied Thomasina. 'Sir Charles Hearle told me he intends sending the cargo to the Mediterranean – to Leghorn, I believe. He's had information that any ship bringing in pilchards would be welcome there, even though Napoleon has banned English ships from trading.'

'My first cargo will also be pilchards and is destined for the same area. It's quite probable that Claude Coumbe has the same information as Hearle. But only the first ship to reach Leghorn will be able to command a high price for its cargo.'

Making up his mind, Abel said, 'I'm afraid this calls for a change of plan, Thomasina. I'll call to one of the Mount's boats and send you ashore before I turn the *Edward V* around. I need to go to Falmouth and tell Claude Coumbe what I've seen here. It will probably lead to me being given new orders.'

'You have no alternative,' agreed Thomasina, 'but can you give me a few minutes? I'd like to pen a quick letter to Zachariah Bennett. Perhaps you would have it delivered for me. It won't take a few minutes.'

Below deck in her cabin, Thomasina wrote to her solicitor confirming all that Abel would report to the shipbroker. She stressed the importance of ensuring that Abel loaded his cargo as quickly as possible and reached Leghorn ahead of the *Celestine*. Zachariah was to inform his brother-in-law immediately.

Sealing the letter carefully, she gave it to Abel.

Then, before climbing down the ladder to the waiting boat, she surprised and delighted Abel by giving him an affectionate kiss, thanking him once more for his kindness on what had been a very difficult mission for her.

She waved to Abel from the boat and had her gesture acknowledged, but by the time the St Aubyn boat bumped against the stone steps set into the harbour wall, the *Edward V* had cast loose the pilot boat and was shaking out sail in preparation for a fast run to Falmouth.

28

Thomasina was not pleased to find Sir Charles Hearle waiting for her at the top of the harbour steps. He too was unhappy.

Handing her up the final, high stone step, he said, 'I presume that the ship you have just left is the one under the command of Sir John's late boatman?'

'That's right, he took me to Newhaven.'

'Had you asked me, I would willingly have put the *Celestine* at your disposal. It would have assured you of a passage in a reliable ship, with an experienced captain.'

'I have no complaints,' Thomasina replied. 'The *Edward V* is an exciting ship and Abel as fine a captain as you're likely to find anywhere.'

Sir Charles scowled. 'It was foolhardy of you to put your reputation at risk by spending nights at sea with an ex-employee of Sir John. Especially one who might have felt you owed him something more than gratitude because he had saved your life not once, but on two occasions.'

Thomasina was extremely angry at Sir Charles's unwarranted insinuations, but she kept a firm rein on her temper. 'I suggest that my reputation was far safer on the *Edward V* than it would have been had I taken a voyage in *your* ship,' she said. 'Anyway, my reputation is none of your business. Now, if you'll excuse me, I wish to go to my home.'

Turning away from him, she called down to the men in the St Aubyn boat, who were making no attempt to hide their delight at the conversation they had just overheard. Sir Charles's reputation with women was well known to all of them.

'Bring my trunk to the steward's house, please.'

Falling in beside her as though no harsh words had passed between them, Sir Charles said, 'I am glad to have caught you before the *Celestine* sails, Thomasina. I shall be away from England for some time.'

Taken by surprise by his words, and her anger with him temporarily forgotten, Thomasina said, 'You're going with the ship? I thought you were an army man, not a sailor.'

'You are quite right, I am a landsman,' agreed Sir Charles. 'But a great deal of money will be changing hands on this voyage. I trust Captain Carberry, of course, but in order to ensure there are no misunderstandings with the authorities, I feel it might be better if I were to carry out the negotiations in Leghorn. I speak fluent French, you know?'

Sir Charles Hearle was the last person with whom

Thomasina would have chosen to hold a conversation, but the movements of the *Celestine* were important to her. 'When do you sail?'

'It was to have been tomorrow,' replied Sir Charles, flattered that Thomasina should be showing an interest in his activities, 'but we have been unable to find a full cargo here. We will need to take on more from Newlyn.'

Newlyn was a very busy fishing port on the western shores of Mount's Bay.

'Does that mean you'll be around for a few days yet?'

'Probably, but we must not leave it too long. We have good reason to believe we will be welcome in Leghorn at the moment, but things in Europe can change overnight.'

'Of course,' Thomasina agreed. By now they had reached the steward's house and she said, 'Thank you for walking me home, Sir Charles. I trust you will have an enjoyable voyage to Leghorn.'

'Thank you, Thomasina – but won't you at least invite me in for a drink?'

'No, Sir Charles,' said Thomasina firmly. 'I am very tired after my own voyage and have much to discuss with my housekeeper. Good night, sir.'

Thomasina let herself into the house. Resting with her back against the door, she breathed a sigh of relief when she heard the sound of the baronet's footsteps as he returned to the harbour. Verity would not have known when to expect her return and was not in the house, but Thomasina had not wanted Sir Charles to know that she was there alone.

Thomasina did not remain alone for very long. News travelled amazingly fast on the island. By the time the St Aubyn boatmen were carrying her trunk upstairs to her bedroom, Verity had learned of her return and hurried to the steward's house.

Her first words were of 'Emma'. Thomasina was obliged to tell the housekeeper the outcome of the voyage and the girl's true identity.

'Well, I never!' Verity said for the third time. 'Fancy that! Her poor mother must have been overjoyed to have her back again, after believing her drowned.'

'She was,' agreed Thomasina, 'but this house is going to feel empty without her.'

'You'll soon find plenty to occupy yourself, my dear. Maisy, housekeeper up at the castle, tells me Sir John and Mistress Vinicombe will be returning to the castle sometime next week. It's to do with an election for Parliament, I do believe. Takes such matters very seriously, does Sir John. There'll be a whole lot of partying and coming-and-going until it's all settled, I dare say – but why hasn't Abel come back with you? I didn't see it myself, but my neighbour said his ship hardly put its nose inside the harbour before it turned around and went back out again.'

'That's right, Verity. He had to go and call upon the shipbroker in Falmouth. Abel is the captain of a ship and a very important man now, and he takes his duties very seriously. Mind you, when Sir Charles Hearle met me at the harbour and walked me home, I wished that Abel *had* returned to the Mount. Sir Charles was at the very bottom of my list of those I wanted to talk to.'

Verity had been expecting Thomasina home throughout much of that day and a kettle had been gently
steaming on the hob. Using the water to make a pot of
tea, she asked, 'Where does Master Humphrey come
on your list?'

'Higher, certainly, than Sir Charles – but he's gone
off to be a parson. Why do you mention him?'

'Because he's not a parson yet – and he's back here,
in Cornwall. He arrived the day you went off in the
Edward V. He's called here at least twice every day
since then.'

'Where is he now? At the castle?' Thomasina wondered what was wrong. She had understood that
Humphrey was to take on a curacy somewhere in
the London area.

Verity made a scornful sound in the back of her
throat. 'Her up at the castle hardly tolerates any of Sir
John's first mistress's children when their father is at
home. They rarely go there when he's not – and never
when the family is away. No, Master Humphrey is
over at Ludgvan, with his mother, poor woman.'

Curious, Thomasina asked, 'Did you know her,
Verity?'

'I knew her well. Worked for Martha Nicholls when
Sir John first took her to his house at Clowance,
then up to the castle. She was no more than seventeen or eighteen in those days and as pretty a
little thing as you'd find anywhere hereabouts. At
least, she was before she bore five children to Sir
John. She was never built to carry children, that
one.'

'Why did Sir John leave her?' Thomasina asked. It

was the first time she had ever met anyone willing to talk about Sir John's first mistress.

'Because he had fallen for Mistress Vinicombe. He'd had his eye on her since she was a young girl, even paid for her to go to one of the best schools in the country. Soon after young Master Humphrey was born, it was off with the old and on with the new. He moved poor Martha out to Ludgvan and brought Mistress Juliana to the castle in her place. Mind you, I believe he still has a soft spot for Martha. There's many a night when he's home you can see a lamp placed in one of the upper windows of the castle. They say it's a signal to Martha, over at Ludgvan, that he's not entirely forgotten her.'

'It must be very difficult for Martha Nicholls's children, especially if they're discouraged from coming to the castle.'

'It hasn't been too bad for the older ones, I suppose. Sir John has made good marriages for the girls, and James knows he'll be the one to inherit from his father. It's Humphrey I feel sorry for. He's never really known his father and has had to watch Sir John's affection being lavished on his half-brothers and -sisters. He must feel he's been left out of his father's life, for all that he seems fond enough of Mistress Juliana's children.'

'Thank you, Verity, I think I understand the family up at the castle a whole lot better now – but I'm still very fond of Juliana.'

Verity sniffed. 'Well, you know her and I don't. I'm sure she has her good points as well as bad, the same as the rest of us. Now, can I be cooking something for you? I don't suppose you had anything worth eating when you were on that ship.'

In fact, the cook on the *Edward V* had produced some very good meals, but Thomasina did not want to dispute another of Verity's prejudices. 'I won't have anything to eat, Verity. This cup of tea is what I have been looking forward to while I've been away. I'll finish it and go to bed. I didn't sleep well on the *Edward V*, especially on the voyage back. You can go home whenever you feel like it. There's just one favour I'd like to ask of you.'

'If it's something I can do, I will,' declared Verity.

'It's just that . . . if Sir Charles Hearle is seen heading in this direction, you'll hurry here as quickly as you can – no matter what time of day or night it might be.'

'I'd do that without you having to ask,' Verity assured her. 'I heard on the way here that you'd told him off in no uncertain terms. You've posed him a challenge, and from what I've heard that's something he enjoys. At least, it is when it's posed by a woman. I don't think he has the same courage if a man's involved.'

29

Humphrey St Aubyn arrived at the steward's house as Thomasina was having breakfast the morning after her return to the Mount.

She was not dressed to receive visitors, especially *male* visitors. Verity's expression left Thomasina in no doubt of the housekeeper's disapproval when she told her to show Humphrey into the breakfast-room.

He entered the room in a state of considerable agitation and blurted out, 'Thomasina! Thank heaven you are home safe and sound!'

Puzzled, Thomasina asked, 'Is there any reason why I shouldn't be?'

'I was out of my mind with worry when I came looking for you and heard you had gone off somewhere in a ship with Abel Carter – without a chaperon.'

'You're beginning to sound like Sir Charles Hearle, Humphrey, and I'm no happier with what you're saying than I was when *he* said it. You are aware of the reason I made the voyage to Newhaven, I presume?'

'Yes, but . . .'

'There is no "but", Humphrey. I reunited a small child with her mother. The child is the granddaughter of Viscount Pardoe – if that means anything to you. It wasn't easy for me to go at all. I had grown to love her and would have liked to keep her for my own.'

Thomasina had control of herself, but only just. Fortunately, Humphrey possessed the sensitivity to recognise this and apologised immediately.

'I'm sorry, Thomasina. I did not mean to cause you any distress.'

'Then we'll say no more about it – but you haven't explained what you're doing here. I thought you'd gone to London to enter the Church?'

An expression of anguish crossed Humphrey's face. He avoided her eyes as he said, 'After thinking long and hard about it, I have reached the conclusion that I don't have the right temperament to become a priest.'

Giving him a quizzical look, Thomasina asked, 'What sort of temperament do you think a priest *should* have? I must confess I don't have a great deal of experience of parsons and the like, but I wouldn't be at all surprised to learn that they're very much the same as the rest of us. You know, good ones and bad ones; lazy and hard-working ones; clever and dull ones . . . Don't you think you could fit in there somewhere?'

'That isn't what I mean,' said Humphrey uncomfortably. 'To be a priest you need to possess a deep and unswerving faith. I'm not at all certain I have that.'

'What an absurd thing to say!' Thomasina declared, in her best no-nonsense voice. 'My father used to say that only fools have blind, unswerving faith – and you're no fool, Humphrey. Why, even Jesus Christ had doubts at times. You'll make a very good parson. You're gentle, kind and thoughtful. All the things a parson ought to be.'

'It's very kind of you to say so, Thomasina, but a good parson also needs an equally good wife to support him in his work.'

'Of course – and I have no doubt you'll have no difficulty in finding one. Someone from a similar background to yourself, who'll have the respect of everyone, from the pauper to the squire.'

'You could be such a woman, Thomasina,' Humphrey said hopefully.

Thomasina shook her head. 'No, I couldn't. You know absolutely nothing about me, Humphrey. I'm certainly not the sort of woman who'd make a parson's wife.'

'That settles it then. I'll not be a parson. Marry me, Thomasina, and we'll do something else – just so long as we do it together.'

'What do you think Sir John would have to say about that? He would certainly cut off your allowance. What would we live on?'

Once more Humphrey would not look at her. 'I'd find something to do.'

'And until then? Would we need to live on my money, Humphrey?'

When he failed to reply, Thomasina said, 'It's not much of a proposition to put to a woman, is it? No, Humphrey. Go back to London, do what you have to do there, then work as a curate somewhere for a while. After that I'm sure you'll find a parish of your own when the time is right, perhaps here in Cornwall.'

Humphrey felt uncomfortable. Thomasina was echoing the words of his mother when he had told her he did not want to take up a career in the Church.

'I would do that if you promised to wait for me until I returned to Cornwall.'

Thomasina shook her head. 'I will make no promise to any man, Humphrey, and would be very unhappy if I felt you had given up the chance to become a parson because of me. Very unhappy indeed. You are a very dear friend and I hope you will write to me from London.'

'I haven't said I will go back there,' Humphrey said sulkily.

'No, you haven't,' she agreed, 'but I think you should, certainly by the time your father arrives here.'

Startled, Humphrey said, 'He is coming back to Cornwall? When?'

'Next week. He and Juliana – the children too, I expect. It's something to do with an election. I don't know how long they'll be staying.'

'It will be for at least a month, possibly two.' Despite his earlier bravado, Humphrey sounded concerned.

'You *will* return to London before he arrives, Humphrey? I don't want to be the cause of a disagreement between you and your father.'

'I suppose that if I'm not welcome here, there's no reason for me to stay.'

'That's a silly thing to say.' Thomasina was speaking to him as she would to a naughty child. 'You'll always be welcome in my house. Anyway, the Mount is more your home than it is mine. All I want is what will be best for you – and I'm convinced that is a career in the Church.'

'There's no one else in your life, Thomasina? You *would* tell me if there was? You mentioned Sir Charles earlier – there is nothing between you and him?'

'I think you had better leave before you insult me any more, Humphrey. There would be nothing between Sir Charles and myself if we were the only two people left on earth.'

'I'm sorry, I really didn't mean to insult you.'

Thomasina smiled at him. 'I know you didn't, Humphrey. You're a dear, and I really am very fond of you. But, please, don't do anything silly on my account. Go back to London, enter the Church and make me proud of you.'

'All right, if that's what you really want, but I haven't given up hope that you'll marry me one day.'

'I am extremely flattered, Humphrey. Now, you really must go. I haven't finished my breakfast yet and I need to dress for the day. You too will have a busy day making the necessary arrangements to return to London.'

At the door he hesitated and said, 'I believe the last time we said goodbye you kissed me.'

'And I intend doing so again.' She was making good her promise when Verity entered the room with the second course of breakfast. Thomasina could see by the housekeeper's expression that she was shocked by what she saw.

She was not surprised when Verity returned to the room after she had shown Humphrey out and broached the subject immediately.

'You might tell me it's none of my business, Miss Thomasina, but I'm a woman who is used to speaking her mind, and I can tell you I won't stay working in a house where there are any "goings-on".'

'I am very pleased to hear it, Verity. There will be no "goings-on" in this house. That's why I asked you to make certain you put in an appearance if ever Sir Charles Hearle is seen coming here. What you saw – or thought you saw – just now was not "goings-on". It's not every woman who needs to turn down a man's proposal of marriage before she's even eaten her breakfast. I was merely trying to make my refusal as kindly as possible.'

Thomasina had not intended mentioning Humphrey St Aubyn's proposal to anyone, but Verity's objection to 'goings-on' had left her with no alternative. She was the mother of Abel, and Thomasina did not want her character blackened to him.

The knowledge that this mattered came as a surprise to her and she thought about it for much of the day.

30

The *Edward V* unexpectedly returned to the Mount three days after Humphrey's proposal and departure for London.

The ship's arrival was so unexpected that Thomasina sent Verity to greet Abel when he came ashore, fearing that something had gone wrong.

She was particularly concerned because the *Celestine* had sailed from Newlyn bound for Leghorn the day before. It already had a full twenty-four hours head start on the *Edward V*.

The sailing had been witnessed by many of the Mount fishermen, the news being relayed to Thomasina by Verity, who included it in her daily résumé of Mount gossip.

It turned out that Abel had called at the Mount in order to collect some clothes he felt he would need on the voyage. He also took the opportunity to offload a hogshead of cured pilchards for Verity and Thomasina, which he accompanied to the steward's house.

There were some three thousand fish in the oversized barrel and he said, 'You won't want to use them all. Share them out with anyone you feel might benefit from them. It's one of five barrels the Mevagissey fisherman gave me as a present for taking the whole of the stock he had in his cellar. I got the cargo for a reasonable price. It should make a good profit when I reach Leghorn.'

'Only if you can beat Sir Charles and his ship there,' Thomasina pointed out. 'He set out a day ahead of you.'

'True,' Abel grinned at her obvious concern, 'but he's sailing in a ship that should have been beached and scrapped before ever putting to sea. I have the fastest ship that's ever been seen in these waters. I could give the *Celestine* four days' start and still be in Leghorn a full twenty-four hours before she called for a pilot to enter the harbour there. I'll be offloaded and out of Leghorn before the *Celestine* arrives.'

'What about a return cargo?' Thomasina queried. 'Will you be taking it on board in Italy?'

Abel shook his head, 'No, it would be too risky. I'll offload, collect my money and get out of Leghorn as quickly as I possibly can. Napoleon would make life very difficult if he were to learn that an English ship had landed a cargo in a port he controls. I'll sail to a Spanish port and pick up a cargo there. Marble, fruit and some wine, perhaps. All in all, I think this should prove highly profitable for everyone connected with the *Edward V.*'

'The owner will be very happy about that,' said Thomasina, speaking with less authority than she felt. 'I wish you a very successful voyage.'

'Thank you.' Peering at her more closely, he asked, 'Are you feeling more settled now about giving up Maria?'

'Yes. You were quite right, Abel. There was no other course I could have taken. It was the best thing for Maria.'

'I never doubted it,' said Abel. 'I admired you for what you did then, and still do. It wasn't easy for you to part from someone of whom you were so fond. It never is.'

Thomasina sensed a deeper meaning behind his statement – and it had nothing to do with Maria. She believed he had come closer than ever before to declaring that he cared for *her*.

In an attempt to lighten the moment, Thomasina said, 'Who am I going to be able to turn to when things go wrong while you're away, Abel – as I've no doubt you will be for a great deal of the time in the future?'

'Humphrey St Aubyn, perhaps? Ma told me he called on you. She also said he proposed marriage to you.'

'That's right, but I persuaded him to return to London and follow Sir John's wishes that he take up a career in the Church. He left the same day.'

'He'll be back. Humphrey isn't right for the Church. He's a romantic who is constantly dreaming up ideas for novels and thinking of himself as one of the characters in them. Still, he's a nice enough young man for all that.'

'Yes, he is, but he's not a man I would choose for a husband.'

Once more the glance that passed between them said more than the words, and once more the awkward silence that followed was broken by Thomasina.

'I envy you the voyage you're making, Abel, but take care and return safely.'

'I fully intend to. I shall also be happy in the knowledge that Sir Charles Hearle is on his way to Italy, so won't be around to pester you. Take care of yourself, Thomasina. With luck I will be back within the month – and with some fine wine for a present.'

'We'll share it over a celebratory meal. I would like that.'

When Abel had gone, Thomasina felt happier than she could remember feeling for a very long time. They had only *half*-said so many things, but she believed even this had taken them an important step closer to one another.

A week after Abel had set sail from the Mount, Verity was dusting the sitting-room in the steward's house while Thomasina sat at a desk checking tradesmen's bills.

As was usual when the two women were in the same room, Verity was bringing Thomasina up-to-date with the latest Mount gossip.

'I expect young Agnes Collins will be getting married very soon. At least, she will if she doesn't want to stand before the altar with William John's baby in her arms instead of in her belly. She needs to hurry up about it. William's been putting the wedding off for so long that people are beginning to talk. They're saying he's spending all the hours God's given him out there fishing, in the hope that the press-gang will take him up before poor Agnes does.'

Thomasina smiled. 'He wants to be careful it's not a French man-o'-war or a privateer that takes him up, instead of the press-gang.'

'If he was really unlucky he would be picked up by the French, have his boat taken away – then be rescued by the English navy and brought back in time for a wedding. Mind you, he wouldn't enjoy it very much if he wasn't rescued and was held prisoner for as long as them Mevagissey men that Abel heard about.'

Thomasina looked up at Verity in surprise. 'What Mevagissey men, Verity?'

'Didn't Abel tell you? I expect he had other things on his mind. I wonder where he is now? Do you think he's arrived at the place he was heading for?'

'Leghorn? No, it'll probably take him another day or two yet – but you were telling me about the Mevagissey men . . .'

'So I was. Abel said it was a wonder the women in the cellars there were able to get the pilchards packed in time. It seems one of our men-o'-war took a French ship, somewhere off the French coast, and found it full of British sailors. Some had been held by the French for years and none had been able to let their families know they were safe. They'd been in some small prison way up in the mountains close to the Spanish border. Wellington's army was getting close, so the French were moving them by boat to another prison, close to Paris. Seven or eight of 'em were Mevagissey men, so the man-o'-war that got them back dropped them off there. Abel said there should have been more, but things were so bad in prison that two had killed themselves and one of those brought back was completely out of his mind. Sad the way some men treat others, isn't it? None of them from Mevagissey were fighting men, either. Most were just ordinary seamen; others were fishermen.'

As Verity was talking, Thomasina became very excited, so much so that she had difficulty containing it. When she had left the house of her Aunt Mary, more than two years ago, there had been no more than five Mevagissey men who had vanished at sea – and her father had been one of them. True, there would undoubtedly have been more since then, but Verity had said some of the released men had been prisoners for years.

She wished Abel had mentioned the incident to her when he returned to the Mount. She would have been able to question him more closely. As it was . . .

Suddenly and unexpectedly, she made up her mind. She had thought of her Aunt Mary and Dolly often of late. She would go to see them again, if only just the one time.

Abel's news gave her the excuse she needed. She would pay her aunt a visit. It was possible her father might be one of the released prisoners . . .

Thomasina did not allow herself to think of what she might do if he were, or of the risk she would be taking.

31

When Thomasina boarded the Penzance to Falmouth coach the following morning it was crowded with West Cornwall clerics. They were on their way to meet the Bishop of Exeter, who was paying a rare visit to this outpost of his extensive diocese.

Listening to them talking among themselves, it seemed to Thomasina that they were almost equally divided into two separate groups, each with a different view of their anticipated meeting with the bishop.

The first group comprised relatively simple men of God, who were greatly excited at the thought of meeting a man who held such an authoritative position in the hierarchy of their Church. For others it offered a rare opportunity to impress the exalted pastor, in the hope that he might one day help them to enjoy similar eminence.

Remembering Humphrey, Thomasina had a momentary feeling that a career in the Church might *not* after all be a suitable career for a man like him.

But she had other matters to think about during the hours before the coach reached the bone-juddering cobblestones of Falmouth and brought sustained thought to an end.

Excited though she was at the possibility of her father being alive, it posed many problems for her and her present lifestyle.

Her father would want to know details of her life during his absence. She would need to think of a very plausible story to explain the wealth she had acquired. Thomasina felt that Malachi would provide an answer. A rich, lonely old man with no close relatives, who had befriended her and become a father figure . . .

But that could wait for now. First, she had to find her father.

Once in Falmouth, Thomasina put her small trunk in the care of a young, barefooted boy with a handmade wheelbarrow. They walked together to the house she had once shared with Malachi.

Along the way the boy chatted happily about the ships in the harbour, but told Thomasina he intended becoming a soldier when he was old enough.

When they reached the house the boy carried her trunk upstairs to her bedroom and she rewarded him with double the sixpence he asked for his services. Overjoyed, the boy blessed Thomasina with a fervour that would have put to shame most of the clerics with whom she had so recently parted company.

It was still early afternoon, so Thomasina decided to call on her solicitor before going shopping in the town.

It would be inappropriate to visit her Aunt Mary dressed as befitted a lady. She would need to purchase the sort of clothes a housemaid might choose for her best walking-out attire.

Thomasina felt a thrill of excitement whenever she thought that her father might be at her aunt's cottage at this very moment. It had been almost eight years since he had set sail, never to return. She was concerned that he might not recognise her after all this time, but he too must have changed . . .

She brought herself down to earth with the reminder that it was by no means certain her father had been among those prisoners taken off the French ship.

In order to take her mind off the disappointment she would feel deeply if this were so, she began to think about Aunt Mary, and her cousin Dolly. The young girl would be about sixteen now and Aunt Mary would have her working.

The bitterness Thomasina had once felt at being forced to take employment at Trebene House had faded somewhat, but she doubted whether her aunt had changed her belief that girls should be put out to work as early as possible.

That afternoon, when Thomasina was shown into Zachariah Bennett's office, the solicitor immediately sent for his brother-in-law.

Claude Coumbe was able to give Thomasina full details of the purchase of the *Edward V*. He also confirmed that Abel had taken a cargo of five hundred hogshead of pilchards from Mevagissey, paying for them the sum of seven hundred pounds.

'I had no hesitation in taking the money from your account, my dear,' put in Zachariah. 'It really was a very, very good transaction. Your captain bought at the lowest possible price.'

'Are there any rumours of what Sir Charles Hearle paid for his cargo?' Thomasina asked.

'I can tell you exactly,' said Claude Coumbe smugly. 'His ship has a larger cargo capacity than yours and he purchased eight hundred hogshead at thirty-five shillings each. A grand total, if my arithmetic is accurate, of one thousand, four hundred pounds. Exactly twice the sum you paid – and for only three-eighths of a cargo more.'

Beaming at her, Coumbe added, 'But then, Sir Charles was not aware that the man from whom he bought the bulk of his cargo is the uncle of his ship's captain. Had he employed me – or any other shipbroker – he would have been informed of the fact.'

'He didn't employ a broker? I'm surprised, especially when he has so little knowledge of the shipping business.'

'I am not,' said Zachariah. 'Sir Charles Hearle was bequeathed money in the will of his aunt. Soundly invested, it should have kept him fairly comfortably off for the whole of his life. Unfortunately, very little that Sir Charles does comes under the heading of "sensible". After paying off his gambling debts – and running up more – he chose to invest his remaining money in a ship no one else wanted, and a cargo that will give him a good return only if he can deliver it thousands of miles away before anyone else beats him to it. I might add that I am breaking no confidences by telling you this. It is common gossip, not only in the taverns of Falmouth, but throughout Cornwall. The same rumours suggest that Sir Charles has left himself so short of money that neither the *Celestine* nor its cargo is insured.'

Thomasina gasped in disbelief and Zachariah Bennett said, 'That is utter madness in such uncertain times.'

'I fear all times are uncertain for Sir Charles Hearle,' commented Coumbe. 'And I have a feeling they are going to get worse for him, rather than better. Sadly, I find it difficult to sympathise with him. Now, changing the subject, Miss Varcoe, do you have any ideas about future cargoes for the *Edward V*?'

32

Thomasina departed on a very early coach the next morning, leaving Falmouth at seven-thirty. Carrying mail from a packet ship which had arrived late the previous night, it reached Truro in time for Thomasina to transfer to a Plymouth-bound coach, which dropped her in St Austell, the nearest town to Mevagissey, at eleven-thirty that same morning. Here she booked accommodation at the White Hart Inn.

Too excited to contemplate a midday meal, Thomasina had her small trunk taken to her room, then set off to walk to the small cottage she had left two and a half years before in order to take work as a lowly housemaid.

Walking along the valley road which would take her to her destination evoked many memories for her.

She passed within a short distance of the great

house she had always admired so much as a small
child, when her father would bring her to St Austell
for the Summer Fair.

Then, at the hamlet of London Apprentice, she saw
the blacksmith at work in the smithy where she had
watched with her father while a horse was shod.

Farther on were the tin-stream workings, now only
a shadow of former years.

Just past Pentewan village a wide break in the cliffs
offered a fine view of St Austell Bay. From here, on a
clear day, it was possible to see the coastline all the
way to Rame Head and watch ships of the King's navy
working their way in to the port of Plymouth.

It was here, too, among the grass-covered sand
dunes of the 'Winnick' that Jeffery had first made
love to her.

The thought of Jeffery and the fate he had met
caused tears to spring to her eyes. Brushing them
away, she began the long climb to the top of the hill
where Aunt Mary's cottage was situated.

Once in sight of the small thatched cottage, which
also held many memories, albeit mostly unhappy
ones, Thomasina for the first time entertained doubts
about the wisdom of what she was doing.

It would all be fully justified if her father was one
of the Mevagissey men rescued by the Royal Navy, of
course, but if not . . . ?

Despite such misgivings, Thomasina continued on
her way. There could be no turning back now.

At the cottage gate she paused. The front flower
garden was neat and tidy – neater than she remembered it being before she left. What could be seen

of the vegetable garden was well tended, too, and
stocked with a wide variety of vegetables.

As she took stock of the garden, a woman appeared
in the doorway. Seeing Thomasina, her expression
registered disbelief. It was her aunt.

'Hello, Aunt Mary.' Thomasina spoke first.

'You! What are *you* doing here?'

Her aunt made no attempt to leave the cottage
doorway and come forward to greet the niece she
had not seen for more than two years.

'I've come to see you. To ask if you have any news
of my pa.'

Opening the gate, Thomasina walked up the path
to the house. Still her aunt did not move, and now
her presence barred Thomasina from entering the
cottage.

Stopping uncertainly, Thomasina said, 'Well, now
I'm here, can I come in?'

Without moving, Mary said, 'I'll have no thief in
my house!'

'Thief . . . !' Thomasina was taken aback for a
moment.

'That's what I said. I heard all about your dismissal
from Trebene. You were lucky not to be taken before
the magistrate, so I was told.'

'You were told wrong,' said Thomasina angrily. 'I
never took a thing from Trebene House.' Even as
she made the declaration, she knew it would have
no effect. She had been dismissed from the house of
'gentry'. It had to be *her* who was in the wrong.

'That isn't what I was told – and if you've come here
expecting to be taken in, then you're out of luck. I'm

not a widow-woman any more. I'm married to Harry Mitchell, gardener up at Heligan. It's a good job and I'll not have it put at risk by word getting about that he's related in any way to you.'

Thomasina remembered Harry Mitchell as a stern, unbending Methodist who had been married to a very sick wife. It seemed she must have died.

'I have no intention of staying. The only reason I'm here at all is because I heard that some Mevagissey men who were prisoners of the French had been rescued. I wondered – I was hoping . . .'

Now the moment had arrived, Thomasina found it difficult to put the question to this cold, unfriendly woman who showed no sign of affection towards her.

'If you're asking whether your father was one of them, the answer is . . . yes, he was.'

'Pa's alive?! He's come home? I can't believe it!' All Thomasina's resentment of her aunt's attitude towards her dropped away in an instant. 'Where is he, Aunt Mary? Has he tried to find me? What . . . ?'

'He's in St Austell, in the workhouse – and if you have any sense you'll leave him there and forget he ever came home.'

Mary's callous reply brought Thomasina up short. 'In the workhouse? But . . . why? How could you let him go there? Even if he's lost his boat, he can work. He's a good sailor.'

'Not any more. I don't know what they did to him while he was a prisoner, but whatever it was has turned his brain. He's insane.'

Horrified, Thomasina cried, 'But . . . he'll get better

now he's back home with us, Aunt Mary. How could you allow him to be taken to the workhouse? He was the husband of your only sister. What would she have thought?'

'I've told you, girl, I'm married again now and need to put my husband first. I couldn't expect him to put up with having a lunatic in the cottage. It might have been different, had Dolly still been here, but since she upped and married Billy Kivell we've got used to having the place to ourselves.'

Open-mouthed, Thomasina asked, 'You let Dolly marry Billy Kivell? Why, she's barely sixteen and he must be getting on for fifty!'

She remembered the occasions when she and Dolly had joked about marrying Billy in order to inherit his father's farm. She looked at her aunt in disbelief. Had she always been so callous and uncaring? Thomasina thought she probably had.

'Billy Kivell may not be much of a catch as a man,' retorted Mary, 'but the farm goes with him – and that's a lot more than you'll ever have, I'll be bound.'

Thomasina wished for just a moment that she could tell her aunt of her present lifestyle, but that would lead to too many questions being asked. Instead, she said, 'I'm not so poor that I haven't been able to send you twelve guineas a year for the last couple of years – or did you believe the money was a heaven-sent gift?'

Thomasina had been sending the money each Christmas without disclosing that it came from her.

'As you're married and don't need it any more, I'll

spend it on my pa instead,' Thomasina said bitterly. 'And just in case you were thinking of paying him a visit in the workhouse, don't bother. He won't be there. I'll go there now and take him out. Goodbye, Aunt Mary. I'm sorry not to have seen Dolly, but I wish her well. You needn't worry about your new husband and his work – I won't be coming back here again.'

Thomasina turned about and walked away from her aunt and the cottage that had once been her home.

She did not look back.

33

Thomasina returned along the road to St Austell a great deal faster than she had walked the other way. At times, when she thought about her father, she felt she wanted to run.

She had very confused feelings about him. First and foremost was incredible joy that he was alive, but she was concerned about his mental state. She nursed a desperate hope that his reason would return when he saw her, but she did not know what to expect.

The workhouse was a large and grim, grey-stone building, occupying a prominent position on a hill overlooking the small town of St Austell. Thomasina had seen it many times, but had never taken a great deal of notice of it before today.

She shuddered at what she saw now. It had more the appearance of a prison than of a building intended to succour the poor and needy.

The woman who answered the door to Thomasina informed her that the occupants were busy going about their various chores, as well as carrying out work intended to bring money in to the workhouse. Visitors were not allowed at such a time. Indeed, unless they had a special reason for calling, visitors were discouraged at all other times, too. She added that the inmates found it disturbing to have callers from the outside world.

When Thomasina told the woman she was there not to visit, but to remove one of the inmates, the woman became less officious. 'You'd better come in and wait in the office while I find Mr Skinner. He's the master here. What's the name of the person you wish to take out?'

'Henry Varcoe. He's only been here a short while.'

At the mention of the name, the woman gave her a look which Thomasina found difficult to interpret. 'I see . . . well, I'd better go and find Mr Skinner.'

She was away for about ten minutes. When she returned she was accompanied by a man Thomasina would not immediately have associated with the post of workhouse master. Small, plump and jolly, he held out his hand to her and shook it warmly.

'Good afternoon, Miss. I understand you wish to relieve us of Mr Varcoe? I am pleased. Very pleased indeed. You are a relative, I presume?'

'Yes, his daughter.'

'Splendid! It is always gratifying when responsibility for one of our inmates is taken over by a close relative. We do our best for them in here, of course, but it is never the same for them as enjoying personal care. When do you wish to remove him?'

'As soon as I can . . . but may I please see him first? I only learned yesterday of his return to the country. For years I had thought him dead.'

'You mean . . . you have not seen him since his return?'

'No, I no longer live in the area.'

Skinner and the woman employee exchanged concerned glances before the workhouse master spoke to Thomasina again.

'Are you aware of your father's mental condition? He is certainly not the man you would have known when he went away.'

'My aunt told me that something had happened while he was in a French prison to turn his brain. I'm hoping that when he sees me it might help his recovery.'

The workhouse master shook his head sadly. 'Oh dear. Oh dear! I feared that was what you might be thinking. I am afraid that is not so, my dear. We are fortunate enough to have the services of a great many local physicians, given free to those in our care. One worked in Bedlam, in London, for twenty years. He has seen your father and pronounced him incurable.'

'May I see him, please?' Thomasina was trying hard to hide the dismay she felt at the master's words.

'Of course – but it will be necessary for me to accompany you. We have had no trouble with your father yet, but the physician says that violent conduct cannot be ruled out in his particular condition.'

The more that was said, the worse it became, but Thomasina still nursed a hope that he would be proven wrong. That when her father came face-to-face with the daughter he had adored, at least a degree of normality might return.

'I'd like to see him now, if you please.'

'Come with me.'

Thomasina followed the master through the building, walking through large rooms where women knitted or crocheted busily and passing a room where other women were washing clothes.

Inmates were busily engaged everywhere they went, but the thing that Thomasina found utterly uncanny was the silence in each of the rooms. It was only later that she learned that speaking was banned while the inmates worked. It was felt that talk would affect their work.

Eventually, the master came to a door fitted with a stout lock. Choosing a large key from a ring attached to his belt, he inserted it in the lock, turned it with some difficulty and opened the door.

The first thing that assailed Thomasina was the stench. The second was the noise. Quiet as the rest of the workhouse had been, it made the noise in here all the more startling.

It was gloomy inside, the only light entering the room from small barred windows set high in a stark, whitewashed wall. On the other side of the long, almost bare room were eight or nine men, all chained to stout rings set in the wall.

'Keep close to the wall when you walk through here, then they won't be able to reach you.'

The need for Skinner's warning became apparent when they were no more than a quarter of the way along the length of the long room. With frightening suddenness, one of the chained men leaped at Thomasina.

Terrified, she flattened herself against the whitewashed wall, but the precaution was unnecessary. When the frenzied man reached the end of his chain, it jerked him off his feet. He crashed to the floor two arms' lengths away from her and lay there screaming in pain and frustration.

Thomasina was still trembling when the master reached back and took her hand. 'It's all right, none of them will be able to reach you – as long as you stay close to the wall.'

Appalled, Thomasina wondered whether this was how her father would be. As though reading her thoughts, Skinner said, 'These are the worst of them. Your father is at the far end.'

Thomasina saw him long before they reached him, but for some moments failed to recognise him. He appeared to have shrunk and his hair was far longer and greyer than she remembered.

Then he turned listless eyes in her direction and she saw it was him.

'Pa! Pa . . . it's me, Thomasina!'

Releasing her grip on the master's arm, she ran to her father, oblivious of Skinner's warning to stay close to the wall.

Reaching him, she flung her arms about him, aware momentarily of how thin he was. Indeed, there seemed to be little flesh on his body.

For a moment there was no reaction. Then she felt him begin to tremble – and the screams began.

Startled, Thomasina released him. He promptly turned upon her, striking out and shrieking obscenities. She was rescued by the master, who pulled her to the safety of the whitewashed wall as her father fought against the restraint of the chain to get at her once more.

Crouching against the wall in the arms of the master, Thomasina was aware that it was not only her father who was shrieking now. It seemed that his attack had aroused every other man in the room to a frenzy. She found their cries terrifying.

'That's what I was afraid might happen. Come, we must go quickly, before some of them injure themselves.'

'But, my father . . . ?'

'We'll talk about it in my office, but we must get out of here now!'

It seemed to Thomasina that the screams and shouts of the men in the lunatic wing of the workhouse followed them even when the door to the room had been locked behind them and they were far away.

Suddenly and unexpectedly, Thomasina began to cry. She sobbed uncontrollably for a long time. It was the way she had cried the day she was told her father's ship was overdue and he had disappeared without trace.

The difference was that then she had been left with hope, albeit seemingly in vain as time went on. Now there was none. The man she had just seen was her father in name and body – but nothing else. It was as though she had been wiped from his mind.

'I am very, very sorry, my dear,' said the kindly master. 'I feared that might happen, but desperately hoped it would not. So often, when the mind goes in a certain way, the object of their violence is those they once loved the most.'

When Thomasina felt there was no more anguish left in her and her sobbing had subsided, she said, 'Will it always be like that? Will he ever get better?'

'I wish I could give you the answer you want, my dear – but I cannot. I doubt if your father will ever regain his sanity, and his reaction to you is always likely to be one of extreme violence.'

Sadly the master added, 'Now you have seen him, I presume you will want him to remain with us here?'

'No . . . Oh no, I don't want that. I can't leave him here, chained up like a rabid animal. I will take him away. Take him somewhere where he has all the comforts of a good home, at least. It's just . . . I will need a few days to arrange things. In the meantime, may I give you some money to ensure he enjoys a few luxuries? Whatever you can get for him?'

'It will be gratefully received and used as you wish.' The workhouse master looked pityingly at her. 'I am so sorry, Miss Varcoe. I wish things might have been otherwise, but at least your father has someone who cares enough to bring some comfort into his life. Most of the others here have no one – and I can do only very little.'

'Thank you for your kindness, Mr Skinner. I don't know how long it will take me to make the necessary arrangements for someone to care for my father. It should not take more than a few days.'

'We will look after him – but on no account should you try to care for him on your own. You are the one most at risk because, as I said before, you are the one he loved most of all. Take what comfort you might from that.'

34

Travelling between St Austell and Falmouth, Thomasina fought hard to come to terms with all that the past few days had brought into her life.

After so many years of believing her father dead, she had found him again – only to discover that he was insane and have him attack her.

It was a nightmarish situation to which there seemed no solution. Only one thing was certain. She would take him away from the horror of the insane ward of the St Austell workhouse as soon as was humanly possible.

She shuddered violently at the thought of what she had seen, causing the nervous, gaunt spinster seated beside her to edge an inch or two along the seat away from her. The extremely plain woman was rewarded with a lewd smile of misunderstanding from a middle-aged purveyor of patent 'cure-all' medicines, seated on her other side.

By the time Thomasina arrived at Falmouth she had formulated the outline of a plan. First, she needed to speak to Edith Hocking, the woman who had cleaned Malachi's home for so many years and whose husband tended the garden.

Thomasina was aware that Edith had a married daughter living with her. The daughter's husband was a seaman on an East India Company ship and was rarely home. Nevertheless, Edith complained that even such infrequent visits came around too often, because some nine months after each homecoming her daughter would give birth to another child.

The Hockings now shared their house with this particular daughter and six grandchildren.

Thomasina felt she had a solution that might suit the whole family. If the two Hockings agreed, Thomasina would have her father brought to her own house. The two older Hockings could then move in and give him the constant supervision he would need for the remainder of his sad, twilight life.

As it was a day when both Hockings were working at the house, Thomasina was able to put her proposition to them, giving them as much of the background story as she felt they needed to know.

Edith's first thought was for Thomasina. 'You poor soul! To find your father alive after all these years, only to learn he's lost his reason. It's enough turn your own mind.'

Arthur Hocking was more practical. 'What form does this madness take? Is he violent with it?'

'The workhouse master told me he isn't – although

he did try to attack me . . .' She choked on the words, but recovered quickly. 'I was told that sometimes happens, even with the most docile of them. They'll attack the one they love most.'

'That's perfectly true, dear,' said Edith knowledgeably. 'You remember your Florence, Arthur?'

To Thomasina, she said, 'Arthur's sister was married to a man who went mad. He gave her a very hard time before he had a fit and died. The doctor treating him said it was because he couldn't cope with all the love that filled his poor, scrambled brain whenever he saw her.'

'We'd want to meet your father before we made up our minds,' said Arthur cautiously. 'And we'll have to talk it over with our daughter.'

'Of course,' agreed Thomasina. 'I would, of course, pay you both well – and I'd like you to come to a decision as quickly as possible. I can't bear the thought of him staying in that terrible place for a minute longer than is absolutely necessary.'

Once more her voice broke as she recalled the scene in the long room filled with chained lunatics.

'Don't you upset yourself, dear,' said Edith kindly. 'We'll speak to our Sybil this evening and let you know in the morning what we've decided.'

'Thank you, Edith – you too, Arthur. I'll write to the workhouse master this evening and let him know what's happening. I'll make certain, if you go to St Austell to see him, that he's brought down to the office for the meeting. I wouldn't want you to go up to the room where I saw him.'

*　　*　　*

Edith returned to the house later that same evening, as Thomasina was preparing for bed.

She explained her intrusion by saying, 'I thought I'd come round right away to put your mind at rest, dear. My Sybil is delighted with the thought of having the house to herself for a while. The longer the better, she says. So, if Arthur and I feel we can cope when we meet up with your pa, we'll take on the task of looking after him, here in your own house. That'll be much better for him and will put your mind at rest.'

'Bless you, Edith. Bless you both. When do you think you'll be able to go and see him and, hopefully, bring him back here?'

'Well, if we carry a few of the more essential things to the house tomorrow, we could go to St Austell the day after. How would that suit you?'

It was more than Thomasina had hoped for, and she said so, adding that she would stay on in Falmouth and accompany them on their journey to St Austell.

'That's all right then,' declared Edith, pleasurably embarrassed by Thomasina's gratitude. 'We haven't said we *will* take him on, but if he's not likely to be violent, then I can't see there being any problem.'

As Arthur Hocking must have weighed at least fifteen stone, and her father less than ten, Thomasina thought there would be no problem, even were her father to prove a little difficult on occasions.

It should be a most satisfactory arrangement. Her father would be living in a caring and comfortable environment and she would continue living at the Mount, close enough to enable her to pay regular visits to him.

484 E. V. Thompson

Hopefully, as time passed, he would become less aggressive towards her and be able to appreciate the love she felt for him.

35

Thomasina travelled with Edith and Arthur Hocking on the regular mail coach as far as Truro. Here she hired a carriage and driver. Her motive in changing the mode of transport, and not employing anyone from either the Falmouth or St Austell area, was to make it more difficult for her aunt – or anyone else who might be interested – to trace her.

The interview between the Hockings and her father took place in the workhouse master's office in Thomasina's absence and proved satisfactory to all concerned.

Outside, Edith told Thomasina that she and her husband had no qualms about taking on the task of caring for the tragic figure who had been mentally destroyed by his years of internment.

It was agreed that they would return to Falmouth with him immediately, the couple riding inside the carriage with Edward Varcoe, Thomasina riding on the seat beside the driver.

On the return journey they travelled by a more direct route, taking a ferry from the Roseland peninsula direct to Falmouth. Thomasina remained in the background on the ferry when the Hockings allowed her father to alight from the carriage. She gained a great deal of pleasure from his obvious delight at being allowed to stand on the deck of the vessel with the wind and sun on his face.

It also increased the sadness she felt that she could not be included in such a simple pleasure. Edward Varcoe had looked in her direction once or twice during the short voyage, but gave no sign of recognition. Thomasina took comfort from the fact that he did not automatically become aggressive towards her.

She hoped his earlier outburst might have been brought on by his surroundings and not by her presence.

It was with great relief that Thomasina returned to the steward's house on St Michael's Mount, after an absence of seven days.

It had been a period of great stress, not least because of the need to keep her earlier life separate from the one she was now leading.

Thomasina believed, rightly or wrongly, that if her relationship with Abel was to progress beyond its present tentative state, then the less he knew, the more chance she would stand with him – and she now admitted to herself that this mattered to her. One day she would tell him as much as she felt he needed to know.

Verity seemed as relieved to see her as Thomasina was to be home.

'Mistress Vinicombe has been asking after you,' she said. 'All I could tell her was that you had gone to Falmouth and I had no idea when you would be back.'

'That's all right, Verity, she'll understand. Has she brought the children to the Mount with her?'

'Only the baby – and it has a nursemaid now. She's left the other children in London. With an election in the offing there'll be a great deal of partying up at the castle. They won't want children getting under their feet.' Verity shook her head perplexedly, 'I don't know what it is that makes Sir John and all them others so keen to get a seat up there in Parliament. It costs them a fortune to get the votes to put 'em there, that's certain.'

Juliana came from the castle to visit Thomasina that same evening. She looked fit and well and gave Thomasina a warm hug by way of greeting.

'I heard you'd returned to the Mount and thought I'd come down and satisfy myself you were well. Verity was concerned about you being away for so long. Is everything all right?'

'There were some things I needed to attend to, that's all.'

When Thomasina made no attempt to amplify her brief explanation, Juliana asked, 'Is there a man involved?'

The question bordered on rudeness, but Thomasina did not take offence. 'Yes, but not in the way you're thinking.'

'Now I'm thoroughly intrigued,' declared Juliana. 'But I'll ask no more questions – for now. One thing I *do* know: it has nothing to do with Sir Charles Hearle, for I've heard that he's sailed with his boat. Abel's at sea, too – and I was beginning to think for a while there might be something between you two. It can't be Humphrey, because he's in London, learning how to be a deacon, or a curate, I'm not quite sure which. If there's a man involved, it must be someone I know nothing about.'

'I *hope* Humphrey is in London,' said Thomasina, refusing to rise to Juliana's probing. 'He was here a little over a week ago and proposed marriage once more.'

Thomasina was not being disloyal to Humphrey. She was telling Juliana nothing she did not already know, or would not learn in the next day or two. Humphrey's visit to the Mount – and to Thomasina – was common knowledge in the village and she had already confided in Juliana about Humphrey's offer of marriage, passing it off as an infatuation on Humphrey's part.

'You refused him once more, I presume?'

'Yes.'

'Thomasina, if you *did* decide you wished to marry him, I could guarantee Sir John's approval . . . eventually.'

Thomasina smiled. 'I don't need anyone's approval, Juliana, because I have no intention of marrying Humphrey. I don't love him and have no need of his money.'

'In that case I am afraid the poor boy has nothing

else to offer,' said Juliana. 'Well, now that is settled, let me tell you the plans Sir John and I have for entertaining at the castle. I am relying upon you to help me receive the guests.'

Startled, Thomasina said, 'I can't do that, Juliana. I wouldn't know what to do. I'm all right with you, but I couldn't mix with the sort of people you'll be entertaining at the castle, really I couldn't.'

'Thomasina, you could charm the Prince Regent if you put your mind to it, and you really need not worry about being out of your depth. The men invited to the Mount during an election campaign are, in the main, those who have a vote to cast. Not all of them are "gentlemen", I am afraid. Even the few who are will be so intoxicated after an hour or so they won't know whether they are beggars or dukes – and nothing about their behaviour is likely to enlighten you.'

Thomasina smiled once more. 'All right, I'll help you out as often as I can, but I'll need to go into Falmouth at least once a week.'

'Thank you, Thomasina. I'll have a boat put at your disposal. It's a quicker way to travel and I know you don't mind going on the water. Mind you . . .' she cast a sly look at Thomasina, 'this time there's no handsome head boatman to take you.'

'True,' agreed Thomasina, 'but if my calculations are correct, Abel is likely to return from the Mediterranean during the next few days.'

'You and he get along well, don't you?'

'Yes, we do,' agreed Thomasina, unwilling to commit herself to any greater degree.

'Hm! Well, he's a go-ahead man. Handsome, too, but you could do a lot better for yourself, Thomasina.'

'As I'm not looking for a husband, it doesn't really matter.' With this statement Thomasina changed the subject. 'How are the children?'

Juliana gave an amused laugh. 'I gather I am intended to take that as a very firm "Mind your own business" – and you are quite right, of course. But come up to the castle tomorrow morning. We'll take tea and have a good chat about all that's going on – everything, that is, except the men in your life.'

When Juliana had left, Thomasina wondered what she would have thought had she known the truth about the 'men in her life'.

She felt that Juliana might have understood about her father and sympathised with her, but Thomasina believed that unpicking just one single thread of her tangled life might very easily lead to the unravelling of the whole of the respectable new image she had built up around herself.

36

The first party to take place at the castle on St Michael's Mount was a great success. It was held for vote-holding traders in Sir John's constituency. The invited guests were somewhat overawed by their surroundings and on their best behaviour. They were also forced to leave at a reasonable hour, in order not to be caught on the island by the tide.

When the last of them had gone, Sir John thanked Thomasina for her contribution to the party, adding that she had done much to ensure its success and, hopefully, his re-election to Parliament.

He was chatting to her for so long that eventually Juliana crossed the room to them. Linking her arm with that of the baronet, she declared that she was becoming jealous but added, 'You were no doubt telling Thomasina of your meeting with Major the Honourable Hugh Pardoe?'

'Good Lord, no! I forgot all about it,' said Sir John. 'This election business is driving all other thoughts from my mind.'

Admonishing him, Juliana explained to Thomasina, 'Sir John met Hugh Pardoe at the War Office in London when he went there to enquire about one of his sons-in-law, who has been wounded in Spain. Pardoe had been newly promoted and called to the War Office to discuss a new posting. When he learned that Sir John had a home here, in Cornwall, he told of how you and Abel had rescued his daughter and taken her to Walkden Hall. He was absolutely delighted when he discovered not only that Sir John knows you, but that we are all friends. He thinks you are absolutely marvellous, Thomasina. What is more, he will be coming to Falmouth to board a ship when a fleet has been assembled. He has been appointed Lieutenant Governor of the convict colony at Botany Bay, in Australia.'

'That's right,' said Sir John. 'It is unforgiveable of me not to have mentioned it before. I have invited Major Pardoe to spend a few days at the Mount while he is waiting for the fleet to assemble. We must have a little celebration when they arrive.'

Thomasina was delighted and said so, adding, 'I still miss Maria – or "Emma", as I called her then. I sometimes wake in the morning and think I can hear her stirring in her room.'

'That is because you have no children of your own,' declared Juliana. 'When you have, you will wake in the morning and pretend you do *not* hear the sound of your youngest, craving attention. Now, everybody has finally gone, but there is still a quantity of champagne left. Shall we sit on the terrace and enjoy it? It is a surprisingly mild evening – and the moon is absolutely magnificent. It is an evening to sit and dwell upon the magic of the Mount.'

Twenty-four days after Abel had set sail from the Mount, bound for Leghorn, he brought the *Edward V* back to the St Michael's Mount harbour.

Sun-tanned and jubilant, he called at the steward's house, scarcely able to contain the pride he felt in what had been achieved with the *Edward V*.

He brought presents, too. For Verity there was a fine collection of Spanish lace. It included a bedspread, tablecloths of various sizes and cushion covers.

While she marvelled at the workmanship of them, he handed Thomasina a black velvet box. Opening it, she gasped in disbelief. It contained a necklace of gold filigree, set with a collection of cut green stones resembling emeralds. Abel told her they came from a group of Spanish islands, known as the 'Fortunate Islands', off north-west Africa.

Taken aback by his gift, Thomasina said, 'Abel! I can't accept this. It's far too generous.'

'I didn't have to pay full price for it,' Abel lied. 'I struck a good deal with a Spanish trader for a cargo and he let me have it cheap. I thought it was just right for you.'

Hoping to make her forget the value of the necklace, he said, 'You'll never believe the price I got for the pilchards in Leghorn. Nine pounds a hogshead – and they paid me in gold coin! That's a profit of seven

pounds and twelve shillings on each hogshead – and
I was carrying a cargo of five hundred! Imagine,
a profit on one voyage of more than three thousand, five hundred pounds! Then I sailed to Spain
and took on a cargo of marble, lace and wine. By
the time it's sold, I'm confident I will have made a
profit of more than five thousand pounds on a single
voyage.'

'That's absolutely marvellous!' said a delighted
Thomasina. She meant it. A ship's captain received
a share of the trading profits and it was more than
most could expect to make in a full year's trading.
'And this necklace really is a wonderful present,
Abel. I've never been given anything like it before.
Thank you.'

The kiss she gave Abel was meant to express no
more than her gratitude for his gift, but it caused
Verity's eyebrows to rise to unprecedented heights.
For some minutes Abel's grandmother forgot all
about her own gift.

Aware that she had shocked Verity, and confused
by her own emotions, Thomasina said, 'Did you see
anything of Sir Charles Hearle's ship on your voyage?'

'There was not a sign of it, but I hope it wasn't too
far behind us. Although we were allowed to land
our cargo without trouble, the authorities in Leghorn
weren't too happy at having us there. They were
contemplating taking action against us. We got in
and out with no problem, but the next ship probably
won't be so lucky.'

If the Italian authorities arrested Sir Charles Hearle,

Thomasina would be delighted, but she said nothing and, instead, returned her attention to the gift Abel had brought home for her.

Later that day Sir John St Aubyn displayed his approval of his ex-head boatman's new venture when he came down from the castle to the harbour and had Abel show him over the *Edward V*.

Suitably impressed, he delighted Abel by purchasing half the ship's marble to use in the building work being carried out on the family home of Clowance.

Thomasina felt that the visit from Sir John, and his unstinting approval of Abel's new status, pleased the *Edward V*'s master quite as much as the success of his maiden trading voyage.

He sailed for Falmouth that evening a very happy man.

Abel and his ship had been gone from the Mount for five days when the *Celestine* entered the small harbour.

It was the evening of another of Sir John's electioneering parties, this time for a more affluent group of voters than on the previous occasion.

Present at the gathering were the High Sheriff, the Lord Lieutenant and a number of Deputy Lieutenants. Many would be staying overnight at the castle.

Thomasina had promised Juliana she would be present to help out, although, had she been given time to think seriously about it, nerves might have got the better of her.

She had been to see her father the previous day and found him in an unexpectedly violent mood towards her. This had upset her a great deal and occupied her thoughts for much of time.

Fortunately, most of Sir John's personal friends were charming. He and Juliana never tired of recounting the circumstances of Thomasina's arrival on the Mount and her subsequent adventures, when she helped to rescue first Juliana and then Maria. As a result, Thomasina found herself at the centre of a great deal of unexpected attention.

This was quite flattering, until she discovered that one of the most attentive of those about her was none other than Francis Vincent, son of the late Henry and Harriet Vincent.

Francis had inherited Trebene House and its extensive estates. When he issued an invitation to her to pay a visit there, Thomasina wondered wryly what he would have thought had he known that she had once been a servant in the house – and the circumstances leading to her dismissal.

There was to be another link with Trebene House later that evening. As night fell, Juliana came to Thomasina and informed her that Sir Charles Hearle's ship had just berthed in the Mount's harbour.

Remembering Abel's words about the authorities in Italy, Thomasina said, 'I wonder if he managed to offload his cargo in Leghorn?'

'I think he must have,' said Juliana. 'The servant who brought the information said his ship was riding high in the water.'

'Then he's either carrying a very light return cargo

or he's come back empty,' mused Thomasina. 'That's not very good trading practice.'

'Well, you should be able to ask him about it very soon. Sir John has sent down an invitation for Sir Charles to join us here.'

37

The thought of meeting Sir Charles once again gave Thomasina no pleasure, yet she was unprepared for the appearance of the baronet when he entered the Chevy Chase Room, where the party was being held, and Thomasina was not the only one to be shocked.

Sir Charles's clothes were creased and untidy and looked as though they were in need of a wash.

Many of those present were associated with ships and the sea. They were aware that it was well nigh impossible to keep clothes in pristine condition when a ship was at sea for weeks at a time, but one look at his face was sufficient to make the observer immediately forget the state of his clothing.

Sir Charles seemed to have aged by twenty years in the few weeks he had been away.

His cousin, Francis Vincent, saw it and was one of the first to greet him, intercepting him when he had taken only a few paces into the room.

'Charles! Is everything all right? Have you had a difficult voyage?'

'No, everything is *not* all right, cousin. Everything is all *wrong*. It's been a bloody awful voyage – and I stand before you a ruined man. Ruined . . .'

It was apparent from Sir Charles's speech that he had been drinking before coming to the castle – and drinking heavily.

Francis Vincent looked around in some embarrassment and Thomasina came to his rescue. Crossing to him swiftly, she said, 'Bring Sir Charles with you. I'll take you to Juliana's study. He can tell his troubles to you there.'

She led the way from the room and, with an arm about the shoulders of his cousin, Francis Vincent followed her.

When they arrived at the small room used by Juliana to write her letters and balance the castle accounts, Thomasina showed the two men inside. To Francis Vincent she said, 'Is there anything I can bring for you?'

It was Sir Charles who replied, 'You can bring me a drink. A large one. A *very* large one.'

'I think you have had more than enough to drink, Charles. It would have been better had you declined Sir John's invitation and sought me out tomorrow. In this state you are an embarrassment to him – and to me.'

'I've always been an embarrassment to everyone, Francis, you know that. Isn't that why Grandfather left everything to the Vincents and not to the Hearles?'

He couldn't prevent me inheriting his title, but he made damned certain I got nothing more.'

When Francis Vincent tried to say something, Sir Charles drunkenly waved him to silence, 'Oh, I know your mother took pity on me and remembered me in her will. I'm grateful to her, don't think I'm not. Not only that, but I'd have made a handsome profit, had everything not gone against me – thanks to a rogue who is a friend of yours, Thomasina. I'm talking of that damned boatman who was given command of a fancy ship. You know what he did? Do you know?'

Without waiting for a reply, he proceeded to tell Thomasina and his cousin.

'He took on a load of pilchards for Leghorn – the port for which I was heading with the *Celestine*, carrying a similar cargo. Not only did he get there before me and flood the market, but he stirred up a hornets' nest among the Italian officials. No sooner had we unloaded than we were warned that soldiers were on their way to arrest us all and confiscate the ship. They actually reached the harbour as we were leaving. We had to brave a whole fusillade of musket shots on our way out. Two of our seamen were wounded, one so badly that he died soon afterwards. I lost the whole cargo, Francis – and with it every penny I'd sunk into the venture.'

'Are you saying you unloaded a full cargo in what was basically a hostile country, before you'd seen the colour of anyone's money?' asked Thomasina. 'What sort of a captain do you have who would allow you to do such a thing?'

'A damned fine captain,' declared Sir Charles defensively. 'One of the best. We had planned a return cargo, too. However, thanks to that boatman, we had no money to pay for it and had to return home empty – to ruination. Where's that drink you were getting for me, Thomasina? I am in urgent need of one.'

'What you need is to sober up and start thinking of ways in which you might recoup your losses,' said Francis Vincent firmly.

'No I don't . . . I know what I want – and so does Thomasina.'

'I am sorry you had to witness this, Thomasina. Will you please give my apologies to Sir John and promise him my fullest support in his campaign. I will take my cousin back to his ship and proceed on my way from there.'

Taking a firm grip on a loudly protesting Sir Charles, Francis propelled him outside the study. Thomasina preceded them, opening doors, and the two very different cousins made their way from the castle.

Later that night Thomasina was telling Sir John and Juliana what Sir Charles had said. Neither had seen Sir Charles enter the Chevy Chase Room. Sir John thanked Thomasina for her part in ensuring that the drunken baronet left the reception before he caused a disturbance.

'It was Sir Charles's cousin who took him from the room so promptly,' Thomasina said. 'He sent his apologies to you, but said that I was to tell you he would give you his full support in your election campaign.'

'Francis Vincent and Sir Charles could hardly be more different, for all they are cousins,' Sir John commented. 'How much truth do you think there is in what Sir Charles said about Abel beating him to Leghorn and stirring up the authorities there?'

'Abel certainly arrived there before Sir Charles,' Thomasina replied. 'Even though the *Celestine* sailed from Cornwall a full twenty-four hours before the *Edward V*. As for the rest . . . I'd say Sir Charles has only himself to blame for what went wrong. He put every penny he owned into buying a ship that had been laid up for so long that prospective buyers had stopped looking at it. Then he took on a captain no one else would hire and spent more than he could afford on a cargo that was only likely to make a worthwhile profit if he got there before anyone else. The man's a fool! Aware that the port was in a country controlled by Napoleon, he should have insisted that money was put into his hands for the cargo before offloading a single item. Even if the military hadn't turned up, the cargo could have been whisked away without payment being made. There would have been nothing he could do about it.'

'You're more than just a pretty face, young lady,' Juliana commented. 'It's a pity Sir Charles didn't consult you when he was looking for an investment for the money his aunt left to him.'

'Sir Charles would have had no help from me,' Thomasina declared. 'I don't like to see serious trouble coming to anyone – but if it's going to, then I can think of no one I would rather see it happen to than Sir Charles Hearle.'

38

The morning after the party at the castle, Thomasina had only just awakened when she heard Verity let herself into the house.

Calling out, she said, 'Verity, it's highly likely Sir Charles Hearle will come calling some time today. If he does, I want you to stay near at hand – *very* near. You understand?'

'I think I do. But I don't think you need worry too much about him. Not today, anyway. His ship sailed early this morning, and him with it. I don't know what went on at Sir John's party, and it's none of my business anyway, but the men on the harbour are saying that Sir Charles was put on board roaring drunk last night and orders to sail at first light this morning were given to the captain by Sir Charles's cousin.'

'Good! Where have they sailed to, Verity? From

what Sir Charles was saying last night, I wouldn't imagine he had any money to spare for harbour dues.'

'That I don't know, but he's not on the Mount, so you don't need to worry about him. If it's all the same to you, I'll cross to Marazion and pick up one or two things we're going to need before very long.'

Thomasina thought the *Celestine* had probably sailed for Falmouth. Once there the ship would no doubt anchor in the Carrick Roads, in order to avoid harbour dues.

But the *Celestine* would not be able to remain there for long. Sir Charles would need to pay his captain and crew – an impossibility if he really had no money. The only way quick money might be made by a ship-owner was by smuggling. It was a precarious means of earning a livelihood at the best of times. Right now it was doubly so.

The Revenue Service was making a determined effort to stamp out the illegal but profitable trade. In addition, a smuggler had to run a gauntlet of British and French men-o'-war – not to mention predatory privateers operating from ports and harbours in both countries.

If Thomasina thought smuggling was the only option open to Sir Charles, then she would soon learn this was not so. The alternative the baronet had in mind was something that would never have occurred to her.

The timing of his visit also took her by surprise. She and Verity had both been looking to the *Celestine* to give them a warning of his presence.

When Sir Charles crossed the causeway on horseback a few evenings later, they were both caught off guard.

Thomasina was preparing for bed where there came a knock at the front door. Frowning, she wondered who would be calling at this time of the evening? She decided it must be Verity, probably returning to the house for something she had forgotten earlier.

Opening the door, Thomasina was taken aback to see Sir Charles Hearle standing outside. Her hand went immediately to the low neck of her dressing-gown.

'What do you want? I'm about to go to bed.'

'I would like to speak with you on an important matter, Thomasina, but first may I apologise for any embarrassment I might have caused you the other evening? I had spent days trying unsuccessfully to come to terms with financial ruin and . . . and I wasn't myself.'

'The only person likely to find the answer to his financial problems in a brandy glass is the man who makes the brandy, Sir Charles – and it isn't me to whom you should be apologising. It was Sir John's party, held for those who are important to him in the election. He's the one you should be calling upon now, not me.'

'I shall be calling on him when I leave here.'

Sir Charles spoke far more sharply than he had intended. He was angry at being lectured on his manners by a young woman – especially one from an inferior social background.

He curbed his anger very quickly. Right now her pedigree was of little consequence. He was in serious financial trouble. She could provide him with a solution to his problems.

'Look, we can't talk out here. May I come in?'

Although more than a little curious about his motives for calling on her at this time of night, Thomasina had no intention of asking him into her home without someone else being present.

'I'm sorry, Sir Charles. I am alone here at the moment. I have no intention of putting my reputation at risk by inviting you in.' Beginning to enjoy the conversation, she added, 'You will recall that I have experience of your behaviour when no one else is around.'

Although she was referring to the occasion when she and the children had paid a visit to the *Celestine*, she also recalled another time and place. One that Sir Charles did not remember.

She had not forgotten – could not forget – but she would never remind him of what she had suffered at his hands.

Sir Charles looked pained. 'That was an unfortunate misunderstanding . . . most regrettable. I can assure you my intentions this evening are entirely honourable.'

At that moment Verity came hurrying towards the house. A neighbour had called at her cottage to tell her that Sir Charles had crossed the causeway and gone straight to the steward's house, where she knew Thomasina was home alone.

With her employer's strict instructions in mind,

Verity hurried off to the steward's house. She was relieved to find that Thomasina had kept the baronet talking on the doorstep.

'Hello, Miss Thomasina. I heard you had company and thought you might have need of me.'

'That is very kind of you, Verity. Sir Charles says he has some business to discuss with me. I wouldn't allow him in, because I was alone in the house, but now you're here . . . Perhaps you could make tea for us. I believe Sir Charles has had a long ride. He must be thirsty.'

Thomasina was well aware that something stronger than tea would have been more to the baronet's taste, but the drink she had in the house had been given to her by Abel. She had no intention of wasting any of it upon her uninvited visitor.

Once in the sitting-room, Thomasina seated herself before motioning Sir Charles to another armchair.

'Thank you.' He inclined his head to acknowledge her gesture. 'If it is all the same to you, I would rather stand.'

Thomasina shrugged her shoulders. Seated or standing, it made little difference to her. However, when Sir Charles began pacing the room she wished she had insisted that he sat down.

As he paced, the baronet started talking. At first, what he had to say made little sense to her.

'As I have already told you, Thomasina, I have recently had a bad run of luck. However, such luck does not last for ever and I already have plans to overcome my problems.'

Thomasina failed to see what his plans had to do with her, and she said so.

'Ah! But you are a very important element in my plans, Thomasina. Together we can not only come through this, but go on to achieve great success.'

'Together? What have *I* to do with any plans you've made?'

'That is what I have come here to discuss with you, Thomasina. I am convinced that together we could have a very successful business.'

'A *business*? Doing what?' Thomasina was puzzled.

'Why, trading, of course. Carrying merchandise to all parts of the world and returning with exotic – and profitable – cargoes.'

'But . . . I thought you were a ruined man? Had lost all your money?'

'That is so – for the moment. But I still have a ship, Thomasina. A very good ship.'

'I see. You want me to put up the money to buy cargoes and pay the crew of the *Celestine*, is that so?'

'Yes, Thomasina. I can assure you that time will prove it to be an excellent investment.'

'I'm sorry, Sir Charles. Quite apart from any other consideration, *you* are not a good risk. I can invest my money elsewhere and get a guaranteed return.'

Sir Charles was silent for a few minutes, then he said hesitantly, 'I am prepared to offer you something you will not be able to obtain from any other investment, Thomasina.'

'Oh! And what might that be.'

'I have already told you of the esteem in which I hold you. To prove it, I am asking you to marry me, Thomasina. In return for your investment in me, I will marry you and make you Lady Thomasina Hearle.'

When Verity entered the sitting-room a few minutes later she was carrying a tray upon which lay two cups and other items for tea. She appeared confused.

'I thought . . . ? I just passed Sir Charles in the hallway. He almost knocked me over – and I won't tell you what his reply was when I said I had brought his tea! It certainly wasn't what I'd expect from a gentleman.'

'Sir Charles may lay claim to a number of titles, Verity – but "gentleman" isn't one of them.'

'Why did he leave so suddenly – and in such a foul mood?'

'He asked me to marry him, Verity. Said he wanted to make me Lady Hearle.'

Verity succeeded in straightening the tray before everything fell from it to the floor. Hastily placing it on the table, she asked, 'What did you say to him?'

'Nothing, Verity. I just laughed. I was still laughing when he stalked out of the room.'

'Well! Well, I never! I certainly don't blame you for refusing him, Miss Thomasina, not for a single moment, but Sir Charles is not a man to cross. He can be very, very spiteful.'

'There's little you can tell me about Sir Charles that I don't already know, Verity, but I must admit his proposal took me by surprise – even though I am

aware he was only after my money. But it's the second
proposal I've had since coming to the Mount. They
say things happen in threes. I wonder who will be the
third man to propose . . . ?'

39

When Abel left the London docks after delivering his cargo, it was late in the day and the *Edward V* was obliged to anchor for the night in the River Thames, off Deptford.

As it was the mate's birthday, Abel took him ashore to an inn for a celebratory meal and a few drinks. The inn he chose was the Admiral's Arms, not far from the Royal Navy victualling yard. Here, he met up with a couple of Royal Marine officers with whom he had served many years before.

Both, like Abel, had left the service and were now employed by the transport service – both on victualling duties.

As well as becoming an extremely convivial evening, it was also to prove a profitable one. Many of the ex-marine officers' friends joined them for a drink or two. One such man was responsible for provisioning the fleet being assembled to carry convicts to Australia.

When Abel mentioned Major Pardoe, and the part he and Thomasina had played in rescuing and returning the major's daughter from the sea off the Lizard, it was deemed an additional cause for celebration.

By the time Abel took the mate back to the *Edward V*, he had struck a deal to deliver a full cargo of cured pilchards to Deptford, as food for the convicts during their long voyage to the convict colony. The price would not equal that obtained by Abel on his voyage to Leghorn, but it was sufficient to ensure that he would make a handsome profit on the deal.

In order to secure the cargo of pilchards, Abel put the *Edward V* in to Mevagissey harbour on his return journey to Falmouth. It had been a good season for the pilchard fishermen and he had no difficulty in purchasing all the cured fish he required.

While the cargo was being loaded, Abel sent the mate off to Falmouth in a hastily hired fishing boat. He would inform the shipbroker of his movements and obtain the money with which to pay the Mevagissey fish-cellar owner.

During the loading Abel would occasionally stop to have a conversation with the Mevagissey man and it was during one such conversation that he asked him about the sailors who had returned to the village after having been prisoners of the French for so many years.

'Have they all settled back to normal life?' he asked.

'For most of 'em it's as though they've never been

away,' said the man. 'Almost all of 'em are back at sea right now.'

Chuckling, he added, 'Mind you, it wasn't such a fine homecoming for Harry Avers, or his wife. She'd been wanting to be rid of him long before he went, and when he'd been gone for three years without a word, she gave him up for dead and married again. He come back to her to find another man in his place and three young maids that he hadn't fathered. At the moment they're all living in the same house – his house. The vicar spends more time there trying to sort it all out than he does in his own church, but then, so he should. He's the one who married 'em. She was a Wesleyan till she wanted to marry again. The minister wouldn't marry her, so she turned to the vicar. He was happy enough to do it for 'em then, thinking he'd put one over on the minister. I don't think he's so happy now!'

Abel gave the other man a wry smile and agreed that it was a very tricky situation. Then he asked after the seaman who had lost his sanity during his imprisonment in France.

'Edward Varcoe?' The fish-cellar owner shook his head, not noticing the start that Abel gave at the mention of the insane fisherman's name. 'His is a sad case. He'll never go back to sea again, that's certain. He's right off his head, so much so that his sister-in-law had him put away in the workhouse, in St Austell. Mind you, I hear his daughter has turned up and taken him out now.'

'I know a Varcoe,' said Abel cautiously, 'but I'm not sure whether or not she came from this part of

Cornwall. What is the daughter's name?'

'Thomasina. Edward wanted a son, and was convinced his wife was going to have one. Had even chosen a name for him. Thomas. Unfortunately, the good Lord decided to give him a daughter instead, so Edward called her Thomasina. Bit of a wild one too, she was. Used to spend a lot of time at sea with her pa and, from what I've heard, she could handle a boat as well as any man. But that didn't stand her in any good stead once he'd gone. She could hardly go to sea as crew, could she? The result was that she couldn't settle down to anything after Edward went missing. Eventually her aunt put her into service over at Trebene, with the Vincents, but there was some scandal there and she was thrown out. No one heard of her then for a couple of years. In fact, not until she turned up to take her pa out of the workhouse. Then it seems she disappeared with him, just as mysteriously as she arrived. Mind you, there's nothing unusual in that, not for Thomasina. She wasn't one for staying in one place for long and I don't suppose she's changed. She can't be all that far away though, or she'd never have heard so quickly about her father coming back home.'

The fish-cellar owner prattled on for some time about Thomasina, her family and the other men who had returned to the village, but Abel was not listening. He was remembering that he had told his grandmother of the return of the Mevagissey men after being freed from captivity.

He believed he had the answers to many of the fish-cellar owner's queries. There was little doubt in his mind that the Thomasina Varcoe he had rescued from the sea at St Michael's Mount and the Thomasina of whom the Mevagissey man was talking were one and the same person.

Her employment and mysterious dismissal from Trebene could also explain her apparent intense dislike of Sir Charles Hearle. Abel was well aware that Sir Charles was a nephew of the late owners of Trebene House.

But why should she have remained so secretive about her past life? He thought of an answer to his unspoken question almost immediately.

Thomasina had come into money – probably a great deal of money. She was also now a companion to Juliana Vinicombe and accepted as such by Sir John St Aubyn and his friends. She would hardly want it known that she had once been a servant in the house of Sir Charles Hearle's aunt and uncle.

But each answer he found only served to pose yet another question. If she knew Sir Charles at Trebene, why had he failed to recognise her when he first met her on the Mount? Or had he . . . ?

There were a great many things Abel wanted to know. Finding the answers to his questions would not be easy, but he would need to try. Since Thomasina had come into his life he had found it increasingly difficult to get her out of his mind. He had felt recently that she was beginning to feel something for him, too.

While she was a friend of Sir John and Juliana, and he a St Aubyn boatman, their relationship could never move forward. But if she was indeed the Thomasina Varcoe of whom the cellar owner had spoken – and there was little doubt in Abel's mind – then things might be very different now that he was master of a ship.

First, he would need to find some way of having *her* tell him the truth about her past – and Abel suspected that was not going to be a simple matter.

40

When Thomasina paid the next visit to her father, she was shocked at the change she found in him.

On days when he was quiet he was allowed to roam around the house, all the outside doors being locked, but the housekeeping couple told her that he had suffered violent mood swings in recent days. As a result they were keeping him confined to a locked bedroom, the window of which had earlier been fitted with slim iron bars.

Thomasina looked in on him twice during her visit to the house, but on both occasions he rushed at her as though intent on attacking her. Fortunately, perhaps, Edward Varcoe had also grown increasingly fragile and Arthur Hocking had been able to hold him off until Thomasina left the room.

Distressed, she asked the couple whether anything had happened that might have triggered off this change in him.

Arthur shook his head. 'We followed your instructions and called in a doctor. He told us that, in his experience, such behaviour wasn't at all unusual. Unfortunately, he fears that your father is going to get worse and not better, Miss Varcoe.'

As if this news was not bad enough, the housekeeper who had cared for Malachi and his house for so many years informed Thomasina that, if Edward Varcoe's condition deteriorated any further, she would be unable to continue to care for him. She had reached an age when most women were allowing others to look after *them*. Caring for a violently insane man was more than she felt able to cope with.

Thomasina had all this on her mind when she returned to the busy harbour to board the St Aubyn boat for the return journey to the Mount.

There was still half an hour to go before the time she had told the boatmen she would want to depart. She decided to call in to the office of Claude Coumbe and enquire about the movements of the *Edward V*. The ship had not called at the Mount for some weeks and Verity had heard nothing from Abel.

Coumbe gave her a warm welcome and was delighted to produce the file he held on Thomasina's ship and to lay out account sheets showing an impressive profit on the ship's voyages.

Leaning back in his chair, the papers spread out on the desk between them, the shipbroker beamed at Thomasina. 'It is a very satisfactory state of affairs, my dear, and much of the credit is due to Abel Carter. You made a very wise choice when you put him in command of the *Edward V* – and that is more than I can say for a certain ship-owner who is known to both of us.'

'Are you referring to Sir Charles Hearle?' Thomasina asked.

Coumbe smiled. 'I will mention no names – but we both know to whom I am referring. Word is going around that his ship is being used to land certain commodities upon which duty is not being paid.'

'You mean he's involved in smuggling?' said Thomasina.

'Exactly, and if word has reached *me*, then I have no doubt at all that the Revenue men are aware of his activities – or, rather, the activities of the master of his ship, who has been given a free hand to do whatever he wishes, providing it turns in a profit at the end of the day.'

'Sir Charles Hearle may escape prosecution,' Thomasina said, 'but that won't prevent his boat from being seized – and it's his sole remaining asset.'

'The man is a fool,' declared Coumbe. 'But that need not trouble either of us. You have one of the finest ships this port has seen – and a captain worthy of the vessel.'

The man being praised so highly by Claude Coumbe was at that moment being landed farther along the sea front from one of the *Edward V*'s boats. The ship had returned from Deptford empty, and Abel had anchored in the Carrick Roads, in order to avoid paying harbour dues.

As he walked along the quayside, Abel saw the

St Aubyn boat tied up alongside the quay wall with men he knew seated in it, quietly smoking their pipes.

Greeting them, Abel asked what they were doing in Falmouth. 'We brought that maid in that you pulled from the sea dressed as a boy,' said the coxwain. 'She had some business here, I believe.'

'Thomasina's here? Do you know where?' Abel thought this might be an opportunity to speak to her without his grandmother, or anyone else, likely to interrupt them.

'None of my business,' replied the dour St Aubyn coxwain, 'but it's almost time for her to come back to the boat and for us to return to the Mount.'

'I'll wait for her,' said Abel. 'I'd like to speak with her.'

'I don't know as she's likely to want to talk to the likes of you now, Abel,' the coxwain said. 'She's come up in the world since you were last at the Mount.'

Abel frowned. 'In what way?'

'It looks as though we might all have to call her "M'Lady" before very long. It seems Sir Charles Hearle called at the steward's house specially to ask the Varcoe maid to marry him.'

'Sir Charles Hearle and Thomasina . . . ?' Abel looked at the boatman in disbelief. 'You must be mistaken, surely?'

'It's as true as I'm standing here,' said the coxwain. 'I got it direct from your grandma – and she should know, working in the house as she does. That young girl's a deep one, and no mistake, but it's my guess that she'll be Lady Hearle before she's many months older.'

*   *   *

Abel was stunned by the news given to him by the St Aubyn boatman and was at first inclined to dismiss it as no more than Mount gossip, but the man would not have lied about his grandmother passing on the news.

He was still trying to digest this when he came within sight of the shipbroker's office of Claude Coumbe. To to his amazement he saw Thomasina leaving.

Suddenly everything fell into place – and his world tumbled about him. Ducking back behind a jumble of rigging and spars piled on the jetty, he made certain she did not see him.

When she had passed by he hurried to the shipbroker's office. Ignoring the protests of the clerk in the outer room, he flung open the door to Coumbe's inner office. He had not thought of the questions he would ask the shipbroker, but questions proved unnecessary.

The answers were spread out on the desk in front of the shipbroker: accounts made out by himself; various manifests describing the cargoes carried by his ship; and, completing the story, the file on which in thick black letters was the name *Edward V*.

He was employed by Thomasina.

Abel left the office as hurriedly as he had entered it. Rushing back along the quayside, away from the St Aubyn boat, he tried to reject the obvious – but he could not. Everything made far too much sense.

Something must have occurred between Sir Charles and Thomasina when she worked at Trebene House and she had been stung by his refusal to acknowledge her when they met up again.

Whatever lay between them must have been serious because, having come into money, she had bought the *Edward V* with the sole intention of putting Sir Charles out of business and bringing him to the brink of bankruptcy. It explained to Abel why he had been instructed that he had to beat the *Celestine* to Leghorn at all costs.

Ruined financially, Sir Charles would be more inclined to heal his rift with Thomasina. Whatever she had once been, she now possessed a great deal of money – and Sir Charles was desperate enough to offer marriage to her in exchange for her fortune.

The more Abel thought about it, the more sense it made. He was both distraught and appalled by what he had learned about her and the manner in which she had used him in her schemes.

He had thought a great deal about Thomasina since speaking to the Mevagissey fish-cellar owner. Much of the mystery that surrounded her had been made clearer as a result of their conversation, but there had still been some puzzling gaps in his knowledge of her. He wished he might have been able to leave it that way.

Abel was deeply hurt. In recent weeks he had allowed himself actually to contemplate marriage to her. What a fool he had been! It was quite obvious now that Thomasina Varcoe had her sights set on someone far more illustrious than a boatman she had promoted to master of a ship merely to achieve her own ends.

41

Unaware that the cocoon of secrecy in which she had hidden for the past two years had finally been peeled away, Thomasina returned to the Mount with a great deal on her mind.

The good news was that the *Edward V*, under the command of Abel, was proving far more profitable than she had ever thought possible. It showed what Sir Charles Hearle *might* have achieved, had he commenced deep-sea trading in a workmanlike fashion, with a suitable ship and a first-class captain.

However, uppermost in her mind at the moment was the problem of her father. She was honest enough to admit to herself that she still nursed a forlorn hope that one day he would wake and find that his sanity had miraculously returned.

Such a hope would linger for her just as long as he lived, but she was forced to concede that his condition was worsening. She was also faced with the additional problem of finding someone to look after him. Someone she could trust.

Thomasina was still pondering the problem when the boat arrived at the St Michael's Mount harbour.

Entering the steward's house, Thomasina found Verity in a state of happy excitement. 'You'll never guess who I've just had in the house,' she said, hardly giving Thomasina time to step inside the door before hurrying forward to impart her news.

Without waiting for a reply, she said, 'It was little Emma – or Maria, as I suppose I must learn to call her. She's staying up at the castle with her mother and father. They came here looking for you. I said I'd send you up there just as soon as you arrived home from Falmouth.'

'Thank you, Verity,' Thomasina said resignedly. 'I'll get cleaned up, change my clothes and go off to the castle to see them.'

As she took off the clothing she had worn in the boat, Verity chatted through the doorway of the bedroom to her about Maria, her 'lovely mother' and the 'fine-looking gentleman' who was her father.

In truth, Thomasina would have preferred to have a quiet evening at home, thinking over the problem of her father – but she did look forward to seeing Maria once more.

The reunion with Maria was as warm as Thomasina might have wished. Contrary to her expectations, the little girl recognised her as soon as she entered the castle room where the family were seated with the St Aubyns.

She ran to Thomasina and, when she was picked up, flung her arms about Thomasina's neck and gave her a warm hug.

'Well!' exclaimed Thomasina happily, 'that's the most loving greeting I have ever received from *anyone*!'

As she set the small girl down upon the ground once more, Juliana said, 'Thomasina is being modest. She has received two proposals of marriage since she came to the Mount – the latest from a baronet.'

'I am hardly surprised,' said Maria's mother. 'What a remarkable story you have to tell! It would also seem that the sea captain who brought you and Maria to Walkden Hall had a part in rescuing *you*, too. Is he around, by the way?'

'No, but he could be home any day now.'

'Splendid!' Major the Honourable Hugh Pardoe, a tall, good-looking man, limped across the room to shake Thomasina's hand. 'We haven't met before, but I am truly delighted to make your acquaintance. May I call you Thomasina? My wife and I owe you a great deal and we are very, very grateful.'

'Maria's grandmother, Lady Pardoe, is very grateful too,' said Lavinia Pardoe. 'In fact, she has sent a present for you. Give it to Thomasina, Maria.'

The small girl took a small jewellery box from her mother. Carrying it with exaggerated care, she took it across the room to Thomasina.

Thanking her, Thomasina opened the box and expressed delight. Inside was a cameo brooch of finely worked gold filigree.

She looked up at Lavinia Pardoe in search of an explanation, but it was Major Pardoe who spoke. 'It's a family heirloom and would eventually have gone to Maria, but my mother wanted you to have it. She said, quite rightly, that had it not been for you, Maria would not be here today to inherit anything. As a reward for that it is a very small "thank you".'

'But – it rightfully belongs to Maria. I can't possibly accept such an expensive gift.'

'Maria will receive a very substantial inheritance,' said Lavinia. 'However much it is, it cannot compare with what you have given to her. The gift of life itself. The debt we all owe you can never be repaid.'

Moved by the gift and the thought behind it, Thomasina gave Maria a warm kiss and was rewarded with another hug.

Thomasina spent a pleasant few hours at the castle. Lavinia Pardoe was a gentle, quiet woman, who adored her husband and daughter, and Thomasina decided she liked her very much.

It was late evening when she left. Major Pardoe and his family were to depart from the Mount on Sunday. Embarking on their ship at Falmouth, they would sail with the convoy carrying convicts to the penal colonies of Australia.

Juliana accompanied Thomasina halfway down the path to the village. On the way she told her that Sir John proposed a small farewell gathering at the castle for the departing officer and his family.

'You will be invited, of course,' Juliana said. 'But I thought I should warn you that Sir Charles will also be there. He is at the moment staying nearby on the mainland, at the home of a distant relative. Sir John met him early this morning, when he went out riding.'

'I really don't know what Sir John and Sir Charles have in common,' said Thomasina. 'Except, of course, that they are both baronets.'

'There's rather more to it than that,' Juliana explained. 'Sir John and Sir Charles are both Freemasons. So too is Major Pardoe. It is possible one or two more senior Freemasons will be at the castle, too. But if they do come I will insist that they bring wives and daughters to the party.'

Thomasina did not relish the thought of meeting up with the wives and daughters of Sir John's Freemasonry friends, but then she thought of Juliana's own difficult situation in the company of such women . . .

'Don't worry, I'll be there,' she promised.

42

It had been dark for a few hours by the time Thomasina reached her home, but Verity was still in the house.

'There was a letter came for you this evening,' she said immediately. 'Delivered by a special messenger who'd ridden all the way from Falmouth with it. I'd have brought it up to the castle, but it's a long climb up there for my old bones and I was expecting you to be home earlier than this.'

Thomasina's first thought was that the letter contained news of her father. She tore it open in a state of near panic.

It was not about her father, but after scanning the contents she paled and sat down heavily on a chair before reading the letter in more detail.

'Is something wrong, dear? Bad news?'

Thomasina nodded. 'Yes . . . but it's nothing to worry about. It's business, that's all.'

Thomasina was lying. The news contained in the letter *was* something to worry about, for both of them. It had come from Claude Coumbe. He told her of Abel's unexpected and abrupt arrival in his office only minutes after Thomasina had left. The ex-St Aubyn boatman had seen all the papers spread out on his desk and must also have seen Thomasina leaving the shipbroker's office.

The ownership of the *Edward V* was a secret from the ship's captain no longer.

Coumbe said that Abel had left the office without a word after viewing the evidence. The shipbroker had been unable to give him any explanation.

Thomasina bit her lip as she read his words. It had become increasingly apparent to her in recent days that she would not be able to keep secret her ownership of the *Edward V* for ever. She would have to tell Abel the truth very soon, but had hoped to be able to choose her moment.

There was worse to come. An hour after he had left the office, Abel had returned. In the outer office he handed in a letter in which he declared he would no longer be used by Thomasina in her schemes, adding that since she had already succeeded in her aim she would need neither him nor the *Edward V* again. He had therefore resigned his command of the ship, which was currently anchored in Carrick Roads.

Although Thomasina did not know what Abel meant by a great deal of what he had written, there was no doubt that she had a disaster on her hands, and it was one she could not solve from

St Michael's Mount while Abel and the *Edward V* were at Falmouth.

Sir John had told her when she first came to the island that she might have use of the St Aubyn boat and its crew without reference to him. It was time to take advantage of his offer yet again.

'Verity, on your way home, will you tell the boatmen I would like to go to Falmouth again, at first light tomorrow? I have some very urgent business to attend to there.'

Upon her arrival in Falmouth, Thomasina hurried off to the shipbroker's office, but Claude Coumbe was unable to throw any additional light upon the letter handed in by Abel.

'Do you have any idea where Abel is now?' she asked.

'None,' replied Coumbe, 'but one of my clerks thought he saw him at the King's Volunteer, on the sea front, last night. However, I don't think you should go there. It's not the place for a woman. At least, not a *respectable* woman.'

'Then I'll try not to stay there long enough to lose my reputation,' Thomasina said. 'Thank you for your information, Mr Coumbe.'

Thomasina was halfway to the inn when one of the shipbroker's clerks caught up with her. Breathless from hurrying, he said, 'Begging your pardon, Miss Varcoe, but Mr Coumbe sent me after you. He says *I* am to go inside the King's Volunteer to see if Captain Carter is there, while you wait outside.'

'That's very kind of Mr Coumbe,' said Thomasina

gratefully. She would not have thought twice about going inside the inn during the days when she was masquerading as a young man, but the tavern was frequented by foreign seamen. A woman inside such an inn would be there for only one purpose.

The clerk went inside while Thomasina waited on the quay, looking out over the busy harbour.

She was watching a particular ship when the shipbroker's clerk came out of the tavern.

'I'm sorry, Miss Varcoe. Captain Carter was there last night, but he isn't there now and the landlord was unable to help.'

'Were you the clerk who saw him in there?'

'Yes, Miss.'

'Was he drunk or sober?' The clerk seemed reluctant to reply to her question, but Thomasina insisted, 'Surely you know? What state was he in?'

'I'm no expert on such matters, Miss Varcoe,' the clerk said diplomatically, 'but I would say he might have been drinking elsewhere before coming to the King's Volunteer.'

'Thank you.' The reply was what Thomasina had been expecting. She felt that Abel was hurt and unhappy because she had not trusted him sufficiently to tell him *she* was the owner of the *Edward V*. But she had her reasons and she would try to convince him they were valid ones – once she found him.

However, something else had captured her immediate attention.

'How good is your eyesight?' she asked the clerk. 'Can you read the name of that ship coming in – over there?'

She pointed to a ship making slow progress towards the quay. It had attracted her attention earlier.

'I don't need to see its name, Miss Varcoe. I recognise the ship. It's the *Celestine*, Sir Charles Hearle's ship.'

'That's what I thought, but aren't the men on board wearing some kind of uniform?'

The clerk peered at the ship, which was being pursued by a grey curtain of drizzle, before saying excitedly, 'They're Revenue men, Miss Varcoe. There have been rumours going around for a few days of what the *Celestine* was up to. It looks as though the Revenue men heard them too and have caught up with Captain Carberry – at last.'

Thomasina did not miss the meaning in the clerk's words. She wondered whether Sir Charles would be involved in any prosecution that might follow the arrest of Captain Carberry and the detention of the *Celestine*.

She decided she would speculate on Sir Charles Hearle's problems later. Mention of Captain Carberry and his employer had given her an idea of where Abel might be found.

Taking a shilling from her purse, she handed it to the young clerk. 'I am most grateful to you for saving me from possible embarrassment. Please thank Mr Coumbe for his kindness. Tell him I will be speaking to him about the future of the *Edward V* as soon as I have settled one or two matters.'

Thomasina had recalled the inn, the British Marine, where she and Abel had lunched together. The landlord was a friend of his and an ex-marine colleague.

If he was still in Falmouth, Abel would most likely be there.

It was not yet lunchtime and the inn was fairly quiet. When Thomasina entered, the landlord recognised her immediately – and guessed the reason for her visit.

'Hello, Miss Varcoe. I'm pleased to see you again. I'll be even more pleased if you tell me you've come in search of Abel.'

'He *is* here, then?'

'That's right. I'm not in the habit of telling tales about my customers, but seeing you're a particular friend of his . . . He had something on his mind last night and went on a jag that would have put lesser men on their backs in half the time. I've known Abel for a great many years, but I've never known him do anything like this before.'

'Where is he? Will you take me to him?'

'Of course.' The landlord unfastened his leather apron, folded it and set it down upon a keg standing in a corner of the room. 'Come with me.'

Thomasina followed him from the public room and along a dark passageway that led to a steep, narrow staircase. At the top of the stairs was another passageway, but this one had a number of doors leading off it at regular intervals.

'He's in number three.' The landlord stopped at the numbered door and tapped on it. When there was no reply he tapped again, with no more effect.

'He doesn't seem to be answering,' said the landlord. 'But he won't have gone out or I would have seen him.'

'Can you open the door?'

The landlord detached a large ring of keys from his belt and, after peering at them, selected one. Inserting it in the door, he tried to turn it and then swung the door open, saying, 'It's not locked.'

The blinds were drawn, but in the light that filtered around them Thomasina could see the figure lying on the bed under the bedclothes. There was a strong smell of stale alcohol in the room.

'Would you leave us alone for a while?' she asked the landlord. 'When I've woken him we are going to have a long chat. He might feel like something to eat afterwards. Although, if he was as drunk as you say, he might not be able to face food for a while.'

'I'll go off and mix up something that will make him feel a little better,' promised the landlord. 'But I have a feeling you're the only one who can *really* help him. I wish you luck, Miss, I really do. Abel is a good man, one of the very best. I didn't enjoy seeing him the way he was last night.'

43

When the landlord left and closed the door behind him, Thomasina crossed the room and drew back the curtains. Then she opened the window, allowing the stale air to escape, at the same time letting in sounds from the busy street outside.

As she turned her attention to the bed, Abel changed his position, disturbed by the noises entering the room. Thomasina could see now that he had gone to bed fully clothed except for his soft, buckled shoes. She stumbled over one in the middle of the floor; the other was lying at the foot of his bed.

Shaking Abel by the shoulder, she said, 'Wake up. Wake up, Abel. I want to talk to you.'

It was a full minute before she had a reaction from him, then it was a purely automatic one. He sought to shrug off her hand, at the same time mumbling unintelligibly.

'You might just as well wake up and speak to me, Abel. I'm not going to go away.'

Eventually it was her voice rather than her actions that got through to him. Turning his head, his eyelids flickered open to reveal bloodshot eyes. Wincing at the brightness of the light from the window, he closed them again. Then, struggling clumsily to sit up, he winced once more. This time the source of his discomfort was the pounding inside his head.

Trying to marshal an array of disjointed thoughts, not the least of which was wondering exactly where he was, and how he had got here, Abel said, 'What . . . ? What are you doing here? What time is it?'

'I doubt if you even know what day it is, Abel. As for my being here . . . I had an urgent message from Claude Coumbe. He informed me that you intended resigning as captain of the *Edward V*.'

Abel's thoughts began to assume some sort of order and he remembered. Leaning back on his pillows, he closed his eyes once more. 'Claude got it wrong. There was no *intention* about it. I resigned when I delivered my letter to his office.'

'Why, Abel? Why didn't you come and see me and talk about the things that were troubling you?'

'Why didn't *you* tell me you were the owner of the *Edward V*?'

'I had my reasons.'

'I don't doubt it. I have a very good idea what they were.'

'I don't think you do, Abel. You might *think* you know, but whatever ideas you have are probably very wrong.'

'I doubt it.' Abel wished his head was clearer and his brain not quite so determined to batter itself into painful insensibility against his skull. 'You see . . . I picked up another cargo from Mevagissey. While we were loading I got talking to the owner of the fish-cellar. He told me of a certain Edward Varcoe, captain of a small ship, who'd been captured by the French many years ago and returned to Mevagissey only recently. Sadly, he is incurably insane . . . But you'd know all about it because my grandmother would have told you.'

Abel suffered a bout of throaty coughing, the action aggravating the pain in his head. When it passed, he continued.

'This Edward Varcoe has a daughter named – yes, you've guessed it – Thomasina. Thomasina Varcoe. She was the apple of her father's eye, it seems, and would often go to sea with him. She knew as much about sailing a ship as any man, so I am told. Of course, when her father went missing it wasn't possible for her to go to sea as a deckhand, but she couldn't settle to anything else. She became "a bit of a wild one", according to the cellar owner. Then she was put to work at Trebene House, home of Sir Charles Hearle's aunt and uncle, to whom he was very close.'

When Abel turned bloodshot eyes upon Thomasina, his expression hurt her.

'This is where I need to bring my imagination into play a little, I'm afraid. The way I see it, while this Thomasina was working at Trebene, she got to know Sir Charles Hearle – a man well known to have an eye for a pretty girl. It's certain that something happened between them, but I won't speculate on what it might have been. Whatever it was must have been pretty serious – at least, I think it was for *her*. When Thomasina was dismissed from Trebene in mysterious circumstances, she left bearing a huge grudge against Sir Charles. Some time later, when she's been left a lot of money by an uncle, she meets up with him again. When he doesn't even acknowledge her, she gets very angry. So much so that, when he stupidly sinks all his money into a venture involving a ship, she thinks of a plan to *make* him take notice of her – and it's a very elaborate plan. She buys a fast ship, employs a gullible captain and gets him to do her dirty work for her. Mind you, it's worked, hasn't it, Thomasina Varcoe? Worked very well indeed. Sir Charles Hearle has come to heel, just the way you planned it. He's come running to you begging for forgiveness. More, he's asked you to marry him. You've probably got far more than you ever believed you would. A title. Lady Thomasina Hearle. Not bad for a girl who was in service in the house of her future husband's aunt. I have to admire you, Thomasina, I really do.'

Abel's voice was choked and Thomasina realised he was terribly hurt. Almost as hurt as she was by what he had said about *her* – but Abel had not finished talking.

'Now you've got what you want, you won't need a captain for the *Edward V* – and I certainly wouldn't work for Sir Charles Hearle. Besides, he has his own captain. If he has any sense now, he'll sell the *Celestine* at the earliest opportunity and use the *Edward V* to carry his cargoes. I wish you both well. Who knows, if I'm lucky Sir John St Aubyn might even take me back as a boatman. We might see each other occasionally then, you and I, when you and your husband visit the Mount. If we do, I promise I'll remember my place and be sure to call you M'Lady.'

The bitterness in Abel's voice cut into Thomasina like a sharp knife, hurting her far more than it should. Speaking very quietly, she hit back at him.

'Do you really believe all those things of me, Abel? That I'd use you in such a manner?'

'Are you denying that all the things I've said are true? That you haven't used me to get at Sir Charles Hearle?'

'No, I'm not denying that – but I haven't done it in the way you think, nor for the reasons you believe. In fact, were I to have told you the real reason why I wanted to bring him down, you would have helped me willingly, of that I'm certain.'

'Then why *didn't* you tell me? Didn't you trust me?'

'I trusted no one with the story of my life – the true story, that is – nor will I. Anyway, you've already been told enough to know what I've been and where I come from. Something *did* happen at Trebene involving Sir Charles Hearle and me – but certainly not in the way you think. What's more, his lies about me not only had me dismissed, but might well have had me hanged! Yes, I set out to ruin him. I've succeeded too, and I'm not sorry.'

Abel looked at her scornfully. 'If all that's true, then why are you going to marry him?'

'Who told you that story? I wouldn't marry Sir Charles Hearle if he brought the crown of England with him as a wedding gift. Yes, he asked me to marry him. Not because we'd ever meant anything to each other, but because he thought I'd jump at the chance to become Lady Thomasina. Then he would have used my money to get himself out of trouble. I didn't even bother to give him an answer. I laughed at him, Abel. If you don't believe me, I suggest you speak to your grandma about it. She was in the house at the time. But I don't think Sir Charles Hearle is likely to trouble anyone again for a long time. I've just seen his ship being brought in by a Revenue crew. It seems the *Celestine* has been caught free-trading.'

This news was sufficient to penetrate the fog in which Abel's brain was operating.

'Is all this true, Thomasina?'

'The *Celestine* is probably moored at the Customs quay right now.'

'I don't doubt *that*. We all knew what Carberry was up to, even though the *Celestine* is too sluggish for such a trade . . . But that isn't what I meant. I was asking about all the other things you've said. Are *they* true?'

'Would you believe me if I said they were, Abel? It's quite obvious from what you've accused me of today that you have a very low opinion of me, but I haven't lied to you.'

Thomasina was aware she had not told Abel the *full* truth, but her statement was accurate, as far as it went.

'If that's so, why didn't you tell me in the first place that you were the owner of the *Edward V*? Why keep it a secret?'

Just for a moment Thomasina thought of making up a story to explain her actions, but she had been honest with Abel thus far, she would keep it so.

'There were three reasons, Abel. The first was that, had I told you I was determined to bring Sir Charles Hearle to his knees, you would have wanted to know why – and it's a story I've never felt like telling to anyone.'

Abel digested this for a few minutes before saying, 'The other two reasons?'

'One doesn't really matter, now that you've made it so clear what you think of me – but I'll tell you anyway. I thought that if you knew I was the *Edward V*'s owner, you'd have thought twice about becoming its master. You'd have believed you were being offered the captaincy, not because I was convinced you were the right man to take it on, but out of gratitude for saving my life. You see, during my time on the Mount I've got to know you a little, Abel. I've come to realise that you're a very proud man.'

Abel nodded, apparently satisfied with this explanation, at least. 'Perhaps you should tell me the third reason?'

'That's rather more personal. You see, as well as getting to know you, I've come to respect you, too. I liked the way things were between us. I was afraid that if we became employer and employee, things would change. I didn't want that.'

Thomasina decided she had already said more than she had intended. 'Now you've been told all you need to know about me. It's far more than anyone else knows, so I'll leave you in peace. If you decide you still want to be captain of the *Edward V* . . . well, the ship is where you left it. If not, then tell Claude Coumbe and I'll have the ship put up for sale.'

The unexpected strain of unburdening herself to Abel had left Thomasina with a feeling that she had been drained of energy, both mentally and physically. She wanted only to get away from the inn and be alone for a while.

Hurrying from the room, she was on the stairs when she heard Abel call to her. She did not pause and, by the time she passed through the public room where the startled landlord was serving a customer, she was running.

Moments later she was outside, lost in a mist that had swirled in off the sea.

44

After wandering aimlessly about the quayside for almost an hour, Thomasina sat down in the lee of a small dockside store to gather her thoughts.

She had been stupid to overreact in the way she had to the situation back at the inn. She now felt both foolish and apprehensive. Abel knew far more about her than she had wanted *anyone* to know, but running from the room had served no sensible purpose.

She had set the record straight with Abel, only to hand him back the initiative by allowing emotion to override all other considerations.

Then Thomasina became angry with herself for entertaining such a thought. It was as though she regarded Abel as an antagonist. Someone from whom points were to be won, or lost.

A gust of wind invaded the lee of the building where she sheltered, bringing cold rain with

it. Wet and windy weather had replaced the mist
and drizzle she had experienced earlier. She began
to shiver.

Thomasina's thoughts went to the St Aubyn boat.
She had sent it straight back to the Mount in anticipation of deteriorating weather, intending to return
to the Mount herself by coach. The boat was not very
large, and she hoped it would reach its destination
in safety.

She shivered once more. If she remained here for
very much longer she would become chilled through
and through. Fortunately, she had put on a hooded
cloak to keep her warm on the boat trip. It proved to
be very practical.

There was only one place she could go now and that
was to the house she still thought of as 'Malachi's',
where Edith and Arthur Hocking were caring for
her father.

Thomasina made her slow way to the house. Climbing the steep hill from the harbour, she used one of
the many alleyways leading from the main street of
the port.

Had she chosen a different one she might have met
up with Abel, hurrying back down the hill, having
been to the house hoping to find her there.

Unaware of how close she had come to meeting
him again, Thomasina tried to shift her thoughts
away from him by thinking of what awaited her at
the house.

She hoped her father would be in a less aggressive
mood than when they had last met. She was not

optimistic. It had been a horribly upsetting day so far. She had a premonition that it was not going to improve.

She realised her misgivings were justified the moment she reached the house. It was unnaturally quiet and the curtains were three-quarters pulled at the downstairs windows.

Puzzled, Thomasina opened the door and went inside. The silence was even more in evidence here. Convinced that something was very wrong, she felt the hairs on the back of her neck begin to rise.

'Edith . . . ? Arthur . . . ? Is anyone there?'

There was no reply. She wondered if perhaps they were resting, then immediately dismissed the thought. It was lunchtime, not an hour when anyone would be taking a rest. Besides, there should have been someone about to listen out for her father.

Her father! Thomasina ran through the house to the room where he was kept.

The bolt on the door was not pushed home. Lifting the latch, she cautiously opened the door and peered inside. The room was empty. Not only empty, but it had been thoroughly cleaned and tidied.

Extremely disturbed now, Thomasina considered the possibility that she had entered the wrong house by mistake. She pulled herself up quickly. She knew it could not be. Her key had unlocked the front door and everything in the house was as she remembered it.

Then another thought came to her. Perhaps Edith and Arthur had moved her father to another room and for some reason had not heard her call. It was unlikely, but she was prepared to clutch at any possibility now, however remote it might seem.

She searched the house from top to bottom, peering inside every room. The result of her search was what, in her heart, she had known it would be. The house was empty. Her father had gone. So too had Edith and Arthur Hocking.

Thomasina sat down in the kitchen and tried to think of what she could do now. She realised there was only one solution. The Hockings had to be found.

She could not remember the actual address of their house, but it should not be difficult to find. She had gone there on a number of occasions in the past, to let Edith know when she and Malachi returned from a voyage.

She decided she would go there now.

At first, it seemed Thomasina would be no more successful at the Hockings' home than at the house she had just left. Then, when she had almost despaired of receiving a reply to her persistent knocking, the door opened and a harassed-looking woman stood before her. From somewhere at the rear of the house Thomasina could hear the cries of a young child.

'Yes, what do you want?' the woman asked Thomasina. Then, in the next breath, she called over her shoulder, 'Be quiet, Simon. I'll be with you in a minute.'

'I'm looking for Edith and Arthur Hocking,' said Thomasina. 'I'm Thomasina Varcoe.'

'Oh! I'm sorry. I'm Sybil, their daughter. Mum and

Dad aren't here right now . . . but you'd better come inside.'

Thomasina stepped in through the doorway, then followed Sybil to the kitchen. Here an infant of about fifteen months sat in a puddle of his own making, proclaiming his unhappiness to the world.

Picking him up and bouncing him in her arms with teeth-rattling zeal, Sybil asked uncertainly, 'Would you like a cup of tea?'

'What I would like are the answers to some questions. First of all, where is my father?'

An expression of utter dismay appeared on Sybil's face. 'You mean . . . ? You don't know? Oh, my God! I know Mum said she had lost your address, but I thought she must have found it and got someone to read it for her. Neither she nor Pa can read, you see, and I can do little more than write my own name . . .'

'Sybil!' Thomasina's patience ran out and she brought the other woman's nervous chatter to a halt. *'Where is my father?* I want to know.'

'I'm sorry, Miss Varcoe. Very, very sorry. He's dead.'

'Dead?' Suddenly the room seemed to swing about her and Thomasina looked at Sybil in horror. 'When . . . ? Where . . . ? How?'

'Sit down. I'll tell you while I make that cup of tea – but first I'll put my little one to bed. He's over-tired and should have been asleep an hour ago.'

Thomasina felt like screaming, but she had realised that Sybil was a very simple girl. She managed to curb her frustration while the child was put to bed.

When Sybil returned to the room, both women tried to ignore the child's intermittent crying, but, as Sybil began to put out the teacups, Thomasina's patience broke.

'Sybil! I'm waiting for you to tell me what's happened.'

Flustered now, Sybil said, 'It should have been Mum or Dad telling you this, but they were so upset by the whole business that Dad has taken Mum to her sister's, up by Padstow, until she's got over it . . .'

'Sybil, if you don't tell me what happened, I'll throttle it out of you, I swear I will.'

'Well, it happened when they took your pa out for a walk . . .'

'For a *walk*?'

Thomasina echoed the words in disbelief. 'They took a man in his state for a *walk*?'

'Yes, but they had a long chain padlocked around his waist . . . It was only a light one, you understand,' Sybil explained hastily, 'with Pa holding the other end.'

Trying hard to shake off the image of her father being led through the streets of Falmouth on the end of a chain like some wild animal, Thomasina said, 'Go on.'

'Well, as it was a nice day last Tuesday, Mum and Dad thought your father would enjoy going out. They took him along the cliff path towards Maenporth. He seemed to be enjoying it, too – then this dog came along the path towards them. Suddenly your father jumped at it, shouting, and the animal went berserk. When my dad tried to drive it away, it turned on him, causing him to drop his end of the chain. The dog bit my dad three times on the legs and Mum once on her hand, before someone came along and drove it off. By then your father had disappeared. They searched for him until it got dark, then went back the next morning with a whole lot of people from round about. That's when they found him – but by then he was dead.'

'How did he die?' Thomasina felt numb with shock, but it was a question she had to ask.

'One end of the chain – the loop Pa used to hold – was caught on the branch of a tree that grew out of the cliffside, but part of the chain was looped around your father's neck. At first everyone thought he'd committed suicide, but at the inquest the coroner decided he'd slipped over the cliff and that the chain had got caught up as he fell. He said it was an accidental death.'

Sybil looked at Thomasina sympathetically. 'Your father was buried in the churchyard down by the docks, the day before yesterday. All of us went to the church. So did some of those who'd helped search for him. It was a lovely service.'

Strangely, now that she had been told the circumstances of her father's death, Thomasina felt no urge to cry. She just thought it terribly sad that her father should have died in such a tragic fashion after all he had suffered at the hands of the French.

'Do you think you could show me his grave?' she asked Sybil.

'I'd like to,' said the other woman apologetically, 'but it sounds as though Simon's just dropped off to sleep. I can't wake him up and take him out in this weather.'

'No. No, of course not,' agreed Thomasina, dull-voiced.

'You won't have any trouble finding him,' said Sybil. 'There hasn't been another new grave there for more than a year, so the gravedigger said.'

'All right,' said Thomasina. 'Thank you, Sybil. I'll go down there now.'

'But . . . aren't you going to stop for a cup of tea? I'm just about to make it.'

'I really don't think I could drink one. I'll leave you now.'

Thomasina bought some flowers close to the church and placed them on the grave, which was as easy to find as Sybil had predicted.

Then, head bowed against the blustery wind, she murmured a prayer that was as brief as it was meaningless.

She did not feel that the grave held her father, even though the tombstone she would arrange to have erected on the site would say that it did.

Her father had been lost at sea, all those years before. Lying in the ground here, in the Falmouth churchyard, was a stranger. A man who had not been capable of recognising his daughter and who could recollect no links with his past life.

Even his own name had not been familiar to him. Yet the name would be carved on a tablet of stone, for the living to see, in order that others might know – better than he – that the body lying here was that of Captain Edward Varcoe.

45

When Thomasina returned to the Mount she had forgotten the farewell dinner due to be held that evening for Hugh and Lavinia Pardoe.

She was reminded when Juliana came to the house late that same afternoon. When Thomasina told her she did not feel she could cope with such an event, Juliana protested vehemently.

'You *must* come, Thomasina. Lavinia will be so disappointed if you are not there – and so will I. You and Lavinia will be the only interesting people there. Sir John has invited a couple of generals and admirals who fought battles that everyone has long forgotten, together with wives who resent the fact that their husbands were not raised to the peerage for deeds-that-never-were.'

'I know how you feel, Juliana, but I really don't think I can face them – Sir Charles in particular. Not today . . .'

'You won't have to put up with Sir Charles,' replied Juliana triumphantly. 'He won't be there. You won't have heard, but his ship was boarded by Revenue officers and found to be loaded with undutied goods. The ship's captain is to be put on trial, together with those of his men who haven't opted to serve in the Royal Navy. The ship, of course, has been impounded by the Revenue Service and will be sold. There's no doubt that if they find Sir Charles, he will be put on trial too – but they won't find him.'

Despite the many other matters she had on her mind, Thomasina was curious. 'Why are you so certain he won't be caught?'

Enjoying the opportunity to impart some really exclusive gossip, Juliana lowered her voice conspiratorially. 'Because tomorrow he'll be on his way to Australia with the convicts.'

Thomasina was confused. 'But you said he hadn't been caught – and wouldn't be.'

'That's right, my dear. You see, he is not going there as a convict, but as an administrator. Hugh Pardoe says Sir Charles will be allowed to use his militia rank there and will probably be placed in charge of one of the smaller convict settlements.'

'Heaven help the convicts!' Thomasina exclaimed. 'Sir Charles certainly won't. I hope for their sakes no women are among them. But why should Major Pardoe do this for Sir Charles, for he knows next-to-nothing about him?'

'He doesn't need to, Thomasina. They are both Freemasons, as is Sir John. When one of them is in trouble, the others will do all they can to help.

Besides, this is Cornwall. Getting the better of Revenue men is one of life's little pleasures.'

Thomasina thought that having Sir Charles go to Australia was the finest possible result she could have gained from her campaign against him. There had been many times when she had wished him dead, but his death might have weighed on her conscience.

This way, he would be banished almost as effectively as if he had been convicted and transported. It was the first piece of good news she had received after suffering a couple of days of anguish and misery.

'So, you see, you won't *have* to be nice to Sir Charles. Besides, you've come back from Falmouth looking absolutely ghastly. I don't know what you have been up to there, but a soirée is just the thing to put some sparkle back into your life. It is always possible that some of the fogeys will bring a son or two along with them. That reminds me, Sir John received a letter from Humphrey today. It would seem the dear boy has finally accepted the Church as his vocation. He has taken a post in a London parish. Judging by the tone of his letter, he could even be contemplating taking an oath of celibacy, but I believe that is not uncommon among sensitive young men who have been spurned by the object of their affections.'

Thomasina succeeded in producing a wan smile. 'Poor Humphrey, but I would be wholly unsuitable for him and his career. One day he'll thank me for turning him down.'

'Perhaps – but promise you'll join us this evening, then I'll go away and allow you to relax for a couple of hours.'

'All right, I'll come.'

'Splendid! I knew you wouldn't let me down, Thomasina.'

Thomasina hoped Juliana might feel the same when the evening was over. She had reached a decision of which the other woman might not approve.

The gathering was a very dressy affair and for the first time since she had been attending Juliana's 'evenings' Thomasina felt very much an outsider. She wore the necklace given to her by Abel and felt it attracted far more attention than she did herself.

This, and Juliana's obvious affection for her, meant that Thomasina was not ostracised altogether, but it was made obvious that she would never be considered a suitable guest in the houses of those present.

Lavinia was aware of Thomasina's feeling of isolation and sought her company whenever she could. She tried her best to draw her into general conversation with others, but the events of the past few days had left Thomasina feeling disinclined to exchange small talk with anyone.

When the party had been under way for a couple of hours, Thomasina felt the need to escape. Believing her absence would not be noticed, she slipped quietly from the room, making her way outside to the small South Court, to escape the monotonous buzz of conversation.

But her departure had not gone unobserved. A few minutes later she was joined on the terrace by Lavinia.

'Aren't you cold out here, Thomasina?'

The night air was decidedly cool, but Thomasina said, 'No, I was finding it a bit hot and stuffy inside.'

'You're quite right. I felt it, too.'

Moving to stand alongside Thomasina, Lavinia looked out to sea, to where a storm was passing eastwards along the English Channel. Flickering lightning would occasionally illuminate the horizon, with a dull rumble of thunder following in its wake.

'Mind you,' said Lavinia, 'I would rather be here than out there in such a storm.'

'A storm at sea can be very exciting,' said Thomasina. 'You feel part of it and that somehow makes it seem less frightening.'

'You must have had a great many interesting experiences during the years you spent at sea with your uncle,' Lavinia said. 'Juliana has told me a great deal about you while I have been on the Mount. She is very fond of you.'

'Juliana has been very kind and took good care of me after Abel rescued me.'

'Ah yes, your handsome sea captain. I was hoping to see him while I was here. Maria has a small gift for him. If he doesn't put in an appearance, Juliana suggested I should give it to you to keep for him.'

'I'm afraid I don't know where he is – or whether

I'll ever see him again.' Thomasina's voice revealed far more than she realised.

'What a pity. He has such an honest, open face and gentle manners. He appeared to be very fond of you, too.' When Thomasina made no reply, Lavinia asked gently, 'Have you and he quarrelled?'

'No!' It came out too vehemently and Thomasina felt obliged to add, 'We've had a misunderstanding, that's all.'

Lavinia put out a hand and rested it on Thomasina's arm. 'Misunderstandings are far easier to right than are quarrels. I will give you the present and a letter for him. I feel quite certain you will be able to deliver them for me.'

Lightning lit up the sky over the sea once more and Lavinia continued, 'I hope the storm will have passed on by the time we board our ship tomorrow. I am not looking forward to the long voyage, but it is wonderful to know I will have Maria for company, thanks to you. When I think of what happened . . . !'

She shivered and said, 'I fear it is too cold for me out here. I grew too used to the sunshine of Spain. Will you come in with me, or do you prefer to remain here?'

'I'll come in with you,' Thomasina said. 'I just needed to be somewhere quiet for a while, to put my thoughts in some sort of order. I believe I've done all the thinking that's necessary now.'

46

Thomasina made the result of her thinking known to Juliana early the next morning when they and Lavinia were all taking breakfast together.

Her opportunity came when Juliana said, 'You're looking very serious this morning, Thomasina. Are you still feeling the effects of last night's soirée?'

'No, it has nothing to do with the party, although I must admit that in many ways it helped me to reach a decision about my future.'

Juliana paused, a piece of toast held halfway between plate and mouth. 'What is there to decide? You have a home here, can come and go as you wish – not to mention suitors who call in regularly to propose marriage! What more could any woman want?'

'I've been very happy here, Juliana, and couldn't have wished for a kinder, or more thoughtful, friend, but I feel it's time I moved on and did something else with my life.'

'What has brought you to this decision?'

Thomasina shrugged. 'A number of things, not least of which has been watching Lavinia and Maria prepare for their new life in Australia.'

'Are you quite certain, Thomasina? Nothing has happened to upset you?'

'No, it's just a feeling that my life is going nowhere at the moment.'

'But what will you do?' Juliana was genuinely upset at Thomasina's announcement.

Thomasina shrugged once more. 'I'm not quite certain. I'll first move to my house in Falmouth and make arrangements to sell the property. Then I might have a look at one or two other countries before I finally make up my mind. I've always wanted to visit Canada. I'd like to spend a little time in America, too, now that it seems the trouble between our countries will soon be over.'

'You could always accompany Maria and me to Australia,' Lavinia suggested hopefully. 'We would both love to have you with us.'

'I don't think Australia will be one of the countries on Thomasina's list,' Juliana declared. 'Sir Charles Hearle will be there with you. He is one of her most unwanted suitors. I will be very, very sorry to lose your company, Thomasina, but I must respect your wishes, of course. Sir John and I will be returning to London any day now. Do you have any idea when you might leave?'

'Yes. Now I've made my decision I'll leave as

quickly as possible, in case I'm persuaded to change my mind. I would like to accompany Lavinia and Major Pardoe to Falmouth, this morning. I've left Verity packing my things at the steward's house.'

Juliana was taken aback. 'So soon? My dear, I will hardly have time to say "goodbye" properly!'

'It's better this way, Juliana. You and Sir John have been very good to me, and you are the best friend I've ever had. Leaving you and the Mount will be a wrench. I don't want to make it any harder.'

'Of course. I *do* understand.'

Juliana was an emotional woman. There were tears in her eyes as she stood up. 'For the same reason I'll say goodbye to you here and not come down to the harbour. I don't want to make a fool of myself in front of the villagers. Goodbye, Thomasina. I am going to miss you very much indeed.'

When Thomasina also rose to her feet, Juliana gave her a warm, uninhibited hug, then without another word turned and hurried from the room, leaving Thomasina fighting back her own tears and Lavinia looking on sympathetically.

Once clear of St Michael's Mount harbour, the boat carrying Thomasina and the Pardoe family steered eastwards, riding easily over the submerged causeway.

From the ramparts of the castle, a number of figures could be seen waving wildly to send them on their way. It was impossible to make out any particular figure, but Thomasina knew Juliana would be one of them.

Before long they were so far from the Mount that waving became futile and Thomasina looked shorewards from the boat, seeing very little.

'Any regrets about what you are doing?' Lavinia put the question from her seat, close to Thomasina.

'Doubts, yes. Regrets . . . ? I'm not certain. They might well come later.'

'It's still not too late for you to decide to come with us to Australia.'

'Thank you, but that really isn't on my list of options . . .'

At that moment Maria complained that the movement of the boat was making her feel sick, and Lavinia and Thomasina both turned their attention to the small girl.

The dour boatman who had once before conveyed Thomasina to Falmouth was in charge of the boat, but he had allowed the youngest member of the crew to take the tiller.

Suddenly the older man said to the helmsman, 'Put her over to starboard and keep well clear of the ship that's coming towards us. She's travelling fast, so give her a wide berth.'

At his words Thomasina glanced up briefly – then looked once more. The ship was a schooner, an American-rigged 'clipper'. A vessel she would have recognised anywhere.

It was the *Edward V*!

Excitedly she watched as the schooner altered course to give them a wider berth. On the upper deck she could make out a number of men, one of whom was studying them through a telescope, the polished brass of which reflected the rays of the weak sun.

The *Edward V* sailed past the St Aubyn boat before turning in a tight, leaning arc until it was steering the same course and closing on them. It was sailing to windward and soon its greater bulk took the wind from the smaller boat, leaving its sails flapping untidily.

As the *Edward V* edged still closer, Thomasina saw that Abel was on deck. He must have decided to remain in command of her boat.

It was he who now hailed his successor as the St Aubyn head boatman.

'Cyrus, where are you bound?'

'Falmouth,' was the shouted reply. 'I've passengers for the convict fleet, bound for Australia.'

There were a few moments of silence before Abel's reply came back to them. 'Come alongside and transfer your passengers to me. I'll have them there in half the time and in far more comfort. There's an easterly blowing and the sea's rough on the far side of the Lizard.'

The dour boatman seemed in doubt about what he should do, but Thomasina said sharply, 'Do as Abel says.'

Her tone of voice brooked no argument and the head boatman moved to comply.

From the thwart where she sat with Maria held close to her, Lavinia asked with a smile, 'Can I presume from this that the "misunderstanding" between you and Captain Abel is over?'

'Not yet,' Thomasina replied. 'But with any luck

we'll have sorted things out by the time we reach Falmouth.'

She was feeling happier than she had for many days. She had not yet spoken to Abel, but the fact that he was once more in command of the *Edward V* was sufficient reason in itself for jubilation. It meant he had accepted her explanation of events.

The transfer of passengers and luggage took twenty minutes, then the *Edward V* surged through the choppy waters to the west of the Lizard peninsula, quickly leaving the St Aubyn boat far behind.

On board, Major Pardoe would have engaged Abel in conversation. However, Lavinia gently, but firmly, insisted that he take her and Maria to the mate's cabin, put at their disposal for the short voyage, leaving Thomasina and Abel together on the upper deck.

When they had gone below, Abel said, 'Why, Thomasina?'

'Why what?' Thomasina replied innocently.

'Why are you going off to Australia?'

'Is there any reason why I shouldn't?' she countered.

'I can think of a great many reasons. One is that you have persuaded me to stay on as captain of your ship, yet you are now going to the farthermost corner of the earth and leaving us behind. What's going to happen to your ship – and to me?'

'I've thought about that,' Thomasina said seriously. 'You're an excellent captain, Abel. You deserve your own ship. I've decided to instruct my solicitor to make the *Edward V* over to you . . . No, I don't want to hear any protest. You've already provided me with more profit than I spent to buy the ship. She'll be yours as soon as we reach Falmouth. What's more, if you have problems paying for your first cargo, I'll have him pay for it on my behalf. When the voyage is over you can repay my money and put the profit towards your next cargo. Perhaps that will atone for the way you think I've used you in the past.'

'I can't take the *Edward V*, Thomasina – and what *was* I to think . . . ?'

'Only you can answer that, Abel. You're the one who made the allegations about my motives in buying the *Edward V* and putting you in command of it. I'm merely trying to show you that your allegations were unfounded. Anyway, what are you protesting about? You have nothing at all to lose.'

There was a long, thoughtful silence before Abel said quietly, 'I have a great deal to lose, Thomasina. The only reason I returned to the *Edward V* was because of what you said to me. Because I believed you wanted me as *your* captain. If that isn't what you meant, then I want no part of the *Edward V*.'

Thomasina looked at him in astonishment. 'I've offered you a ship – the finest you'll find anywhere – and guaranteed you a profit on your next voyage. What else do you want, Abel?'

'Something that means more to me than money or a ship, Thomasina. I've been asked to take a cargo of mine-engines from Hayle to Mexico. It will be a long voyage, one that will need to have the approval of both owner and shipbroker.'

'So? I've told you I'll transfer the *Edward V* to you.

That will make *you* the owner, and I've no doubt Claude Coumbe will give you his blessing.'

'I'm quite happy to make the voyage, Thomasina, but before I do, I would like a blessing from a much higher authority first.'

'You're talking in riddles now, Abel. What do you mean?'

'The blessing I want is from the Church, Thomasina – on you and me. I know you've had two offers of marriage since I pulled you from the sea. Well, I'm making it three and hoping it will be third time lucky. Think about it, Thomasina. You love the sea and I've learned, albeit belatedly, that I love you. We could make the trip to Mexico our honeymoon. Once the cargo is delivered, we could sail anywhere you wish – and for as long as you want. I promise you'll enjoy it far more than a voyage to Australia on a convict transport. What do you say?'

Suddenly, in the course of little more than half an hour, Thomasina's life had gone from accept-ance of defeat to the prospect of a new and happy future, but she would not allow her guard to drop immediately.

'Your offer is the best I've had to date, Abel, but I suggest we go down to your cabin. If my estimate of the *Edward V*'s sailing qualities are correct, that should give you an hour and a half to convince me that it's an offer I can't refuse . . .'

Author's Note

Thomasina was neither the first nor the last woman to pass herself off successfully as a man in an exclusively male environment.

It is on record that a highway*man* was taken, convicted of highway robbery and sentenced to transportation. Her sex was not discovered until she had been on a prison hulk for many months.

Similarly, a young woman named Christian Davies enlisted in an infantry regiment, was wounded and taken prisoner, exchanged and then returned to active duty. Her sex was only discovered when she was seriously wounded once more. Three times married, she was buried among the Chelsea pensioners.

Another woman, Phoebe Hessell, enlisted as a private in the Fifth Regiment of Foot and was discovered to be a woman only when she was wounded at the battle of Fontenoy. She went on to live to the age of a hundred and eight.

There are many more such examples on record.

In 1812, during the Napoleonic Wars, the guns of the Mount successfully took on a French man-o'-war, driving it ashore in the bay.

Of Sir John St Aubyn's fifteen children, all illegitimate, a number entered the Church – with mixed success. (John) Humphrey St Aubyn was forced to resign the living of Crowan, being cited as co-respondent when Sir John Tyrrell divorced his wife, Elizabeth.

Sir John St Aubyn eventually married Juliana Vinicombe in 1822, when most of their children were adult, and St Michael's Mount was inherited by their son, Edward, who became a baronet in his own right and was the father of John, First Baron St Levan.

John St Aubyn, Fourth Baron St Levan, and his wife Lady Susan are the present occupants of St Michael's Mount, continuing a family occupancy which goes back for almost three hundred and fifty years.

The Mount itself is now in the ownership of the National Trust. During its very long history it has been a church, priory, castle and private home – but the full story of the tidal island that is St Michael's Mount is lost in the mists of time.

It is believed that traders from the Mediterranean came here centuries before the birth of Christ. Indeed, one of the island's many legends has it that a young Jesus himself set foot here, on a trading voyage with his uncle.

St Michael's Mount is a magical place for all whose heart is in this south-western corner of the land, where the winds of fortune still blow.